KNOT all IS LOST

THE COMPLETE DUET

International Bestselling Author

ELIZABETH KNIGHT

Knight, Elizabeth
Knot All Is Lost: Complete Duet
Editing: Swish Editing
Cover artist: Emily Wittig Designs
Formatting: Creative Wonder Publishing

Dear Readers,
Knot All Is Lost is a book that contains subject matter that could be triggering to some people. If you feel like this could be a problem for you, please protect yourself. No work of fiction is worth your mental health.
The full detailed list of content warnings is available on my website.
https://geni.us/omegaverseCW

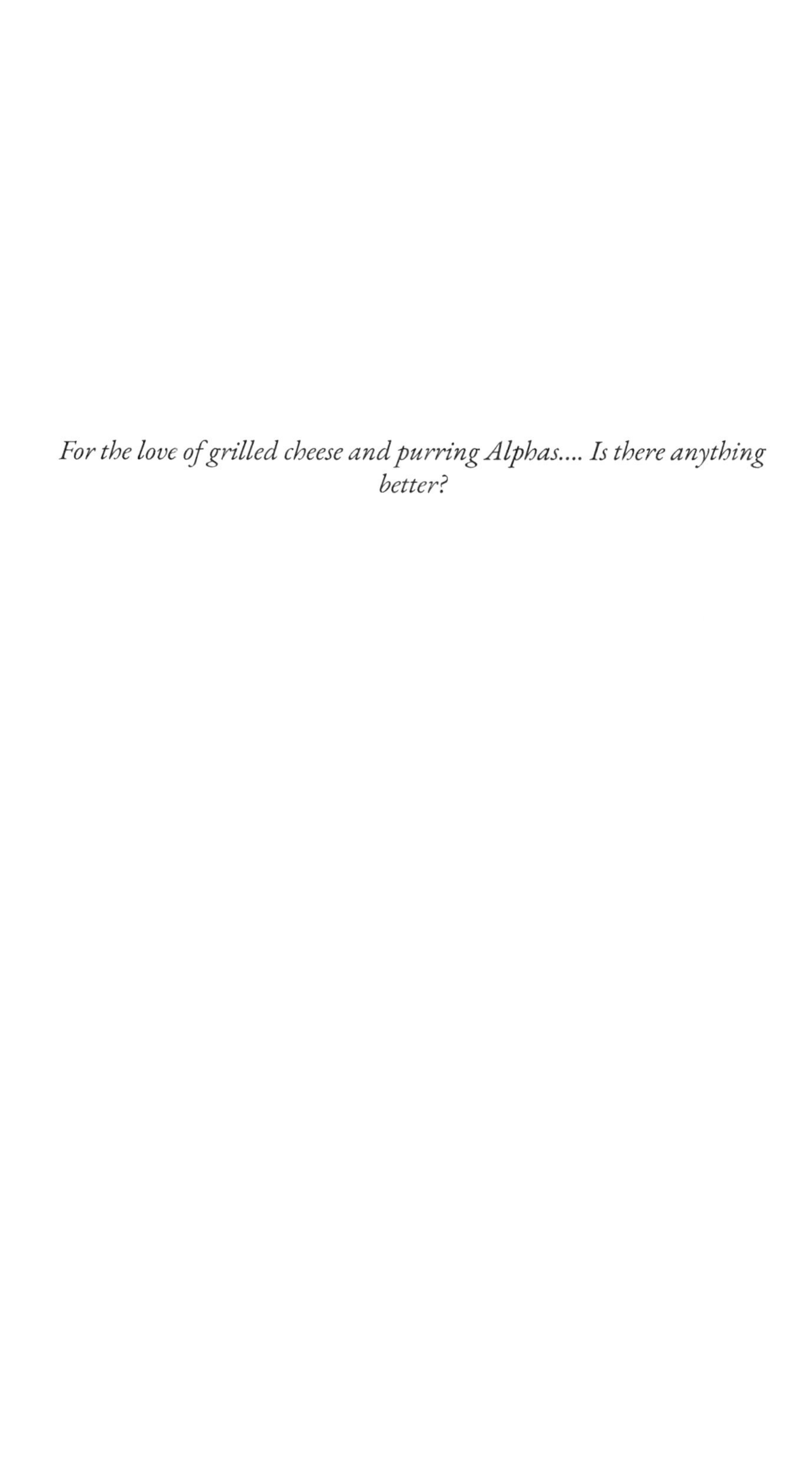

For the love of grilled cheese and purring Alphas…. Is there anything better?

CHAPTER 1

Cambrie

My world is small, dark, and filled with nothing resembling happiness.

That all vanished when my mother died eight years ago. My father had always been a drinker but when she wasn't there to stop him anymore it became so much worse. When things didn't go his way, I was now the one he took it out on. It became so bad that I couldn't hide the marks anymore, and instead of getting visits from social workers, we moved. He never let me go back to school and lied if people asked, telling them he was homeschooling me.

"Oh Cambrie, how are you today, darling?" Peggy, the head librarian, a sweet Beta asked as I entered the building.

The one bright spot in my life was the library. Father would be home all day since he was on his three days off from the warehouse, and he'd come home in a foul mood last night muttering about a shipment going wrong. Of course, he took it out on me when he found out we didn't have any beer in the fridge. Thankfully, he remembered not to hit me in the face and settled for tossing me across the room, followed by a few swift kicks. I didn't want to spend today, of all days, holed up in my room waiting for him to remember I existed when he woke up hungover.

"Today is actually my birthday, so I figured what better place to spend it but here with you," I answered, giving Peggy a bright smile as I tucked my wild blonde hair behind my ear.

Today I was turning sixteen, the age when your designation revealed itself. Everyone talked about how they knew what their children would be all along. Most of the time I'm sure they were right, most were kind of obvious to pick up on. Alphas were always confident, natural born leaders, drawing people to them left and right. It's why they became politicians or other influential people. Then there were the Betas, the diligent workers who truly ran our world and made up most of the population. If we no longer had Betas nothing would ever get done and our society would be a fraction of what it was. The government, in all their wisdom, had already almost caused one designation—Omegas—to go extinct, and the world was still recovering from that.

Peggy clapped her hands together as she burst out of her chair. I couldn't help but flinch at the sudden movement even though I *knew* Peggy would never hurt me. Years of abuse trained my mind and body to act first and process later... if ever.

"That's so exciting!" Peggy gushed as she held herself back from giving me a hug. I'd never outright told her what was going on, but it didn't take a private eye to figure it out. "We'll have to do lunch together, my treat since you're the birthday girl."

Peggy and her co-worker Diane have looked after me like I was one of their own for the past five years I've lived here. They were the ones to talk me into getting my GED and helped if I got stuck. There was never any judgment, just patience as they guided me through the problems. My plan right now was to find a college that would take me far, far away from Father and his anger. I'd been trying to find a way to make some money but that was far more challenging being so young. Now that I was sixteen it opened up a lot more doors and gave me a glimmer of hope.

"Now, birthday girl, where are you hiding for the day?" Peggy asked, leaning against the front desk giving me plenty of space with her hands calmly at her sides.

The whole walk over I'd been trying to decide that very thing. Did I want to be productive and work on my GED stuff, or did I want to toss responsibility to the wind? "I'm going to spoil myself and go for fiction."

"That a girl," Peggy said with a wink. "I have your bean bag chair in the office, give me a moment and I'll grab it."

As I waited, I slipped out of my patched up bomber jacket that was far too light for the chilly day but it had a beautifully stitched Japanese style dragon on the back. I'd found it in a clothing bin where people put clothes they don't want anymore. It had a huge tear down the sleeve but I stitched it together with silver thread so it looked like it was supposed to be that way, instead of hiding the flaw. I might need to forage for my clothes, but I did my best to create my own style with what I found.

"Here you are darling, I'll find you when it's lunchtime, and we'll go to that café you love down the street, hmm?" Peggy offered, handing me the giant bright teal bean bag chair.

Teal was my favorite color, and the chair was a gift from Peggy and Diane for Christmas a few months ago. Hugging the bulky ball of squishy beads, I headed to the second level and wandered past the Young Adult area and went straight to the Adult Fiction section. It was here I could find a book about the way things had been in the past, when packs were a normal way of life and full of love for each other, whether it was familial love or as a lover. A pack formed from a blend of men and women who fit together perfectly, no matter their designation. It gave me hope that somewhere in the world that still existed, and one day I might stumble upon it for myself. I let out a huff of laughter. This was the real world. Nothing like that would ever happen for me. Not for the poor girl who lived with a father who one day might get mad enough to kill her by accident. That's where books and daydreams come in.

"Oh, going for a re-read I see," Peggy commented as she looked at the book I was reading. "That's one of my favorites too, that Cameron though," she said, fanning herself, giving me a salacious grin. "I'm not even going to comment on the fact we told you not to read from this section until you're older but I guess there isn't really any harm in it now, is there? Packs who think like those are so rare it's best to believe they're only in fiction. Oh, listen to me getting all weepy on your birthday. Come on, let's get something to eat."

The thing I loved most about Peggy was that she was a hopeless romantic. She was in her late fifties and never settled down or had kids. She always told me the kids of the library were who she was meant to look after. I quickly placed the book back in its spot and chuckled at the name of it *I Think Knot*. While a knot was something everyone wanted from an Alpha, it also gave for a great amount of play on words for authors. Jogging to catch up to Peggy, I slipped on my jacket and we headed out.

The café was just down the street and had the best soup and sandwiches in town, not to mention their baked goods. It was small, and many people did to-go orders or delivery to their work, making it fairly quiet inside. This helped me relax and enjoy my meal since I didn't do so great around strangers.

While I tried my best to hide the aftereffects of living with an abusive father, being around a lot of people in a small space just wasn't something I could do comfortably. It made me mad that even when he wasn't around he controlled my life and how I did things. I let out a sigh when we walked in and there were only two other people in the place and the table in the back corner was empty.

We settled into our seats, and a waitress came over to take our order. "Hello ladies, what can I get for you?"

"I would love a turkey club with that yummy tomato soup," Peggy ordered. "Oh, and an iced tea."

The waitress turned to me and Peggy gave me a warning look. She knew I hated feeling like a charity case but this was different in my brain, it was my birthday. "I'll have a large bowl of cream of chicken and rice soup with a full roast beef sandwich, please. Water to drink would be fine."

"Lovely, I'll get this in and it should be out shortly," our waitress chirped and headed back to the kitchen.

Peggy slowly reached out and patted my hand, that was resting on the table. "Bless you child for actually ordering what you wanted. You know I can't stand how skinny you are."

"You do so much for me already, and don't think I don't know that you pack far more than you can eat in your lunch just so you can share with me," I pointed out, giving her a mock glare.

She had the grace to blush but refused to comment. The waitress returned shortly with our meals and I dug in, humming at how good the soup tasted. As we ate, we chatted about my GED progress, the latest books we'd read, and Peggy told me stories of her traveling days before she settled here.

"How is it that you have been all over the place, and you settled on Cheapstow of all towns?" I asked, bewildered.

Tilting her head in thought she let out a sigh. "I thought I'd found someone to spend the rest of my life with here. We dated a short while and he'd just asked me to move in with him, but before that could happen he was shot trying to stop a man from kidnapping an Omega. Timothy had such a pure heart and was always looking out for others, the perfect white knight if there ever was one. After he died I couldn't bring myself to leave, his family let me take over his apartment and that's where I live to this day. It's how I can stay connected to him even though he's gone."

In this dark world, Peggy's story wasn't all that different from many I'd heard on the news or read about. This world was in shambles, and no one was stepping up to do anything about it.

"Well, we best be getting back to the library. I talked Diane into letting me take a longer lunch since it was a special occasion and all, but I don't like to leave her alone too long. You know how she gets if anything on the computer goes wrong." Peggy chuckled as we got up to leave.

As I stood, a wave of dizziness hit me and I stumbled into the table, almost crashing into it. Peggy reached out and grabbed my arm to steady me but I recoiled from her on instinct, slamming into another body. The sound of dishes smashing on the ground followed by a man swearing up a storm told me I'd taken out the bus boy I'd seen running around. Scrambling off him while panic clawed at my throat as I desperately needed to get away from having that much contact with a person. I was better with women but men, men were a whole different story.

"Fucking bitch, watch where you're going!" the man snarled.

Panic clouded my vision so I still couldn't see straight, and another sensation tingled all over my body. Terror the likes of which I've never known before sank deep into my bones, as a new perfume in the air around me was proof that my designation had reveled itself. In a twist of cruel irony, when we come into our designation, we learn the truth the same way others did upon picking up our personal scent. My scent of heady vanilla, that was sweetened by a hint of nutmeg, screamed Omega.

"Cambrie," Peggy called, her voice filled with urgency. "You need to get up *now*."

Breathing was hard and what little air I could get into my lungs did nothing to ease the burning I felt. Tears spilled down my cheeks and I let out a whine that only an Omega could make, which was the worst possible thing I could have done. Alphas might be powerless to resist an Omega's whine, but Betas felt the pull as well, just to a lesser degree.

"Cambrie, we need to get you out of here this instant and I'm going to have to touch you," Peggy whispered harshly as she grabbed my arm and yanked me to my feet with surprising strength.

My vision started to clear as she dragged me out of the restaurant. Looking back, I saw three men watching us with a look that would have crippled me if it wasn't for Peggy. Walking as fast as our legs could move, we headed for the safety of the library, or at least I thought that's where we were going. It was almost too late when I saw Peggy was bringing me to the police station. It was protocol that all Omegas were removed from their parents and placed in a secure location until a pack was selected for them. The Omega didn't get a say in the matter, even if there was no connection to the pack they were placed with, it was all decided by the government.

"No!" I screamed, jerking away from her. "I won't. I won't let them lock me away until I'm whored out to some pack. I'd rather take my chances on the streets than be forced into the life of a breeder."

"Cambrie, this is for your protection," Peggy pleaded, her eyes begging me to understand. "If you don't do this something worse could happen. What if the black market dealers find you? They will sell you off just the same, but it won't be to someone who gives a damn about you and your wellbeing. Being placed with a pack is the best you can do in this world."

Tears flowed down my cheeks as I kept shaking my head. "Don't make me do this," I begged.

This time, when I tugged my hand from hers she let me, and I didn't question it as I bolted down the street. I ran as fast as I could back home, where I was going to pack up my meager belongings and disappear. I didn't know how I was going to do it or where I was going to find suppressors, but I wasn't going to be used. I'd been my father's punching bag most of my life. I wasn't going to let a group of strangers tell me what the rest of my life would be like.

The front door slammed as I entered, making me flinch and internally scolded myself for making such a stupid mistake. I needed to get my head on right or I was going to get caught before I could even make a run for it. Quietly, I padded down the hallway to my room making it past my father's slightly ajar door.

I paused to listen.

The room was silent, maybe he wasn't even home and he'd gone to the bar. I prayed that was the case and I would be able to get out of this hell hole before he returned. Finally in my room, I snatched up my backpack and started to jam in the two shirts and one other pair of pants I owned. Lifting my mattress, I grabbed the two hundred dollars I'd managed to save over the past year, keeping the leftover change from buying beer.

"Where the fuck do you think you're going?" Father snarled from behind me.

I froze. The sound of his voice had my body locking up against my will, unable to convince it to do anything. There was a long deep intake of breath as father caught my newly acquired scent and was quickly followed up with a husky laugh. "Seems keeping you has finally become beneficial to me for once."

Ever so slowly I turned to face him, and the look on his face told me I wasn't going to leave this house, not on my own two feet that was.

"Did you think you could just run away and live out in the world on your own as a fucking *Omega*? How stupid could you be? Good thing I caught you before you threw away your life to the government without making me some kind of profit. All I have to do is wait for you to turn eighteen when your heat starts and I'll sell you off to the highest bidder. Finally, something is going my way and I'll be set for life."

Lunging forward, Father grabbed my throat and dragged me to him. His breath reeked of stale beer. "Don't worry, Cammy, I'm going to take such good care of you and make sure no one finds you until the time is right."

Sliding his hand to the back of my neck and fisting my hair, he dragged me after him. We came to the door of the basement. A whimper escaped my lips as I knew what awaited me down there. This was his favorite punishment, making me feel like I was nothing more than a worthless dog. He pulled the door open and tossed me carelessly down the stairs. Tumbling down the steep steps, I landed at the bottom on the hard, cold, concrete floor.

"Welcome to your new home, Cammy. I know how much you've enjoyed your days down here. I'm off to get some suppressants, can't have someone walking by the house and smelling you, or risking an early heat now can we? Wouldn't want you to be taken before I can get my profit out of you," Father informed me as he cackled to himself, slamming the door and locking it with the five deadbolts.

Listening to them each slide home sealing my fate took all the fight out of me. I didn't bother to get up off the floor and find the moldy mattress that was down here. What was the point? It's not like it would make any of this better. Instead, I curled around my backpack that I'd managed to hold on to and sobbed. I should have listened to Peggy. She was right, there were worse things than being at the whim of the government. Unfortunately, I'd made my choice. Now I had to live with it until I could escape—because mark my words, I would not be sold off and make that bastard any money. It would be my final revenge, but it would take careful planning.

CHAPTER 2

Cambrie

TWO YEARS LATER...

The sound of five deadbolts being unlocked woke me from my fitful sleep filled with strangers chasing after me with clawed hands. Although I couldn't say being awake was much different from the nightmares, in some ways it was worse, since I knew it was real. The lights flicked on, followed by the stomping of heavy feet as Father made his way down into the basement I'd been locked in since my sixteenth birthday.

"Do you know what day it is, Cammy?" he asked, his tone showing how pleased he was with himself.

He'd taken great delight in making sure I was fully aware of the countdown to my eighteenth birthday and how much money he would make. There was a bidding war between three Alphas, and he'd been holding the winner back until today—my birthday. I refused to answer him, using my silence as my only weapon, knowing he wanted me to beg and cry. Those first few months that's all I did, and the beatings never stopped. It drove him wild that no matter how badly he hurt me I didn't make a sound when I'd finally decided to wall off my emotions. The thrill was lost and he found other ways to punish me: by withholding food, leaving me in the dark, and finally, chaining me to the wall with only a ten foot radius to move. That also could have been because I'd managed to pick the old locks and almost got out of the house. For that, I got a broken leg and chained to the wall, he also replaced the locks with deadbolts that could only be opened from the outside.

"I'm going to bring you a bucket to wash in and a new dress for you to wear. We can't let your new owner see you look like a caged rat, now can we?" Father scoffed as he tossed me a bag. "We only have an hour before I need to take you to the meeting place so don't take too long, or I'll make your last moments with me the worst you've ever experienced," he warned, and sparked the taser he always kept with him after I bit off a chunk of his ear.

Going to the utility sink, he filled a bucket brought just close enough to me to reach and stepped back. While I was his captive, I'd learned how to get my jabs in when I could. I refused to let this break me. This was the moment I'd been plotting for since I knew what his plans were. If I wasn't going to draw attention to myself I needed to look clean, so I didn't fight this order. The water was tepid but at least it wasn't freezing like I thought it would be. I yanked off my oversized t-shirt and sweatpants that had been hanging off my body that wasn't much more than skin and bones.

I took the washcloth from the bag and got my skin wet before using the shower gel that was made specifically to remove all scents from my body, allowing my natural scent to be strongest. While I'd have to do something about my scent later, I just wanted to be clean at this point. Quickly, under the watchful eye of the bastard who calls himself my father, I cleaned my body and pulled on the loose flowing mustard yellow sundress with a floral pattern. Did it matter that it was the end of March and I'm sure to be far too cold to be wearing this? Of course not, because my father's goal was to make me look like the pure innocent Omega of any Alpha's dreams. Now that I was clothed, I washed my hair and dried it as much as I could with the towel that was little and riddled with holes. My blonde hair was now all the way down to my butt and with how wavy it was, I tended to keep it braided, so that's what I did now.

"Times up, let's go," Father ordered gruffly as he walked up with a pair of zip-ties he'd made into cuffs. "No funny business or I'll knock your ass out, and you'll wake up in your new home as someone else's problem."

That was something I couldn't let happen. If I was going to get away I needed to be awake the whole time. Even though it crushed my soul to let him bind my hands, I did, then he wrapped me up in a trench coat so no one could see my hands. He made sure the taser was ready as he unlocked my ankle cuff. I couldn't blame him, since this was how he'd lost the tip of his ear. I remained perfectly still as he tossed away the chain, grabbed my arm, and dragged me up the basement stairs. We had an old beat-up sedan he shoved me carelessly into the back seat of. This was what I'd prayed would happen, that he wouldn't put me in the front seat next to him. He pulled out of the drive and headed down the street like all was right with the world and he wasn't about to sell his daughter off.

"Would you like to know who bought you?" he asked, looking at me in the rearview mirror. "I'll only tell you if you ask nicely."

Fucker knew I wasn't going to say a damn word to him, but it gave him the joy of leaving me in the dark.

"He's a very powerful man who will be able to give you a life you never dreamed of, but they say his tastes in the bedroom tend to be too much for most people. So what if the man likes to cut his women up? I'm not one to judge what gets a man off if he's willing to pay a million dollars for it," Father rambled.

Tuning him out, I let him believe he was scaring me with all this information on how twisted the man was, while I listened to the road sounds. I needed us to get on the highway so my plan could work. If we stuck to city streets it'd be too easy for him to pull over and catch me. I needed to use the fact he was on the highway and the flow of traffic to keep him from coming after me. Living trapped and starved in a basement for two years left me with little stamina, even though I did what I could to keep from getting too weak. Basic exercises could only get you so far when you had no cardio to build endurance.

YES! I felt the car speed up and the roar of traffic around us got louder. Now the trick was getting out of the damn car alive once I hit the road. I needed him to stay in the right lane, and with this

POS I felt like that was a safe bet. Last I knew, this damn thing couldn't go over sixty without making your teeth rattle. The car fell silent as Father got bored trying to get me to talk. I tried to keep as still as possible so he had no inkling of what I was planning. I didn't know where we were going but one of the few reasons you took the highway was to get to the city. If this person was as rich as Father was making him out to be, then he would live near the heart of the city.

When I felt the car slowing, I risked peeking out the window and saw it was just some traffic merging onto the highway. It was the perfect time for me to make a run for it, we were slow and I was near an off ramp, providing an escape to disappear. Taking a deep breath and psyching myself up I hooked my barefoot on the door handle and pulled. The lock on that door had been broken for years and I knew Father wouldn't remember since he never sat back here. The door released with a snick. Pulling my legs up to my chest I propelled myself forward, crashed into the door, popping it open, and dumped me onto the road. I rolled a few feet, the sound of screeching tires, and horns filled the air as I came to a stop. Turning so I was on my stomach, I scrambled to my feet and ran without looking back. We'd gotten further down the highway than I'd expected and I could see the towering building of the city not far away.

This just meant I had even more places to hide in the swarms of people packed into these city neighborhoods. My feet slapped on the asphalt as I ran, flinching as the gravel and other debris cut into my feet but that pain was nothing compared to what I would suffer if I got caught by my father. I was ruining all his chances of getting out of the shitty life we'd lived in since Mother died. Once upon a time, I'd thought about finding out who my grandparents were, to see if they would take me in. Though that would be hard having never met them, they'd disowned Mother when she chose to be with Father. Can't say I blame them, but it made me think I wouldn't be welcome if I came knocking on their door.

So, with two years to sift through all possible outcomes and no other options left, here I was running barefoot down an on-ramp as people gawked at me. Making it off the ramp, I found myself on a busy road in an area I knew nothing about. Trusting my gut, I turned left heading closer to the city proper, figuring there was a better chance at a shelter or something similar. Luckily, from the basement I'd been able to hear the TV Father had blaring as he slept in front of it most nights.

Last year a new official, Marius Stone, was elected to the Council of Four. Official Marius was big on helping those less fortunate and providing a helping hand to get them on their feet. Everyone was saying he was a man of the people and his win had been a landslide, blowing away his competition. People wanted change, they craved hope that their world could get better, and Official Marius was fighting to do just that. His plan so far was free shelters for the homeless, that provided a meal and a place to sleep. Apparently, someone in his pack had been running a successful shelter somewhere in the city, proving it could be done. Knowing they existed helped give me direction, making it my one and only goal to find a shelter and make it through the night. If I could do it once that meant I could keep doing it.

Feeling I was far enough away from the highway to pause a moment, I ducked down an alley. Leaning against a building's brick wall I tried to calm my heart, which felt like it was going to burst out of my chest at any moment. My wrists throbbed where the bindings bit into my skin, reminding me I needed to get them off before leaving this alley. Looking around the space, I found a fire escape ladder with a broken rung that I could use to break the plastic zip-ties. Using my entire meager body weight, I begged for them to snap, and just when I didn't think they would, I fell to the ground in a heap.

"Yes!" I cried out in joy, rubbing my wrists to get the circulation back into them.

Now that I was fully mobile, I pulled on the trench coat properly, wrapping it tightly around me, then secured the tie trying to trap as much body heat as possible. The summer dress wasn't what I would have picked for this mission but it was what I had and far better than the nasty clothes I'd been wearing for months. My next plan needed to be finding something to wrap my feet up in and the location of one of those shelters. The last thing I needed was to get an infection and die before I could even get away.

If I couldn't find something before getting to the shelter, I prayed they might have something I could use, even if it was a pair of cheap ass flip-flops. Turning up the collar and hunching my shoulders, I walked out the opposite side of the alley just to be safe and headed deeper into the city. The sun was still high in the sky giving me hope I should be able to manage it before it got dark.

CHAPTER 3

Cambrie

Having never spent time in the city before, it was a lot to take in. The sounds of honking cars filled the air, people bustled to and fro keeping their heads down on a mission, or talking on their phones, ignoring everyone around them. I had no idea what day it was or even the date, only knowing it was close to my birthday. Thankfully, I passed by a bank where a sign was hanging from the building that gave the time as early afternoon, on a Friday, and the date turned out to be a week after my birthday. There was something oddly empowering being armed with knowledge, no longer was I in the dark, kept hidden from the world. While I was free-ish, I still needed to be sure I didn't draw any attention, landing myself in a new kind of trouble.

As I wandered, I noticed an older man stacking magazines at his newsstand. I paused to watch him for a bit weighing the risks of asking him for help. As others passed him, he didn't really bother to look up, keeping to his task, minding his own business. The newsstand looked like it had been there for a long time, and my hope was he knew where the shelter might be.

Taking a deep breath, I steeled myself to interact with this stranger, praying it was worth the risk of him scenting me. As long as he didn't get too close or touch me I felt I could manage to ask my question and be on my way with him none the wiser.

"Excuse me," I called, leaving a good two feet between us.

He didn't look up and kept doing his task as if he hadn't heard me. Hesitantly I took a step forward, and he caught sight of the movement and met my gaze.

"Hello there, young lady." He smiled. "Did you need something? You'll have to forgive me and speak up, my hearing isn't what it once was."

I could have hugged him for asking. Now I was freed from having to make the first move. "Yes," I started, then cleared my throat when he cupped his ear and spoke louder. "I'm looking for a specific homeless shelter. The one they talk about on the news run by Official Marius's pack."

The man slowly straightened and took a good look at me. I'm sure some of the bruises my father had given me showed on my face since that was the only place the coat didn't hide. While I might look a weakling in this man's eyes, I wouldn't be ashamed of what I'd survived to get to this point.

"Now why would you need to find a place like that?" he questioned, his brows furrowed. "Looks to me like you need to go to the police instead of a shelter. Who's been hitting you? Your old man or a boyfriend? They have laws against that nowadays, and they can help you find a safe place to stay."

While I knew he was right and I should go to the police and tell them about my father and what he had planned to do with me, I just couldn't risk them not believing me and sending me back to him. While Father might be a drunk, he also had this magical ability to get people to like him. It's how he managed to keep his job all these years when they absolutely should have fired him.

"Thank you, but I really am just looking for the shelter," I answered with a shake of my head, my hand fisting around the coat's collar.

Everything in me told me to run now that this man brought up going to the police. What if he turned me in? Then they'd find out I was an Omega and place me in the Omega Preservation Project more commonly called, Care Centers. Doing that would make me an easy target if my father had been telling the truth about this man who wanted to buy me being powerful. Once in the system it would make it all that much easier for him to get to me, and my guess is it would be cheaper too.

The man grumbled something to himself and shuffled off into his stand leaving me standing there utterly confused.

Just as I was about to leave and continue my search, he returned with a flier, thrusting it at me, along with a few other things. "Here is some change for a pay phone, call this number, and they will pick you up and bring you to the shelter. It's not safe for you to be wandering around the city alone and dressed the way you are. I can't help with the shoes but I always keep a pair of extra wool socks for days it rains. It's not much, but it will give you some protection and keep them from catching frostbite."

Stuffing the flier and the change into a pocket, I slipped on the socks relishing the warmth they provided, instantly helping me feel better. "Thank you, this is more than you needed to do and I'll be forever grateful."

"None of that now, people need to look after each other in this world," he said, waving off my thanks. "I'll call us even if you promise me one thing. Don't ever go back to whoever you got away from, no matter what they say. Bastards like that will never change. You're a pretty little thing. I'm sure you'll do alright for yourself if you just keep looking forward."

I couldn't help but smile at this old man worrying over me as if I was his granddaughter. "I promise there's no going back for me, only forward." I turned to leave but paused and looked over my shoulder. "I'm Cambrie by the way. One of these days, I'll come back and let you know how things turned out."

"I like the sound of that, Cambrie, but if you ever need a reminder about what I said, old Charlie will be here to give it," he grunted, shooing me away.

Now that I had the information I needed, locating a payphone was my next goal. It took me a few blocks to find one that worked and then I had to figure out how to use it. With cell phones being the norm, payphones were going to be a thing of the past. Thankfully, there were still some around or I'm not sure what my next plan would be. Inserting the change like it told me to, I waited for the dial tone and typed in the number.

"Open Arms Shelter and Resource Center, this is Clara," a chipper woman answered.

"Ah, hello... I... um..." I started suddenly unsure of what to even say.

"It's alright sweety, take your time. I'm not in a hurry. What's your name? Do you need help?" Clara asked, her tone patient and sincere.

"I'm Cambrie. The old man, Charlie, at the newspaper stand told me you could come pick me up? I... I don't have anywhere to go tonight," I shared as I clenched my free hand into a fist, my nails digging into the flesh of my palm, irritated at myself for sounding so weak.

"He was right, we most certainly can come to pick you up. Can you tell me where you are now? If you're not sure, then I'll take whatever cross streets you see," Clara instructed.

I looked around and I couldn't see any street signs where I stood, I'd have to set the phone down and walk down the street to the intersections. None of the buildings were helpful either with a business name I could give her. "I need to put the phone down to look, will you wait?"

"Of course, Cambrie, I'll stay on the line," she assured me.

Setting the phone down on the metal shelf I darted out of the little box and hurried to the intersection. I took a good look around to see if there was a good spot to meet up in eyesight but it seemed I was in a part of the city with only skyscrapers and large amounts of traffic flying by.

Hurrying back to the phone, my breathing labored from all the running, I gasped out my answer. "Fifth Avenue and Kenzington, I tried to look for a landmark but it's just tall buildings all around."

"That's alright, looks like you're in the financial district," Clara said as I heard her typing. "Well, what do you know, I have one of our staff in a meeting down that way who can pick you up sooner than we could get the van to you. Now normally we don't do this since we like to make sure you feel safe and the van is clearly marked with our name on it. It's up to you, we can have someone to you in ten minutes or it could take a half hour for the van to arrive."

Looking up at the sky, I couldn't see if the sun was on its way down since it was already hidden by the skyscrapers. The suppressants I'd been taking while trapped in the basement wouldn't last much longer since Father didn't give me another this morning. If I started to perfume out here in the open before finding more I was fucked.

"Is it a man or a woman that's already out here?" I asked as I chewed on my thumbnail.

"It would be a man, an Alpha, his name is Nixon. He's actually the man who founded this rescue and runs it with his Beta partner, Spencer. I know you don't know me from a hill of beans but I wouldn't have suggested he come get you if it wasn't safe. Being on the streets at night for a young lady is not something I would wish on anyone," Clara cautioned.

"Okay..." I whispered. "He can pick me up."

"That's a smart choice, Cambrie, I'll have someone give Nixon a call. What I want you to do is not to move from that spot, do you hear me?" Clara asked, her voice brokering no argument. "I've found the payphone you are calling from and sent him that location. He has a black sedan and his license plate is A-five-eight-B-nine-three-two. Nixon will get out of the car and introduce himself. Then he will ask you if you like classical music. Now what response should I tell him you will give so we ensure he's picking up the right person?"

"I've never listened to classical before, so I don't know if I like it or not," I answered truthfully.

Clara gave a hum of approval. "That will work perfectly. We'd do this same procedure even if we sent the marked van to pick you up. With all that's going on in the world you can never be too careful. He has all the information and should be leaving shortly. Do you want me to stay on the line with you? I'm more than happy to."

"Thank you, but I don't want to take up your time if someone else calls in," I answered, even though deep down I wanted her to keep talking to me. Her voice was soothing, and she reminded me of Peggy from the library.

"Don't you worry about that. We have five people here whose job it is to answer the phone for situations just like yours," Clara chided. "Now Cambrie, do you mind if I ask how old you are? We like to keep some records on file here at the shelter since we also offer many resources for getting people back on their feet."

Did it matter if she knew how old I was? I'd already given her my name, if they wanted a last name, I would just make something up so they couldn't connect me to my father.

"Eighteen, I just had a birthday," I shared.

"Well happy belated birthday! The big one eight, that's a major deal you know. Did you already graduate from high school or is that happening this year?"

My mouth went dry at this question, I'd been so close to completing my GED, but my father took that from me as well. Now here I was an eighteen year old woman who didn't have anything to show for herself.

"No, I haven't graduated," I answered, not giving her more details.

"That's not a problem, I'm sure we can figure something out to help with that. It's not the first time we've come across this," Clara commented as she typed down more information. "Now, I know you said you don't have any place to go tonight but what about tomorrow? We can help you reach out to other family or friends if you need us to. Now that you are eighteen it gives you the freedom to choose what you want to have happen in your life."

"I just need a place to stay tonight that is safe so I can sort out my next move. I appreciate the offer, but I think I can manage on my own," I countered, not ready to trust they wouldn't just lock me up when they found out I was an Omega.

The fact that the suppressants were still working was a miracle, and I didn't know how much longer that would last. I knew some Betas took them to keep their designation to themselves or if they worked in risky jobs where they couldn't risk going into heat. What

I didn't know was if they would just give them to me if I asked or if a doctor had to give them. Father bought them off a dealer but I didn't have any money to go that route.

"Okay Cambrie, we'll come back to that question later," Clara murmured, clearly not liking my answer. "Alright, Nixon should be with you in just a minute or two, so I'll let you go. When you get to the shelter I'll meet you at the front and we'll get you settled. Sound good?"

"Yes... thank you, Clara," I whispered before hanging up, not waiting for her reply.

CHAPTER 4

Nixon

"Josh, come on, we've been friends since college. I know you can do better than that. Our existing shelters run fully off donations and help from government assistance. We need a loan this time because our newest shelter will have to be built from the ground up," I argued. "Having that high of an interest rate is ridiculous, not to mention you want it paid back in ten years."

"We both know if you wanted to you could pay for the building out of your own pocket and use it as a write off," Josh argued. "You want the loan to prove to the government you need the assistance when you don't. Banks aren't as willing to extend to non-profits as they once were, with how many have gone bankrupt and shut down. If you wanted to ask for the loan under your personal name, then I can give you a much better deal."

I raked my hands through my hair trying to keep my irritation from showing. "Everyone knows the CoF is doing a huge push for these shelters to be in place and we are the example for the others to follow. If you won't give me the loan, what will you do when one of them walks in here?"

"Nixon, first of all, they won't come to this bank. We wouldn't let them in the door, seeing as we only work with clients in a certain income bracket. If you want to be the everyday man on this, then you need to try with another bank or take the loan out personally," Josh answered, shrugging his shoulders. "To be honest, I shouldn't have taken this meeting, knowing you were going to ask for this, but the partners thought it was only fair to explain this to you in person."

No longer able to fight against my Alpha nature, I snarled at the Beta across from me. "Next time, do us both a favor and just tell me over the phone. It's clear I've wasted both our time so I'll take my leave," I got to my feet, fixed my suit jacket, and headed for the door. Reaching for the door handle I paused and looked back. "Let the partners know if they are unwilling to help Marius and myself in this project, then we might need to find another bank to do all our dealings with."

I caught a glimpse of Josh's stricken face as he sat behind his desk, my threat doing exactly what I'd hoped it would. Marius and I have worked for years to make this dream come true, first with our shelters, and then with him getting elected to the Council of Four. These were the steppingstones to helping our people find balance again.

After the attack by the terrorist group known as Equality for Betas or EQ, killing thousands of Omega mothers and babies in one fell swoop with a massive batch of a tainted serum, our country was left reeling. The terrorists believed Alphas and Omegas were treated far superior to Betas, given more privileges and cared for more lavishly. In removing Omegas, they hoped to create more reliance on Betas since now Omegas were so rare.

What we found out from this catastrophic attack was that Omegas were so much more than breeders. In doing what they did, the once common practice of having a bonded pack was fading out of existence. It was no longer feasible for Alphas to bond with their Beta partners since an Omega was required to be part of their pack. This, of course, didn't stop people from taking Beta partners but the pack dynamic was lost and became something far less common.

The vibration from my phone in my pocket snapped me out of that train of thought back to what was happening around me. I found myself standing in front of the elevator, having yet to push the button to go down. Looking at the screen, I saw it was Spencer, my Beta and manager of our flagship shelter.

"Hey, what's up?" I answered. He'd known I would be in and out of meetings so this must be important.

"Look I know today is crazy for you, but we have a situation," Spencer explained. "There's a young girl who called in asking for a pickup. It would take the van a half hour or more with evening rush hour to get to her. You are only ten minutes or less to her location. I was listening in on the call with Clara, and I think we need to get to her sooner. She agreed if you were available to get her."

"Spence...," I hesitated, rubbing my forehead trying to decide what to do. "The meeting with Purity Holdings didn't go well and I lost my temper, threatening to pull all our money from them. In twenty minutes I have a meeting with the zoning commissioner on permits for breaking ground."

"And? I'm telling you, Nixon, I wouldn't have made this call if I didn't think we needed to get to this girl. Something in my gut as I listened to her tells me leaving her alone for much longer is going to be trouble. I'm sure Marius could talk to the commissioner and smooth things over about canceling at the last minute. If we can't use our connection to an Official that shares our bed, then what's the point?" Spencer teased.

Groaning, I knew he was right. "Okay fine, where am I going? Also, you're the one who gets to tell Marius why he's sucking up to the commissioner."

"He better not be sucking anyone but me!" Spencer said indignantly.

"Spence," I answered with a warning growl.

He let out a heavy sigh. "You can be so serious sometimes, Nixie. Learn to laugh a little or you'll have wrinkles making you look far older than you really are." I growled louder, reminding him to get to the point. "Right, so Clara already sent you the information. She's staying on the line with Cambrie, that's her name by the way, until you get there. Her answer to the question is also in the message."

"Thank you, Spencer," I said sarcastically, shaking my head at the antics my Beta got up to.

He was right though, Marius and I were both driven, goal focused, and didn't take much time to smell the roses. Maybe that's why we both fell for the fun-loving Beta who wreaked havoc on our perfectly planned lives the past five years.

"Love you, see you both when you get here," Spencer chirped before hanging up.

Pulling up my email, I found the information Clara had sent me and was shocked to see she was indeed just down the street. It would take me longer to get to the garage and into my car than to arrive at her location. Another email pinged giving me the intake questions. The poor thing was only eighteen. I tried to remember back twelve years ago when I was first starting college with Marius. The biggest struggle we had was that Oscar, another Alpha in our pack, was going to a different school after we'd become family during our six years together at boarding school.

Sliding into my car, I hit the start button causing it to purr to life. The classical music I'd been listening to filled the space, making me smile. It would seem if her answer were truthful about never hearing it before I would cross that off her list in the first few moments of our meeting. Pulling onto the road, I had to double back a few streets with all the one-way roads but soon enough I pulled up to the given location.

I put the car in park, made sure the doors were unlocked and got out. When I spotted her over the top of my car, my Alpha instincts were on high alert. Clothed only in an oversized trench coat, blonde hair mussed with wisps blowing around her face as she hunched against the cold with no shoes, only socks, was the girl I was sent to pick up. Large azure-colored eyes met mine for a moment before falling to the ground. The color was made brighter by the bruises on her sunken face, making me snarl. I couldn't catch a clear scent to pick up on her designation, but my guess was she was a Beta. Outrage flared inside me at the mistreatment of this girl and I wanted nothing more than to scoop her up and protect her.

Knowing I couldn't approach her until my anger was under

control, I took a few deep breaths and unclenched my fists, then approached. "Hello Cambrie, my name is Nixon. Clara said you were looking for a ride to the shelter for the night. Do you like classical music? It's what I've got playing right now, but I can change it if you'd like?"

As I spoke, her body hunched, trying to make herself an even smaller target. She shuffled on her sock covered feet, almost as if she was thinking of running. "I don't know..." she whispered. "I've never listened to it before."

I offered her a gentle smile and cocked my head to the side trying to pick up anything off her, but still got nothing. "Alright, I'll leave it and you can tell me whether or not you like it. How does that sound?" I asked as I pulled open the door to the backseat and stepped away so she didn't feel crowded.

Cambrie chewed on her bottom lip which was still full despite how skinny she was. Gripping her jacket tighter around herself she took one tentative step forward. "Can you open the window? I—I need to know I have a way to get out if I need to."

My heart shattered at her request. What had this poor thing been through to even have to consider leaping out of a car through the window to get away? Her hands had scuff marks on them as did her chin, which looked fresh. Could it be that something similar had already happened?

"If that will make you feel more comfortable, I can do that. I'll make sure to crank up the heat so you stay warm as well," I offered as I stepped back to the door and rolled down the window. I wanted to prove to her that nothing was blocking her.

Trusting my gut, I walked around the back of the car and got into the driver's seat. Cambrie needed to know this was her choice and I wasn't going to force her to come with me if she wasn't comfortable. Fiddling with the heat, making sure it was blasting and that most of it was directed to the back kept me from watching her every move.

Everything in me cried out that I shouldn't take her to the shelter, but right to our home where we could keep her safe. Of course, that would only backfire, she'd been told I'd take her to the shelter and that's what I *should* do to prove I'm a man of my word. I glanced in her direction and found her peering into the car taking in the situation like there might be something hiding, waiting to snatch her.

Grabbing my phone off the holder in my car I sent a message to Spencer. He'd been right to make sure I was the one to get her. While I trusted all the people that worked for us I wasn't convinced they would have had the patience needed for someone like her.

ME:

Make sure one of the private rooms in the back is ready for Cambrie. She can't be put in the community space.

SPENCER:

I thought it might be bad. I'll get right on that. She with you now?

ME:

We're still working on getting in the car. Think abused animal situation. I'm letting her come to me when she's ready.

SPENCER:

The whisper of fabric on leather told me she'd finally made a move to enter the car. Peering into the rearview mirror I found her tugging the door shut. Reaching for the door exposed more of her arms and they were covered in new and old marks. Once the door was closed, she balled up against the door clinging to the windowsill.

"Cambrie, before we get moving would you mind putting on your seatbelt?" I requested. "I'm an excellent driver, never been in an accident, but I don't ever want to put you at risk of getting hurt. It seems to me you've suffered enough for one lifetime."

Her gaze flicked up to meet mine for a moment, surprise was present in her eyes before they dropped once more. While I couldn't scent her, she definitely wasn't an Alpha, but anyone that was abused would come across as weak. It took her a few moments but she did as I asked when I didn't move to drive. Now that she was safe in my care, I pulled out into traffic and headed toward the shelter. The ride was silent except for the music but I didn't feel it was the best move to push her to talk. Reaching out and asking for help, getting into my car, and trusting I would take her where I promised was enough. Tonight, I'd talk to Rafael about meeting with her, knowing without a doubt she was going to need therapy. No, she needed more than just therapy. She needed a pack.

While packs had become less common, when I thought about doing life without mine, I couldn't imagine it. Marius, Oscar, and I had known each other the longest, growing up together. Then when Marius and I both fell for Spencer, it made sense for us to become a unit. Oscar came to us after college when his family refused to claim him as their child. He'd suffered an illness that destroyed his vocal cords and left him mute. The thing about Oscar was he made up for it in so many ways as a talented musician. His family was old money and they'd hoped to use their son to climb the political ladder but what good was a son who can't speak?

We had no problems claiming our childhood friend as part of our pack. Oscar was one of the kindest souls known to man, and while some see that as weakness in an Alpha, we knew it was a testament to his strength. To be that kind and selfless when you've been abandoned and ostracized took far more character if you ask me.

Rafael, the final Alpha in our pack, came as a surprise, but when you click with someone and they fit into your family so seamlessly, it's hard to ignore it. A renowned therapist, who had his own practice that was sought after by the elite in this world, shut it all down to come work with us. His long-time partner, a female Beta, died in a tragic accident, leaving Rafael to take stock of his life. When he approached working with us full time, traveling between the shelters, helping people get their lives back, we thought he was joking. Having lost the love of his life, he wanted to do something she would be proud of.

Him coming alongside us and working with the people who

come into our shelters had been monumental. It changed the way everyone perceives the shelter and now we could also refer to it as a resource center. We now focused on helping those who entered our doors to one day never have to come back ever again. Most governments see it as a waste of money, but we've made it our mission to prove it can be so much more.

One of the patients Rafael helped in an odd set of circumstances has become the last and newest member of our pack—Bodhi. He is the picture-perfect representation of an angry abandoned boy, with such a warm heart that he's locked away. Bodhi is beyond gifted in musical talent and his voice is one that hits you right in your soul. The music he writes and sings makes you question everything as he pours all his hurt into it. Rafael thought Oscar would be a perfect influence and would bring him over to work with him.

Then one day, he just never left, having been adopted by us all. Bodhi and Oscar became best friends, they were exactly what they each needed. While Spencer is convinced they might one day be something more, I believe if it's meant to happen, it will. For now, I'm just happy to see how our entire pack was built on the fact that we all needed each other. Marius always wanted to run for a place in the CoF and I believe seeing what a healthy pack can do in the world kept him working toward it. Having a career in politics is never fun and they always try to find a way to destroy you from the inside out, but our pack had been through so much they didn't have anything left to scare us with.

I let out a sigh as I saw the massive Open Arms sign at the entrance to the warehouse sized building. Glancing back, I found Cambrie still curled up but at some point she'd drifted off to sleep. Her face looked so innocent and young, full of unlived life. My anger flared and I gripped the steering wheel so tight my knuckles turned white. How could someone do something like this? My money was on it being a parent since she'd just turned eighteen. Well, now that she was in my care, there wasn't a chance in hell I would ever let them get their fucking hands on her again.

I pulled into my reserved spot right up front and shut the car off. I sent a message to Spencer letting him know we were here, then shifted in my seat to face Cambrie. "Cambrie," I called softly. "We're here."

At the sound of my voice she woke with a gasp and started to thrash against the seatbelt. Panic was written all over her face as she clawed at the restraint, desperately trying to get out of the car. Not wanting her to get hurt in the struggle, I reached back and hit the button releasing the seatbelt. Seconds later she was out the window crashing into Spencer.

"Let me go. I won't let them take me!" she screamed. "Don't make me go back!"

Scrambling out of the car, I looked at my Beta's panicked face as she fought against his hold. Clara hurried over, motioning for Spencer to let her go.

"Cambrie, it's Clara. Open your eyes for me, sweet girl, you're safe. Whoever had you isn't here," she murmured, stroking Cambrie's back as she clung to her. "I need you to look at me, you're having a panic attack. Tell me what you see around you. It can be anything, colors, shapes, words, something to help your brain understand you're not where it thinks you are."

Cambrie gasped for air as she tried to do as Clara requested. "I'm outside," she managed to blurt out.

"Good, what else?" Clara pressed.

"You, you smell like apple pie and sunshine," Cambrie mumbled as she hid her face in Clara's shoulder. "Please, you can't let my father find me. I got away. I finally got away."

"Cambrie, I vow to you we won't ever let your father touch you again," Clara promised, her voice hard with conviction as she met my gaze.

While Clara was a Beta by designation, when it came to protecting those who had been abused like she had once been, she could have easily been mistaken for an Alpha.

"Come on sweet girl, let's get you inside where we can clean you up and get you in something warmer. It's far too cold to be wearing something so thin, and where are your shoes?" Clara rambled as she led the girl inside.

Spencer came to stand beside me, taking my hand and gripping it tightly. "Please tell me you're willing to do whatever it takes to make her feel safe in this world again."

"If I didn't think it would do more damage to have taken her to our home instead of the shelter, I would have," I shared, leaning in to kiss him on the temple. "It's going to take the right people to help her, Spence, but something in my soul tells me our pack can do it."

Spencer rested his forehead on mine. "I think you're right, somehow we were meant to be the ones to find her. Let's just hope she agrees, because this is going to be a long road."

"All the best things in life are worth working for," I agreed, pressing a kiss to his lips. "Come on, let's go call Rafael. We're absolutely gonna need his help."

CHAPTER 5

Cambrie

Being wrapped up in Clara's sweet, soothing, apple pie scent helped keep me from falling back into my panic. Waking up to find myself trapped in a car with an Alpha I didn't know, who had the strong scent of sweet tobacco and scotch, made me panic. Half asleep, I didn't remember I'd gotten away from my father and chosen to be in that car. No, my brain believed I was being taken away by the man who'd bought me and would hurt me worse than my father ever had.

Inside the shelter, I was greeted with a large open area filled with people sitting on couches reading, playing games at tables, or working on computers along one wall. It reminded me of the library in a way, a safe place to spend time. There was a large counter with three people working. They waved to Clara, giving me warm smiles as they buzzed us in through a set of double doors.

I dug my heels in and fought against Clara's hold. "No, I won't be locked away again! You can't keep me here against my will!" I screamed, my voice echoed through the quiet space.

"Cambrie, we are not trying to lock you away. The sleeping rooms are back here and we keep them locked to ensure no one can break in and steal people back. We do this so whoever hurt you can't get to you. Anyone can come out of those doors at any time, day or night. We just want to make sure we know who goes back there," Clara explained, holding my shoulders and forcing me to look at her. "I don't know what's happened to you, and clearly it's been hell, but *we* are here to do all we can to keep you safe. You are now eighteen Cambrie, which means no one but you can dictate what happens to you from this day forward."

My whole body shook and I kept looking around trying to find a way out. All I saw were faces of people in shabby clothes looking at me with pity and understanding. Then I heard someone behind me, and I caught a whiff of spicy sandalwood and hints of vanilla. I knew by that scent this person was an Alpha. The last thing I wanted was, for him to be at my back. Right now between Clara and this unknown man, Clara was the safer option.

Spinning on my heel, I broke Clara's hold on me, I was now faced with an older distinguished gentleman. His hair was short and neat, dark brown with white coming in at his temples and moving further back. Wrinkles that only came from someone who smiled more often than not accented his face and framed his blue-gray eyes. He wore a pair of horn-rimmed glasses making him appear to be highly intelligent. His face was clean shaven and with the untucked button-down shirt and high end jeans it gave him a more relaxed look.

"Hello there," he greeted with a smile that made it all the way to his eyes. "I'm Rafael, I work here at the shelter with Clara."

The fact that he wasn't doing anything but standing here, relaxed, with his hands in his pockets smiling at me seemed to settle me. Nothing gave me any indication that he was going to try and grab me or force me to do something. He was simply greeting me as a newcomer to the shelter.

"Hello…" I managed, my hands still shaking as the adrenalin drained my body.

Rafael's smile grew wider at the sound of my voice. "Welcome to Open Arms…" he started to say, letting the sentence drift off, and I realized he was looking for my name.

"Cambrie, that's my name," I offered.

"A lovely name at that, it is nice to meet you Cambrie, and we are all happy to have you here. I believe that Clara and Spencer prepared a room for you. They felt it might be best to have one to yourself, but we do have a group room where all our guests can sleep communally. This means men, women, and children all share a larger room full of cots with lockers to keep their things in," he explained. "Now, out of those two options which would make you feel more comfortable?"

Chewing on my lower lip, I thought about that for a moment. While I didn't think either option would keep them from holding me against my will, the fact they were offering helped prove it wasn't their goal. At first, I was going to say the common room, then others would be able to see if they did something fishy, but I had no idea when my scent might come back.

"I think a room to myself might be better," I answered.

"Great," Rafael said, clapping his hands together as he headed for the double doors. "Now I'm going to hand over my access key to Kyle here, and he's going to let me in. Then I'm going to come back out again just to make sure you feel confident you can leave whenever you want to. You can even do it yourself once or twice if that will help."

The man did just as he said, handing over his card and getting buzzed in. Once the doors locked there was a moment or two before one of them swung open and the click of a release bar from the inside sounded. Then Rafael walked out and gathered his key card.

"What do you think Cambrie, you alright to head back? There is no rush at all," Clara murmured from where she stood next to me.

I nodded and walked up to the doors. Neither Rafael nor Clara reached for the door as the buzzer went off letting me do it myself. Yanking the door open, I looked over my shoulder and found Nixon standing next to another man, watching as I entered. Nixon gave me a smile and a nod of encouragement almost as if to show he wasn't upset with me for leaping out of his car. Turning forward, I walked down the hall until it came to a T.

"If you go to the right that is the common sleeping room and the single rooms are beyond that. To the left is the cafeteria where we serve breakfast and dinner for everyone staying with us," Clara shared as she stepped ahead of me leading us toward the right. "After we check out a room, if you're hungry we can talk about how you want to approach dinner. Typically, we have everyone eat at the same time. It's one of our rules, you have to be here by the time we check everyone in for dinner if you plan to stay the night. We do another wave of meals, but those are served outside in the pavilion for those who are just in need of food."

Hearing Clara chatter about things made me relax slightly as we passed through a giant room with rows of simple, clean cots ready for use. At one end there were rows of lockers for people to keep their things in just as they'd told me. Entering into another hall there were doors with small windows in them showing simple rooms with a bed, nightstand, and locker for personal things. They led me to the end of the hall where the door was ajar and the light was on as if it was waiting for me.

"This is the room we got ready for you if you choose to take it," Clara shared.

When I stepped in to look at the space I was struck by how cold and impersonal it was, but this wasn't a place for people to stay long term. The hope was they could move one to someplace more permanent. I caught the lingering scent of something almost tropical with coconut and bright hints of lime. My brain told me I'd smelled it somewhere else recently. Then I remembered leaping out of the car and smacking into someone with this same scent. He was a Beta that came out with Clara and caught me.

Shame bloomed in my chest with how I reacted to him helping me. He'd only been making sure I didn't get hurt and I'd lashed out at him. It made me wonder if there would ever be a point when men didn't scare me so badly. Right now, things were so much worse, as it'd been two years since I'd interacted with people outside of my father.

Walking to the bed, I took a seat and it sank under my slight weight revealing just how soft it was. Smoothing my hand over the clean white sheets I couldn't help but smile thinking how such a simple thing could bring me so much joy.

"Cambrie, can I leave Rafael here with you while I get you some warm clothes?" Clara asked, making me jump as she reminded me that there were still people in the room with me.

Looking over, I saw he was leaning on the door frame and wasn't trying to enter the room so I nodded in agreement.

"Alright sweet girl, did you have any preference for what kind of clothes you'd like? Are you more of a jeans and t-shirt girl or would you like something more feminine, since I see you're wearing a dress," she inquired.

My instant reaction was to wrinkle my nose at that last suggestion, which made Clara chuckle. "No," I answered. "Jeans and a t-shirt would be fine. I'm not really that picky."

"Do you have a favorite color?"

"Teal, or any shade similar," I said with a smile, looking down at my dirty, scuffed up hands. "Is there a place to clean up a little?"

Clara hesitated a moment looking at Rafael but he waved her off. "I'm sure Cambrie and I will be able to manage without you for a few moments."

She gave me one last look with a teasing wink and left to find me clothes. Rafael came into the room, took a seat in a folding chair near the door, and crossed his legs before settling his hands in his lap.

"Do you mind if I ask you a few questions, Cambrie? If you don't feel comfortable answering them you can tell me and I will leave it alone, sound okay to you?" he asked.

Everything about him was soothing, the sound of his voice, his scent, even the way he carried himself. Nothing about him gave you the impression he would ever be a threat to you. After needing to protect myself from a predator all my life, I felt I became a good judge of reading people. So far, Rafael hadn't given me any reason to doubt his words.

"Can I ask some?" I ventured, proud of myself for asserting a request.

"I would rather enjoy that if you did, Cambrie. Feel free to ask me anything," he answered, a smile tugging at his lips. "Would you like to go first?"

I thought about that for a moment, then shook my head. What I wanted to know was about the suppressors, but I felt like it would be better if I got to know him a little better. I didn't know the rules on things like that, and I didn't want to upset him right away.

"Very well, then I'll start off with something simple. I know now that teal is your favorite color, what about your favorite kind of music?"

Why was everyone so interested in what music I liked?

"I don't really have a favorite," I answered simply.

"Is that because you like all music or could it be that you haven't gotten a chance to find a favorite?" Rafael inquired.

That made me scowl as I thought about his question. Did I like all music? No, I didn't like the stuff blasting out of our neighbor's house that was all yelling and angry. When I was in the grocery stores they played some music I enjoyed, but I didn't know what type of music it was. Father never let us have a radio, saying that music always reminded him of Mother. She loved country music and used to sing it all the time doing chores around the house.

"After Mom died, I wasn't allowed to listen to music. I'd hear songs around town or in stores that I liked, but I didn't really pay attention," I offered.

"I'm sorry to hear your mother died. Was that recent?"

"No." I shook my head. "That happened ten years ago, everything changed from that point on." I looked up to meet his gentle blue-gray eyes that seemed to see into my soul. "My father became so angry at everything and took it out on me every chance he could. It was almost as if he thought it was my fault that she died, so he took everything away from me. Then, when I tried to get away after my designation came in, he locked me away for good."

Rafael sat up a little straighter at this information, his eyes narrowing. "What is your designation, Cambrie?"

Tears welled up in my eyes. "If I tell you, will you help me? Please, please don't send me away. I can't let him find me, or the evil bastard who was going to buy me." The more I spoke, the faster the tears came pouring out of me. "All I want is to be free to live a life of my own. I've never been free."

Rafael slid to his knees and crawled over to me slowly, making sure I was okay with him coming closer. The tears just kept coming, and breathing was getting harder as my lungs tightened making me gasp. Rafael started to reach out for my knee, going slowly so I could stop him if I wanted to, but I didn't. For once in my life, I just wanted someone to hold me and tell me everything would be okay. His scent wrapped around me as he gently tugged me forward so my head was resting on his shoulder as a hand ran up and down my back.

My knees touched his thighs but he made sure that there was minimal contact between us as he comforted me. Before I knew what was happening, a whine escaped my lips as I nuzzled into his neck, and his body grew stiff. The next second I was wrapped up in his arms, cradled against his chest. My fear spiked and my first response was to fight him, but then this sound unlike anything I'd heard before rumbled in his chest. The rattling purr cut through my fear and I was finally able to take a deep breath, flooding my nose with his sandalwood and vanilla aroma as it acted like a balm to my nerves. Something in my brain, on a base level I've never experienced before, told me I was safe. For the first time since my mother died, I was in the arms of someone who would protect me.

Curling myself into a tight ball I tried to get as close as I could to the sound emanating from his chest. It did things to my body and brain that I didn't understand. It was as if I craved it. Rafael paused in his purring as my scent started to pour off me, filling the room with my perfume. I could feel his chest expand as he took a deep intake of my scent before I was lifted and carried off. My normal response would be to panic but there was something different about this, something that my broken mind couldn't fight. All I kept thinking was, I'm in the arms of my Alpha, and he would keep me safe.

CHAPTER 6
Rafael

She's an Omega!

This precious gift curled up in my arms, beaten to hell, was none other than an Omega. Some bastard had raised his hand against her repeatedly, for way too fucking long. The second her scent hit me, my Alpha urges took over and I needed to get her someplace safe. That room was too exposed, it was too close to the other people in the shelter. My little diamond in the rough was covered in bruises, fresh cuts on her face and hands, and her scent had been blocked for a long time if the strength of it was any indication.

Now her claims of her father trying to sell her made sense. I saw Nixon and Spencer in their shared office talking and I kicked the door open and slammed it closed with my heel, causing my precious bundle to whimper and curl tighter within herself.

"Shh, Cambrie, you're alright," I whispered to her rubbing my cheek on her head, marking her with my scent.

Lifting my gaze, I met the stunned expression of Nixon and Spencer as her perfume hit them. Nixon took a step forward, reaching out for her but stopped and looked at me, worried. I knew more than anything right now she needed a pack to ground her, so I nodded. "Cambrie, I'm with Nixon and Spencer. They are members of my pack and I trust them with my life. All we want is to help you.”

She lifted her face looking at me with bloodshot, puffy eyes filled with shadows of past hurt. Giving me a sniffle, she fisted my shirt as she looked over at Nixon, who was standing right in front of me, gently resting a hand on her arm.

“Hello again, Cambrie, this is Spencer,” Nixon shared, gesturing to his partner. “As Rafael said, we are all pack, who are here to look after you if you’ll let us.”

“Can you keep them from taking me?” she asked, her voice raspy from crying.

Nixon’s eyes flicked up to mine as his jaw clenched tight, the only sign showing how upset he was. “Cambrie, I vow to you we will never let someone take you against your will.”

She nodded and turned to bury her face once more in my neck. I took a seat in one of the office chairs and looked at my fellow pack members. “We need to tell the others, because there is no way in hell I’m leaving her here tonight.”

Nixon nodded as Spencer pulled out his cell and started typing something out to the others.

“How did I miss this, Rafael? She was a few feet from me for twenty minutes. There’s no way I would have missed the fact she was an Omega,” Nixon muttered as he squatted down next to me, wrapping a hand around her ankle.

Cambrie shivered in my arms but Nixon was already on the move, heading out of the office. Spencer pulled a chair next to me so he was near her head. He gently tugged her long, braided hair out from under my arm and started to loosen it.

“Cambrie, I find when Marius, my other Alpha partner, is upset he likes it when I run my fingers through his hair. Would you like me to brush yours? If you decide it’s too much, I’ll stop. You just say the word,” Spencer explained as he took the brush from his lap and started at the end of her blonde hair.

He worked on sections of her hair, trying not to snag it too much but it was clear it hadn’t been brushed all that often. As it brushed against my hand it felt dry and brittle, not looked after. I relaxed my hold on her slightly and noticed the trench coat had opened to reveal her legs mottled with bruises. Reaching down, I ran my hand over the socks wanting to make sure they weren't wet, causing her to feel colder than she clearly already was.

They were a little damp. I didn't think they were too bad until I looked down at my hand. The dampness was from blood. It had been seeping into the wool but must have stopped since she didn't leave bloody footprints everywhere. Slipping a finger into the top of the sock I started to push it down. Cambrie flinched and jerked her foot away.

I wanted to smack myself for acting without explaining what I was doing. "Little One, it seems your feet have been bleeding. I would like to take a look at them, and clean them up to make sure they don't get infected. Then we can wrap them and get clean socks and maybe some shoes. Will you let us do that?" I asked, looking at Spencer who'd stopped brushing as he listened to what I said.

Cambrie lifted her head, this time she seemed more settled. "He didn't give me shoes when he dragged me out of the house. I had to run. There was no other choice, I couldn't let him sell me."

"You did the right thing, Little One," I murmured, as my thumb caressed her arm. "The hard part is over, you got away, and now we will look after you. No one in my pack will cause you harm or do anything you don't want them to. Like Nixon promised, we won't let anyone take you unless you want to leave."

She studied me with her haunted eyes, as if she could tell the truth of my words by what was written on my face. I'd seen this kind of self preservation skill before in people who'd suffered long term abuse. They became masters at reading body language and reading between the lines of what people said and what they actually meant.

"Everyone knows that I'm an Omega. What do I do now?" she asked, letting her body sag with the weight of the unknown. "I planned to stay here tonight and find more suppressants so I could hide, but I don't think I can do that now that you know, can I? You have to tell them about me and send me away to one of those government places because it's the law. They won't give me a choice where they send me, will they?"

"Let's take this one step at a time, Cambrie," Nixon interjected, having heard enough of Cambrie's worries as he entered the room. "We have some connections with the CoF that might help us. I've made him aware of what's happened so we will see what he thinks when we arrive at our home."

I noticed Nixon not only had a blanket but a first aid kit as well, it seems Spencer was on top of things. The Alpha knelt before Cambrie, opening the kit and slipping on some gloves before he addressed her again. "Can I remove your socks?"

She nodded, but carefully watched what he was doing, hissing as the sock stuck to sections of raw flesh. Now that both socks were off and I could see the condition of her feet, I was shocked she could walk on them as well as she had been. There were tiny bits of gravel, glass, and other debris embedded in the wounds, while the rest of her skin was black from how dirty the ground was.

"Spence, I think it would be more comfortable for her if we could get a bucket of warm water to clean her feet with," Nixon instructed, sending off his partner to gather what was needed. "Now Cambrie, what I'm going to ask next you might not like but I just want to make sure you aren't hurt anywhere else. Can we take off the jacket?"

Cambrie recoiled in my arms, almost as if she was going to climb out of my lap and over my shoulder to get away. *Has someone done more to her than just hit her? No, she said she was to be sold, and a pure Omega would sell for more money than one that had been used.*

"Easy, Little One," I cooed. "Nixon is not asking for anything more than to remove the jacket, besides the blanket will be far warmer for you. None of us would ever dream of touching you or anyone else in that way if they haven't consented, Cambrie."

Stilling, she took a shaky breath and seemed to consider what I said. "Let me do it myself."

Nixon moved out of the way, even though it made me cringe to see her standing on those poor torn up feet as she did so. My first instinct was to pull her back to me when I saw how her hands shook as she reached for the knot holding the coat closed. Everything was screaming at me not to make her go through this but I held myself still, knowing a victim like Cambrie wouldn't appreciate being smothered.

Biting on her bottom lip, she struggled with the knot but finally worked it free, then slowly she undid each button. In an interesting turn of events, it almost seemed by taking control of doing this helped her gain more confidence. Her hands steadied, shoulders straightened, and while she wouldn't look at either of us, she wasn't turning away or trying to hide.

Survivors of abuse tended to respond in a few different ways, either feeling they will always be a victim or the other end of the spectrum, where they become fighters, never allowing themselves to be a victim again. Now, I hardly knew Cambrie or her story, but something told me she wasn't a quitter. She might not be a fighter per se, but I don't see her becoming a doormat either. The fact that she was standing before me now showed me just how tough she was.

When the jacket slipped down her arms and dropped to the ground Nixon and I were faced with all the evidence we would need to know her life had been anything but loving. Covering her arms and legs in an array of colors from deep purple to a sickly lime green, were bruises. Around her one ankle were signs she'd been chained and the cuff had rubbed her skin raw. The mark that nearly sent me over the edge was the shadow of fingerprints on her neck from someone either trying to strangle her or pinning her against something.

After you got past the marks on her, the other glaringly obvious problem was how skinny she was. Her bones were clearly visible and I could only imagine what her body must look like under the dress being that malnourished. She was the poster child for abuse victims, how had no one seen this or done anything about it?

"Cambrie, I noticed your hands were pretty scuffed up, did you fall?" Nixon asked.

Just as she was about to answer, the office door opened making her scramble to hide behind one of the desks. Spencer froze, looking at us both for direction. I waved him in, knowing that dealing with things like this would be a common occurrence in the near future. It was going to take time for her to believe she was safe and for us to learn her triggers. Dealing with PTSD took equal work on the victim and those around them.

"Spencer has come back with water to wash your feet, Cambrie," I shared. "Take your time, come back and join us when you feel ready. There shouldn't be anyone else coming to this office tonight."

Cambrie peeked over the desk finding it was indeed just Spencer. After a moment, she came around the desk, eyes cast to the floor as if she was ashamed of her reaction. A sharp intake of breath from Spencer had me giving him the side eye, ensuring he didn't say anything about her appearance. The last thing she needed was to feel guilty about how she looked, even though none of it was her fault, but abuse victims didn't always have the ability to view things in the correct light.

"I'm sorry I scared you," Spencer apologized. "I should have announced it was me before just walking in and surprising you."

Worrying her poor lip, she glanced at Spencer and nodded, then turned to Nixon. "I jumped out of the car."

Nixon frowned, cocking his head to the side. "I'm sorry, you did what?"

"I didn't fall, I jumped out of the car," she repeated, lifting the dress just enough for us to see her knees.

There was asphalt gouged into them and little trickles of dried blood down her legs. Just when I didn't think things couldn't get worse, she told us something new.

Spencer set down the bowl of water and pulled out a folding chair for her to sit on. "Cambrie, will you sit here for me? I need to get some more rags but I want to soak your feet so we can clean them without it being too painful for you."

Dropping the fabric she'd been holding, she shuffled over to the chair and tugged it so her back was to the wall and she could see the door. The amount of conflicting feelings coursing through me left me at a loss of how to act. One side wanted to hunt the man down who dared lay a finger on this girl, while the other just wanted to wrap her up in my arms, purring for her. Clearly, there was no way I would leave her to go after this man, so I had to content myself with finding another way to take care of her.

"Are you hungry at all? As I mentioned earlier, dinner is just about to be served so I can bring something back for you." I offered.

Glancing up at me she nodded slightly, wrapping her arms around her stomach.

"All right, you soak your feet like Spencer asked and I'll be back with food. Nixon will be here with you to make sure nothing happens," I explained, wanting to drive home that none of us were going to leave her alone, and if we had something to say about it, she would never be alone again.

CHAPTER 7

Cambrie

The water felt so nice and warm as I slipped my feet into the basin Spencer brought. I couldn't remember the last time I'd had the chance to wash anything in warm water. Feeling it now made me realize just how cold I was and a shiver wracked my body, clattering my teeth at the force of it.

"Are you cold? Here, I grabbed a blanket and forgot to give it to you," Nixon muttered as he shook out the soft looking blue fabric. "Here you go, Cambrie, I'm an idiot for not making sure you were warm after I made you take off your jacket."

He started to move as if he was going to place the blanket around my shoulders but stopped as my head ducked down to avoid the blow my brain assumed was coming. Nixon took a step back, letting me have some space until my body relaxed somewhat.

"Would you rather me hand it to you?" he questioned, his brow creased as if he was trying hard to solve this problem.

Licking my cracked lips, I sat up a little straighter forcing myself not to shy away from his gaze as I looked at him. "I'm sorry, I just wasn't ready for it."

Pity crossed his face for a moment before he wiped it away, just looking sad. "You don't need to apologize, Sweetheart. I should have asked before acting. You have every right to feel or respond in any way you do. Life so far hasn't shown you there is much kindness out there to experience. Now would it be easier if I stood beside you and put the blanket around you?"

"I guess we can try," I answered with a shrug.

Moving slowly but with purpose, Nixon stood beside me and draped the blanket around my shoulders, making sure it covered all of my back. The whole time he made sure not to actually touch me. Having him this close, I got a good whiff of his scent, I couldn't help but take a deep breath. Closing my eyes, I let the sweet, smoky scent surround me, making me think of the olden days when men went to cigar clubs and drank scotch, playing cards while chatting with their fellow men.

One way I survived the cold, dark basement for so long was by reliving all the books I read and creating stories of my own. By allowing my brain to live in the fictional world, blurring out the reality I survived. In my stories though, I was the heroine fighting the dragons, going on quests, being the chosen one to save the world, and falling in love with dashing men who loved me.

My head made contact with something soft and warm, while the intoxicating aroma got stronger. Instantly my eyes snapped open. While I'd been lost in my own thoughts my body had gravitated toward Nixon and my head ended up in his lap. He sat on the edge of the desk my chair was backed up to and I was now sitting sideways so my head could rest on his thighs. I started to lift my head but a hand softly stroked my hair followed by a purring that instantly put me at ease. My feet were no longer in the warm water but it didn't matter, not while Nixon purred for me.

Images of things I've read in books popped into my head, of sweet moments like this between Omegas and their Alphas. I'd never once expected to find an Alpha who would purr for me. I'd always believed that Alphas in this day and age didn't care for their Omegas, only seeing them as an object of status or power. We were to be bred and produce more Omegas, while allowing a pack to bond and grow their power through the magical connection we created. Yet here I was having experienced two separate Alphas treat me with kindness and care, gracing me with the gift of their purr.

What would happen next? They wanted to take me to their home where it sounded like more men lived. Did I have a choice in the matter? The way they talked made me think I didn't. Nixon had said one of his pack members had a connection to the CoF, which meant they would have to send me away to a government facility. It was the law and to break the law meant death.

After the attack by the terrorists the CoF cracked down on any kind of perceived rebellion to ensure something like that never happened again. These men had been kind to me so far, I wouldn't want them risking death if it was found out they were hiding me. No matter how relaxed my body was, my mind raced with worry, flipping through every horrible thing that could happen. Nothing about this escape had gone how I planned, not that I had much choice. The number one goal though had been to escape the notice of Alphas—clearly, I'd failed in that endeavor.

A soft knock sounded on the door, the sound had me snapping my head up and out of the relaxed state I'd been in. Nixon stood and placed his hand on the back of my neck stroking a thumb along my throat. "It's all right, Sweetheart, it's just Spencer and Rafael returning."

Feeling his touch should have triggered me with how alert I already was, but it didn't. In fact, my instinct was to lean into it so I could nuzzle my cheek along his bare arm now that he'd rolled up his sleeves.

In walked Rafael with a bowl of something that smelled amazing, and hot if the curls of steam were any signal. Spencer shut the door behind him and locked it making me panic, my breath coming quicker, as the fear of being locked away in here took over my brain.

"Sweetheart," Nixon murmured, moving his hand to cup my chin and forced me to look at him. His eyes searched my face, his frown grew deeper.

Had I upset him?

Would he hit me now?

Did they really intend to help me or had they been lying to get me to let my guard down so they could trap me into a bond with them?

"Cambrie," Nixon barked, making me flinch, recoiling from the command. "I need you to take a deep breath, in through your nose out through your mouth."

What?

"Please don't make me use my bark on you again, Sweetheart. In through the nose…" Nixon instructed, taking a deep breath.

Keeping my eyes locked on him I followed his example. When he exhaled I did the same, together we did this three or four times until the tightness in my chest eased.

Had I been so panicked I wasn't breathing?

"There's a good girl," Nixon praised, giving me a soft smile and letting the back of his finger brush down my cheek. "Can you share with us what triggered that panic attack?" he asked, coming to kneel next to me.

Licking my lips I glanced at the others, who seemed just as worried about what just happened. "He locked the door. I was trapped again. What if I can't get out for another two years? I don't think I could survive being imprisoned like that again."

Spencer slowly approached to squat next to his Alpha. "Oh Cambrie, I'm so sorry. I thought I was helping to make you feel safe knowing that no one else could get in here. Would you like me to unlock the door?"

"Please, I… I just don't feel I can trust a locked door right now," I answered, my bottom lip quivered as I fought back my fear.

"That explains your reaction to the doors earlier," Rafael muttered, staring into the bowl. "Were you only with that man for two years?"

My face scrunched up at the question. "He's my father, I've been with him my whole life. It was only after he learned I was an Omega that he locked me away until he could sell me."

All of the men froze, staring at me intently, shocked by what I'd just told them.

"Your father is the one who has been hitting you and locked you away?" Spencer questioned, with a look of almost disbelief.

Nodding, I couldn't quite figure out what they found so shocking. I wasn't the only kid that got smacked around by their parents. It's one of the reasons we lived in the neighborhood we did. People kept to themselves because they didn't want any attention drawn to their own shit. Peggy once mentioned she should alert the authorities that I wasn't in school, but once I started working toward my GED, she let it go.

"Do you know when this started or why your father told you he felt the need to hit you?" Rafael inquired as he handed me the bowl. "Please be careful, that the soup is very hot."

Using the blanket, I shielded my hands as I grasped the bowl and set it in my lap. Vegetables and what looked like chicken floated around in it, making my stomach voice its excitement. Lifting the spoon I slurped some, testing the temperature, and found it hot but not so much I couldn't eat it.

"My mom died when I was eight, he didn't drink as much as he does now, but when he got drunk he would hit her. She would lock me away in her room so he couldn't do anything to me but I knew what was happening. After she was gone Father drank any chance he could. It took me a while to learn if he didn't see me he would forget I was there. At first, I tried to take care of him like Mom did, all that got me was more bruises and a broken arm. After I went to the hospital they called the authorities on him so we moved to the slums where no one gave a shit," I explained in between bites of soup.

"Then he locked you away when your designation revealed itself?" Nixon asked.

Mouth full I nodded wiping my mouth with the back of my hand. "I tried to run, Peggy from the library wanted to turn me in to the police but I begged her not to. When I went home to get my stuff so I could run, Father caught me. I'd been locked in the basement before for one reason or another but this time he kept me down there for good. Once I almost got away, so he chained me to the wall, forcing me to take suppressants so no one would find out I was down there. When he came for me earlier today, he told me he'd sold me to the highest bidder and today was the day I would be given to him. That's why I jumped out of the car while we were on the highway, making it harder for him to come after me."

It would seem that after so long of being silent and alone, once I got started telling my story I couldn't stop. People needed to know what happened to me.

It was wrong!

No one, no matter their designation, should be treated the way I was. I didn't think being locked away for so long had changed me as much as it had. Up until I was sixteen there had still been a flicker of hope for the future, the knowledge that I wouldn't have to live my life this way forever. Then in the blink of an eye, the reality of the world reared its ugly head and snuffed out all vestiges of hope. Now life was about survival, just making it one more day.

The men didn't press for any more information, letting me eat my meal in peace while Spencer washed my feet. While I tried not to react, the zings of sharp pain when he had to pluck something out of my foot had me twitching. Father seemed to enjoy it more if he knew how badly what he did to me hurt, it seemed to fuel his rage. So I quickly learned that being silent helped to make things end sooner. It might be more violent as he tried to get me to cry out but the drunk bastard would soon run out of steam.

"I'm sorry, Cambrie, there are some pieces of glass that got really stuck in there. I'd hoped the soaking would keep this from being so painful but I'll try to be as fast as I can," Spencer said, giving me a reassuring smile.

I nodded and bit my lip to keep my whimpers to myself. A hand settled on my head making me flinch, but I caught the scent of sandalwood and knew it was Rafael. Slowly, he stroked his finger through my hair, effectively distracting me from what was happening to my feet.

"Let's give those a little break," Spencer suggested after a bit. "Can I take a look at your knees?"

Nixon took the empty bowl from me, and I scrunched up the fabric of my dress and tucked it tightly around my thighs so I wouldn't flash more than I was willing to show. Father had never touched me like that, even though he'd threatened to sell me sooner as a whore if I couldn't behave. He knew I'd sell for more money as an untouched Omega. Thankfully, money was the one thing he wouldn't risk losing.

I watched Spencer as he started at my ankle gently pressing the rag to my raw skin from the cuff, letting the water wash away the dirt and grime. Then he moved up the leg with smooth, consistent strokes keeping it professional, never once making me feel uncomfortable.

"You have two Alpha partners?" I asked, wanting to fill the silence. My world had been quiet and lonely for too long. I craved conversation with someone, even if I wasn't good at it.

Spencer's eyes moved to mine and he grinned. "I do, Nixon and Marius. We've been together for just a little over five years, and I love them both very much."

"Did you meet them at the same time?" I ventured, curious how two Alpha males came to share one Beta. I always assumed they would be too jealous to share their affection with more than one person.

"Nixon is who I met first, he interviewed me to work here at the shelter. That interview went from him being all serious and focused on the needs of his business to more of a twenty-questions game. I teased him that he put the ad up for employees as a farce to interview for a boyfriend, not a front desk associate," Spencer shared, the warmth and love in his voice telling me how he felt about his Alpha. "I got hired of course, but I'll have you know I was way too overqualified for the job, but I'd been looking for something of meaning to do with my life."

Nixon snorted at this, drawing my attention. His chocolate brown eyes glowed with humor as he smiled at his partner, crossing his arms as he leaned back in his office chair. "Overqualified my ass. You told me you were a front desk manager for a hotel but what you didn't say was that the hotel was so small it only needed one front desk employee a shift. You would have stayed there too if it hadn't shut down."

Spencer glared at him. "Everyone knows to pad your resume to put yourself in the best possible light. I didn't lie, it just might have been silly to say that I managed myself on the dayshift. As for the part of wanting to do more with my life, that was absolutely true. I just didn't know I'd fall for the two men who want to change the world."

He must have seen the confusion on my face as he patted my calf reassuringly. "My other partner is Official Marius Stone, the newly elected fourth member of the Council of Four. When we said we had a connection to the government, really, we meant we had a direct line."

My jaw dropped at his words before snapping my head over to Nixon, who nodded that what I'd been told was true. "Marius has been my best friend my entire life, guess it seems fitting we would fall for the same Beta. Oscar, the last Alpha in our pack, went to boarding school with us so you could say that the core of us have been together for what seems like forever. The only other person we haven't mentioned is Bodhi. You could say we adopted him almost two years ago. He was one of Rafael's patients from the shelter. So, us bringing you home isn't going to shock anyone," he added reassuringly.

"Now, we just have to finish getting your feet cleaned up and we can all call it a day," Spencer announced. "I shouldn't be too much longer. I got most of it, I just hated seeing you in pain."

"It's okay, I've dealt with worse," I shared, wanting to ease his worry. "Do what you need to. I won't move, promise."

Spencer gave me a halfhearted smile as he picked up the tweezers. "Why don't one of you find some shoes for her? I believe Clara also had some clothes as well. We can have Cambrie change into those once she has a proper shower at the house."

"Agreed, I don't want her using the open shower here," Nixon muttered as he left the office.

CHAPTER 8
Cambrie

Spencer made quick work of my feet, dried them, treated them, and wrapped them before putting on clean socks, then a pair of soft slip-on flats. Rafael held out a hand for me and I reached out slowly, curling my fingers around his as he pulled me to my feet.

"Tell me if it's too painful to walk and I can carry you," he offered.

Blushing, I ducked my head. "Thank you, but I... I can manage. I don't want to be any trouble to you guys."

Rafael squatted in front of me forcing me to look him in the face. "Little One, you are not any trouble. How about you and I make a deal?"

Curious, I nodded wanting to hear his offer.

"If I offer something to you like I just did, I will only do so if I truly want to do it. Not under obligation, or feeling forced, but simply because it makes me happy to offer. That way you know it's no trouble or bother for me," he said, giving me a look that told me he expected an answer.

"Deal, but you have to follow the same rules if I offer to do something for you too. Things need to be fair," I announced. He might be an Alpha and I might be an Omega, but in life I could pull my own weight. I always have and I always will.

"That sounds fair to me, Little One," Rafael agreed, smiling as he stood. "Do we have everything we need?" he asked, directing his question at Spencer.

Spencer pulled a massive tote bag over his shoulder. "I can't think of anything else we need, but if I missed something we can always run to the store."

As they moved to leave the room, I paused looking over at Nixon. "Don't you need me to take a suppressant or something to hide what I am? If I walk around as I am now with my scent blooming everyone will know."

Nixon slowly put his arm around my shoulder allowing me to pull away if I wanted to. Instead, I let him pull me to his chest in a light hug. "I can't even imagine how afraid you must be of being an Omega. The world paints Omegas as such an ugly picture these days it's no wonder all you want to do is hide." Taking a deep breath he hugged me close for a moment. "No, you don't need to take something to hide what you are, Sweetheart. We will keep you safe. You no longer have to handle this all on your own."

I peered up at him, tears threatening to spill over at his words. Finally—I had someone on my side. For how long? I don't know, but I was getting so tired of surviving through all this alone. "Okay."

Keeping me tucked at his side, Nixon guided me out of the office and through the halls back to the main lobby. There were tons more people now in the common space, scattered in groups doing various activities. Fear of someone coming after me the second my scent hit the air had me gripping Nixon's coat tightly. His purr started, keeping the panic from winning but I didn't start to feel better until we were outside, away from all the strangers.

Rafael opened the door of the car Nixon brought me here in, the same classical music played. I slipped into the seat and before I could even move to do it myself Nixon buckled my seatbelt. "I would have done it," I voiced.

"Sorry, the need to make sure you're safe in my car won't allow me to let you. I need to *know* the seatbelt is on and secure, the downside of being an Alpha, I guess," he answered with a sheepish smile.

"Thank you for making sure I'm safe," I said, meeting his gaze, and held it for a moment before letting my eyes drop to my hands.

Rafael slid next to me while Spencer took the front seat next to Nixon. This shocked me. How would an Alpha let a Beta take his spot in the front? Turning to Rafael I searched his face but I didn't see anything that told me he was bothered about this occurrence.

"You don't mind sitting back here?" I asked, unable to keep my thoughts to myself.

He cocked his head in confusion. "With you, you mean?"

"No." I shook my head. "Spencer is in your spot, he should be back here with me."

"Why is that, Little One?" Rafael asked, his tone curious.

Licking my lips, I looked forward and saw Nixon and Spencer had turned to hear my answer. "He's a Beta..."

"Yes, he is, but why would that mean he has to sit in the back?" Nixon inquired.

"Because Rafael is an Alpha, his place is at the top of the pack. Spencer shouldn't be allowed to sit where an Alpha would... right?" I asked, looking for confirmation from any of them.

"Cambrie, while other packs might view their designation as equal to their status in life, our pack isn't of that same mindset. Nixon is Spencer's partner in life, so I feel it's only right he should sit next to him. Me sitting back here with you doesn't make me any less of an Alpha, in fact, I think I'm getting the better side of the deal," Rafael shared, a smile tugging at his lips.

"Why would you be getting the better end of the deal?" I inquired.

Rafael cautiously lifted a hand, and when I didn't move he tucked some hair behind my ear, letting his smile bloom on his face. "That's because I get to sit next to you. I don't doubt the others would eagerly change places with me if I gave them the chance, but I won't."

Heat crept up my cheeks as I couldn't help but bite my bottom lip in embarrassment. A hand gripped my chin and the thumb pulled my lip from between my teeth. "It's not good for you to be so mean to your lip. The poor thing will start bleeding if you keep chewing on it."

My gaze lifted to meet Rafael's, ensuring he wasn't angry at me even though his voice was calm and even. His expression was neutral with some slight concern but nothing that would have me believe he was upset. "I'll try. It's a bad habit of mine."

"We all have them, but such pretty lips shouldn't be so abused," he added with a wink as he dropped his hand, which landed on top of mine. He didn't move it like I assumed he would. Instead, he curled his fingers around my palm to hold it as Nixon pulled away.

"Our house isn't too far away but it's in a special district for members of the CoF and other important officials. There is a gate around the whole property to ensure no one comes in or out that shouldn't be there. Since you are with us there will be no problems, as I said before, it's not the first time we've taken home someone from the shelter," Spencer explained as we pulled out on the road. "When we come to the guard shack, I think it would be best if you placed my coat over your lap to hide some of your scent." Seeing my eyes widen in panic he quickly waved it off. "Cambrie, we are not doing anything wrong by bringing you to our home. What I hope to prevent is others gossiping about how we have an Omega staying with us. It is none of their business and I don't want it to lead back to your father or the man he was going to sell you to."

What he said made total sense, allowing me to relax and gaze at the city I'd never visited before. The tall buildings started to shrink, changing to brownstone homes, schools, and parks where families were more prevalent. Then I saw the gated section we were coming up to with bright lights and a towering ornate fence that no one would be able to make it over without being noticed.

A jacket was placed on my lap and instantly I was hit with Spencer's tropical coconut and the bite of lime scent. I hugged it to my chest, needing the extra assurance as we pulled to a stop at the guard shack. "Good evening Mr. Hayes, Mr. Wells. Official Stone managed to beat you home tonight, must have something special going on to pull him away from work so early."

"We have a guest joining us for dinner tonight, one of Mr. Leshem's patients from the shelter," Nixon shared, showing no signs of being on alert or worried about what he was saying.

The guard peered into the car as Rafael draped a protective arm over my shoulders. While I didn't want to appear as afraid of this man as I was, I couldn't fight the urge to turn into the comfort Rafael offered.

"Poor thing looks in pretty rough shape. I hope you're able to help her as you've done so many others. You all have a good night now," the guard said, saluting before he stepped back and hit the button to open the gate.

Rafael leaned down to nuzzle his cheek on the top of my head. "You did good, Little One. In time, you will learn that the world has some decent people in it. They're just harder to find."

The homes in this gated community were all massive, sprawling things made of brick, stone, and some were even all wood. The styles seemed to change depending on the street we drove down as if they were added at different times. Nixon turned down the drive of a beautiful home with lots of stonework and white walls. The lush green yard that stretched out before it made it seem like it was out of an advertisement in a magazine. Ivy climbed up the stone adding character to it and showing its age. People didn't build homes like this anymore, mostly they were simple two or three bedroom houses crammed together so people could afford them. That or an apartment building, giving you a box to live in with no chance of a yard.

There was a garage with three wide doors, but Nixon curved around the drive circle to stop in front of the main entrance. Spencer got out and offered his hand to me as Rafael released me from his hold. Letting him pull me from the car, I stood in awe at what I saw before me. Even the air here seemed to smell different, cleaner, fresher, almost as if we'd been transported to another world.

"This is where you live?" I asked.

"Yes, we've been here for almost a year. The CoF insisted we be part of the community for as long as Marius is in office. Although we still keep our penthouse in the city that we use from time to time," Spencer said, leading me up the stone steps to the front door.

I'd expected him to pull out a set of keys to unlock the door, instead, he typed in a code and used his thumbprint to let us in.

Seeing my expression he let out a sigh. "The price we pay for Marius being someone important, they go overboard on all the security measures. The Official that Marius replaced was killed by the EQ so they stepped up security on all fronts where they could. Just to be clear, it didn't happen on the compound, he was at a public speaking event and was shot."

He spoke about it so calmly like he wasn't worried that his lover was now in the same position. "Aren't you worried the same thing will happen to him?"

Spencer shoved open the heavy wooden door and ushered me through, leaving it open for the others to follow.

"I'm terrified that something like that will happen to him, but it was one of the risks we knew would be part of our lives if he ran for the position. It's been his dream since he was ten years old. How could I stand in the way of that?" Spencer admitted, his expression showing just how much it bothered him.

"He's downplaying it for you," a smooth, silky voice cut in. It surprised me so much that before I knew what I was doing I'd darted behind Spencer, hiding my face in his back.

"Mari," Spencer scolded. "Cambrie isn't someone you can sneak up on like that." Reaching around, Spencer gently tugged my arm pulling me to his side and kept me close. "Cambrie, I would like you to meet my other partner, Marius."

Marius was a stunning man, his skin was perfect, showing no signs of aging. He had bright green eyes that observed me with vivid intelligence, but not in a cruel way. His deep brown hair was styled up and away from his face but almost in a relaxed way like he combed his fingers through it often. He had a neat beard that was trimmed close to his face, adding to the whole polished feel I was getting from him. Even his hands seemed elegant, as one hung at his side while the other was tucked into the pocket of his slacks.

"Hello Cambrie, welcome to my home," he said, with a warm smile until it morphed into a scowl. "What happened to you? Who did this? I demand you tell me now!"

My hands gripped Spencer's shirt tightly, fighting the urge to bite my lip as the anger in his words made me want to run. Marius's scent was a heady bergamot and clove, that seemed to wrap itself around me holding me in place. It added to his already clear dominance as an Alpha pushing me to submit, a useful tool for someone in a position of power. Everything about it made me nervous that he might hurt me if I did something wrong or upset him, which I clearly had.

"Little One, what's the matter?" Rafael asked, crouching in front of me.

It was only then I realized I was shaking, my fear having decided to show itself visibly. Releasing Spencer, I let myself drop into Rafael's open arms, and I curled up in his warmth. "Is he safe?" I whispered.

"Marius?" he asked as if shocked by my question.

I nodded my head not wanting him to hear me questioning him in his own house. Rafael didn't respond, instead he picked me up and carried me out of the room. "Spencer, call the others down to the family room now," he ordered with an edge of bark to his tone.

"Rafael, I don't know what's going on, but you will not speak to him that way," Marius said, a growl rumbling in his throat.

A whine slipped out as I burrowed closer to Rafael. His arms tightened and his purring started, instantly soothing something on a soul level. Instinctively, I knew I could trust him, that he would protect me.

"She's an *Omega*!" Marius bit out in a harsh whisper.

"Spence didn't tell you?" Nixon asked. "That little shit, he was supposed to warn you about that. I told him to tell you and the others so when we showed up something like this didn't happen."

"Rafael, please know I would have handled that all differently...I wouldn't have come on so strong." Marius said, his voice so close he had to be standing in front of us. The odd part was that his tone was tinged with pain. "I didn't know... God, how did I not pick up her scent until now?"

"Spencer thought it was best to muddy hers with his as we passed through the gate," Nixon answered.

"Is someone making cookies? It smells like fucking snickerdoodles in here for some reason," a cocky voice called from somewhere in the house.

Even though every sense of mine was on high alert, I didn't like that I couldn't see. Yet part of me believed that child's lie if I couldn't see them, they couldn't see me. More footsteps sounded on the wood floor telling me that more of them had arrived. I felt him lower us so we were sitting against something soft. The need to evaluate my surroundings finally won out over the fear.

Lifting my head, I discovered we were in a room with a wall of built-in bookshelves made out of a rich dark wood, filled to the brim with old looking books. There was also a large couch where I found five people watching me, some with curiosity and others with concern or boredom. Marius looked like he was in pain, his face was pinched, and his hands kept opening and closing like he wanted to do something but couldn't.

Two new faces were among those I'd been introduced to. A man who seemed closer to my age, with tousled brown hair with random vibrant red streaks. His hazel eyes washed over me with indifference and slight curiosity. From his pine and fresh rain scent, I could tell he was a Beta. He must be the one they said also came from the shelter. Looking him over intently, I couldn't see any signs of him being mistreated, or even a hint of fear wafting off him sitting so close to Marius.

That left who should be the fourth Alpha of the pack. He had sleek blond hair that came to his shoulders, making his bright blue eyes stand out against his tanned skin. He gave off a warm energy, his scent was that of caramel and cinnamon, making me want to smile. It pulled me back to the days when Mom took me to the fall festival and we made caramel apples and stuffed ourselves full of cinnamon doughnuts. It was the last happy memory I had before she died.

Shifting me off his lap so I sat next to him instead of curled up in a ball, Rafael introduced me to the room. "Everyone, this is Cambrie, she's an Omega who will be staying with us for a little bit."

CHAPTER 9

Cambrie

From where I was now seated on a soft velvety loveseat filled with pillows, I spotted one in a royal blue color. I snatched it up and hugged it to my chest, needing to hold onto something as I waited for their reactions. Nixon smiled and gave a little snort as if I'd done something cute, but I couldn't evaluate that right now. I was more concerned about what everyone else thought.

The fourth Alpha, I couldn't remember his name, tapped Spencer's shoulder, then signed with his hands. While I didn't know what he was saying, I'd seen others use this sort of communication before. Did that mean he was deaf? Wait, no one had been signing to him, ah maybe he could possibly read lips.

"Her father," Spencer answered, his gaze flicking to me. "Oscar is asking who hurt you. That bastard beat her on top of locking her away for the past two years, then tried to sell her. I'll warn you though, Cambrie's no wilting flower, she's braver than any of us. That woman jumped out of a car on the highway to get away. Not sure I would have the balls to do that."

"What?" Marius bit out as he shot to his feet.

Seeing the anger flash through him, I curled up behind the pillow and tried to sink into the couch. Marius noticed and instantly sagged in defeat. Spencer reached out and squeezed his hand, reassuringly nudging him to do something. Nodding, Marius started to approach me but stopped a few feet away and sat on the floor looking up at me.

"Cambrie, I'm sorry," Marius said, then paused as if conflicted about what to say next. "Not many people know this...I once had a sister, her name was Kimberly. She and I were so close, born only eighteen months apart, we were inseparable. When her designation revealed itself, we assumed she would be a Beta, but turns out she was an Omega. While my family was well off and moved in the upper class circles, we had to follow the same rules as everyone else. She was sent away to a government facility."

The pain I heard before in his voice was back and so thick it almost made it hard for him to speak. I sat up a little straighter, watching as his scent got stronger, more overpowering, as he struggled to continue.

"They failed my sister, I failed her, everyone failed Kimberly." he snarled, lifting his eyes to meet mine. "They were transporting her to a new secure location when they were attacked and she was stolen, never to be seen or heard from again, no matter how hard we looked. Two years later, we'd done everything we could, even hiring a private investigator to find her. Then she was discovered, beaten, raped, and dead on the banks of the Wynboro Canal. While I've always wanted to be a politician, one of the driving forces of that is to ensure nothing like what happened to my sister happens to anyone again."

A single tear rolled down his cheek that he brushed away angrily, it was almost as if I could see the horrors of that day replaying in his mind.

"When I saw you standing there covered in bruises, scared, clearly malnourished, and your feet all bandaged, it brought me back to seeing my sister's lifeless body." Taking a few long deep, controlled breaths, I could feel his dominance shrinking. "A flaw that I have is when my emotions get the better of me, which only happens when it comes to my sister or the sight of abuse, I lose control over my Alpha nature. I'm incredibly aware that I'm far more dominant than many other Alphas, I know it can be too much for some people, especially Omegas."

Marius scooted closer and slowly placed a hand on my knee that peeked out from the pillow. Hearing his story and seeing how he reacted telling it, I came to the decision to give him a chance, a small one.

"Cambrie, you have no reason to believe me or any of us in this room, but please hear me when I tell you this. There will never be a second, a blip in time, that I would ever dream of letting myself, any member of my pack, or the government hurt you. If you will let us, I'd like to consider you now under our protection."

Having no idea what to say to everything I heard, the only thing I could think of was to nod my head. My heart wanted to believe that these were good men, that I didn't just walk myself into a new hell. On the other hand, my brain wasn't nearly as easily convinced, time would tell if I'd made the right choice — I just hoped it wouldn't be too late.

Marius shifted so his back was leaning on the edge of the loveseat in front of where I sat as if to guard me. His powerful scent coiled around me once more but with the combination of Rafael's it was comforting.

"Spencer," Rafael spoke, his tone sharp. "Why didn't you warn Marius about Cambrie? None of this would have needed to happen if he'd been made aware of the *real* situation."

The Beta in question sat up straight and met Rafael's challenge head on. "I appreciate you are an expert in the human mind and behavior, but you are not an expert in Marius's behavior. He is my partner, a man I love deeply, that I know inside and out. If he knew all about Cambrie when I asked him to come home, it would have been much worse for her." Spencer pointed at his partner calmly sitting before me with a raised brow. "He would have driven straight to the shelter to address the matter himself. That would have caused far too much of a stir. If you thought her reaction to him here in our home was bad? I can promise you, given the state she was in back when I was supposed to call him, it would have been a disaster. Her being with us isn't going to escape notice, but I was damn well going to do all I could for her safety."

Part of me wanted to run to Spencer to tell him not to argue with an Alpha, to just admit he was wrong and maybe they wouldn't punish him. Rule number one is never anger someone stronger or more dominant than you. It will only end in pain. I'd learned that my whole life, experiencing and seeing it firsthand. I swallowed trying to combat my dry throat knowing I needed to defend Spencer. I fisted Rafael's shirt and tugged once.

He looked down at me questioningly. "What is, Little One?"

"Please don't be mad at Spencer," I pleaded, my voice a little raspy so I tried again pushing to be stronger. Having spoken more now than I had in two years, my voice was getting rough. "I know he didn't do as you instructed him and it's your right as an Alpha to punish him, but don't do it. He did what he did because of me, I should be the one in trouble, not him. Please don't hurt him because he was looking out for me."

The room went silent, no one moved but to breathe, all eyes fixated on me. Everything in me wanted to crumble under their weight, but Spencer was kind and he had stood up for me more than once. I could do the same for him.

"Cambrie, you lovely dove." Spencer sighed as he walked over to us and motioned for Rafael to get up. To my shock, the Alpha did as asked, but stood nearby arms crossed watching the situation.

"Now listen to me, look me in the eyes as I say this alright?" He paused waiting for me to do just that, when I did, he continued.

"I'm not in trouble, Rafael would *never ever* hurt me or anyone else, no matter how upset he got. Not only because Marius and Nixon would never allow it, but because that's not how you treat people. Rafael and I might not see eye to eye on how this should have been handled, and that's okay, it happens all the time." Spencer glanced over at the looming Alpha and pretended to whisper hiding behind his hand. "If we're being honest, he's not a good gauge to go off right now on how to behave properly. His Alpha instincts are in overdrive right now when it comes to you."

My brows scrunched up at this. "What do you mean? Why do I have anything to do with how he's behaving? You're the one who keeps upsetting him." Everyone in the room laughed, making it clear I'd missed something.

"Clara mentioned you didn't graduate high school yet. How close were you to graduating?" Spencer asked, his tone careful as if he didn't want to offend me.

"Two years ago I was working toward getting my GED, but then my designation appeared. Before that, Father pulled me out of school when I was ten, I think," I answered trying to remember back that far. "It was the same time we moved out of our old neighborhood, social services were called on him by the school. He was too drunk to remember not to hit me where people could see."

The atmosphere in the room went cold and growls erupted from all angles. Flinching, I hid behind the pillow as Spencer reached out to stroke my hair. "Ignore them, it's a side effect of them being Alphas in the presence of an Omega that has been mistreated."

Peeking out from the pillow I noticed no one had moved, even though their expressions were unhappy ones. "Does every Alpha react that way to an Omega?"

"Ah..." Spencer started, but stopped. "I believe that is a question that an Alpha should answer for themselves."

"*Teh*," Oscar uttered as he waved for my attention. He tapped the Beta's arm he was sitting next to and signed something.

"Yeah, it's cool," he answered. "Um, I'm Bodhi, by the way, and Oscar has a few questions he'd like to ask." Oscar nodded, giving me a warm smile as he raised his hands but Bodhi stopped him. "Look, I want to make one thing perfectly clear. There is nothing *wrong* with Oscar, he has no vocal cords because he got super sick, so he can't speak. Everything else about him is just fine, he's not slow or anything so don't treat him like he is."

Oscar whacked him on the back of the head and signed angrily at him, his disapproval over what Bodhi just did incredibly obvious.

"No, don't be upset with him Oscar, he was protecting you. I will never fault a person who looks out for those they care about. In fact, I'm glad he told me. I wasn't sure how to ask if you were deaf or how I should interact in a way that would be best for you…" I cringed and covered my mouth looking at the others. "Was that rude of me to say?" I squeaked out.

Oscar shook his head and touched his chin, then lowered his hand palm up.

"That means thank you," Bodhi shared. "If you're going to be staying here, you're going to need to learn how to sign. For Oscar, that's how he feels most comfortable being able to communicate, other than email, but that would be stupid in the same house."

My lips twitched trying to hide my smile, even though I could hear the humor in Bodhi's voice. "What questions did Oscar have for me?"

Bodhi waited a moment as Oscar shared this question and Bodhi responded as if to confirm something. Confident, he nodded and they both turned to me. "What do you know about the importance of scent between an Alpha and an Omega? His second question ties into that as to what you actually know about being an Omega."

If I got them wrong would they ask me to leave? Was this a test? How do I even begin to try and answer these questions? Is there supposed to be a right answer? I told them I didn't go to school, should I have learned that by the time I was ten?

"Dove, take a breath," Spencer said, his voice cutting into my spiraling thoughts bringing me back to the moment.

"Cambrie, can you tell me what just went on in your head?" Marius asked, having turned to face me.

I dropped my eyes and bit my lip, ashamed that I lost myself so easily to my fear. *Is this who I was now? To be turned into a quivering mess the moment I thought someone might be upset with me?*

"Hey, don't get lost on me," Marius cautioned, his hand resting on mine. "Can I… would it help if Rafael sat with you again? As an Omega, to have an Alpha close by can help ground you, make you feel more secure if you trust them. Spencer is wonderful at being comforting and soothing, but I think you need a little more than that right now," Marius shared, having seen me glance at Spencer and guessed my thoughts.

"I have a better idea, instead of sitting on the floor, why not just join us up here? Then she gets the best of both worlds, a cuddly Beta buddy and the overprotective Alpha," Spencer suggested.

Marius looked at me hopefully, as I realized they were letting me decide what I wanted to do. "I would like Spencer to stay, and I think you'd feel better sitting up here with us instead of letting Rafael be so close to your partner."

"Little One, have you ever done a selfish thing in your life?" Rafael asked.

"Once," I answered, looking up at him. "I tried to run on my sixteenth birthday. I was going to be selfish and live my own life instead of doing what I should have. If I'd been the daughter my mom raised me to be and followed the rules instead of dreaming of a life out of a storybook, I wouldn't have been locked away for two years."

Sadness filled Rafael's expression as he regarded me. "None of that is true, Little One. It's not your fault. None of this has ever been your fault. Your father is in charge of his own actions. Nothing you did would ever warrant him treating you that way. Instead of taking you out of school, hurting you, belittling you, and making you feel unworthy, he should have loved the beautiful person you are. I've only just met you, and I can see how pure your heart is, despite all you've been through. Give us time Cambrie, we will show you what it means to be cherished and cared for."

How I ached for that to be true. There was nothing more I wanted in life than to have a pack like those I've read about in books. At first glance, this group of men seemed to be the type that could make that happen with all their kind words and comforting gestures. What scared me even more was not knowing if I could stay with them.

Marius stood and, without preamble, scooped me up so he could sit on the loveseat, and placed me so I was half sitting on him and half on Spencer. I waited for my fear response to kick in seeing as our initial meeting wasn't all that great, but it didn't. My feelings were cautious of what was going on but not scared or panicked. Spencer snuggled against Marius and placed a chaste kiss on his partner's lips before adjusting me into a more comfortable spot with his arm behind Marius, playing with his hair and another over my hips.

"Yes, this is perfect, isn't it, Dove?" Spencer asked, looking pleased.

"Now back to Oscar's questions, Cambrie," Marius interjected, bringing us full circle. "This is just so we understand what you know about yourself, Alphas, and packs. It could be knowledge you already possess so we don't go over things unnecessarily."

Nodding, I looked at Oscar, seeing as he was the one who'd asked. "You asked about scent. I know that it is one thing we use to identify each other since they are unique to each person. They also match personality, designation, and give us a sense of whether or not we will like them. If you don't care for their scent, I've found you don't care for the person in general."

Oscar nodded and seemed to think about my answer before signing. "The basics of what you said are correct, that is how most people use and perceive scent in the world. When it comes to an Omega, there is another layer tied to a deeper level of emotion. If you don't mind me asking, has our scent impacted you differently than others?" Bodhi translated.

Unconsciously, I chewed on my thumbnail as I decided how I was going to answer. *Do I risk being honest? What if this is how I react to all Alphas and not just them? They are the first Alphas I've spent time with since I discovered I was an Omega.*

A hand grasped mine, gently tugging it away from my mouth. Marius intertwined our fingers as he pulled it back to kiss my poor, gnawed on, digit. Shifting, I glanced at him as he just held my hand with his lips pressed to the skin.

When he saw me staring, he gave me a rueful smile. "I couldn't watch you hurt yourself any longer, I'm sorry." He didn't pull my hand away so as he spoke his lips brushed my skin, making an odd tingling sensation in my stomach.

Clearing my throat, I pushed aside that feeling as I answered. "The only Alphas I've interacted with since becoming an Omega have been the four of you. Nixon set me at ease even though I was so afraid to get in his car." I spoke to him as I said this, wanting him to know. "As I stood outside the open door of that car, not knowing what would happen once I got in it, the pull of his scent is what convinced me it was the right choice." Then my gaze moved to the Alpha still standing guard beside the couch. "Rafael... he's just safe. From the moment I met him, even though I didn't show it, and every time he holds me it's as if nothing in the world can touch me. It's a feeling I don't know that I've experienced since Mom died."

Pausing, I decided to shift my attention to Oscar, he was easier to explain. "You and I don't know each other at all, but your scent tells me you will be someone special to me. Everything about your scent reminds me of the happiest moments of my life. It's warm, inviting, and for some reason, I really want a hug from you. I don't normally like when men touch me, even by accident."

Now that left me with Marius, the man whose lap I was sitting on while he held my hand. Lifting my gaze to his, I could see how desperate he was to hear what I had to say. "While we didn't get off to the best start, your scent was always honest about who you really are. It's strong, dominant, and all encompassing, like the roar of a lion, yet makes me feel like I'm wrapped up in a warm wool blanket. It will battle the cold, keeping me safe and warm while knowing I can trust you to lead the way."

Bodhi let out an impressive whistle as he sat back against the couch. "That's wicked impressive Cambrie. By their scent alone you all but pegged their personalities to a T. When I catch their scents I get most of what you're saying, but nothing near the level of depth you clearly have."

"Do you know why that is, Sweetheart?" Nixon asked.

"No, I didn't know I could smell something different from anyone else," I admitted.

Nixon smiled and nodded. "That makes sense since it seems you haven't been educated on what it's like to be an Omega. Back before the attack by the EQ, Omegas were allowed to pick their packs. There would be interviews, and packs would send in scent cards for the Omegas to smell. With that alone an Omega could tell if they were a good fit or not. They would either find it appealing or imme-diately turn up their nose." He grimaced and ran a hand through his hair in irritation. "Of course, now there is no choice, so that practice has been done away with. The interesting thing is that Alphas respond the same way the Omegas do. When your perfume finally came out, it hit Raf and I like a ton of bricks, in the best way possible."

CHAPTER 10

Marius

Hearing Nixon speak about Cambrie's scent and how it affected him was exactly the situation I was in now. Here I was holding her hand like it was the most treasured possession I'd ever had. With Spencer at my side and Cambrie nestled against us, I didn't know my life could feel this complete. What scared me most about this was how clueless Cambrie was about how her perfume drew us to her like a drug. In this room were four powerful Alphas that had good standing in our world, and money to care for her in the lifestyle that befits an Omega.

If we'd been in a day and age like Nixon spoke about we'd be sending her gifts, courting her, and showing how we would be good providers for her and any offspring she decided to have. Now, all of that ceremony and wooing was tossed to the wayside. The government placed Omegas, correction, I now helped place Omegas into packs that had been cobbled together by how advantageous they could be to each other. Men and women might not even like each other, but on paper, they show in the best way possible.

While the other men of the CoF might not choose to meet with the packs on the waitlist for an Omega, I did. I wanted to see the nest room, if they created an environment that would help foster a loving relationship with the people the Omega would be required to mate with. Once a bond was put into place there was no way to remove an Omega, no matter how much we wished we could.

Without thought, I rubbed my thumb along the back of Cambrie's hand, craving contact between us. It wasn't sexual, more like the need to show affection that she clearly has been lacking. An Omega's nature thrives on casual touch, kind words, and gifts of various kinds to show them they are valued. They want comfort, security, and the knowledge they are wanted by the pack. Cambrie had gotten none of this for almost all eighteen years of her life. It sounded like things were a little better when her mom was alive but that was a drop in the bucket of the attention she needs.

Nixon and Oscar kept chatting with her about scent and how it relates to Alphas and Omegas. They transitioned that into delving into how and why Omegas are coddled and cared for the way they are, creating resentment in Betas. I knew Spencer and Bodhi didn't feel that way, it was just how Omegas were wired, and there was nothing they could do to change it.

Glancing at Spencer, I could tell he was already taken with Cambrie. He watched every move she made, trying to preemptively figure out what she needed. He was amazing like that. It was one of the many things about him I loved so dearly. His heart's desire to care for others was so large that I'd never once felt I was getting the short end of the stick sharing him with Nixon. Spencer cared for us in different ways, showing us each how much attention he paid to our every move.

The feel of his hand on the back of my neck as he massaged the tight muscles made me want to moan, but I knew Cambrie wouldn't feel comfortable with that. From everything she told us, it was clear her father didn't touch her or allow others to touch her that way. Of that, I was thankful for whatever gods might be listening. The physical and mental abuse was more than enough for anyone to handle but to top it off with sexual abuse, it would break anyone.

Spencer caught my eye and gave a slight head tilt asking if I was all right. I smiled and nodded, reaching up to grab his hand from my neck to kiss his palm in thanks. With me being a political icon, we had to learn to share our emotions and affection in small ways that wouldn't cause ripples in the media. Typically, when we were home that stopped but having someone new in the house, I just didn't want to put her on edge more than I'd already done. Part of me wished Spencer had given me the heads up, but he was also right that I would have caused one hell of a scene.

"Marius," Rafael called, making me aware that I'd zoned out of the conversation.

"I'm sorry, my mind drifted off. What did I miss?" I said, looking at the others.

Cambrie shifted and looked at me, her beautiful blue eyes trapped me in a hold that seemed almost magical in its effect. "They were explaining Omega nature and that typically once an Omega found a pack they liked, no other scent would be as appealing. I asked if that were to happen with me and a pack would I be able to stay? I know I haven't met many Alphas besides the four of you, so I can't really know if I react this way to everyone or not. But, if I did find people the old way will the CoF let me stay?"

That's the question of the century now, wasn't it?

"Cambrie, I would love to tell you I have an answer for you, but I won't lie to you, ever. In the past ten years there hasn't been a situation like this. Typically, either the black market snatches them up, or they are given to the government by the parents. You're one of the first to be out and about on their own, meeting Alphas in a casual setting," I explained. "This is a matter I'm going to have to do some research on, but I will find an answer for you. As we've already promised, we won't let anyone take you if you don't want to go. You are welcome here in our home for as long as you like."

"Trust me on this, they're serious when they say that," Bodhi interjected. "I was coming over on the weekends while Oscar was teaching me how to play piano and guitar. Then the next thing I know, I live here with these guys. If they give you their word about something, then trust it will happen."

I could tell by the looks on the other's faces they were stunned to hear such a thing come out of Bodhi's mouth. That Beta was one tough person to read, the only one who truly understood him was Oscar, and they'd become inseparable. He'd aged out of a foster home when he stumbled his way into the shelter, beaten up by a group of thugs that ran the streets. Bodhi had tried busking to make money, and they made it clear that he wasn't welcome on their turf. From the bits and pieces we've all learned over the years, the group foster home wasn't doing their job and they were only in it for the money. Kids were jammed in any available space and school lunches were the only meal they got.

If anyone in this room understood Cambrie in the slightest, it would be Bodhi. I would be curious to see what he would do having someone younger to look after instead of being the kid of the group. Rafael, of course, was the oldest being almost forty, while the rest of us were young to mid-thirties, leaving Bodhi at twenty-one, almost twenty-two, if I remember correctly.

"Okay, I'll stay, just until we know what happens next," Cambrie conceded.

My heart leaped hearing her say that she would stay with us. I knew she didn't say it would be forever, but everything in me told me she wouldn't leave as long as we didn't fuck this up.

"What do you say we find you a room to sleep in?" I asked, squeezing her hand. "Then you can change into something more comfortable and get a good night's sleep. Unless you're hungry? I'm sure we could whip something up by the time you get settled."

"I get a room?" Cambrie asked, surprise ringing in her voice. "I figured I would just sleep on the couch or something. I don't want to put anyone out."

"We have plenty of open rooms for you to pick from," Spencer assured her. "This place has space for I think ten people. There are even two open rooms with an attached bathroom. I think we should look at those first to see which one you like."

"Any room will be fine, I'm not picky. I've been locked in a basement, anything else is going to be better than that," she pointed out.

Spencer tucked a strand of hair behind her ear, giving her a soft look. "Would you humor me, so I feel better knowing I showed you both rooms? It's a bad habit I have to mother everyone in this house, and it would make me worry less if I knew you at least got to see them."

I couldn't help but grin as Spencer worked the magic he did on us all. That Beta had a way with words and used them to bend us all to his will, without us realizing it right away.

"I don't want you to be worried or cause you any discomfort because I wouldn't look at the rooms," Cambrie said, then started chewing on her lip. It was obvious this was a physical representation of her feeling like she said or had done something that might upset one of us.

Rafael glared at her lip like it personally offended him, making me raise a questioning brow at him. He gave me a dismissive look and swooped in to pull Cambrie off our laps so she was now standing before him as he pulled her bottom lip down so it was free of her teeth.

"Little One, if I catch you doing that again, I'm going to find a different way to remind you that those lovely lips are not for chewing," Rafael warned, with raw heat in his voice betraying what he had in mind.

This was a side of the good doctor I'd never seen before. He exuded calm professionalism always, now here he was letting his Alpha nature get the better of him. All that heat came to a standstill when Cambrie gasped and fear flooded her face. She hadn't understood that what he'd said wasn't a threat of violence as much as one of passion. The man wanted to kiss the hell out of her, not harm her.

"I... I won't do it ever again... I'm sorry, Rafael," Cambrie stammered.

Rafael took a deep breath through his nose, no doubt drowning in Cambrie's sweet sugary scent as he calmed down his urges. "No Cambrie, I'm the one who should apologize. I never should have said something like that to you and it wasn't how it sounded. While I know we've said this often, no one in this pack will lift a hand against you. Forgive me for even having you think that could be an option. I'm incredibly out of practice having a woman around, let alone an Omega whose scent is so pleasing to me."

"You think I smell good?" she asked, blinking at the man.

I had to bite back a groan. This woman had no idea what she was doing to us Alphas. Her scent was so intoxicating I wanted to shove my face into the crook of her neck and lick her skin to see if she tasted just as sweet. When visions of marking her started to fill my head, I clamped a hand on Spencer's leg, needing to ground myself. This wasn't the time or the place for such thoughts. Cambrie had a long way to go before we could even broach marking her as ours. Then there was the small matter of the CoF and how they would react if I sidestepped the rules.

Spencer placed his hand over mine, intertwined our fingers, and gave me a questioning look. I let the physical need I was feeling show in my gaze as I looked at him, warning him of what was happening tonight. He smirked and gave me a sassy wink, letting me know he was more than happy to help me with my issue.

"Yes, Little One, your perfume is one that I enjoy. It speaks to my Alpha nature and pushes me to take care of you in a more demanding fashion than I normally would," Rafael answered in an incredibly diplomatic way. "Come, let's get you settled in a room. Ah yes, Marius asked if you were still hungry, was the soup enough, or would you like something more?"

"I think I'll be fine until tomorrow. I don't want you to make something just for me," Cambrie countered.

Bodhi stood and stretched his arm above his head with a yawn. "Then it's a good thing I haven't eaten yet. How about I just double what I was going to make and I'll share it with you?"

Cambrie shifted from foot to foot as she thought about his offer. "If it isn't going to be too much trouble?"

"Nah, I always make too much as it is. Normally I pawn it off on Oscar, but now I have someone else who can help me out," Bodhi explained, stuffing his hands into his low slung baggy jeans.

Everything about that man was the persona of a careless musician. His shaggy hair he constantly swished out of his face, the vintage band tee, and the holey jeans he simply added more patches to. The one thing Bodhi never could be was wasteful. He'd learned how to rub two pennies together and make it last a week. Not once had he made too much food he couldn't eat, and if that was the case, he'd force himself to finish it. Waste wasn't tolerated. There was always something you could do with it.

What he was doing for Cambrie showed me just how much we'd managed to rub off on the guy. He wouldn't let her go hungry or make it seem like she was putting us out. The man was a genius, and I couldn't be more thankful there was one person in this house that understood what Cambrie needed in a way none of us from well off backgrounds, who'd never struggled in life, could.

"Now we have that settled," Spencer said, pulling his hand from mine to stand and clap his hands together. "Let's have a house tour, you'll need to know where you can find us in case you need something."

Swooping by, Spencer grabbed Cambrie's hand and charged up the stairs with her all but dragging along in his excitement.

"One of us needs to go with them," Rafael pointed out.

Nixon stood and raised his hand. "I'm on it. I'll try to keep him from overwhelming the poor thing." Quickly he jogged up the stairs after them. "Spencer, stop yanking her about like that, remember her feet."

I frowned, hearing him yell that down the hall, looking to Rafael for answers. "When she jumped out of the car she didn't have any shoes on. They got cut up pretty badly, but we cleaned them up and made sure they were bandaged before having her put on shoes. The little thing doesn't seem to be bothered by them at all. It's like the pain isn't bad enough for her to care, which worries me more than anything."

Oscar waved for our attention. "*Tell me we're going to find her father and make him pay. What he's done to her is worthy of the death penalty, and you know it.*"

"Oscar, you know it isn't that simple. If I go to the police with this information, then I have to disclose that we have her *here*. I know she isn't going to stay hidden for long, but I'd like the chance to come up with some kind of reasoning for why she needs to remain with us," I explained. "While I'm part of the CoF, I'm not the deciding vote, there are three other senior members to contend with. My plan is to do some research into the matter and find a way to prove what I've been saying. An Omega who chooses their pack will have a better quality of life, leading to better chances of breeding."

"*You want us to breed her?! She's just turned legal age, Marius. How could you even think of such a plan? There has to be another way.*" Oscar said, all but growling at the idea.

I walked up to my friend, resting a hand on his shoulder. "That isn't what I meant. You know I've been fighting for the placement of Omegas to be done away with. It isn't healthy for them and a large majority of them won't come into heat because they don't feel safe or cared for. What I'd like to try, is saying this is an experiment since we are drawn to her, and she is clearly drawn to us. If I can show them that allowing nature to take its course will do more good, they might let her stay and eventually help other Omegas in the future."

Oscar crossed his arms and gave me an uncertain look, like he wasn't sure he agreed.

"What would you suggest instead? I'm open to all ideas if you have any," I shot back. "None of us want to see her forced to be with another pack just because they're next in line. I promised her I would do whatever it took to keep her safe, and that's exactly what I'm going to do."

My old friend ran a hand through his hair and nodded. "*I don't have any ideas either. I'm sorry I'm being an ass. I've never been around an Omega before, and the urge to rip out her father's throat is all I can think about.*"

Hearing this my brow shot up. Oscar was one of the most loving and merciful people I knew. He even chose to forgive his own family, who cast him aside for something he couldn't change. "Trust me, I understand what you're feeling. It's wild isn't it when your Alpha instincts show themselves in unexpected ways. Even though my sister was an Omega, I didn't get much time around her before she was sent off. This is somewhat new to me too."

Bodhi backed out of the kitchen with a tray that had two bowls of tomato soup, and grilled cheese sandwiches. He caught us staring and shrugged. "She needs something light, right? I had a late lunch so I'm not super hungry. This will hit the spot. Besides, I'm not letting her suffer just because none of us eat like normal people at the same time or place. That girl's had enough of a person controlling her life, seems fair she can change ours instead." Pausing, he tossed his head to get his hair out of his face. "That being said, I'm making breakfast tomorrow at eight. She won't eat if one of us has to make it for just her, which means we will be implementing family meals. If you can't make it, then you have to make your own food."

Having made his point he headed upstairs, leaving us to figure out what magic Cambrie had to get that type of reaction out of Bodhi. The only person he wanted to spend time with typically was Oscar. While we all got along, none of us had found a way to connect with him the same way. It seemed just having an Omega in the house created changes in the pack for the better.

CHAPTER 11

Cambrie

"Here at the top of the stairs is Nixon's room. He and I share a Jack and Jill bathroom so I'm the next door over if you ever need anything," Spencer informed me, pointing to each door as we passed. "Next, we have one of the spare rooms I wanted to show you. It puts you next to me and Rafael is on the other side."

He turned the handle to the door, pushed it open, and flicked on the light. "I think the room is nice, but for an Omega I feel like it's a little small."

The room was bigger than any I'd had before, along with the size of the bed. The walls were painted a warm yellow with every-thing else in creams and tan. It was a lovely room, but I wrinkled my nose at it and already turned to leave the room before I spotted Nixon hiding a smile behind his hand.

"Did I do something wrong?" I asked, confused at the reaction.

"Not at all, Sweetheart. If it's not the right fit, then it's not the right fit," he answered. "Come on, there's one more on this floor, then we can look at one on the second floor. I think that's going to be the winner, but one never knows."

We left the yellow room and headed down the hall that ran widthwise of the house. As we passed the next door, I caught Rafael's scent remembering Spencer had mentioned that. This time

Nixon opened the following door to reveal a soft seafoam green room. It had white lace curtains and felt like something out of a fantasy book. While it was much prettier than the last room it still didn't feel *right*. I couldn't explain it, but there was something that urged me to move on.

"Really? I thought for sure this would be a winner," Spencer mused as we walked out. "Seems Nixon has picked up on your taste faster than I have, and that's saying something."

The smell of melted cheese caught my nose, and my stomach growled loudly in excitement. Turning, I found Bodhi walking up to us with a tray of food.

"Looks like I got here just in time. No go for these rooms?" he asked.

Spencer said something but my whole focus was on the golden brown sandwich with cheese oozing out of it.

"Earth to Cambrie," Spencer called, waving his hand in front of my face.

On instinct, I jerked back and dropped to the floor covering my head as I curled into a ball.

"What the fuck, man!" Bodhi snapped. "Take this."

"I'm sorry, I didn't think. She'd been doing so well... I just didn't think," Spencer rambled as someone moved closer.

My brain finally caught up to my body as I realized what happened. I tried to calm my breathing as my heart felt like it was going to burst out of my chest while adrenaline coursed through my veins.

"Cambrie, it's Bodhi. I'm not going to touch you just sit next to you, alright?" Bodhi shared, his voice low and soothing. "Take your time, catch your breath. There's no rush."

My stomach grumbled as if it mourned the loss of being able to have the grilled cheese sandwich. How could these men want to keep me around when I reacted like this? This wasn't normal for anyone, let alone an Omega. They were supposed to be cuddly and loving toward their pack, craving touch, but I freaked the second someone made a wrong move.

"Nix, hand me a plate with a sandwich," Bodhi instructed.

When the aroma of the food registered in my brain, pushing past my fear, I slowly lowered one arm. Bodhi indeed was sitting close by but where I could easily see him. He took half a sandwich and bit into it. The crunch of the bread and the strings of melted cheese that stretched as he set it down again got me moving. Carefully, I watched the other two who stood against the wall on the other side of the hallway. Spencer was now holding the tray of food, looking thoroughly upset.

"Here," Bodhi said as he slid the plate closer. "It's obvious you're hungry. No sense in wasting food that's been made."

Keeping my back to the wall I pushed myself up and pulled my knees close to my chest. I noticed the trench coat I still wore had fallen open to reveal the ugly yellow dress. *Would they let me change before I was asked to leave?*

"Come on, you don't want it to get cold, or it ruins the taste," Bodhi urged. "I'm sure you'll feel more settled with some food in you. From what it sounds like, you haven't been too active in the past few years. Jumping out of a car and running for it, that would wear me out."

Bodhi continued to talk, his tone neutral and slightly bored as if what happened hadn't been that big of a deal. I started to reach for the plate but paused, double checking to make sure it was alright. He just glanced at me and gestured with his hand to help myself to the food. Gingerly, I lifted the portion he'd taken a bite from, leaving him the whole half.

"Cambrie," Bodhi said, stopping me with a warning tone in his voice. "Take the other one, I already claimed that half."

Biting my lip, I snatched up the whole half and brought it to my mouth. The smell of the creamy butter and melty cheese was as decadent as a steak dinner to me. I love cheese, all kinds, and it was something Father withheld any time he was upset. He'd say it was too expensive or I ate it too fast, wasting money. This would be the first taste of cheese in almost three years. I slid a corner of the sandwich into my mouth and bit off a small chunk savoring it. My eyes fell shut when the sharp tang of the cheddar mixed with the gooey goodness of the mozzarella. Bodhi knew how to make an excellent grilled cheese, and he put plenty of cheese on.

"Taste good?" Bodhi asked, causing me to snap my eyes open to look at him. "Sorry, didn't mean to take you out of the moment."

"This is amazing," I praised, giving him a shy smile before I took another bite and sighed. "I love cheese."

Bodhi flashed me a wide grin showing off his teeth. "I'll make sure to keep that in mind. I'm making breakfast for everyone tomorrow, so it sounds like cheesy eggs need to be a thing. Unless you don't like eggs."

"I like pretty much all food," I answered, my mouth full of food. Cringing, I covered my mouth and looked over at the others to make sure I didn't offend them by talking with my mouth full. Mom would have been so upset with me.

Spencer and Nixon were sitting on the floor talking quietly to each other as Bodhi and I ate our food.

"Don't worry about them, they might look prim and proper but they aren't stuffy about the rules. Pretty sure the only thing I've gotten in trouble for is staying out one night and not telling them I wouldn't be home. They got super worried, even sent the police to look for me," he shared.

My eyes grew wide at that, thinking how awful I would feel to make them worry so much. "What happened when you got home?"

Bodhi rested his head against the wall looking up at the ceiling. "I showed up the next morning before the sun was even up, and there they all were in the front room, sleeping, waiting for me to come back. Oscar scolded me and biffed me upside the head, which I deserved. It's been so long since I had people give a shit about where I went I just didn't think about it, you know?"

"After Mom died, I tried to be gone as much as possible. If Father caught sight of me and he'd been drinking I knew what would come next. When he noticed I wasn't coming home he started to lock me in the basement for a day or two, so I would hide in my room with the door locked. Well until he removed the door, pissed that I locked him out," I shared, pausing in my meal. "It was like I couldn't do anything right. Something always upset him. I would be quiet, I'd do my chores, he never taught me anything so I didn't have homework. No matter what, everything made him mad."

"I had a foster parent like that. He'd fly off the handle at the stupidest shit, always changing the rules so you couldn't win. People like that are just fucked up in the head, and there's nothing we can do about it but survive long enough to get away," Bodhi shared.

He stuffed the last part of his sandwich into his mouth before he stood, brushing off the crumbs on his pants. Pausing a moment he looked at me uncertainly, then reached out a hand to me palm up, making sure it looked in no way like he was trying to hurt me. Clutching the half I still hadn't finished eating to my chest, I took his hand letting him pull me to my feet.

"You don't need to guard that, I'm not gonna take it, and there is a whole other sandwich if you want more. I also heated up some tomato soup if you want to dip it in that," Bodhi commented, motioning to the tray by Spencer. "Let's have you see the last room, and if you like it, then we can eat the rest there. It's spacious enough you shouldn't feel too claustrophobic."

"Clastro... what?" I asked, not understanding the term.

"It means you don't like small spaces or feeling trapped," he answered, leading me up the second flight of stairs, still not having let go of my hand.

I thought about that for a moment and wondered if that was why I didn't like the other two rooms. They were bigger than my old room, but there was so much stuff in them it felt cramped, even though they were nicely decorated. When I reached the top of the stairs the third floor opened up into a wide area with a comfortable looking leather sectional sofa and a big screen TV. It looked like the space was used fairly often and had a much more relaxed feel than the rest of the house.

"Oscar works from home and I help him with a bunch of stuff, so this is our space just to relax and chill. He has a whole production studio out back in a separate guest house. That way when he comes here work is over and he can just be home. Of course, the others use it too, since it has the best sound system and the video game console," Bodhi explained when I paused to take it all in. "The room is over here opposite Oscar's and mine. We haven't done much to it other than put a bed in there, so if you like the space we can make it into whatever you want."

"Oh, that's not necessary, I don't have any way to pay for things and I don't know how long I'll be here," I said hurriedly, not wanting them to think I was looking for a handout. "I just need a place to stay until Marius figures out what the best plan is for me."

Bodhi harrumphed at that as he flicked the light on in the room. It was empty but for a bed on the floor just like he warned but that was perfectly fine with me. Everything else about the room was perfect. Pure white painted walls with a ceiling that came to a peak with two large skylights right above the bed. Wooden beams showed how the roof was supported but also adding character. The carpet was soft underfoot and a pretty gray-blue color. I had the strangest urge to take my shoes off so I could feel the texture of it.

Not wanting to act stranger than I already had this evening, I settled for sitting on the mattress and brushing my hand over the carpet. It was just as soft as it looked, making me smile. Then I tilted my head back and gasped as the stars winked at me from above. Before I realized it, I was lying flat on my back, hugging my half of grilled cheese sandwich, gazing at the stars.

"I can't remember the last time I looked at the stars... have they always been that bright?" I asked, not really expecting anyone to answer.

"You're lucky, tonight there aren't that many clouds," Nixon commented, reminding me I wasn't alone.

I scrambled to sit up and my sandwich tumbled off my lap onto the carpet. "Oh no!" Quick as I could I snatched it up and used my coat sleeve to dab where it landed. "I'm sorry I shouldn't have even brought food in here."

Nixon knelt in front of me and slowly reached out to place a hand on my arm. "Sweetheart, it's okay. There is no harm done and all of us eat in our rooms from time to time. Trust me when I say you're not the first one to spill. In fact, Spencer knocked over a glass of red wine in my room once."

"That was all your fault," Spencer mumbled, his cheeks turning pink.

Nixon just winked at his partner, then returned his gaze to me. "Accidents happen and there's always a way to clean things up. Now take a deep breath for me, because no one is upset in the slightest."

I did as he instructed, just as Rafael had told me, in through my nose out through the mouth. It was surprising to see how much that helped.

"Would you mind if I traded you this tray with a full sandwich and soup for the half you dropped?" Nixon asked.

Blinking a few times, confused, then I looked down at my hand seeing the sandwich was squashed and some carpet fuzz stuck to it. "It's fine, I'll still eat it."

"No, you won't," Nixon ordered, holding out his hand. "I understand not wanting to waste food, but I'm not going to allow you to eat that when there is no need."

Meekly, I handed over the battered food item, watching the crumbles land on his pants. I moved to clean them up but a hand rested on my shoulder.

"It's alright, I was going to change out of these clothes into something more comfortable for the evening. They need to be washed anyway. Speaking of, after you finish your dinner we should get you set up with things to take a shower and clothes to sleep in," Nixon instructed, turning his attention to Spencer. "Do you mind, Spence?"

"On it! We also need sheets and things for the bed," Spencer answered cheerfully and headed out of the room.

"Cambi, why don't you join me out in the rec room? There's a coffee table we can eat at," Bodhi suggested.

"Cambi?" I asked as I trailed after him.

Bodhi just grinned. "Yeah, you're like *Bambi*, all sweet, inno-cent, and a little awkward. I think it fits, don't you?"

"Who's *Bambi*?" I asked, still not understanding what he was talking about.

"Seriously?" Bodhi blurted, looking shocked. "Even with my shit childhood I watched a few Disney movies. In fact, it was the default for some foster parents to just turn on a movie so we would stop bothering them on the weekends."

"Mom didn't like me watching TV. She always told me to go outside and play. She used to say it would foster a better imagination. Personally, I think reading did that more, but I couldn't read at that point," I shared. "Of course, I know about the movies and I've read the original stories but I don't think I know *Bambi*. Is it good?"

Bodhi set the tray on the coffee table and grabbed two pillows from the couch. He placed them on the floor and pointed to one, making me assume he wanted me to sit there. He plopped down on the other, grabbed a bowl of soup, and slid the rest over to me.

"Hmm, that's a tough question to answer. It's got a lot of real life moments that it deals with, not all of them happy," he mused. "What do you think, Nixon? Would you say *Bambi* is good?"

"Oh god, I haven't seen that movie in forever, all I remember is the beginning of him as a kid and maybe the ending..." Nixon answered, taking a seat on the couch behind me. "I'm sure we can find it somewhere and watch it. Allow you to make up your own mind."

"You would watch a kid's movie?" I inquired, surprised.

Nixon grinned at me. "Some of the best movies are meant for kids. They make you laugh and take you out of the real world for a few hours. What's not to like about that?"

I nodded understanding that completely, it was how I felt about books. Turning my attention to the food, I stirred the soup, the bowl was still warm but not too hot. I tested the spoonful and found it perfect for gobbling down. Now that food was available, and it all tasted so good, I realized just how hungry I'd been. Trapped, unsure of when the next meal would come, I had to keep from dwelling on it and just trained my mind to find it unimportant.

With the soup gone, I could now relish the grilled cheesy goodness. I took one half and slid the plate over to Bodhi. "Here, I hope you don't mind. I picked first this time."

"If you're hungry eat the whole thing. Finishing off the soup has me rather stuffed," Bodhi said, patting his stomach. "I promise, it's fine if you eat the rest."

Glancing over my shoulder at Nixon, I pointed to the food. "Do you want the other half? I'm not sure if you ate dinner or not yet with me crashing in on your day."

"God, you really don't have a selfish bone in your body, do you?" Nixon murmured, giving me a sad smile. "I'm fine, Sweetheart, once I finish getting you settled I'll reheat some leftovers. You enjoy the sandwich since I took half of the other one away from you."

"If you're sure, I'm happy to share," I assured him.

Nixon leaned forward resting his elbows on his knees. "How about a bite then? You claimed this was rather amazing grilled cheese. I suppose a sample might be in order."

I grabbed the half from my plate and held it up to him. Instead of taking it from me like I thought he would, Nixon held my gaze as he grasped my wrist gently to take a bite of the sandwich. His lips closed around the bread and the crunch told me he'd taken a bite. When he pulled back cheese followed but he let go of me and grabbed the strings licking them off his thumb.

Watching this made my mouth go dry and flutters started in my stomach. There was something about what he did that had my heart beating faster and wishing he would do it again. Everything he did, like Marius, seemed so elegant it made me feel clumsy. A rumble started in Nixon's chest calling to me, my body listing toward him.

"Nix," Rafael's voice called out. "Could you please come help me for a moment?"

Nixon's soothing rumble suddenly changed into a growl as he glared at the man standing at the top of the stairs.

"Please, Nixon," Rafael stated, his voice laced with something reminiscent of a command. "Spencer and Bodhi can look after Cambrie for right now. I *need* you to come with me."

With a grunt, Nixon finally stood but he paused and looked down at me, carefully reaching out to brush a caring hand over the top of my head. "You need me just call, I'll be right downstairs."

Unsure of what to say I nodded, watching him stride over to Rafael and exchange a few sharp words before descending. I glanced over at Bodhi, who just shrugged, "Alphas do some weird things sometimes."

CHAPTER 12

Cambrie

With my belly full to the point of being a little painful for the first time in what seemed like forever, I unwrapped my feet. Spencer had come back with towels, a toothbrush, toothpaste, clean clothes, shampoo, conditioner, and a hairbrush for me to use. He bustled me into the bathroom and showed me how to turn on the shower before leaving.

"When I see you next you better be showered and in those clean clothes. Take your time, there's no rush. This is your bathroom, no one else needs it. I'm going to make the bed so when you come out you can snuggle up and sleep," he informed me. "Is there anything I missed that might help you feel more comfortable?"

I shook my head vigorously. "No, you all have done so much for me already. This is overwhelming and more than I ever expected."

"Bodhi is in the rec room playing video games if you need anything. If he's not there, then feel free to knock on any of our doors, and we'll handle whatever it is," Spencer assured me before backing out of the bathroom, shutting the door.

Quickly I locked it, needing the reassurance that no one would be able to sneak up on me while I was showering. Taking a shower, or anything to do with removing my clothes, made me feel so vulnerable. Even though Father never once touched me in that way,

I could feel his eyes linger when I changed or washed up. With all my attempts to run he refused to take his eyes off me if I wasn't securely locked behind all those deadbolts. Sometimes, I think he knew I hated it so he did it just to make me uncomfortable.

Looking at my feet, I grimaced at how rough they looked but I was glad they did little more than ache. I removed the trench coat, the one item that had been able to hide my abuse. I caught a glimpse of myself in the mirror and cringed. My eyes looked like sunken saucers in my face, with my cheekbones protruding out sharply. Blonde hair hung in a wild mess around my head, the wave in it having gotten out of control with them brushing it while dry. The bright canary yellow of the dress made all my bruises stand out in stark contrast. It was as if Father picked it to show them off, like he was proud of the beatings he gave me.

Refusing to shy away from the person I was staring at in the mirror, I pulled the dress over my head. My shabby underwear hung off my hips, and since I had no breasts to speak of there was no need for a bra. Scars where he'd beaten me with objects other than his fist littered my skin. It was as if my whole life story of abuse was forever etched into my skin, never to leave or allow me to forget. I looked down at my wrist, brushing a finger over the one and only self-inflicted scar.

At a low point after a beating so bad I didn't think I was going to live, the pain was so bad I decided it was better to end my life on my terms. In an odd way it was good I didn't know the best way to cut myself to do the most damage. The nail I'd tried to use wasn't sharp enough to do much damage, but it had been bad enough that Father was scared I'd get sick. It was the one and only time Father allowed another person to know of my existence and treat me while I was in the basement.

I'd gotten a reprieve from the beatings as I recovered and was given food on a somewhat more regular basis for a week or so. That all ended once he knew I was going to be fine, and the first beating was just as bad as the one that caused me, for a moment, to give up hope. I learned from that experience that I didn't want to die. I might not have known how I would survive, and that moment solidified that I wasn't going to let my father win, but I knew it wouldn't be at the expense of my own life.

Tears welled up as the feelings of that time started to overwhelm me. Shaking my head, I turned on the shower and tested the water to find the best temperature. It had been ages since I had a hot shower but I wasn't sure my body was up for more than warm. I glanced at the claw foot soaking tub that sat on the other side of the bathroom. Part of me craved to submerge myself in clean water, but I knew the bucket I washed in this morning hardly removed all the grim from my skin. Maybe another day, but right now I just wanted to scrub away the two years of captivity.

Gingerly, I stepped into the shower, my feet slightly more tender since I didn't have them wrapped. The stone floor of the shower didn't help but it was nothing I couldn't manage. The feeling of the water coating my skin, weighing down my hair, and dribbling down my face was a sensation I wasn't sure I'd ever feel again. I just stood there a moment fighting back tears once more, as the reality that I wasn't trapped sank deeper into my consciousness.

Once I had enough of soaking in the moment, I grabbed the shampoo. It was labeled for men and smelled of mint, but I liked it. Everything about it was fresh and invigorating, making my scalp tingle with a clean feeling as I scrubbed. I washed my hair twice, feeling that once was just not going to cut it, then I worked in the conditioner and used the brush to battle the tangles that I'd tried to keep from getting worse. When the bristles ran smoothly through my locks, I knew another piece of evidence I'd been locked away was gone.

Finally, I took the washcloth and scrubbed my skin harder than I should have, but the *need* to be free of anything that could cling to me was too strong. The parts that weren't bruised were bright pink from my abuse but that was a color I hadn't seen in a long time. Shutting off the water, I wrung out my hair as best I could knowing it would take forever for it to dry with how long and thick it'd gotten.

The towel was soft and fluffy, gentle on my skin as I dried off. Wrapping it snuggly around me I looked over what they'd brought me to wear. There was a simple gray T-shirt that smelled like Rafael and sweatpants that carried Spencer's scent. That made sense, he was the thinnest out of the bunch to even come close to something that would fit me. Soft white socks were also included in the pile. They didn't carry a scent, almost as if they were new, which made me curious. Then I remembered they had collected things for me at the shelter. It would make sense people would donate items like socks for them to give out to those in need.

Dressed in my warm, wonderfully scented clothes, I peeked out the door to see if anyone was in the room. It was empty, but a few more things had been added to the room. A small lamp near the bed that was now made with several pillows piled at the head. The sheets were pulled back and a warm cream colored fluffy blanket was added for warmth.

A sigh passed my lips as my feet landed on the carpet, it was so perfectly soft. Placed on the end of the bed were two books, one was a classic fairy tale I'd read a long time ago, and the other was a book titled *A Little Princess*. I could tell it was old by the color of the pages and the leather of the cover. There was something about the smell of an old book that made it all the more special. When I opened the cover I saw a note had been tucked inside.

It was mentioned you liked to read, so I thought I would share these with you. These stories were always a favorite of my sister's. She made me read them to her all the time. I hope you find enjoyment in them. I think she would have liked for someone like you to have them.

Sweet Dreams, Marius

I clutched the book to my chest and this time I couldn't stop the tears from leaking out. For him to give such a precious gift to me made no sense. Even from the little he'd told me of his sister I knew how important she was to him. *Why would he give them to me?*

Turning off the main light I padded over to the bed, curled up under the covers, nestled myself against the pillows, and opened to the first page of *A Little Princess*. Instantly, I was captivated by Sara's story of how her life was full of joy, love, and imagination only to be crushed at the hands of a person who only saw her as an object. I don't know how long I read, until I couldn't keep my eyes open any longer and drifted off to sleep dreaming of the little princess.

THE BED SHIFTED CAUSING me to wake instantly, I froze as terror seized my body. My ears strained to pick up any noise, trying to determine just why my father was down here and why I didn't hear him stumble down the steps. The blanket shifted and no longer was I frozen. The moment had come that I feared where Father decided he wasn't going to wait to get his money from me. I scrambled off the mattress to get as far away from my father, or whoever was down here, as the chain would allow. When nothing stopped me I ran into a wall with a *thud* and crumbled into a ball.

"Please, please, don't do this," I begged.

Then a scent hit my nose and the terror abated slightly, allowing me enough of a clear mind to realize I knew that warm caramel and cinnamon scent. There crouching before me, sadness etched on his face, was Oscar. When he noticed I was truly seeing him he sat back on his heels and pulled out his phone. His nimble fingers flew over the object doing something he was incredibly intent on. Then he surprised me as he placed the phone on the carpet and slid it over. He gestured for me to pick it up, making sure not to move any closer.

Slowly, I unwound myself and leaned forward to take the phone. There written on the screen was a note.

"I'm so incredibly sorry, Cambrie. I didn't mean to scare you like that at all. I was checking the house before going to bed and noticed your light still on. When I peeked inside, I saw you asleep with your

light on and your face sleeping on your book. I should have let you be, but I just wanted you to be comfortable. Please forgive me for not real- izing this would upset you."

"Thank you," I whispered. "Thank you for checking on me, it was incredibly sweet of you."

Oscar frowned and shook his head, clearly not agreeing with me.

"It's not your fault that I'm broken, Oscar," I pointed out. "Sleeping is always scary, I never knew what time of the day it was, but I tried to sleep when he was at work. It wasn't ever a deep sleep, that would be too risky, so I learned how to keep aware of my surroundings. This scared me because I was truly sleeping soundly. I didn't hear you enter the room like I should have."

An odd grunting sound came from Oscar as he motioned for me to hand him back the phone. Instead of sliding it across, I crawled over and sat next to him knowing he didn't pose a threat. He took the phone, careful not to touch me, which I appreciated more than he knew. After coming out of panic attacks was the worst time for me to be touched. Although I was quickly noticing wasn't the case with the Alphas of this pack.

Oscar's scent this close was intoxicating and all I wanted to do was curl up against him. I could hear his fingers moving and the phone's vibrations as it confirmed what he'd pressed. My eyes drifted closed and my head landed on his shoulder. Both of us froze for a moment before I started to pull back. Instead, he placed a gentle hand on my head urging me to leave it where it was. My body was too tired to fight and my mind was finally quiet as I rested here.

Maybe he wouldn't mind if we stayed like this for a bit.

A soft melody filled the air, it carried echoes of sadness in the notes that pulled at my heartstrings. It was as if whoever wrote this song was lost and alone, but as it continued it seemed to blossom into something that had more happiness. It wasn't like the classical music Nixon was listening to, this had more soul as if someone's raw emotions were poured into it. The pain, sadness, and loneliness that they felt translated into music. Then as this person found their way, the pain lessened, they weren't alone anymore which lifted the sadness. There was still that lingering pain that I'm not sure anyone would be able to be rid of but there was hope.

"That's beautiful, what kind of music is that?" I murmured.

A tap on my arm had me opening my eyes to see the screen of his phone. There, scrolling along the bottom under the title of artist was Oscar's name. Shifting back, I looked at him in amazement. "You *wrote* that?"

He nodded, a smile tugging at his lips. Shifting the screen to a list of names I realized were songs that he'd written. I trailed my finger across the screen to scroll through the list, but it went on and on. Some were written by him alone, while others had a few artists listed.

"Can we listen to them all?" I asked, scrolling back up to the top. "I want to hear everything you have to say."

That had him pause a moment flipping to his notepad to write out what he wanted to say.

What do you mean you want to hear what I have to say? There are no words in these songs, only instruments.

"You don't need words to hear when someone puts their heart and soul into a song," I pointed out. "That song I just listened to, did you write it before coming to live here?"

He nodded, watching me intently, searching for something in my expression.

"It might not be obvious to everyone, but someone who has felt all those feelings as intensely as you and I have, understands them even without words. There's no way I couldn't hear what echoes in my own heart, I just hope one day I'll get to the second half where hope exists again," I sighed, curling up against him, needing the knowledge I wasn't alone right now.

Do you want me to stay?

"I couldn't ask you to do that. You need to get sleep. I'm sure there's lots you have to do tomorrow. Besides, I think I've disrupted your lives enough for one night," I answered, yawning, trying to find the will to pull away from him and get back into bed.

Then his phone was nudged into my hand.

How about I stay till you fall asleep, then I'll go to bed. I just want to make sure you feel safe.

"Okay, just until I fall asleep," I answered.

Oscar tucked his phone into his sweatpants and scooped me up. He settled me into bed pulling the covers up, tucking me in like Mom used to when I was little. Turning off the lamp, he sat beside me leaning on the headboard, tucking an extra pillow behind his back. I curled up on my side so my head was resting against his hip as I tucked my hands under my chin letting out a tired sigh. His fingers gently brushed my hair out of my face as I nuzzled into his warmth.

"Goodnight Oscar," I murmured.

Before drifting off I could have sworn I heard him whisper. "Goodnight, Little Star."

CHAPTER 13

Spencer

Hearing the *snick* of the bathroom lock eased my fears as I left Cambrie's room. Not that I had any fear that someone here would do anything or cause her harm, it was more that I think she needed time to herself. Since Nixon had picked her up she's been surrounded by new people, strange places, and having to manage her anxiety at every turn. I could have kicked myself for what I'd done earlier.

How had I thought it was a smart idea to wave a hand near her face? You'd think seeing a body covered in bruises would have given me a clue how she'd react. Standing outside her room I gritted my teeth, trying to keep from allowing my own personal demons of negative self-talk to seep in. On the outside, no one would have a clue about the darkness that I've fought my way out of to be where I am today.

No!

I couldn't allow my mind to go back to those days. They were over and I had two Alphas that loved me, knowing all the baggage I carried. They saved me and I knew they could do the same for Cambrie, our little pure dove, who didn't realize the hope she represented for our pack. Taking a deep breath, I shook out my hands and shook off the memories that seeing her abuse had brought back.

Bodhi was absorbed in his video game, ignoring my meltdown, which gave me the chance to believe he didn't notice. All of us had wounds from our past, and over the years we've come to respect the moments we struggle with them.

Heading down the stairs, I almost crashed into Marius as he came up. "Sorry babe, I didn't see you, lost in thought," I apologized.

"It's all right," he answered, wrapping a hand around the back of my neck, pulling my head down to touch his forehead. "If you're up for it, will you stay with me tonight?"

"Of course, I don't really feel like being alone tonight either. I'll warn you though, Nixon might be joining us too," I answered.

Marius smiled and shrugged. "You know that doesn't bother me. He's the one who gets uncomfortable when I get added to the mix, since we aren't interested in each other romantically. We used to have sleepovers as kids all the time, so what if it happens now we're adults?"

"I think it's the naked part, maybe also the fact his best friend fucking his Beta. You know he struggles with the views his family hammered into him," I pointed out.

"But we always have so much fun on your birthdays when the three of us play together." Marius purred into my ear. "He knows I love him but not in that way. We share you, and you share us. Why can't we share together occasionally? I'm careful to only touch you."

My knees started to go weak as my cock went from soft to hard in two seconds. I had to grab the railing to keep from stumbling. "You know what that does to me," I muttered.

"Good," he answered, pressing a kiss to my lips. "I'm going to drop these books off for Cambrie, then I'll be more than happy to fix the problem I've caused."

He jogged up the stairs, leaving me to steady myself before hurrying my way to Nixon's room. I knocked and seconds later I was yanked inside and plastered against the wall with my other Alpha's tongue down my throat. Need oozed off Nixon as he growled and ripped off my shirt.

I pushed him back, looking at my clothes and scowled. "That was a new shirt, now I have to find all the buttons and sew them back on."

"It's fine I'll buy you a new one, but my Prince, I *need* you right now," Nixon said, all but begging me as he ran his hands down my chest.

Grabbing his hands, I stilled them before they got to my pants. "Marius needs me too. I said I would sleep with him tonight as long as he knew you'd be there too."

Nixon paused for a moment as if he wanted to argue but he nodded and rested his head on my shoulder. "Cambrie's done something to me, made me more possessive than usual and all I want is to steal you away for myself right now. Marius and I share you, that's how it's always been and will stay. We made a promise to *never* make you feel like you had to choose because neither of us wanted that. Now I fear I'm going to have to share someone else with him... with all of them."

I wrapped Nixon in my arms, hugging him tightly. "Our Little Dove is an Omega, which is entirely different from how things are between the three of us. Cambrie is already handling the whole situation perfectly and she isn't even aware of it. Give her time. Once she understands what she feels being with us and how we feel about her, it's going to be magical. Omegas are meant to pull a pack closer through their love and affection toward every pack member, not just one. You saw Bodhi, when have you ever seen him smile that much?"

"My brain knows you're right, but my heart is so worried she might not pick me," Nixon admitted. "I know how hard you fought for things between the three of us, and it was my fault for being a stubborn ass and not trusting you could love us both the same."

"Enough now," I chided. "Cambrie's wounds, her story, seeing her like that, has brought up a lot of old memories for us all. We've risen above who we used to be and have become better versions of ourselves." I nudged him to stand upright and grasped his face. "You know without a shadow of a doubt that I adore you, without you in my life part of my heart would be missing forever. Yes,

Marius holds the other part and I have a feeling soon Cambrie will take another for herself. But that doesn't make what you hold any less than the others."

The moment I finished speaking his lips were on mine feasting, showing me through actions that he understood what I'd said. Our relationship might have started with a few bumps in the road but now we were a family who fought for each other. A knock on the door interrupted us and Nixon pulled away.

"It could be Cambrie," he murmured as he strode across the room to open the door.

It wasn't Cambrie and I didn't think she'd be brave enough yet to bother one of us. Instead, it was Marius with a sheepish smile on his face. "I figured you'd distracted him when I didn't find him in my bed. Would you rather us stay here in your room? Or share mine? I'm fine with either, I'll just need to grab a few things."

"No, we can use your room, besides you have the bigger bed to fit all three of us. With mine, someone is bound to fall off the edge with how bad Spence hogs the bed," Nixon answered, giving me a wink.

"So hateful," I huffed. "You ruin my shirt, you call me a bed hog, what's gonna happen next? I snore?" Both of my partners looked at me tight lipped as if I did actually snore. "Do I?"

"Do you what?" Marius asked.

"Snore."

He ran his hand through his hair dropping his gaze. "Well, I wouldn't call it snoring, more like you sigh in your sleep." My jaw dropped, Marius lifted his hands as if to stop me from speaking. "Hold on, don't do that. I think it's adorable, so I didn't feel the need to tell you about it, alright? It only happens when you are first falling asleep and I didn't want you to be all self-conscious about it."

"He's right, it is really cute, Prince," Nixon agreed, giving me a smirk. "It's like you're so content with us you just can't help but sigh."

"Ugh, hate you both right now," I groaned. "I'm going to sleep in my own bed where my sighing won't bother anyone."

As I tried to walk past Marius, he grabbed me around the waist pulling me to his chest. "Now babe, that isn't at all what we said." I pretended to struggle in his arms but when his teeth bit down around the shell of my ear I melted. "Now that I have your attention, listen closely. Both of your partners find your sighing positively adorable and endearing. It does something to our Alpha nature to hear you so contented in our beds."

All thoughts of leaving had now flown away with the renewed raging hard on I had pressing at the seam of my zipper. "Can we go to bed now? I think I'd like to get out of these clothes."

"I love the sound of that," Marius purred, releasing me from his hold, and smacking me on the ass. "Get to it."

With no other encouragement needed, I raced out of Nixon's room, to the opposite end of the hall to the master bedroom Marius used. Seeing as this house was given to those who were part of the CoF it made sense he'd have the biggest room. He also just so happened to have ordered an Alaskan king size bed that filled the ostentatious room perfectly. This was one reason that on special occasions when the three of us came together we used his space. Not that Marius didn't always offer to be in Nixon's, he was so considerate like that.

Marius's room was something you would see in a magazine advertisement for the *power male's den*. It was all leather, earth tones, and dark wood accents which, when you added in his scent of heady bergamot and spicy clove, made the whole thing work. Of course, the room had been done by a designer, part of the perks of being an official. Most of the first floor was done for us but many of the guys wanted to make their rooms their own. Bodhi refused to let anyone but him and Oscar touch anything on the third floor, but we'd expected that.

I slipped out of my already ruined shirt and laid it on the leather bench at the foot of the bed. Marius hated messes, so I tried my best to leave things in a neat pile that wouldn't drive him crazy. While I was detailed in my life and work, I might tend to be a bit of a slob in my personal space. It was almost like I needed one part of my life I didn't feel judged on and that was my bedroom. Marius would sleep in there with me, but I would make an effort to make it presentable enough not to unglue him. That, in my mind, was an act of true love.

Hands stopped me as I started to remove my belt. "Let me," Nixon said in a low voice, kissing along my neck as he pulled my belt loose and dropped it on the floor.

I made a worried sound as I tried to bend down to pick it up, but Nixon stopped me. "Don't worry about it. Marius will be distracted soon enough not to care about your clothes littered on his floor."

His hands brushed along the top of my pants, slipping his fingers in just slightly, making me moan. When he reached the clasp, he undid it slowly but stopped before getting to the zipper. Turning us both so we faced Marius, who'd already stripped down to his boxers. "If I remember, this is your favorite part," Nixon commented as he nibbled from the crook of my neck to my shoulder.

Marius closed the space between us, quickly dropping to his knees and gripping my hips in his hands. Leaning forward, he bit down on the zipper pulling it down until he could slide my pants off. The sight of my Alpha on his knees before me was something I could never get over and was always my undoing. Marius was a powerful person in every part of his life but when we shared our bodies we were on equal footing.

Kicking off my pants and boxers, I was now exposed to them and their growls filled the air around me making me shiver with delight. "Is it strange that I'm glad we don't do this all the time? Both of you together are overwhelming in the best way and I don't ever want that feeling to go away." I sighed.

Nixon's hands were on my chest, playing with my nipples, stroking my skin, and keeping me upright as Marius took my cock in his mouth. The feeling of his tongue lapping up my shaft like it was his favorite treat was one of the best feelings in the world. Marius's hand shifted to cup my ass, kneading it in his hands as he took me deep down his throat.

"Oh fuck," I cried out, grabbing onto Nixon. "If you keep this up I'm going to be spent way too fast."

"Hmm, is that a challenge, Prince?" Nixon purred, rubbing his body on mine.

Feeling that he still had his clothes on I reached behind me to help him get them off. Seeing what I was up to, Nixon shifted out of reach making me grunt in irritation. "Just wait my sweet Prince, we'll get to that soon enough. For now, we just want to spoil you before we ravage you and our Alpha nature takes over, rutting into your perfect ass."

"Yes, god yes, that's what I want," I whimpered, feeling Marius probing my asshole. "I want you to use me, even though I know your cocks are begging for a pretty Omega sleeping upstairs."

That got their attention, Marius pulling away to stand, grabbing my jaw. "Is that what you want babe? To claim her as our Omega, to share her between the three of us?"

I bit my lip and nodded as much as his grip would allow. "Yes Alpha, that is what I want."

Marius purred as his lips crashed into mine in a bruising kiss as he took both our cocks in hand, stroking them against each other as Nixon stepped back. I could hear the rustle of clothes and I relaxed realizing he wasn't walking away. When he returned to us, I felt the cool sensation of him pouring lube on the peak of my ass only to spread it down the line to massage my asshole.

"This is going to take patience, trust, and understanding from us all to make that happen," Nixon added as he continued to prep me. "If we make Cambrie ours, we're going to have to fight for it. The CoF isn't going to just give her to us."

Marius broke our kiss, allowing me to answer as I leaned my head back on Nixon's shoulder to stare into his eyes. "She is ours already, and all of that comes with any relationship worth having. Cambrie is our pack's Omega, that's all there is to it, fuck the CoF and anyone else who tries to take her from us."

Nixon grinned at me. "Such a smart Prince we found ourselves, didn't we Marius?"

"Yes, we most certainly did," Marius agreed. "Now I think our Beta deserves a reward, don't you?"

"Absolutely, he's all lubed and ready," Nixon assured, scooping me up and tossing me on the bed. "Now you're going to return the favor to Marius while I pound that juicy round ass of yours."

Knowing exactly what he wanted me to do I got on all fours and wiggled my ass at him playfully. His eyes flashed with hunger and I knew his careful control had shattered. With a growl he pushed his cock into me, easing his way until his hips met my ass. Reaching under he stroked me as he gave short strokes letting me relax into the fullness of him. It had taken us a long time for me to take him to the hilt and I could only do it at the start, once his knot began to swell I couldn't manage it. No matter how we tried, my body just wasn't meant to take it the same way an Omega could. It didn't make our sex any less mind blowing but I knew it was something all Alpha's craved that I couldn't give.

Marius crawled his way up to me looking like a lion on the prowl and I was his next meal. Instead of presenting his cock to me the way I thought he flipped onto his back and slid under me. Nixon released my cock as he realized what Marius was doing, freeing him to focus on one thing. Making me lose my mother fucking mind as he rutted into my ass. Bending down, I gobbled up Marius's dick that lay hard and already dripping with pre-come on his stomach. In a mess of limbs, mouths, and hands we feasted on each other's bodies.

Nixon kept up with his deep power strokes for as long as I could take it, then backed off as things got too tight. Marius was relentless with his attention to me, cock licking, sucking, humming, and even using a hint of teeth around the crown making me twitch at the sensation. Just as I felt Nixon's knot start to swell he pulled out, flipped me off Marius, and climbed on the bed to straddle my face.

"I want to finish in your pretty mouth, my Prince. I want to watch you drink my cum as you squeeze my knot," Nixon ordered, his voice laced with a growl.

This is one of the ways we'd worked around me not being able to take a knot. If they finished in my mouth I could squeeze their knot with my hands, giving them their full release. They could finish with no knot, but it wasn't as pleasurable as it was when that added pressure was given. This was the struggle for all Betas, women bore children so their bodies could take more, but I wasn't willing to stretch that far if there was another way.

I gripped Nixon's cock, dragging him closer so I could take as much of him as I could, deep down my throat, Marius was entering me on the opposite end. Both of my Alphas fucked me like they owned me and there was nothing that made me happier. I pictured Cambrie joining us riding my dick so that all of us could be in a chaotic love orgy. Her soft moans adding something more to the melody of slapping skin, grunting men, and my moans of pleasure. It would be perfect when it happened and I prayed that it would be forever when it did.

"That's it, Prince, squeeze me good and tight as I come between those pretty lips of yours," Nixon groaned as he dropped onto his hands, unable to keep himself upright.

Marius's knot was knocking at my door but it wouldn't be able to enter, as much as I wanted it to. Soon, hot cum shot down my throat and I wrung that knot of everything it had, gulping down his seed to the last drop. Marius roared as he finished inside my ass his own hand gripping his knot as he gave short thrusts, acting as if he was in an Omega.

Nixon rolled off me while Marius grabbed my cock and timed his thrusts with his hand pushing me over the edge to my own climax. As I cried out my release I felt hot strings of cum land on my stomach but it didn't sit there long as Marius cleaned up after the mess he made. His hot wet tongue gliding over the ridges of my abs. It was one of the sexiest things I've ever seen him do. Marius didn't hide his true self from me, there had even been occasions he'd wanted to be the bottom and let me top him. Just because he was an Alpha didn't mean he couldn't give up control every so often. It wasn't common but to me, those times were precious, showing me how much he loved and trusted me.

"Holy shit, you guys." I sighed, covering my face with my arm. "That was amazing."

Nixon brushed a hand down my arm tugging it away from my face so I could look at him. "I wasn't too rough with you, was I? It's not like me to lose control like that."

I gave him a lazy smile as I caught his hand and kissed the back of it. "No Nixie, that was hot and I know you would never hurt me. If it was too much I would have said something and you would have stopped. Change is good and you hardly ever go Alpha on my ass... literally." I teased, trying to hold back the laughter at my own joke.

Marius lay down on top of me, not bothering to keep his weight from pressing me into the mattress. After sessions like this I liked to be grounded, reminded that when all was said and done love was at the root of all their actions. He kissed along my neck and nipped at my ear, making me squirm.

"Is someone not satisfied yet?" Marius asked.

Shaking my head I brushed a hand through his hair. "I'll never get enough of either of you, but I was picturing her here with us too."

"Cambrie?" Nixon questioned.

I rolled my eyes. "Is there another female that we've recently met I would want to drag into our bed? Yes, silly." The joy it brought me to tease Nixon when he got all broody was unhealthy but it kept him from getting too hum-glum so I kept doing it.

"What did you imagine?" Marius asked as he started to purr.

The vibrations of his purring sent little sparks of electricity through my body making me shiver with pleasure. "We were in the same position with Nix in my mouth and you fucking me while she rode my cock. All of us together, not knowing where one started and the other ended, it was like the best sex dream a person could have."

Now both Nix and Marius were purring thinking of what I'd just shared. We lay there for a bit then the three of us retreated to the bathroom to clean up. Marius finished first and left me with Nixon who got me all dirty again before crawling into bed. I was in the middle being little-spooned by Marius as I sprawled over Nixon's naked body. This would only be better if Cambrie was snuggled up in our puppy pile. One day, one day my dreams would come true.

CHAPTER 14

Cambrie

The world's most soothing noise surrounded me. It called to my soul and told me everything was alright. I was safe and right where I belonged. The aroma of spicy cinnamon made me think of the roasted almonds my mom used to make in the fall. They were a favorite snack of mine that died when she did. Refusing to wake from this dream and face the reality of my hellish life, I snuggled deeper into the warm fluffy blanket.

It was only when the sound got louder, and the blanket moved I realized it wasn't a dream. My eyes popped open, and I sat up to find Oscar sleeping next to me, his body wrapped around mine, with my face nestled into his chest. I didn't know what to do.

Do I stay until he wakes up? Would he be mad if I left the bed while he's still sleeping? What if I wake him up?

In my experience, no man liked to be woken before he was good and ready. Father would come out swinging if I was too noisy or I would even end up locked in the basement so he could get his goddamn rest. The purring came to an abrupt stop as Oscar opened his eyes to meet mine. He seemed just as surprised as I was to find me here.

"Good morning?" I said hesitantly. "It seems you fell asleep last night when I did and didn't leave."

His face morphed from confusion to panic as he released me and sat up. His hands were moving so fast but I couldn't understand anything he was trying to tell me. Running a hand through his hair he growled in frustration and climbed out of bed to storm out of the room.

I gazed after him, utterly confused as to what had just transpired. Was he mad at me because I couldn't understand him?

Moments later, Oscar was back dragging a bleary-eyed Bodhi with him. "What the fuck is going on? God, I've never seen you this pissy first thing in the morning. Why am I being dragged into this?"

Oscar clapped his hands loudly in front of Bodhi's face, shocking the poor Beta into wakefulness before signing furiously at him. Bodhi watched carefully until his brows shot up and his jaw dropped. "You *what?* How could you do that? God, I knew Nixon was having a tough time keeping himself in check but *you?*"

Oscar snarled and pointed to me, then to himself, and signed what looked like he was telling Bodhi there was no chance of something happening between us. *Were Oscar and Bodhi partners? Did he think I'd done something to cause problems between them? Oh god, I had to fix this.*

"Bodhi," I cut in. "Nothing happened, he came to turn my light off and scared me. When I calmed down he offered to stay with me till I fell asleep. Nothing else, if he is your partner I'm sorry, I didn't mean to overstep or ask him to do something that would cause problems. It's clear Oscar is upset about staying here all night and I just want to make it clear that *nothing* happened. I would never ever come between someone's relationship."

Bodhi gaped at me like I'd grown a second head. "Cambi, what on earth are you babbling about? God, it is too fucking early for this, and I haven't had a drop of coffee." He drove his fingers into his shaggy hair and scrubbed at his scalp in irritation. Then he took a deep breath and dropped his hands and turned to face me. "Start from the beginning for me please, Cambi. Numbnuts over here isn't making any sense, or I'm still half asleep. Either way, I'm not following what went down and why he's upset and why *you* think we are in a relationship."

I crawled to the end of the bed and sat cross-legged, clutching a pillow. "Marius dropped off some books for me to read and I got so sucked into the book I didn't realize I'd fallen asleep. Oscar noticed my light was still on and came to turn it off. He startled me and I had a panic attack, but he calmed me down. He shared some music of his with me, then offered to stay until I fell asleep. When I woke up this morning he was still here... I think it surprised us both. Then he stormed off and grabbed you."

"Okay, now some of what he was saying makes sense, but that doesn't explain why you think he or I are upset? Also, for the record, we are best friends, not lovers. Not that I don't love him because I do, just not in *that* way," Bodhi clarified.

Oscar didn't seem convinced about that but didn't comment as he waited for my answer.

"He said something that got you mad, then he motioned to me then him in what I took as a clear sign of not interested," I explained.

Bodhi rubbed his face a second before walking over to sit next to me. "Cambi, that is not at all what that meant. He was trying to tell me he didn't do anything inappropriate with you while he was in your bed. Oh god, why am I left to explain this? Rafael should be the one to go over the Alpha, Omega, birds, and the bees."

"What does this have to do with sex?" I asked my brows scrunching together. "I might not have gone to school and gotten that talk, but you read a romance book or two and it's not hard to learn what you need to know."

"There is a difference between knowing something in your brain and your body reacting to a situation happening in the moment. An Omega's perfume is like crack to Alphas, especially an Omega that is the right fit for their pack. The Alphas smell just as addictive to the Omega, drawing them closer together. When that happens sometimes an Alpha can go into rut, a phase where they become hypersexual and the only way to fix it is to have sex... lots and lots of sex. It's somewhat the Alpha version of going into heat for Omegas," Bodhi educated, his cheeks turning a rosy color with his embarrassment.

I blinked at him a few times as my brain sifted through that bit of information, then when it finally made sense I gasped covering my mouth. Bodhi flinched a little as if he felt guilty for telling me.

"Wait, so you think Oscar was in danger of going into rut just by spending the night with me?" I asked, dropping my hands.

Bodhi scratched the back of his neck as he nodded. "Nixon was showing signs of it, so was Rafael last night. Marius had an Omega sister, so he knew what to expect but Oscar's never spent time with an Omega. So, I got mad he would put himself in a position that could have potentially upset you. He was telling me off and explained nothing happened but sleep, the best night's sleep he'd ever gotten I should add."

Now it was my turn for my cheeks to heat up thinking I might have helped with that. I couldn't think of a time I slept as soundly as I had last night. I didn't even dream I was so deeply asleep.

"The real reason Oscar woke me up and dragged me in here is because he was worried he'd overstepped and wanted you to know he was sorry. He wasn't trying to be forward, he had every intention of going to his own bed but fell asleep," Bodhi added, placing a hand on my knee. "I'm sorry your first morning with us turned out to be so chaotic. We aren't used to having a woman around, much less an Omega. So forgive us men as we blindly stumble about trying to do the best we know how."

I couldn't help but smile at them. "There is nothing to forgive, it was just a whole bunch of misunderstandings, and my lack of being able to communicate with Oscar correctly." Pausing, I covered Bodhi's hand with my own, shocked at how small it was compared to his. "Will you teach me sign language? Then there won't be any more misunderstandings and we won't have to drag you out of bed."

Bodhi nodded, then nudged me with his shoulder, his gaze catching mine. "Sure thing Cambi, but until you can manage on your own, feel free to come to me when you need help. No matter what time it is," Bodhi demanded, pointing a finger at me. "I'd rather be there to help than have you take something the wrong way like you did today."

"I can do that," I answered with a shy smile and my cheeks flaming hot. Then my stomach decided that was the best moment to voice its need for food. Apparently, giving it two meals yesterday had reawaken it, and I was *hungry*.

"Guess now would be as good a time as any to get breakfast started," Bodhi said with a sigh. "What time is it anyway?"

Oscar held out his watch for him, Bodhi gasped and grabbed the Alpha's wrist. "That has to be wrong, it is not seven in the morning!"

His shoulders shook with silent laughter, Oscar signed something to Bodhi that had the Beta swearing under his breath.

"Yeah, yeah, yeah, must be nice you got to cuddle with the adorable Omega and get lots of good sleep to be so chipper, asshole," Bodhi muttered as he got up from the bed, then reached out a hand for me. "Come on Cambi, looks like I'm making breakfast for everyone since I'm awake at the crack of dawn."

Giggling at his misery, I gripped his hand and let him pull me off the bed. He didn't let go, so I trailed after him as he trudged down the steps. When we made it to the second floor, I spotted Nixon sneaking out of what I think was Marius's room.

He froze as he spotted us, his brows shooting up. "Ah... everything okay?"

Bodhi just grunted and tugged me along. I twisted to face Nixon as I called out. "We're going to make breakfast, are you joining us?"

"To believe it, I'm gonna need to see it," Nixon chuckled. "Yeah, I'll be down once I get ready for work."

I gave a wave before I had to pay attention to what was in front of me, since Bodhi was determined not to slow down. He paused a moment before we got to the stairs and I crashed into him with a squeak.

"Good morning, everyone," Rafael's voice reached my ears.

I peeked out from behind Bodhi and saw the Alpha walking upstairs holding a mug of coffee.

"Good morning, Rafael," I answered when Bodhi once again

didn't speak. I poked him in the ribs making him jump and look down at me.

"What?"

"It's polite to say good morning when someone says it to you, in case you forgot," I whispered as I tilted my head in Rafael's direction.

"It's all right, Little One, Bodhi doesn't speak to anyone so early in the morning. In fact, it's rather a miracle that he's awake since it's normal for him to sleep till almost noon," Rafael informed me.

My jaw dropped as I spun to glare at Oscar. "You dragged him out of bed this early when you knew he needed more sleep?"

Oscar grinned, pulled out his phone, typed something, then handed it over.

The man sleeps the day away all the time. He doesn't need to sleep that late, he just likes to because he stays up playing video games. It will do him good to see a morning once in a while. Don't let the grumpiness fool you, he just doesn't like to show people how he really feels about things. He's happy to be up to make you breakfast.

"If you say so," I said not convinced but handed him back his phone.

Bodhi looked between me and Oscar, eyes narrowed. "I'm not gonna ask because you clearly didn't want me to know, but don't go saying unnecessary things, Oscar." Bodhi's tone was cold and unfriendly.

At his words Oscar looked hurt and dropped his gaze. "Bodhi!" I snapped. "Don't you ever speak to him like that!"

"Cambi—"

"No," I said, cutting him off. "Oscar is your best friend, right? A person who knows you well and would respect you enough not to tell secrets to a stranger?"

Bodhi paused for a moment looking at Oscar behind me. "Yes..."

"Then trust he wouldn't betray you like that. I scolded Oscar for waking you up thinking you needed sleep, badly. He was telling me that wasn't the case, you just like to stay up late by choice. Then you go and say mean things like that to him. If you should be mean or grumpy to anyone it should be me, I'm the reason you got yanked out of bed." I ranted, anger that I hadn't felt in a long time rose within me. "People who care about each other don't tear each other down. At least not in front of me they won't."

Bodhi opened his mouth to say something, then stopped and looked around. At some point during my tirade, everyone had come out of their rooms to see what was happening. My cheeks burned with embarrassment as I yanked my hand out of Bodhi's grasp. Panic overwhelmed me as I realized I'd just yelled at one of the few people who'd been kind to me in years. Fight or flight hit me and I ran. I ran right down the hall past Oscar, Nixon, Spencer, and Marius to fly up the stairs and run to the room they let me use. I closed the door but didn't lock it, not wanting to anger them more, then dove into bed and pulled the blankets over my head.

Shivering with anxiety I waited, my ears straining waiting for any noise that would tell me what my fate might be. There was no way they would let me stay now that I'd been so disrespectful to Bodhi. This was the problem I ran into with my father all the time, I didn't know when to keep my mouth shut when I thought someone was being treated unfairly. It didn't matter that I couldn't really change my life, but I wasn't going to let someone else experience what I did day in and day out.

Even at the library, if I saw kids picking on others I would step in trying to defend them. Sometimes it meant I went home with new bruises but it wasn't like I had anyone around who cared or noticed. Hearing Bodhi go that cold toward Oscar when he'd been nothing but wonderful just rubbed me the wrong way and I couldn't let it slide. Now because of that I was going to be dropped back on the streets to fend for myself.

Why? Why couldn't I just behave like Mom always tried to teach me?

I don't know how long I lay there before there was a soft knock on the door. I didn't say anything, it's not like I could stop them from coming into a room in a house they owned. When I didn't answer another knock sounded slightly louder, but I wasn't going to invite their wrath in here. No, if they wanted to punish me or kick me out they would make the first move, I wasn't going to make it easy for them.

"Little One?" Rafael said, his voice muffled by the door. "Can I come in?"

My mind flashed back to my father beating down my door. *You little bitch! How dare you lock me out of a room in my own house! You better open this right now or I'm kicking it down, then beating your ass for being such a disobedient cunt like your mother.*

"Cambrie?" Rafael's voice pulled me out of the memory only to realize I was sobbing under the blankets. The mattress sank as Rafael sat and moved the blankets back to reveal my face. When he saw me it was almost as if my sadness hurt him as he slowly reached out to cup my cheek brushing away the tears. "Little One, what's wrong?"

"I'm so sorry." I sobbed, sliding onto the floor ready to beg for forgiveness like Father always made me do before he hit me. "I didn't mean to be disrespectful and say those mean things to Bodhi. Sometimes, the words come out before I can stop them. Mom tried to teach me to be a good obedient girl but I could never mind my tongue. I'll leave now, I don't deserve to be here after doing that."

"Cambrie, you're not going anywhere," Rafael announced. "Please come back up here and sit with me, there is absolutely no need for you to beg on your knees to me or anyone else, ever."

He reached out a hand for me to take but I just couldn't believe he wasn't upset. Why? Why had everyone else in my life found me lacking and yet these men seemed to find no fault whatsoever?

"Why?" I whispered. "Why aren't you mad at me? Why do you care so much when you don't know me? No one treats people this way."

Rafael studied me for a moment, then joined me sitting on the floor stretching out his legs, resting his hands on his lap. "You know why, you said it not five minutes ago to Bodhi. People who care about each other shouldn't tear each other down. Believe it or not, Little One, I unequivocally care about you in a way that I don't fully understand yet. It ruins me to think your parents have made you believe that you're anything less than perfect being who you are."

I scoffed. "I'm far from perfect, I could never follow all the rules Mom tried to teach me. When she died, Father told me it wasn't even worth trying to improve the worthless daughter he had, so why should I bother going to school? I thought I could show him how wrong he was by getting my GED, going to college, and getting out. Then I failed at that too by becoming an Omega. Maybe my mother knew what I would be and tried to teach me how to behave so when the government took me I could fit in with a pack like yours."

"Do you know why you got mad at Bodhi?" Rafael asked.

My gaze flicked up to his, confused by his question. "He was being cruel to Oscar when he didn't deserve it. That tone he used he wanted his words to hurt Oscar and I wasn't going to let him do that."

"Is that something you do often, defend those around you? Or is it only people you know?"

I knew the answer right away, but I took a moment to appreciate Rafael's question. "Everyone deserves to have someone on their side, whether you know them or not. If I can do something about it I will try because then the other person knows they're not invisible to the world around them."

"Do you feel invisible?"

Leaning my head back I looked up at the skylights at the blue sky with the puffy clouds. "Before meeting all of you... I know I was invisible. I could be covered in bruises, cuts, getting skinnier by the day, and no one cared. They had their own problems to deal with so why bother with someone else's?"

"Cambrie, will you look at me please?" Rafael requested.

I did as he asked, meeting his blue-gray eyes, shielded by his glasses, but piercing into my soul just the same.

"You are not invisible to me, or anyone in this pack. We see the pain you've been through marked all over your body, watch you as you struggle to be stronger than your mind will let you be as it is filled with lies, and what you did for Oscar meant the world to him." He paused letting his words sink in for a moment. "When he lost his voice, the world he grew up in considered him damaged goods. His family and most of his friends walked away, abandoning him to face this life altering change by himself. For you to protect him like that, having just met him, and after all that happened this morning, is something he will never forget."

"But Bodhi—"

"Deserved the lashing you gave him," Rafael said, cutting me off. "Bodhi has been through hell in many similar ways as you have, but instead of choosing to see the good in people, he hardened his heart. Yes, Oscar is his best friend, and I think he might be the first real friend Bodhi has had. Sadly, his first response is to assume someone is going to betray him and lash out first before he can get hurt. He was upset Oscar told you something without him knowing what it was, so he assumed the worst."

"Doesn't he want Oscar to stay his friend? Saying cruel things will only push him away, not encourage him to stick around," I asked, trying to understand. "If I had someone who genuinely wanted to be my best friend I would do anything to make sure that person was happy with that choice."

"Hmm, see there is trouble in that way of thinking too. Bodhi chooses to cut people off who get too close so he doesn't get hurt. Oscar and Bodhi have had many fights, then once they've both cooled off they find a way to reconcile. With what you said, I'd worry about you doing things that aren't healthy or you'd do anything just to make the other person happy. Relationships of any kind go both ways. Each person needs to give one hundred percent to the relationship for them to stay strong. The moment someone pulls back that's when things start to crumble. You can't be the only one working to keep the friendship alive, it has to be both of you," Rafael explained.

Everything he said made sense but went against most of what I'd been taught all my life. Mom always went the extra mile while Father provided for us, that was the roles they lived by. My duty was to be a good obedient daughter who reflected well on her parents... but I never seemed to be able to do that.

"What if both people don't understand that's how friendships work? Like I didn't and I wouldn't have expected the other person to either," I argued.

Rafael nodded. "You make a valid argument, Little One. We learn by what we see and who we spend time around. When you don't have a good example of a healthy friendship it's hard to get it right. This is when *you* decided to be the change and teach someone else how to be a better friend and person. When people realize that every relationship takes work you find out quickly who's worth the effort. Some will stay, others will leave, but let them leave because they aren't worth the effort. Remember it's not fifty-fifty it's one hundred and one hundred."

"So does that mean you and I are best friends now because we both know how to be good friends to each other?" I asked, tilting my head to the side.

Rafael smiled so brightly that I wasn't sure it was real. "Little One, I would be honored to be one of your best friends."

"You can only have one," I countered.

"Now why would you choose to limit the love you can share? You said you protect anyone whether you know them or not, so why can't you develop deeper friendships with more than one person?" Rafael challenged. "A healthy pack works best when everyone is friends. Yes, some might be more than friends and develop into lovers, but at the core of every couple is friendship. If you don't have that foundation when you get into hard times, relationships shatter, and you can't put them back together again."

As he spoke I could see old wounds casting shadows in his eyes, and sadness lingered in his words. Moving closer I placed my hand over his hands in his lap. "I'm sorry."

He frowned. "For what, Little One?"

"That you had someone shatter your heart," I answered. "You have the same look on your face as my friend Peggy does when she talks about her fiancé that died."

"You truly have a gift for reading people like a book, don't you? It's astounding you can see others so clearly down to the depths of their soul after all the world has given you is sadness," he murmured as he gently tugged me to his side, where he wrapped his arms around me. "No one who has a heart as big as yours could be anything but perfect. I am so glad we found you Cambrie. Things will be hard as you learn to trust us and we learn who you are under all these lies people have slipped into your beautiful mind."

Rafael tucked his hand under my chin and lifted it so I looked up at him. "The first step to being a better friend is for you to learn that conflict is not always bad. There will be times when you will need to stick up for yourself and we want you to, without question. Your voice is welcome here and we want to know what you have to say. On the other hand, so is everyone else's, in this house, in our pack, things are decided together. You know what we all decided unanimously before I came up here?"

I shook my head, my throat was too full of emotions to speak.

"That an Omega by the name of Cambrie Price will have a home here for as long as she wants and that all of us want to be your friend, family, and pack," Rafael announced.

My eyes watered and spilled over, dripping onto his hand. "All of you want me to stay? What about the government? Won't they make me leave?"

"Those are worries for another day. For today, we just want to know your vote. Do you think that Cambrie Price will accept our offer?" Rafael asked as he wiped away my tears with both his thumbs as he cupped my face.

"If they really want me to stay, and Bodhi isn't mad at me." I licked my lips and cleared my throat. "I would really love to stay here with all of you for however long that may be."

Rafael pulled me close and pressed his lips to my forehead. "The answer to that is forever, Little One, you belong here with us."

CHAPTER 15

Cambrie

"Bodhi is working on breakfast so why don't you take some time to get ready for the day before you come down?" Rafael suggested as we both got to our feet. "That will give you a moment to collect yourself before joining us. I brought up the clothes we gathered at the shelter, but we will get you others since you can't live with only one set of clothes."

My eyes grew wide. "I can't pay you for anything. I have no money right now. I'll find a job soon and then I'll be able to get some more clothes. I can make it work with what I have now and whatever the shelter gave me."

Rafael crossed his arms and looked down at me with disapproval. "Little One, I understand this concept is going to be a hard one for you to accept, but we are a pack. Half the money we earn goes into a communal fund to take care of things needed within the pack. If any of us are short on money or need something and can't afford it, then we pull from the pack fund. You have been asked to be part of this pack and if you truly mean what you said about joining us, then that fund applies to you."

Fidgeting, I looked down at the floor and worried my lower lip. Rafael cleared his throat and I instantly stopped, knowing he wasn't happy about it. "You said everyone puts money in, then they can take money out... I haven't put any money in."

"Bodhi doesn't put money in either right now. He works with Oscar, does chores around the house, and pitches in where he can because he chooses to go to school instead of working. He's getting a degree in audio production so that he can partner with Oscar, and one day they will both run the business together," Rafael shared. "I believe that is what we will suggest for you, to finish getting your GED and then see if maybe college might be something you're interested in."

My head snapped up, my mouth hanging open in shock. "Can I really do that? I thought Omegas weren't allowed to go to college, that they had to stay with their pack."

"Get ready for the day and we can talk about it over breakfast. There are many ways to work around things. What I want you to promise me is that you will keep an open mind and think about what you want to do with your life, other than being an Omega. It is your designation, but not your whole identity, Cambrie." Rafael pointed out as he gave me a warm smile and headed for the door. "We'll also need to get this room set up for you to use. This is your space now to do with as you please," he called out as he shut the door behind him.

I sat down on the end of the bed stunned by what just happened. *They wanted me to stay! I could really have a pack, a family of my own. Does that mean Marius talked to the CoF and got them to approve me to be here? How could he have gotten an answer so fast?*

Shaking my head, I decided not to worry about it, they asked me to work on trusting them. This was a good place to start and take them at their word. I wandered into the bathroom and brushed my teeth, combed my hair and braided it, then looked over the clothes the shelter had given me.

I found a pair of black leggings that I slipped on, they were a little loose but I'm not sure anything would fit how skinny I was. Next, I pulled on the white tank top and a giant striped sweater in grays and teals. It was clearly meant for a person more filled out than I was, but the softness on my skin had me instantly loving it. The sleeves went well past my fingers, but I just bunched them up until they were free. It hung to mid thigh so it was almost like wearing a dress. It made me smile, knowing that I wasn't going to be cold. Lastly, there was a pair of white soft looking slippers with floppy bunny ears.

I picked one up and looked and then giggling at how cute they were, there was even a little pink nose right at the toe. *These couldn't have been at the shelter, they look far too nice. Did someone go out and get them? When would they have had time to do that?* Regardless of how they got to me, I was delighted to wear them. They fit perfectly and the sturdy bottoms on them protected my poor feet from any more damage. Ready as I was going to be for the day, I headed out of the room... Stopping, I turned around and looked at the space before me.

This was mine.

Rafael said this could be *my* room to do with as I wanted. Never had I been given the chance to decorate a room before. It had always come down to what we could afford or what we found others were throwing out. But this time I might actually be able to find a few things to put my mark on the space.

A warm feeling filled my chest as I walked down the stairs, almost like I was in a daze. How in the world did this happen? In less than a day, I went from living each day praying I might survive, to the next to thinking about what future I wanted. They were encouraging me to get my GED and possibly go to college. What would I want to do?

I halted at the base of the first floor stairs, stuck on that thought. Once, so long ago, I remember my mom asking me what I wanted to be when I grew up. Of course, I'd told her I wanted to be a princess like the books I'd read, but after Mom died I don't think I dreamed like that anymore. The future at that point was making it to the next day, week, turning eighteen so I could get away. Now it seemed like everything was possible again.

"Cambrie?" Marius called, bringing me back to reality. "Are you alright? You seem a little lost."

"Oh... ah...," I faltered, tugging at the sleeves of my sweater, dropping my gaze to the fluffy slippers. "I...I'm sorry for how I behaved this morning. It was wrong of me to yell at Bodhi like that."

I felt him coming closer, his heady scent getting stronger. Now that I knew what to expect, it wasn't nearly as overwhelming as it had been last night. A finger slid under my chin and pressed upwards urging me to look at him.

"There you are," he said with a soft smile. "Don't hide those beautiful eyes from us, Princess, they help us know what you're thinking."

My cheeks flamed with heat at his words and the look he gave me. The feeling people talk about where it's like butterflies in your stomach had to feel like this. Something about feeling *seen* by these Alphas had me feeling all sorts of new emotions.

"Now, as to what you were saying about Bodhi. While I understand that you're apologetic for the situation, I believe he's the one you need to talk to, not me," Marius pointed out. "Come on, let me show you where he's at," he offered, holding out his hand.

Part of me felt it was a little odd that they always wanted to touch me, but another craved the feeling. I slid my hand into his and let him show me through the living room we'd been in last night, past a swinging door into a giant kitchen. Everything was oversized, stainless steel, and professional looking. There at the stove, wearing a black apron, was Bodhi flipping pancakes.

"I'll leave you to it then," Marius whispered in my ear as he squeezed my hand and left the same way he entered.

"I told you I don't need any help with breakfast," Bodhi snapped. "You want to be helpful Spencer, go find out if she likes chocolate chips or not. I'm sure Rafael will manage to fix the fuck up I've made out of this morning for the second time." He slammed down a pan making me jump. "God damn it, why can't I ever be fucking normal? Why do I have to lash out at people like that? You know what, don't answer that, I don't need another therapy session right now."

"It's been years since I've had chocolate chips in my pancakes," I whispered, not moving from where I was, in case I needed to leave quickly. "I think it would be fun to have them again, I remember liking it, but who doesn't like chocolate?"

Bodhi froze, then slowly turned around to look at me letting his gaze linger over my body. "Cambi…"

"Wait please," I cut in, holding out my hand to stop him speaking. "I need to apologize for what I said to you. While I don't approve of how you treated Oscar, there was absolutely no reason for me to yell at you the way I did. My temper gets the better of me when I feel someone is being bullied. I know you care a lot about Oscar, and Rafael is trying to help me understand that not all fighting or arguments between people are bad. I know I have a long way to go but I would really like to work on being someone who could be a good friend to you… if you want me to be your friend." Now that I'd said everything I needed to, I felt awkward and picked at my sleeves.

I heard the clattering of some pans, followed by the slap of bare feet on the tile floor, then arms surrounded me pulling me against an apron covered chest. I waited for my body to react to betray me and freak out at this clearly well meant interaction, but nothing happened. His clean fresh pine scent surrounded me, making me feel like I was out in a forest after the rain had purified the world from its grime. Excitement welled up as I returned his hug, making him stiffen a moment before he rested his head on top of mine.

"The one who needs to apologize is me," Bodhi whispered. "The guys were right, I'm not a pleasant morning person but I wanted your first morning with us to be a good one, and I ruined it. I know Oscar would never do something to hurt me, but in my broken brain I was so worried he might say something to make you think poorly of me. I'm not a great friend to have but I would love to try and be the best friend I can be for you."

Bodhi's words resonated deep in my heart, echoing what I'd just been saying to Rafael moments before. "We can work on it together, because I'm not sure I'm a very good friend either. I never know how to keep my thoughts to myself and tend to cause trouble for others."

Bodhi chuckled, nuzzling his cheek against my hair. "We're quite the pair, aren't we?" Releasing me, he took a step back and ran a hand through his hair ruffling it. "So that was a yes to chocolate chips?"

With my heart lightened knowing Bodhi wasn't mad at me, I gave him a bright smile. "Who says no to combining dessert and breakfast together?"

He grinned in return shaking his head. "You make a good point Cambi, a very good point." Bodhi returned to the stove and poured batter into the frying pan. "The others are in the dining room if you want to join them. I've got a few more to make, then I'll be in with them. I've already brought out the cheesy eggs and bacon."

I gasped at the mention of the cheesy eggs. "You really made them?"

Bodhi nodded, a pink tinge blooming on his cheeks. "Yeah, you seemed so excited about the grilled cheese I couldn't not make them after I offered."

Rushing up to him I tossed my arms around his neck and dragged him down to plant a kiss on his cheek before getting embarrassed and rushing out of the kitchen in the direction he pointed. Everyone looked up from there what they were doing when I burst in, causing me to freeze.

"Goodness Dove, you look bright as a strawberry, did Bodhi say something inappropriate?" Spencer asked, setting down his phone, looking worried.

I shook my head furiously and took the seat next to Marius, hoping they would let the matter drop. "Bodhi said something about cheesy eggs?"

"Yes, and we were forbidden from having any until you got what you wanted first," Nixon answered, folding up his newspaper and grabbing a covered dish.

He walked over to me, pulled off the lid, and scooped a mountain of fluffy eggs covered in cheesy goodness onto my plate. Done with the dish, he passed it to Marius who helped himself and sent it down the line.

"Sweetheart, what would you like to drink? We have coffee, orange, apple, or grapefruit juices," Nixon asked.

My face scrunched up as I tried to decide on what sounded good. Father never bought anything but basic ingredients or frozen meals he could microwave. Nothing could affect his ability to buy beer when he wanted it, so all luxuries went to the wayside.

"We always keep these in the house so if you want to try something different every day you can," Marius pointed out.

"Apple please," I decided.

"Coming right up," Nixon said, heading back into the kitchen.

"Oh," I said anxiously. "I should have gotten it while I was in there, he didn't need to go get it for me."

"It's alright Dove, part of being a pack is looking after one another," Spencer assured me, then nodded to my eggs. "Better eat your fill before they get cold."

Pushing up my sleeve, I picked up my fork and stabbed it into the fluffy egg. When I popped it into my mouth I couldn't help but do a little happy dance at how good it tasted, humming a little tune as I went in for more. After a few more bites, I looked up when Nixon set down a glass of juice for me.

"Sounds like everything is tasting good to you," he said with a chuckle. "I don't think I've ever seen anyone so excited over cheesy eggs before."

Setting my fork down I picked up the glass and took a sip. The shock of how sweet it was caught me off guard that I gave a little gasp. "Wow!"

Soft laughter made its way around the table and I looked up to see all the guys watching me with warm expressions.

"I forgot how sweet it was," I shared, so they understood my reaction.

"That's why I personally prefer orange or grapefruit," Rafael said, pointing to his glass of pink liquid. "I don't mind something sweet every so often but tart tasting things are a favorite of mine."

"What about you Oscar, are you more of a sweet or sour fan?" I asked since he was sitting next to Rafael.

Oscar held his hand up to his chin and moved it downward with a smile.

"I'm going to say that means sweet," I guessed.

Oscar nodded and clapped in approval. Then he took his pointer finger and put it where someone would have a dimple and twisted it making his face pucker a bit.

"Sour?" I asked.

He nodded and gave me a thumbs up, filling me with a sense of excitement that he was taking the time to teach me. I wanted so badly to be able to talk to him the way he was most comfortable speaking. He was being kind, writing all that out for me last night, but this was his home and I didn't want him to feel awkward because of me.

"Alright everyone, we have pancakes," Bodhi called as he burst through the kitchen door with two platters. "We have plain and chocolate chip to choose from. Cambi, which would you like?"

"Hmm, one of each I think. If the apple juice is super sweet I might not be ready for chocolate," I said as he placed them both on my plate. "Just so you know, these eggs are the best I've ever had. You're a wonderful cook, Bodhi."

Bodhi flushed slightly and almost dropped one of the platters at my words. "Ah... thanks, Cambi. I try to help out where I can around here, and cooking is something I like to do."

"Rafael is another who is skilled in the kitchen," Marius pointed out. "He can make amazing Italian food, his homemade sauce is the best I've ever tasted."

My eyes grew wide as I looked at the man giving Marius a knowing look. "You're just saying that because you'd like me to make some and you know if Cambrie asks I would."

"Oh, you don't have to if you don't want to or don't like cooking. Maybe one night I can cook for you guys instead? I don't know how to make a whole lot of things, but I picked stuff up from cooking shows here and there. Although I'm a little out of practice," I murmured to myself as I realized it had been two years since I cooked anything.

"Why don't you help me, then?" Rafael offered. "Then the three hour job will be far less tedious."

"Three hours? It must be really good if it takes that long to make. I would absolutely love to help you, and it will help me learn where things are in the kitchen," I said, liking the idea more and more.

The guys passed around butter and syrup for the pancakes but I didn't think they needed anything. When it got to the point where my stomach was so full if I ate another bite I might burst, I paused. There was still half a plate of food left, but I knew I couldn't manage to eat it all. Why did I ask for two pancakes? Wiggling in my chair, I tried to find a more comfortable position to sit as I forced the rest of the food down.

"Princess, are you feeling alright?" Marius asked, placing his hand on mine where it lay on the table.

Slowly, I put another bite of pancake in my mouth and nodded as I chewed and chewed and chewed, hoping I could convince my body not to reject this next bite.

"Stop," Marius barked.

My whole body froze as my hair stood on end with the command of an Alpha. My whine instinctively slipped out distressed that I'd done something to upset my Alpha.

A napkin covered hand appeared in front of me. "Spit it out."

I glanced at him, eyes wide at his order. *He wanted me to spit this chewed up food into this napkin?*

"Don't make me bark at you again, Cambrie. Spit the food out for me, please," he instructed, his voice commanding but not harsh.

Embarrassment made me close my eyes as I leaned my head forward and released the ball of pancake I had been holding onto. I knew he pulled his hand away but I couldn't bring myself to face any of them, so I kept my eyes shut and just sat there. He'd known, somehow Marius knew I couldn't finish my plate and decided I didn't even deserve the food I already had in my mouth.

Abruptly, my chair was dragged until I was now sitting in front of Marius. He reached out and grasped my chin, forcing me to look at him even though I tried to struggle out of his hold. I didn't want to look at him as he told me what I'd done wrong or that he was disappointed in me. My heart couldn't take seeing that type of look on his face.

He didn't give up but he wasn't at all rough with me, unlike everyone else in my life so far. "Princess, please be good for me."

The croon in his voice had me surrendering and lifting my gaze to look at him. He cupped my face with his hands as he stroked my cheeks. I didn't realize I'd started crying. I hadn't dared shed a tear in over two years but now it seemed the waterworks happened in an instant.

"Will you please share with me why you were forcing yourself to eat when you were already full?" he asked.

I sniffed and licked my lip tasting the salt from my tears. "You don't leave food on your plate. It's a privilege to have a meal so you must eat everything you're given."

"I see," he murmured, releasing me from his hold. "Then that would be our fault now, wouldn't it?"

My brow scrunched at that. "Why would it be your fault?"

"Nixon is the one who filled your plate with so many eggs and I added bacon, then we also encouraged the pancakes. You have been without regular meals for a long time and I'm sure that's made your stomach a lot smaller. We served you what we would eat and that is far more than you could handle," Marius explained. "Here in this house, we have different rules. When you are full, regardless of what's left on your plate, you can be done eating. We like to have leftovers in the fridge since we all work at various times of the day. While we'd love to have family meals all the time, it doesn't always work out."

I nodded with another sniffle, unsure how to feel. Everything they did was the opposite of what I expected. Had my life been so different from everyone else's? Could it be that what I knew as normal wasn't at all? Bodhi understood some things, but even in what we understood about each other he had access to, things I only dreamed about.

"Marius," I whispered.

"Yes, Princess?"

"I think I'd really like a hug," I said, leaning toward him, reaching out but he moved far faster, scooping me up.

CHAPTER 16

Cambrie

He settled me on his lap so my legs straddled him as I twined my arms around his neck, burying my face in his neck. The feel of him pulling me close to him just felt so right and perfect, the fear of knowing this happiness and losing it was something I didn't know if I could survive. Tears streamed down my face causing me to hiccup as I tried to break through them.

Then Marius started to purr, the deep rumbling sound drew my Omega nature out unlike anything I'd felt before. I whined as I clung tighter to him, and without understanding why I let my head roll to the side so my hair fell away and my neck was exposed. Instinct rode me hard right now and I knew I was offering something important, but I didn't really understand what it meant.

"Cambrie," Marius whispered, a tightness in his voice as if he was fighting to be able to talk. His lips landed on my neck in a soft kiss. I went limp in his arms in an act of perfect surrender to my Alpha.

"You honor me by offering up your neck, but I haven't earned the right to claim you just yet," Marius said, his lips brushed my skin igniting a fire deep in my belly. "One day, my Princess, you will be ours in every way but for now you must wait a little longer."

Another whine was on the tip of my tongue but it stopped

when he locked his mouth around my neck catching the skin and sucking it roughly. My hand convulsed as euphoric pleasure I've never experienced before flooded my body sweeping me into the clouds. Only in heaven could something feel this good.

"Marius," Nixon's voice cut out.

Slowly, Marius pulled back and cradled me to his chest, his purr kicking up a notch as I sat there trying to remember my own name.

"Sweetheart," Nixon murmured, brushing a hand over my forehead causing me to open my eyes to look at him. "Come here, we need to let Marius finish getting ready for work but he's not going to move from this spot with you in his arms."

I hummed my understanding, turning to press a kiss to Marius's neck where he'd kissed me before letting Nixon pull me from him. While my brain understood that Marius left the dining room with Spencer in tow, I didn't seem to have the energy to worry if I'd done something wrong with how light I felt.

"Holy shit, he blissed her out good, didn't he?" Bodhi said as he lifted a glass of water to my lips. "Here Cambi, this should help."

"He's a better man than me, I'll tell you that," Nixon muttered. "I don't think I could have done that without marking her for real."

Rafael snorted. "Oh, I'll say he marked her. That's as clear as you can be about your claim on an Omega without doing the deed."

"Hey, Sweetheart," Nixon said, tracing my face with a finger. "You alright?"

"I had no idea that someone could do something to a body that felt so good," I shared, lifting a finger and brushing it down his nose. "You have beautiful eyes, did you know that? They are so deep and remind me of the ocean."

Nixon playfully nipped at my finger. "You're one to talk, with those shimmering aqua orbs sitting in your face. They are like gazing into a crystal ball, you never know what they might say about your future."

"No, I'm not nice to look at like all of you are. Everyone who lives here is so handsome. I'm all bones, bruises, and marked up with scars," I said, brushing off his compliment, reaching out with both hands, placing them on his cheeks. "You're scratchy today," I shared, rubbing my hands along his scruff until I realized what I was doing and yanked my hands back to my chest. "Sorry."

Nixon laughed, and a bright, happy smile appeared on his face as he brushed his cheek against mine. "Haven't shaved yet, Sweetheart, don't worry I'll be smooth faced in a bit. Speaking of getting ready, I need to get going on that. Do you think you're gonna be alright if you stay here today with Oscar and Bodhi?"

Hearing him say that made me realize they wouldn't be able to stay with me all day. I nodded slowly, keeping my feelings to myself as the euphoric cloud started to dissipate. "You have to work. All of you do incredibly important things for everyone. I'll be just fine if you need me to stay here."

Nixon kissed me on the forehead, stood, then settled me in his spot next to Oscar. "Don't worry, we'll make sure to say goodbye before we leave, alright?" I smiled reassuringly as he headed upstairs.

"Guess that's my cue to get myself ready since we all drove home together. I left my car at the shelter, so I'll need to catch a ride with them," Rafael informed us as he picked up his plate and carried it into the kitchen.

I looked at the table and saw all the food that was left and was amazed. Clearly, Marius hadn't been kidding when he said they liked leftovers.

"Cambi, do you mind helping me clean up the table?" Bodhi asked. "It's part of my chores since I don't work just yet doing school, but and it will help familiarize you with the kitchen if you need anything. No matter the time of day you are welcome to eat or drink whatever you find here and no one will care."

"Okay," I answered, getting to my feet.

Now that the amazing feeling I'd gotten from Marius was gone, it almost felt like I might be hollow inside. After feeling *so* much all at once, now I was left... empty. Never in all my memories could I remember having felt something so powerful and so warm. It was hard to find the right words to describe what Marius had made me experience.

Numbly I gathered plates, stacking them and placing the silverware on top before walking into the kitchen. Spotting the sink, I set them on one side and started the water, turning it to hot as I grabbed a sponge. I couldn't find any dish soap but when I tested the dispenser it came out blue. I guess in fancy kitchens you hide the common things like dish soap. I got lost in thought as I started on the silverware, gazing out at the backyard.

"Cambi, you don't need to actually wash them," Bodhi commented as he stood next to me. "We have a dishwasher right here. You can toss them in."

He pulled open the silver door next to the sink, pulling out the wire rack that already had some dishes in it. "Silverware goes in these baskets, the cups go up top, and the rest just find the best place they'll fit. Once we put all of it in, we'll run it, and put it away later."

"That sure makes things easy, doesn't it," I said, placing things where he instructed. "With it just being Father and me, we didn't have much to clean up."

"Makes sense, I never used one either until moving in here, but the way these guys eat and cook, this is a lifesaver. There's a lot in this kitchen I never knew existed but now that I've gotten used to them it's gonna be hard to go back," Bodhi rambled.

"Why would you need to go back? Isn't this your home?" I questioned.

He sighed, shutting the dishwasher and leaning on it. "We only get to live here as long as Marius is an Official. That could be a year or ten years. Life's just taught me not to get too attached to things that can get taken from you."

That was something I'd learned myself firsthand. Things were easily given and taken away at the whim of others.

"Do you think they'll really keep me?" I asked, that gnawing empty feeling creeping up again.

Bodhi didn't say anything, he just pulled me into a tight hug. "If I knew the answer to that about myself I would tell you, but I ask that question all the time. They've never given me a reason to think they would abandon me, but when it's happened once you always fear it will happen again."

"Cambrie!" Nixon called. "We're heading out."

Bodhi released me and nudged me toward the living room door. "Go say goodbye, you'll be sad if you don't."

Trusting his judgment, since he had more experience than I did with this new pack dynamic, I headed to the front door. There the four of them stood, ready in their work clothes, faces shaved, hair done, looking even more handsome. Then there was this awkward moment when I realized I had no idea what to do at this point. I always avoided my father whenever possible but Bodhi was right, I wanted to see them off. So, as we stood there staring at each other for a moment I wracked my brain for what to say.

"Have a good day at work," I blurted, remembering what my mother used to say to my father. "I'll be here when you get back."

They all smiled at that, waving and saying their goodbyes as they left, shutting the door behind them. Hearing the door latch triggered something in me as I stood there. It almost felt like everything wonderful I ever felt in my life left with them. Here I was left behind when all I wanted was to be with them. Tears flooded my eyes and I crumpled to the ground, feeling void of anything close to happiness.

Oscar jogged down the stairs and came to an abrupt halt in front of me. He crouched and reached out to place a hand on my leg, letting it rest there until I looked up at him. His brows were knitted together as he looked over my body.

Knowing we couldn't really communicate well I leaned forward and let my head fall against his chest. "Why do I feel so empty?" I whispered. "It shouldn't matter that they left for work, I hardly know them."

Oscar gathered me in his arms and carried me into the kitchen, where he set me on the counter, catching Bodhi's attention. "What happened? She just went to say goodbye to them."

Oscar and Bodhi carried on a silent conversation as I sat watching, trying to make any sense out of what they were saying through my tears that wouldn't stop. Their hands moved so fast and every so often they would get irritated and their motions became more aggressive. As the conversation came to an end, Oscar returned to me with a warm smile as he tucked some of my hair behind my ear. I leaned into the touch, feeling the need to be touched which had never been something I wanted. Gently, he pulled me off the counter and I wrapped my legs around his waist, then my arms around his neck as if I was a koala.

We left the kitchen and headed upstairs to the third floor where he set me on top of my bed. He motioned for me to wait there as he backed out the door, making sure I wasn't going anywhere. Noticing the pile of pillows, I crawled over and surrounded myself with them so I was in the middle of the pile. It didn't have the weight I wanted but it was starting to help a bit. I caught faint whiffs of Oscar's scent since he'd spent the night, but I needed more.

"Cambi?" Bodhi called.

Peeking out from under the pillows, I saw him entering my room with blankets and something else tucked under his arm.

"Wow, you burrowed, *way* under there, didn't you?" he commented with a chuckle. "What do you say about upgrading your pillow fort to a blanket fort?"

Sniffling, I wiped at my nose with the cuff of my sweater as I sat up straighter. "I don't know how to make one."

"Then it's a good thing you have me. I used to make them all the time for the kids in our group home," Bodhi shared. "Oscar went to find more but I think we can start with this."

He dumped the blankets on the bed and quickly headed back to the game room and returned with chairs, rope, and clothesline clips. Oscar showed up with more chairs and blankets.

"Did you steal those chairs from the dining room?" I asked, curious, drawn by the scent of all my Alphas. "Wait, are these blankets from their beds?"

"Don't worry, we checked with them and they don't mind at all that we're using them," Bodhi assured me as he placed the chairs. "Off the bed, we need to pull the mattress off the bed frame."

Sliding off, I moved to the side as they pulled the mattress off and on the floor in the middle of all the chairs. Fascinated, I watched as Bodhi confidently created a little hut out of such basic things. Oscar did whatever was asked and seemed as excited about this as Bodhi did.

"What do you think?" Bodhi asked, hands on his hips, a proud smile on his face. "Don't just stand there and gawk at it, go on in. Let me know if there is any place that looks like it might fall or is sagging too much."

Pulling back the front blanket, I peered in. The space was dim but I didn't feel like I was trapped, and the scent of all the men in the pack filled the air. Crawling on the mattress I smiled, loving the feeling of being wrapped in their warmth. The emptiness I'd been feeling started to lift some as I sat.

Light shone through as Oscar entered, arms full of pillows, handing them to me. Taking them from him I set them beside me and noticed he'd brought the teal pillow from the living room. "Did you mean to grab this for me?"

Oscar nodded, brushing his hand upward on his chest in a sweeping motion twice with a smile.

"He's saying the pillow made you happy, so he grabbed it," Bodhi shared as he entered with a laptop. "Others might have differing opinions, but I'm pretty sure there's a rule that you have to only watch kids movies in a blanket fort. Cambi, we have a lot of catching up so we better get started right away."

Oscar clapped his agreement with two thumbs up as he scattered the pillows around the bed. He motioned me over, patting the teal pillow with his palm. When I reached him, he wrapped an arm around my middle and tucked me to his side so when he stretched out on his stomach he was half lying on top of me, my head rested on the teal pillow. Bodhi sprawled on my other side but didn't touch me, leaving space between us as he set up the laptop for the movie.

"Now, you said you like to do a lot of reading, so I'm guessing they are fantasy fiction?" Bodhi asked, glancing at me.

"Fairy tales are my favorite but I love anything with a happy ending," I shared.

Bodhi grinned and clicked play, allowing the movie's music to fill the space. Soon, the title of the movie appeared: *Beauty and the*

Beast. It took seconds for me to be completely sucked into the story and lost in Belle's world. As I wiggled further under Oscar he started to purr, stroking his fingers through my hair that he'd unbraided at some point, now falling freely around me.

When I got scared toward the end at the battle between the Beast and Gaston, Bodhi moved close and I clutched his shirt sleeve. When the Beast was shot I cried out. "No! He can't die!"

"Easy Cambi, you said you like anything with happy endings and this one definitely has one," Bodhi assured me. "I wouldn't make you watch something that would make you feel worse than you already were."

Nodding, I grabbed his hand and held it to my chest needing the reassurance he offered. "Okay, I'll trust you, we're best friends after all."

Bodhi snorted and grinned at me. "Yeah, and best friends look out for each other, right?"

Oscar started to get upset about something pointing to himself then to me. It took me a second, but I figured it out. "You want to be my best friend too?"

He nodded while using a closed fist motion that I assumed meant yes.

"Rafael said I can have as many best friends as I want so you can absolutely be one," I announced. "Does that mean I get to be one of your best friends?"

Oscar's body shook in his version of laughter as he pulled my head to him kissing the top of it before he put his lips to my ear. "For now, Little Star."

Hearing him speak even though it was so faint, softer than the quietest whisper, stunned me. "You just spoke!"

Bodhi looked at us, his brows so high they were hidden under his shaggy hair. "Wow, he must have had something important to say."

"I thought you couldn't talk at all?" I questioned, frowning at the Alpha.

Oscar shook his head and turned my face back to the movie which Bodhi had paused so I didn't miss the ending. Clearly, my

Alpha wasn't ready to share that part of his story, but I couldn't blame him. No one likes to share the darkest parts of their life with someone they don't really know. We were new best friends after all.

"You ready for your happy-ever-after I promised?" Bodhi asked, pressing play. "After this we'll watch one of my all time favorites. I think you'll love it."

Of course Bodhi was right, Belle did have a happy ending with her Beast, who'd finally become a man after learning to love. It made me wonder if all people who act like beasts were just misunderstood people who were being swallowed by pain or self-hatred. Then my thoughts drifted to my father and I couldn't remember a moment where I'd ever seen him happy. Even when Mom was alive he still yelled, smacked her around, and felt like life had wronged him. There had to be something about him that my mom fell in love with, right? Both of them were Betas, they didn't have anyone telling them how to live their lives or to stay together. Mom could have left at any point but instead she didn't. In the end, it killed her.

"What did you think?" Bodhi asked, sitting up cross-legged, looking at me expectantly.

"Do you think all beasts can change?" I asked.

He blinked at me a few times, clearly not expecting that question. "Damn Cambi, you don't pull any punches, do you?" he said, running his hand through his hair. "I don't know the answer to that, I'm not sure anyone would. People make choices about their lives. They can either choose to make it better or live with the shit that got dumped on them."

Oscar sat up, taking me with him so I sat in his lap as he sighed while Bodhi translated.

"*Like Bodhi said, people can choose to be mad about their life or circumstances, or they can rise above. You are a perfect example of that. From what we understand, it sounds like your father hated his life, always trying to take the easy way out, which landed him in bigger trouble. He decided that if life was going to be cruel to him, then that is how he would treat others.*" Pausing, Oscar shifted me so I was sitting between them and could see his face as he spoke. "*Then there is you, a person who has been treated in the most barbaric way for almost their entire life. Yet you would never dream of treating someone like that. Instead, you did whatever it took to get away and have such a drive to protect others from that same fate. People decide how they will let the world treat them and how they will react.”*

“That’s how you see me? As a protector?” I questioned, not at all sure how he came to that conclusion.

“You protected me from Bodhi this morning and last night you didn’t want Spencer to get in trouble, taking the blame yourself. My Little Star, you shine so bright in the world with how big your heart is, but it shines brightest when you defend those you believe have been wronged.”

As if my body only had one way to deal with the ever changing emotions, my eyes watered as I flung myself into Oscar’s arms, hugging him tightly. “Thank you for seeing me that way Oscar. I’ve never been good enough for my parents, but the way you all talk about me, it’s like you can’t see any of my brokenness.”

“Cambi,” Bodhi stated, then paused so I turned to look at him. He sat there staring at me as if unsure how to say what he was thinking. “Look, I didn’t have the greatest life growing up either. I’ve got my own damage and fucked up way of viewing life. The small bits that we’ve heard from the others lets me know it’s nothing close to what you’ve been through. I might understand some things, but how you aren’t screaming at the world for wronging you so badly, I don’t get. I’d be tracking that son of a bitch who dares to call himself your father down and killing him for how he hurt you. Somehow, the universe knew you needed every ounce of goodness for you to survive. How you are and the way you care about others... none of it makes sense to me.”

Once more sitting in Oscar’s lap, I grabbed Bodhi’s hands and clasped them in mine. “What good does it do any of us to fill the world with more hate and anger? Do I ever want to see my father again? No. Do I want him dead?” I shrugged.

“What would that change? If you found him and killed him how would that make you feel any better about yourself? My father is now in the past. I’m free of him and can choose how I want to live my life. You, Bodhi, and the others of this pack, are my future for as long as this lasts. Being with all of you is terrifying. I've never felt so safe, warm, or cared about than I have in the past twenty-four hours. While I don't know how long it will last, I plan to soak every bit of it up so I never forget what it feels like ever again."

Oscar tightly wrapped his arms around me, as he hid his face in my neck, purring, while Bodhi wrapped us both in a hug. We stayed like that for a bit, then we all pulled ourselves together, and started the next movie. This time, I found myself in the middle of a puppy pile. Oscar wrapped around my back as Bodhi rested his head on Oscar's hip with his legs tucked up by my chest so it was hard to tell where one of us started or ended.

Bodhi's choice of movie was *Treasure Planet* and I loved every second of it. *Beauty and the Beast* was great, but this was full of adventure, pirates, and a sense of freedom I always longed for. Not to mention, the most adorable pink blob that had me laughing my head off. It felt good to be happy, to smile, laugh, and know it wasn't a dream I made up in my head. It was real, these men were here and taking the time to make me feel better after my meltdown this morning.

Everything they did was genuine, full of heart and I knew if I ever had to leave them I might not survive. None of it made sense. After being abused for so long how could I just trust? But some things in life you can't explain, and these men were quickly becoming my whole world. I just hoped I fit into theirs the same way.

CHAPTER 17

Marius

Shutting the door and walking away from the house had never been as hard as it was that morning. I couldn't believe I'd almost marked her for real. There she was in my arms desperate for comfort and stability, and she offered herself to me in the most trusting way an Omega could. I knew from everything I learned about Omegas that I couldn't let the offer go unacknowledged, but there was no possible way I could accept what she was asking me to do.

With one bite I would be bonded to her for life. We would have a soul connection that was deeper than anyone could understand. Or that's how my grandmother explained it to me as a child. Her pack was created the old-fashioned way, before everything fell apart during my parents' lifetime. I'd grown up hearing stories of the good old days and watching the love my grandparents had for each other.

My father and mother loved each other in a way. They enjoyed each other's company and chose to marry, committing to spend life together, but it wasn't how I saw my grandfathers look at my grandmother. When we found out about my sister grandma was there to comfort her, but when she was taken from us it broke my grandmother, because she passed away a few months later. Her men soon followed, seeing no point in living when she wasn't.

Having Cambrie enter my life, I could easily understand their thinking. When someone so special and perfect walks into your life it's almost as if you see the world in a whole new light. Now, I needed to leave her home while I went off to work for the same people who would want to take her away from us. She'd already made an impact on each and every person in my pack. The rag tag members Nixon and I collected through the years had the same vision as us for the future and was the bond we all shared. Then comes a blonde haired, blue eyed little princess that gave us a reason to become a real family.

"Love," Spencer murmured as he rested a hand on my back. "You sure you're okay?"

After I almost marked Cambrie and Nixon sent me upstairs, I'd taken Spencer up against the wall in my bedroom, like a brainless rutting Alpha. My options were to mark her, fuck her, or fuck the shit out of someone else I loved, or I was going to do something I couldn't take back. Poor Spencer had a bruise of my teeth on the back of his neck where I held him as I fucked him. Thank god he enjoyed every moment of it as much as I did, or else I would feel even lower than I already was.

"I'm sorry, I just can't believe how out of control I've been." I turned and cupped his face, loving his smile as he turned into the touch. "I don't ever want you to feel like I'm using you or treating you as an outlet for my needs and ignoring your own. I don't want you to doubt my love and desire for *you* just because Cambrie's come into our lives. What I did upstairs was wrong and I know it."

Spencer scowled and slapped my hand away. "Wrong? What you did..." He took a deep breath and glared at me. "I'm sorry, are you talking about the amazing quickie we had ten minutes ago where you fucked me like you thought I was going to leave you? Where you left a claiming mark on the back of my neck telling anyone who sees it that I have an Alpha who owns my ass? That, that's what you're telling me is wrong?"

His words were like a slap to my face, as was the hurt in his eyes.

"Did you think I wasn't as fucking turned on as you were watching you almost mark Cambrie? God, all I could think about was how I wanted to be right there, with you holding her between us as you claimed me right after her, making us a truly bonded pair. I didn't know if there would be a chance for that to happen for us, but now because of her, I can see our future together. One where I could proudly display two marks from both my Alphas while holding an adorable Omega that I get to call mine as well. Don't you ever fucking say shit like that again, Marius!" Spencer snapped.

A car horn honked, making him sigh as he pressed a kiss to my cheek. "I love you. I'll see you after work, alright?"

I stopped him and pulled him back for a real goodbye kiss before I let him go. "I really don't deserve you, do I?"

"Damn right, and don't you forget it, mister," Spencer quipped.

Another quick kiss and I stepped back. "Thank you for setting me straight, I love you too. Have a good day, and I'll see you tonight at home."

"Promise you won't let them take her from us? I don't think anyone else in the world could fit our pack the way she does," Spencer said as he walked backwards toward where Nixon and Rafael were waiting for him.

"I won't let them take her, Spence," I vowed. "I gave Cambrie my word and you know how seriously I take that."

He nodded, understanding firsthand just how far I would go to keep my promises. With a quick wave, he slipped into the car's backseat and the three of them drove off. With a heavy sigh, I tossed my briefcase into the passenger seat and got in. The benefit of living here was that I was close to the new Capitol Building. The Capitol Building was built twenty years ago when it wasn't safe to have it in the middle of the city anymore. Too many attacks by various groups unhappy with the way things were being handled forced the CoF to relocate. The building they constructed was rather opulent in my opinion, and a waste of taxpayer money. Now it's where I went to work every day.

I pulled up to the gleaming white marble building that looked more like a Greek palace than a Capitol Building. A spire of gold-plated metal rose high into the sky, the sun glinting off it, blinding you if you stared too long. From what I read in records, the officials at that time wanted to ensure that anyone in the city could find their way to justice by simply looking for the spire. All I thought of when I saw it was how many people that money could have helped.

"Good morning, Official Stone," Tommy, the valet, greeted as he opened my car door for me. "Decided to take a leisurely morning?"

It was comments like this that told me I work far too much and that I would need to change if I wanted to spend time at home.

"Might be something I do more of, it was nice to have the morning with my pack," I shared, clapping Tommy on the shoulder. "While my work is important, if I have nothing to come home to, what good is it?"

Tommy was a young kid recently out of high school and working at the Capitol for a year to save up for college. He was hardworking and I never had any trouble with my car when it was in Tommy's hands. Cars were the one thing I indulged in and spent far more than I should on a vehicle. This newest sports car was bright red and could fly like a bat out of hell. This led to having a few issues with the other valets that worked here.

They didn't think I noticed when they took it for a joy ride. They only did it once after I chatted with them. The world was harsh and I didn't want to be another person telling them they were screw ups. Yet, on the other hand, they also needed to understand I wouldn't stand for it and it was an abuse of their power. So now only Tommy drove my car. When he goes off to college I'm not sure what I'll do, but that was a drop in the bucket of problems I had to deal with right now.

"Marius, odd to see you coming in at such a reasonable hour. Did your alarm not go off?" Official Fredrick McCoy called from behind me as I started up the steps.

I paused and waited for him to join me. He was a kind man and loved to tease me for being the youngest member of the CoF and having far too much gumption as he called it.

"No, I decided to take your advice," I answered as he caught up. "Enjoy life and stop trying to change the world overnight."

"Ha, ha, ha, that a boy," Fredrick said, his booming laughter rattled my ears. "Now, let's see if you can actually leave at a decent time. That will be the real test to see if my words finally hit home."

Fredrick was a brilliant mind when it came to numbers and systems, but he was incredibly lazy and didn't involve himself in anything more than he had to. He was a puppet for Yoram, the longest standing member of the current CoF. If Yoram needed something to be passed he would always have Fredrick's vote. When it came down to a split vote, which hardly ever happened, it would then get put before the City Magistrate, Willem, for the deciding vote.

Of course, like Fredrick, Willem was in Yoram's pocket as well. The only support I had was Alton, the fourth of the Officials. He is the second longest standing Official and hates Yoram with everything he is. I feel like he would have stepped down a long time ago if he didn't think he was the only thing stopping Yoram from changing things into a dictatorship. The moment I was voted in Alton took me under his wing and showed me the truth behind the curtain. That the CoF was a sham, Yoram was the puppet master and all the dreams I had of changing the world would never happen with him in power. Sadly, Alton had become extremely ill and hadn't been able to work as much. I feared they would vote him out, but it seemed they were content to leave him be since he's not causing trouble.

Knowing the truth about the CoF made me question why I should even keep trying day in and day out, getting here early, staying far into the evening when none of it mattered? Because one day I would find that smoking gun that would help me to get Yoram removed from his position. Nixon and Spencer knew the truth of things, but I kept it from the others, not wanting to crush their ideal before I had *something* that could change things. On my sister's grave I vowed I would change the world so no one else had to suffer through what she had.

Now Cambrie lands in my lap, having survived so much cruelty just for being an Omega. I was going to fight even harder because she would be a daily reminder that what I was fighting for could have changed her whole life. I might not be able to remove all the shadows from her eyes, but I can damn well make sure it won't happen to someone else. It had to end.

Once through security, I split off from Fredrick and headed for the stairs. My office was on the fourth floor but the City Records department was on the second floor. Not wanting Yoram's shadow to know what I was doing, the stairs were a safer bet, Fredrick would never use them. This was a trick I learned early and used often, giving me the ability to move more freely.

With all the research I was doing, Bethany, the head of records, and I had become friendly. Spencer was under the impression she wanted to be more than friends, but I disagreed. Sure, she was a beautiful woman, but I never gave up hope of our pack one day having an Omega at its center. Most female Omegas wouldn't take well to having another female in the dynamic, so I never let the thought cross my mind. I had Spencer, and was content with our relationship until things needed to change.

"Oh, good morning, Marius," Bethany greeted, her green eyes lighting up at my appearance. "What can I help you with today?"

"Do we have a section dedicated to the laws pertaining to Omegas?" I asked, setting my briefcase on the counter.

Bethany frowned at my request. "That depends, what part of the laws are you looking for? Inactive laws that are no longer practiced or the current ones?"

"Both, I'm trying to put together a proposal to allow Omegas and packs to pick each other instead of being assigned like they are now," I explained as broadly as I could. "My hope is to compare pregnancy rates from then to now."

"Well, that won't do you any good," she huffed. "The laws changed once the attack happened, and people were snatching Omegas off the streets all willy-nilly. It was clear that the packs weren't able to protect them so the government had to step in and ensure a pack could keep them safe."

"Thank you, Bethany, I did get the same education you did in school. I know what they tell us, but now we have far more information on present trends as well as the past. I just feel like things aren't progressing and this is the only thing I can think of to make some real changes. None of the women nowadays have ever been exposed to the drug used in the attack. Which means we are back to normal methods of reproduction like they were in the past," I argued.

"So does that mean you want information on the births of Omegas for the past sixty to eighty years as well?" Bethany asked, her tone resigned.

I flashed her a bright smile. "That would be amazing, I know you keep that information locked away."

"You can't take it out of the research room. There can be no copies or pictures taken," Bethany warned, giving me a stern look.

I grabbed my briefcase and nodded. "Alright, I will keep that in mind."

"No, Marius, I don't think you understand what I'm saying," Bethany said emphatically. "You are allowed to know this information because of your status as an Official but no one else can. Not even I can know what these files say."

Now I was utterly confused. "What files, the laws?"

"The birth records," she snapped. "The files are in sealed envelopes, and I have to write on them who is checking them out and when they did. If anyone finds out we gave them to someone who shouldn't we'd be put in jail. Everything to do with Omegas is highly guarded and isn't to be taken lightly."

What she was saying did the opposite of what I'm sure she was intending. It made me want to investigate them all the more. Clearly, something was hidden in these records that the government didn't want the world to know.

"Thank you for making that clear for me, Bethany. I promise not to get you in any trouble and respect the rules you've laid out," I assured her. "Can I use the same document room that I always use or do I need to be elsewhere?"

"Your room should be fine. I just brewed a new pot of coffee as well, so help yourself. I know how you get once you're on a project," she answered, dismissing me to get the requested files.

While a lot has been transferred to digital, being the government, they always kept paper copies and that is what I requested to look at. Anything can be altered in digital form, but paper wasn't as easy to tamper with.

Entering the simple room with a desk, chair, and computer I set my briefcase down, then headed for the coffee maker. Bethany had been right about that I was a bit addicted to the stuff, it's what kept me going with the early mornings and long nights. Even though today I'd had a much more leisurely morning, a lot had happened, and the caffeine would help.

My phone buzzed in my pocket, making me frown. Typically, the guys didn't contact me about things during the day unless it was important. Glancing at my phone I saw it was from Rafael.

RAFAEL:

Cambrie seemed to be experiencing Omega Drop once we left the house. I talked to Bodhi and they have a plan, just wanted you to be aware.

ME:

Thank you for letting me know, I'm closest if they need me to come home during lunch.

RAFAEL:

To have you come only to leave again so soon wouldn't help. She will be fine, it's just something young Omegas can experience when they experience an Alpha high.

Fuck! I'd done that to her. Nixon told me she'd been majorly affected by my almost marking her. I should have known it would be too much and stopped sooner. I doubt she'd ever experienced something like that in her life, being so young. Here I am seventeen years her senior and I'm acting like a novice teenager. She's the eighteen year old and I'm the adult who should be looking out for her so things like this didn't happen.

"Marius, are you alright?" Bethany asked.

My head snapped up from my phone to see her standing next to me, arms full of files and peering at my phone. Locking the screen, I stuffed it back into my pocket.

"Everything's fine. Rafael was just updating me on a shelter kid who will be staying with us for a bit," I answered, trying to control my anger at her trying to read my phone. If something happened to Cambrie because of Bethany's need to know everything I'd ruin her life.

Clearing my throat, I grabbed a mug from the shelf and filled it with coffee like nothing out of the ordinary was going on. "Are those the files?"

"Half of them, I need to get the rest of the birth records," she said, following me back to the room I was using. "Figured you could get started with the laws while I get the rest."

"Thank you, once you've brought me those it might be best to leave me to it. I wouldn't want you to accidentally see something that could get you in trouble." She didn't look happy about the suggestion but she nodded and left. Leaving me to start the task of finding a way for Cambrie to stay with us forever.

CHAPTER 18

Rafael

"Mike, it sounds like things are going well, you made it through the interview and they asked to have you come back in," I reassured the Beta.

He'd been in and out of our shelter dealing with alcoholism and finally decided to go through rehab. Instead of going to the rehab center for his continued counseling, he requested that I help him here. Before shutting down my private practice I dealt with so many of the rich and the addictions that seemed to come when you had money to burn. Of course, none of them really wanted to change, they just found being in therapy was better to say than they weren't giving up their habit.

"It's just been so long since I've held down a steady job, I'm not sure I can handle the pressure," Mike argued. "This isn't just cooking at a fast-food joint, it's a family run business, and I don't want to let them down."

I leaned back in my chair, watching the man before me. He'd been part of a pack who tore him apart when he decided to leave law school and become a chef, an incredibly good one by the things he's made here at the shelter. That didn't matter though, because if you ever wanted to become an official pack with an Omega, you needed the right credentials. If Mike couldn't become a five-star chef cooking for the officials themselves, it was menial work that put them at a disadvantage.

He didn't give in to them though, but it cost him everything. For a while, his passion was enough until it wasn't, and he started drinking. The voices in his head telling him he'd never be good enough, that his job and talent were worthless. Now clear headed and sober for the first time in ten years, he was getting a second chance. A friend I knew needed help in the kitchen, so I set up an interview for Mike. I'd given him the tools, it was his turn to use them.

"What makes you so sure you'll let them down, you haven't even gotten the job yet. The only way you can mess things up for yourself is not going to that second interview tomorrow morning. I can't make you believe in yourself, but we've done a lot of work on clearing up the lies your old pack ingrained in you," I reminded him. "You loved to cook so much you walked away from that life for this dream, this is the chance to live it. Go tomorrow, hear what they have to say, then make your choice. Don't go in thinking you don't deserve it."

Mike shot to his feet, hands fisted at his sides and determination in his eyes. "You're right, if I had the courage to give it all up for doing what I love to do, then fuck them for not believing I could do it. This is the break I've been looking for, real work in a kitchen that feeds hard working Beta's, not some yuppy Alphas." He paused and looked at me. "No offense."

"None taken, I would much rather eat at Trudie's than some of the stuffy places we go for CoF dinners," I confided in him. "Food tastes way better and bigger portions."

I glanced at the clock and noted our time was up so I rose to my feet and clapped Mike on the back. "I want you to call me tomorrow and let me know how things go. If I don't answer, leave me a message and I'll get back to you when I have a moment."

"Thanks, Doctor Leshem, you saved my life ya know getting me into rehab. I'm not sure I could have survived on the streets living like I was," Mike shared, shaking my hand. "You'll be hearing from me tomorrow, that's a promise."

Since I didn't have another session right away, I walked with him into the main lobby and watched him leave. I wished with everything in me that he went tomorrow, I already knew they were going to offer him the job but Mike needed to learn to fight for himself.

"Excuse me, do you work here?"

I turned to find a rather stocky man with mussed shaggy graying hair, a beard that looks like it grew out of laziness, and a blush of broken blood vessels over his nose and cheeks. He wore weathered jeans, a button down work shirt with a major warehouse logo, and a warm mechanics jacket. While he was certainly a drunk—if the blush and stale beer scent pouring off him was any indicator—I didn't think he was looking for our services.

"Yes, what can I help you with?" I asked.

It wasn't unusual for people to come in looking for some person or another but it was our policy never to admit who was or wasn't making use of our shelter. Too many battered women and men running from bad relationships to ever trust someone who came knocking on our door.

"Yeah, thing is, my daughter's missing," he admitted, scratching his scalp looking around nervously. "We got into a fight and she ran away. The problem is, she's real sick and needs her medicine. She didn't come home last night so I thought I'd check here to see if she turned up."

"I'm so sorry to hear that, how old is your daughter?" I inquired, my gut telling me this man wasn't telling me the truth.

"Ah... oh eighteen, just had a birthday two weeks ago," he answered, telling me he wasn't that close to his daughter if he forgot her age.

"If you give me a description I can leave a note at the front desk and ask around. We have a lot of people coming and going at all hours of the day. I'm a counselor here so I don't deal with the intake process," I explained.

If we did have the person here he was looking for, I wanted to make sure our staff knew someone was trying to find them and to proceed with caution.

"Right, description, good idea," he muttered, pulling a flask out of his coat pocket and taking a swig. "Let's see um, she's got blonde hair, skinny, green no, sorry, blue eyes like her late mother. Doesn't talk much but likes to read, always got her nose in a book, neglecting her chores, damn kid."

"I think we're getting a little off track, do you know what she was wearing when she ran away?" I redirected as a sinking feeling washed over me. If he said what I prayed he didn't, I wasn't sure what I would do.

"Yeah, you know what I sure do because I got her a real nice yellow dress for her birthday, had flowers and shit on it. Even gave her my old trench coat too, ungrateful brat," he rambled, taking another swig. "You know, you put all this work into looking out for them and then they just throw it in your face. When her mom died, I could have shipped her off to some group home, fucking kid ain't even mine, but I looked after that little bitch all the same."

My blood ran cold as I realized the man standing before me was none other than Cambrie's father. The bastard who dared to hurt my Little One for years, locking her away until she could be sold to pad his sleazy life.

"If she's eighteen and not really your child, why bother looking for her? Seems like you're free of her now," I ground out through clenched teeth.

Maybe if I could get this useless sack of shit to forget about Cambrie it would be one less thing for us to deal with.

"I told you already, she's sick and needs her medicine," he retorted, narrowing his eyes at me. "You know what, why don't you just take down my name and number. That way you can call me if she shows up, no need for someone like you, donating their time to the less fortunate, to get your hands messy with my business."

The urge to throttle this man was becoming almost overwhelming but I somehow managed to control myself. "Fine by me."

"Daryl Minks," he said, then rattled off his phone number. "I don't have a cell phone so just leave a message on the answering machine. Was hoping I would find her before my shift starts tonight but looks like that's not gonna happen."

"Yes, so it seems," I said, snapping the pencil I was holding at my side in half. "I'll make sure this information gets into the right hands."

"Sure, sure, I've got one more of these damn shelters to stop at, no way she could survive on her own," he rattled on, waving me off as he trudged out the door.

"Rafael, who was that?" Clara asked as she returned to the front desk.

Calmly I tossed the pencil into the trash and faced her. "I need you to ask security to print the clearest picture they can of that man and post it on the watch out bulletin board. Then I need it to be sent to all the other branches of our shelters as well, he's trolling them all."

"Of course, who's he looking for?" she inquired.

"No one, because he's never getting her back," I said, a growl lacing my words as I walked toward the main offices.

Nixon's door was open and he was at his desk, so I rapped on Spencer's window and motioned for him to follow me as I walked by. The moment I stepped into Nixon's office he looked up, then his face hardened with suspicion. "What happened? Is Cambrie alright? Is she still having trouble getting over what happened this morning?"

I held up a hand as Spencer joined us. "Close the door," I barked.

Spencer did as he was told and walked around the desk to stand next to Nixon. I knew my Alpha nature was in control right now, but I didn't know how to calm it down without it involving killing the man who dared call himself Cambrie's father.

"Rafael, you need to tell me what's wrong," Nixon said, his voice commanding.

I slammed the note with his name and phone number on his desk. "He came looking for her," I managed to say anger making my hands shake so I clenched them into fists.

"Who is..." Nixon looked at the note. "Daryl Minks?"

"Cambrie's father, who's not even her real father. The bastard knew it all along and kept her around as his whipping boy to take his anger out on. He dared to come here and demand we give her back to him. SHE'S OURS!" I roared, slamming both fists on the desk. "He lost his rights to her the day he lifted a hand against her. My Little One will carry scars inflicted by him the rest of her life!"

Both of them stared at me in stunned shock, from my outburst or the news I gave them, I'm not sure but I had never felt fury like this ever before. I suppose it's because I never had someone I wanted to protect and care for as much as I do for Cambrie. With every passing moment I spent with her she was resurrecting my dead heart and I wasn't sure if I was going to survive it at this rate.

"He was here and you let him walk away?!" Nixon demanded. "You should have called the police and had the bastard arrested not let him walk out the front door."

"Did you want me to put out a sign in flashing lights that she was here and we know who you are?" I snarled. "If I did anything other than what I'd just done it would have been to rip out his throat right there in the lobby, not calling the police. They probably would have congratulated him and forced us to give her back or taken her for themselves, never to be seen again."

"Okay guys, you two need to calm down," Spencer interceded. "The Alpha waves going off in this room might make people take notice and we can't have that. Rafael did the right thing, if we even hint we have her or know anything about her, shit hits the fan. We still don't know who he was going to sell her to in the first place. It could be anyone, even the chief of police."

Hearing Spencer siding with me and not Nixon helped to calm me down. I'd done the right thing by my Omega, I protected her the best way I could and no one was going to tell me otherwise.

"Now that you two have processed that realization, Rafael please sit, tell us exactly what happened," Spencer requested as he rested his hip on the desk, getting comfortable.

The Beta was right, we needed to calm down and think about this logically to keep Cambrie safe. I pulled over one of the chairs I pushed out of my way in my rage, took a deep breath, and sat down.

"I'd just finished with a session and walked him out. While I was there, this man approached me about his missing daughter. I managed to talk him into giving me a description so we had a heads up if she was one of our people. The man reeked of stale beer and I could easily tell other signs of being an alcoholic, so I was leery of his intentions. Not that we would ever give out that information anyways," I started, crossing one leg over the other in a pretense of calm.

"About halfway through the description, I had a gut feeling it was Cambrie. It wasn't until he described what she was last wearing that I knew for sure he was talking about her. He'd started to drink something much stronger that he had in a flask and he became more agitated as he went. That's when he let slip he wasn't her father. Apparently, her mother got with this guy already pregnant or something else happened along the way. That, he didn't share. When I suggested he let her be since she's eighteen and not even his, he shut down. It was almost like he realized he was saying too much and I might not tell him if we found her or not," I mused as I stroked my chin, analyzing the interaction now that I didn't have to fight the urge to kill him.

A groan of wood had me glancing at Nixon gripping his office chair's arm so hard it threatened to splinter. "What else," he asked through clenched teeth.

"He gave me his name and number, told me he was checking at the other shelters but he had a shift tonight. He wore a uniform shirt for one of the major warehouses on the outskirts of the city. Must be what job he was referring to," I added. "It explains why Cambrie couldn't ever figure out what time it was or when he would go to work. Those places do twelve hour shifts three or four days in a row."

Spencer stood up and pushed Nixon aside pulling up something on the computer. "Good, looks like you already had someone inform the other shelters about him. There's no way he could be Cambrie's father. They look nothing alike." He shifted the screen so Nixon could see.

The Alpha leaned forward, memorizing every feature just as I had. The protectiveness of an Alpha was no joke, there is a reason we were considered fearsome leaders and held prominent positions. We defended what was ours till our last breath.

"I had Clara print that photo out and put it in the back room for all the shelter employees to see. I didn't have her say who he was looking for, only we were to deny any and all knowledge of anyone he asks after," I shared.

Nixon leaned back in his chair, biting the end of the pen he was now holding. "This just got a whole lot more complicated."

"Did we really think he wouldn't come looking for his life changing payout?" Spencer reasoned. "We need to keep an eye out for this guy but no one knows *we* have Cambrie. I'm going to have a contact I know in one of the security companies people hire for Omegas wipe her information from our system."

"Is that wise?" I questioned. "Wouldn't that draw more attention if he knows?"

"Nah, Savo is a good guy, and it wouldn't be the first time we've had him do this favor. He did it for Bodhi when we were worried about that witch foster mom of his trying to go after him for 'assaulting' her husband," Spencer said using finger quotes.

The woman was crazy, and her husband got what was coming to him after all he put Bodhi and the other kids in that home through. Tough love was one thing when you have a house full of problem children, but verbally abusing the kids until one of them committed suicide was another. Teach them discipline and responsibility but going so far as to make them believe they were worthless is never acceptable. Bodhi's last act before leaving was to break the man's jaw so he couldn't speak for at least a month.

"Savo is an immigrant who once worked in intelligence in the military back home. It got too dangerous for him to be there, so he left and now is doing cyber security. Occasionally, he will do full time security but only if he likes the person. Dude's in high demand but won't take just any job. He's picky," Spencer rattled on. "Although he told me he got pulled by the government for a job so we'll see if he even has time to help."

Nixon gave Spencer a quizzical look. "When the hell did you meet a person like that? I've never heard you talk about him before."

"Oh, we met at one of the campaign dinners, you know how bored I get at those things. He was working security and saved me when I locked myself out on the roof. Said he saw me on the cameras and came to the rescue," Spencer explained.

If that wasn't the most Spencer thing I'd ever heard. I had to fight to keep a straight face. Spencer never met a stranger and even though he didn't like the highbrow parties, he always managed to find friends in the wait staff, hotel employees, and now security.

"How many people has he removed from our records?" Nixon demanded once that part of the conversation finally hit home.

"Ah..." Spencer drawled. "Do you really want to know the answer or just trust that I do it when necessary?"

Nixon held up his hands. "You're right, I don't want to know. With everything else that's going on I really don't need to know." He paused for a moment, then lowered his hands. "Do you think he would work for us? To look after Cambrie? We can't keep her in the house forever. She will need to step outside at some point."

"Like I said, he got pulled in for a government job but I'll find out when I ask about removing her information," Spencer said as he headed for the door. "You two going to be alright if I leave?"

I waved him off. "Go do what you need to, we'll be fine, but thank you for handling that situation so well."

"With two Alpha partners you get used to dealing with the hot-headed moments," he said over his shoulder, shutting the door behind him.

"That Beta is lucky I love him as much as I do." Nixon sighed, running his hands through his hair. "So, what do *we* do about this? Should we tell the others?"

"My gut response is no, let's just keep it to the three of us, watch and see how things go, then if we need to involve the others we can. Right now, there's nothing they can do except worry," I reasoned.

Nixon grunted at that. "Is there really nothing we can do right now except worry?"

"Yeah, make sure that bastard never finds her," I stated.

CHAPTER 19
Marius

I spent half my day in the records room and didn't get through a third of the information. There was so much information I'd never seen before or knew existed. The laws regarding Omegas changed almost weekly for a while after the attack. Some were good ideas, others were trash, and I'm glad they got thrown out. Then they started to develop the system we have today but instead of just placing them with a pack who met the criteria they had them apply. Omegas still had a choice in the matter but the packs that passed and didn't have the money to stay in the game started to riot.

That was when they took choice out of the equation altogether. Now it was which pack was next in line. How much money did they donate? Who were they related to, and what benefit could they bring to the members of the CoF?

Of course, that wasn't how it was written on paper, but I could read between the lines. It wasn't hard to see those that got favored or even moved up the line when they greased the wheels. As a member of the CoF, I'm entitled to an Omega joining our pack, but the problem lies in the fact I can't choose the Omega. They give out whichever Omega was ready to begin breeding. When their designation appears at sixteen they are collected, they are then trained, educated, and prepared for a life to be pampered and produce offspring that will hopefully be Omegas.

If Cambrie went into the program, I had no idea if she'd be the one we'd be given or if it would be another eligible Omega. You'd think we'd be sending them out to packs as soon as they were ready but no, according to the report we currently have ten Omegas that can be paired with a pack, but none of the applicants could entice Yoram's attention with a bribe. Everything I learned about this whole situation was just asinine.

A knock sounded on my actual office door. After lunch, I'd come up here to get some real work done. Even if I couldn't deal with the major problems, we still had day to day issues to deal with keeping the city running. "Come in," I called.

There was only one person my secretary didn't alert me to and it was the devil himself. Yoram opened the door and stepped in, closing it behind him. He was tall and slim with a head full of neatly styled white hair, with a full silver mustache. Every suit he wore was simple and classic, with everything in its place and pressed with sharp seams. The only pop of color he had was his tie and pocket handkerchief which was a bold fuchsia today. His belt always matched his shoes, which were shined so you could see your reflection.

The old Alpha had a backbone of steel and never once slouched or had a momentary lapse of bad posture. He was rigid in his appearance as he was crooked in his politics. For him to feel the need to visit me in my office meant I did something he didn't like. Which meant I saw him at least once a day, but the look on his face told me I'd really pissed him off and I think I know what it might have been.

"Marius." He nodded in greeting. "Hard at work I see. Is that the petition for the low-income housing to go up on the west side near Bril Point?"

"Yeah, they've got good backing and they are partnering with a few other local organizations to offer support in the area. It's a decent proposal and they already have plans to ward off issues that arise with low-income sections," I shared, looking it over once more.

"Good, good, let it pass to the next stage to let them know

they're doing a good job, then I'll have the Zoning Commissioner deny them," Yoram instructed as he pulled the sheets from my hand, looking them over. "This group just won't give up. It's the fourth time they've tried in two years."

"I don't understand. It was an excellent idea that would cost the city or the taxpayers hardly anything. People need an alternative to going homeless when they fall on hard times. This would help support those people and keep them out of the city funded shelters," I argued, frustrated that once more Yoram was going to try and strong arm me into doing things his way. "Besides, the zoning angle won't work, they've already gotten approval."

Yoram's lips thinned as he tore up the petition and dropped it in the garbage. "Why should we support those who aren't doing their part? If they were working hard at their jobs, providing for this city and the other people in it, then there shouldn't be this problem."

I sat back and placed my hands in my lap, keeping my expression neutral as Yoram showed the vile sack of flesh that he was. "What if they work for one of the many companies that just filed for bankruptcy and shut their doors? They don't have a job to work hard at."

Yoram scoffed. "They weren't working hard! If those employees did their jobs right the company would have been making money and never would have had to file for bankruptcy."

"So, it would have nothing to do with the recent tax increase on sold goods within the city?" I countered. He knew I tried to fight it but with Alton out and deemed unfit to vote, the City Magistrate was brought in to replace him. Which meant... I was on the losing side every time right now. Which reminded me, I needed to check on the old coot to make sure Yoram hadn't had him killed without me knowing.

"You made your feelings quite clear in your voting," Yoram said, brushing off the fact that I made the argument that this very thing would happen if we raised the taxes.

"I'm sure you didn't come here to deal with the low-income housing matter," I remarked. "So what is it that I can do for you?"

Yoram stepped in front of my desk and took a seat in one of the chairs as if it were his throne. Clearly, this wasn't going to be a quick matter or he would have just come right out with it. No, it was obvious he needed to maneuver carefully around whatever he was going to say… or rather not say.

"It was brought to my attention that you made some odd requests today in the records department. I felt it was best to come and speak with you directly to find out what possible reason you could have for looking into the birth records of Omegas for the last sixty years," Yoram said so eloquently you'd have no idea how furious he really was.

No one had alerted him, he must have some protocol in place that notified him when people request information he didn't want them to have. Bethany might be a busybody but she wouldn't tattle on me. Instead, she'd have denied me the information and told me to beat it. By Yoram doing this, it told me far more about *him* than he realized.

"While I believe the system we have in place now was right for a time, I don't think it's the best way. We haven't seen an increase in Omegas being born, in fact there are fewer births overall since we started pairing them together. When Omegas don't have the choice in their pack or who they bond to, they don't prosper. The ones in packs now have fewer heats and only one out of ten conceive from a heat when they do happen," I explained. "If we want this city to recover, grow, and become prosperous once more, something needs to change."

"So you think it's the Omegas that are the problem?" Yoram inquired.

"Yes, in a way," I pulled out a sheet I made notes on. "I looked at birth rates from Betas and Alphas that have chosen their partner and they are having kids five out of every ten. That is exponentially more than what is happening with our Omegas. The chances of them being an Omega out of that type of union is once every ten but since they are having more kids they are producing more."

"That can't be true. We don't have nearly that many in our government Care Centers," Yoram argued.

"Yes, why would anyone be reluctant to give up their child to the government, never see them again, and have no idea what kind of pack they end up with?" I mused, thinking of how Cambrie viewed being an Omega. "A child's worst fear nowadays is to find out they're an Omega. So it stands to reason not all of them are coming forward voluntarily."

"How could you possibly know that from looking at a bunch of old records?" Yoram blustered, his mustache twitching, the only sign he was enraged.

I leaned forward on my desk, resting my elbows on the edge and clasped my hands together. "Did you forget that my best friend and partner run the largest shelters in the city? It's not hard for me to find out information like that."

"Are you admitting to me that your shelters harbor and hide Omegas from the government?" Yoram snapped.

"Not at all. I'm merely sharing what the average layperson says in regards to being an Omega," I countered, realizing I was on a slippery slope here. "If people don't feel it's in their child's best interest to be taken to one of our Care Centers, then they won't. There are other countries for them to live, granted, many of them are far worse off than we are or in constant battle over land and power. It's the reason we've become the pillar of our kind, showing that you can live free and love who you want."

"So you deny ever having helped an Omega hide from the government?" Yoram demanded.

I frowned at the man. "Why would I do that? I am the government."

"Yes, well I'm glad you realize that," Yoram said with a grunt. "As for this project you are working on, I don't see the need for it, this plan has been working for forty years. Why fix the wheel that isn't broken?"

"But is it really working?" I snapped. "If our city and nation that depends on us is dying, then what good does it do? Fewer Omegas are being born, not more, the only thing that's getting bigger is the city's treasury that we used to build ridiculous buildings like this."

The thunderous expression that fell over Yoram's face at my

outburst told me I'd said enough for one day. "You are young, full of ideals, and that is what got you into this office but I would tread carefully if you want to stay in this office. New faces are always exciting but once the novelty wears off who knows where that might leave you."

His threat was clear as he stood brushing out the nonexistent wrinkles from his clothes as he exited my space. Once the door latched behind him, I dropped my head to the desk knowing I'd just made matters so much worse. Now, I needed a new plan. There was no way that Yoram was going to accept the argument I just made. Not after that defiant display of mine, he'd throw it right in the trash next to the housing plan. Glancing at my watch, I saw it was still early afternoon but I needed to get out of here and talk to someone I could trust. Shoving back from my desk I hit the speed dial for the valet.

"Valet, Tommy speaking."

"Hey, it's Marius, I'm heading out for a meeting. Can you bring the car around?" I said as I gathered my research, not wanting to leave it out where someone might see it.

"Of course, Official Stone, I'll have it up by the time you come down," Tommy promised and hung up.

Checking my desk, I made sure I didn't miss anything that was important and headed out the door. It was days like this that I wondered how it was possible that I made it into this position. Yoram had to have hand-picked someone else, my guess was Kenneth, my opponent through most of the race. The elections were intense because once an Official was voted in they didn't leave unless they committed a crime or the other Officials lodged an investigation of being unfit for the job.

That is what I'd feared they would do to Alton, but he was far too respected and had as many connections as Yoram. The two were well matched in many regards, like two boxers in a ring fighting for the role of champion.

"Sarah, I'm running out for a meeting, I should be back later but I'll call if something comes up," I said as I passed my secretary.

Sarah was a good egg but she came with the office, I didn't hire her so I never really trusted to tell her much of anything. "Understood, Official Stone," she said, not even bothering to look up from the book she was reading.

Guess that explained why Yoram could just walk right into my office; she must not have even seen him arrive. I used the stairs, feeling the need to be as careful as I could not to have people tracking my movements. I knew there were cameras everywhere but the ones in the elevators had sound. Alton warned me right away about that, among many other traps one could fall into when they least expected it.

I gave Tommy a wave as I slipped into the car and headed off. Now that I was safe to speak, I called Alton's home and spoke to his wife, letting her know I was coming by.

"Bless you, Marius, he's been in such a foul mood the past few days and the rest of us are about to chuck him into the yard," Marla said, waving her arms dramatically.

Marla was a Beta and bonded to Alton for over forty years. Their pack came together from the first wave of the program of Care Centers, when Omegas could still pick their packs. Phillip, their Omega, was perfect for them, he was calm, collected, and could cool Alton's and Marla's tempers. There was another Alpha, Eric, and his bonded Beta but I didn't see them much since they hated everything our government was doing. They avoided anything to do with politics, preferring to keep to themselves. Since Eric was also bonded to Phillip, they would never leave the pack so they divided the house into two halves with joint spaces in the middle for them to spend time together.

Something like that happening to my pack was my biggest fear, but since most of us found each other due to our common interest in fixing what's wrong with our world, my hope was commonality would always stay the same.

"Alton, you'll never guess who popped in to see you," Marla called as she entered the library.

There was a bang as a book missed her and hit the wall. "Why the hell would I want to see anyone, woman?! Let an old man die in peace, Yoram's finally got what he wanted, no one to stand up to him."

"Alton!" Marla snapped. "You knock that shit off right now, I've tolerated enough of this. You are not dying, stop saying it or you'll make it happen with wishful thinking."

If there was a love language for arguing these two would be the poster couple. I don't think I've witnessed two people make an argument out of the simplest things like they do. Most observers would assume they hated each other but they didn't see the tender moments when they apologized, kissed, and made up. This was why Phillip was so important to the pack, he made sure no one went to sleep angry or with misunderstandings.

"Oh, wouldn't you just love that, to be rid of me so you can leave this city with the others? I know I'm the one holding you all here like a ball and chain," Alton grumbled.

I peeked my head in and found Marla fretting over Alton, making sure his blanket was tucked in around his waist and collected the empty teacup. "Now you two have a nice chat, and I'm gonna make a fresh pot of tea."

"Ah, so Yoram hasn't decided to oust you yet I see," Alton cackled as I walked over and sat across from him.

"Depends, I might have tied my own noose today," I shared with a sigh as I leaned back in the overstuffed armchair, crossing my leg over the other. "Tell me, how badly do you want to remove Yoram from the CoF?"

My question caught him off guard but quickly drew him in. "What did it for you? He must have had you cross some line you weren't willing to for you to come asking me that question."

"It's not him, well it is, just not in the way you're thinking," I explained, grabbing my briefcase, and pulling out the papers with the information I collected today. "Look at these."

Slipping on his glasses he turned on a lamp as he looked over my work. He slowly shuffled through the papers pausing at some to go back and double check something. "How can this be? This doesn't make sense to what other reports have shown us. Did Yoram see these?"

"No, he didn't. I told him what I was working on though because he came to confront me about being in the Omega birth records," I explained. "There's another part to this but I need to know that I have your word that what I'm about to tell you will never be spoken of outside these walls."

Alton pulled off his glasses, looked at me for a moment, held up a finger to his lips, and gestured for me to follow. Slowly, he got up from his chair letting the blanket fall to the ground not bothering to pick it up. Once he was upright he started to cough, a deep hacking cough that shook his whole body. I hurried over and grabbed his arm to steady him when he looked like he might fall over. When the fit passed, he waved me off and headed for a bookcase on the other side of the room. He flipped open the cover of a book and entered a code, the bookshelf slid to the side showing a room behind it. Alton looked back and motioned with his head for me to follow.

Behind the bookshelf was an office, one with filing cabinets along the wall and a corkboard with papers tacked all over it. Glancing at it I found news reports, laws, memos from the Capitol Building, and other random bits of information. "What is all this?"

"You asked me how far I was willing to go, it's the one thing I've been working on since my third year in office. That bastard has been gaining power year after year. The only win I've gotten past him was you," Alton confided. "Now sit and tell me everything, and I mean every last detail. You never know what could be the nail to hammer it home."

"I found an Omega, and I'm not giving her up."

CHAPTER 20

Cambrie

That night I helped Bodhi make dinner while Oscar went off to do some work he had to finish. It was quiet in the house but it didn't feel lonely at all, even with how huge it was. This place was a home and the people who lived in it left their impression, giving it personality. We both wore aprons, and I happily chopped up ingredients while he put everything together.

To have someone around all the time was a new feeling, but I decided I liked not having to be alone. Bodhi and I didn't feel the need to talk. We were just comfortable in each other's presence. He would tell me to grab something for him or if I needed to chop something differently but we found a natural rhythm. When a door banged open I startled, causing me to accidentally cut my finger as I brought the knife down on a carrot.

"Ah," I hissed, popping my finger into my mouth to stop the bleeding. Looking at the cutting board it didn't seem I'd bled on anything too badly but I was going to need to clean up this mess. Keeping my finger in my mouth I moved off what was safe and carried the rest to the sink.

"Sweetheart, did you cut yourself?" Nixon asked as his eyes fell on the cutting board.

I nodded, not wanting to remove my finger, knowing it was still bleeding.

"Cambi, why didn't you say anything?" Bodhi chastised, coming over to me but Nixon beat him to it.

The Alpha gripped my wrist and tugged gently for me to release my finger. Slowly, I let him pull my hand over the sink and under the running water. "It's better to clean it with soap and water. Your mouth isn't a very clean, it could get infected."

He pulled it out from under the stream of water to look at it. The cut was deep but only a quarter inch long on the side of my pointer finger. I reached for a paper towel to wrap it with since it was still seeping a little but Nixon had other plans. He hoisted me up on the counter as Bodhi placed a first aid kit next to me, pulling things out.

"It's not that bad, once it stops bleeding it will be fine," I assured them.

The looks I got from them told me to keep my mouth shut and let them do as they pleased. Like a doctor and his nurse, the two of them cleaned, medicated, and bandaged my finger as if it was a life threatening gash. Now my finger couldn't really bend with the gauze bandage they'd made.

"This seems a little much…" I offered hesitantly. "I'm sure a simple band aid would work too."

"I think you've done your part to help with dinner, why don't we let Bodhi finish while you help me and Spencer with another project?" Nixon decided.

Placing a hand on Bodhi's arm I drew his attention. "Are you okay with finishing on your own? I did say I was going to help you."

"It's fine Cambi, you did all the hard work prepping everything, now I just have to toss it all together," he replied, giving me a crooked smile. "Go see what Nixon's got up his sleeve, he seems a little too eager for just having worked a long day."

That had me looking at Nixon for what Bodhi had noticed that I didn't. His blue eyes glinted with something I couldn't quite place, that had to be what Bodhi had noticed. Nixon lifted me off the counter and set me on my feet, letting his hand rest on my back as he directed me out of the kitchen.

"I hope you don't mind, but Spencer and I went to the home goods store to get you some things for your room. It's one of the few rooms we hadn't set up but in hindsight, I suppose that's a good thing. Now you can create your own space. I'll have you look through some websites to pick out things you'd like to have. We just got the basics and tried to guess what you might like," Nixon rambled as we walked up to the third floor.

The giant bags of things set outside my bedroom door had me pause. "This is the basics?" I blurted, feeling like my eyes were going to pop out of my head.

"Maybe I should have explained what that means to Spencer," Nixon answered, rubbing the back of his neck. "It's one of his favorite things to help someone feel like they belong, it's how he shows he cares. Sometimes he gets a little out of hand, but he was so excited I didn't have the heart to stop him." He caught my eye and gave me a stern look. "If there is something you don't want or don't like we will return it. Just because we picked it out doesn't mean you need to keep it, capeesh?"

I nodded, then ventured forward to find Spencer peeking into our blanket fort. "How cool is this?!" he called out, stepping all the way in. "I don't want to take this down, nothing we got is as awesome."

When he popped back out he spotted me, and a bright smile lit his face. "Hey there Little Dove, this is a pretty cool nest. Seems like you had a way better day than I did, watching movies with the others."

"It was a pretty wonderful day, best one I've had in a long time," I answered, returning his smile. "Don't worry about the fort, Bodhi is an expert, I'm sure he can make another one all of us could fit in."

"Who would have guessed that for a hidden talent?" Spencer mused as he came the rest of the way out and walked up to me with open arms.

I leaned into his embrace hugging him back, loving how simple a thing it was, but how much affection went into it. Spencer nuzzled the top of my head and pressed a kiss to it before releasing me. "Wanna see what we picked up?"

"Sure, but Bodhi was almost done with dinner so we might need to come back to it," I warned.

"No problem, I'm really ready for dinner so you won't hear me complaining," he answered, grabbing a giant bag and dragging it in. "This is bedding so we can start here, and if you like it we can make the bed so it's ready when you want to go to sleep."

"Why is the bag so big if it's just bedding?" I questioned as I started to pull things out. There were tons of decorative pillows in teal, soft pink, cream, and gray. Each a different shape, size, and texture that had me running my hand over them all. One cream pillow felt scratchy like coarse wool, and I scrunched up my nose at the feel.

The pillow was snatched from me and tossed across the room. "Not that one, it got the nose wrinkle," Spencer called as Nixon caught it and set it outside the room. "Keep going, Dove, there's lots to see."

Curious about his reaction, I continued on until I found a pink pillow that squished in the most amazing way. I pressed it again and the feel of the soft buttery fabric made me smile. *How was it so squishy? It felt like marshmallows stuffed in a pillow.* Continuing, I kept this one in my lap not wanting to misplace it. Only a few pillows were discarded by the time I was through, and there was a growing mound of them next to me.

"I know I went crazy on the pillows, but I had no way to know what would feel right to you," Spencer explained as he put the pillows I hadn't hated or loved back in the bag. "I'm going to send these back, and we'll keep your pile of treasures."

Looking down there had to be ten pillows next to me. "All of them?" I asked. "I get to keep them all?"

"Of course, it's hard to build a nest without the proper items now, isn't it?" Spencer reported as he dragged another bag in. "These are all blankets and sheets. I knew you liked teal, and yellow seemed to be a no go but other than that, I made guesses. Since you like the gray and pink pillows I'm hoping I went in the right direction."

He pulled out two large plastic encased squares that had pictures of beds on them. One showed a bed covered in a white comforter with teal geometric shapes and color blocking with gray. It was beautiful but when I saw the second one, I gasped. It was also a white base, but this looked like it had been painted with watercolors. Each area of color bloomed out fading into the white or one of the other colors. The pink was so soft compared to the teal and the gray seemed to tie it all together.

"This one," I whispered as I pulled the image closer. Then I paused, cocking my head slightly to look at the size of the bed. "I think this will be too big, my bed is about half this size."

Spencer's cheeks started to turn pink and when he opened his mouth to answer, nothing came out. He closed it and looked past me to where Nixon was watching everything as he sorted through bags. Nixon didn't seem to notice Spencer was at a loss and kept searching for whatever it was he'd lost in the mass of things.

"Hey, dinner's ready!" Bodhi hollered up the stairs.

Spencer blew out a breath as he jumped to his feet, startling me into falling backward clutching a pillow. "Shit, sorry Dove. I need to be better about moving too fast around you," he muttered as he crouched next to me, offering a hand. "Can I help you up?"

I smiled, wanting to reassure him I wasn't afraid of him, it was just a response I couldn't really control. He grasped my hand and pulled me to my feet, then frowned. "Did you cut yourself? Clearly you did, but who on God's green earth put this bandage on you?"

"Nixon and Bodhi," I answered. "I told them a band aid would be fine but they disagreed."

Spencer snorted and shook his head. "I'll bet they did. Would you like me to put a band aid on it so you can use that finger to eat dinner? I feel like you won't be able to hold a knife."

"She's not touching knives for the rest of the night. If she needs something cut we will do it for her," Nixon grumbled. "Come on, let's go eat. I'm starving."

Laughing, Spencer took my hand and we headed out after

Nixon down to the dining room. When we got to the first floor, I saw Rafael was home hanging up his jacket.

"Welcome home, Rafael," I said, beaming at him when he saw us. "Did you have a good day at work?"

He smiled but I noticed it didn't quite reach his eyes and he looked almost sad. "It was an interesting day, but I think overall it was good."

His tone made him sound tired and everything in me felt like I needed to do something to help make him feel better. I thought about how nice it was to have a hug from Spencer when he got home, so I walked up to Rafael and wrapped my arms around his waist. "I'm sorry something happened today to make you feel sad."

Rafael let out a breath as if he'd been holding the weight of the world on his shoulders. Curling his arms around me, he held me tight and rested his head on mine, taking a deep breath. "Thank you, Little One, this is helping immensely. It's nice to be welcomed home with a hug and someone who smells as yummy as you," he added with a wink as he pulled back. "I believe I heard Bodhi call for dinner, let me wash up real quick and I'll be in."

"Alright," I said, then froze as Rafael kissed me on the cheek before heading to the hall bathroom.

I lifted my hand to touch the spot and could feel the heat of my blush. The fluttery feeling returned to my stomach and I didn't quite know what to do with myself. I turned and walked into the dining room letting my hand slowly drop from my face. Why had that kiss seemed different from the other times he's kissed my head like my mother used to? Was it the feel of his lips on my skin and his scent wrapping around me like a warm blanket?

"Cambi, come sit by me this time, there's no assigned seats," Bodhi said, then paused. "Okay, no assigned seats but for the fact that Marius always likes to sit at the head of the table. Other than that, sit wherever you like."

"Sorry Bodhi, but you and Oscar have had her all day, I saw the pillow fort. Now you have to share," Spencer challenged, then looked at me patting the chair next to him. "Have a seat Dove, we need to talk about what we're gonna do about clothes for you."

Unsure of what to do, I considered what Spencer said and felt he was right. I'd spent all day curled up with Oscar and Bodhi, it was smart for me to spend time with Spencer and the others. Walking around the table I took a seat and was promptly given a tablet.

"Here, look through the catalog and pick out what clothes you like. I mean anything and everything because all you have is this one outfit and that isn't gonna fly. You need socks, undergarments, pajamas, jackets, pants, shirts, swimsuits for the summer, and so on," Spencer instructed.

"There's a pool?" I inquired. "I can't remember the last time I've gone swimming!" I bounced excitedly in my chair just thinking about the idea.

"We don't have one in the backyard, but there is a pool in the community that we can use," Nixon shared. "Not many people use it so when it warms up we'll probably have the place to ourselves."

Everything about this was so exciting, I couldn't remember the last time I could plan ahead for my life, or dare to dream it would be possible. Something as simple as going to the pool sounded like heaven and I couldn't wait.

"What is this about a pool?" Rafael asked as he joined us.

"They were telling me we could go when it's warm enough, so I'd better look at buying a suit," I offered, scrolling through all the choices. "Oh, look at this one. It's teal with all kinds of sparkles on it." I turned it to show Spencer and Rafael.

Spencer's eyes widened and Rafael let out a snarl, making me jump. I looked at the picture trying to figure out what about the suit they didn't like. It wasn't too expensive and it said the pieces were buy one get one half off.

"Let me see, Sweetheart," Nixon asked, who sat across from Spencer.

I showed it to him and he had almost the same reaction as Rafael, only not quite so aggressive. He cleared his throat and drank some water before he spoke. "That is a lovely suit, Sweetheart, but maybe it might be best to see the color better if there was a little more of it."

Looking at it with new eyes, I could see how the bottoms might be smaller than a pair of underwear and the top was only large triangles to cover your boobs. Not that I had any to worry about, but then the thought that wearing this would show off too many of my scars I decided maybe it wasn't right.

"Yeah, I think I need something with a little more coverage. Who knows if I'll have gained enough weight back," I said, setting the tablet down. "Better leave that for after dinner, it's rude to ignore those at the table with you."

Bodhi walked out with a large pot of steaming yummy goodness and set it in the middle of the table. "Oscar should be in any minute. Has anyone heard from Marius?"

"Last I knew he was going to visit Alton, so I'm not sure if he's going to stay there for dinner or not," Spencer shared. "You know Marla when she lays down the law."

Nixon shivered. "I don't know if I've ever met a Beta who terrified me as much as she does. That man is a strong one to have been bonded to her for so long."

"Well then, we won't wait," Bodhi decided as he set the last few things on the table.

Oscar walked in through the kitchen holding a basket of rolls that he set down before taking a seat across from me. He gave me a wink which made me smile as I took a sip of water, then nearly choked on it when he grabbed my injured hand. He looked at it then at Bodhi knowing he would have the answers.

"Battle wound while making dinner, she's going to be fine," Bodhi assured him. "Helped to bandage it up myself."

"You mean half mummified her finger? How much gauze did you think was really necessary?" Spencer asked as he leaned past me to see Bodhi.

Bodhi glared at Spencer. "It was still bleeding. I wanted to make sure it didn't bleed through. We'll change it before she goes to bed to make sure it's stopped, otherwise we'll take her to the hospital."

A shockwave of fear slammed into me at the notion of going to the hospital. "No, no hospitals," I blurted. "Please, no matter what happens I can't ever go there!" Everyone gaped at me so surprised by my outburst that I shrunk down in my chair. "Mom made me promise I would never, ever go to a hospital no matter what. If I did, then they would take me away forever."

"What do you mean, Little One, who would take you away?" Rafael asked, his voice calm and soothing to my nerves.

"She never said, only that going to a hospital would be the worst thing for me. I went once when I broke my arm, they asked me so many questions and I heard them talking about taking me from my father. Once the cast was on I ran, I couldn't let them take me," I whispered.

"Sweetheart, I think your mother was talking about if they found out your father was hurting you. Then they would take you away, put you in a foster home to make sure you were safe," Nixon said, reaching out to place his hand over mine. "You don't have to worry about that now, he's never going to get you back, and they can't take you from us now that you're eighteen."

Once the fear subsided I thought about his words. He was right, I knew about child services and how they took kids from bad homes. It's why we moved and I couldn't go to school. They would notice and take me from Father.

"You're probably right, things are different now that I'm older. They can't take me and I trust you won't let my father take me either," I said, giving them all a weak smile as I pulled myself together.

My stomach growled loudly, stirring everyone into motion as my plate was taken and food was placed on it. When I got it back, I realized they put small servings of everything on there for me. Even the roll was cut in half, ensuring I wouldn't have too much food on my plate to feel guilty about.

"If you want more of anything you speak up, alright?" Bodhi commanded, pointing a finger at me.

"Promise," I said, picking up my fork. "I'm super excited to try everything. It all smelled so good as you were cooking."

"Just so everyone knows, Cambrie helped me prepare dinner so this meal is a joint effort," Bodhi stated, everyone then promptly started to eat.

CHAPTER 21

Cambrie

We'd been eating for a little while when a door opened and shut, drawing my attention. From where I was sitting I couldn't see who'd come in but my guess was Marius. Sure enough, a few moments later he appeared with a bakery box in his hands.

"Hey everyone, sorry I'm late but I had to stop at Harner's to grab something and it took way longer than I expected," he explained, setting the box on a side table, then dropped a quick kiss on Spencer's lips and my head before taking his seat at the table. "Everything smells amazing, it seems you've outdone yourself tonight."

"It wasn't just me, Cambrie helped, even got a battle wound for her efforts," Bodhi said, giving me a wink.

Marius's head snapped in my direction as he looked over what he could see of my body. I raised my left hand and waved it at him to show off my wrapped finger. "It's nothing, I just got startled and wasn't cutting with my fingers tucked under like I should have."

"You're still not picking up another knife tonight," Nixon reminded me.

I smiled and looked down at my plate of creamy chicken and rice with lots of cheese coating the top of it. "Thankfully, this meal doesn't need any so I'm safe for the time being."

The table fell silent, then Bodhi snorted, causing all the others to give in to their laughter. Even Oscar's shoulders shook as he placed a hand on his chest to control his laughter.

"It wasn't that funny," I muttered, popping in another mouthful of food as I pouted.

"Oh, don't take it too hard Dove, we all poke fun at each other," Spencer said, jostling me with his shoulder. "It's how boys show they care when they pick on each other, it's all meant with love."

The guys fell into conversation about their days as Spencer asked about Alton who Marius went to visit. Rafael shared about a patient he was working with that was able to get a lease on an apartment for the first time in years, while Nixon complained about dealing with bankers. I didn't understand half of what they were discussing but having everyone together made me feel whole. This could easily become something I was addicted to, and I didn't understand why more people didn't want to live as a pack.

"Tell me, Princess, what did you do all day?" Marius asked when there was a lull in the conversation.

I froze for a moment as everyone's eyes turned to me. It was a little overwhelming to have everyone's attention all at once when I'd gone unnoticed for eighteen years. "Um…, Bodhi made a blanket fort in my room, first one I've ever experienced. Then we watched movies for most of the afternoon, took a nap, and made dinner while Oscar got some work done. Then Nixon and Spencer came home with massive bags of stuff for my room," I paused and turned to look at him. "We need to switch out that bedding, right? Since you got one that was too big."

"Yes, Nixon about the *bed* situation," Spencer deflected, looking over at his Alpha. "You were going to share that fun bit of news, weren't you?"

Nixon paused, his fork almost entering his mouth as Spencer addressed him. He closed his mouth and lowered his fork, setting it on his plate before addressing whatever Spencer was alluding to.

"Yes, the bed," Nixon started, then paused to clear his throat and take a gulp of water. "Since you are now part of this pack, and we want you to stay forever and be as comfortable as possible we... I thought it would be best to think about the future."

I frowned, looking between him and Spencer trying to figure out what in the world he was trying to say. "The bed that's there is comfortable, there's no need to change for my comfort."

Nixon's face started to redden as he looked down at his plate and rubbed the back of his neck. "I'm glad it's comfortable, but it's a little small."

"Oh, for goodness sake," Rafael muttered, pulling my attention from the Alpha who clearly was struggling with something. "Little One, there will come a time when it's right, and we will bond together as a real pack. Eventually, you'll have a heat, and in those situations where there might be one or more partners in your bed, it would be best to have one that can accommodate them all. By no means are we rushing this or forcing it upon you, but this is the future we see with you."

Now it was my turn to blush bright red as I understood his meaning. It made perfect sense, I knew what being the Omega to a pack meant and that someday heats and bonding would happen, I just hadn't thought that far down the road. "Right," I squeaked out.

"Back when Omegas could pick their packs, it was customary for the Alphas to shower their prospective Omegas with gifts, courting them. I suppose you could say that's what we're doing, in our own way, as we help you set up your room and provide for you in other ways," Nixon explained, seeming to have regained his composure. "All of this is happening a little backward, since things are so different now in our world. We want to show you just how much we desire you to be with us, as a best friend, and hopefully more, much more when it's right."

Were they confessing they had feelings for me? We've only just met. How could they possibly know so quickly about something like that?

"Dove," Spencer said, resting a hand on my thigh. "Take a deep breath for me."

As he said that, I realized I wasn't breathing with all of this catching me so off guard. I took a long slow breath and let it out as I looked over the men at the table. Of course, I'd always dreamed of a pack and the happy ever after it could bring. The men who loved me and I loved them just as much. I'd read the spicy scenes and knew that love and passion mixed together would be something absolutely amazing. What I hadn't counted on, was it actually happening to *me*!

"Do you all feel this way? That you want me to be your pack's bonded Omega?" I asked, thinking there was no way all of them could feel that deeply.

Yes they'd been kind, thoughtful, and attentive, but Spencer already had two Alphas. Rafael was the oldest out of the group and couldn't possibly see me as anything but a child. Marius and Nixon had Spencer so why would they need someone else they would have to share with even more people? Bodhi was my best friend, and Oscar was someone who exuded warmth and just cared about people in general. How could it be that six men could want me in a way that a man wants a woman? I was damaged goods that freaked out at the worst moments over the silliest things. Not to mention my father could still be out there looking for me. What about the CoF? Would they let this happen? Could I trust they wouldn't take me away?

Someone grabbed my face and turned it to them but with the panic flooding my body my eyes wouldn't focus. Then the softest lips I could have ever imagined pressed against mine. I gasped at the touch as the velvet touch of a tongue swiped along my lower lip. A sound I'd never made before slipped out, causing whoever was kissing me to deepen his efforts, a purr rumbling in his chest.

The next thing I knew, I was straddling him, my arms wrapped around his neck as he gently clasped my throat. His other hand was on my lower back pressing me to his chest so I could feel his purr through my whole body. The scent of caramel and cinnamon engulfed me, and my brain seemed to switch back on as the panic subsided and something else took its place. Need and heat filled my body so when the tongue brushed past again I opened up allowing him in. Having no idea what I was doing, I tried to reciprocate what

Oscar was doing to me, kicking his purr up another level. Gently he pulled back, pressing our foreheads together as we caught our breath.

"That's one way to end a panic attack and answer the question without having to utter a word," Bodhi commented.

Hearing him talk made me remember we were at the table with *everyone* still sitting there. Oscar shifted to hold me tightly against him, a warning growl in my ear. When I calmed down and stopped fighting he turned me so I was sitting on his lap, arms around my waist, and his nose running along my neck. His purr started again, easing some of the tension I was feeling due to the wish of digging a hole and hiding in it after that display.

"Is it that hot when you watch me making out with one of you?" Spencer asked his Alphas. "Because I don't think I've ever seen anything more beautiful or sensual in my life."

My cheeks grew hotter at his words as my stomach did excited flips of joy. Oscar had just kissed me! My very first kiss and it was amazing! I lifted my hands to my lips and felt how swollen they were, proving that what just happened wasn't a dream.

"I'm fairly certain I can speak for us all, if we had any doubts of our interest in you it's no longer there," Rafael stated. "Little One, there is nothing I want more than to pull you into my lap and show you why those lips should never be chewed on again. There are far more enjoyable things that can be done with them."

"Raffie!" Spencer scolded the Alpha. "Don't talk like that to her, you're going to scare her away from the idea. I, for one, would like to ensure that I get a chance to taste her lips and if you go all dirty old man on her it will never happen."

Rafael lifted his nose and scented the air. "I'd say by her perfume she's anything but turned off by what I said."

Bodhi shot to his feet. "Okay, I think everyone needs to take a walk to cool down, then come back to the table so we can finish our meal. I think Cambi is now well aware of how we all feel about her, so let's give the girl a break."

Oscar nuzzled into my neck taking a deep breath before releasing me so I could return to my chair. The other three Alphas did as Bodhi requested, got up from the table, and headed into the kitchen. A few moments later they returned with short glasses filled with amber liquid and ice. By the smell of it I could tell it was liquor of some sort, but I wasn't worried about things getting out of hand. Unlike my father, they only had a mouthful or two instead of a bottle to drink.

"Princess," Marius said as he once more had the bakery box in his hands. "I believe you told us it was your birthday not too long ago and I had a feeling you never got to celebrate it." He flipped open the lid and there was a beautiful round cake with white frosting and brightly colored flowers. Written on the cake in cursive was *Happy Birthday, Cambrie!*

Gasping, I covered my mouth as I took in the sight of the cake. I hadn't celebrated my birthday since I was eight. Mom always tried to do something special and she always made sure there was a cake with candles.

"Hold on," Bodhi blurted and rushed into the kitchen. Quickly, he was back with candles and stuck them in various places that wouldn't destroy the design. There were only five but it didn't matter, it was the thought that counted. "Are we singing?"

"If you call what comes out of some of our mouths singing, then yeah. It's not a birthday without a little embarrassment, right?" Spencer reasoned. "Bodhi, you lead and sing as loud as you can since you're the one with the talent here."

"One, two, three..." Bodhi counted down, and out of his mouth came the most amazing sound.

While I knew the others were singing along, Bodhi had me transfixed with the slight rasp in his buttery tone. It slid against my skin like silk and all I wanted to do was be wrapped up in it. All too soon the song was over and I had to shake myself out of a daze as everyone waited for me to blow out the candles. Taking a deep breath, I did my best to get them all in one go, which I did for all but one. It fizzled out and then popped back to life again. I blew again, same thing, it went out, then came back.

I sat back a moment staring at it like I could figure out how this kept happening. I gave it one more shot but when it burst back to life again I looked at the others for help. Each of them were trying to hold back laughter but I had no idea what was so funny. This darn candle wouldn't blow out.

"Am I doing something wrong?" I asked, glaring at the candle.

"Yup, I don't think there could ever be a more perfect Omega to have in our lives," Nixon said, licking two fingers and snuffing out the candle. "It's a trick candle, Sweetheart. They are made so no matter how many times you blow it out, it will come back."

"Sorry, Cambi, I didn't know there was one in the bunch. I just grabbed what I could find in the drawer," Bodhi apologized.

I smiled at him and shook my head. "No need to apologize, it was a good trick, now I get why all of you were laughing." I looked down at the cake before me and pouted a little. "It's so pretty I almost hate to cut it."

The cake was instantly snatched away. "What did I say about knives?" Nixon scolded. "One of us will cut it up and then you won't have to feel so bad about it."

Chuckling, I sat in my seat and watched as Marius and Bodhi argued over the best way to cut the cake. Spencer pulled my chair closer to him and wrapped an arm around my shoulders so my head rested on his chest. "Happy belated birthday, Dove," he murmured in my ear. "But I have to say I think we got the gift, having you walk into our lives."

My cheeks flushed as I cuddled closer to him, taking in his refreshing citrus and coconut scent. It made me think of what spending time on the beach somewhere tropical might smell like. Maybe one day I might find out, every other dream I've had so far has come true.

AFTER THE CAKE WAS EATEN, and dinner was cleaned up and put away, I found myself in my bedroom looking through more bags. Apparently, the new bed and other furniture they bought would be here Monday since they didn't deliver over the weekend and tomorrow was Saturday. Everyone would be home for the next two days and I was trying not to bounce with excitement.

"Dove, what do you think about painting the walls?" Spencer asked, lying on his back looking around the room. "With all the color we've added into the space I feel like the plain white walls just aren't right."

"But wouldn't that make all the color we added get lost? Right now it's so bright and cheerful because nothing is competing with it," I countered.

New curtains had been hung, the blankets and pillows had been placed to the side waiting for the new bed, and a beautiful woven swing was hanging from the ceiling for me to read in. Spencer and I looked through tons of pictures of bedrooms, oohing and ahhing over various things.

"You make a good point and the plan I have, inspired by your blanket fort, is going to be a showstopper," he admitted, sitting up and facing me. "So how do you feel about going shopping with me tomorrow?"

"For what?" I asked, feeling like there couldn't be anything more he'd need to buy for the room.

"You, clothes remember?" he teased, booping me on the nose. "What do you say? A date with you, me, Marius, and Nixon."

My eyes went wide. "A date... like a real one?"

Spencer's eyes glowed with happiness as he smiled. "Yeah, Dove, a real date with three men who are extremely interested in this one stunning Omega with beautiful blue eyes and blonde hair."

"You think I'm pretty?" I blurted, then slapped my hands over my mouth embarrassed at my outburst.

Spencer crawled over, closing the space between us until I was sitting between his knees, his body leaning over me. He reached out and gently tugged my hands away so he could see my face, running a finger along my jawline.

"You, my sweet Dove, are gorgeous inside and out," he whispered, leaning in to brush his nose along the shell of my ear. "Do you want to know a secret?"

I tried to say yes but it came out more like a squeak than a word, but Spencer took it as agreement.

"When I'm with them, I picture you there too," he shared, his lips brushing my cheek, sending a shiver through my body. "You've already stolen a piece of my heart, Cambrie, and I wouldn't have it any other way."

When he finished speaking his lips hovered over mine. Hesitating, almost unsure if I wanted him to kiss me when I wanted nothing more in the world than to know what his lips felt like. After my kiss with Oscar, it's almost as if a switch had been flipped and I wanted to know more—feel everything these men had to offer. When he still didn't make his move, I decided for him and went for it.

I might have been a little overzealous as I slammed my mouth to his, knocking him back slightly, but it didn't slow him down for long. Wrapping his arms around me he fell back, pulling me on top of him as he slid a hand into my hair, and the other landed on my butt keeping me from falling off him. The combination of his coconut and my spicy nutmeg permeated the air as our scents blended as he tasted my lips.

Spencer was in no hurry as he moved his lips against mine, tilting my head to allow him better access as I allowed him in. While Oscar had been powerful and assured in his kisses, Spencer was slow and methodical, almost as if he wanted to know every inch of my body. The hand on my butt grabbed tighter, pressing me against him and I felt something harden under me. I'd studied anatomy, I knew the differences between men, women, and Alphas, but to feel it with only clothes between you was another matter.

My hands fisted into his shirt as I fought against the urge to rub against him like a cat seeking out a person's touch. Needing to change something, I let my legs fall to the sides so I was straddling Spencer, my pelvis pressing tighter against him. A moan escaped him as he bucked under me.

"God almighty," Spencer groaned as he hugged me firmly and ground into me. "You feel so good, Dove. I love the way you respond, molding to my body like you were meant to be there."

A knock came at the door. "Spencer? Sweetheart? Everything alright in there?" Nixon called.

"Come on in, *Alpha*," Spencer answered, clearly not intending for us to move as he stopped me from sliding off. "No, Dove, there is nothing to be ashamed of. Neither of us are doing anything wrong, and trust me when I say Nixon is about to be incredibly jealous."

The bedroom door opened and a deep guttural groan could be heard. "Spencer, you naughty Beta, you knew exactly what I would be walking in on," Nixon said, his voice lower and rougher than normal. "Fuck, Sweetheart, you're perfuming like crazy, has my Prince been taking care of you?"

As he spoke, I heard him coming closer until he stood next to us looking down, raw need glowing in his eyes. Spencer let his hand slip from my hair as he tucked it behind my ear so I could see the Alpha looming over us better. Peering up at him, I wasn't sure how to respond to his question but I knew he wanted an answer.

"Spencer always takes good care of me," I said, pushing up slightly on Spencer's chest so I could sit up.

Spencer grunted as he grabbed my butt with both hands holding me still and grinding against me. "Dove, you're killing me."

I gasped and looked down. "Did I hurt you? I'm sorry I should have been more careful. I don't really know how to maneuver around a man whose penis is erect," I stammered, trying to move off him, but he held me fast.

"Trust me, you are not hurting me at all, Dove," Spencer assured me as his breathing picked up. "I'm incredibly happy to keep my penis right where it is, with you sitting on top of it."

I looked up at Nixon to find his eyes laser focused on me, a low rumbling growl in his chest. "Tell me, Cambrie, what do you know about sex?"

My whole body flushed at his words as a mixture of embarrassment and arousal caused me to fill the air with even more of my scent. As an Omega, I would never be able to hide when I felt desire, a biological assurance that my need wouldn't go unmet.

"I..." My mouth went dry and I had to swallow and lick my lips before I tried again. "I've read about it in books, seen pictures when studying, so I understand the basics."

"Hmm, then I think it might be time for you to further your education," Nixon suggested. "Would you like to show her a thing or two, my Prince?"

Spencer looked at Nixon then at me. "Only if you are comfortable with this, Dove. I don't want you to feel we are rushing things or pushing you for more. What Nixon is asking won't involve you, he means only for you to watch. While we won't refuse you if you decide to interact, I need you to understand it's not expected." He paused to search my face. "Say the word right now and we will both leave and I'll deal with him in our own space, not intruding on yours."

His words seemed to snap Nixon out of his Alpha induced need, shaking his head and taking a step back. "Holy shit, what am I doing?" He turned his back to me holding his head. "I'm so sorry Cambrie, your scent mixed with Spence's nearly sent me into a rut. This shouldn't be happening. I'm a horrible Alpha for even asking you what I just did, fuck!"

Nixon turned to rush out of the room and this time when I moved to follow Spencer helped me to my feet. "Nixon, wait," I called, rushing after him, grabbing the back of his shirt. "Don't leave please, I can't let you walk away from me that upset."

He stopped but refused to look at me, his body tense under my touch as if he was trying to keep himself from doing something he shouldn't. "Cambrie, it's not safe for me to be here right now," he said his voice gruff with emotion. "I promised nothing would happen to you, that I would protect you and right now I think I need to protect you from me."

My heart broke at the self-loathing in his words, I walked around so I was facing him. His eyes were closed, hands balled into fists, body practically vibrating with the need to run.

"Nixon," I said, reaching out to brush my hand over his. He flinched at my touch but I didn't shy away, instead I wrapped my arms around him, letting my head rest in the middle of his chest.

It felt like if I didn't break through he would never trust himself around me again and I couldn't let that happen. "Please don't leave me," I whispered. "You might not trust yourself but *I* trust you. There isn't a doubt in my mind that you won't keep that promise you made to me."

His whole body shuddered as he hesitantly placed his arms around me, dropping his head so his nose was nestled in my hair. "I'm not always a strong man, Sweetheart, especially when it comes to something I want so desperately, like holding you in my arms. Seeing the man I love passionately making out with the woman I am falling for more and more each moment was everything I never knew I wanted."

Hearing his words had me melting into him unable to resist him if I wanted to. "Will you stay with me tonight?" I leaned back looking into his shocked eyes. "Just to sleep, Spencer too, the three of us together. That's what you wanted, right? Because that's what I want too and someday it will be more than sleep, but for now I just don't want you to leave."

"Okay," Nixon answered, pressing a sweet kiss to my lips before hugging me close. "I'm not going anywhere."

CHAPTER 22

Nixon

Agreeing to be in the same bed as Cambrie right now was one of the stupidest things I'd done in a long time. I knew the control I had over myself and the need to bury my cock deep within her pussy until I knotted her good and tight was holding on by a thread. Her bed was a queen and while for two people it was enough space to manage... three was another story. Looking down, I saw her face tucked against my chest. The moment she fell asleep she cuddled in close with a deep happy sigh that made me want to fight the world to keep her safe. Right now, the person I needed to fight was myself.

Spencer was at her back with a hand draped over her hip brushing against the skin right above my cock. It was so hard I could feel it pulsing against my leg. I'd tried everything to distract myself but when the best smelling fucking snickerdoodle cookie was curled up against you it was impossible to forget about the dessert within your grasp. I knew I needed to fix this and if I couldn't fuck her, then I was gonna need to fuck the only other person who made me lose control like this.

Grabbing his wrist, I drew his hand to my cock, rubbing it along the outside of my boxers I was sleeping in. It took a minute but slowly Spencer cracked open an eye and met my gaze. We'd been together long enough all I had to do was cock one brow at him and he knew what I wanted. He frowned and shook his head slightly, looking down at Cambrie.

Fuck, he's right. There's no way we could fool around with her in the bed. That was crossing more boundaries than I could even imagine. No, we needed another option, but I'd promised I wouldn't leave the room, so that left us with the floor or the bathroom. I gestured for him to get out of bed first, and he carefully extracted himself from around her body. He headed straight for the ridiculous pile of pillows, grabbed a pink one, and brought it over to me.

"Tuck this in front of you so when you move she has something to cuddle," he whispered as he handed it over.

When I took it I understood why he picked this one, it was squishy as shit in the best way. I almost had the urge to cuddle it myself. It felt so nice, but my need wasn't going to let that happen, so my sweet little Cambrie would hang on to it for me. Slowly, I slipped one leg out of bed and then the other, keeping low like I was a burglar trying to get out unnoticed. Kneeling on the ground beside the bed, I looked up at Spencer.

"Will you be a good boy, my Prince?" I asked as I pulled out my cock. "Your Alpha needs a good boy right now who can help with this problem."

Spencer's pupils blew wide as he dropped to his knees and crawled forward, licking his lips. "Yes Alpha, I'm a very good boy who would love nothing more than to ease your pain."

I stifled the growl those words elicited from me. There was nothing sexier than my Beta with his ass up and mouth watering to take my cock in his mouth. God what a mouth it was, as his hot breath brushed against my tight needy cock. His tongue flicked out, lapping up the pre-cum that was leaking out of me. I knew it wouldn't take me long to cum. The question was if I really was in rut, would once be enough?

Biting my fist, I groaned as Spencer's lips wrapped around the tip of my cock while his hand squeezed the base where my knot started to pulse. *Fuck*, just picturing what it would be like to have

Cambrie wrapped around my knot was almost enough for me to blow my load and we hadn't even gotten started yet.

"What a good Prince, let me in, let me fuck that glorious mouth of yours," I cooed, letting my hand slide to the back of Spencer's skull. The perfect place for me to control just how deep he took my cock. "That's it, take it all, let me into your throat, feel you swallow around me. Just like that, *yes*."

I knew I was talking too much but I couldn't stop myself. When I was with my partner I wanted them to know what I wanted and just how much they pleased me. Some people didn't like or understand dirty talk or praising their partner, but I never wanted them to have doubts.

The beautiful sounds of Spencer gagging on my cock as I pushed it just a little too far made me shiver. His hand gripped my thighs but he wasn't giving me the signal I was being too rough so I went with it. Watching his eyes water as he looked up at me, my cock ravaging his mouth, did something to me on a primal level. He trusted me to know what was too much even though he had the power to end this in a second.

Knowing that coming in his mouth wouldn't take the edge off like I'd hoped, I eased up on him before pulling out of his mouth completely. Grabbing his throat, I drew him up to me and kissed the hell out of him. My tongue chased after his, wanting to taste him even knowing he'd just had my cock in his mouth. A man who was afraid to kiss someone after they sucked their cock didn't deserve the pleasure. They ought to be kissed right after in gratitude, no matter what.

Spencer clung to my arm, whimpers leaking out of his mouth, telling me he was in as much need as I was. Of course he was. The lucky bastard had been getting some heavy petting in with our Omega before I joined the party and fucked it all up.

"What do you need, my Prince? Tell me and I will give it to you," I murmured against his lips.

"Fuck me, Alpha, I need your cock inside me, *please*," Spencer begged.

My lips slammed against his, rewarding him for being honest as

I reached out and stroked his cock that was poking out of his boxers. "How do you want me to fuck you?"

"I want you to hold me as you fuck my ass, Alpha," Spencer said, wriggling out of his boxers before climbing into my lap.

"We don't have any lube in here, my Prince," I warned as I lubed my finger up with spit.

Spencer grabbed my hand and signaled for me to give him a moment as he got up and raced to the bathroom. He returned with a jar pure of coconut oil which he scraped out a good chunk and worked over my cock. It melted into a smooth, silky lube that would do just the trick. I took some and massaged it into his asshole, dipping a finger in ensuring he was prepared. The last thing I ever wanted was for sex to be uncomfortable for either of us.

My sexy Prince climbed back onto my lap, holding himself up as I gripped my dick, making sure it was steady for him to settle himself on. Spencer eased my cock inch by inch, warming himself up until he could finally take my whole shaft up to my knot that had started to expand. His arms twined around my neck as he pulled me into a kiss while he rocked against me. I let him pick the pace to start with since we hadn't taken the time to stretch him to take me. Splaying my hands wide on his back I supported him as he moved, then once I felt he was loose enough I thrust into him. A gasp escaped him as he tossed back his head in ecstasy, fanning the flames of my male ego, because I was the one who was causing him to make that face and it felt amazing.

Shifting my hands lower to grip his hips more firmly I sped up my movements, pressing him down, making him take everything he could. While some Betas worked at being able to take an Alpha's knot Spencer had chosen against it, which I didn't mind. I love how tight he was, clinging to my cock, milking it when I came inside him. There was so much more to us than having my knot wrung out. The love we shared completed us, with or without that. Besides, now we have Cambrie, and one day, hopefully not in the too distant future, she would be the first to ever take my knot.

Spencer faltered in his movements. Thinking I'd pushed him too far, I slowed, tucking my face into his neck where I grabbed the skin right as his neck met the shoulder. Gently I nibbled on it with my teeth, the place I craved to one day mark him as mine forever. I'd seen Marius's claim and it made me desperate to leave my own, so that's what I did. This drove Spencer wild, his hips moved faster, then he slipped a hand between us to stroke his cock, telling me he was close. My own climax was building, and the way Spencer was clenching tightly around me I knew I wouldn't last much longer.

With a moan Spencer came, his hot come spurting on my stomach as he clamped his mouth on my shoulder to keep quiet. With another thrust, I too exploded, filling his asshole with my mark, claiming him in the only way I could right now, ensuring my scent would linger on him for a good long while. We clung to each other as we caught our breath, and I scattered kisses over whatever skin I could find, whispering how much I loved him in his ear.

"You hold my soul, sweet Prince," I murmured. "But I hope you don't mind sharing my heart with another?"

"Not as long as you don't mind me sharing mine with yet another," he answered, sitting back so I could see his face. His eyes glittered with mischief that had me a little worried. "Seems we weren't that quiet."

Glancing over at the bed, I saw Cambrie sitting there hugging the pillow I'd given her with wide eyes. I could tell from the perfume wafting off her she'd enjoyed watching the two of us together. Spencer gave me a slow drawn-out kiss before he stood up, winked, and headed to the bathroom with my cum leaking out of his ass.

"Is that what you wanted to show me earlier?" Cambrie asked, her voice breathy, drawing my full attention.

Had we turned our little Omega on? Did she even understand what she was feeling right now? What the fuck was I supposed to do now?

CHAPTER 23

Cambrie

Hushed words, soft moans, labored breathing, and an overwhelming heady scent I'd never experienced before drew me out of sleep. Opening my eyes, I found I was alone in bed, clutching a pillow instead of being curled up with Nixon and Spencer. Panic spread through me as all the worst case scenarios ran through my head, urging me into a sitting position. Looking around the room I didn't see either of them but a groan had me whipping my head to the left.

I froze, bewitched by the sight of Nixon and Spencer naked, clinging to each other, panting as Nixon fucked his Beta. As I'd told them before, I might not have seen sex in action but I'd read enough books to know what they were doing. Part of me felt like I should lie back down and pretend I hadn't woken up, yet I couldn't take my eyes off them. It was one of the most beautiful things I'd ever seen.

There was a look of pure enjoyment on Spencer's face when he met my gaze and made me wish I was the one Nixon was doing that to. When he realized I was watching he faltered, fear and shame clouded his face where it was blissful moments before. Not wanting to take this moment from them I shook my head and tried to signal for him to keep going, urging him to ignore me. I started to turn around to give them privacy but Spencer called out.

"No, don't stop," he pleaded, causing me to turn back to see him holding Nixon's head tighter to his neck. "Yes, that's what I want, just like this."

I knew he was talking to me since his gaze was locked on mine, a slow satisfied smile on his lips as he stroked himself. Nixon began to get more forceful and slightly more erratic in his thrusts until Spencer tossed back his head, crying out. "I'm coming, fuck yes, come inside me, Alpha!"

Nixon let out a snarl as he clamped down on Spencer, thrusting up into him in short bursts, as if he was knotting Spencer. I could see he wasn't as I watched the thick band of muscle pulsing just outside Spencer's ass. My whole body shivered, knowing that one day that would be inside me. I would somehow manage to fit all of that and be locked to my Alpha until he was finished with me.

When I first discovered I was an Omega, the thought of a knot tying me to a person for possibly up to an hour was terrifying. Now as I watched the love they had for each other, kissing and whispering sweet words... I wanted it. Not just the knot, no I wanted it all. The love, caresses, promises of a life together, and knowing I was claimed. Marked to be theirs forever, that is what I never knew I'd always wanted in my life. To be an Omega claimed, marked, fucked, and loved for the rest of my life.

Seeing Spencer get up and head to the bathroom I turned my attention back to Nixon, and my question blurted out of my mouth before I could stop it. My brain was still fuzzy from all the scents in the air, including my own, betraying just what I was feeling at the moment. It had an edge to it that I'm sure told Nixon how much I'd enjoyed seeing them together. *God, I hope they don't hate me for watching them.*

"Not exactly, Sweetheart," Nixon answered, reminding me I'd asked him a question. "My thoughts were geared toward something a little tamer, but I can see from your expression and your perfume that you didn't mind this interaction at all." He smiled as he stood, grabbing his boxers and pulling them up to hide his thick penis.

"Don't look so disappointed, Cambrie, there will come a time you'll be able to examine it all you like. Tonight is not that night," he shared, climbing back on the bed and gathering me in his arms, shoving his face into my hair. "God, you smell so good. I just want to bury myself between your legs and eat you right up."

"Why would you want to do that?" I asked, not understanding what he was saying at all. "Wouldn't that be gross?"

"I thought you said you read dirty romance books? Are you telling me none of them ate their woman out?" He chuckled. "Seems I'm gonna need to get you some new books... for educational purposes, of course."

My brain raced through the books I'd read and realized they had indeed covered many moments of men with their faces between a woman's or man's legs. "I... I didn't realize that you were talking about oral sex," I mumbled.

"Ah, so you have read about it," Nixon teased, nipping at my neck, making me squeak. "What a dirty girl you've been, learning about things before an Alpha has the chance to teach you properly. Don't you worry, Sweetheart, I'll make sure you learn all about it someday soon. For now, we need to go to sleep, the four of us have a date to go on," he purred, laying us back down and pulling the blankets up.

The bed dipped as Spencer joined us but when he didn't slide in, I looked up to see him staring at us with the strangest face. "What's wrong?"

"Nothing Dove, absolutely nothing. I love seeing you two curled up together and how happy he is with you nestled in his arms," Spencer shared as he snuggled against me so I was sandwiched between them.

"You're not mad he's holding me after you two just had sex?" I asked, biting my lip and waiting for his answer.

He leaned in, kissing me softly until I freed my lip. "No Dove, mad is the furthest thing from what I'm feeling right now. It's hard to explain, but seeing someone I love happy, even if I'm not the one making him feel that way at the moment, means everything to me. But knowing it's *you,* a person who also makes me happy, it's practically euphoric. Now, go to sleep. I have a big day planned."

Nodding, I closed my eyes and let the rumble of Nixon's purr echoing through my chest lull me to sleep.

"YOU BETTER MAKE sure that she eats lunch, we need to get some weight on her and skipping meals isn't going to help," Bodhi instructed as he helped me put on a borrowed jacket of his.

In fact, I was wearing a shirt of his too since he was the closest to my size. I wore the leggings again since I didn't have another option unless I wanted sweatpants. It was nice to be wrapped up in Bodhi's fresh, pure scent that reminded me of that smell you get right after a rainstorm.

"Seriously Bodhi, do you think we're incapable of taking care of Cambrie?" Spencer demanded as he glared at the fellow Beta. "Marius's sister was an Omega, and Nixon also has two siblings he managed to keep alive while growing up together. Between the three of us, I'm sure we'll manage just fine, unless you were gunning for an invite."

Bodhi scowled as he zipped the jacket all the way up to my chin. "No, I wasn't trying to come with. I'm just reminding you because my money's on the fact that Cambi here won't tell you she's hungry."

Looking between them, I couldn't tell if they were really mad at each other or not. "Please don't argue, not about me. I promise to tell you if I'm hungry if we don't stop to eat before I reach that point."

"We ready to head out?" Marius asked, jogging down the stairs and noticing the standoff. "Uh... Did I miss something?"

Nixon was leaning against the garage door watching this whole thing go down with a smirk. "Nope, just two possessive mother hens fighting over their chick. Come on Sweetheart, let's leave them to it and the three of us will have a good time instead."

"*Nix*," Spencer gasped. "I'm the one who came up with the idea in the first place, like hell you're leaving me behind." With that said, Spencer took my hand and led me into the garage.

Four beautiful cars were parked in the garage, the bright red one caught my eye as Spencer guided me over to Nixon's sedan. "Whose car is that?"

"That would be Marius," Spencer shared, taking in my shocked face. "I know right, you never would have guessed he had a love for sports cars, but he does. I'm sure he'll take you for a ride if you ask."

"Oh, I wouldn't want to impose," I said automatically.

Spencer reached out and cupped my cheek, making me look up at him. "Trust me when I say it would never be an imposition to spend time with you." His thumb stroked my cheek gently before he pulled it away to open the door to the back seat. "I know you two haven't had much time together yet but that's why I planned today. He'll be around all weekend but taking you out so it's just the four of us will be nice. Then we don't have to compete with the others."

I climbed in as the two Alphas joined us and we were underway. Nixon waved as we passed the guard at the gate and I instinctively ducked down, not wanting to be noticed. Being in the house with them almost made me forget the dangers of the world and what that meant for me as an Omega. One would think being with three people, and one who is an Official, would make me feel safe but it didn't. Not because I didn't trust them to look out for me, it was more about everyone else. I knew firsthand how cruel the world could be and I couldn't go back to that.

The drive to the mall was much longer than I would have guessed, and we took the highway the whole time to get there. Watching the city pass us by was fascinating as all the tall buildings started to shrink into suburban houses. I recognized a park as one I used to play in before Mom died, making me think we might be in my old neighborhood. Nixon pulled off the highway and down a few streets until we arrived at a massive shopping mall. Signs for the major stores were listed on the outside of the building and the parking lot was full of cars, even though it was late morning.

"This is supposed to be the best mall with all the best stores for what we need," Spencer shared as we drove around the outskirts of the mall. "The places by us are way too fancy and fussy. I knew you wouldn't like anything in them or let us spend that much on you."

"About that," I ventured, then stopped talking the moment Marius looked over his shoulder at me.

"What was that, Princess?" he asked, knowing he'd heard me.

I licked my lips nervously, then decided to say my peace. "I know you told me not to worry about the money and that the pack looks out for each other, but I need you all to know that you don't need to do this for me to like you."

There, I said it. Part of me wondered if all the nice things they've been doing, like getting stuff for my bedroom and now this shopping trip were to make sure I liked them. That if they bought me enough stuff I would be happy, and they didn't need to do that at all. I was the happiest I'd ever been in my whole life, and it was because of them.

Nixon pulled into a parking spot that he'd managed to find close to one of the main mall entrances. He placed the vehicle in park and turned to look at me like Marius was. "Sweetheart, do you really think we are doing all this to buy your love and affection?"

"I... I just wanted you to know that I do like you, but not because of your money, or the things you give me," I babbled, feeling insecure. "All of you have been so good to me and I'm not really sure what I've done to deserve it but you guys just being you is more than enough to have me like you. Maybe even more than like you... I... I've never been in love before so I have no idea what that feels like. But I do know that even if you didn't have a penny I'd still like you and want to be with you."

Marius's expression seemed to melt into something that was equal parts sad and hopeful. "Princess, I love that you feel that way about us and I hope we deserve that affection you give so willingly. As for your concerns about us spending money on you, it is because we believe you deserve to be showered with gifts. You may not have been raised as an Omega, but this is exactly what Alphas are supposed to do. It is our job to make sure you are provided for in every way, and right now you are in need of some provisions."

"Sweetheart, you don't have anything to your name but that yellow dress and trench coat. Everyone deserves to have clothes to wear, a bed to sleep in, food to eat, and a roof over their head. Right now, we are dealing with getting you clothes and other personal items to live life day to day. You owe us nothing other than being happy and healthy in our care," Nixon added. "Now, let's go enjoy our afternoon and see what we can find, alright?"

Having settled that matter, we got out of the car and headed for the mall. Marius took one hand while Nixon took the other and Spencer led the charge. I think out of all of us he was the most excited. When we entered, I was overwhelmed with all the stores, I don't think I'd ever been to a mall before. Spencer directed us to a store overflowing with clothes, shoes, undergarments, and so much more. It was even two levels, women on one and men on the other.

It wasn't long before I was set up in a dressing room with clothes lining the walls for me to try on. It was mind-boggling to me that there was so much to choose from, having shopped mostly at second-hand stores. Now if I liked the shirt but not the color there were three other options. It was hard to pick a size because I knew I was far too skinny, and even with the few days I had regular meals, my bones weren't sticking out quite so much. So while the extra small might fit now I'm not sure it would in a few weeks. So with the other's opinions, we settled on some smalls and some mediums as I filled out.

Shoes were easier because even if I'm skinny, feet stay close to the same size. While I thought I was just going to get a pair of shoes that I could wear with almost everything, the men decided on a different answer. I couldn't even look at something too long before they snatched it up and added it to the pile.

"I think this was a successful first round, don't you?" Spencer asked as we waited for Marius and Nixon to load the bags into the car.

Looking up at him I gaped like a fish. "What do you mean, first round? That is more clothes than I'll ever be able to wear."

"My sweet, sweet Dove, that was just the basics. Now we need to get the fun stuff, like swimsuits, dresses, coats. We should probably stop by a beauty store to get you stuff for your hair too," Spencer rambled as I slowly started to freak out.

Then suddenly, I was knocked to the side as someone entered

the mall in a hurry. The shove was so hard I slammed into Spencer, letting out a yelp of surprise.

"I'm so sorry… Cambrie?" a strange voice called out making me whimper, hiding my face in Spencer's shirt. "Cambrie, is that you? Your father has been looking everywhere for you."

CHAPTER 24

Cambrie

"Sir, I don't know who you are, but you need to take a step back," Spencer ordered, his voice sharper than I'd ever heard. "You're mistaken, this isn't the woman you're looking for, she is a member of our pack and doesn't do well with strangers. I would ask that you move along."

"That's her. I know it is," the man argued. "Have you kidnapped her? I'll call the police on you if you don't let her go."

The sound of heavy feet came closer before a deep voiced man with a slight accent spoke. "Do we have a problem here?"

"Savo," Spencer greeted, his tone telling me this Savo person was a friend of his. "This man seems to think that our Omega is someone a friend of his is missing. I tried to tell him that wasn't the case but now he wants to call the police on me."

As Spencer talked he wrapped his arms tightly around me keeping me safe in the shield of his body. *Why wouldn't this man just leave us alone? How in the world did he know who I was, Father didn't have any friends that I knew of. No one ever came to the house, there's no way he could know who I was.*

"Sir, I'm with government security, and I can tell you that this man here, who is Official Stone's Beta, isn't lying to you. Now, I'm going to need you to move along before I'm forced to arrest you for harassing a member of the political party," Savo explained, his words clipped and to the point his accent growing heavier, making me think he might be more upset than he let on.

"You have to be kidding?" the man yelled. "Why would you arrest me when they're the ones who have the girl?"

"It is my duty to protect the members of the CoF and their pack so, no, I'm not kidding you. Official Stone, as a member of the CoF, is entitled to add an Omega to his pack regardless of your feelings on the matter. You say that someone is looking for her. Are you telling me there was a man harboring an Omega, refusing to do his duty by handing her over to the government Care Centers?" Savo inquired, every word filled with a veiled threat, making me shiver. I was beyond grateful he was on our side.

The stranger spluttered and let out a string of swear words as he stormed away. All I wanted was to go home, back where it was safe and no one wanted to take me from my new family. Yet I didn't want to take away from this special day that Spencer and the others were excited about. So, I took a deep breath and turned my head to the side to look at the man who'd come to protect us.

He wasn't a man, he was a giant, towering over me with his deep forest green eyes pinned right on me. The muscles that bulged out of his shirt made me wonder if it was going to tear and the leather jacket over it did nothing to hide what was under it. Jeans and what looked like black biker boots gave the complete image that he was a man I never wanted to cross paths with in an alley at night. Savo's hair was cut tight on the sides so that I could see his scalp, then slightly longer on top, showing it was a dark red-brown color. His full beard was well maintained and neat but only added to the vibe that he was a gangster or something equally terrifying.

"How is it I always find you in trouble, Spencer?" Savo asked, a frown making him even more intimidating.

That other man must have been crazy to argue with the Hulk. If he'd told me to leave I wouldn't have asked twice and ran.

Savo's eyes fell back to me as Spencer loosened his hold. "Dove, this is my friend Savo. He works for a security company and the government when it's needed." Spencer paused and looked up again. "Speaking of, didn't you have a job starting this weekend?"

"Supposed to but the person I was to be in charge of never showed. They're trying to track down what happened so until then, I'm back to life as usual," he shared with a shrug. "What about you? What brings you all the way out here from fancy pants land?"

I turned so my back was to Spencer and I could face Savo better, not craning my neck back so far. "They're shopping for me," I answered, my voice so quiet I wasn't sure he heard me.

He narrowed his gaze, then something like recognition sparked in his eyes as he glared at Spencer behind me. "She's—"

"An Omega, yes," Spencer cut off smoothly. "She's the newest member of our pack, just as I explained to that man. Dove has only been with us a few days and we were just getting settled before any sort of big announcement. Once everyone knows about her there will be no more casual mall outings like this for a while."

"I would imagine," Savo muttered.

"Savo, fancy running into you here," Marius greeted as he returned with Nixon. "Doing some shopping on your day off?"

"Unexpected day off as it were. Thought I'd make use of it," Savo answered, shoving his hands in his pockets. "You need to be more careful with her," Savo scolded. "Found these two arguing with a man in a case of mistaken identity between your Omega and a missing girl named Cambrie."

Marius stood up straighter and the comfortable air about him was gone. Nixon didn't look all that happy either as he stood closer, almost shielding me with his body.

"As you said, case of mistaken identity," Marius agreed, his tone telling Savo not to push the matter.

Savo nodded. "These are dark times we live in. You never know what might happen or who might snatch an Omega right out of your grasp. If you decide you need security you let me know, I'll make sure she stays safe."

Each of the men around me relaxed as if a cord had been cut hearing his offer. Nixon pulled me from Spencer and tucked me against his side, pressing a kiss to the top of my head. Now I too was relaxed, knowing that both Alphas had returned.

"Thank you for the offer. I'll keep that in mind," Marius said, reaching out a hand to Savo. "I have a feeling it's going to come in handy one day, but for now we plan to keep her close at home while we settle into things."

I felt Savo's eyes on me, and I turned my head to see him staring at my arm. After trying on all the clothes, I wasn't as cold so I'd left my jacket off. The short sleeve shirt I was wearing showed off the still fading bruises that littered my body. They were in that ugly yellow green color that seemed to draw more attention than when they were dark and purple.

"What would you say if I joined you while you're at the mall? I'm not looking to butt in, but as security. There was already someone after your Omega and it's my job to keep them safe. Let me give you a sample of my work as it were, so if you decide to work with me you'll know what you're getting." Savo offered, not taking his eyes off me as if he was trying to see beyond my clothes to what other evidence of my past might be there.

Nixon glanced down at me, then over to Marius. "It would be stupid not to accept an offer like that now, wouldn't it? Thank you, we are willing to do whatever it takes to keep Cambrie safe."

I saw out of the corner of my eye Spencer flinching at my name and realized in all the conversations he'd called me Dove. Pulling away from a begrudging Nixon I held out a hand to Savo, hoping he wouldn't feel lied to when he heard I was the person that man thought I was.

"Thank you for keeping me safe and chasing that man off," I said, letting my hand dangle in the air waiting for him to take it.

Savo slowly reached out and, with gentle care, grasped my hand. "Did your father do this to you?"

Meeting his gaze, I refused to be embarrassed about what I'd survived. I wasn't that girl anymore, I was free with a pack of my very own to start a new life with. "Yes, he's beaten me my whole life but it got worse when he found out I was an Omega. That's when he locked me away until I could be sold." I gave him a bright smile and clasped my other hand over his as I watched his eyes glitter with anger. "That's all in the past now, I have a new family with Marius, Nixon, Spencer, and the others back home, so don't look so upset, Savo."

Now that I was this close to him, I could pick up on his scent, marking him as a Beta. Smooth black coffee with the musky scent of leather twined around me, making me want to take a deep breath. His hand tightened on mine slightly as if he could sense my enjoyment of his personal signature.

"Snickerdoodles... Those are my favorite cookies," Savo shared, giving me a half smile.

"Well," Spencer cut in as he lightly placed his hands on my shoulders.

It still made me flinch, but I recovered and leaned back into him so he didn't think I was upset. Savo noticed, his eyes narrowed, and I could have sworn I heard the faint rumble of a growl.

"Sorry Dove, I should have spoken first so you knew I was behind you before touching you," Spencer apologized. "Shall we continue on our date?"

Tipping my head back so I could see him, I grinned. "Is there any way I can talk you out of buying me all the things you listed?"

"Not a chance," he answered, dropping a kiss on my forehead. "Now off we go."

We made it through three more stores, picking up various things here and there that were deemed a necessity by the others. Savo, for as a giant of a man as he was, seemed to blend into the background. He was always within sight but somehow he never attracted attention, it was almost as if your eyes just glanced right over him. When we had too many bags to carry Savo contacted the mall, and they had a staff member set them aside for us to pick up later instead of any of them having to leave. It was quite a handy experience, one of the perks of Marius being who he is apparently.

"Let's see, where to now?" Spencer mused, looking over his list tapping the pen on his chin.

"If I might interject," Savo said, drawing our attention. "You might want to consider getting *Keksík* some food."

"Who?" Marius asked just as my stomach let out an unhappy grumble. The four men looked at me, a little surprised, then Marius chuckled. "It would seem that Bodhi was right. You didn't tell us you were hungry, Princess."

My cheeks heated. "I wasn't, but the moment Savo said something about food my stomach decided to weigh in on the vote."

"How much more do we need here?" Nixon asked Spencer.

"Truthfully, we could be done and go somewhere nicer than the food court for a late lunch. Most of the stuff left I can order and have shipped to the house. I figured if we could find it here then we would, but I started with the important things first so if she got tired we'd settle for what we got," Spencer informed us.

Marius took a critical look at me, then nodded his head. "I say be done shopping for the day. We'll do lunch, then head back to the house and we can work on that list of movies you made with the others."

Hearing him say that made me breathe a sigh of relief. It had been a long time since I'd walked this much and I was getting tired. The thought of having to come back and do more after lunch made me want to cringe, but we were all having such a good time I didn't want it to end. Then an idea popped into my head.

"Savo, you said you had the day off, right?" I asked and he nodded in response. "Would you like to join us for lunch and a movie? I'm learning how to be a better friend to people, and I feel like you've been so amazing at looking after me when you didn't have to on your day off. So it's only right, I should offer something fun in exchange for making you work," I reasoned.

Then I realized this was a date and I'd just invited someone else to our time together. "I mean..." I glanced at the others as I started to wring my hands. "If that's okay with everyone? This was supposed to be our time together on a date. Now here I am making my own plans, adding someone when Spencer worked hard to make today special."

"Sweetheart," Nixon cooed, grasping my hands in his. "Look at me for a sec," he requested, so I did. "Take a deep breath in, then let it out after the count of three."

Together, Nixon and I did the breathing exercise helping me think a little more clearly and not be so worked up. Without being prompted, I did it a few more times until I heard my heart rate starting to slow.

"There you go, good girl," Nixon praised, making me smile and blush. It was odd how much I wanted them to praise me, tell me I was doing good at something. For most of my life I'd never received much of it and now I craved it. Cupping my cheek, Nixon lifted my head once more, letting his thumb stroke my skin. "If you would like for Savo to join us we would be happy to have him. He is a friend of Spence's as well, so I'm sure we will all get along just fine. There will be many more dates between us, so I'm not worried about sharing. Now that we have that settled, do you have a taste for something to eat? Anything you want, just say the word."

"Anything I want?" I asked.

"Just ask," Nixon assured me.

"Can we go home so Bodhi can make me a grilled cheese?" I requested. "I'd really love to have another one, it tasted so amazing."

The group of men around me chuckled and Nixon pulled me into a hug. "If that is what you really want, then we will go home and you can have your grilled cheese."

Now that we had everything planned, we collected the bags we'd placed with the staff and headed back home. I had a bag in my lap that I was quite excited about and kept peeking in it and smiling. When we'd passed by the bookstore an idea struck me, and I was thrilled to find they had what I was looking for. The fatigue of the afternoon caught up with me, and I snuggled against Marius, who'd decided to sit in the back with me. I glanced in the rearview mirror and spotted Savo in his big black truck following us. It made me smile to think I'd made a new friend. After the whole situation with that man, I wasn't sure I would like many people outside my pack. Seems I might have jumped the gun on that assumption.

"Close your eyes, Princess. I can see how hard you're fighting to stay awake. I promise nothing will happen between now and home that you'll miss," Marius murmured, lifting a hand to stroke my hair as he pressed a kiss to my head. "I'll protect you while you sleep so nothing bad will ever have the chance of happening to you."

I got the sense when Marius promised something he never offered it lightly. He struck me as a person who took promises as seriously as knights did oh so long ago. Once a vow or promise was made he would do whatever it took to keep it. I didn't sleep, but I let my eyes shut and just enjoyed having Marius close to me. Now that I'd gotten to know him a little better his scent wasn't as over-powering as that first night. It was just as strong but instead of being intimidating, all it made me think was how safe I was.

"Welcome back, Mr. Hayes," the guard at the gate greeted. "Is the gentleman in the truck with you?"

"Yes, he's a friend, also works for government security so he's already got clearance," Nixon said.

The guard looked back at the truck a little uneasy. "What's his name?"

"Savo Bakal," Spencer answered, leaning across the center console.

That had the guard snapping his head back to us. "Bakal, you said?"

"Yeah, is there a problem?" Nixon demanded, his tone losing the friendliness to it.

"Nope, and he's more than got clearance. Official Yoram has him down as authorized personnel. I'll make sure to get him the proper sticker so we can avoid this happening again. Once I'm through with him I'll send him your way," the guard shared with a salute and backed up waving us along.

"Why would Yoram give Savo that kind of clearance?" Nixon asked, looking at Spencer.

The Beta shrugged. "Look, we're friends but not best friends who tell each other everything about our lives. How the hell should I know why the man gets special treatment from the devil?"

"Why is he the devil?" I asked, incredibly confused.

Marius sighed and paused in his mindless stroking of my hair. "He's not really the devil, it's more that everything he does is about what he can get out of it. Yoram is another member of the CoF but in reality, he controls most things, has all the connections, and is incredibly hard to beat when he wants something to happen that might not be for the best of everyone."

"So... he's a really bad friend," I said, trying to make sense of what Marius was trying to say.

"You could say that again," Spencer muttered. "The man is as selfish as it gets. If he can't make a profit from it, then fuck everyone else who stands in his way."

"Spence," Nixon admonished as we pulled into the driveway. "Don't swear like that in front of Cambrie."

"It's fine, my father swore so much that I don't really notice it anymore," I interjected. "I know that words can be hurtful, but I also know sometimes you need the right word to express how you're feeling. If that's how Spencer feels about it, then really, he's sharing his emotions which everyone should do."

Nixon looked at Spencer with a frown. "Just because that made way more logical sense than it had any right to doesn't mean you should start swearing more." Spencer gave his Alpha a grin then a quick peck on the lips before getting out. "He's totally going to ignore what I just said, isn't he?"

"One hundred percent," Marius agreed, shaking his head. "Come on Cambrie, let's round up the others and see if we can get all these bags up to your room. Then we can get the things that wouldn't fit out of Savo's truck."

Sliding out of the car I looked at the overflowing trunk. "I told you guys it was too much. It's going to take me forever to wear this many things."

"Good thing you have a big closet in your room then, isn't it?" Spencer reasoned, giving me a wink and grabbing as many bags as he could carry.

I reached out to take a few but Marius grabbed my wrist, keeping his touch light. "Go find the others. We will deal with this."

"There's no reason I can't help, Marius," I argued.

Marius caught my chin with his hand, telling me I'd done something to upset him. "Cambrie, while I understand your need for independence and to take care of things yourself, which I respect, there is also a time when you need to hear what I'm saying and listen. Sometimes our requests might not make sense, but I promise there is a reason we ask these things."

Meekly I lowered my eyes, and when he released my chin, I nodded, "I'll go find the others."

Before Marius or the others could stop me, I ran into the open garage and into the house. Peering into the living room I didn't see anyone, so I ventured into the kitchen. It was dark and silent so I peered out the back door and saw the light on where Oscar worked out back. Setting my one shopping bag on the counter, I headed off through the yard over to the little house. The French doors had paned glass in them so I could see Oscar sitting at a piano with headphones on.

I didn't want to bother Oscar, but if I didn't, then Marius would be more upset with me than he already was. The handle turned easily allowing my entry into his space. The soft clack of the keys as he played totally oblivious to me standing there. Knowing how I would prefer to be approached, I stepped to the side and waved my hand in front of my chest. That way he could see the motion but it wouldn't be taken as a threat.

Instantly, he stopped and smiled pulling off his headphones. He waved in greeting and opened his arms inviting me in for a hug. After the incident with Marius, I needed the kind of hug Oscar could give me. It was everything wonderful in the world. I let him hold me for a moment, then I pulled back and looked him in the eyes. "Marius would like your help with carrying things in, he sent me to find you."

Oscar nodded and made a few clicks in a program that was running on a computer next to him. Then he stood and held out a hand to me but I shook my head. "No, he doesn't want me to help just to find you three. I was gonna look for Bodhi upstairs, but I'm not sure where to find Rafael."

He gestured for me to wait a moment, then grabbed his phone. He typed something and when the phone pinged he showed it to me. Oscar had texted both of them, asking for them to come out and help with bringing things up to my room. Shoving his phone back in his pocket, he took my hand and led me out to the front yard through a gate I hadn't noticed before. When we got there the other two were already helping and Savo was grabbing things out of his truck.

"Cambrie," Marius barked, making me freeze. "Didn't I tell you to go inside?"

Oscar tucked me behind him and I could see his arms moving as he talked to Marius. I'd known coming back up front was going to make him mad but Oscar seemed sure it was going to be fine. Tears started to prick at my eyes, hating that I'd ruined the whole day because I couldn't do as I was told. Mom had always said I had a stubborn streak that was going to get me in trouble if I wasn't careful. Seems she was right once again, I just couldn't do things right.

"What the hell, Marius?" Bodhi demanded. "Why are you barking at her like that? She wants to help, tell me what is wrong with that?"

"Don't argue with me, not on this, not when it comes to her safety," Marius growled, making me flinch even more. "Savo, could you please take Cambrie inside with you and ensure she stays there."

"Who the fuck is the brick wall and why the hell is he going anywhere with *our* Omega?" Bodhi challenged.

"Calm down Bodhi, I'm sure there is a reasonable explanation for all this, right Marius?" Rafael intervened.

"That will be addressed once Cambrie is inside the house," Marius ordered, his tone one that I imagine he used being one of the leaders of our government.

"Come on *Keksík,* show me where to bring these bags," Savo encouraged, herding me into the house.

I led him up the stairs to the third floor and pushed open my bedroom door. "This is my room."

Wandering in, I looked around the space but it didn't seem as warm and inviting anymore. It seemed I might have to say goodbye to it now that I had made Marius so incredibly angry with me. I knew he told me to stay in the house and I didn't listen, so there is no one to blame but me.

"Where do you want to put these things, looks like most of it is shoes and some stuff for the bathroom," Savo inquired.

Was there a point in unpacking any of it? If they weren't going to keep me, then it should all be returned. Marius and Nixon bought this for their Omega and I wasn't sure that's what I was anymore. Tears burned my eyes as I tried to hold them back, but since they'd been freed, I couldn't seem to stem the flow.

"*Keksík*, don't cry," Savo rumbled in his deep voice. "Hey, I'm sure he's not as upset as you think." He knelt in front of me so we were closer to eye level.

Hesitantly, he reached out and tried to wipe away my tears with his thumb but that just made me cry harder because he was being so sweet. Seeing his plan wasn't working, he shrugged off his leather coat, exposing the T-shirt underneath and revealing his tattoo covered arms.

"Can I hug you, Cambrie?" Savo asked, his voice as soft and gentle as he could make it, being so deep. I nodded and reached out my arms to him, needing someone to hold me as the world I was starting to build was crumbling around me.

Savo didn't just hug me— he scooped me up in his giant arms like I was a child and tucked me against his chest. He walked over to the bed and I heard it groan as he sat. For how large and strong he was, every touch was incredibly delicate as he handled me. I fisted his shirt and hid my face in the crook of his neck, letting the silent tears soak into the material.

As he held me he started to sing in a language I didn't know but sounded soothing if a little sad. "*Sivé očká, čo plačete? Však vy moje nebudete. Budete iného šuhajíčka švárneho.*"

When he finished the song he stopped rocking almost as if he hadn't realized he'd been doing it. "Sorry, I used to sing that to my *malá sestra*, little sister, when she was upset."

"You have a little sister?" I asked, lifting my head to look into his dark green eyes that were filled with sadness. "I'm sorry for your loss. You must miss her a lot. I know I miss my Mom every day, I try to be the woman she always taught me to be. But as you saw today, I just keep messing it up because I'm far too stubborn."

"Stubbornness is a good trait, *Keksík*. It will keep you alive no matter what happens to you," Savo ran a finger down my arm. "Seems like you might already know that, though."

An odd growling sound started and I shifted to see Oscar setting down a bag and marching over to me. He pulled me out of Savo's grasp and tucked me against him, flipping Savo the bird as he marched out of the room.

"Oscar?" Bodhi asked as we stormed past him.

Oscar stopped long enough to point to my room before heading for his. When we entered it was almost as if I was in the sky. Everything was white, with soft blues and grays making the space seem so comforting. If I didn't already like how my room was coming together, I would have moved in here with Oscar. He finally came to a halt at the unmade bed that smelled so strongly of him I wanted to dive into it. Which apparently Oscar agreed with since he plopped me into the middle of it and built up pillows and blankets around me until I was cocooned. He took a step back, looked at his work, and signaled for me not to move and to go to sleep.

Satisfied with what he'd accomplished, he left the room, closing the door and leaving me to take a nap, apparently.

CHAPTER 25

Oscar

Watching Cambrie be led away by that unknown Beta made me grind my teeth. How could Marius speak to her like that? I'd brought her up front with me, figuring since she did as she was asked to, it would be fine. The one who should have been yelled at was me, not her, never her. I saw the crushed look on her face as she entered the house. Things were so new and fragile with her, I knew without a doubt she would take Marius being upset with her badly. Now none of us could go after her. Because of that I wanted to throttle our so-called leader.

Once Cambrie was inside and couldn't see what I did next, I walked up to Marius, shoved him in the chest and gave him a few choice gestures that anyone could figure out. Spencer stepped between us, always the most loyal to his partners, as he should be. It was just hard when it became three against two, well now with Bodhi, it was a tie since he seemed to always side with me.

"Oscar, just give him a moment to explain himself," Spencer pleaded. "The last thing we need right now is a fight brewing between us."

This wouldn't be the first time we'd had fights as a pack. Some were worse than others but, in the end, we always managed to work things out. When it came to Cambrie, I wasn't sure there would be any such resolution if one of us fucked up royally. I took a step back then motioned for Marius to explain himself with an inquiring cocked eyebrow for emphasis.

"There was an incident at the mall," Marius began.

"I *knew* it," Bodhi snapped. "Didn't I tell you taking her to that part of the city was stupid, that she probably grew up somewhere near there?"

Marius looked at him and waited for him to stop speaking. "Are you going to let me finish telling you what happened? Or should I just forget the whole thing since you were right?"

I blinked at the harsh tone Marius was using. Clearly, whatever happened had rattled him far worse than any of us expected. He was never one to crack, even with all that went into getting elected, he took it with grace and a smile. One mishap with Cambrie under his watch and he snaps. Bodhi grumbled something but let Marius speak without any further interruption.

"There was a man at the mall who *knew* Cambrie," Marius announced. He turned to Spencer and gave him the floor.

"While the other two went off to drop off bags to the car, Cambrie and I waited in the mall by the door. This guy entered, almost took Cambrie out, and when he apologized, got a good look at her and freaked out. He kept going on and on about how Cambrie's dad was looking for her and that we'd kidnapped her. Thankfully Savo, my friend who works for a security company and the government providing protection, stepped in and got rid of the guy. He stuck with us for the rest of the trip to ensure there wasn't any other trouble and Cambrie, being Cambrie, invited him back for lunch and a movie. So don't be an ass to him, he kept our girl safe," Spencer informed us all.

I felt bad for not liking the man, but I just couldn't stand anyone else touching or spending time with *our* Omega. We were the ones who were supposed to keep her safe, granted most packs did hire people like Savo to safeguard Omegas but there was something about him I just didn't trust.

I waved a hand, drawing everyone's attention as I looked directly at Marius when I signed. "*Why were you so insistent on her being in the house? You took her to a mall. What does it matter if she's in the front yard helping us?"*

"The problem is, if word gets out that she's *here* with us it will make it easier for her to be found. We haven't announced her existence to the CoF and that means they could charge us with hiding a fugitive. While the CoF hasn't gotten rid of the death penalty, we just don't choose to use it, but if I know Yoram, he would be more than happy to dispose of me after the research I've been doing," Marius explained, muttering that last part to himself.

This was the first time I'd ever heard him talk like this about work. Normally, he was so optimistic, had it all been an act?

"There needs to be a more in-depth discussion about this, but here and now is not the time to have it. Soon, we all need to take a trip and see Alton, then I can explain the reality of our situation. After that, then you can argue with me about keeping Cambrie out of sight for now. It won't be forever, I'm working on a solution but it's far more complicated than I realized," Marius disclosed, his shoulders sagging.

"We better get up there, you know Cambrie isn't going to handle upsetting you well. I'm sure at this very moment she is trying not to cry and assuming we are going to do something dramatic like send her away," I pointed out.

Everyone mumbled their agreement and headed for the trunk. I grabbed some bags from the ground and hurried inside. I didn't like leaving her alone in her room with the Beta. Her perfuming had been getting stronger each time one of us interacted with her in a more intimate fashion. I feared her first heat might be right around the corner. I'd done some research on the subject after I kissed her and my body reacted so much stronger than I ever imagined.

Was it just because she was an Omega, or was it something else?

There was no real gauge on when they got their first heat after turning eighteen. It seemed more to be based on if they were around Alphas they found pleasing or not. No one in this house denied they found her pleasing and if what I've seen and heard going on around the house she felt the same about us. I knew from what they taught us about being Alphas growing up that when an Omega got closer to being in heat, which happened at most twice a year, our urges would become stronger and harder to control. On top of that, we can become more territorial, aggressive to those outside the pack, and have a much higher sex drive.

That one I'd already been dealing with for about the past year to six months as Bodhi and I got closer. If anyone told me I would be attracted to another man the way I wanted to lick Bodhi from head to toe, I'd have laughed. Women had always been my preference or so I thought, but possibly it was more about slowly falling in love with Bodhi that it snuck up on me. I hadn't been looking for it, but it found me anyway. Rafael first brought him over as a way to connect with the surly young man who hated the world and everyone in it. Slowly through his love of music and learning from me, he started to talk.

Over the years, I'd learned to be content with being a good listener since it was much harder to interact with large crowds or the average person when I couldn't speak. Typically people felt uncomfortable and tried to fill the silence with their own words. For Bodhi it was different, he spoke through songs and music like I did. We worked on writing a few and he sang them while I played the instruments. Then we graduated from just me playing to him learning to play. He was gifted and picked it up like he was born to give life to music the same way I felt I was.

Then one day I knew I didn't want him to leave, he was too important to me. If he left and never came back my heart would break. That's when I knew I was in love with him. It was obvious to me that he didn't feel the same way, he cared about me, but not the same way I did. There was no way I could blame him, I myself had never considered falling for a man but it just happened. Now we have Cambrie, the last piece to the puzzle of my life to feel complete. She stole my heart when we sat there listening to music and she *heard* me. I don't know why I picked that song, in particular, to have her listen to. It was one I wrote a few months after coming to live here with the guys when my family kicked me out.

I wasn't sure I'd find a place to belong when after my illness left me mute—well, basically mute. I could occasionally whisper even though it felt like someone was stabbing me in the throat when I did it. Suddenly, people no longer knew what to do with me— like, just because I couldn't talk, all of a sudden, I was an alien. They'd talk louder or slower, treating me like I was stupid. My hearing was just fine, thank you very much. At school I had to do everything through email, messenger, or text while I was learning sign language. The problem with that is everyone automatically thinks you're deaf, and the things they say when they think you can't hear are vile. That all changed once I found my place here with my childhood friends. Each of them took the time to learn sign language, and I could easily communicate with my whole environment. It was life changing.

As I entered Cambrie's room, I came to an abrupt halt as I saw her cradled in this stranger's arms. Bodyguard or not, he wasn't allowed to touch what wasn't his.

Are those tears in her eyes?

I *knew* it, Marius was too harsh on her and got her so upset she'd cried.

Neither of them noticed me but when I saw him stroking her arm and the look in his eyes, I snapped. Charging forward, I snatched Cambrie up and tucked her close to my chest. I gave the Hulk the one gesture no one needed to be taught and stormed out of the room.

How *dare* he feel free enough with Cambrie to touch her so casually. She was *our* Omega and he had no right to do that. Cambrie was too trusting, too pure, she would believe anything anyone said, even if it was all lies. No, we, as her pack, needed to protect her and I was going to put her somewhere safe.

In the fog of my Alpha driven intent, I vaguely remember Bodhi calling out to me, but I couldn't stop. Cambrie needed to be nestled away in my room where no one could touch her. Settling her on my bed I stepped back a moment to look at her closely. I could tell she was still upset, her eyes were puffy from crying and yet they drooped in a way that told me how tired she was. What could I do to comfort her while I handled things with the Beta, who I was going to throttle no matter how gigantic he was.

Pillow nest!

The guys used to joke that my room was fit for an Omega rather than an Alpha, but I like my space to be comfortable. I got used to hiding in my room at school, because of that I found exactly how I like my environment to be. So what if I had a lot of pillows and too many blankets? I was happy and that's all that mattered. Besides, now it came in handy as I smothered our Omega with everything I could get my hands on.

When basically only her head showed above the pile, I took one last look and decided it was good enough for now. I caught her eye and motioned for her to stay put and try to get some sleep. The last thing we needed was her getting sick on us. She was still recovering from two years of being locked away. I was amazed she lasted so long with those three on a shopping trip. That was something I tried to avoid at all costs.

Shutting the door behind me, I pushed up the sleeve of my sweatshirt and prepared to take down a giant. When I got to the room Savo was still sitting on the bed with Bodhi glaring at him from where he leaned against the wall near the closet. Rafael was there as well, hands in his pockets looking between the two Betas who were in some silent war I didn't understand.

I tapped Rafael's arm. "*What did I miss?*"

"How should I know? You were the one storming out of here with Cambrie. I had to stop Bodhi from clobbering the man," Rafael answered. "Care to fill us in on what got you so upset and where you took our Omega?"

"*She's in my room. I got her settled to try and get some sleep before coming back here. I was right, by the way, Marius was too harsh and upset her to the point of crying,*" I shared.

This had Rafael glancing out the door as if he would much rather abandon me to deal with the situation and help Cambrie. I raised a hand to stop him from even trying.

"*Give her some space, she's exhausted and I wouldn't be surprised if she's conked out or close to it by now. Poor thing pushed herself too far,*" I said, then turned my attention to Savo. He'd been watching my hands, and I wasn't sure if it was out of curiosity or if he understood me. *"Why the hell would you think it's okay to be so casual with an Omega in her own pack's home?"*

"You aren't her pack yet," Savo stated. "None of you have marked her so your claim to her is nonexistent. If I was a real prick, like you seem to believe that I am, I would be calling the Care Center to come pick her up."

Rafael and I both growled at him, sensing the threat in his words. But now I knew he could understand everything I said.

"I didn't say I was going to, only that I could," Savo pointed out. "Cambrie is too precious to go to a place like that, but you're all handling this situation like there's no possible way someone could take her from you. Until she is marked for your pack by one or all of your Alphas, she can be plucked from your hands in an instant."

"You better not have said shit like that to her," Bodhi snapped. "The last thing she needs is to feel like her world is falling apart."

Savo shifted his gaze to look at him. "Your Alpha did a good enough job at that before I ever stepped foot in this house."

"Then maybe you should leave," Marius ordered as he entered the room. "If you don't like how I take care of my family you don't need to be here."

"Cambrie asked me to stay and hang out, if she tells me to go, then I'll go," Savo announced, crossing his arms, settling in like it would take a bulldozer to move him.

Marius stepped forward but I grabbed his arm, pulling his attention. *"Cambrie is in my room, hopefully sleeping. Let's not get into a fight that wakes her up."*

While I was fucking pissed about this Beta's audacity to speak to Marius that way, I had to admit I was impressed. Not many people can stand to be in his presence when the full weight of his Alpha nature is released. Savo sat there and took it without batting an eye, all because he didn't want to disappoint Cambrie. *That* was the part that had me worried. If he became fixated on her this could blow up in our faces.

"I can make you leave," Marius threatened.

"Actually, you can't," Savo countered. "Remember the guard

needing to get me a pass? Turns out, it's an enforcement level badge. So if you called someone to remove me, it would be me that answered."

Panic welled up in my stomach. *"You can't, you can't take her from us, Savo. Please don't make this a war between us. The only one who will get hurt is her."*

There was a flash of shame before it vanished behind a stony expression. "I just want to say goodbye to her before I leave. It would upset her if I just left, she's not used to people caring enough to make that effort. Like you said, causing trouble between us will only hurt her, which is the last thing I want to do."

"Guys..." Cambrie's trembling voice called out. "I don't feel so good."

Rafael was next to her in an instant, brushing back her hair to feel her forehead. "You're burning up, Little One. Tell me what else is bothering you?"

"My skin feels so sensitive. I'm hot, and... and... I'm..." She leaned in close and lowered her voice. "I'm leaking... between my legs."

Nixon and Spencer just entered the room when she said that and Nixon dropped the bags he was holding, staring slack jawed at her. Then it hit me, I'd been too concerned to notice right away but it hit me in the face like a ton of bricks.

Holy fuck, Cambrie was going into heat.

"Get out, Savo," Marius growled. "Say goodbye and get the fuck out."

Turning back to the Beta, I saw he was still as a stone statue, his eyes were closed and he was gripping the mattress like it was the only thing keeping him on the ground. Slowly, with jerky movements he stood and took a breath, then stopped. Opening his eyes, he looked at Cambrie, then ran out of the room faster than I ever expected someone his size could. She made a move to follow after him, but Rafael's grip on her shoulders prevented it.

What were we going to do now? There was no way we could leave her, a heat for an Omega can be tortuous when left unattended. In some cases, it could cause actual physical pain as they moaned and begged for an Alpha to knot them.

Why did it have to be sex? Not that I didn't want Cambrie in that way more than the breath in my lungs, but was she ready for that step? Were we ready for that?

The chances of making it through a heat without any of us marking her were going to be slim. Nixon had been fighting off rut, and so had Rafael. If what I knew was correct, I didn't think I was that far off myself with how obsessive I'd been about her. This heat might just throw everyone into a mess of sex-drugged animals.

"Rafael, is Savo mad at me?" Cambrie asked, her body shaking slightly as the *need* started to grow within her.

"No Little One, he is not mad at you," he assured her, then turned her to face him. "Do you have any idea what it is that is happening to you right now?"

She shook her head, tears glistening in her eyes. "Am I dying? I feel like I'm going to burn up from the inside out, and I ache between my legs like if I don't get something to put there, I'm going to die."

"My room," Marius instructed. "I have the biggest bed and room to deal with this. The master bathroom will be nice too, I'm sure, when we need a break."

"Are we really doing this?" Nixon asked, stunned. "No one's even told her what's happening, I'm not doing anything until she understands what it means. Once I go there with her, I can't go back if she changes her mind. It would ruin me."

"Someone needs to tell her. Leaving her in the dark is a stupid idea," I agreed.

Spencer pulled Cambrie from Rafael, who was reluctant to give her up and sat on the end of the bed together. "Dove, you're going into heat, or by the looks and sounds of things, already there. Do you know what that means?"

"It's when an Omega is most fertile, and they become crazed and delirious for anywhere from three to five days. The only thing that can help them through their heat is to be knotted by an Alpha, but sex regardless will help lessen the discomfort," Cambrie responded, almost as if she was reading it out of a book and not truly understanding it.

"That's correct, but there are other ways around this if you don't want to have sex," Spencer explained, soldering on even as we Alphas snarled at him for offering her another solution when we were more than willing. "We can get you a substitute to use on yourself instead of having a real Alpha. Or I've heard of pills that will help ease the discomfort as you ride it out alone in your room."

Cambrie looked up at him, her lip quivering. "You don't want to help me? Or is it that you don't want to fuck me because you prefer men?"

Hearing the word fuck come out of Cambrie's mouth made me instantly hard. Granted, I was almost there by her scent alone but now I could chop wood with my boner. I hadn't been this hard ever in my life, to the point of almost being painful, pressed against my jeans.

The sharp laughter that burst from Spencer pulled me out of my head and back to what was happening around me. I watched as he reached out to her, cupping her face as he closed in for a kiss. Not just any kiss, this was him practically fucking her mouth with his tongue as he pulled her flush to his body. A warning growl from Marius had Spencer bringing the kiss to an end but they were both panting like they'd run a marathon.

"Cambrie, there is nothing more I want in the world than to fuck you right now. Okay, maybe I might want to fuck you as one of my Alphas fucked me into you, but that's semantics. I want my cock buried so deep inside you that you scream my name," Spencer stated bluntly.

The image of what he described flashed through my brain and it was fucking hot. *What would it be like if that was Bodhi and me instead of Spencer and one of the others?* I quickly slammed the door on that thought knowing it wasn't good to put myself in that place when Bodhi had shown no interest.

Marius stepped forward and looked down at our Omega. "Cambrie, I need you to tell us your answer. Do you want us to help you, or do you want to try one of the other methods? None of us want to push you into something you're not ready for."

She looked up at him with her big blue eyes filled with hope as she asked him. "Am I not your Omega anymore? Did I ruin it by not listening to you?"

That woman had a strangle hold on my heart and I desperately wanted to set the record straight on that matter, but I wasn't the one who needed to give the answer.

"Princess, you are the only Omega I want from now till forever," he answered, reaching down and picking her up. "Come on, my sweet Princess, we're gonna help you through this as a pack should, together."

As Spencer followed those two out, I looked at the others. "*Any of you going to join them?*"

Bodhi looked at me like I'd just asked a stupid question. "Didn't we all say we wanted her? Why wouldn't we help her through her first heat?"

My gaze landed on Nixon, knowing he might view that differently. "I won't be strong enough to stay away, not with Spencer in there with her. I just pray to God that I'm not too much. I know how I get when I lose control."

Rafael walked over and gripped his arm. "We won't let you hurt Cambrie or yourself, that's what packs do. They look after each other, even if that means stopping them from hurting themselves."

"Thank you, I trust you to keep your word," Nixon answered, returning the gesture before heading downstairs.

Rafael looked at me with a raised brow. "You coming?"

"*Wild horses couldn't stop me,*" I said, taking one last deep breath before I lost myself to experiencing my first heat with our Omega.

CHAPTER 26

Cambrie

I was so hot, everything inside me was burning up, and I felt itchy. No, that wasn't the right word... tingly? Whatever this feeling was, I knew I needed something to make it stop but I didn't know what that was. Spencer had tried to explain this to me, but I wasn't truly able to understand what he was saying. My mind felt like it was in a fog, nothing seemed to make sense but for the feeling of *need*.

"I've got you, Princess," Marius whispered as I let out a whine. "Just hang in there a little longer, we need to get you to my bedroom. Spencer, run down to the kitchen and grab anything you think we'll need for the rest of the night. We have no idea how intense this is going to be."

Everything about Marius smelled so good I just wanted to get lost in his scent. *I wonder if he tastes as yummy as he smells?* Marius snarled the moment my tongue met his flesh, as I dragged it along his collarbone that was peeking out from his shirt.

"Princess, you need to behave, or I'm going to lose what little control I have and fuck you right here in this hallway," he bit out, his arms tightening around me. "I want this experience to be perfect for us, not all of us losing our minds and ravaging you," Marius added as he shoved open the door to his room.

His scent was everywhere. The heady aroma of bergamot with the bite of clove enveloped me, making me squirm. Everything about this space screamed Alpha and *that* was what I needed desperately. I was lucky enough to have a pack with four Alphas, all with glorious knots to fill me. Just the thought of it had me gushing between my legs. I'd thought I was leaking badly before, but now I was sure I'd soaked through the pants I was wearing.

Marius deposited me on the bench at the end of the bed, and started yanking off pillows, pulled back the sheets, and turned on the bedside lamps, filling the room with a soft warm light. He knelt before me, holding my face in his hands as he tried to get my attention. "Princess?"

"Yes, Alpha?" I murmured, trying to focus my eyes.

"Cambrie, I need you to try and hear me, alright? When I ask this question there is no judgment at all. I just need to understand what you might have experienced before coming to us," Marius said, his eyes intense. "Have you ever had anyone touch you in an intimate way before? Under clothes, over clothes, kisses?"

I shook my head and pointed a finger at Oscar. "He was my first kiss, and it was amazing."

Nixon swore and turned away from me. "Fuck, it's like she's drunk. How is this okay? She doesn't *really* know what we are asking or understand what she's giving consent to. This is a bad idea. I shouldn't be here for this."

Panic shot through me at the thought of Nixon leaving me. "No!" I lunged forward, trying to get past Marius. "Don't, please don't leave me. I want to be your Omega, to live with this pack. You can't leave me. I have nothing else but you in this whole world." The last bit came out as a desperate sob, but I couldn't let him leave.

Something inside me was breaking at the thought of him not wanting to be here for this. That I wasn't good enough or I didn't please him in some way tore me apart. Whimpering whines poured out of me making everyone in the room take a step closer. Everyone but Nixon.

"Shh, Princess," Marius soothed, pulling me to his chest. "It's going to be alright, we can't force someone to join in this if they aren't ready. I know you can't understand this right now, but this is a massive step for us as a pack. Even though we won't be claiming you with a bite during this, it's almost the same thing. We haven't been together long and everyone is ready to commit at their own pace, so if Nixon needs time, we will give him that."

I hiccupped a sob or two as I nodded my understanding. Then out of nowhere, I got slammed with a stabbing pain that tore up my spine, starting in my low back and making me scream.

"Enough of this. We need to help her," Rafael ordered. "Those who are going to stay, stay. Anyone else, get the hell out and let us help our Omega through her first heat."

There was a flurry of movements as my shirt was pulled over my head and pants slipped off my legs. I should have felt embarrassed, but right now I didn't give a rat's ass I was naked, as long as they were going to help me. Rafael, who was shirtless, scooped me up and carried me to the side of the bed, where he sat and settled me deeper on the mattress. I reached out a hand and let it drift through the curls of salt and pepper hair on his chest that led down to a V on his stomach as it lightened.

That was when I realized he wasn't wearing any pants either. There resting between his legs was a penis, a real live penis just sitting there hard, red, and apparently jumping for joy at my attention. I was so incredibly curious I reached out a finger and brushed it from tip to base.

"Little One, be careful what you touch," Rafael warned. "Your Alphas are trying incredibly hard to be good, but if you do things like that, we might not be able to."

My whole body shivered at the growl in his voice as he spoke, but I didn't remove my hand. Instead, I wrapped all my fingers around it, or as much as I could, feeling the pulse moving through it. My actions were brought to a screeching halt as a hand drifted across my naked stomach traveling up toward my breasts. Snapping my head to the left, I found Oscar's ocean colored eyes watching me with heat, and yet vulnerable, as if he wasn't sure his touch was welcome.

Removing my hand from Rafael, I placed it over Oscar's and

moved it so he was over the small mound of flesh that made up my breast. "It's okay, I want this," I whispered as his thumb drifted over my nipple, making me gasp.

Rafael's hand rested on my stomach, and he ran his fingers from my belly button down to the crest of my mound between my legs. Then he'd stop, then drifted back up, repeating this over and over again until I instinctively shifted my legs apart. I needed him to get closer to where I craved to be touched, but I wasn't brave enough to ask. Oscar's attention on my breasts had my breath catching as he let his fingers wander in patterns around one nipple, then over to the other, until both were peaked begging to be touched.

Oscar shifted closer and started to kiss up my neck, starting at my collarbone. His lips were so soft, followed by little nips that had me letting out whimpers and I wriggled under the attention. When he finally reached my mouth, he cupped my cheek, and our lips met just as Rafael finally slid his fingers between my legs. I cried out at the shockwave of pleasure, unlike anything I'd felt before, flowed through my body. It was almost as if every nerve ending in my whole body was being stroked, and it was amazing.

A finger circled what I knew to be my clit, but he didn't touch it full-on like he had a second ago. My hips started to shift, chasing after him, begging with a whine for him to make that feeling happen in me again.

Then he did.

If Oscar had not been holding my head and his upper body resting on me holding me down, I would have sat straight up.

"Did that feel good, Little One?" Rafael asked, his gruff voice sounded so sexy to my ear. I wanted to hear him talk more.

Oscar released my lips to let me respond as he worked back down my neck. "Yes, Alpha, I need more," I pleaded, hoping his answer would be yes.

"What would you like me to do more of?" Rafael asked, holding my gaze with his knowing eyes. I didn't want to say. "Through this heat you're going to need to tell us what your body is demanding or we won't be able to help you the best way we can."

"I need more," I begged. "Please touch me between my legs and my breasts, my body wants to be desired by you."

"Good girl," Rafael purred. "We can do that for you. Do you care what we use to touch you?"

I shook my head vigorously. "No, my body is craving to be used, wanted, fucked." Saying the word hit me instinctively. "Yes, that is what I need, to be fucked, my body filled with your cocks. Please, will you do that for me?"

"Like anyone could say no to an offer like that," Bodhi muttered, somewhere close above my head.

Tilting my head back, I found him keeling behind me. I reached out a hand to him, which he took tentatively. "Will you kiss me, Bodhi?"

"Yes Cambi, I would very much like to kiss you right now," Bodhi said, his voice sounding strained as he moved closer to Oscar.

Seeing Bodhi join us, Oscar moved down slightly making room as he returned his attention to my breasts. Only this time he didn't use just his fingers. The feel of Oscar's mouth wrapping around one of my nipples had me moaning as Bodhi's lips captured mine. Finally, my body was getting what it yearned for tenfold as Rafael returned his attention to my clit.

As these men enveloped me in sensations I've never experienced before, I felt almost like I was leaving my body as an explosion of ecstasy slammed into me, making me arch and scream into Bodhi's mouth.

"It's okay Cambi, you just experienced your first orgasm," Bodhi explained as Rafael lightened up his attention but didn't stop, causing my body to shiver and twitch. "Don't worry that will be the first of many, my sweet Cambi. By the time we're done with you, your body won't know how to live without at least one orgasm a day."

I licked my lips and smiled as my breath came in quick pants. "I think I'm going to enjoy this whole heat thing."

"Not more than we will," Rafael shared as he let his fingers slip over the opening to my vagina. "I'm going to check how ready you are for me, Little One. Just relax as I slide my fingers inside this perfect little pussy of yours."

I loved the feeling of him rubbing his fingers in my slick, getting them wet before he gently pressed into me. I could feel how big two fingers were inside me, but it didn't hurt as he moved them in and out, inch by inch moving them deeper into me. Then the tips of his fingers scraped along a spot that had me mewling, grabbing onto Oscar's arm as he watched me with awe as I writhed.

"That, Little One, is what we call your G-spot," Rafael shared as he pushed in deeper, letting more of his fingers run over it as the palm of his hand rubbed against my clit. "This is just a sample of what it will feel like when I knot you up. The base swells locking you in place right where I want you, Little One. You'll be tied to me, filled with my cock until I'm done wringing out every last bit of pleasure from your body."

"Please Alpha, I want your knot more than anything," I begged, rolling my hips to get the friction I needed from his fingers, since he'd stopped moving them.

"What my Omega needs, my Omega gets," Rafael whispered as he removed his fingers, which had me crying out at their loss.

Rafael shifted closer, moving my legs wider until he was nestled against my body. He grabbed his cock and ran it through my folds, ensuring it was well lubed with my slick. Pausing, he leaned forward so he was stretched out over my whole body, resting on his forearms on either side of my head to keep his weight off me. He was so large it made me feel so tiny compared to him but instead of feeling intimidated or scared, I had never felt safer. My Alpha was here, and he was going to give me what my body was screaming for. He was finally going to claim me as his own. Our bodies were going to learn each other on a level that Omegas were born for as they connected to their Alpha through their knot.

My eyes stared into Rafael's as he brushed his nose along mine before our lips came together in a moment of perfect trust, as his cock nudged its way inside me. His hands curled into my hair as he slowly sank into me, our kiss becoming more urgent as I was finally getting the feeling I'd been searching for. My body had been craving the feeling of being filled, and Rafael's cock was doing just that as he finally managed to fit all of himself into me.

"You take me so good, Little One," he murmured against my lips. "What a good Omega you are, taking your Alpha's cock down to the root."

Pleasure at pleasing my Alpha had me wrapping my arms around him as far as possible, wanting to touch him as they'd touched me. My hands wandered over his back, noticing it didn't have the same hair that he did on the front, it was incredibly smooth. As the feeling of my channel being so tight relaxed, Rafael started to roll his hips slightly, getting me used to the movement before he pulled out and thrust back in. Each time his movements became bigger, thrusting in deeper, pulling moans from my mouth that he swallowed up as he kissed me.

As the pace sped up, I buried my face in his neck, holding on as the sensations grew more and more until I was sure I'd explode. When I finally tipped over that edge I screamed, digging my nails into his back as my legs clung to him, trying to hold him steady to give me a moment to let my brain handle the assault of ecstasy that shot through me.

"Yes, Little One, scream for me. Let the others know how good I'm making you feel right now," Rafael demanded as he curled his arms under me and lifted me so I was sitting in his lap.

In this position I slid further down on his cock, to the point I could feel it hitting places I wasn't sure it should be. Squirming I tried to adjust, but his hands gripped my hips and shoved me down, making me groan and toss my head back. Releasing one hand, he wrapped it around the back of my neck and supported me as I rested in his hold. This allowed him to capture one of my nipples in his mouth, making me whine at how good it felt.

A body approached and moved in behind me, allowing Rafael to return his hold to my hips so he could lift me up and down on his cock. My head lolled on their shoulder, but the clove scent told me it was Marius. Opening my eyes, I saw his jaw covered in scruff, his body vibrating as he purred, sending rumbles through my body making every other sensation even more pronounced.

"Princess, do you know how sexy you look riding Rafael's cock like that? I couldn't keep my hands off you a moment longer," he shared, his hands running up my ribs until they cupped my breasts. "Are you going to be a good girl and take his knot? I can tell he's getting close to filling that pussy of yours with his cum, claiming it as ours."

His words had my eyes rolling into the back of my head as he plucked at my nipples.

"Did you hear me, Princess? Your Alpha asked you a question," Marius asked, pinching one of my nipples sharply enough to make me gasp.

It didn't hurt with the flood of endorphins I had flying around from Rafael's cock ramming into me, but it gave me enough of a jolt that I could think more clearly. "Please knot me Alpha, your Omega wants to be owned by you and this pack," I cried out pulling myself to cling to Rafael's neck. "Fill my pussy with your seed so everyone knows I'm yours."

Rafael snarled, his mouth clamping down on my neck, not breaking the skin but it would absolutely bruise. I didn't care about that, wishing it was the real thing. I wanted to be his in every possible way. To have his mark on me for life would be something I'd display proudly everywhere I went.

He slammed into me once more, shoving my hips down tightly against him as I felt something growing inside me. My eyes flew open and I started to panic slightly as his knot continued to grow, pushing the limits of what I believe my vagina could handle. I let out a concerned squeak as I started to wriggle, trying to get away from the feeling of being locked in place.

"Easy, Princess," Marius soothed, kissing my other shoulder, running a hand over my back. "You're an Omega, you're built to take our knots. I know it must feel strange, but just relax and trust that Rafael would never hurt you."

I took a deep breath and forced my body to acknowledge we were fine. Rafael's body seemed to curl around me, not releasing his hold with his teeth as he growled. This had me tensing again, thinking I was doing something wrong. Instantly the growl turned into a purr and I went limp as a noodle. The feel of his knot vibrating in my core was mind blowing and chased away any and every concern I had about what was happening. As if he knew what his purr was doing to me, he sped it up, making me moan and thrust against him.

"Little One, you do that, and I'm going to use this knot in a way I'm not sure you're ready for," Rafael warned, releasing me.

That warning had the opposite effect and I did it one more time and added a swirl of my hips, loving how his knot hit me in all sorts of places. Rafael slammed us to the bed with a roar as he rutted his hips into me in short quick bursts that had me screaming in pleasure. The walls around his knot squeezed even tighter and I felt his seed being milked from his cock, filling me up. The second it hit deep inside me a wash of relief flowed through my body, cooling the heat I never thought was going to dissipate. There was still a long way to go before I felt remotely normal but it was like running an ice cube on the back of your neck in the summer heat. It didn't last but it felt amazing.

"More," I whispered, my voice cracking. "I need more."

And more is what I received as Rafael let me pull every drop from him, until he flopped to his side, his breathing labored like he'd been running. My own mimicked his, sweat drenching our bodies as we lay there looking into each other's eyes.

He reached out with a hand letting it brush along my jaw, then down my neck to the tender spot where he'd bitten. "This might not be permanent yet, but don't you think for a moment you aren't mine, Little One."

I grasped his hand and kissed the back of it, clutching it to my chest as I closed my eyes to rest for a moment.

CHAPTER 27

Bodhi

Watching Rafael take Cambrie for the first time was a sight I'm going to have playing on repeat in my head forever. She was so small compared to the bigger man but he handled her so gently, encouraging her every step of the way. I found myself stroking my cock more than once but I wasn't going to bust a nut with my hand when I had an Omega begging to be dicked down.

The way Cambrie begged had to be the most erotic thing I'd ever heard. Her soft voice breathy with need mewling out her request, followed by a whimper, had me almost coming without even touching myself. For a moment, I was sure Marius was going to pounce on Spencer before he joined in at the end. Not that the Beta looked like he would object, the way he rubbed his ass all up on his Alpha.

While I knew Nixon and Marius shared Spencer, other than kisses and cuddles on the couch, they were incredibly respectful when around us. Yes, there were times we heard them making him scream at night, but who were we to tell them not to enjoy their lives together? When you find someone you love, you damn well hold on to them tightly so they never leave. Not that I had much ground to talk, since the person I was half in love with didn't really see me that way. Seeing the way Oscar was with Cambrie told me that he didn't feel the same way about me.

Granted, I'd never let on that I had feelings and when Cambrie asked about it the other day I panicked. It would have been the perfect chance for me to say something that made it sound like it could be possible. Instead, I made it that much fucking harder, just like I do with everything in my life. Glancing at him where he lounged on his side, running his fingers through Cambrie's hair while she was knotted to Rafael made me slightly jealous. Not in the sense that he was doting on Cambrie, fuck knows that girl needed all the love this world could give. Hell, she turned me into a mother hen when I'd never given a shit about anyone before these guys.

No, what I wanted was Oscar to be knotted to her, and I would be in his place showering love on our sweet angel, Cambi. I'd heard so many old people talking about the good old days and how the love of a pack was unlike anything you've ever experienced. Looking around this room, I had to agree with them. Never did I think I could sit in Marius's room, buck ass naked, and not feel weird about it at all. Not saying this would be an every weekend thing, but I didn't feel embarrassed, threatened, or judged sitting here sharing in the afterglow.

Once Cambi had started to convulse in pain with her heat not being addressed, and Rafael had taken the lead, none of us argued. She was *ours* and he was the perfect person to coach her through her first sexual experience. How often had she said he made her feel safe? That was what she needed in that moment, when her brain was lost to the fog of her heat she needed someone to take care of her.

Sliding off the bed, I slipped on my boxers and went to go grab my guitar. It seemed Cambi liked the music Oscar and I worked on, so why not work on some things between waves of heat. The woman only had three holes and I didn't think we'd be stuffing them all this quickly. Maybe by the end but not now, she'd almost panicked when he knotted her. Imagine how that would go if she had two knots going on. Maybe an Alpha and a Beta would be better to start off with.

Opening the bedroom door, I found Nixon sitting in the hall with his head in his hands. After Rafael ordered him out of the room, he fled. "You alright man?" I asked.

Nixon just shook his head. "I thought getting out of the room would help, but just the fucking sound of her has me going crazy."

"Do you have a place you can leave to? Family or anything? I know you said your parents were in the city somewhere," I suggested, feeling for the guy. I didn't understand a fucking thing about what he was going through but if he didn't feel it was safe for Cambi I wasn't gonna argue.

Nixon finally lifted his head and looked at me. "Are you kicking me out of my own house?"

"Whoa, bro," I said, holding up my hands in defense. "You're the one who keeps going on and on about how you're too aggressive and you can't be trusted with her. Isn't that the whole reason you're in the hall? If it's too painful to hear her, the smartest thing to do would be to leave. Try Oscar's studio, maybe it's far enough, you're not gone but not here either."

"Why are you so chill about this?" he asked, narrowing his eyes at me. "Are you trying to get her to like you more? Ice me out of this pack?"

"Fuck you, Nixon," I snapped. "Here I was worried about your ass, and you sit there accusing me of being an asshole? Nah man, you can deal with whatever psycho bullshit you've got going on in your head. While you're doing it, stay the hell away from Cambrie, the last thing she needs to hear is that kind of vile talk."

Nixon sat there stunned, watching me storm up the stairs. That perfect prince of a ken doll can suck my balls for being such a prick. Here I was just trying to be thoughtful and nice like Rafael always tells me I need to be and what do I get? Fuck-all that's what. When I reached my room I took a moment to take a few breaths, knowing I couldn't go back in there when I was all heated. I'd be no better than Nixon. Picking up my guitar, I headed back down and Nixon was no longer in the hall. I hope he'd listened to my advice but if he didn't, well that was on him.

Slipping back into the room, I stopped dead in my tracks to find

Oscar face first in Cambrie's pussy, with his ass facing right at me. His cock dangling between his legs so I got the full picture of a man I had lusted after for almost the full two years I'd been with them. Oscar wasn't what you'd call a super fit muscular dude who went to the gym all the time. He wasn't at all overweight but he wasn't toned. He was soft in the best way possible, just like the rest of his personality. Warm, inviting, kind, and fuck did I want to snuggle the shit out of him as we sucked each other's dicks.

"Does that feel good, Princess?" Marius asked as he leaned down to nibble on her neck, which she bared to him without hesitation.

"It feels amazing," she sighed, then gasped arching her back as I watched Oscar slide three fingers into her.

Slowly, I approached leaning my guitar against the wall, clearly not at all interested in playing. I was drawn to the end of the bed where I could see Oscar's face glistening with her slick as he feasted on her. He wasn't at all bothered by the fact that Rafael's cum was leaking out of her as his fingers thrust in her. My dick ached as I watched, shifting to see Cambrie's eyes glaze over with euphoric happiness, her hands clutching the bed sheets.

I couldn't take it anymore. I needed to be a part of this with Oscar, we always found our rhythm together flawlessly. Kicking off my boxers I crawled on the bed over to our sweet writhing Omega. "Cambi," I whispered, leaning in, letting my fingers trace down her breastbone.

Her face was already tilted in my direction, so when she opened her eyes they found mine right away. Immediately, she reached for me and I went to her like a moth to a flame, it might burn me up but fuck it would be the best way to go. Our lips met and she opened for me right away when I traced my tongue along the seam. The tentative nature was only that much more endearing as she learned, mimicking what I was doing. It surprised me when she sucked on my tongue drawing it into her mouth, making me groan.

"Cambi, you're going to be my undoing," I muttered as I nuzzled into the crook of her neck, showering her with kisses until I reached her breasts.

They were pert little handfuls with soft pink nipples that

begged to be played with. I let my teeth scrape over one ever so gently, gauging her reaction. When her hand fisted my hair and shoved my face closer, I got the feeling she enjoyed it. Feeling the need to tease her, wondering what kind of sounds she'd make, I flicked my tongue quickly a few times over the tip making her breath hitch.

I can do better than that, she's totally lost in what Oscar's doing, not even noticing my work.

This time, I wrapped my whole mouth around everything that was pink and sucked it into my mouth, swirling my tongue at the same time. Cambrie shuddered as she cried out my name, making me swell with pride in more ways than one. I released that one and went right for the other, not wanting it to feel left out. I repeated the attention on this one while my hand flicked the other, making her wriggle under my attention, causing Oscar to growl at me.

Pausing, I looked down her body at him, and he sat back signing his intentions.

"I want to flip her over and fuck her from behind while you teach her to suck your dick," Oscar instructed.

My jaw fell open at his suggestion. *Was this really, Oscar? My Oscar, who hardly ever ordered people about, and when he did, he felt guilty about it?* Must be the scent of Cambrie's heat that was getting to him, because holy shit it was hot to be ordered around by him. I wouldn't take it as well from the others, but Oscar had earned the right to make those demands after working as hard as he did to gain my trust.

"Cambi, can you open those beautiful eyes and look at me?" I asked cupping her cheek, my thumb stroke the skin that was finally starting to get some fullness back into it. She did as I asked, blinking a few times to focus but she got there eventually. "Oscar wants you to roll onto your stomach so he can fuck you from behind. Then I'm going to teach you another way you can please your Alphas."

"Hmm," she purred as she rolled over, looking up at me through her lashes. "I want to please all the men in this bed, not just the Alphas."

Fuck me sideways. This fucking woman was going to kill me with this kind of talk.

Once she was on her stomach, Oscar took hold of her hips, lifted, and Marius shoved a pillow underneath for support. She was still so skinny and she'd been exhausted by the shopping trip. I was amazed she was conscious, but apparently, her heat didn't give a rat's ass. I sat in front of her, my legs splayed out on either side, leaning against the headboard, then pulled her up to be close enough to reach my dick.

Oscar got himself situated and nodded for me to go ahead, which made sense. It would be better to teach her when she wasn't getting my cock shoved down her throat with his thrusts. "Cambi, do you know what a blow job is?"

The blush that flooded her face made her look so fucking cute I wanted to smother the shit out of her with kisses. "I put your penis in my mouth and suck on it."

Why did that sound so innocent and erotic at the same time?

"When we are in moments like this I'd call it a cock, or dick works too," I suggested. "Penis is too... formal."

Spencer snorted on the other side of the bed, trying to cover up his laughter with coughing. I flipped him the bird and turned back to my sweet girl. "Now, you got the basic part right but you don't have to suck on it, you can stroke it with your hand, lick it, whatever feels right to you."

"So... pretend like it's a popsicle that's melting?" she asked, cocking her head as she examined my dick.

"If that is what you imagine it being to make yourself feel more comfortable, then I'm just fine with that. The only things that won't feel good is a dry hand and probably teeth," I explained.

"Oh, you've just never had someone use their teeth right, I can speak from experience that can feel fucking amazing," Spencer interjected. "Nixon is a master."

"Let's say for right now no teeth," I instructed. "If you want to talk to Nixon for pointers, then you can practice on Spencer, since he knows what it should feel like. We want to start with the basics like riding a bike with training wheels before we graduate to other stuff."

Cambrie reached out with a hand and let it lightly slide down my shaft. "That's something I've always wanted to do."

"What's that?" I said through a clenched jaw, not catching what she said.

"Learn to ride a bike," she explained, then stuck out her tongue and licked me from root to tip like I was a fucking popsicle.

Realization that I might not survive this hit me as my eyes met Oscar's on the other end of our Omega. This is what I'd just been dreaming about... in a way. The two of us would get to share this moment with Cambrie, but did it mean the same thing to him as it did to me?

All thoughts came to a halt when Cambrie started to kiss up my shaft with little licks until she kissed the very tip. My whole body shuddered with how good it felt. I hadn't had anyone touch me like this in longer than I cared to think about. Granted, none of it meant anything other than a means to an end. If I wanted a distraction from my life, sex was a sure fire way to lose yourself for a bit. Anything between Cambrie or Oscar couldn't help but be more intimate since I was half in love with Cambrie and teetering on the deep end with Oscar if I could ever get the balls enough to say something.

It wasn't manly to pine after someone you live and interact with on a daily basis but here I was, trapped in a hell of my own doing. More than anything, I wanted to lean over Cambrie with my cock down her throat and kiss the hell out of Oscar as he fucked our girl. One day it would happen, but right now this night was about Cambrie and getting her through this first heat.

Looking down, I watched as Cambrie explored me with her hands and mouth, trying to figure out what to do. Reaching out I slid my hand into her hair and encouraged her to take my cock into her mouth. She looked up at me with such trusting eyes as I felt the tip hit the back of her throat. There was a cough as she adjusted, tilting her head down to take it in even deeper. I groaned at the feel of her hot mouth wrapped around my dick, her tongue tasting me as I pulled her head back.

Once she caught onto the rhythm I was setting she needed less encouragement, but I kept my hand there, wanting to be connected to her in every way. I couldn't bond with her the way an Alpha could, so touch was the closest I would get. A moan burst from her, causing her mouth to vibrate and send shockwaves up my spine.

"Holy fuck," I grunted trying not to thrust deeper than she could handle right now.

Looking up, I saw Oscar had finally entered her and was now balls deep in our girl. We were in this moment connected through our Omega. Cambrie was our conduit and it was fucking amazing. Oscar smiled as he pulled back and slowly slid back inside her, making sure not to jostle her as she figured out how to handle us both. Cambrie was a quick study, and soon she was taking us both like a champ, using a hand on my thigh to keep from getting shoved into me.

As much as I loved watching her mouth gobble down my dick, looking past her I got to see Oscar with his head tossed back, his hips pumping into her, and his breath coming in harsh gasps as various sounds exited his mouth. He couldn't speak but some noises didn't need to come from your vocal cords, they came from deep in your soul. Dropping his head, he placed a hand on the center of her lower back, with the other he reached around to play with her clit. Her cry had me lurching forward, shoving her head down by accident but she swallowed me down. Quickly, I let up and she gasped for air.

"I'm so sorry, Cambi, I didn't mean to do that," I apologized and brushed her hair out of her face. "You okay?"

She lifted her mouth off my dick and looked at me with saliva dangling off her chin and eyes glazed with pleasure. "Amazing," she said with a grin as her eyes began to focus on me. "Everything feels amazing. Am I making you feel good?" she questioned, concern in her eyes.

"Cambi, you are making me lose my mind," I whispered before I grabbed her chin and slammed my lips to hers. Thrusting my tongue in, I kissed the hell out of her as my other hand slid down her chest to pluck at a nipple. She moaned and I drank it down like it was the only thing I could live off.

Drawing back, I offered my cock to her again and this time she gripped it in one hand as she got right to work matching the pace Oscar was setting. "God yes, Cambi, just like that, keep doing that and you're going to make me come so hard," I panted.

Through slitted eyes, I saw Oscar watching what Cambrie was doing with a look that could only be desire. *Was Oscar wishing he was the one sucking my cock? Have I entered some alternate reality? He couldn't possibly want me like that... could he?*

Cambrie's other hand slipped under my cock and brushed my balls. "Holy fuck," I gasped. "Cambi, you need to be gentle with those, they're incredibly sensitive."

Her response was to brush the back of her hand over them like she was petting them. I could feel them clenching under the attention and if she kept it up, I would be shooting off into her mouth in five seconds. Opening my eyes, they locked on Oscar's and there was no mistaking the heat and desire he had directed right at me. He lifted a hand and crooked a finger at me.

Like an idiot my jaw dropped and I froze. That was until Cambrie's hand around my cock squeezed, holding me steady as she deep throated me. "Oh god, I'm gonna come," I wheezed.

Oscar's movements started to get quicker and deeper, making me think he was beginning to knot up our little Omega. Once again, he gave me a pointed look and motioned for me to come to him. Grabbing Cambrie's hair, I paused her movements, got on my knees, and thrust deep into her mouth as I leaned over her. Oscar grabbed the back of my head and slammed his lips to mine, making me cum instantly, shooting down Cambrie's throat. Oscar growled into my mouth, refusing to let me go as he owned me in a way only an Alpha could.

Not wanting to choke Cambrie, I managed to slide my hips back enough so she could free herself from my cock. Oscar must have realized what I was doing and released me, only to pull Cambrie onto his lap, then grabbed my arm to pull me in. With

Cambrie sandwiched between us Oscar resumed the act of sucking the soul from my body as he kissed the ever-loving fuck out of me. If I hadn't come harder than I had in years, I would have come again.

Sliding a hand between us, I started to rub Cambrie's clit just to ensure she knew we were well aware she was between us. Her arms wrapped around my middle as her head rested on my shoulder while Oscar made quick, short thrusts with his knot, making her whimper. When she came her body shivered as she screamed, her nails clawing into my back. I didn't think it was possible but I came again, my cum spurting onto her stomach, marking her with my scent. I wasn't sure there could be a more perfect moment.

Oscar let me go, pressing another soft kiss to my forehead before he had me help him lay Cambrie down on the bed. He wrapped her in his arms and he pressed his lips to her ear and whispered something. It made her smile, and her cheeks blushed as she snuggled into him and motioned for me to join them. Taking the front, I let my arm drape over both of them and let this moment be ingrained in my brain for all time. I had no idea what this meant for us once we stepped outside of this room, but I was going to take what I could get now.

CHAPTER 28
Cambrie

I'd lost the sense of everything including time, and how many times I've come between all my Alphas knotting me, filling me with their cum, and if I'd eaten at all. Spencer and Bodhi both teased me with their hands and mouths, then taught me the finer points of how to give a blow job. My mind was spinning with all the new sensations I was experiencing and I couldn't get enough of it. I remember at some point water and food being offered, but I didn't get much time before the next wave of need hit me. Now that I'd been shown this new world of pleasure, I don't think I'd ever get enough of it. Luckily for me, it seemed neither could my pack, based on the way they would steal me as soon as a knot released me.

One moment I was resting and the next I was begging for someone to fuck me. Which is how I ended up crawling on top of Marius and begging for him to knot me, like the good girl I was. "That's it, my precious Princess," Marius praised as I settled myself over his cock. "Your Alpha wants to see you ride him."

Resting my hands on his chest I lifted my hips and slammed them down, creating a slapping sound that made me smile. I did it again and when Marius grunted, his hand gripping tighter on my hips, I knew I was doing a good job.

"That's it, just like that," Marius encouraged. "Take what you want Princess, you have my permission to be selfish."

Feeling the need to have more friction on my clit I leaned lower grinding my pelvis into his, being granted with the stimulation I'd been looking for. Hands brushed up my back and Spencer's scent wafted around me, making me moan. I loved when my Betas didn't shy away from interacting with me just because I was with one of the Alphas.

"Do you want to know what I'm thinking right now, Dove?" Spencer murmured in my ear.

My movements slowed as he draped himself over my back, rubbing his cock between my ass cheeks. "Yes," I breathed.

"I want to fuck this pretty ass of yours while you ride our Alpha's cock. I want to feel his dick sliding in and out of you while I rut into your ass," Spencer shared as he kissed along my neck and shoulder. "Do you think you'd let me do that, Dove?"

"Will it feel good?" I asked, a little concerned.

Spencer hummed, then bit my ear. "I can say from personal experience it's fucking amazing. But there is no pressure, if you're not ready for it yet there are other things I can do for you to see how you feel about it."

Pausing, I turned to look at him and reached out to cup his cheek with my hand. "Will it make you happy?"

Spencer smiled and kissed me softly. "That's not how this works, Dove. I'm happy right now, watching you please our Alpha and taking the pleasure you want from him. Didn't he say to be selfish?" I nodded. "Then you will only say yes to things that will make *you* happy, even if that means saying no to one of us."

Biting my lip, I thought for a moment.

"Little One," Rafael said in a warning tone. Instantly, I let go of my lip knowing if I didn't then Rafael would be over here—*putting my lips to better use*—as he would say.

Looking into Spencer's face I made my choice. "I want to try. How will I know if I like it or not if I don't experience it?"

"If that's what you truly want, and you're not just saying that to make me happy," Spencer challenged, giving me a serious look.

Kissing him deeply, I wrapped my arms around his neck and hugged him tight. "Yes, this is what I want," I murmured against his lips.

"Then my sweet, sweet, Dove, that is what you will get. If you don't like it or you want me to stop, just say the word. No one will be mad or upset with you, this is your body and you get to say what happens to it no matter what," Spencer stated, booping me on the nose. "Now turn around, lie down on Marius's chest, and leave the rest to us until you say otherwise."

Doing as I was instructed, I let myself sprawl over Marius's broad chest. I was grateful to Oscar for saving the day when he pulled my hair into a messy bun on top of my head. I'd said something about cutting it all off and they all freaked out, then Oscar offered this solution. Marius ran his hand up and down my back soothingly as he started to move his hips, thrusting up into me. It was a slow rhythmic movement, as if he had all the time in the world to fuck me.

Spencer's hands rested on my butt cheeks as he pushed them apart. I squeaked when I felt cool liquid run over my back entrance. "Sorry, Dove, I should have warned you this was coming. I'm not going to do anything but massage the area, let you get a feel for what's gonna happen. When I feel you relax we'll move to me sliding a finger inside okay?"

"I'm fine, it was just cold," I shared, not wanting him to think for a moment he should stop. I was getting tingles up my spine as he applied pressure, circling the area he wanted to relax.

Marius must have decided I was getting too distracted because he sped up slightly, making sure to thrust all the way in hard enough that his balls slapped against me. He also slipped a hand under my chest to play with my nipple, making me moan. I put my hands on either side of him and lifted slightly so he could use both hands as he fucked up into me.

"Tell me what it feels like, Princess," Marius instructed. "I want to know what's going on in that beautiful brain of yours."

Spencer nudged just the tip of his finger into the hole, then resumed swirling. He was teasing me and he knew it, I wiggled back, shoving Marius deeper as he thrust but also creating more friction with Spencer's touch.

"It's hard to describe," my voice catching as he pressed the finger in again. "When he prods at the entrance it feels like electricity shooting up my spine, making me quiver. Everything feels so odd yet amazing."

Marius started to purr as he was pleased with me. "Are you enjoying it, Princess? Is our Beta making our Omega feel good?"

Spencer added more lube and worked it into my ass a little more, taking the strength right out of my body. I crashed to Marius's chest as an orgasm rocketed through me. "Oh god, I'm coming! Don't stop, please don't stop!"

"Ah fuck, what are you doing to her Spencer? She's squeezing the life out of me and I haven't even knotted her yet," Marius groaned, gripping my hips tightly as he halted his movements.

Spencer leaned over me so his face was next to mine, grinning at Marius. "I'm just doing what you used to do to me when we first met, babe. I've told you that your fingers are gifted and I'm glad I took notes, it's sure coming in handy. Our sweet Dove is opening up for me beautifully." He planted a sloppy kiss on my cheek before sitting back up and continuing his work.

This time, instead of just the tip, more of his finger went in. My breathing was labored as I tried to hold on to Marius as the pressure built in a strangely delicious way. Part of me wanted to push him out because it shouldn't be in there in the first place, yet as he gently used his other hand to rub my lower back I relaxed.

"That's it my beautiful Dove, don't fight the feeling, even if your body is screaming it's wrong. Just accept that it's different and breathe through it," Spencer encouraged.

"Good girl, Cambrie," Marius rumbled in my ear as he smoothed a hand down my back. "I can feel him moving inside you, his fingers fucking that tight little asshole."

I wanted to sob with how good my whole body felt with Marius's cock in my pussy, and Spencer now sliding two fingers into my ass. Every time these men wanted to 'teach' me something new I just needed to say yes, because I'd never felt so much pleasure in my life. As my body adjusted, Marius and Spencer fell into an alternating rhythm that made my mind go blank. I felt everything, my skin felt like it was on fire and I didn't think I'd survive much longer without selling my soul to these men to fuck me like this forever.

My scream filled the room as I came again, my whole body convulsing so much that Spencer removed his hand, and Marius had to lie me on my side. Marius didn't pull out because apparently what set off the explosion was his knot swelling, tossing me over the edge into ecstasy. Nothing in the world mattered right now but the feeling of these men wrapping me in their arms, whispering how much they cared about me. Never in my life did I believe this could happen outside of a storybook.

"What a good girl you are, Princess, you came so beautifully on my cock, taking my knot deep inside you," Marius purred as I felt his hips flexing as his cum filled me.

Spencer was humping my back, the feel of his seed shooting over my skin as he moaned in my ear. "Our sweet Dove, making me cum just by the sound of her voice and watching her get fucked senseless by our Alpha as I finger fucked your ass, simply beautiful."

Every touch had me writhing and gasping for breath clamping harder on Marius's knot.

"Cambrie, if you keep doing that I'm going to claim you right here, right now," Marius warned as he nuzzled his face against my neck. "I want to leave my mark on your skin showing the world we possess the most incredible Omega in existence."

His words seemed to knit broken shards of my soul back together. Each of these men, every day I'd been with them, had slotted another piece of my shattered puzzle back in its rightful spot. While they kept saying it wasn't the right time for them to claim me there was nothing I wanted more.

"Alpha," I whispered. "Will you mark me? I know you keep saying to wait, that it's too soon, but I know without a shadow of a doubt I won't be able to survive this without all of you."

Marius clung to me tightly, his teeth scraping over the skin of my neck, then bit down and stopped just before it would break the skin. He didn't move, just held me as if he couldn't bring himself to do it yet, causing hot tears to roll down my cheeks. *Why wouldn't they mark me?*

"Little One," Rafael murmured, taking Spencer's spot. "Don't cry, please don't be sad. You are ours, mind and spirit, you belong to each and every one of us. The only reason we don't claim you right now is we need to address it with the government first. Once that is all settled and they know we've chosen you, I promise we will claim you the second we get home."

I sniffled, relaxing into Rafael's larger body slightly more reassured. "When will you talk to them?"

"When your heat is over, we will hand in our petition and make this all official," Rafael stated.

Marius's body tensed and he removed his mouth from me and looked at the Alpha behind me with anger in his eyes. "Is that so?"

"Yes, there is no reason for them to deny us the right to have an Omega. We fit all the qualifications and you're an Official, the matter should be simple," Rafael challenged, a warning note in his tone.

"I don't think this is the right time to be talking about this," Marius said, brushing a hand along my cheek. "Let's not worry about such things while we are enjoying this time together. You absolutely are our Omega and there is no one who could replace you. Things will happen as they are meant to, and will end in us creating a life together."

Completely soothed by their reassurances I rested in the arms of two of my Alphas as the heat began to cool. It wasn't done with me, but I was getting more coherent moments. My stomach rumbled and I couldn't help but giggle as everyone looked at me expectantly.

"Bodhi, is there any chance I might be able to talk you into making me a grilled cheese? I really wanted one when I came home from the mall but then this happened," I asked as he appeared behind Rafael.

"You got it, Cambi, one grilled cheese coming right up," he said, giving me a wink before he took off.

"That Beta is wrapped around your finger like nothing I've ever seen before," Rafael chuckled.

My mind drifted back to that moment sandwiched between him and Oscar. "I don't think it's just me he's like that with."

"Can't say I'm surprised," Spencer shared with exasperation. "About time you made a move, Oscar. I thought I was going to have to do something drastic for you two to finally realize you've been mooning over each other for at least a year."

I assume Oscar had something to say but caught between Marius and Rafael I couldn't see. As I lay there connected to Marius in one of the most intimate ways a person could be, my mind drifted to Nixon. *What was he doing? Was he alright? Did he hate me for stealing his whole pack for the past two days?*

"Princess, what has you thinking so hard? You've got wrinkles in your brow from concentrating so deeply," Marius asked as he used a finger to smooth out said wrinkles.

"Nixon," I murmured.

"Hmm," he answered, pressing a kiss to my forehead. "Worried about him?"

I nodded curling up closer to him, hiding my face in his chest. "Why didn't he want me?"

Marius slid a hand under my chin and forced me to look up at him. "That is not what happened. Nixon cares about you deeply, that is the reason he's not here."

"That doesn't make sense to me," I argued. "If he cares he would be here with me during my first heat."

"Little One, do you know what it's like when an Alpha goes into rut?" Rafael asked, running a hand down my back.

I peered over my shoulder remembering what Bodhi told me. "They get sex crazy."

"That is part of it, but they become possessive, out of control, and in some cases, they can harm their own pack in the desperate need to keep the Omega to themselves," Rafael expounded. "Nixon is fighting falling into rut, and he tends to be a little more assertive when it comes to sex. He is incredibly worried that if he were to be that way with you it would scare you or he might hurt you, when that's the last thing he wants."

"So, he's staying away to keep me safe?" I questioned, thinking it still seemed backward to what I'd think he should do.

Rafael nodded. "Nixon is doing this to keep us all safe. He wouldn't like all of us touching you, holding you, or fucking you while he's in that state. Rut brings an Alpha to their baser logic, where need trumps all other rational thinking. It could also lead to him marking you when that wouldn't be the best approach right now."

I let out a heavy sigh, accepting that I was going to have to deal with things as they were. Marius's knot relaxed enough for me to roll onto my stomach and curl around a pillow. My stomach grumbled again but the sound of the bedroom door opening alerted me that a grilled cheese might be close at hand. Sitting up as quickly as I could, I spotted Bodhi walking over in just his boxers. His lean muscled chest made my mouth water at the idea of licking every dip and ridge. As if sensing my attention, his gaze met mine, and it brought him to a screeching halt.

"Cambi, you can't look at me like that right now," Bodhi warned, his tone husky. "There needs to be a break long enough for you to eat this, and right now I'm not sure I have the strength to say no."

Oscar slid off the bed and approached Bodhi, took the plate, then handed it to me, kissing me on the forehead as I took it. The smell of the sandwich held my full attention as I snatched up one half and promptly bit into it. Humming, I did a little happy dance as the cheese melted on my tongue. This simply had to be the best food in existence.

Opening my eyes, I nearly choked on my food as I found Oscar on his knees pulling Bodhi's cock out of his boxers and licking it from balls to tip.

CHAPTER 29

Cambrie

The sandwich fell out of my hand back to the plate with a *thunk,* drawing their attention. Oscar smiled and gave me a wink before he signed something, then returned to what he was doing.

"He said for you to watch and learn as he gives him a blow job," Spencer whispered in my ear as he settled himself behind me. "Now eat your food, Dove. We can't have you fainting from hunger now, can we?"

I looked down at my grilled cheese that I loved so much, but my appetite was now entirely focused on something else. If I could gain nourishment from the sexual desire coming off both men, I would be stuffed full right now. Instead, Spencer picked up the sandwich and put it to my lips. Mechanically, I took a bite and chewed, unable to pull my eyes away from the looks and touches these two men were giving each other.

"Here, drink some water," Marius ordered, handing me an already opened water bottle.

He didn't use a bark but the tone wasn't up for negotiation, as I gulped down half of it in one sitting. I'd been far thirstier than I realized. Between the two of them I managed to eat the rest of the sandwich and finish the bottle of water, but if they hadn't hand fed me I'm not sure it would have happened.

Oscar had Bodhi's boxers around his ankles, his cock down his throat, and a hand cupping his balls as he bobbed his head up and down. The moans that were coming out of Bodhi's mouth made my whole body vibrate with need. I wanted so badly to be there, helping Oscar, making Bodhi come again, having his cum in my mouth. The need was so strong a whine burst from my chest.

"It's alright Dove, I'll help you," Spencer assured as his hand slid between my legs and two fingers entered my pussy. "Don't look away, keep watching as Oscar finally claims his Beta for the first time. We've all been waiting for this moment but it's happening because of you, Cambrie."

I leaned back into Spencer, letting his words and touch bring me higher as I kept my gaze riveted on these two men. The look of sheer joy in Bodhi's eyes told me how much he'd wanted this to happen. Oscar had his eyes closed, giving his full attention to the man he was giving pleasure to. I watched as his hand slid further back and Bodhi's breath hitched.

"You're gonna want this if you're gonna start down that road," Marius said, then tossed a bottle of lube to Bodhi. "Trust me when I say, *that* is going to be your best friend forever and always."

Oscar took the bottle from Bodhi and put some on his finger before resuming his work.

"Wait," Bodhi grunted as he placed a hand on Oscar's shoulder. "I want to taste you as well."

Nodding, Oscar lay down on his back and motioned for Bodhi to get on top of him. I had no idea what they were trying to do but when they got into position it made perfect sense. Now each of them could suck on the other at the same time. Oscar poured some lube on Bodhi's ass like Spencer had mine and massaged as he worked him with his mouth.

Spencer's fingers sped up, keeping in time with those two as if I was a part of this moment with them. It felt amazing but his fingers weren't going to be enough. Leaning back, I looked up at him meeting his bright green eyes. "I need more Spence, please give me your cock."

Spencer's lips descended on mine, his hand cupping my jaw to keep me in place as he showed me just how much he loved that idea. When he released me, he put me on all fours so I could continue to watch the two men losing themselves in each other. I looked over my shoulder at Spencer and decided to be bold and ask for what I really wanted. "Will you fuck me in the ass, I want to know what it feels like."

"Your wish is my command," Spencer answered as Marius pulled open a drawer and tossed another bottle of lube to Spencer. "He wasn't kidding about his obsession with making sure we have enough lube to go around. Run out one time and the man gets a complex."

"Whose job was it to buy some and forgot when he was at the store?" Marius countered making me giggle at the look he gave Spencer.

"Don't you dare blame me when you were sending me dirty texts and getting me all riled up," Spencer shot back. "Now if you'll let me get back to the moment, I'm about to blow my little Dove's mind."

It seemed that our conversation had done nothing to distract the other two, who were now adjusting so Oscar could fuck Bodhi. Our Alpha kissed down Bodhi's back, smoothing his hands over his ribs, using his body to let Bodhi know how much he cherished him since he couldn't use words. I'd always been a believer in actions speaking louder than words. Spencer resumed what he'd been doing before, massaging his fingers around the entrance and pushing in one until I was relaxed enough to take two. Somehow, Spencer and Oscar timed it just right that they started to introduce their cocks simultaneously, but Bodhi raised his hands to pause.

"Wait," he said, then turned to me, reaching out a hand. "I want us to do this together."

Spencer patted my butt, letting me know I could go to him as he followed right behind. With Bodhi and I facing each other, Oscar behind him, and Spencer settling himself behind me, they both started to enter us. My arms went weak and I dropped to the pillow my elbows were resting on, keeping my ass up in the air.

"That's it, Dove, take deep even breaths and relax. I'm not going to force anything, the more you relax the easier you'll accept me," I heard Spencer coaching. "Such a good girl opening up like that for me, taking me in your ass, giving me your anal cherry."

I shivered at his words, loving the praise and soaking it up as I felt him sink deeper into me. The feeling of fullness was slightly overwhelming, but soon my body started to receive him as something that was supposed to be there. Everything happened slowly, his hands gently stroking my body, murmuring words of encouragement and love. Then as if my body figured out what was happening a feeling of immense pleasure started to build and Spencer could move more easily.

"Yes, that's my good Little Dove, I can feel you loosening up for me," Spencer purred as he bent down and kissed the back of my neck. "If you can, I'd look up if I were you, those two are erotic as fuck," he murmured into my ear so the others couldn't hear.

Spencer lifted himself off my back, allowing me to push up on my arms. The embers of my heat flared into overdrive as I found Oscar holding Bodhi against his chest, pumping into him from behind, as he stroked Bodhi's cock with his other hand. My mouth went dry as I gaped, enamored by the look of pure bliss written over their faces. Before I knew what I was doing, I pulled away from Spencer, moved Oscar's hand, and took Bodhi deep into my mouth. Knowing that Spencer was right behind me, I wiggled my ass hoping he would catch the signal.

I shouldn't have worried. Within seconds I was filled with cock once more and he thrust into me deep and hard. I moaned, pushing back into him as Bodhi's hips bucked, forcing him deeper into my mouth. The four of us moved in perfect harmony as we fucked each other. If there was a way that I could take a mental picture of this moment to celebrate that my pack truly loved each other, I would have. In all the daydreams I had, this was far better. These men were a family, they loved one another, and while some didn't on a physical level, like Rafael, I knew he would do anything for them.

Spencer's hands tightened on my hips as Bodhi's hand fisted into my hair. The air around us was filled with grunts, moaning, and the sound of heavy breathing as we all exploded at once into a moment of pure orgasmic joy. Spencer slammed deep into my ass, bending over to wrap his arms around me as he thrust his cum as far as it would go. Bodhi once more found his way down my throat, feeding me his cum, which I swallowed happily while I could feel Oscar rutting into Bodhi.

Pulling me off Bodhi, Spencer held me against his chest, sitting up as I watched Oscar kissing his Beta tenderly, removing his cock. I noticed he hadn't knotted Bodhi and realized that he couldn't, just like Spencer couldn't take Nixon's. I kissed Spencer with slow unhurried kisses before I left him to go to Oscar. Both he and Bodi pulled me into their arms, putting me in the middle. I climbed on Oscar's lap and slid down on him 'til I butted up against his knot. It wasn't a full knot as if it knew it couldn't be used. Oscar hissed as I rubbed against it.

I cupped his cheek, drawing him to look down at me. "Let me take it for him." I looked over my shoulder at Bodhi. "Will you help me fit it in?"

"Cambi, you can't. It's already expanded, there's no way you can take his knot now," Bodhi argued.

"That's not a full knot, I can take him. I just need you to help me," I explained.

Bodhi didn't seem convinced, but he trusted me as I lifted up and when I dropped down I relaxed and let Bodhi's added force pop me right past that half-mast of a knot. Oscar made a strangled sound as he curled around my body thrusting his cock into me as his knot swelled to full size, officially locking me to him and his cum filled me.

I smiled as Oscar purred and held me tucked against his chest, his face hidden in my hair as he kissed my neck lovingly. Relaxing in his arms, I rested my head on his shoulder as we enjoyed our bodies holding each other.

"Holy shit," Bodhi swore. "I thought he was going to tear me apart and it wasn't even the full thing!?"

Spencer patted him on the shoulder. "If you want to take your Alpha's knot that's going to take a lot of work and I myself didn't really enjoy it. You might, but that's going to take some practice and effort on each of your parts. Unlike an Omega, we aren't naturally that... stretchy."

"Yeah, I think we might keep it simple for a bit, that was fucking amazing and totally overstimulating at the same time. I'm not sure I could handle more just yet," Bodhi shared, rubbing the back of his neck like he was embarrassed. "So, I got distracted before, but did Cambi eat her grilled cheese?"

"It took me and Marius hand feeding her but yeah she ate it," Spencer shared leaning back against the padded bench at the foot of the bed. "I got to say, you two were made for each other. I've never seen two people fit together like you and Oscar did just now."

Bodhi looked at Oscar, who'd lifted his head at Spencer's comment. Bodhi had a sappy smile on his face as he ran his hands through his hair. "Yeah, it makes me kind of pissed that I didn't make a move sooner. If I knew it would be like that, I would have risked it the moment I knew I had feelings for him. Guess the cat's out of the bag now."

"Dude, that cat's out of the bag, adopted, and purring in someone's lap already. Next time I tell you that two people need to be together, don't doubt me," he boasted, lacing his fingers behind his head.

"Is there someone else you think is harboring hidden feelings for another one of our pack members?" Marius asked, ruffling Spencer's hair.

All eyes turned to Rafael who was getting up from the bed making him pause as he looked at us. "Oh no, you guys are great but the only person I want to love and hold for the rest of my life is my Little One," he shared as he walked to me.

He squatted and tucked my hair behind my ear as he stared deeply into my eyes. "Now that I've had you, there will never be another who could compare. You, my Little One, are everything I've ever wanted or needed, it seems the universe knew I needed to experience some life before I could love you properly."

My cheeks exploded with heat as his words melted my heart. This man, and all the others of this pack, were going to ruin me to the point I wouldn't be able to survive without them. Rafael reached for me and I went to him willingly, knowing that Oscar's knot had subsided enough to release me. Wrapping my arms around his neck, I peppered his face with kisses as he carried me into the bathroom.

"Bless you, I would love to take a shower," I sighed as he turned on the water.

I thought he'd set me down so I could clean up but that was not at all what he had planned for us. Without releasing me, he stepped into the shower protecting me from the water as it fell from the middle of the ceiling. Gently, he settled me on the tiled bench of the gigantic shower, grabbed a few things from the rack in the corner, then returned.

Tilting my head, I watched as he wet washcloth and ran it over my skin, soap sudsing up as it moved. "You know, I could do this myself," I commented.

"I'm aware," was his cryptic answer. "It's clear that your heat has broken after three days but I'm not ready to give up keeping you close... and naked," he admitted. "All I want right now is to take care of you. We used and abused your body, even though you loved it, but right now I *need* to make sure you're alright."

"Rafael, thank you for always making me feel so cherished," I whispered, dropping my eyes to watch his hands working over my body, washing every inch of my skin.

He paused and squatted in front of me so I was once more looking into his blue-gray eyes. "Cambrie, you are the most enchanting woman I've ever met and I had no idea I could fall this hard and fast in love with someone. You've stolen my heart, so how else could I treat the woman I want to spend the rest of my life treasuring?"

Blinking at his words, one just kept replaying over and over in my brain. "You... you love me?"

"You must have been lost during your heat, because I'm pretty sure I've said it before," Rafael chuckled as he caught my lips with his in a tender kiss. "Unless I've just been saying it in my head as I treasure each moment with you... but now you know."

Unable to do anything but sit there in wonder, I let him wash me from head to toe, feeling more lightheaded than I did through my whole heat. When Rafael pulled me to my feet and led me under the water, I closed my eyes and let it wash over me. Here I was after my first heat with one of *my* Alphas that loved *me*—Cambrie—the girl who'd been told all her life she was useless, good for nothing, and a waste of space. Not to them, not to this pack, I was a woman who was loved and valued not for what I could give them but just for being me. Tears trailed down my cheeks, mixing with the water, but they didn't go unnoticed by Rafael.

"Little One, did I get shampoo in your eyes?" he asked. "I'm sorry, this is the first time I've done this for anyone."

I shook my head as I smiled at him. "No, it's not that, I just never thought this would happen to me. No one since my mother died, has ever told me they love me and it really hit me that I might love you too, or at least I think I do... I'm not really sure what that feels like to be honest," I trailed off realizing I was rambling.

Rafael swooped me up and I reflexively wrapped my arms and legs around him. Slowly, he settled me down over his cock, filling me slowly as I sighed nuzzling my face into his neck, nipping where I could feel his pulse.

"Little One, you make it so hard for me to be good and do this the right way. There isn't anything more in the world right now that I want to do but mark you as mine, put a baby in that belly, and grow our perfect family together," Rafael whispered in my ear as he just held me, the two of us connected as closely as humanly possible.

The sound of having a child made me squirm a little. One day I might want that but not yet, I hadn't grown enough myself to be any sort of mother to a baby, even if I did have a pack of men that would be amazing fathers.

Gasping, I clung to him tighter as he slowly moved, pumping in and out of me agonizingly slowly as we clung to each other. Surprisingly, neither one of us lasted long, already bubbling over with emotions. He didn't knot me this time, making my face scrunch up as I looked at him. "Be calm Little One, the point of the shower was to get you cleaned up. After hearing you say you love me, I couldn't not bury my cock in you, but now it's time for you to rest. I can feel your body growing tired after all it's been through these past few days."

"I guess that makes sense," I said, pouting at not getting that feeling I've now come to crave.

Maybe Spencer was right, after this, I don't know if I'll be able to go a day without one of them knotting me. Somehow, I'd turned into this wanton needy Omega whose body yearned for her men, because it wasn't just the Alphas my body cried out for.

CHAPTER 30

Cambrie

Rafael carried me out of the shower, wrapped me in a towel, and set me on the counter in the middle of the double sinks. As if he had a sixth sense, Bodhi walked in wearing sweats, with excitement shining in his eyes as he approached me with his hands behind his back.

"So, remember during our movie day we talked about doing something fun with your hair?" Quickly, he displayed a small box to me.

Cocking my head I read the label, and my eyes went wide. "Really? Can I really do that?"

"No one is going to stop you if you want to do it, Cambi," Bodhi assured me. "Only if *you* want to, though. If you're not ready for something like this we can wait, there is no rush at all."

Hopping off the counter I rushed over and grabbed the box. "Can we do my whole head, or is it something we can only do in chunks like yours?" I asked, reading over every detail.

"I got three boxes in case you wanted to do your whole head, but now that I'm looking at how thick it is I'm not sure that will be enough," Bodhi answered with a chuckle. "This is the perfect time to do it though, since you already washed your hair."

I squealed with delight and ripped the box open, and pulled

everything out. Rafael kissed the top of my head as he left the bathroom with the warning not to make a mess. Bodhi and I read the instructions, donned the gloves from the boxes, and got to work. Thankfully, Marius had a black T-shirt I pulled on so it wouldn't stain as my hair fell around my shoulders.

"Thank you, Bodhi," I whispered, turning to face him once the color was all over my head. Grabbing his face, I pulled him down for a simple kiss but soon I was pressed up against the counter and then hoisted up.

"You got to taste me, but I haven't gotten to taste you yet, and it's been driving me wild," he murmured as he snagged the instructions. "Hmm, looks like you need to wait thirty minutes for this to process. I suppose I can work with that."

Before I could ask him what he meant, Bodhi shoved open my legs and buried his face between them. "Oh my god," I yelled as his tongue slipped inside me.

"Nope, just little old Bodhi doing the Lord's work," he corrected, his hazel eyes shining with mirth.

That made me burst out laughing until he resumed his work that was blessed by some god that I wanted to thank. His hands on my thighs kept them open as I tried to squash his face when it became too intense. Just when I thought I was going to come, Bodhi would move away from my clit or pull back all together, letting me cool off as he kissed other places in the area that made me shiver. Sweat trickled down my back as time went on. My hands gripped the counter as I tried to hold myself up when all I wanted to do was lean back against the stark white wall behind me.

"Please, Bodhi," I whimpered, my eyes closed, trying to hold on as I felt myself reaching the edge of the climax once more. "Let me come this time, please, please, please," I pleaded a whine accenting the last please.

Fingers flicked at my nipples, making my eyes open, and there was Oscar with a wicked smile. He stood to the side and dipped his head to capture one of my nipples in his mouth as he toyed with the other with his hand. Whether Bodhi wanted me to come or not, there was no way I could hold back at this point with the added stimulation. Oscar's tongue swirled around the raised bud, then he nipped it, rocketing me into a climax that had me screaming long and loud as Bodhi never gave up his quest between my legs. My arms gave out and I almost crashed into the wall, but Oscar caught me, laughter now written all over his face as his shoulders shook. I wanted to be irritated at him for laughing at me but I was floating through clouds of bliss at the moment so he was saved from my scolding.

"Oscar, would you help me carry her to our bathroom so I can wash her hair out? I don't think Marius would appreciate me doing it here," Bodie admitted. "I'm sure he's not in here freaking out simply because it's Cambi that's coloring her hair."

With a nod, Oscar opened his arms, and I fell into them, wrapping myself around his body. I waved to Marius and Spencer, who were talking as they changed the sheets.

"What the hell?" Spencer called out, catching a glimpse of me. "Oh, you are so lucky Marius didn't know what was going on in there."

"I did," Marius grumbled. "Don't look at me like that. Were you gonna tell her no with that smile on her face? At least Bodhi is taking pity on me and washing it upstairs in his color explosion of a shower."

Spencer just laughed, giving me a wink as I was carried out of the room. As we reached the top of the stairs, I caught a glimpse of Nixon slipping into my bedroom but I decided not to call out to him. If I was being truthful to myself, I was hurt he walked away from me. My brain knew it was for a good reason but as much as these men had helped to start mending the pieces of my heart it was still very much broken. Him choosing not to be present felt like total rejection, and I didn't know how to feel about it after everything else he'd said to me. One thing I wasn't good with was mixed signals.

Oscar paused as if sensing my mood change, and looked to see what I was staring at. Not seeing anything he just started to purr and kissed the side of my face. Appreciating the reassurance, I nuzzled him back, making sure to keep him color free. When we entered the bathroom they shared, I understood what Marius meant and why he was worried. The once white walls of the shower were now tie-dyed with splashes of various colors. It would seem that Bodhi didn't just stick with red, but might have done every color of the rainbow.

"Okay Cambi, this water is going to be cold but we don't want to lose more of it than we have to, so I'll be as quick as I can," Bodhi explained. "Now come kneel here and we'll flip all this hair into the tub. The extension comes off the wall so it makes it easier, and you don't have to suffer the cold water everywhere."

I yelped when the icy water hit my scalp, my toes curled with the shock. Bodhi's hands moved efficiently as he washed my hair until I saw the water starting to run clear, only the barest hint of color tinted the water. When he was finished, he wrung it all out, and Oscar helped to wrap it up in a turban. When I lifted my head the guys looked at me in horror.

"Um..." Bodhi started to speak but Oscar cut him off with a hand telling him to wait a moment.

I looked between them as Oscar rummaged through the closet, clapping when he found what he was looking for.

"Oh, thank god," Bodhi sighed. "I totally forgot you bought those the last time this happened to me. I didn't think about it, with how long her hair is," he muttered as he pulled a wipe out of the container and scrubbed my cheeks, ears, and hairline. "All that hair, of course, it would bleed everywhere. Could you imagine what the others would say if she came out looking like Smurfette?"

"Anyone gonna tell me what happened?" I inquired.

Oscar started to sign but then paused and grabbed his phone from his sweats' pocket. He took a picture of my face then showed it to me. I gasped, hands covering my mouth as I saw the teal staining all over my skin from it hitting my face as he washed it out. My ears were totally covered, as was my front hairline. Peals of laughter fell came out of my mouth as I held the phone, taking in that image of myself. Offhandedly, I noticed my bruises had finally faded, and my skin had more life to it.

"What the hell is going on in there?" Nixon's voice asked from the other side of the bathroom door.

I froze, not ready to face him just yet after how beautiful the past few days had been. Panic started to claw at my throat as I tried to prepare myself for him to tell me he'd changed his mind about wanting me to be his Omega.

"Sorry, you don't get to see until we have the finished product," Bodhi announced as he scrubbed at my face. "We'll have the grand reveal shortly."

My gaze met his, and I gave him an appreciative smile.

"Alright, guess I'll have to wait for Cambrie to see the surprise I've got for her then too," Nixon taunted, making my brows shoot up.

"A surprise?" I called.

"Oh no, Sweetheart, you have to wait just like I do for the grand reveal," Nixon pointed out as I heard him walking away.

I looked over at Oscar, and he just shrugged. *Of course, he wouldn't know, he's been with me the whole time.* Now I just had to wait.

Losing track of time, I sat as the two worked at removing the color from my skin. For the tough spots Bodhi had to pull out the rubbing alcohol and cotton balls to get the last of it off. Once finished, he began the arduous task of combing through my hair. It was thick and wavy, but now that I'd been using much better shampoo and conditioner, it was getting softer and more manageable.

"How do you feel about me giving you a trim?" Bodhi asked. "I've been doing it for Oscar since I moved in. It's easier for me to do it since he can tell me what he wants directly. If you're not interested though that's fine, it was just an offer."

Looking at him, I tried to remember the last time I'd had my hair cut by anyone other than my mom. "Sure, it's been forever since it's been looked after, so I'm sure it needs some help. Just, please don't take too much. I like my hair long."

"We like your hair long too," Bodhi said, kissing my cheek. "Selfishly, I wouldn't have cut more than an inch or two off even if you'd asked me to."

Reassured that he wasn't going to go crazy, I sat backward on the toilet and let him work his magic. He clipped up part of my hair, and the *snick* of the scissors lulled me into a trance as I enjoyed the feel of him playing with my hair. Once he was done, Oscar took over with the blow dryer and diffuser after he scrunched in some mousse. Never in my life had I felt so pampered as I did right now. These men were taking care of me in ways I didn't know I'd been starving for. Touch used to be the one thing I feared the most in life, never having had a good experience with it. Now, with these five men at least, it was all I wanted, never getting enough.

"Nice work Oz, you magical wizard," Bodhi murmured before pecking the Alpha's lips.

Oscar seemed to glow under the attention, a smile grew before he caught Bodhi by the back of the neck and kissed the hell out of him. It was clear that while these two didn't know exactly where they stood, they wanted each other desperately. When they broke apart, breathing heavily, grinning like fools, I couldn't help but chuckle.

"How is it you managed not to realize you loved each other before now?" I asked, spinning around to stare at them.

Bodhi blinked at me, a little confused, then looked at Oscar. "Wait...hold on here. No one said anything about love, we haven't even decided if we're dating. This could just be lusting after each other... right?" Bodhi asked, looking back at me.

Reaching out a hand to him I let him pull me to my feet, then wrapped my arms around his waist. "I get how scary it is to admit that you have deeper feelings for someone. Rafael told me he loved me today, and I didn't know what to say or even if I truly understood what love meant. Then as I looked at him, I imagined him out of my life, never being able to see him again, and it broke something in me." I peered up at Bodhi. "That has to be what love is, right? To feel you won't ever be whole without that person in your life."

Hazel eyes gazed down at me full of fear, excitement, and hope. "You think so, Cambi?"

I shrugged and twisted to look at Oscar. "What do you think?"

He smiled at us with eyes glowing with happiness as he signed his answer. Bodhi's sharp intake of breath told me Oscar wasn't holding back on how he was feeling anymore. That wall had been broken between the two of them and they were in a new section of their relationship, but I knew there had to be love involved.

"He said that's exactly what he thinks love is like, finding yourself becoming a better person just because they are around. Challenging each other and knowing no matter how badly you quarrel they would be willing to mend things in the end," Bodhi translated, his words filled with the awe I myself was feeling.

Bodhi swallowed hard and he looked down at me. "If that's what love is, then I think I might be falling in love with more than one person."

"I might be falling in love with five," I whispered. "It's a really strange feeling."

Bodhi grinned and hugging me tightly. "Okay, enough of the mushy, let's get out of here and get you dressed for the big reveal."

Oscar swung the bathroom door open, and when we stepped out, I found a pile of clothes on the ground with a note.

> Sorry sweetheart, you can't go into your room without all of us.

It didn't take much guessing to figure out it was from Nixon. The message made me think of spotting him going into my room as we headed up. *Is the surprise in there?* Shaking my head out of my daydreams, I picked up the clothes and stepped back in to change. The white leggings were so soft and the top was a soft blush pink with flowy ruffles. It was so soft and feminine looking I wasn't sure I could wear it. Stepping in front of the full-length mirror on the back of the bathroom door, I gazed at myself and gasped.

My hair fell in soft, shiny, teal waves down my back and over one shoulder. The pink accented the teal perfectly and added warmth to my skin. With the shirt being so flowy you couldn't tell just how skinny I was, even though in a week you couldn't see my bones as easily. In the mirror stood a woman, not the girl who'd escaped her father, eyes wide with fear, covered in bruises. This is what an Omega who was cherished by her pack looked like and I couldn't hold back my smile.

Flush with confidence I wasn't sure would stick, I headed out of the bathroom and into the loft space. The guys all sat on the couches fresh from showers and in clean clothes with a hint of tiredness in their eyes. A tiredness that fled the moment their eyes landed on me and my new look.

"Holy fuck," Nixon exclaimed.

Unsure if that was a good or a bad sign I paused, dropping my gaze the courage I felt fleeing just as quickly as it came. *Could I have made things worse between Nixon and me?*

"Don't just sit there," Spencer snapped. "Fix this."

There was a grunt as if someone had been pushed, harsh whispers, then footsteps approached. When Nixon reached out, I reflexively stepped back, my body deciding to act defensively at the unknown outcome. The hand froze, then dropped as a throat cleared loudly from farther back.

"Cambrie," Nixon said, his tone making it sound like a prayer falling from his lips. "Will you look at me?" he pleaded, as he dropped to his knees before me.

Unsure, I glanced up, then dropped my gaze again, my hands wringing each other nervously. "It would be easier for me if you just told me straight out if you didn't want me anymore. I'll be able to handle it better if you don't beat around the bush. The last thing I need is mixed signals. Just say the word, and I'll accept that you changed your mind."

"What?" Nixon asked in disbelief. A hand gripped my chin firmly and forced me to look him in the eyes. They were swirling azure pools and they told me he was livid. "Who told you I didn't want you anymore?" Nixon barked out, making me flinch.

Licking my lips, I whispered my answer. "You did."

That had not been what he expected to hear, and jerked back like he'd been slapped. "You're going to need to break that down for me, Sweetheart, because I'm not following. How in the ever-loving fuck did I make you believe I didn't want you?"

Tears gathered in my eyes as I thought about that moment he turned and left the room. I hadn't remembered it right away with the haze of my heat drowning out anything that wasn't someone fucking me.

"You left me," I whispered. "Rafael said whoever wasn't going to stay needed to leave, and you did," I choked out.

"Rafael also said he explained it." He glared at the other Alpha. "Clearly, he didn't do a good enough job."

Rafael made to defend himself but I cut in first. "No," I snapped, grabbing Nixon's wrist. "He explained his reasoning for why you left, something you should have done yourself."

Now I was getting angry. *How dare Nixon be upset with Rafael, who had done his best to defend his friend?* "If a man was going to walk out on a person, then he should have the balls to say it for himself. Not let some friend smooth things over for him."

Nixon blinked at me, taken aback by my tone. "Cambrie, I couldn't be in there with all of you. Even being outside the room almost had me losing myself to the rut. Ask Bodhi I ripped into him in the hallway, for which he rightly chewed my ass out for doing, by the way. My only thought was to keep you and the others safe. It was your first heat and you needed to be able to explore that with men who could give selflessly to you, and that wasn't me. There would have been nothing selfless or gentle about how I would have taken you. Even in my right mind I like control and to push my partner to the edge."

My hands balled into fists as anger bubbled over, spilling into my wounded and broken heart. "Then you should have at least said goodbye so I knew you hadn't abandoned me like everyone else important to me. You asked me to give you so much of myself, my story, my heart, and you *left*," I yelled the last word before a sob broke out of my chest. "You left."

Understanding broke over Nixon's face as he pulled me to him, wrapping me in his arms. Slowly, he rocked me as I slammed my hands against his back not willing to give in just yet. "I'm so sorry,

Sweetheart," he crooned. "You're absolutely right, I should have made sure you understood I wasn't turning my back on you, and I am absolutely gutted that you even had that thought. Clearly, I haven't been doing a particularly good job at making sure you know just how much you mean to me, Cambrie."

Picking me up as he stood, I just hung there, forcing him to slide an arm under my ass while the other held me tightly to his chest. How could I trust he wasn't lying, just saying what I wanted to hear so I wouldn't be upset with him anymore? Even an Alpha who wasn't bonded with an Omega didn't want them to be distressed. The others watched as Nixon carried me in the direction of my room and kicked open the door.

He set me down on my own two feet and turned me so I faced into the room. I wanted to be stubborn and refuse to look at what he wanted to show me, but a soft, warm glow caught my interest. Lifting my head I gasped, hands lifting to cover my gaping mouth as I took in the space.

Cambrie

The walls had been painted a soft blue-gray that matched Rafael's eyes and brought out the new bright white furniture.

There in the middle of the space was a bed, but it wasn't like any bed I'd ever seen before. It was hexagon shaped with raised padded edges in soft velvet pink. The middle was slightly lower so it almost resembled a shallow bird's nest. Pillows filled half the space, leaving the other side open to reveal a plush teal blanket that I wanted to curl up on. The whole thing was surrounded by gauzy fabric that had twinkle lights sewn into it, which is where the glow was coming from.

A waist high section of shelves ran along one wall filled with books, fresh green plants, candles, and other knickknacks. The swing chair was still where we'd hung it with a cheerful teal rug under it and a step stool to help me get in and out of it. More twinkle lights ran along the ceiling, framing the large skylights and in the fading sunlight it felt like they were stars. Finally, a light cream couch was along the back wall where the bed had once been. It looked like something I could sink into if I wasn't careful, draped with blankets, and oh so inviting.

Stepping forward, I couldn't stop taking in all the little details that had been added. There was a sound system with speakers around the room and a handheld device that was loaded with all of Oscar's music. Picking one at random, the room was flooded with the soft lilting sound of a piano. The closet door was ajar so I peeked in, finding the whole thing reorganized and new shelving to work more efficiently for my things. There was even a shoe wall for all the pairs Spencer made me buy so I could easily see them.

Exiting back into the room, I found Nixon watching me like a hawk, frozen as he waited for my verdict. Drifting over to the bed I pulled back part of the curtain and brushed my hand along the blankets, nearly groaning at how soft they were. If I had ever dreamed of a room that I one day wished to have this would make everything pale in comparison. This, this was an act of love. One that wasn't forced or manipulated in any way, because I knew he'd done it all by himself. He'd never risk allowing anyone in while my heat was happening.

I faced him, tears once more threatening to spill down my cheeks as I tried to speak. "You do love me," I gasped, unable to stop the inevitable waterworks as my emotions got the better of me.

Nixon in two swift strides snatched me up and slammed his lips to mine, a possessive growl rumbled deep in his chest. "Yes Cambrie, I do love you and never again will I make you question that, because I won't leave your side ever again," he murmured against my lips, kissing me every so often. "You light up my world like a bright northern star, guiding me home to the ones I love and my family I treasure."

He nuzzled his nose against mine, making me giggle before stealing the sound away with another kiss. My hands curled into his hair, loving the feeling after having missed him the past few days. Even though I was lavished on by the others, it felt like a part of me had been missing, and it was the part of my heart Nixon held.

"Do you like it?" Nixon asked, his voice betraying how nervous he was as he put me down.

I grabbed his face and beamed. "I love it almost as much as I love you." I got another breathtaking kiss before I pulled back trying to speak. "How did you do this all by yourself?"

"I took the advice Bodhi gave me and put my pent-up energy

into something useful," he answered, looking over my shoulder where I assumed the man he was referring to stood. "I'm truly sorry, Bodhi, you didn't deserve what I said to you and I didn't mean a word of it."

Twisting in Nixon's hold I saw all of them were in my room taking in Nixon's hard work.

"We're all good, man," Bodhi assured him, waving it off. "This is impressive, hell of a lot of work for just three days."

"I had plenty of energy to burn off," Nixon sighed. "I don't know about all of you, but I could kill for a pizza right now. What do you say we order in and have a movie night?"

Spencer whipped out his phone and started to dial. "Are we all getting the usual?"

"Yeah, but make sure to add extra wings since we have Cambrie," Marius reminded as he turned his attention to me. "What do you like on your pizza, Princess?"

Bodhi snorted. "My money is on cheese."

My jaw dropped as I looked at him. "How did you know?"

All of them burst out laughing but I wasn't getting the joke. How was what I said funny?

"Cambi," Bodhi said, walking up to me and cupping my face. "Your love affair with cheese is well known in this house. Spence, you might want to tell them extra cheese and to make sure it's good and melted but not brown. That perfect gooey stage, I'm sure Saul can manage it."

Spencer shot him a thumbs up as he was talking to the person on the other end of the line.

"Who's Saul?" I asked as I let Nixon and Bodhi lead me out of my room back out to the couches.

Nixon sat down in the corner of the longer sectional and pulled me down next to him, tucking me under his arm as if he couldn't bear for there to be any space. "He's the owner of our favorite pizza place. It's not super close to here but we pay him whatever he asks for so they will deliver. Saul's pizza is the best this city has to offer, and we've tried them all."

"He's not exaggerating," Rafael added. "I was skeptical when they kept boasting about it but then they ordered it and I was hooked. It has to be the sauce, or the crust, there is something about it that just makes it perfect."

With all the talk about food my stomach let out a grumble, sharing how excited it was at the prospect of dinner.

Nixon smiled and kissed my head as he started to purr, nuzzling into my hair. "I have to admit I didn't think you could get cuter, but this teal hair really does something for you. It's almost like it matches the bright life you have hidden inside that only we get to see."

My cheeks heated at his compliment. Even after going through my heat and having rolled around naked with these men for days, their sweet words had such an impact on me. "Thank you, I'm glad you like it," I whispered.

"I have to agree with him," Marius said, taking his place on my other side, running his finger through the curls that fell over my shoulder. "It's absolutely stunning, Princess." He took a chunk of hair and lifted it to his lips in a kiss. Who knew that could be so romantic?

"Alright everyone, pizza and wings are ordered," Spencer announced as he joined us. "I'm gonna run down and grab some drinks, who wants a beer?" Everyone but myself and Bodhi raised their hands. "I figured as much, Bodhi, Dove, do you want soda instead or something else?"

"Soda, whatever kind you have as long as it's not grape," I answered, my nose wrinkling at the last soda I'd had ages ago. "It tastes like medicine."

"Who drinks grape soda?" Spencer asked, looking horrified. "Never mind, that isn't something you're going to need to worry about in our home," Turning he went down the stairs still muttering to himself. "Grape soda? Why even create such a thing?"

The chuckle that escaped from me at Spencer's ramblings made Nixon's purr resume stronger than before. "I love hearing you laugh, Sweetheart. It does something to me in the most delicious way."

Having no idea how to respond to that, I just snuggled deeper against him, placing my hand on his chest so I could feel his purr.

"Let's work on picking a movie," Bodhi suggested pulling out his phone. "So, do we have any suggestions? Otherwise, I made a list of movies Cambi needs to see. It covers all the cult classics and some of my favorites because well, I made the list."

Rafael held out his hand and Bodhi handed the phone over so he could read the list. "*Pulp Fiction*, really?" Rafael commented looking at Bodhi. "Don't you feel like might be a little too close to home?"

Bodhi shrugged. "There are so many movies on that list I figured by the time we got around to the grittier ones it might not be so tough. *Schindler's List* is on there too, so I covered the gamut of emotions."

Rafael grunted, then passed the phone to Marius. "I vote for *Princess Bride* or *Monty Python and The Holy Grail*."

"Those are both good choices," Marius mused as he scanned the screen. "Tonight, I think I'm going to add my vote to *Princess Bride*, so many quotable lines in that movie."

"Agreed, it's a great movie," Nixon added. "Let's start with that, then we can go from there."

"As you wish," Bodhi said with a dramatic bow as he winked at me. The guys all let out a huff of laughter as Bodhi set things up.

Nixon brought his lips to my ear so when he spoke they brushed the shell of it. "You'll get the joke right away, Sweetheart, don't you worry about being left out."

Shivers from his touch and his warm breath on my skin ran all over my body. My heat might be over but whatever they unlocked in me had my pussy slick with anticipation. Nixon froze as he took a deep breath, my perfume filled the air around us.

"Nope," Marius snapped as he yanked me out of Nixon's arms. "We are going to have a movie night, with all our clothes on, and actually watching the damn film," he ordered as he looked down at me. "Behave Princess, give us one night to recharge, then we will happily answer your needs starting tomorrow."

Rafael gave a dark chuckle. "Who knew a bunch of older men

would end up with an Omega in her prime and a sex drive that pushes us to our limits in the best way possible. Thank god we have Spencer and Bodhi who might be able to keep up with her."

Frowning, I reached out and took Rafael's hand. "You're not *old*," I corrected him. "You're perfect just the way you are, and I love the silver in your hair, it matches how wise you are." A snort drew my attention to Bodhi who was covering his mouth to try and stifle laughter. "Did I say something wrong?"

"No, Little One," Rafael assured me, stroking my cheek with the backs of his fingers. "You just speak your mind no matter what and I love that, thank you."

I pouted, sinking back into the couch. "That absolutely means I said something wrong, but you think it's cute."

"Correct on all accounts, I do think you are cute," Rafael agreed, kissing me until I was smiling once more. "There, that's better. For the record, I always want you to be honest with me, speaking your mind as you see it. Your view of the world is refreshing and a good reminder there is always a bright side to things."

"If you say so," I relented just as Spencer returned with the drinks.

"Oh, *Princess Bride* I fucking love that movie," Spencer cheered as he handed out beers to the guys and soda to me and Bodhi. Once he flopped into the spot between Nixon and Marius that I'd been pulled from, the movie started.

It was an amazing night as the guys quoted their favorite parts of the movie loudly, making us all laugh. At one point, Spencer got up and pretended to sword fight against the man with six fingers.

"Prepare to die!" he proclaimed just as the doorbell rang.

Bodhi paused the movie as Spencer and Nixon ran down to get the pizza. When they said it was the best in the city they weren't wrong. The perfectly melted cheese complimented by the sauce and the golden flaky crust was utter perfection. Each bite I took I did a little happy dance, unable to sit still as the cheese pizza restored life to my body.

"Is that what she looks like when she comes?" Nixon asked, watching me in wide-eyed amazement.

"Close, she's incredibly vocal when she shatters in your arms," Marius answered, making my whole body blush bright red.

"Oh, I'm incredibly aware of how vocal she is," Nixon grumbled. "You have no idea how many times I had to stop working to rub one out or my dick was going to explode. God, just listening to her was amazing, I can't wait until I can experience the real thing."

I rubbed my legs together, a puddle of turned on and embarrassed emotions swirling around in my body. Unsure if I wanted to hide from them as they talked so bluntly about me coming or if I wanted to drag Nixon into my room to test out my new bed.

Oscar clapped his hands loudly and signed something once he got their attention. By the expression on his face, he was telling them to shut up so he could watch the movie. I smiled gratefully at him as the others settled down and resumed eating. When I was done with my slices I crawled over to Oscar and he pulled me into his lap, purring for me as he stroked the outside of my thigh soothingly.

We made it through one more movie before I drifted off to sleep in Rafael's arms, having rotated from member to member of my pack for cuddles. It would seem a high sex drive wasn't the only thing these men created in me. Now my need to be as close to them as possible was stronger than ever. I soaked up every second like it would be my last, because the world had taught me nothing was forever.

THE NEXT MORNING, I woke up with all of them wrapped around me in my new bed. It felt like I was sleeping on a cloud, which explained why I hadn't even noticed so many bodies around me. Marius was awake and reading something on his phone that made him scowl. I reached over Spencer's head to brush my finger through Marius's hair. He flinched in surprise, but a smile quickly followed when he saw it was me.

"Good morning, Princess," he greeted. "Did you sleep well?"

I nodded and kept my voice low so as not to wake the others. "I slept the sleep of the dead, not sure that I've ever slept that soundly in my life."

"That's what we like to hear," Nixon's rough morning voice rumbled from behind me. "Glad to hear the bed meets with your approval, I had them switch it at the last minute when I discovered this bed even existed."

Wiggling around until I faced Nixon, I gave him a peck on the lips, trying not to scare him with my morning breath. "Thank you for all of this, I know if I say I don't deserve it you'll tell me I'm wrong, so I won't. But just know that I'm a little overwhelmed with gratitude for such an amazing gesture."

Tugging me close he seared his lips to mine, not at all caring that I hadn't had a chance to freshen up as his tongue slipped over my lips, asking to deepen the kiss. I gave in to the request willingly and a moan escaped as his hands roved over my ass. Another body covered my back pressing his lips to my shoulders, making me realize I was naked in this bed with my lovers. That sent a bolt of lust through me, and my perfume filled the air at my excitement. I pulled away from the kiss which didn't slow Nixon down one bit as he moved to kissing my neck.

"Oh, fuck," Bodhi groaned. "Waking up to that is going to take some getting used to. God, I think I'm going to be rock hard all day," he muttered as he sat up, Oscar grunting his complaint at his movement, having been wrapped around him.

"While I would love to say we could be lazy and have a morning orgy, if we want to meet with the other CoF members, then we need to get a move on things," Marius reminded. "The mornings are slow and they will have time to see us right away."

That sold it for me and I shoved my growling Alpha away and squirmed out from between Nixon and Spencer. Rafael was already standing and offered me a hand to help me out of the bed. Pressing a quick kiss to his lips, I hopped out of the bed and ran to the bathroom. No way was I going to meet the CoF without making sure I looked my best.

Quickly, I washed my face, scrunched my hair, applied the most basic of makeup I knew how to use, then headed for the closet. Pulling on my undergarments, I selected a simple yet elegant dress and slipped it over my head. Shoes in hand, I walked out to find Marius dressed in a dark gray suit waiting for me on my new couch.

"I just need to put my shoes on then I'm ready," I shared beaming at him. "Do we have time for breakfast or is there a time crunch?"

"No, Bodhi is making you breakfast as we speak," Marius answered.

His words gave me pause as I went over them in my head. "Did anyone else want breakfast? I realize not everyone likes that meal and many skip it. He didn't need to cook just for me if no one else was going to eat."

Marius held out a hand to me, making me frown.

"Please come here, Princess," Marius requested but his tone told me it wasn't one I should ignore.

Slowly, I walked over and placed my hand in his. He grasped it and pulled me to sit on his lap, looking down at me with worried eyes. "What is it?" I asked, now feeling uneasy about the whole situation.

"Since we've had you here with us for about a week, I'm worried the other Officials will be displeased with us. They would have expected us to come forward right away that we had found you and possibly even put you in a Care Center." He paused to take a deep breath. "Do you trust me, Cambrie?"

If he's using my name, this must be something incredibly serious to him. Did he believe they would say no?

"Yes, Marius, I trust you," I answered knowing my words rang true.

For the first time in what seemed like forever—I had people I trusted to look after me.

He leaned in and kissed my forehead. "Thank you for that trust, and I'm going to ask that with this next request you understand it's for your safety." I nodded as our gazes met once more. "You aren't going to come with us, I need you to stay here at home where it's safe."

My eyes went wide in shock. "I'm not coming?"

"Please know that I want you to be with us, to announce you to the world as ours, but as one of your Alphas, all I can think about is keeping you safe. What would be safest is to have you stay here, in our home, not in the Capitol Building where they might take you from us," he explained, making my heart sink.

"Why would they take me from you? You're an Official and allowed to have an Omega," I challenged, remembering Rafael's words.

Marius smoothed his hand over my head as he pressed his forehead to mine. "In a perfect world that would be the case, but this world is far from perfection. Darkness lurks at every turn, and I *won't* put you in harm's way."

"Okay," I answered meekly, knowing I wasn't going to win this argument. "If you tell me this is what's best, then I trust you."

"Thank you," he whispered, kissing all over my face. "My perfect little Princess, I won't let them take you from us, you are ours. Never forget that."

"I won't, because you're mine too," I stated, slamming my lips to his in a fierce kiss.

Marius chuckled as he set me on my feet and we walked hand in hand down to the kitchen. Bodhi had food already set for me. Oscar was writing out something with single minded intensity.

"Pancakes, my lady, but this time I made them with blueberries," Bodhi shared. "Also, a meal you didn't need a knife for because Nixon never would have allowed it," he teased the Alpha, who glared at him.

"I don't have to worry because I locked them all away so she can't get to them while we're gone," he announced with a haughty grin. "Now my girl will be safe and sound until we return."

Laughter bubbled out of me at their antics as I took my seat and picked up my fork. I glanced over to see what Oscar was doing, and when I read the first part I snorted. He was writing out care instructions on how to take care of me like you would for a babysitter. All their phone numbers were written down. Instructions on how to work the TV, what the alarm code was for the house, and extra keys to the cars if I needed to get away quickly.

"Oscar," I said, drawing his attention. "Just how long are you planning on being gone?"

He held up two fingers, then shrugged and put up a third.

"I'm fairly certain I can manage to keep myself alive for two or three hours. I've been doing it since I was eight," I reminded him. "Although I have to admit, knowing how to work the TV upstairs will be helpful, there are so many buttons."

Oscar smiled softly and stroked my cheek with a finger before he resumed his work. Meanwhile, the others made simple meals or smoothies to eat, all dressed in business attire except for Bodhi, and I bet he didn't have anything remotely close to *business* style clothing. The clock struck eight, and Marius waved at the others to follow.

"Oscar, we're taking your wheels since we can all fit," he announced, then kissed me breathless, leaving behind the taste of his coffee. "We will see you soon, don't answer the door and the phone will tell you if it's one of us. If it doesn't say our name let it ring, they can leave a message."

"Got it," I answered with a sharp nod.

With kisses from all my other men, they left, leaving me alone for the first time in a week and it took everything in me not to run after them. I looked down at my pancakes and suddenly they didn't taste as good. Not wanting Bodhi to think I didn't like them I made myself eat them. Once finished I washed, dried, and put my dish away giving the kitchen a once over before heading up to my room to lose myself in *The Little Princess* once more.

CHAPTER 32

Spencer

The drive over to Capitol Building was a quiet one. Nixon had informed the other Officials that Marius had been sick for the past three days, ensuring he was covered. Now we were about to go in there and explain that not only had he not been sick, but we'd been fucking an Omega they didn't know about through her first heat.

From what I understood, in the Care Centers they medicated them through a heat if it happened before they found a pack. For all we knew Cambrie could be knocked up, since none of us took any precautions when she was the most fertile. With heats only happening once or twice a year, it was the prime objective of the Alphas to get that Omega pregnant. Granted, we hadn't had that intention but, well, that girl was knotted more times than I could count over the past few days.

"What are we even going to tell them?" I asked, unable to keep the question to myself any longer. "They're going to ask us where we found her and why we didn't hand her over right away."

Marius let out a sigh so heavy I knew he was beyond stressed. "My gut says to be as honest as we can be, but then another side of me says to lie so there's no way they could take her from us."

"What lie would that be exactly?" Rafael asked with a raised brow.

"I don't know, she's pregnant, bonded, or something equally desperate to show they can't take her from us," Marius offered.

Rafael pinned him with a look that I didn't want to be on the receiving end of, it was so intense. "One or both of those things could have been the truth if you'd let me mark her instead of stopping all of us from doing it. I know Oscar wanted to mark her just as badly as I did."

Marius snarled at Rafael, angry at himself as much as he was at the situation. "Don't you think I know that? Tell me, Raf, if we had done that, marked her, filled her with a baby and they still took her from us what would that do to her? They don't give a flying fuck about her, they only care about what they get out of it."

Now Oscar was the one glaring at Marius from the rearview mirror, signing as fast as he could while we were at a stoplight. *"Why didn't you tell us things were this bad? We could have been more aware and possibly handled this situation better. Maybe we could have found a place to keep her safe that wasn't at the house. Now you've just cut our legs out from under us."*

"Whoa," Bodhi cut in. "That's not fair, Oscar. I get you're upset just like I am but I would bet almost anything that none of us would have changed how we've interacted or cared for Cambrie up to this point. She is our Omega, that's a fact. No other Omega will fit into our pack the way she does, but if she heard us talking like this, accusing each other, we'd have our asses handed to us."

That seemed to silence the accusations as we pulled into the Capitol Building parking lot. A young man, Tommy, ran up to the car waving at Marius in the passenger seat.

"Whatever we do needs to be done as a unit. Do you all have enough trust in me to handle this the best way possible? I know these men, who they truly are under the masks, and I am willing to do whatever it takes to make sure Cambrie stays with us," Marius stated as he looked at the rest of us in the car.

I gave him a reassuring smile and reached out to squeeze his arm. "You know I'll stand behind you no matter what." His hand rested over mine for a moment, then he turned his attention to the others.

The rest of our pack gave their agreement, which also signaled for us to get out of the car and hand over the keys. Marius spoke to the young man, clapping him on the back before joining us. As a unit, we entered the building, moved through security, got our badges, and were escorted to a waiting room.

"I'll be right back once I tell them what this meeting is for. They will want to do this as normal as possible, even if I'm an Official," Marius explained, then he leaned in, keeping his voice barely above a whisper. "Do not say anything you don't wish them to hear, there are eyes and ears everywhere."

Well fuck, this isn't going to go well at all, is it?

I leaned back in my chair, letting my hand rest on Nixon's thigh needing his reassurance he was in this with me. A woman came in asking if we wanted coffee or water but we all declined after the warning Marius just gave. Wouldn't want them to drug the beverages or something equally heinous. My leg started to twitch restlessly as we waited for what seemed like ages for Marius to return.

"Sorry, there were a few things that needed to be dealt with right away since I was out at the beginning of the week. If you want to follow me we can head into the meeting hall," Marius said, gesturing for us to follow.

I'd been to his office on occasion but never without an escort and without venturing into these sort of behind the curtain halls. The staff bustled about with papers and cups of coffee, looking nervous about something. Nothing in this whole building ever puts you at ease, it had been built for the sole purpose of making you understand your place in the world. That we were all well and truly under their control, is what it told me.

"Good morning," Frederick greeted, his boisterous voice echoing in the vast room.

A man I didn't know was seated in a fifth spot, so by deduction, I assumed it was Willem, the City Magistrate, who filled in for Alton in certain votes. I figured they would need another person present since it would have only been Yoram and Frederick who weighed in. Not that it mattered since Willem was Yoram's man.

"What brings you boys here to see us?" Frederick carried on like he didn't already know the answer to that, but this was a formal request, so it appeared he wanted it to be *formal*.

"My pack would like to petition for an Omega," Marius announced.

Yoram shifted in his seat as he looked over all of us standing there in a neat row before them. "I see, as you are well aware as an Official you are entitled to bring an Omega into your pack. Did you have a timeline for when you wanted this to happen?"

It took everything in me not to let my eyes wander to stare at Marius impatiently waiting to see what his answer to that would be.

"Immediately," Marius answered succinctly.

Yoram blinked twice, the only sign that Marius might have surprised him. "I see, unfortunately, that isn't how that works. We need to see what Omegas are ready to be paired with a pack and to pick one we believe would be most beneficial by what your pack has to offer. Those within the Council of Four need to have an Omega that can withstand what comes with a life of being in the limelight."

"That won't be necessary, we already have an Omega picked out," Marius admitted. "She is exactly what our pack needs and completes it in ways we never realized."

This had Yoram sitting up straighter— if that was even possible, eyes locked on Marius. "Am I to understand you already *have* an Omega in your home?"

"Yes and I wasn't sick, she went through her first heat and that is where I was needed," he answered quickly. "She was found in one of our shelters. I took her in planning to bring her to the Care Center once I found out her history. One thing led to another and she is the Omega we will be keeping."

"Is that so..." Frederick mused. "What makes you think we will allow that?"

Marius frowned at them. "Didn't you hear me say that she just completed her heat? All of my pack participated in managing it, which means that she needs to remain with us for at least a few months regardless to find out if she's pregnant. If she is with child, it's the law that she remains with us as the mother of our offspring."

I could see Yoram's jaw muscle twitch at this news. "Say she isn't with child, have you marked her?"

Fuck, fuck, fuck. Rafael was right, he should have just done it and saved us all the trouble.

"No, because that would have broken the law. My pack has acted within the letter of the law as it is written today," Marius answered.

Something about what he just said had me curious what obscure law he'd found that was going to be our magic loophole.

"That," Yoram spat, pointing a finger at Marius. "Is not true and you know it."

"What part of the law have I broken?" Marius shot back.

Yoram dropped his hand, then folded them both neatly in front of him himself. "A few, one of them being that once discovered, the Omega should have been given to the Care Center. Second, keeping the Omega hidden in your home. Third, an act of treachery against the Council of Four by harboring a fugitive and lying to the government."

"I have done none of those things," Marius cut in before anyone could panic. "It is the law that if we find an Omega over the age of seventeen, we must first discover who their family is and arrest them for hiding them away. I needed her to gain information to that end. During which time her heat arose. There again it is the law to offer all options to the Omega in heat and allow them to choose which way their heat is to be handled. She specifically requested for my pack to aid her through her heat. Then that brings us to the law of children produced during times of aid. We all know the only way to quell a heat is for an Omega to be knotted and filled with sperm, it's a biological design for breeding."

He paused for a moment to let that sink in. "Furthermore, you keep saying I was hiding her, but that was never the case. The guards at the gate have seen her, we even took her shopping for clothes since she had none, and all Omegas are to be provided for by their government until such time as they are permanently with a pack. As you keep reminding me, *we* are the government so I felt it was only fitting to provide for her. Now that her heat is finished I am informing the CoF of her existence in my home and a petition along with it for her to remain with us as our Omega."

Holy fucking shit, how did he have that all prepared? Did he know her heat was coming? Had he done something to induce it? Fuck it, who cares as long as it works to let us keep her.

Yoram steepled his fingers as he watched Marius with a calculating gaze. "That is a blend of laws Marius and not all of them apply anymore."

"Then you'll need to show me where a new law making that rule no longer valid is, because I've gone over them a dozen times to make sure as an Official I was upholding the law I vowed to protect in my acceptance inauguration into this role," Marius countered.

Frederick shifted in his seat, grabbing his glass of water and chugging half of it. He clearly knew that Marius had played the game well, but was it enough?

"While you may have stuck to the letter of the law, there is a matter of intention and no one can truly know what that was," Willem spoke up. "I believe this case will not be as cut and dry as you hoped it would be. We need to think about what is in the best interest of the Omega. Did you find her family?"

Shit, he can't make us send her back to him. She's over eighteen.

"In fact we did, but after looking into who he was it was made clear to me her safety was in jeopardy so I didn't tell the man we had her. When we took her in it was clear she'd been beaten, starved, and mentally abused. There was no way any of you would send her back to that man, but I have his information if the government wishes to press charges against him," Marius explained, handing over a sheet of paper with Cambrie's father's picture and information.

Damn, Marius was just so sexy when he got like this. When he made a promise to someone he would do whatever it took to keep it. Made me love him all the more.

Yoram took the sheet and he glanced over it almost as if he

wasn't interested in what it said. How could a man who demanded they give up their children the moment they were found to be an Omega not care that she was hidden away and beaten? That should have caused him to send an army out after him.

"As Willem stated, I believe giving us time to consider all this information before giving you an answer would be wise. We ask that you remain in the building while we do so in case we have more questions," Yoram announced. "If you wish to gather in your office Marius, that would make it easier for us to find you when we have a decision."

Everything in me wanted to argue but when he simply nodded and led us out of the meeting hall, I followed. Silently lost in our own thoughts we headed to Marius's office taking the elevator to the third floor. Once inside his space, I flopped into one of the armchairs at a loss of what to do next. Marius closed the door and held up a finger to his lips as he pulled out a small device from his pocket and flipped a switch so a small green light appeared.

"Now it's safe to talk," he said, taking a seat in his office chair.

Oscar scowled at the little device and started to sigh furiously. *"What's with that? Are we in some James Bond type shit with these guys? How could you not tell us how bad things really are in general?"*

Clearly, Oscar wasn't going to let this go, but I understood his feelings. If Marius had lied to me about what life was like here and I found out in a situation like this, I would be furious. While I got the reasoning behind keeping it quiet from the rest of the pack, it should have been handled differently.

"I'm sorry I've dropped this all on you now, but we can deal with that part of things after we figure out what's going to happen with Cambrie. This scrambler is just a precaution. I make sure to check my office but since I've been gone for two days I didn't want to take a chance. Alton made sure I had one for situations like this, he was also the one to help me break down all the rules where it concerned Omegas." Marius paused when the other started to growl at him. "He's on our side and is doing everything he can to help get Yoram out of power, along with helping us keep Cambrie."

"I don't like any of this," Rafael snarled. "If you'd explained things to us I never would have promised Cambrie those things."

"If I felt we couldn't figure a way to keep her I would have stopped you," Marius pointed out. "She needed to know how we truly felt and I already had this argument prepared. The mall was a calculated risk that I feel backfired in some ways and helped in others. I needed to make sure they didn't think we were outright hiding her but knowing her father might come forward freaked me out. We should have had a pack meeting then and there but I was overconfident."

"You, overconfident? Never," Nixon teased, trying to lighten the mood but I scowled at him and shook my head slightly. "Right, so worst case scenario if they tell us no today, then what? Do we have to give her over to a Care Center and try another petition?"

"That would guarantee we would never see her again," Rafael said, his voice rough with emotion. "They would never just give her back to us after denying our request. It would be a power move to prove they are the ones in charge and we broke the rules."

"*Guys we can't think like that, we have to have faith in what Marius said to them. Corrupt or not, what he stated was the law and even they can't just ignore it,*" Oscar reasoned.

Bodhi rested a hand on Oscar's shoulder from where he stood next to him. "I would love to have that kind of blind faith but if what Marius says is true, then it doesn't matter. They break the rules every day, this will mean nothing to them other than teaching Marius a lesson."

"*So we're just fucked?*" Oscar challenged.

"No, but I think we need to be realistic that this is going to be a fight, and we might need to play dirty to keep our Omega," Bodhi said, with a determined look.

Marius shook his head. "No, we will do everything we can to keep her with us but we won't stoop to their level. If I have to break this whole government into pieces, then I will, but I refuse to be like them. They will either abide by the law or I'll tear the law apart proving it never worked. We'll share it with the world and let the people destroy the rest when they find out all their suffering has been to line their greedy pockets."

"Damn," I said, then whistled. "You are sexy as fuck when you talk world domination." Marius and Nixon both shot me warning looks. "What, can't a guy pay his partner a compliment?"

"Not the time," Nixon scolded, poking my leg with the tip of his shoe. "Later, when you tell Cambrie how much of a boss he's been today would be better."

A beep from the phone on the desk had us all jumping. Marius just shook his head at us, turned off the scrambler, and hit the intercom button on his phone. "Yes?"

"They are ready to see you now," Sarah informed us.

"Thank you, Sarah, we'll be right down," Marius answered and looked at the rest of us. "Ready?"

"I think I'm going to puke," Bodhi said, bending over at the waist, his hands on his knees.

Oscar stood and rubbed his back affectionately. *God, what were we going to do if they said no*? Shaking myself out of my worry, I clapped my hands together gaining the attention of my pack.

"If we go in there already believing we have no chance, then we don't. So buck the fuck up and put on your game faces. Cambrie needs us to fight for her so that is what we are damn well going to do," I ordered, placing my hands on my hips.

That seemed to do the trick as their faces hardened with determination, and they rose. I turned on my heel and looked at Marius. "Lead the way, Alpha."

"Now I get why you think Marius was so damn hot," Nixon whispered in my ear.

A shiver went down my spine at his words but I elbowed him in the gut hard enough to make him grunt. "Not the place for that kind of talk."

Nixon just chuckled as he slapped my ass, walking past me to head out of the office. "Rude!" I yelled after him charging out of the office. If he wanted to get me riled up for a fight that sure did the trick.

Once again, we were lined up facing the three men holding our fate in their hands. Yoram looked a little too pleased for my liking, but Frederick looked almost sick, while Willem looked as unemotional as ever. This wasn't going to go how we wanted it. I just knew it.

"While you presented a compelling argument, I feel it is in the best interest for the Omega to be brought to the Care Center. If she is found to be with child, she will be placed back into your home provided we do a DNA test to ensure it is truly yours. During the time she is waiting to find out the results, she will be looked after and ensured she has been given the proper education all Omegas get while at the Care Center. I would hate for her to have a disadvantage since her life has been so hard up to this point," Yoram announced.

Yoram's words hit me like a punch in the gut. He was going to take her from us until we found out if she was pregnant or not. What were the chances of that? Even though she was young and it was her first heat, Omegas didn't produce the same way they used to, even before the attack.

"So what now?" Rafael asked, his voice completely neutral, not at all betraying the rage I could see making his body shake.

"Seeing as Omegas tend to be rather emotional right after a heat, we will give you the remainder of the week with her before we send a team to pick her up. Did you already make arrangements for security?" Yoram inquired.

Marius just nodded. "We have someone willing once we were given the verdict."

"I suggest you enlist this help for the remainder of the week, if *anything* happens to her it will be on your head. You didn't follow the guidelines in place for situations like this. While we might not be able to punish you for what's occurred so far, we can now we know she is in your care," Willem explained, giving each of us a searing look of hate. "Don't give us a reason to punish you all, because you are walking a fine line here boys."

Rafael scoffed under his breath at the term boys but held it together.

"Are there any other matters you wish to discuss?" Yoram asked.

When we all shook our heads, he turned to Marius. "You will remain home for the week as is the custom for all pack members during an Omegas heat. If there is anything urgent we will have the staff reach out."

Dismissed, we exited the room trying to hold in our anger until we stepped outside and got back into the vehicle. Once we were on the road, the car erupted with anger and all the things we left unsaid.

"Those rat bastards just couldn't let things be, could they? They had to make a point of slapping me on the wrist for not following *their* rules. None of us broke any laws, strictly speaking," Marius sneered as he ran his hands through his hair.

Rafael slammed his fist against the car door, swearing. "Fucking pricks, the lot of them." It was strange to see the man who exuded calm and rationality at all times lose his shit. He pointed at Marius, his whole body vibrating. "We are taking them down. Those three shouldn't have the power they do. There was no reason whatsoever for them to tell us we couldn't keep her. This whole goddamn thing is a sham."

"I couldn't agree more," Nixon muttered. "Everyone is just too scared of what they will do in retaliation for speaking out."

"Too bad they're doing the one and only thing that would stop me from ripping them a new asshole," Bodhi interjected. "As long as we have each other and Cambrie in our lives, nothing else matters. Let them do their worst because I've already survived hell. I'll do it again for her."

"Here, here," I cheered. "I'm with Rafael and Bodhi. It's time those bastards learned they won't be able to stay at the top of the food chain forever."

All eyes turned to Oscar as we pulled up to a stop light. He looked over his shoulder to look at us and signed. *"Let's hit them where it hurts and make them pay for all they've done. It's time for anarchy and a fresh start."*

"Then it's decided," Marius agreed grimly. "I'll reach out to Alton and let him know he just gained some new members for the collapse of the CoF mission. We will bring the fuckers down and make this place a world we want to start our forever in."

The car was filled with shouts of agreement as we pulled into the gated community. There was a flurry of activity outside the guard hut like something awful had happened. Oscar rolled down his window, and the guard on duty looked panicked as he searched the car opening the back passenger doors of the SUV. "Official Stone are you in there?"

Marius popped off his seatbelt and leaned forward to see the man. "Yes I'm here, what's happened?"

"Someone broke into your house, and we've been trying to contact you. When none of you answered we assumed the worst—"

The guard didn't get a chance to finish what he was saying as Oscar peeled away down the street. I grabbed the door and slammed it shut as it felt like we turned on two wheels onto our street. There was our house, front door kicked in and hanging on its hinges oddly. The car hardly stopped moving before we all stumbled out, rushing inside. It looked as if there was a struggle with things strewn across the floor making panic claw at my throat.

"Cambrie!" I bellowed, flying up the stairs. "Cambrie you better answer me *now*!"

The others were quick on my heels as we made it to the top floor and found her room in disarray like she'd been in bed and whoever took her hauled her out of it spilling pillows all over the place.

"No," Marius gasped, dropping to his knees. "This can't be happening, please god tell me this isn't real. I promised her she would be safe here, that I wouldn't let anything happen to her."

Far too numb to think properly, I moved to her closet, then her bathroom. When I couldn't find her there, I started to look in every room of the house calling her name, the desperation clear in my voice. When I got back to the front door, I noticed nail marks on the door frame. She fought with everything she had not to leave us, and we'd failed her. A sob escaped from my chest as I ran my fingers over the marks.

"Where have you gone, my little Dove?" I whispered. "You can't leave us, we need you just as much as you need us."

Then I spotted something in the dirt next to the steps. I bent down and picked it up, realizing it was one of the books Marius had given her— *The Little Princess.* Turning back, I found the others gathered by the front door, looking as lost and stunned as I was.

"She's gone."

CHAPTER 33

Savo

Grunting under the weight of the bar I was bench pressing, I shook away the sweat that was rolling into my eyes. The past four days had been hell, my body begged me to go back to that house and claim what was mine. Her scent had been intoxicating, calling to me like a siren. My grandmother, the superstitious old bat, kept telling me that when I met my soulmate it would be like this. They would invade every part of your mind leaving you utterly useless until you gave in and accepted it.

Accepting wasn't my problem. It was the fact she already had a pack she fit with, and I was the outsider. No one ever talked about what happens when you fall head over heels for an Omega you can't have. With a roar I shoved the bar up and racked it as I heard my phone ring. Unfortunately, with my assignment with the government falling through, I didn't have another lined up to drown myself in for distraction.

Not bothering to see who it was I slid my thumb across the screen and growled. "What?"

"Fuck Savo, you have to stop doing that. You're going to make me shit my pants with how scary you can sound," Rick, my boss, muttered.

I grabbed the towel I'd hung to the side and wiped my face. "Did you need something?"

"Let's not forget who the boss is here," Rick warned.

He was a good guy, he gave me work without questioning my past or how I came to be here. All Rick cared about was that I was fucking good at my job and kept out of trouble. While we had our moments of butting heads about certain approaches, he was willing to let me speak my peace before telling me to go kick fucking rocks.

"Yeah, yeah boss man, what you got for me?" I grumbled, knowing when not to push the boundaries.

"Seems that the old job you had is back on. They need a specialized bodyguard who can keep his mouth shut and questions to himself while keeping the charge alive and safe," Rick answered. "You still the man for the job?"

"Do I have a choice? Last I heard, it was take the job, or I would regret it," I countered.

Rick let out a heavy sigh. "Yeah, this job is coming directly from the top of the food chain, so if you want to remain here in the city when they say jump, I'd ask how high. I'd really hate to lose my best guy over something stupid like this."

"How long is the job for? They never said," I asked as I shoved to my feet and headed for the shower.

"Until they don't need you," Rick stated, which translated to they didn't tell him either.

"Send me the info. I'm assuming they want me over there ASAP?"

"You know the type, never fast enough or good enough for them. I'll text you the address, they are expecting you," Rick said as a ping sounded in my ear, letting me know I got the information.

I pulled the phone down to double check and grunted as I saw it was on the outskirts of the city. "Got it, now I'm gonna clean up and head out. Anything else I should know?"

"Just one, if it's any of the CoF who is behind this, that is a fight you do not want. They will ruin you faster than you can blink. I guess what I'm trying to say is, be fucking careful." With that, the call ended.

Fucking hell, this is the last thing I need.
I've managed to stay under the radar for so long.
Why does it have to go to hell now?

Rushing through my shower I got dressed in the typical body-guard uniform of a simple black suit with a white shirt. I double checked my gun was secured in the holster under the jacket and headed out. My truck rumbled to life under me, and I smiled. It was one of the things I'd dreamed of owning when I finally got out. Let's hope I could do this job without ruining everything I'd worked for.

It was a forty-five minute drive outside the city straight north. Once upon a time this area had been filled with affluent families and their children. Then when things got more dangerous they moved closer to the city and the safety the government had to offer them in protected communities. They gave up backyards and pools for security. While I couldn't blame them, things had calmed down considerably. They could move back out here, freeing up some space for everyone else.

The house I pulled up to was a massive old mansion with marble pillars holding up the awning that covered the front door and part of the circle driveway. It screamed old money, like ancient old money that came from the blood, sweat, and tears of others. That was a world I knew all too well back home. Everyone was always fighting tooth and nail to survive, throwing others under the bus just to get ahead. It didn't look like anyone had lived here for quite some time, but I'm sure they had staff looking after it, that's what money can buy you.

Rapping on the door it was yanked open a few moments later by a man dressed as a butler. Or at least pictures that I'd seen of them or how they were portrayed in books. "We've been expecting you, Mr. Bakal. Right this way if you please."

Not bothering to see if I was following, he shut the door and took off at a speed that didn't make sense for how old he was. Most people assumed with how big and muscular I was I couldn't move quickly, but I was light on my feet. The life I led, you'd be dead if you couldn't get out of the way fast enough. The butler took me up a flight of steps and down a long carpeted hallway into a sitting room where a man stood in front of a fireplace. The flames flickered casting shadows over his face making it hard to decipher who it was.

"Please have a seat," the man said, gesturing to a pair of armchairs near the fire. "Care for a drink?"

"No thank you, I find it's best to keep a clear head while on the job," I answered as I sat.

He nodded and turned to face me. "Wise of you, it seems all the talk of your skill wasn't just hot air. Do you know who I am?"

"Yes, Official Dubois, I do," I stated as my gut warned me to be incredibly careful with anything I said to this man.

"I need a bodyguard for someone extremely important, but what I need more than that is discretion. You see, no one knows about her, and I intend to keep it that way. Which is why I keep her here in this home away from prying eyes. There is a whole security team that watches the grounds and the staff aren't allowed to leave. If they do or manage to get information out they are killed," Yoram informed me without batting an eye. "While that might seem extreme, it's not, you see this child holds the key to what we need to survive. She managed to slip through my fingers and was taken from me years ago, and now I have her back, I won't let that happen again."

"Sounds pretty straightforward to me," I answered, knowing that refusing would mean I too would be killed now that I knew about this place.

Yoram nodded after he studied me for a moment. "In case you have any grand plans to go behind my back and do something foolish, just know I know exactly *who* you are, Savo Bakal. To betray me would be your demise and any hope you had of living a free life. You will be able to live freely here ensuring the future of our kind doesn't come to any harm. If she does, you will be held personally responsible. Do I make myself clear?"

"Crystal clear," I answered.

"Good, Arthur will remain here with you, tending to your needs. My people will pack up all your things from your home and deliver them here tomorrow. Welcome to my staff, your country thanks you for your service." Yoram drained the last of his glass and then chucked it into the fire. "Oh yes, her name is Cambrie."

To be continued in Part 2...

PART

TWO

CHAPTER 34

Cambrie

Nightmares plagued my dreams.

Monsters chased me through the house, their clawed hands reaching for me. I could feel their touch grazing my skin as I tried to escape. No matter what I did or how loud I screamed, no one came to save me.

Once more—I was all alone.

Gasping, I sat up, sweat soaking my body as my chest heaved, trying to suck in all the air it could. As I looked around, the panic only grew as I didn't recognize anything in the room. Everything about it was cold, harsh, and unwelcoming, the complete opposite of my room back home.

What happened? How did I get here? Why does my head feel like someone slammed it into a wall? Had my father found me?

I looked around wildly, shoving away the blankets and looking down at my clothes. They were the same leggings and sweater I'd put on after the guys left. The *guys*! Rushing to the door I assumed led out of the room, I tried the handle. It was locked. Panic flooded my body as it threatened to pull me back to the days of being trapped in the basement.

"No," I sobbed, slamming my hands on the door. "No, this can't be happening again. Marius?! Spencer?! Bodhi?!" I screamed, beating my fists on the wooden door, praying someone would hear me and tell me what was going on. "Someone, please, let me out!"

When that didn't work, I hurried over to one of the other doors, flinging it open to find a bathroom. Spinning on my heel, I moved to the next, a closet. There was one more I hadn't tried, and I begged whoever might be listening that it would be a way out. Closing my eyes, I grasped the handle, but it didn't budge—it was locked.

"This can't be happening again," I wailed, sliding to the floor, and banging my head against the door, praying it would be hard enough to knock me out.

I'd survived this once, but I knew there was no way I could do it again. Yes, this might be a nicer prison, but that was exactly what it was, a jail cell for me to waste away in. Then, a horrifying thought struck me. Had my father told the person who was going to buy me where I was? I'm sure that man at the mall had told him what he'd seen and who I had been with. It wouldn't take much work to find out where I was staying, and if a person could pay a million dollars for me, they had to be wealthy enough to send a goon squad after me.

Memories of them breaking into the house flashed through my mind. I'd been in my room reading when the sound of the door being kicked in had paralyzed me. My panic had frozen my ability to act fast enough, and I didn't have a chance to hide before they grabbed me. Men in all black with angry faces snatched me out of my bed and tossed me over their shoulders. Lifting my sweater, I saw the bruise from where the man had elbowed me in the gut after I'd kicked him in the balls.

Unlike when my father tossed me in the basement, I wasn't going to be a meek little victim. This time I was going to fight with everything I had. That blow had knocked the wind out of me, but I'd managed to grab hold of the front door's frame in a last-ditch effort to keep them from taking me. I wasn't going to let them steal from me the chance at truly being happy and having the family I'd always wanted. Yet it wasn't enough, because here I sat in a strange room, with no idea what lay beyond either door.

Tears rolled down my face and dropped onto my hands which were clenched in my sweater, as I tried to hold myself together. I couldn't let them win, whoever it was that stole me from my new life. They would look for me. I knew in my heart they wouldn't abandon me, so I had to be strong. Even as I told myself this, my tears came faster and a whine filled with all the heartache I felt poured out of my mouth.

Curling up in a ball, I wept, afraid that even with all the words I could tell myself, it wouldn't be enough. Surviving those two years had nearly broken me, and I wasn't sure I could do it again. Not after knowing what happiness and love looked like. It was too great a loss, and my heart wasn't nearly as strong as I thought it was. The men who were holding my heart together weren't here to help me through this.

So, what now?

The first door I'd tried rattled as someone unlocked and pushed it open. A man dressed in a formal-looking suit entered with a covered tray. He paused when he noticed the bed was empty and scanned the room. When his cold, mud brown eyes met mine, his brows pinched together.

"What are you doing on the ground? That is no way for a lady to behave. Get up this instant," he ordered.

I could tell he was a Beta, though his tone didn't leave room for argument. Taking a moment to wipe my face with my sleeve and give a good sniffle, I stood right where I was.

"Goodness, you have the manners of an animal. It seems we will have lots of work to do in your education," the man muttered as he walked over to a small table with a single chair. "I've brought you breakfast. Seeing as the tranquilizer kept you asleep for quite some time, you must be famished." He lifted the tray lid, and the smell of bacon and eggs filled the air.

My stomach growled, but I remained where I was. "Where am I, and why did you take me from my home?"

The man turned to look at me with irritation evident on his face. "That wasn't your home, *this* is your home, and you're right where you belong."

"Nothing you're saying makes any sense," I argued. "Those men broke into my pack's home and took me from my bed. How can you tell me that wherever this place is," I paused, waving my hands about, "is my home?"

"I see you have your father's stubbornness. How delightful," he muttered. "You will be told everything in the proper time. Right now, you are going to sit, eat, and then bathe. I'll have clothes laid out for you when you're finished. Once you've accomplished that, I will go over your lesson schedule. I was informed that you stopped going to school at age eight. Can you read and write?"

Shock and anger warred in my body. *How did he know that about me? What kind of lessons is he talking about, and why does he think I am illiterate?*

"I can read and write incredibly well. I planned on taking my GED when I was sixteen. Unfortunately, events happened making that impossible," I explained, not willing to let this man think I was a simpleton.

He walked over to me and looked me up and down, then reached out a hand, making me jerk backward. His hand paused, then retreated. "Can I assume those events were the man claiming to be your father?"

"Exc... wha... my father... he wasn't my father?" I stuttered, stumbling over my words as my mind reeled from the information this man had just carelessly stated.

His lips pursed as he took a step back. "It seems I've spoken out of turn. My apologies, Miss Cambrie. Off to the bathroom with you. We have much to do, and dawdling won't be tolerated."

"Wait," I blurted as he headed for the door. "What do I call you?"

Turning sharply on his heel, he looked horrified. "Has he told you nothing?"

"You're the first person I've seen since I was dragged out of my home," I shared. "Who would there have been to tell me anything?"

This seemed to make him increasingly uncomfortable as he adjusted his cuff and cleared his throat. "You may call me Arthur. I will attend to your education and well-being during the time you remain in this house. Since you were never brought to a Care Center, there is a gap in your knowledge that all Omegas are given during their time there, preparing them for life with a pack. The only other person you will be interacting with is your personal bodyguard. I'll leave him to make introductions. He will be arriving later today."

"No one else is in the house but us?" I questioned, perplexed.

Arthur gave a sharp shake of his head. "No, Miss Cambrie, other than a cook, two maids, grounds security, myself, and soon your bodyguard, there is no one else. That is to ensure your safety. As I said before, all things will be made clear in time. I'll be back momentarily with your attire."

I watched the man leave, locking the door before I heard his footsteps retreat down the hall on what sounded like tile floors. The smell of food reminded me that he'd brought breakfast. Standing, I picked at the food, eating the bacon and toast, but the eggs were bare. Bodhi always made sure to sprinkle cheese on mine since it was the only way he could get me to eat them. I wasn't a fan of the texture of eggs, but the cheese was never to be wasted.

Knowing Arthur would be back soon and displeased if I wasn't in the bathroom with the water running, I headed in that direction. *How had he known about my past, and what in the world did he mean about my father? There's no way he couldn't be my real dad, Mom never talked about there being someone else in her life.*

As I turned the water on, my head swirled with a myriad of thoughts, one more outlandish than the next. This shower was all glass walls, stark tile, and rigid fixtures. Everything in the space screamed that I wasn't welcome and not to make myself at home. It made me miss my room so terribly, knowing it had been built for me by the men I cherished. Tugging the sweater over my head, I was once more reminded of how thin I was. The week I'd been with my pack had helped fill me out enough that I didn't look like a skeleton, but I had a long way to go until there was any softness to my features.

On the bathroom counter next to the sink was a stack of white towels that were soft, thankfully. I grabbed one, not liking how open this space was and knowing anyone with a key could get in. While this was to be my space, I wasn't in control of it. Part of me hated myself for submitting and doing as I was told, preparing myself for whoever my new jailer was. Yet, there was a stronger instinct of self-preservation that told me to go along with this until I knew what was going on. The truth that fighting back only got you hurt had been beaten into me my entire life.

I knew my men were different. They saw the world for what it could be rather than what it was now. Their dreams of a better life fueled them to create change, which they did in all areas of their lives. The water was hot on my skin, making me hiss. I realized I didn't even check it before getting in. My brain was so jumbled with everything that had happened.

"Now, Cambi, when you wash your hair, you can't use hot water or it will make the color bleed, fading it faster. If you can stand it, use cold or at least lukewarm," Bodhi's voice echoed in my head as imaginary hands brushed through my hair.

I reached out and turned the handle until the water was bitterly cold, letting it shock my body. Nothing about this could be enjoyable. I was a prisoner trapped in a gilded cage, and I couldn't allow myself to forget it. Before, it had been cold water in a bucket with a rag, and I was denied all comforts. This would be my silent revolt, they might try to gloss over the details, but I would remember. No matter what they said, this wasn't my home, and I didn't belong here.

Steeling myself, I lifted my face to the icy downpour. Everything would be about discovering who brought me here, what they wanted, and how I would escape. Arthur said there were guards on the grounds and soon a personal bodyguard. Those would be new challenges, but I could be a patient woman. Knowledge was power, and knowledge was what I lacked.

When my body started to shiver and my teeth chattered, I hurried through my shower, wrapped myself in the large towel, and walked over to the sink. Testing a theory, I pulled open a drawer and found all the personal items I might need. While I wasn't going to give in to the comforts, I needed to ensure I was healthy for when I got out of here and not drawing attention was crucial, so I used what was available. It was a miracle I wasn't picked up last time looking the way I had, all battered and bruised. If a cop had seen me, I'm sure they would have stopped me.

Wrapping my hair in a towel, as Oscar had shown me, I slipped on the bathrobe I found on the back of the door. This made me feel immensely better about leaving the bathroom to who knows what might be lurking in the bedroom. Cracking the door open, I looked around the space, but there was no movement and nothing out of place. Swiftly, I moved over to the bed and found a stiff black knee-length skirt with a white turtleneck long-sleeved shirt. Undergarments were placed to the side, all in the correct size.

That was easy enough to explain if they took things from my room and used them for sizing. What I found odd was how the stiff, impersonal clothing matched the whole feel of the house. Leaving the robe on, I slipped into my panties, then left it draped over my shoulders and put on the bra. I hadn't been using one since I was severely lacking in that area, but the shirt seemed like it would fit snuggly, and I didn't want any unseemly points to happen. This room had a chill, and I would be utterly mortified if I drew attention to the fact that I was cold.

I hesitated when it came to the shirt, worried that my hair would stain it. Venturing back to the bathroom, I searched and found a drawer of hair supplies and wrapped it up in a bun high on my head. *That should keep it from doing any damage.* Finally, I slipped on simple black flats to complete the outfit. I was unsure what to do now, so I went to one of the armchairs and sat. I took in the room in more detail now that I was more clear-headed than when I'd first woken up in a panic.

To me, it seemed like something out of a museum. The walls were covered in a burgundy and gold filigree pattern, with the ceiling painted burgundy to match. The wood of all the furniture was dark and highly polished, with gold accents. The bed had a massive wooden frame with a canopy made of thick fabric that didn't let in any light. Feeling trapped in darkness would be the last thing I wanted, especially when I was trying to sleep. Nothing good ever happened in the darkness.

Shifting, I looked at the ornate wooden fireplace that didn't have a fire burning but had logs at the ready. They were probably worried I might burn the place down if they lit it. I sat in one of the two tufted burgundy armchairs with a low coffee table between them. They weren't particularly comfortable, had no give, and kept you seated perfectly straight. Maybe it was intended to help with my posture, part of the lessons Arthur kept going on about. There was a sharp rap on the door, pulling my attention.

"Are you decent, Miss Cambrie?" Arthur asked.

Surprised at his thoughtfulness, I answered. "Yes."

The word caught in my throat, and I doubted it could be heard on the other side of the thick door. I cleared my throat and wet my lips before trying again. "Come in."

With the *snick* of the lock, I braced myself for what would be coming next. Only Arthur just opened the door and looked at me expectantly. When I didn't move, he muttered something to himself and motioned for me to come. "Let's move along. We have a lot to cover today. I must establish your education thus far and where it is lacking, absent, or proficient enough not to cover."

Cautiously I rose and headed for the door, still unsure why he would allow me to leave the room. What if I ran? The answer was made clear when I stepped into the hall and found the guard. Spotting him made me pause, and when Arthur touched the small of my back, I shrieked and threw myself against the hall wall.

"Do. Not. Touch. Me." I ground out as I tried to control the panic attack that was trying to overwhelm my mind.

Closing my eyes, I imagined Rafael standing with me, his comforting sandalwood and vanilla scent grounding me. *"Breathe through your nose as deeply as you can, then slowly let it out through your mouth."* I followed the memory of his direction. *"Good Little One, that's good. Now do it again until you can tell me what day it is."*

My eyes snapped open as I realized I wasn't sure. "What day is it?" I croaked.

"The day or date?" Arthur asked.

"Day, what day of the week is it?" I demanded, frustrated that he wasn't helping me as I fought back the panic he had induced.

"Today is Friday. You arrived early Thursday evening," he informed me.

Since that technique hadn't worked, I placed my hands flat on the wall, feeling the texture of the wallpaper, and continued to breathe. Friday meant it was almost the weekend when all my men would be home. I wondered if Spencer had made plans for us to do something fun? Thinking of them helped more than I had expected. I recalled their features, scents, and the feel of their touch that I loved. When I felt the panic slipping away, leaving me exhausted and wrung out, I took one step forward and brushed out my skirt, not looking either man in the eye.

"It would be best if people I didn't know refrained from touching me," I explained, trying to show that I was calm once more. "If you will lead the way, Arthur, I will follow right behind you."

"I apologize for upsetting you, Miss Cambrie, and will ensure the staff knows to avoid any more such incidents," Arthur said, his voice cool and detached. "It would seem both of us were ill-informed about a few things," he muttered more to himself than to me.

He started down the hall, and I swiftly moved to be right on his heels, giving the guard behind us no reason to interact with me. After a panic attack like that, I couldn't handle another one so close. They seemed to get worse when they happened too close together. Arthur didn't venture far, only four doors down, before opening a double door.

This new room looked like a cross between a classroom and a small library, with lots of open space. There was a large wooden desk with a chair behind it and a smaller desk in front that was clearly meant for me. A chalkboard hung on one wall while the others were covered in bookshelves. There was a small round table with two chairs and a loveseat near a fireplace. Fireplaces seemed to be a common feature in this house, though none of them were lit.

"Please take a seat at the desk, and I will hand you some tests. They will cover a gambit of subjects. Please fill out what you know and leave those you don't. Once you are finished, I will look over them as you prepare tea for us," Arthur instructed.

"When you say serve tea, do you mean hot tea?" I asked as I took my seat at the smaller desk.

Arthur set the thick stack of papers in front of me, lifting a brow in surprise. "Surely you've at least had hot tea before."

"My father drank coffee, and so did Mom. Sometimes, Mom would make me a hot chocolate, but all of that stopped when she died," I explained.

"When did she pass?"

I bit my lip and started to pluck at my skirt. "When I was eight."

"You were under that brute's care alone since the age of eight?" Arthur snapped, making me flinch. "Good god, it's a miracle you haven't lost your wits entirely. Let's start with these tests, and I will make a list of etiquette subjects that we can go over. That will help me determine just how basic we need to start."

"Why are you teaching me all these things?" I asked, peering up at the butler.

"All Omegas are taught how to serve their pack in every way possible. Plus, you, dear girl, have no idea where you truly come from. Your family line has been built from greatness. You, the only heir, will also bring greatness to your family with the pairing of an advantageous pack and the offspring you shall have," Arthur shared, making me feel like I was some lost princess or something. "Now, no talking. This will take you as long as it takes to get through all the sheets."

He pulled a stopwatch out of his pocket and clicked it. "Begin."

CHAPTER 35

Marius

A hand ran over my back, stirring with such a gentle touch, I smiled.

"Cambrie?" I murmured as I blinked my eyes open.

The hand paused, and I found Spencer sitting on my desk, looking down at me with sad green eyes. "I'm sorry, love, it's just me."

Groaning as I sat up, my body not happy with me falling asleep in my home office, I reached out and grabbed my Beta's hand. "Don't say that, Spence. Waking up to you is something I always look forward to. Forgive me and my sleep-addled brain."

He squeezed my hand reassuringly. "It's fine, I'm not upset. I would be waking up praying this is a nightmare myself. What were you doing in here all night? I figured you wanted some space, but I didn't think you'd sleep here."

I tugged him onto my lap, which was slightly awkward since he wasn't much smaller than me, but I needed to hold him. After losing my sister as a young man, and now having Cambrie stolen out of our own home, I needed to hold my remaining loved one close. Spencer didn't say anything or push me to talk. He simply wrapped one arm around my neck and held me to his chest. I took deep breaths of his bright citrus and coconut scent that I enjoyed immensely, helping to ground me to reality.

"Alton, over the years, has gathered so much information on the Council of Four and its members. He's convinced that within all the shady deals they've made, there has to be something we can use to get them out of office," I finally shared. "While I have time off from work, I figured it would be best to put it to good use."

"You think they took her while we were at the Capitol Building?" Spencer questioned. "Why would they tell us they would collect her next week and then steal her out from under us? We were going to give her to them."

I looked up and met his gaze. "No, we weren't. There was no way any of us would allow Cambrie to be taken by those people. She is *ours*. No one else will *ever* lay a finger on her once she's home safe where she belongs." I paused and spoke the words that echoed deep in my soul. "When I find out who took her, I'm going to ruin them. Destroy whatever life they have and smash it to pieces."

Spencer leaned his forehead against mine. "Oh, my love, do not make promises like that, because you never break them and one like that might break you in the end. We are not like Yoram and his lackeys, who will crush those weaker under their boots. Everything we've ever stood for has been for people like Cambrie. That's why we are going to do this right, Marius, you hear me? All of us will work together, find the truth and bring it to light where they can't hide in the darkness anymore."

While I knew what he was saying was true, the rage that boiled inside me demanded that I take more drastic action. *How could he say we wouldn't crush them? Was he just willing to let this slide? What if we never got her back?*

"Aren't you angry?" I demanded, my tone sharper than I meant it to be.

While I was slow to anger and could take the hits as needed to a certain point, once I reached that point, my temper was something to be feared. The last time I lost complete control was after they found my sister's body and had no leads to where she'd been or how she'd died. That day, I let the anger win and sent a police officer to the hospital. Embers of that same fury were rekindling, and I feared I wouldn't be able to stop it, or worse— that I wouldn't even want to.

Spencer's hand grasped my face, and for the first time ever, I saw a look of rage that matched my own. "Am. I. Angry? What the fuck kind of question is that, Marius?" Spencer snapped, his tone icy with malice.

I stayed silent, knowing he wasn't finished.

"Do you think you're the only person who's lost others before? Who knows the pain of loving someone only to have them ripped from you? Yes, I'm *fucking* angry, and I want to rip the heart out of whoever did this, but then I wonder... what would she think? Our pure, warm-hearted Omega." His eyes shimmered with unshed tears. "Do you think she'd look at us the same if we acted just like the people who've tortured our sweet girl? No matter how much I want to burn the world down around us until they give her back, I won't. Never will I allow her to look at me with fear in her eyes. That's something I'd never recover from."

"Okay," I answered. "We will be the white knights, even if our hearts are as black as the devil's. She really is our compass, isn't she?" I murmured.

"She's more than that, Marius," Nixon said from the other side of the desk.

Pulling out of Spencer's hand, I looked over to find the rest of our pack standing before my desk.

"*She's the heart of our pack, and without her here to keep it beating, I fear we will all fall into darkness,*" Oscar signed. "*Spencer's right, though. We can't fight this fight the way they do. They know the rules and how to manipulate them. We don't. How we will win this battle is by being true to who we've always been and the men Cambrie chose to love. That way, we can look at her with pride when we say we won the battle.*"

Spencer stood, resting his hand on my shoulder as I took my pack in. These men and I had bonded over our ideals for the future, the world we wanted to create. It was the whole reason I had worked relentlessly to become an Official. The CoF used to stand for more than just themselves, it was time we rebuilt that. But first, we needed to get our Omega back, *then* work on creating a whole new world.

"We need to see Alton. He will be our best ally, and he might know why they took Cambrie. Do we have someone we trust to see if we can locate her father? I'd like to make sure that it isn't being overlooked. I also want to make sure our involvement isn't known," I asked.

Rafael nodded and pulled out his phone. "I've got a friend who's a police in the jurisdiction of the mall. If a man there recognized her, then she must have lived out that way. I still have the information her father left us and the picture. This wouldn't be the first time I've called him about a kid who came to us after being abused. He won't think anything of it." Lifting the phone to his ear, he left the room.

"That's a good start," I mused, rubbing a hand across my forehead, trying to get a clear thought to occur in the jumbled mess of options.

"Babe, you need to take a shower, change, get some food in you, then we'll come up with a plan together," Spencer urged. "Go, we'll start brainstorming."

I grasped his hand and kissed his palm. "What would I do without you, Spence?"

"For starters, be smelly and hungry. Now go. What will the neighbors think if they see you like this?" he teased, trying to lighten the mood.

I gave him a small smile, stood, then dropped a kiss on his lips. "I love you."

"I love you too, Marius," he answered, his eyes full of so many emotions.

Doing as he suggested, I left my office and headed upstairs to my room. When I looked at my bed all I could see were moments from her heat. Seeing her curled up, sleeping, hair splayed out around her like an angel. How could I sleep there, not knowing if she was safe? Did she have a bed to sleep on? Were they hurting her? What about her panic attacks?

Shaking my head, I pushed those questions aside, knowing they would only get darker if I let them go on. Stripping out of my clothes, I let them fall to the floor, uncaring that I had made a mess. My whole world was a mess right now. If I didn't have the others of my pack going through this with me, there's no question if I'd have gone mad or not. They were the only thing keeping me from charging up to Yoram and demanding he gave her back. Which was exactly what he wanted. He'd made it clear that if anything happened to her because we didn't have security, then we would personally be held responsible.

As that thought hit me, I froze. That motherfucker set us up. He knew she was already gone when he set that ultimatum. I walked right into his trap when he set the rules; Yoram let me tie the noose around my neck. If I go back Monday without her, we'll have more to worry about than losing her. We could be executed. The laws regarding Omegas were strict and ruthless in trying and stopping the black market from stealing them.

Fuck, we needed to fix this fast.

The shower was helpful and cleared my head almost as much as the threat of death. I didn't bother to put on work clothes, instead opting for jeans and a polo. When I made it down to the dining room, I found everyone seated, having grown accustomed to our new family meals. It was clear how much Cambrie loved when we were all together, so naturally, that's what we did because we loved her.

Taking my seat at the head of the table, Nixon slid the carafe of coffee over, and I poured myself a cup. I took a few gulps of the caffeinated liquid before dropping the realization I'd had. "We've been set up," I announced. All eyes turned to me, shocked.

"What do you mean? Set up by who?" Bodhi demanded, setting down the bite he was about to take.

"Do you remember what Yoram and Willem said about security and if anything happened to her?" I asked, watching understanding dawn on them.

Bodhi shot to his feet, slamming his fist to the table. "They already had her, didn't they?"

"That is my assumption, which means we have until Monday to

get her back, or else there will be no one left to rescue her," I laid out bluntly. "None of you are going to work until then. All of us will focus on this problem, or else she won't have anything to come home to. While I don't doubt her father was involved somehow, our main point of attention needs to be on Yoram and his men."

"I should call Savo. He'll be able to help us," Spencer interjected.

My instincts told me that Savo was dangerous to us in other ways, but because of that, he would do whatever it took to find her. "Do that," I agreed. "I'm going to reach out to Alton and find out when we can meet with him. However, I don't want that to stop us from running down other leads. Did you get a hold of your cop friend, Rafael?"

"He's off today, but he said he'd get in touch as soon as he runs the name. He asked me if I wanted to press charges." He paused as anger wared in his features. "I told him we absolutely wanted to press charges. When they find and arrest him, that will also give us a chance to talk to him. The idiot was happy to blather on at the shelter, so I'm sure the threat of jail will make him sing like a bird."

"Damn," Bodhi said under his breath. "Rafael, you are one scary dude when you want to be."

Rafael looked at our youngest member and tilted his head slightly. "Those who learn to have control over every aspect of their lives do so because they are hiding something underneath."

"That is equally profound and terrifying to know," Nixon commented. "I would never have guessed that you had that side to you, but I suppose we all have our secrets."

"*So, what do we do now?*" Oscar asked. "*If we know Yoram is the one behind it, and we can't get to her father today, how do we proceed?*"

"Alton," I answered. "We need to speak with him, and he will show you what he's discovered so far. Then form a plan of attack while searching for whatever properties Yoram owns that he'd keep Cambrie at. My gut tells me he didn't take her to a Care Center. That would be the first place we'd look, and if he's purposefully hiding her to fuck us, then he will do a good job of it."

"Not just Yoram," Bodhi interjected. "If I was gonna hide something, it wouldn't be someplace you'd think to ever look. It seemed like Frederick and Willem would be more than willing to offer up a place to stash an Omega. Those two are as big of a problem as Yoram himself."

"You make a really good point, Bodhi. While we know Yoram is the leader, we can't discount his loyal soldiers either," I agreed. "Everyone eat up, we're going to need all our strength and wits about us for this battle."

Marla greeted us all with hugs when we arrived, even Oscar and Bodhi who she hadn't met yet.

"Oh, ever since you came around last week, Alton's been in such a better mood," she gushed, clapping her hands. "Now you brought the whole pack. This is just so good for him. The other Officials just sent gift baskets with his favorite tea and other things to help him get well. Hmph, like they even mean that," Marla grumbled as she led us to the library where I met with Alton last time.

Bodhi leaned in and whispered to Spencer. "Is she always this chipper?"

Nixon snorted and covered it up with a cough, pounding his fist on his chest to add to the effect.

"Marla is like Jekyll and Hyde, you never know who you're going to get or when," Spencer answered. "Just stay out of her way and smile and nod."

When we entered, I found Alton sitting on the couch with Phillip, their pack's Omega, both reading the same book.

"Alton," Phillip scolded in his soft voice. "I wasn't done reading that page. You know I can't read as fast as you do. My eyes are getting worse, and you keep this room like a cave. You know there is a sun outside that will light up this room."

"I keep telling you to get them checked, but you won't," Alton chided. "There is nothing wrong with admitting you need a pair of reading glasses."

Marla cleared her throat, drawing the attention of the men. "Alton, look who's back and brought others with him this time."

"Oh, Marius," Alton greeted, a smile appearing on his face. "You brought the rest of your pack with you. What did I do to owe this honor?"

"It's actually pertaining to the topic we chatted about last time. It was so helpful to me that I thought the others should hear it," I answered, trying not to spill secrets his pack members might not know about.

"Of course, of course," Alton nodded and patted Phillip's thigh. "I'm sorry, Phil, but this is going to cover some Official business, and I know how much you don't enjoy listening to that."

"It's fine, I needed a break from that dry legalistic nonsense we were reading anyway," Phillip said, getting to his feet and holding out his arm for Marla. "Come, my love, let us go for a stroll in the sun. I've been in here so long I've forgotten what it looks like."

I had to hold back a laugh as the two walked out of the room leaving a muttering Alton behind with us. "Doesn't matter how old he gets, that Omega is a cheeky one. Never would guess he's gonna be sixty this year, would you?"

"Can't say I would," I admitted before the smile fell from my face. "Would you mind if I turned on the same music as last time? It was such a good record, and Oscar and Bodhi are both music buffs."

"By all means, let them pick what they like from the collection. I've got some rare ones," Alton offered as he stood, giving me a look of understanding.

I walked over to the record player, picked one randomly and placed it on the turntable. The room was soon filled with the old sound of traditional big band numbers. Brass horns and trombones, and many more I couldn't pick out like I knew Oscar could. It was the perfect cover as we talked in his secret room behind the bookcase. The guys seemed stunned when Alton revealed it and motioned for them to enter. Each looked at me, and with a nod, they followed. Once we were all in the small room, I slid the door shut, cutting off the sound of the music.

"Does someone want to tell me what just happened?" Spencer asked. "Are you a spy or something, covering as an Official?"

A huff of laughter from Alton had them regarding him inquiringly. "If I were really a spy, then I wouldn't be sitting at home wasting away. I would have done that snake in years ago, but looking at this room I might see how you'd think that. Ever since I realized things were crooked in the CoF, I started to find a way to bring it all down and start again." Alton's attention shifted to me. "What happened? Must have been something big to bring all of them."

"They took her, stole her right out of our house. On top of that, they made it clear that if anything happened to her, we would be held responsible," I explained.

Alton glowered. "What's the deadline he gave you?"

"Monday," I answered.

"Roll up your sleeves, boys, we have a hell of a lot of work to do," Alton announced and put us to work.

CHAPTER 36

Cambrie

The stack of papers seemed never-ending as I answered question after question. Part of me was thrilled that I knew the majority, even though there were some that I had no clue what it was asking of me. Math was never my strength, but I muddled through it, using the back of the completed sheets to work out my problems.

When it came to writing the essays, it wasn't that I couldn't do them. More so, the topic they wanted was on classic literature or something history-related that I hadn't learned yet. When it came to the morality questions or a book I had read, letting the words flow was simple. I'd always thought it would be fun to one day write a book. I'd spend so much time lost in them I wanted to provide that escape for others. The world could be falling apart but so as long as you had a book there was always a way out.

My hand was cramping when I reached the end of the page and placed the final period on the last paragraph when Arthur called time.

"That's enough," he announced. "Four hours of work, and you made it through three-quarters of the stack. Impressive."

Massaging my hand, I looked at him, confused. "You said I needed to finish them all."

"No one has ever finished them all. As you progress they get harder and harder, and you've gotten farther than many others. I'd say you would have most certainly passed your GED test. Some of this is college-level work," Arthur pointed out. "While you missed some, it wasn't enough for me to call a stop. Typically, I stop them when they can't answer more than three."

There was a knock at the door before being opened by a guard, allowing an older woman to enter with a covered tray. It was larger than the one for breakfast so I assumed it was for both of us. Without saying a word or even looking at me, she placed it on the table, removed the lid, and left. Rising from my seat, I wandered over to the table and saw a bowl of soup and a basket of bread.

"Take a seat but do not begin eating. We must first go over table manners," Arthur instructed.

I lowered myself into a chair and looked down at the thick green soup that didn't smell all that appetizing. The bread, however, looked fresh and fluffy, leaving me something to eat.

"First, we must place the napkin on our laps, fold it in half and keep the fold nearest to your body," Arthur explained, then demonstrated. "To make things simple, I've selected for us to have an easy single-course meal. Normally, there would be additional courses, such as a salad or another light side before a small main course since it's lunch. The largest meal of the day will be dinner. We will instruct you on how to navigate four, seven, and twelve-course meals like a proper lady."

Nothing he was saying made any sense. *Why would you need so many dishes or courses, whatever he called them? It seemed like such a waste of food, and how in the world would someone eat all that?*

"When eating soup, you will only use your right hand. Your left will rest in your lap unless you need to use your napkin. Meals are to be enjoyed to the fullest, which means slowly, allowing you to experience all the meal has to offer," Arthur droned on. "When it comes to actually eating your soup, one will use the soup spoon like so."

I watched as he scooped away from himself and lightly scraped it on the back of the dish to prevent it from dripping on him.

"If you feel the soup is too hot, you blow on it. There will be no slurping. It is rude and disrupts everyone's enjoyment of their meal," he warned, once more showing me exactly what he meant.

"What if I want to eat my soup with my bread?" I asked, reaching out to grab some.

Faster than I ever would have expected, a ruler snapped against the back of my hand, causing a shooting spark of pain up my arm. "Ouch," I hissed, pulling my hand back.

"A lady never reaches across the table. If you need something out of reach, you request that it be handed to you. Never are you allowed to have your body touch the table at any point. No resting arms, elbows, or allowing your chest to make contact. You will keep your back upright and shoulders relaxed," Arthur ordered.

To be confronted by this man being so demanding and cruel over a simple mistake was shocking. If I couldn't clearly tell he was a Beta, I would have guessed he was an Alpha.

"Is this what I'm to expect from here on out? Any mistake, innocent or otherwise, and I'll be punished?" I questioned. "It seems rather harsh to me."

Arthur looked down his nose at me. Here I'd thought we'd started to find a rhythm but apparently, I'd been mistaken. "Omegas should know their place," was his answer, then he cleared his throat and continued with the lesson.

What seemed an hour later, I was allowed to take my first bite of soup, but only if I did all the steps correctly. Arthur stood beside me and poked and prodded with the ruler every time I messed something up. It was so hard for me to remember not to lean forward. I was so worried I'd spill on my shirt, so I did the logical thing and moved closer to the table.

"Miss Cambrie," Arthur scolded with another tap on my elbow.

This time he hit at just the right spot for my hand to spasm, and I dropped the spoon full of green soup in my lap. Thankfully, it was on the napkin, but that didn't spare me from being disciplined.

"Right hand on the table, palm up," Arthur snapped.

Three hits in quick succession turned my hand bright red and it stung like fire. I bit my lip to keep my silence, knowing he would hit me again if I said a word or showed any hint of obstinacy. While he might not have inflicted the same type of beating my father had all my life, this was worse. He was adding to what my mother had always said about me. I was too stubborn and selfish. If I thought of others before myself, I wouldn't end up getting in trouble. The difference was, this time it wasn't my fault. Tears burned the back of my eyes but I refused to let them fall while this man was lording over his power. He wouldn't get the satisfaction of knowing he got to me. When I was alone, I could let my tears fall, but not now, in front of him.

"Again," he ordered.

Taking a deep calming breath, I picked up my spoon, kept my back straight, scooped it away from me, cleaned off the bottom of the spoon, and kept perfectly still. When the soup made it to my lips it was cold and tasted disgusting. When I finished the spoon full of lumpy, tasteless goop, I set it down in my dish. Then I grasped my water with a firm yet light hold and took a sip, hoping I could wash the taste out of my mouth.

"Seems you can be taught," Arthur commented. "Now, you will eat every drop of that soup just as you did that bite. Next time, incorporate the bread," he instructed, sitting in the chair across from me. "Don't dawdle. Otherwise we will be here until dinner time, and we have more lessons to learn today."

It had to be late in the afternoon at this point. If it had taken me four hours to do the test and we'd been eating lunch for another hour or more at a minimum, it had to be close to three or four o'clock. Taking a moment to look out the window, and sure enough, the sun was on its downward journey. Somehow, I felt like this was worse than living in the basement and taking a beating. Then I had no concept of time or how it was being stolen from me. Now, all I had to focus on was time while following this blasted schedule they had for me.

Soldiering on, I forced all the soup down, even properly tilting the bowl away from me to get the last half spoon. When I was finished, I placed it in the dish and put my right hand back on my lap, waiting for my next instruction. Arthur had been going through my tests, grading them as I completed my meal.

"I'm all done, Arthur," I whispered, doing everything I could to keep the nausea in my stomach from causing me to lose my lunch.

He looked over his glasses at me and then down at the bowl. "Seems we will be in time for dinner, after all. You will head back to your room, and a dress will be waiting for you. I will collect you in ten minutes. I expect you to be dressed and presentable for the meal."

"Will we be eating in here again?" I asked.

Arthur looked at me like I was the most trying being he'd ever encountered. "Certainly not. We will take supper in the dining room, as is proper for a lady."

My heart dropped to my stomach at this news. "Will there be anyone else there?"

"Yes, your new bodyguard. He's been busy with his own training and instruction on your care, which is why he hasn't greeted you sooner," Arthur explained as he rose from his seat, motioning for me to do the same.

Tossing the napkin in the bowl, I hurried after him out of the schoolroom and back into the hall. Arthur unlocked my door and pushed it open for me to enter.

"Just so you are aware, that door," he pointed to the single door on the right, "it leads to your bodyguard's room. He will have a key and the ability to check on you whenever he chooses. If he elects to, he could also leave the door open at night to keep a closer eye on you. He's been made aware of your aversion to physical touch but has been permitted to discipline you as he sees fit."

Before I could even utter a word, Arthur turned on his heel and left the room, slamming the door behind him. Fear gripped me as I stared at the other door my bodyguard would be staying behind. This man, who I hadn't even met, had already been given permission to do as he saw fit. My mind flashed through all the punishments my father had inflicted upon me; punches, kicks with his steel-toed boots, hits with pieces of wood he found in the basement, and then the time he broke my leg.

Earlier, I'd said this was a worse form of torture, and had hoped for the beatings and to be locked away. Now things could be so much worse. *Did they know that I'd already had a heat? That I was no longer pure? Is that what they meant when they said he could punish me as he sees fit?*

My hands started to shake, and I turned to the bed to find the dress waiting for me. The fabric was light blue and simple cut with long sleeves. Mechanically, I undressed, knowing that if I didn't do as I was told, there would be unknown consequences. If I knew what the punishment might be, I might have been willing to risk a small show of defiance. Although the speed at which my heart was beating at told me that wasn't going to happen.

Thankfully, the dress zipped from the side so I didn't have to get someone to help me. I stood in front of the full-length mirror and let my hair down; it fell in looser curls than were natural, having dried in the bun. The black flats still worked, so I left those, not seeing an alternative. It would seem that whoever picked out my wardrobe didn't want me showing any skin except from the knee down. Not that I minded, as I didn't want to draw any attention to myself. I saw a sort of classic beauty in this look. The dress hugged my chest then flared out at the waist giving me the illusion of more curves than I think I've ever had.

"Miss Cambrie, it's time to go," Arthur announced after a quick rap of his knuckles on the door.

Seemed to me that this man was trying to catch me doing something wrong so he could punish me. Thankfully, he didn't try to escort me. He just led the way down the hall at a quick pace. This time, we went much farther, even down a whole flight of stairs. It was hard to keep up as I gawked at this place. Everything was vintage, and the house was gigantic. Clearly, we were only using a small part of it.

Who in the world is the man that bought me? Is this actually that man, or has something else happened entirely? Arthur kept referring to him as my father, but I still wasn't convinced about that. I'm not sure what proof I would need but taking the butler's word for it didn't seem like enough.

Finally, we arrived at an ornate dining room with a table large enough for ten people, but only three place settings were laid out.

There was already a man seated at the table, to the left of the head chair. He was looking down, frowning at something, yet the dim light of the room made it hard to see what he looked like. Then he raised his head, and my gaze clashed with deep forest green eyes that I knew, and hope soared in my heart.

Savo.

He was who they'd hired as my bodyguard. I wanted to shout and clap with joy that I wasn't alone. All the fear that I had about the mysterious bodyguard trying to hurt me blew away on the wind of relief. *Could he get word to the others about where I was? Was he going to help me get out of here?*

When I opened my mouth to greet him, he shook his head slightly. My jaw snapped shut so fast it made my teeth click. If he wanted to keep the fact that we knew each other quiet, then I would do so. Even though our interaction was brief, I knew no matter what, I wouldn't have to fear him hurting me. Whether or not he would save me was an entirely different question.

"Miss Cambrie, allow me to introduce you to Savo Bakal. He is your bodyguard. From this point forward, he will be the one to escort you to classes and meals. As we discussed previously, he had been given the authority to punish you if you do not abide by the rules," Arthur informed me. "Now, please take your seat at the head of the table. We will be having a four-course meal tonight."

My stomach churned at the thought of having to eat more food when I'd just had the bowl of soup not fifteen minutes ago. He had said there would be more lessons, so that might help draw out the length of time as it had earlier. Arthur pulled out my chair for me, and I took my seat, then was startled as he shoved it forward. I tried not to react but a gasp escaped, snapping Savo's attention to me.

Quickly, I situated myself trying to play the whole thing off, not wanting Arthur to know I was distressed. This time the napkin was artfully folded on my plate, and I picked it up and placed it on my lap. *So far, so good. Please, god, don't let it be soup.* The same woman who brought us lunch entered the dining room with a tray and placed a small plate with three little ravioli in front of me.

I went to grab a fork but paused seeing there were multiple to pick from. When the lady returned to the kitchen, I looked at Arthur. "How do I know which one to choose?" I asked.

"You will start from the outside in. There are three forks since we are having an appetizer instead of soup," Arthur explained. "You will not eat the ravioli whole. Instead, you will cut it in half. Take the fork in your left hand then cut with the knife in your right. Once cut, place the knife down and switch the fork to your right hand. All food must be eaten with the right hand, understood?"

Nodding, I reached for my silverware only to hiss as I got slapped with the ruler across the back of my hand. Pulling it back to my chest, I looked at the butler, absolutely confused. I hadn't even leaned forward. What could I have possibly done wrong?

"When someone asks you a question, you will reply with your words," Arthur scolded. "Allow me to ask once more. Have you understood the instructions I've given you, Miss Cambrie?"

I licked my lips, trying to keep the frustration out of my voice. "Yes, Arthur, I understand."

"Good, now you may proceed," he ordered.

Savo's gaze resting on me was like a weight. I knew he wanted me to look at him, but I couldn't. With the shame that I felt burning hot in my chest, it was easier to pretend he wasn't here witnessing all this. Keeping my back straight, I grasped my silverware and cut the ravioli in half, set the knife down, and switched the fork. So far, so good. Now all I had to do was pick up the pasta and eat it.

The sweet taste of the bite had me letting out a contented little moan. It was sweet yet savory with the sauce they'd paired with it. The inside was a bright orange color, telling me it was a sweet potato or maybe a squash. Whichever it was, it was delicious and I was glad that I had to take such small bites to make it last longer.

"Miss Cambrie," Arthur snapped. "What on earth has possessed you to make such a sound at the dinner table?"

I set my fork on the plate looking at him curiously. "I don't understand what you mean?"

Savo chuckled darkly, pulling my attention to him. "The good butler is offended by the sound of you taking pleasure in your meal.

Makes me think he hasn't gotten any pleasure of his own in quite some time." While his words sounded cold, his gaze told me something quite the opposite.

"Mr. Bakal, I understand you are not required to follow the rules of etiquette in this house, but you will refrain from speaking of such vulgar things at the dinner table," Arthur remarked.

Savo raised a brow. "Yet, I'm allowed to treat her as I see fit, correct? Train her in all the ways you clearly would never be able to teach."

"That is not dinner conversation. If you wish to discuss that topic at another time, you may. Not at the dinner table," Arthur ordered.

Part of me was glad to see that the butler treated everyone with disdain, but I didn't like that he was speaking to Savo like that, in the least. The same protectiveness I typically felt for my pack rose in me, pushing me to say something. However, I knew it would only get me in trouble.

"I will keep my thoughts to myself, but only because there is a lady present and she deserves more respect than you're giving her," Savo challenged as he twirled his dinner knife in his fingers.

Spencer had mentioned Savo had been in the military, and seeing how confidently he handled that utensil, I believed him. What had me more worried was what he'd just said to Arthur. Was I mistaken, or did he just say that he had free rein to sleep with me if he wanted? Sex might be a new part of my life, but that didn't mean I was unaware of sexual innuendos.

Savo couldn't be like that, not the man that had held me in his arms and let me cry. No, the person who'd sung to me as he made sure I felt safe wouldn't act that way. The man I'd experienced was the truth, and this was an act. It had to be. My heart wouldn't be able to take it if I didn't have an ally.

Feeling it was best to move on and act as if nothing was wrong, I continued to eat, making sure to keep my noises to myself. When I was finished, the plates were cleared away and a salad was presented. I'd never been one to shy away from vegetables and it looked rather tasty but for fear of getting smacked again, I waited. Sure enough, there was another lesson. Keeping my attention on Arthur, I listened and watched as he explained the complicated nature of eating a damn salad.

No wonder all the fine ladies I saw pictures of were so thin. The effort to eat was so great I'd forgo the activity altogether. Even though the portions were smaller than most, having so much at once was a struggle. Marius's words telling me that I didn't have to finish my plate ran through my brain, but my too-full stomach told me that might not be the case here.

"Arthur," I ventured, not sure if I was allowed to speak.

"Yes, Miss Cambrie?"

"What is the etiquette if you are getting full and unsure if you can eat the remaining courses?" I questioned.

Arthur looked at me, slightly surprised. "These portions are made so they won't be overly filling. There should be no reason you can't finish what's given to you, especially with how emaciated you are. We need to get you looking more presentable before we can ever hope to match you with a pack."

"I see," I murmured and resumed the arduous task of finishing my food.

When the salad was replaced with a petite filet of salmon and a bit of seasoned rice covered in a cream sauce, I panicked. The mere smell of the food had my stomach revolting; there was no way I could finish my whole plate. I knew Arthur was droning on talking about this or that rule, but I couldn't focus on him.

Out of the corner of my eye, I noticed movement where Arthur was seated and it wasn't until I saw the shadow descending that I knew a hit was coming. Instinct born from a lifetime of abuse had me ducking, covering my head with my hands, as the dish of salmon went flying. The blow fell on my shoulder as the sound of a plate shattering echoed in the room. A hand grabbed my arm and hauled me from the chair, but I couldn't act. Everything was frozen in fear, so instead of getting to my feet like I'm sure I was supposed to, I fell to the floor. Shards of the china plate sliced into my bare knees, but I didn't care. My mind had taken me to that place deep inside where nothing hurt and no one could touch me.

CHAPTER 37

Cambrie

A roar like a lion startled me out of my daze, eyes focusing on a sight that didn't make sense. Savo had Arthur by the throat, and he was bellowing at him, spit hitting the butler's face as the words flew out of his mouth.

"You lay one more goddamn finger on her, and I will rip off your fucking hand. Do you understand me?" Savo demanded.

Arthur just gurgled, his hands scrabbling against Savo's grip as his face turned funny colors.

"Don't be rude now," Savo snarled, shaking the man. "You speak when someone asks you a question."

It seemed Savo let up just enough on his hold for the spluttering butler to speak. "Yes," he croaked out.

Savo tossed the man across the room. "Glad we've got that cleared up. Now find a first aid kit and bring it to my room."

Turning on his heel, he marched over to me but slowed when he got close and crouched down, leaving space between us. "Come here, *Keksik*, I'll keep you safe."

Instantly, I threw myself into his arms, not caring that the action drove the shards deeper into my skin. More than anything right now, I needed to feel safe and Savo was just that, my shelter in the storm.

He cradled me to his chest, rose, and then faced Arthur again. "I don't want you to step foot near Cambrie without me present. In the event that should happen, and any harm comes to her, I will consider your life as payment. All I'd need to do is inform her father you tried to kill her. It is my job to keep her safe from any and all harm, including you."

With his threat still lingering in the air, Savo left the dining room and headed up the stairs. I wrapped my arms around his neck and buried my face against his chest, breathing in his leathery scent. It was a balm to my soul, and my whole body shivered as I began to relax.

"It's going to be alright, *Keksik*. I won't let that bastard hurt you ever again," Savo whispered into my ear, then pressed a kiss to my hair. "I should have ended it sooner, but I didn't think he would go that far. Has he laid a hand on you before?"

I nodded, not feeling up to speaking. It was over, the brutal discipline would stop, and that's all that mattered. Though my fear was if Arthur couldn't harm me physically, would he shatter me mentally?

Savo kicked open the door to his bedroom and strode in, setting me down in one of the two armchairs facing the fireplace. His had a fire in it, lighting up the room and casting flickering shadows over the space, making it seem slightly spooky. I wasn't worried, however. Savo was with me, and he'd promised to keep me safe. He flipped on the light, and I was able to see the room as a whole. It was just as cold as my room but in shades of deep green and gold. Other than that, the space was almost identical except for being a replica of mine.

I watched Savo head into the bathroom and returned with towels and a bowl of water. He knelt in front of me, but because of how big he was, he still towered well over my head. Knowing what he wanted to do, I pulled back the fabric of my dress so he could see my knees. I'd done quite a bit of damage to myself.

"Just when the bruises were about gone," I sighed.

"*Keksik*, you need to be more careful," Savo murmured as he squeezed water over my shredded knees to clear away some of the blood. "You're too precious to be getting hurt."

Even though it was just water, it stung as it flowed over my skin and revealed the shards of white china that needed to be removed. There was a knock at his door, which made me flinch and curl back into the chair. Savo glared at the door but took a moment to wrap his hand around my ankle and stroke his thumb over my skin reassuringly.

"No one will step foot in this room, so breathe easy, *Keksík*," Savo vowed and got to his feet. He opened the door and stepped out, pushing whoever it had been back. "Yes?"

"Um... I brought a first aid kit?" A woman's voice quivered, sounding incredibly unsure.

"I thought I'd instructed Arthur to bring it?" Savo questioned.

"Yes, he is, ah," she stumbled. "Unavailable at the moment."

Savo grunted and took whatever the woman handed him, then shut the door behind him. Kneeling once more, he opened the white and red box filled with simple medical supplies. He pulled on gloves and ripped open a packet that held tweezers in them.

"I'm sorry, this might hurt but I will be as fast as I can," he warned, waiting for my acknowledgment before he started.

The smile I tried to give him wavered as I admitted the truth. "This will be nothing compared to what I've endured before. I'll hold as still as I can," I promised.

His eyes flashed with sadness as he grasped my calf and set my foot on his massive thigh to give me something to brace against. "Say the word, and I'll pause so you can take a break. We'll get through this together, *Keksík*."

My heart thumped loudly in my chest at his words. I'd known the harsh man at the dinner table wasn't his true self, but to see how right I was made my confidence in him soar. *Why did I feel this pull toward Savo, like I did with my other Alphas? While I cared and loved Spencer and Bodhi, there wasn't that same instinct-tugging draw I felt with the others of our pack. Savo's scent told me he was clearly a Beta, yet that didn't seem to fit his personality or actions.*

We were both silent as he worked, only the slight sound of

whimpers escaping my lips when he removed a shard that was deeper or larger than others. True to my word though, I didn't move. I held my leg steady as my nails dug into the chair's fabric. My mind drifted to when Spencer had done the same thing to my feet when I'd arrived at the shelter. His touch had been gentle, and with Nixon standing behind me, his reassuring presence bolstered me to handle the treatment. Now here I was with Savo, clinging to his scent and touch as if it was the most natural thing in the world.

"I think I've gotten it all," Savo commented as he scrutinized my knees. "I'm going to take you into the bathroom so I can really wash those cuts out in the bathtub. The last thing we need is for you to get an infection, because I have no idea if they would send for a doctor."

A huff of laughter burst out of me. He looked at me questioningly as he scooped me up into his arms. "Sorry, if only you knew how similar that sounded to my life in general, you would get how ironic it is. I was finally free, and somehow I've ended up right back where I started. Although this prison is much nicer, and it seems I will get regular meals, or maybe not after tonight's debacle."

"With me around, you will be getting your meals," Savo growled out. "Keeping you alive and safe doesn't mean just from dangers of the outside world. There is danger lurking everywhere, but that is nothing for you to worry about. I'm very good at my job."

Setting me down on the edge of his tub, he tucked a towel around my legs, ensuring I wouldn't flash anything or get too wet. He fiddled with the knobs until he got to the temperature he wanted, used a cup to pour water over my knees, then pulled out a bottle of what I assumed was soap from the first aid kit he'd brought along. It was a dark orange color and burned like fire as he did his best to be gentle but thorough. The pain dulled as he rinsed off the soap. Now, it was just a deep dull ache that I hoped sleep would drown out.

Lifting me once more, he settled me on the bathroom counter near the sink and blotted the wounds dry. "How did you learn to do all of this?" I asked. "This seems more advanced than an average person would know how to do."

"When I was in the military, they trained everyone in first aid. I made good friends with one of the medics and helped him when I could. There were always more wounded than there were able-bodied men at the end of the day," he shared. "I'm just glad I learned something useful in my time there."

I watched his expression intensely as he talked, wanting to know everything about this man. It was only because of that that I saw the flash of shame mixed with anger as he spoke. Whatever memory I'd triggered it didn't seem to be a happy one.

"I feel like that's what we all hope for," I mused.

Savo paused as he wrapped my knees in gauze to look at me. "What do you mean?"

"The hope that we've gained something from the pain and awful things we've had to experience. If not, then what was the point of having to go through it? What had we done so wrong that the world would decide to punish us like that? For me, I have to believe, hope, that there was a point to it all in the end," I said, looking down at my hand, picking at the nail that tore when I fought back.

Savo's hand covered both of mine as he gently squeezed them. "I like that way of thinking, it makes it seem less hopeless."

My smile was small, but I felt it reach my eyes as I looked into his. "True bravery is finding the hope to go on when all is hopeless, don't you think?"

A fire burned in Savo's gaze as his hand trailed up my arm and cupped my cheek. The feel of his touch made me want to melt, and I couldn't hold back from leaning into it. I'd felt so alone and despair had almost crept in, but now he was here with me. Together we could survive this until the others came for me, then I would take Savo along with us. He had promised to protect me after all, which he couldn't do if he wasn't at my side.

In an instant change of mood, Savo drew his hand back and resumed bandaging my leg. He dropped his head, and it was almost as if he was trying to put up an emotional wall between us before my very eyes.

"Did I do something wrong?" I asked, my voice squeaking with my fear.

Savo jerked his head from side to side in a no. "I'm the one who did something wrong. You have a pack. Alphas who have claimed you in every way but placing their mark on you. Forgive me. I shouldn't have been so careless with my touch."

His words slapped me in the face as I realized he was right. The men I loved, my pack, the people who rescued me from myself would have been furious with how I was acting with Savo. Yes, he was my bodyguard, and we would be together often, but that moment had crossed a line. Savo had been right to shut it down. When I got back to my pack, I wanted to be able to run into their arms with no reason for them to ever turn me away.

"There," Savo announced, rising to his feet. "All wrapped up for the night. If you're alright with it, I'll carry you to your room. You really shouldn't be walking for the rest of the night."

"Okay," I said meekly.

When he lifted me, I refrained from burying my face in his neck and sat upright. When he set me on my bed, I found a nightgown laid out for me to change into. It was simple and white with no frills or decoration, the fabric wasn't all that soft either. Nothing about it seemed appealing. Part of me wondered if it would be better to just sleep naked. Then I remembered that Savo could enter this room whenever he wanted.

"I'll leave you to change," Savo murmured as he headed back to his room and shut the door between us.

Rubbing my hands over my face, I just sat there for a moment unsure of what to do with myself. All day I'd just been following orders, doing as I was told, and where had that gotten me? Sitting alone in this room, cut up, exhausted physically and emotionally, with a man I was starting to crave but couldn't have on the other side of the door. Pulling the hair tie off my wrist, I gathered my hair up in a ponytail and out of my way.

Gingerly, I set my feet on the floor and stood grimacing at the ache from my knees. Quickly as I could, I got out of my dress and into the nightgown. I was glad to see, even if it wasn't the nicest fabric, it wasn't see-through. Savo had said I shouldn't walk much, but I needed to use the bathroom and I wasn't going to call him to carry me to the toilet. A woman had to keep some of her pride intact and I didn't have much left tonight.

I moved slowly, but once I realized the ache stayed the same and the pain wasn't all that bad, I moved at a more normal speed. Tending to my needs, I then brushed my teeth and headed back to bed. Seeing the dress still lying across the bed where I'd put it had me wondering what they wanted me to do with it. There was a closet, but it was empty when I had last looked. Curiosity had me checking behind the door again to see if that had changed. Peering in, I found it had indeed been filled with a few changes of clothes. There was also a hamper with the outfit I'd worn earlier, which is where I placed the dress.

Feeling better that I had clothes and didn't need to wait for the mysterious person who supplied them, I pulled back the covers. When I looked down, I screamed, stumbling back and falling on my butt. Savo burst from his room, gun drawn, scanning the space before he strode over to me.

"Cambrie, what's wrong?" he demanded, crouching beside me.

I pointed to the bed with a shaky hand. "There's a snake under the blankets."

Savo frowned and moved to the bed where he slowly pulled back the sheets. I heard him swear under his breath then he returned to my side. Without warning, he hauled me into his arms and headed for his room.

"You're going to stay in here until I get that thing out of there. It's a good you saw it because it's incredibly poisonous. One bite and you would have been dead before I heard you scream," Savo informed me.

I stared up at him wide-eyed. "How did it get in my bed?"

"My guess would be someone put it there," he answered. "Someone, it seems, who doesn't like you being here."

When he turned to leave, I grabbed his hand, causing him to look back at me. "Please be careful," I implored.

His eyes softened as he looked at me. "I'll be just fine, *Keksik*. You just curl up under the covers and rest, okay?"

I nodded but wasn't sure that would be possible until I knew the snake was dead and gone. When he closed the door behind him, I got off the bed and pulled back the sheets all the way to the end of the bed. Seeing there was nothing under the blankets, I then pulled back the sheet leaving the comforter off and checking the next layer. No sign of snakes or any other kind of trap, so I placed the comforter back over the bed. I eyed the pillows, wondering if there might be anything hiding under them. It would be more dangerous to snatch those off the bed, but maybe I could find something else to move them.

Glancing around the room, I spotted a fire poker that looked like it had never been used. Taking it in hand, I batted away the first decorative pillow. One by one, I cleared them all, and just to be sure I slammed the fire poker across them. When nothing slithered out or made a sound, I felt they were safe enough to be put back on the bed. Just as I placed the last one in its spot, Savo returned, pausing to stare at me questioningly.

"I had to make sure the bed was safe," I explained.

By the twitch of his lips, I could tell he was trying not to smile. "And is it?"

"Yes, as a matter of fact, it is," I quipped, feeling slightly embarrassed about the whole thing.

"Good. Does that mean you'll get in and lie down now?"

I looked at the bed then at him. "Only if you let me stay here tonight. I don't think I could go back and sleep in that bed, knowing I almost died."

Savo tilted his head and rubbed a hand along his beard-covered jaw like he was considering my proposal. "You drive a hard bargain, *Keksik,* but I accept your terms."

Even though I still felt panicked about the whole thing, I smiled at him. "Let me guess, you were going to tell me I had to sleep in here tonight regardless."

The smile he gave me was bright and full of teeth. "Seems you caught me, now into bed with you. Unless you need me to check under it to make sure they didn't hide something while I wasn't in the room."

My eyes went wide and I gulped, stepping back before I realized what he was doing. Whipping my head around, I glared at him. "That's not funny, Savo."

"I'm sorry, you're right. It wasn't nice of me to tease you when you have every right to be upset about this," he apologized and moved forward to pull back the covers. "Come, *Keksík*, I'll make sure you don't have any bad dreams and fight off any monsters that might try to harm you as you sleep."

Blowing out a breath, I climbed into bed and kept to the middle so if there was something under the bed, it couldn't grab me. Savo pulled the blankets up and tucked me in so I was in a tight little cocoon of warmth. He brushed the hair out of my face and let his fingers glide through the rest of the length.

"I didn't get a chance to tell you before, but I like the new color," he shared, picking up a lock and running his thumb over it. "Makes you stand out from the rest of the world, because a beautiful soul like yours should be seen."

Biting my lip, I curled my hands under my chin as my cheeks heated with embarrassment. "Thank you," I whispered.

"Do you want me to leave the lights on or turn them off?" he asked, letting my hair fall through his fingers as he pulled away.

I looked around the room, seeing the fire was still going strong. "You can turn the lights off," I answered.

He nodded and did just that before heading into the bathroom.

CHAPTER 38

Cambrie

L ying there, I stared into the fire and thought about the time my mom took me to a fall festival. We got to ride the rides, eat yummy food, and at the end of the night, there was a place you could roast marshmallows. I wanted to do it so badly after seeing the other kids enjoying the dessert so much. She shook her head and told me no, we had to get back home.

It was unusual for us to be gone all day like that. Normally Mom made sure we were home so she could make Father dinner. I didn't question it at that point; I was far too excited and having so much fun that I didn't want it to end. Then I asked her on the way home while we were riding the bus why Father hadn't come with us. Mom didn't drive, so it was super rare for us to go and do anything since Father had the car.

"Of course, he couldn't come with us. He had to work," Mom answered. "Didn't you have a good time with it just being the two of us?"

"Of course, Mom, but it would have been fun to have Father join us. He never looks like he has fun doing anything, always working or yelling at you for silly things," I reasoned.

Mom gave me a scolding look. "He doesn't yell at me, he's teaching me to be a better wife. One day you, too, will learn the hard lessons of *what it means to be a woman in this world. If you think your father is harsh, then I fear how you will view the rest of the men out there."*

"You are a wonderful wife and mom," I said, wanting to defend her. "You do everything for Father. All he does is work."

She ran a hand over my head trying to calm my curls. "My dear sweet, Cambrie, always coming to my defense. I wasn't always a good wife. You see, there was another man before your father who was far more cruel and demanding. This is why I teach you what I now know so you can be a good wife and a sweet girl. If you already know and practice what's expected of you, then it will make your husband happy. When they are happy, they don't yell or have a reason to discipline you."

Had she been talking about this mysterious man who claimed to be my real father? Could my mother have run away from him and gotten together with the person I believed to be my father? Flashes of memories came faster as I remembered all the *lessons* she had tried to teach me. Don't put your elbows on the table, keep your back straight, don't run places—that's not very ladylike. Could it be that she went through training like this? Had she lived in this house? Why did the idea of that make me sick to my stomach?

Needing to dwell on something else, I rolled over away from the fire. This had me facing the bathroom door, which wasn't shut all the way, leaving a gap. The light from inside the bathroom streamed out, a stark difference from the warm darkness of the rest of the bedroom. Savo stepped up to the sink to brush his teeth. He wasn't wearing a shirt and his sleep pants hung low on his waist. I watched his muscles ripple as he moved, doing such a simple mundane task, but it still had my body heating up.

The second my perfume flooded into the air, I rubbed my legs together restlessly. Slick oozed out of me, seeping into my nightgown and making it cling to my skin. My heat might be over, but the need of an Omega wasn't something that just stopped altogether. By nature, Omegas tended to be more hypersexual. It was our job to provide offspring and to do that, you needed to have sex. Stifling a moan, I hid my face in a pillow unable to watch Savo and control myself.

There's no way he won't notice that I'm perfuming right now. Oh god, and after he told me he needed to distance himself from me. What kind of horrible person am I? My body is craving him just as badly as I do my pack. Omegas were meant to find their pack, become bonded, and live happily ever after. Or that's how it always went in my version.

The sound of the bathroom door opening had me squirming under the covers and tugging them up over my head. Hopefully, if I ignored what was happening, then he would do the same. It was wrong of me to feel emotionally or physically attracted to him —right?

"*Keksík,* why are you..." Savo started to say until I heard a deep intake of breath.

Then a low rumbling purr started that had my head shooting up to look at him wide-eyed. There he stood next to the bed, his upper body still on display, only now I got to see his powerful chest. He had tattoos running down his left arm, full of shapes and symbols I didn't recognize. His skin glowed bronze in the firelight, making my mouth dry and my pussy weep with slick.

"Are you perfuming for me right now, little Omega?" Savo asked, his purr adding to the sultriness of his voice.

Unable to speak since my tongue was stuck to the roof of my mouth, I nodded.

His green eyes flashed with something primal, possessive, and slightly dangerous. Slowly, he crawled onto the bed as if he was waiting for me to tell him to stop, but that was the last thing I wanted to do. He stopped right before me, reaching out to brush down my cheek making me sigh in relief at being touched.

"Better men might be able to turn away and do the right thing, but that isn't a term I've ever used for myself," Savo said as he pulled back the blankets. "Tell me now, Cambrie, tell me to stop."

His hand started at my ankle and trailed all the way up over my nightgown until he reached my hip. I gasped and arched backwards and rolled onto my back so his hand could touch more of my body. The heat I could feel from where his hand sat on my stomach was so hot it felt like it could sear through the fabric.

That was all that separated him from my skin since I hadn't put on panties.

I met his gaze and saw he was at war with himself. If we crossed this line, I knew there was no going back, no keeping my distance from him. I would crave him like a drug, and he knew it. "Is this what you want?" he asked, his voice barely above a whisper. "I won't do anything that will harm you, Cambrie, even if it means protecting you from myself. So many people have stolen choices from you. I can't let myself be one of them."

This man was going to break me if he walked away again. It was clear to me now that he'd already stolen a part of me when he held me in my room as I cried. Something deep in my soul told me he was mine, and I was meant to be his, but I wouldn't betray my pack. I couldn't let myself be swept away without being honest with them first. Yet knowing all of that, I knew tonight I would need his help. This wouldn't go away unless I got a release.

"I need you, Savo," I answered in a breathy tone. "But we can't have sex."

Savo nodded. "You have a pack, but I'm the only one who can help you right now. I understand."

"No, you don't," I blurted, his words feeling like a slap in the face.

I reached up, grabbing as high up on his arm as I could, and pulled myself into a sitting position. This gave me a better vantage point to pull him down so my forehead was pressed to his. "When I said I needed you, I don't mean in this moment or just for now while we are trapped here. No, Savo." I looked into his eyes so he would know I was telling the truth. "I. Need. You."

His lips slammed against mine, sending us both crashing back onto the mattress. He cupped my face as he worshiped me with his kisses.

This was right.

He was mine, and now I just needed to escape and have my pack accept Savo as one of us.

My gentle giant did his best to ensure he didn't put too much weight on me as he straddled my body. One hand left my face and reached down to my hip yanking my nightgown up. I wriggled, trying to help him remove the rough fabric from my hot and needy body. With the amount of slick happening right now, it made it that much harder to accomplish. A growl seeped from his lips as he pulled back, took the gown in his hands, and ripped it apart. I gasped as the sudden whoosh of cool air licked my body, but the second he was back over me, I was warm and safe.

"I want to taste you, *Keksík*," Savo said, running his nose along mine. "To see if your scent matches your flavor."

My body shivered with excitement at his words, and I nodded. "Please," I breathed like a prayer.

Then there was that sound again, a low rumbling purr that shouldn't be coming from him. The thought was soon lost as I felt his lips caress down my neck, along my collarbone, to the top of one of my breasts. Insecurity had me wanting to cover them, knowing most men like breasts that were fuller than my tiny curves.

The second I started to move my hand, Savo's eyes snapped to mine. "Don't you dare hide yourself from me, *Keksík*. This body of yours has seen hardship, starvation, abuse, and from the looks of it," he paused to trace one of the hickies the guys had left on my breast, "adoration, which is what I fully intend to do here tonight. I will worship this vessel that has kept you alive so that I might one day find you."

His words had me melting into the bed as he traced one finger around my nipple and then moved it across my chest to do the same thing. My breath started to quicken as he wound ever so close to my now pert peaks begging to be touched. He leaned lower so his mouth hovered over one and blew gently, making me gasp and arch at the sensation. How something that didn't have a tangible form felt so amazing had me reeling. Then, with a simple flick of his tongue, he had me moaning, grabbing the back of his neck and trying to force him closer. I needed him to touch me, or I was going to lose my mind.

"Savo," I whined, my fingers on his skin digging in as I willed him to give in.

And he did, as his lips finally wrapped around my nipple and his tongue lapped at it like ice cream. I groaned as I felt an orgasm building; he'd denied me touch for so long that my body was hypersensitive. Every sensation was amplified, and I didn't know how much longer I would last. When he used his other hand to flick in time with his tongue, I shattered. My whole body tensed as I cried out his name.

His lips moved from my breast to my mouth, stealing the breath from my lungs as he swooped his tongue inside teasing my own tongue. Still new to kissing this way, I went with what felt natural, and it seemed to please him as he ground his cock against my thigh. It would seem all his anatomy was in proportion to his body size because what I felt was massive. When it came to that, would he fit?

My worries were swept away as his hand moved lower and lower until it dipped between my legs. Letting them fall open, I welcomed his touch, rolling my hips to encourage him to the right spot. He didn't need my help, though, he found what he was looking for instantly.

"Oh, *Keksík,* look how wet you are for me," Savo whispered in my ear, his beard a contrasting roughness as he nuzzled my neck. "Do you know the torture you put me through when I caught the scent of your heat and had to leave? All I've thought about was you under me, just as you are now, begging for my touch. Then to see you shatter as you come, like watching fireworks explode in the night sky."

He let just the tip of his finger slide into my entrance then pulled it back out. "Savo, please, don't be cruel," I keened.

"No, my sweet one, I will never be cruel to you," he answered as he kissed down my body, coming to lie on his stomach, his face between my legs. "When I'm done with you, *Keksík,* you'll think you're in heaven."

Before I could ask what that meant, his tongue lapped at my pussy. Starting low and licking all the way up to the clit, letting the tip swirl around before his mouth latched on, sucking sharply. Having just climaxed, I was sensitive enough that this sent me right over the cliff crashing into another. This one was so strong I couldn't even make a sound as my body twitched, trying to pull away from the overwhelming sensation.

The grip he had on my hips was powerful. No matter what, I couldn't budge from his hold. He didn't quit as I fell apart. No, Savo was busy working up the next explosion that would happen inside me. His tongue glided in and out of me as if he was fucking me while a finger was playing with my asshole. That finger massaged and pressed, coating the back entrance with my slick. Just as he did with my pussy, he put the first section of his finger inside. When he heard my moan, I felt him smile against my pussy.

He liked that I enjoyed having my ass played with. Was that not a common thing?

As if he knew my mind had wandered, that same finger slipped in deeper the second time he thrust it in. "Yes, more, please," I begged. "It all feels so good."

My body started to shift in its need, craving the fullness of a knot, but I'd already made the rule of no sex, and I wouldn't change it. Savo seemed to know what my body needed before I did, as he added a second finger to my ass and switched to just using his tongue on my clit. Removing any sensation from the inside of my pussy had my want for a knot to fill it lessen. His fingers moved in a steady rhythm, pushing me closer to the point where I would burst from pleasure. When it finally happened, he used his teeth to scrape my clit ever so slightly as he thrust into my ass at the same time. The scream that erupted out of me echoed off the walls of the room, and I didn't care in that moment if someone might have been able to hear me.

A sheen of sweat covered my body as I lay there limp, unable to even consider moving. Savo lifted his face from my pussy, his beard glistening with my slick, and looking utterly satisfied. "I was right, you taste just like a snickerdoodle."

Laughter burst out of me at his words. I reached for him, pulling him to me so I could kiss him. It was easy to taste myself on him, but it didn't bother me because this man was worth every second of it.

"That was incredible," I murmured, peppering kisses all over his face.

"Helps when you are delectable to eat," he teased, nibbling on my neck. "Have they taken you in the ass already?" Blushing, I bit my lip and nodded once. "I thought so from the way you responded to my touch and enjoyed it so eagerly."

"Is that odd?" I asked, feeling slightly awkward for even broaching the question.

Savo shook his head and lay on his side next to me, tugging me close enough that I could feel his hard length on my thigh. "No, not odd, Omegas are built to find pleasure in all areas of their bodies, but few ever explore it."

That had me giving him a questioning glance. "You make it sound like you've been with an Omega before."

He traced a finger along my jaw then tapped it against my nose. "No need to be jealous, *Keksik*. Not all cities and countries are like this one. Some don't put the same value on having Omegas bonded and in a pack. Where I was raised, Omegas are in a breeding house and can be enjoyed by whoever pays for the experience."

My eyes widened in horror. "That's awful," I gasped.

"We are always at war, they need soldiers, and the only way to ensure more will fill the places of those killed is to have more children," he explained. "It's one reason I'm so thankful to have left that all behind. I have no family left to fight for, and I refuse to die for a country that hates itself."

"If you don't mind me asking, who are they fighting?" I questioned.

Savo pressed a kiss to my head and breathed deeply. "Truthfully, I don't think they even know anymore. At some point, there were two people of power who split the country in two equally. Then as time went on, each ruler after them got greedy and wanted to take more land from the other or overthrow them entirely. Since then, there has been no peace, always one side fighting to take back what's theirs. The thing is, I'm not sure anyone knows where the original division was, and they just fight because they don't know how to stop. One of them would have to give up or surrender, and no one is willing to do that. If they did… they wouldn't live long."

"I'm so sorry that's the life you grew up in, but it led you to me, so there is good in this yet," I offered, turning to snuggle into his chest.

While we lay there in the flickering light of the fire, my hand wandered across his muscles, venturing lower and lower. I reached the waistband and tried to slip my hand past it, but he stopped me.

"That is not necessary, *Keksík*," he said as he intertwined our fingers. "I got all the pleasure I needed hearing you scream my name to the heavens above."

"I can feel how hard you are still," I commented, rubbing my body against it to prove my point. "It has to be uncomfortable to leave it like that."

He pushed me onto my back, looming his body over mine as he answered. "If I allow you to do that for me, I won't be able to hold back. Every atom of my being wants to bury my cock deep inside you and claim you as mine. You told me no sex, I will honor and respect that, but you need to respect the boundaries I have as well."

Shame flooded me at his words. He was right to scold me. I'd put my own rules in place and hadn't even bothered to ask him if he had any for me. "I understand," I whispered, dropping my gaze.

These were the moments Mom would tell me I was being selfish, only worried about my needs and not the needs of those around me.

Savo's fingers gripped my chin and pulled me back to look at him. "Now it is you that doesn't understand. I want you so badly, Cambrie, that the slightest touch of your hand would make me lose all reason. If that were to happen, then I know I would break my promise to never hurt you, because having to tell your pack that we went all the way before talking to them would devastate you. As I said before, I will not be one of those people who takes away your choice. Ever."

Tears welled up as I kissed him, clinging to his neck and holding him as tightly as I could to ensure he would never leave me.

CHAPTER 39

Rafael

We spent the day at Alton's and even slept over, not willing to go back to the house without Cambrie there. The information that Alton had on the CoF as a whole was slightly disturbing, but I didn't give a shit. We needed to get our girl back, and it needed to happen fast. Our priority was trying to find a location where he would keep her that was out of the way but still close enough to keep an eye on.

Since all the men we were looking into were government employees, all their information was cataloged and filed. They needed to declare what property they owned to ensure that bribes weren't happening. Clearly, that wasn't working, since we knew for a fact that Yoram and the others were getting money into their pockets somehow. However they did it, though, was hidden well because there wasn't a goddamn trace of it to be found.

"We need access to different records we can't get as citizens," Nixon grumbled. "If only we could get into the Capitol Building without raising suspicion, but they've made it so that's impossible. Spence, have you heard anything from Savo? He's the hacking wizard, right?"

Spencer looked up from the documents he was reading over and frowned. "He hasn't answered, and his phone goes straight to voice-mail. I don't really want to leave a message or text him in case someone else might read it."

"Fuck, this is getting us nowhere," Nixon swore, kicking a trashcan across the room. "Alton's been looking for loopholes for years. How in the hell did we think it would be different just because we read over the same damn things?"

Most of us had gotten hardly any sleep last night, which made for short tempers. All the coffee in the world couldn't replace what we actually needed.

"Wait, I think I got something," Bodhi called, waving us over. "It's not in his name, but a female in his pack owns this property outside the city closer to the countryside. Actually, if you really look at his pack, they only have Beta members and their one Omega that died in childbirth nineteen years ago. Oh, she's the one who had the house. Seems her family was well off and died at an early age, leaving everything to their daughter, who was bonded to Yoram."

Peering over Bodhi's shoulder, I took note of the Omega's name and frowned. "Isabelle Neenan, I read that name somewhere."

I walked back to the newspapers I'd been looking through that had articles about each of the CoF Officials. Flipping through them, I found the announcement of her parents' death. Skimming over the piece, I found what I was looking for.

"So, her parents were from old money. Her grandfather was one of the creators of the fertility drug they used to help pregnancy rates. This was before they twisted it to create more Omegas. This says that after the terrorist attack, the family retreated to the coun-tryside, where they lived out their lives, raised their children, and died in their sleep," I read aloud. "Isabelle's family raised her out there, choosing to keep out of the city life. That's also where they passed away, refusing to seek treatment at hospitals for fear they would kill them for who his parents were. Autopsy shows it was a natural death for them both, yet this reporter challenges that outcome. He reasoned that it would be impossible for them both to die from an illness that destroyed their lungs, drowning them in their sleep at the same time. He called foul play but his words, I'm sure, fell on deaf ears."

"Wait, did you say they died from their lungs being damaged?" Marius asked with a furrowed brow. "Let me see if I can find more information on them. What were their names?"

"Carson and Elise Neenan," I answered, handing the article over to Marius, who sat in front of the laptop Alton had for us to use. "If the property went to the daughter, then it was transferred to Yoram when she passed."

"Do we think it's weird that she died just a few months after her parents did? I know pregnancy is dangerous and all that, but the timing just seems odd, don't you think?" Bodhi asked, leaning back in his chair and folding his arms. "You'd think a man like Yoram would do anything to prove his pack could produce viable offspring. That's more impressive to anyone than how much money or power you have."

The sound of keys clicking as Marius typed filled the silence. "Okay, I found a few articles that agree with that reporter. They said Isabelle's parents bought and moved to that house because they were harassed by the Equality for Betas group before becoming known as the terrorists, EQ. They found the use of drugs to alter women's reproductive system repulsive and an abomination. To them, the fact that children were not being born was more about their sinful nature proving they shouldn't extend their genes than an actual physical issue."

He scanned the article, mumbling to himself until he reached another part to share. "The family as a whole became reclusive after the attack. Hardly ever being seen in society. That changed once Isabelle was bonded to Yoram since he was a big-name government Official. Isabelle was much younger than Yoram, but I'm sure he chose her because of the money, connections, and vitality to bear children, not because he liked her."

Oscar made a grunt before he signed. "*Does he actually have a heart to* like, *let alone love someone?*"

I had to agree with Oscar on that. I'm not sure he could ever care for someone other than himself.

"One reporter notes that Isabelle's parents became reclusive again when the changes to the Omega Preservation Project came into effect, no longer allowing Omegas to choose, but be placed with a pack instead," Marius noted. "Interesting how that changed after Yoram got the Omega he wanted and could ensure that bribes would come flooding in. It wasn't until there was an announcement that Isabelle was pregnant that anyone noted her parents started to fall ill," Marius paused as if something caught him off guard. "That's odd... these symptoms. Oddly enough, they match exactly what Alton is dealing with right now. Every doctor he goes to see just tells him he's getting old."

Bodhi shot to his feet and pointed at the screen. "See, what did I tell you? The bastard probably poisoned them so he could get their money, the house, and whatever else might've been handed down to their daughter." All of us looked at him, confused at his level of excitement. He rolled his eyes and carried on. "Yoram isn't the affluent man people think he is because he covers that shit up so well. Sure, he went to a fancy college, but if you read anything about him, he never once talks about what it was like growing up. To me, that screams cover-up. It's what I'd do."

Feeling the need to move as I filtered through all the information we'd just uncovered, I paced the length of the small room. What Bodhi said was true. People who grew up with a past they were ashamed of never wanted people to know about it. Instead, they'd rather distract you with the things they want you to remember about them. The elite college they went to, the job they hold, a new house they bought, anything for you to stop inquiring about a time in their life they wished never existed.

Everything Yoram had done was about gaining power and prestige. So, what would Isabelle's family have given him? Money—yes, but not the latter. They were reclusive, living in their country home away from prying eyes, always being blamed for the attack. What people couldn't understand was that they didn't originally set out to create the drug that was used to increase the chances of an Omega being born. They wanted to help fertility as a whole...

Could that be it? Could it truly be that simple?

"Guys, what if we're making this too complex," I said, turning back to them. "Bodhi already said it. What gives you more power than just having money?"

"*Omegas*," Oscar answered. "*Her parents probably had access to the drugs, and Yoram would have no qualms about using them to ensure his Omega had an Omega child. Later, we learned that while the basic fertility drug helped, once they started trying to do anything more than that, it put both mother and child in danger.*"

"Oh fuck," Nixon swore, dropping his head in his hands. "You don't think he could be using them on Cambrie, do you? Trying to make sure that if you guys got her pregnant during her heat, it would result in an Omega for him to use, do you?"

While that might be a valid concern, I felt like Yoram didn't have time to play that long of a game. "If you take that logic and apply it to the past... what if the baby hadn't been lost at childbirth but stolen," I mused. "That man, Daryl Minks, claimed that Cambrie wasn't his. Although, he never said if her mother was pregnant when he met the woman or if Cambrie was already born. What if she stole Cambrie?"

Just the idea of that made my heart break for my Little One. All her life, people came and went, but she always had the reassurance that her mother was the only one who loved her. If what I guessed might be true, then even that was a lie. Oh, I'm sure the woman loved little Cambrie and did the best she could to care for her adopted daughter. Now, it just had me questioning who this woman could really be.

"Do any of you know what her mother's name was?" I asked.

Everyone shook their heads, appearing even more defeated than when our Omega was taken from us. Everyone, that is but Marius, who looked utterly distracted by something that had him shoving out of his chair and racing out of the room. Having no clue what might have caused this, we all followed him to the kitchen.

"Where is it? Damnit, it needs to be here," Marius muttered to himself. "*Marla,*" he bellowed for the woman in a fashion that was incredibly out of character.

"Goodness, whatever is the problem?" Marla asked, her eyes

wide as she took in the madman pawing through her kitchen cabinets.

Marius whirled on his feet, charged over to the woman, and rested his hand on her shoulders gently but full of urgency. "The Get Well baskets that come all the time, you said there was a tea in it that Alton drinks every day. Where is it?"

"Oh, well, they come on Sundays and have just about enough to make it through the week. I just made him the last of it..." Marla trailed off as Marius ran past her. "For heaven's sake, someone better tell me what is happening right now!"

Spencer placed a comforting arm around the woman's shoulders. "I wish I could tell you, but he charged out of the study without telling us a thing. Where is Alton right now?"

"Damnit, son, what's gotten into you?" Alton's hollering voice echoed down the hall.

That had us charging off, finding the man in question standing in the sunroom with a shattered cup on the floor. Alton's eye flashed with anger as he glowered at Marius. "You better explain yourself, or I'm going to have you arrested for assault, young man. To think, I invited you into my home and extended my hospitality to have you turn on me like this."

Marius's breathing was heavy, like he'd run a marathon instead of just down the hall. "I'm not attacking you. I'm saving your life, you idiot."

My brows shot up at this claim, making me look over at Nixon, who just shrugged.

"Marius, what are you talking about?" Marla asked as she stood next to her Alpha.

"Please tell me Eric is home and that you haven't tossed out the tea leaves," Marius cut in, ignoring all their questions.

Alton stomped a foot in frustration as his face started to turn purple with rage. "What in the blasted hell is going on, Marius? Spit it out right now or so help me god," the Alpha barked, making Marla flinch at the command.

"They've been slowly poisoning you for years, Alton," Marius burst out. "Fuck, they could be doing it to me, too, for all I know. Marla, I know you don't have a reason to listen to me but please get the remains of the tea and call Eric." She looked at Alton, but when he didn't argue, she left the room to do as Marius requested.

"Are you going to tell me what's going on now that she's gone?" Alton demanded before he lapsed into a coughing fit. Marius helped the man back into his chair and handed him a glass of water, but Alton waved it off. "Only thing that helps with this damn cough of mine is that tea. It gives me some relief."

"Be that as it may, it's also the same thing that's killing you," Marius explained. "He did the same thing to Isabelle's parents."

"That poor thing, she never should have picked Yoram, no matter what he offered her. If the child hadn't killed her, I'm sure he would have eventually," Alton said, shaking his head. "Such a sweetheart, one of the gentlest spirits I'd ever seen. Pity, both of them were lost. The bastard didn't even have a funeral for them. Put them both in the same casket to bury them."

Marius looked at us questioningly yet if Alton could shed some light on the situation from personal experience, it would be more helpful. The others must have agreed with me since he turned back to Alton and laid it all on the table.

"What if the baby didn't die? What if she was smuggled out of the house, away from Yoram? Then was raised by another couple until she turned eighteen and ran away, stumbling right into the last place she should have been to keep herself safe," Marius explained, keeping things hypothetical, even though it was clear what he was suggesting. "If it were even remotely possible something like that might have happened... What would Yoram do if he found her again?"

Understanding lit up Alton's expression. "There was nothing Yoram wanted more than a child who was an Omega. I used to have to listen to him go on and on about the possibilities it would open up for him. Just think what a disaster it would be if that ever happened and he mated her off to some powerful pack in another country. Even worse, if the poor thing was mated to a pack in our own city that added to his control over the government. It's a lucky thing that little girl never had to grow up being turned into the epitome of a subservient Omega like her mother."

Just when I didn't think that Cambrie's life could get worse, it did. Each time Cambrie talked about her mother or situations of her childhood, she always mentioned how she was corrected in her behavior. Being too selfish, not doing as she was told, stubbornness was bad, and to be exactly what your husband wanted. Could this person have been part of Yoram's pack as well or staff in their home?

"Has Yoram ever been able to love again after losing his Omega? I can only imagine what a blow that must be to his pack," I ventured, hoping he would catch on to what I was asking.

"Before Yoram even met Isabelle, he had three other Beta's in his pack. Two lovely ladies who didn't interact with others much and a gentleman who seemed to be in charge of running the house. What was his name?" Alton muttered as he scratched his chin. "I've only met them twice, at Isabelle's baby shower and then again at the funeral. Although, come to think of it, one of the ladies wasn't well enough to attend, so stricken with grief. Ah yes, the chap's name was Arthur, a real stickler for the rules and roles of each designation."

The conversation was halted as Eric and Marla returned to the room. In her hands, she held a small plate with what looked like a tea strainer on it. "I brought what you asked for, but I don't understand what this has to do with Eric," Marla grumbled.

I'd heard Marius talk about the fact that as the years went on, this pack had become divided in their ideology. Where they'd once seen eye to eye, now it was only arguments and pointing the finger at each other. Eric was the other Alpha of the pack, and he had a bonded Beta whose name I couldn't remember but the only thing keeping those two men from moving out was Phillip, their Omega.

"Yes, I would also like to know why I was pulled out of my office so abruptly and without explanation. I have patients to see," Eric sneered.

Marius turned to the man. "Correct me if I'm wrong, but you

were once one of the top biochemists in our country and shifted to working with holistic medicine instead?"

Eric inclined his head. "That's correct, but it still doesn't tell me why I'm here?"

"I know you and Alton have your differences and have drifted apart over the years, but I hope when I tell you he's being poisoned, that might mean something to you," Marius said, not buckling under this man's brusque manner.

"What?" Eric snapped. "Who's trying to poison the stubborn bastard? If anyone was gonna kill him after all these years, it would have been me."

Marius grabbed the plate and handed it to Eric. "There is something in here that is toxic, causes the lungs to break down, fill with fluid. I also believe they've laced it with something to help with his cough, so he continues to drink it regularly letting the poison, toxin, whatever you want to call it, seep further into his bloodstream."

"This is the stuff the CoF keeps sending him, isn't it? Why would they want to knock him off when he's one of them?" Eric pressed, clearly not understanding that Alton was far from being considered one of them.

"Is that what you've believed all these years? If there is one person who is actually fighting for the betterment of our people, it's Alton. Yoram has everyone else in his pocket, but no matter what he's tried, the only option for getting your packmate removed from his position is to kill him. It was thanks to his efforts that I was able to beat out the person Yoram hand-picked to take that seat," Marius stated, his anger at Eric's assumption clear. "Do you even know him at all? For you to believe he would willingly let these men ruin our country without trying to do all he could to stop it, means you haven't been paying attention."

The clenched jaw on the Alpha told me he hadn't been talked to like that in a long time. If there was one person I wouldn't want to tear me a new asshole in the politest way possible, it was Marius. Bonds of a pack were one of the most sacred things to our fearless political leader, and this man was proving he didn't feel the same way. Eric looked down at the plate, then over at Alton as if he was seeing the man for the first time in years. With a grunt, he turned on his heel and started out of the room.

"Stay alive long enough for me to save your sorry ass, Alt," Eric called over his shoulder before he was gone.

Alton blinked at us for a moment before a broad smile appeared on his face. "The bastard hasn't called me that in at least ten years. Maybe the grouch still has a heart after all."

CHAPTER 40

Savo

Holding Cambrie in my arms all night was pure torture. I thought for sure I wouldn't be able to fall asleep, feeling the need to protect her from any harm that might arise. My mind churned with the questions I had about this place, why she was brought here, and what the fuck that bastard who claimed to be her father wanted. There clearly was an endgame to this, but I couldn't even begin to guess what it was with how little information I had.

Then there was the whole issue with Arthur and whoever put the motherfucking snake in Cambrie's bed. Whoever put it there meant for her to die. There was no other reason to interact with a snake whose venom could kill you in seconds. I was able to chop off its head once I got it out of the bed, holding its head with my foot and using my knife to finish the deed. Thankfully, the carpet was a dark color so you couldn't see the blood stain, but I didn't give a fuck. If that pretentious fuck wants to have a beef with me over it, I'll tell him to shove it up next to the stick in his ass. I was doing my job, end of story.

Glancing at the clock, I groaned knowing it was probably time for us to get up. In my training, I'd been informed that breakfast would be promptly at seven, lunch at noon, and dinner at six. If I missed any of those times, I wouldn't be eating. My schedule was her schedule since I'd been instructed to be attached to her side. This oh-so-treasured long lost daughter of his was in danger of being stolen again—yeah, by her goddamn pack. *Fuck, what was I going to do about that*?

Cambrie had been right to tell me we couldn't have sex, no matter how badly I wanted to. God, she smelled so good, and her taste was simply addictive. If I got to spend the rest of my life eating her out, I'd be just fine with that. Her moans and the way she shattered before my eyes as she came were simply magical. This woman had no idea how alluring and sexy she was, with her shy glances and sweet smiles.

No. I had to stop thinking like this, or I was going to have a painful boner trapped in my pants the whole day. While I would happily suffer, it was distracting, and I couldn't afford that right now. Danger was high, especially since I didn't know where it was coming from. Yoram was a powerful man, and if his claim of knowing who I was, was indeed true, I don't know that I could stand the look of disgust I'd get from Cambrie. Telling her as much as I did about my home was risky, but I refused to lie to her about anything I didn't absolutely have to.

My attention snapped down to her as she shifted in my arms, looking at me with a sweet, sleepy smile. "Good morning, Savo," she greeted.

Unable to hold myself back, I kissed her, loving how she melted in my arms. For her to give such trust to me when I wasn't sure I deserved it, made me want to fix all this even more. I had to get her back to the others, they were her family, her pack, and those men loved the fuck out of her. That's where she belonged, not with the trouble I would bring into her life. Until I handed her over to her men, I would treasure every second, knowing they would never accept me into their family, no matter how much she wanted it.

"Good morning, *Keksik*," I whispered against her lips. "Did you get some sleep?"

"Kek-seek," she drawled out the word as if tasting it. "You keep calling me that. What does it mean?"

I grinned at her. "In my language, it means cookie, because you smell like my favorite kind. Snickerdoodles."

"I do?" she asked, her eyes wide with wonder.

I hummed, nuzzling her neck so I could take a deep breath of her delicious scent. "Yes, you smell absolutely edible." I pulled back to look down at her. "Trust me, if we had time, I would taste you again. However, if you want breakfast, we need to get ready."

She gave me the cutest little pout that I just had to kiss away before I begrudgingly slid out of bed. "I'm going to do a check of your room. If you need to use the bathroom, feel free to use mine until I give you the all-clear."

I quickly turned my back, because if she gave me puppy dog eyes I wouldn't be able to say no to them. All I wanted was to snuggle and love that woman, but we weren't in a place I could allow that to happen. The two of us needed to figure out what was going on and how to get the hell out of here. They'd taken my personal cell phone, locking it in a safe in the armory. The phone they gave me to use only had two phone numbers in it, and only incoming calls or messages could be received. If it wasn't from either number, I couldn't use the phone to speak to anyone.

Yoram was brilliant at being a bastard—I had to hand it to him. So, my first order of business was finding a way to let Spencer and the others know she was okay. Then, how to get her the hell out of here?

My eyes scanned her room, spotting the tiny changes telling me someone had already been in here. I didn't like that at all, but it must be a maid since most of it was to tidy up the space, and a new dress was laid out on the bed. Not trusting anything to do with the bed, I picked up the dress and moved it to the back of the armchair. Her closet was the same, except for the dirty clothes gone and the black flats on the shoe rack. The bathroom was unchanged but for clean towels I made sure to check. The last thing I was gonna do was trust anything they provided.

Whoever wanted Cambrie dead or gone from this house knew the rules and schedule. The only people allowed here were hand-picked by Yoram, so that narrowed my suspect pool down.

It also meant it would be harder to catch them in the act, since we were all prisoners here. I knew a prison when I saw it, even if it came with lush carpets and five-course dinners. The hardest part was I was one of the jailors keeping Cambrie locked up. Though too bad for Yoram, I chose her over anything or anyone. Even if it meant I got locked up and sent back to my home country.

Satisfied her room was as safe as it could be, I returned to my own. I spotted her in the bathroom wrapped in a towel, since I had destroyed her nightgown. She'd braided her hair so it fell in a long rope down her back. When I'd first seen the color, I wasn't sure how I felt about it, but the more I stared at it, I approved. Like I told her, it made her stand out like a flower in the desert. She had so much light and life inside her, adding a color to her hair only made her sparkle outside too.

Giving her some privacy, I went to my closet and dressed in there, not wanting to assume she would be fine with it. We might have given in to our desires last night, but now it was time to go to work. During the day, I was her bodyguard. If at night, she wished to be in my bed and my arms, I would gladly oblige. While I was sure whoever cleaned her room noticed she wasn't in there and assumed she was with me, I wasn't going to let them know I *knew* who Cambrie was. The less they could use us against each other, the better.

I needed them to believe I wasn't a threat to their mission, but I wasn't going to allow them to lay a hand on her that wasn't needed. Training and education could be done without beating her. I'd lost my temper last night, but the rage at her mistreatment boiled over, and I couldn't stop myself. Now it was time for me to put on the mask of a soldier doing his duty.

Stepping out of the closet, I found my space empty and went to finish getting ready. I would give her what time I could, but I wouldn't allow her to miss any meals. She needed the nutrition to make up for what she'd lost and keep her healthy and strong. Mental and physical strength were linked in more ways than people like to believe, but each was equally important.

With ten minutes left, I moved to the door and knocked. "Cambrie, are you ready?" I called.

Moments later, she opened the door, wearing a simple forest green dress that hugged her body but was still incredibly conservative. "Yup, let's hope breakfast is something I can manage to eat properly, so it's still warm when it gets to my mouth."

"*Keksík*, when we leave this room, I'm not the same Savo. Here in our rooms, we can be free from the worry of prying eyes. Outside this room, I'm a soldier hired by the man who brought you here to keep you safe. No matter what, I will keep you safe, but I need you to ignore that I exist as you go through your day," I explained, hoping she would understand. "I can only keep you safe as long as they believe I will do my job and won't cause trouble. The last thing either of us wants is a reason for them to remove me from this job."

Cambrie searched my face with eyes that seemed to see into my soul. "I understand. As long as I know you're watching over me, I can do what's needed to make it through this. My biggest fear was having to survive this alone, but I'm not anymore."

Where had this woman come from? How could she have survived what I'd witnessed marking her body and still say things like that to people?

"You'll never be alone, Cambrie. I'm going to do whatever it takes to get you back to your pack," I vowed. "Now, let's head down for breakfast before the nasty butler cuts us off for being late."

She gave me a flash of a smile and headed for the door, which I had to slam shut making her jump. "Rule number one: the bodyguard always goes through the door first."

Her cheeks flushed a pretty rose color as she backed away from the door. "Sorry."

Pulling the door open, I entered the hall, holding up a hand and keeping her where she was. "Rule number two: don't enter or exit a room until I give the all-clear," I explained, then motioned for her to join me as we walked down the hall. "Rule number three: unless you are in danger or I feel it is needed, I will be two paces behind you just off to your right so you can see me out of the corner of your eye. Ignore that I'm here unless you feel you are in danger. If that is the case, you will flash two fingers, which means you feel uneasy. Flash me one finger, and I will intervene in the situation and remove you to somewhere safe. If I feel you are in danger, but you for some reason don't want me to step in, make a fist. This signal will be disregarded if I feel you are making an error in judgment."

"Goodness, I had no idea there were so many rules," she sighed, rubbing the side of her head like she might have a headache.

Everything in me wanted to check on her, ask if she was alright. Did she need meds or something else to help with the discomfort, only I was just a bodyguard and it wasn't my place—for now. That would change if I was given the chance by her pack, but I wasn't holding my breath. Hope was as lethal as it was helpful.

We got down to the dining room with time to spare. She took her place at the head of the table, with me to her left. Moments later, as if the maid had X-ray vision to see through the door, she walked out with a tray and set food on the table. It seemed that breakfast was a less formal meal than dinner. A basket of muffins, a bowl of fresh fruit, and bacon were placed, making me feel like the main course was missing. Moments later, the woman returned with two plates, an omelet on each, and set them before us.

"Can I get you anything to drink?" the maid asked, looking at me.

"Coffee, black, please," I answered.

Ignoring Cambrie completely, she returned to the kitchen. A glass of water was already filled and waiting, so it seemed that was what she would have. We ate in silence, and I didn't see any sign of Arthur until we finished our meal. He appeared on silent feet, almost catching me off guard since he entered through a side door hidden behind a tapestry.

Were there servants' hallways in this house? It would explain how people could enter in and out of Cambrie's room without notice. Now I would need to search her room, and mine, in a whole different way. There's not a chance in hell I was going to allow someone to sneak in on her. Yet, on the other hand, it might be worth checking out where they went if we needed to get out of the house.

"Miss Cambrie, it is time for your studies. Please follow me to the lesson room," Arthur instructed.

Cambrie did as he asked, quietly following the man upstairs and into a small room that seemed to be a mix between a library and a classroom.

"Your reading and math are quite advanced. Where you are lacking is in history, etiquette, and writing. These essays you wrote are riddled with grammar and spelling mistakes. It's obscene," Arthur stated when Cambrie took her seat. "I fear that with all of these areas, we will need to start at the beginning since I have no idea what you do or do not know."

Arthur walked over to his desk, picked up a large stack of books, and dropped them in front of her. "I expect you to read all of these and have them done within the week. It is all the history from the beginning of our culture until now. You will have an hour in the morning to work on them with me here then we will move on to other studies. After dinner is your free time, but I highly suggest you catch up on your education. The faster you do that, the faster you will be out of here and with your chosen pack. They are aware of your... shortcomings and have decided that it's in your best interest to have your education put first."

I could see Cambrie stiffen at the mention of a pack already having been decided. "Do I get to meet this pack or even the man who's decided to keep me here?"

"Your father is an incredibly important man. That's why he's put me in charge of your education. He doesn't have time to worry about your flaws," Arthur snapped, brushing imaginary lint off his jacket in a nervous habit. "Be grateful he's deemed you worthy of all this effort. If he didn't, then he could have just left you with that brute of a man who tried to sell you."

Her face scrunched up in confusion as she turned to face Arthur, who'd taken a seat on the couch near the fire. "Wasn't he the man who bought me, though?"

"Enough questions," Arthur roared. "Get to reading. In an hour, we will begin work on your posture and the hideous way you walk," he ordered, glaring at her with such menace it almost made me take a step forward.

There was something about this Beta that I didn't trust one bit. Why would Yoram put someone who clearly hated Omegas in charge of her well-being? None of this made sense. There had to be a reason all of this preparation was important. Did they really do all this schooling in the Care Centers? The Omegas that I saw at events I'd worked didn't seem anywhere close to what they wanted from Cambrie. It was as if she was being prepared to be sold off to some pack that needed her to act a certain way.

While Oscad had its flaws when it came to Omegas, it didn't need them to be subservient. Now Shearia, a country on the southern end of Oscad, expected their Omegas to be perfectly educated, properly mannered trophies on display. Could it be that Yoram was trying to use Cambrie as a bargaining tool? Something like that wouldn't work with my home country Asturg since there was no leader, so to speak, so it had to be Shearia.

As Cambrie diligently spent the day under the cruel hand of Arthur, she took every criticism, correction, and spite that man had to give with grace. A woman like that should be raised up to be a queen, not a pawn in someone's scheme. I needed to get my sweet girl out of here if she was going to survive. Mental abuse, while it took time to make an impact, sank deep and was nearly impossible to reverse if continued for too long. There was no fucking way in hell I was letting anyone convince this pure Omega that she was anything but perfect. The only way I was going to be able to do this, is to find some way to get ahold of her pack.

After dinner, the bastard was true to his word and left Cambrie to her own devices. Not trusting her to be in her own room, I kept her in mine. The fire was going, taking the chill out of this damn drafty house and making a perfect space for her to curl up in a chair with a blanket.

"*Keksik*, I need you to stay in this room," I instructed. "I'm going to lock both doors while I'm gone to make sure you're safe in here and no one can get to you."

She looked up from her book, blue eyes full of curiosity. "Where are you going?"

"I need to find a way to contact your pack. Let them know where we are so they can come get you," I explained.

While she was safely in here, I planned to check her room for a hidden passage or door, but I didn't want to alarm her for no reason. She was already leery about being in the room since the snake and was more than willing to let me check it before she did anything.

"Please be safe," she whispered when I turned to the door. "You're all I have here."

It was like she'd reached into my chest and squeezed my heart the way it killed me to leave her. I grunted my answer, knowing if I turned to look at her I wouldn't leave the room. *This was for her!* I needed to pull my shit together to keep her safe. That's all that mattered. Locking the door, I tested the handle to ensure it was well and truly locked. I wasn't delusional to think there weren't sets of keys that could open it, however, I needed to know I was doing everything in my power to protect her.

Moving to her room, I started in the closet, feeling like it would be a smart place to hide a secret door. Testing the shelves and knocking on the walls, I didn't find anything. Next, I tried near the fireplace, and wouldn't you know, the bookshelf next to it gave off a strange draft. It took me a bit to find the latch. It was hidden under one of the shelves cut into the wood, so it was recessed back from view. With how gloomy these rooms were casting shadows, it would be nearly impossible to stumble upon.

The passageway was made of stone, just like the outer structure of the house, meaning these were placed in the original construction. I left the door open to give me some light to see by, but there was a soft glow coming further down the way, telling me there was light if I kept moving. There wasn't another door until I reached the one with light glowing around the seams. It made me feel better knowing there was a chance mine didn't have an entrance, since

Cambrie's room was at the end of the path. I listened at the door, trying to hear if anyone was in the room before I tried to open the door.

"Why isn't she dead, Arthur?" a voice asked. The tone was that of an upset child, but it was coming from an older woman with a slight rasp. "I put the snake in her bed. She should be dead, dead, dead." Nervous laughter followed. "He should never have brought her back here. Didn't he know this is where everyone comes to die?"

"Laura, enough. You'll only upset yourself," Arthur said, his voice sounding tired. "I told you to leave the girl alone. Our Alpha needs her to do his work. She is the key to making all our dreams come true. We need her alive for us to be free."

The woman, Laura, shrieked at his words and then there was the sound of things being tossed around the room. "No! It's all lies. Why don't you see it, Arthur, my love? He has been stringing us along, making us believe he's going to keep his word. Look at us. Look at me. I haven't left this house since the bitch took the child and ran. Our Alpha blamed *me*. I shouldn't have had to take Aria's punishment just because we're sisters."

Now the screaming devolved into loud wailing sobs. "Shh, Laura," Arthur soothed in a tone that made me believe he actually cared about this woman a great deal. "Have you taken your medicine?"

"It makes me sleepy. I don't want to sleep anymore," she cried. "He's killing me off just like he's done to everyone else who displeases him."

"Here we go, drink, yes, that's a good girl," Arthur crooned and continued his rambling of reassurances. "Rest now, Laura. I'll make sure that little Omega bitch suffers the way we have over the years. Although we have to be smart. Hiring a bodyguard tells me he knows the danger he's putting her in being here with us. I thought he'd be smarter than that, honestly. You can't create a pack, abuse them, and then abandon them without repercussions."

Just when I thought Arthur was done sharing his thoughts with his apparent packmate, he continued. Only this time, malice coated his words. "For all his power, our Alpha didn't have anywhere else he could hide his precious daughter from the world, did he? Now he needs me to make her perfect for those Shearian bastards, withholding the fact he never marked me so he could send me back. I'll do my part for you, Laura, so he will let us stay together. This is the last chance he has to make good on his promise to us, my sweet Laura. If he doesn't, I'll find an Alpha to mark his precious Omega, and the deal will be finished. Shearian's are superstitious like that. They believe even if the Alpha is dead, that part of their soul lives on in them!"

Turning away from the door, I walked down the path, heading deeper into the house. It seemed Yoram had well and truly destroyed his pack. Ruining their minds to the point I wasn't sure they would know how to live outside this house and its structure. Everything about this carefully constructed environment might be the only thing holding them together. While I might pity them, I knew now to keep an even closer eye on what was happening with Cambrie. They might need her alive, but there was plenty of damage to be done in other ways.

CHAPTER 41

Cambrie

The crackling of the fire, the warm blanket around me, and the dry words of the history book I was being forced to read made it hard to stay awake. Savo had been gone for little over half an hour, and it was making me anxious. Something about this house, in general, gave me a bad feeling in the pit of my stomach.

Lessons today with Arthur had been brutal, but I'd tried to do my best to keep from letting him know he was getting to me. Men like him and my father just wanted to know they could get under your skin. Once they figured out what made you flinch, they would zero in on it until it became a massive target straight into your mind. If Arthur managed to do that even with Savo around, I wasn't sure I would come out the other side of this the same person.

Though my time with my pack had been short, it made me realize just how isolated and ignorant my mom and father had made me. How they viewed the world and explained things to me was so wrong. Even now, as I read about Oscad's history and the other two main countries bordering us, I wasn't sure anyone really knew where we'd come from. It seemed that our leaders nowadays wanted to keep us ignorant so we didn't remember what we once had. A prosperous country, large population, and packs were the norm instead of the exception.

Generations ago, it used to be a part of life to build your pack from a young age, bonding together through life experiences. Then after the age of eighteen, they could start courting Omegas, and they would be wooed into choosing the best fit. This allowed for the best compatibility between Omegas and Alphas, which in turn created a booming population.

How things were happening between my pack and me was considered normal back then. Today it was a crime, and they could be put in jail or killed for bonding with an Omega that wasn't given through the Care Centers. Being forced to read through these books just disgusted me at what our lives had become. No wonder no one was having children. Who would want to inflict this life on them?

Letting out a sigh, I set aside the book and decided to take a bath. I'd been wanting to soak in a tub since I got out of the basement and just hadn't found the chance. Savo promised that I would be safe in here, and there was no way I'd do this in the room they gave me. I'd be terrified that a snake would come up the drain or something. Padding into the bathroom, I shut the door but left it cracked so I could hear when Savo came back.

The tub was massive and more than deep enough to cover my whole body with water. Turning on the water, I found the right temperature and then explored the space to see if there might be some sort of soak or bubble bath to add to it. Under the sink, I found a jar of floral-smelling salts and a bottle of oil that matched the scent of the salts. I added it in, and the room was flooded with the light scent of jasmine and vanilla.

When it was half full, I climbed in letting out a small moan at the feel of the water enveloping me. The way the water seemed to cradle me gave me such comfort. With the tub being so deep, I didn't need to fill it the whole way, so I shut the water off and closed my eyes, soaking in the calming effect it had. This is absolutely what I needed after a day like today.

Letting my mind wander, I thought of my guys wondering what they might be doing right now. Were they upset I was gone? Was Bodhi being a jerk because he was upset? Had he and Oscar had a chance to talk? What about Nixon? He'd been so amazing, making my room so beautiful, but now I wasn't there to use it.

Shaking my head, I cleared out the worries and tried to focus on happy moments. I would get back to them. Savo promised he would find a way to get us out of here, and I believed him. This wasn't the time to get bogged down in sadness, this was temporary. There was hope at the end of the tunnel, and this was going to be an epic adventure I could tell them all about when I got home.

Home, funny to think I had a place for the first time in a long time, that I considered home. It was not the house or the beautiful room. No, it was the men who filled that home with life. As I floated, I dreamed of what our life would be like together as a pack and a family.

The smell of Bodhi's cooking and the sound of him humming some song as he worked. Spencer muttering as he moved about the house cleaning up after everyone, even though most of it was his mess. Marius, in his study, reading or working on something he couldn't finish at work, yet refused to be away from us longer than he had to. Rafael, in the library, reading a book as he drank tea; the picture of refinement. Oscar would be up in the rec room with a guitar, plucking out the notes of a song that had been rolling around in his head. Nixon would be on the phone, pacing through the house and arguing with this business mogul or that bank, demanding the respect his shelters deserved.

There was something missing in all this, though. An element that I longed for. In my mind, I wandered through the house from room to room, the guys all smiling when they saw me. It wasn't until I reached the door to the garage and felt the urge to enter that I found what I'd been looking for. Savo was at his workbench, cleaning off his tools after working on his truck, his gun still in pieces needing to be cleaned before he came in to watch a movie with us. Looking up from the tool he'd been holding, he grinned at me then winked.

"Looking for something, *Keksik*?" he asked.

I shook my head and blushed. "Nope, I found him."

"Sweet girl, I'll always be where you need me to be," he said, walking over and cupping my cheek with his hand. "Didn't I promise you I'd keep you safe, always?"

Yes, these were the men I called home and who held my heart. No matter what, I would get back to them, there was no other option. I would do whatever it took.

***

"*Keksík*," Savo whispered. "You need to get up, you fell asleep in the tub."

Cracking open an eye, I found those deep green eyes staring down at me just like he had in my dream. "You're back."

"I'm sorry it took me so long. I got a little turned around in the house," he apologized. "Come on, up we go."

Savo reached in, pulled the plug, lifted me out, and cradled me to his chest. "No, I'll get you all wet," I cried, trying to shove myself away from his chest.

"Settle down or I might drop you, as you're all slippery," Savo ordered, but there wasn't any genuine threat in his voice. "Being a little damp for a few moments isn't going to kill me. Let's get you dry, then I'll take a shower before bed, so we'll both be wet and clean."

"Oh, I didn't wash my hair, and now it has all that bath oil in it," I grumbled when he set me on the bathroom counter to dry me off.

He paused, then looked me up and down for a moment as if considering something. "Come on, we'll take a quick shower together. No sense in wasting time or water."

My jaw dropped at his suggestion, and my cheeks flamed. "Ah..."

Savo gave me a wicked smile as he placed his hands on either side of me. "Are you nervous to be naked with me after I've had my face buried between those legs?"

"No," I exclaimed. "It's only, the other night, you made a point of making sure I didn't touch you and I didn't want you to put yourself in a position you shouldn't be in," I rambled, unsure if I should have said anything about the matter.

Lips landed on mine, silencing me before I could continue to spew my nonsensical words. A little moan of happiness slipped out of me at the contact. I knew we couldn't act as anything more than a bodyguard and his lady, but my men had gotten me addicted to small touches throughout the day. None of them seemed to be able to be in the same room with me and not touch me in some manner. So to have his lips on mine was filling the bucket of affection that had started to get dangerously low.

He pulled back, desire in his gaze as his hands found my hips. "I want you so bad, *Keksik. I* would fuck you right here on this counter in a second. That being said, we've both agreed sex isn't the best choice right now, so I'll behave as long as you do."

"What does that mean, exactly?" I asked, feeling so new to sex and interacting in an intimate nature. "Before my heat, I'd never had anyone see me naked or been around another naked person, let alone had sex. I don't know all the rules."

"My sweet girl," Savo murmured, kissing behind my ear, then growled. "We need to get this stuff off you. I can't catch a whiff of your scent." Stepping back so I could see his face, he explained. "All that I ask is you keep your hands to yourself. We are taking a shower to get clean, and then it's to bed with you. I kept you up far too late last night, and you need rest to deal with everything Arthur is putting you through."

As if to prove his point, I yawned as I nodded. "Alright, I can deal with those rules."

He pulled me off the counter and set me on my feet. I turned on the water and tested it before entering, letting the water spray onto my face and rinsing off my body. I felt Savo step up behind me, his hard muscular body pressing against mine. He turned me so we switched spots and he was under the water.

"I thought you said to keep your hands to yourself?" I questioned.

He leaned down, and I felt his breath tingle over the skin of my neck. "No, I said *you* need to keep your hands to yourself. I didn't say anything about me."

Looking over my shoulder, I glared at him. "You tricked me."

"How so?" he challenged, humor showing in his eyes. "All I see is you and I taking a shower, with you keeping your hands to yourself. Now hand me that shampoo, and I'll make sure we clean your hair good enough to get that scented oil out of it."

I did as he asked, pausing before letting him take it. "Do I smell that bad?"

"*Keksik,* the scent that I'm addicted to, that I want to bury my nose in all day long, is *you.* This perfume is nice, but what I want can't be bought in a bottle and reproduced because it belongs only to one certain Omega named Cambrie," Savo explained as his fingers massaged the shampoo into my hair, making me moan. "That's right, my sweet girl, sing for me. I love to hear those beautiful noises come out of your mouth."

I couldn't help feeling embarrassed at his words, even though there was no way for me to keep my moans quiet either. His strong hands turned me into Jell-O as they worked over my scalp. Then when it was time to rinse it out, he stepped out of the water and guided me back, tipping my head so the soap ran down my back. When he was satisfied that the shampoo was out, he lifted a chunk of it to his nose. I couldn't help but giggle at how determined he was to make sure none of the scent lingered.

"Did you wash it good enough?" I teased.

He looked at me, eyes narrowing, and swatted my butt making me yelp as I darted away. "So, my sweet little Omega thinks to tease me, hmm? Seems that my plan to make you scream loud enough for the whole house to hear you isn't going to happen anymore, is it?"

My eyes went wide at his words and slick started to seep out between my legs as my scent perfumed the air. "I won't do it again. I'll be good, I promise."

Unconsciously, I licked my lips as if getting them ready to show him just how good I could be, before I remembered the rule— no touching.

"Hmm, we'll see about that," Savo said, motioning me to turn around again. "Omegas are supposed to enjoy being pampered and coddled by their pack, not tease them about it."

This time, I heard the tone in his voice that told me he wasn't upset with me at all. We were playing a game. Trouble was, I wasn't sure what game we were playing or what the rules were. Savo worked the conditioner into my hair, and I realized neither the shampoo nor the conditioner had any scent to them. Had they assumed I might be using his bathroom as well as mine? That worry was chased away as those heavenly fingers once more dove into my hair, massaging my head.

"That feels so amazing," I whispered, unable to keep from sharing.

Leaning into his touch, a moaning sigh escaped when his thumbs started to work on my neck, releasing the tension I could feel there from adjusting to the new posture Arthur had me doing all the time felt like heaven. "I never knew hands could feel so wonderful until I met you and the others. It's like you've all opened a whole new world for me to explore."

"Explore away, *Keksík*. We are more than happy to guide you through it step by step," Savo whispered into my ear as his hands moved from my neck to my shoulders.

My breath started to come quicker as they skipped over to trace along my collarbone, venturing closer to my breasts. "What if I become greedy and need this all the time? That would be incredibly selfish of me, don't you think?" I asked.

"How is it selfish when we want to give it to you? Don't forget we get just as much pleasure in giving as you do from receiving," he shared, letting the backs of his fingers brush over my nipples. "To watch your body respond to me, the way it begs to be touched, is as intoxicating as the scent pouring off you once more, *Keksík*."

I shivered at his touch, mixed with his erotic words, building my desire higher and higher. What would make this moment even more wonderful than it already was, was to have the rest of my pack with me. To feel their eyes on me as Savo worked me up to the point where I was begging to be knotted, then one of my Alphas would reach out to me offering what I craved. For me to be watched was as addicting as watching the others together. How sinfully delightful would it be for me to be taken by Rafael as Oscar took Bodhi while Marius and Nixon shared Spencer? Then I could finally take Savo into my mouth, lapping him like I wanted to.

"What are you thinking, *Keksík*? With how strongly your perfume is pouring off you, I think it's something dirty," Savo asked, nipping at the shell of my ear. "Are you dreaming about your pack as I work your body into a frenzy?"

I hummed my pleasure as he rolled both my nipples between his fingers. "Yes," I answered, my voice little more than a wisp of air.

"Tell me," he urged, letting one hand drift down my stomach and swirl right above my pussy. "I want to know your fantasies, my sweet Omega. What would bring you pleasure?"

My mouth went dry with how much his words turned me on, even more than I already was. "I was wishing my pack was here watching you drive me mad with need. Stoking the fire until I couldn't take it anymore, begging for one of my Alpha's knots. Rafael would take me, but I don't want to be the only one who gets to enjoy this moment. I want the others to relish in the love we share as a pack. Alphas would take their Betas, and I would take you, finally repaying you for the ecstasy you've already bestowed on me."

Savo groaned as he rubbed his cock between my ass cheeks and speared two fingers into my pussy. His breath was panting in my ear as his hips moved in time with his fingers. It was almost as intimate as if he was fucking me, but I needed more, so I wiggled back against him trying to give him something to really press against. He jerked me against his body, thrusting furiously as his free hand gently wrapped around my throat, urging my face up as his lips devoured me.

My body lit up like a firecracker as it exploded around his fingers, clamping down on them so tightly he had a hard time moving them. It was then I noticed something odd about how he was thrusting, almost as if he'd knotted me and was pumping me full of his cum instead of it spurting onto my back. Then I felt it—he did have a knot—Savo was an *Alpha*!

CHAPTER 42
Nixon

It had now been two whole days since Cambrie had been missing from our lives, and it might as well have been two years for how empty I felt. We were working tirelessly to figure out the best way to bring our Omega home. After talking with Alton and doing more research into Isabella and her family, we were ninety-five percent sure that's where Cambrie was being held. Once we found out his remaining packmate lived there full-time, never having been seen since the funeral, it made sense.

Yoram would want to keep Cambrie somewhere he could control, a place that people wouldn't think of or even know about. The property was large, and there weren't many neighbors to notice who was coming and going from the home. As we delved deeper, we discovered there was a full-time set of guards watching the place, paid for by the government. This meant we couldn't just walk up to the house and demand our Omega back. We needed a course of action that wouldn't get any of us killed.

The biggest stroke of luck we got was a strange and cryptic email that Spencer got last night. He didn't see it until this morning, but as we read it I had a feeling it was more important than it seemed. All morning, Bodhi and Rafael had been working on trying to solve whatever riddle this person was using. The one big hint that ensured we didn't gloss over this was the comment about snicker-doodle cookies. Each and every one of us knew instantly that it was referring to Cambrie's scent. We'd all commented on it at least once or twice when we met her.

Those two were applying every code-breaking skill they could find on the internet while the rest of us were brainstorming the exit plan. What we really needed was a person on the inside to tell us how they were using the guards. Were they patrolling the grounds? Did they have more guards inside, ensuring that no one left the house? Yoram's pack hadn't been seen in well over fifteen years. That didn't happen without someone ensuring they never stepped foot outside that house.

Could they be locked in?

No, that wouldn't make sense. There were tons of windows they could have broken out of if it came to that. That is what made us fairly certain the guards weren't there to keep them safe but to ensure they stayed locked away. Why even have a pack if you didn't want one? These were supposed to be people you wanted to build a family with. Then again, when I thought of Yoram, a family man wasn't at all what I considered him to be. What would it have been like if Cambrie had grown up in that home versus the one she ended up in?

That had me spiraling down a whole other rabbit hole of thought. Who was the person who got her out? The woman who she called mother? How would Cambrie take it when she learned that her biological father was evil and her mother was dead... both of them? How could someone so sweet and kind have been born from a man who was anything but?

"We got it!" Bodhi hollered, leaping up from his seat, hands in his hair. "Holy fucking shit, we actually figured it out."

The rest of us abandoned what we were doing and came over to see what the note said.

> This is Savo. I was able to find a computer to
> send this note. I fucking hope you can figure it
> out because Cambrie needs you to get her the
> hell out of this place. Yoram took her. He's her
> real father and wants to sell her off to Shearia.
> I'm here with her, they hired me as her
> bodyguard. I'll keep her safe until you can come
> get her. Use the same code and get back to me
> ASAP.
>
> 1539 Sulter Lane

"You have got to be kidding me," Spencer blurted. "This is the job that Savo was hired for but fell through suddenly. The job fell through because Cambrie ran away and ended up with us. Her bastard of a father was going to sell her to her real father. How fucked up is that?"

Marius nudged me aside so he could read the uncoded message Bodhi had written out on a pad of paper. "What the hell does he mean Yoram is going to sell her off to another country?! If that twisted fuck thinks he can use our Omega to gain more power and make some kind of deal with them, he's more fucked in the head than I figured."

"*Excuse me, what?*" Oscar signed after he'd gotten our attention. "*Do we even have that kind of relationship with them to warrant this kind of agreement? They seem more the type to take us over than to make a marriage alliance.*"

"We discovered six months ago that the old king died, and his son has now taken over the country. Yoram suggested we reach out and offer a gesture of friendship. This has to be what he meant. I thought he was going to offer some kind of trade deal, not a fucking Omega to be auctioned off, let alone *our* Omega," Magnus snarled. "If we can find any sort of proof that this deal is legit, then it is grounds for us to remove him from his position. This kind of act violates four or five different laws I can think of just off the top of my head."

All of us looked at each other in stunned silence at that realization. We had our ammo with him poisoning Alton. Now we needed proof of the smoking gun of him trying to sell off Cambrie to broker a deal with another country. Trouble was, how the hell did we do that in two days? Could we risk going after Cambrie, bringing her home, and then facing down the devil himself?

I don't know, but if I had faith in anyone pulling it off, it would be our pack. Since the day we'd joined forces, we'd been waiting for our chance to change the world—that moment had arrived.

"So, what do we do first?" Bodhi asked. "Do we go with the Alton being poisoned angle first?"

"No," Rafael cut in. "It took us half a day to get this message decoded, so we need to answer him back. We have the inside man that we need. If we can tell him our ideas, Savo can direct us to which would work the best. Then, when we have that figured out, we should decide how to get Yoram off our backs."

"Right, that whole coming to get her Monday thing," I muttered. "Still can't believe that bastard set this all up for us to take the fall."

"Then what do we have to lose?" Spencer asked. "There's no way in hell after we get her back we're going to let them take her from us again. I say we take the risk to mark her. Stake our claim. That way, when shit blows up in their face, they can't say she isn't ours when the dust settles."

Spencer had a point. What *did* we have to lose, other than Cambrie?

"What we need is some distraction to keep Yoram's attention on things happening here while we get our Omega," I responded.

Marius started to pace, running his hands through his hair, trying to put it all together. I'd seen him like this when the campaign began, and he had so much to go up against. No matter what the hurtle was though, he always found a way to get past it.

The sound of banging on the door to the private office made us all jump. Oscar ventured over and looked through the peephole. Whatever he saw had him yanking back the door to reveal a stricken Phillip.

"They arrested Eric," Phillip blurted. "The idiot called a press conference to the steps of our home, and he accused the CoF of trying to murder Alton. The police just came and arrested him for inciting a riot and speaking against the government."

Bodhi, who was standing next to me, muttered under his breath. "Looks like we don't need to come up with a distraction."

He was right, but it also meant that Marius would likely get pulled back to the Capitol Building to help settle this. However this played out, we needed to be incredibly careful not to tip our hand too early.

"Phillip, it's going to be alright," Marius assured the Omega. "I will do everything I can to make sure Eric is fine and these charges are dropped."

Phillip's eyes started to tear up, but he held himself together. "Just when they were starting to mend things, he had to go and make a splash. It's so like the bastard."

"At least he was doing it for Alton. He could have been out there saying something about bringing the CoF to an end," Marius countered.

"Oh, he absolutely did that. Saying if they were going to kill off one of the only two honest members, then why have it at all? I told you, a complete idiot, that Alpha of mine," Phillip muttered. "Now, I need you to stop Alton from falling on the sword to get Eric out of jail."

"Shit," Marius swore, and we all charged out of the room. "Where is he, Phillip?"

"Try the front hall. I'm sure Marla's done a decent job of stalling him," he called after us.

Who knew a bunch of old men could be so much trouble? You'd think they would know better, but here we were trying to fix what chaos they'd managed to stir up. When we got to the main entrance, Alton was attempting to wrestle the keys out of Marla's hands.

"Goddamnit, woman, give me the blasted keys right this minute," he barked.

Marla flinched at the order, but not being an Omega, it didn't have quite the same effect on her. "No, he did this to save you, and now you're just going to throw yourself at their feet and beg to have him released. Eric would hate you even more if you gave in that easily," she argued.

Marius and Oscar stepped in and managed to pull them apart as they continued to argue.

"Enough," Marius ordered, raising his voice loud enough that it echoed in the space. "Settle down and tell us what the hell is going on, Alton?"

"Eric found out that tea had trace amounts of hydrangea poison in it. Given enough time, or a bigger dose, it would have killed me, and I wouldn't even know I'd done it to myself. Those bastards hand-delivered my own death to my door for the past month," Alton raged. "Before I could stop the stubborn asshole, he had this whole plan cooked up, and by the time he told me it was too late and the press was here."

We'd known they'd discovered the poison but not what kind it was.

"What's worse is he named Yoram as the mastermind behind this plot to take me out," Alton added, sinking onto a bench in the hall. "I'm not sure there's any way to save him without giving them what they want."

Marius squatted in front of him, resting a hand on his knee. "We learned some incredibly valuable information today, Alton. Let's not give up hope just yet."

"Can it help get Eric out of this mess?" Alton questioned.

"It can do more than that, it can bring them all down, but I need a little time to get proof. We're going to find the best lawyers, and if Yoram calls me in, I'll do whatever it takes to slow down the process," Marius promised. "We need to head back to our home, but I won't do that if you're going to go rogue on us."

Alton waved a dismissive hand at Marius. "If you think you can save him, then I'll let you try. If it comes to naught, I'll do what they've wanted since the beginning and resign. With me out of power they won't have any reason to keep going after Eric."

"Give me two days," Marius requested. "I'm so close to getting our Omega home, and she'll have part of the puzzle I need to drive the final nails in the coffin of their political careers."

"Alright, my boy," Alton answered, patting Marius on the shoulder. "If you think you can save them both, I'll let you try. It might be time to let the next generation step in and take over the hard work from here."

"Don't be talking like that, mister," Marla snapped as she charged over to him. "Eric found an antidote for you to take that will help. You're not even close to giving up. You hear me?"

"Yes, the woman I hear you," Alton answered as he pulled her down for a kiss. "I'm not giving up. Just thinking it might be time to take a step back from being in charge. Haven't you liked having me around more?"

Marla looked up at us, her face determined. "You need to fix this and fast. He's becoming delusional. If he stays home any longer, he'll forget we're not his minions he can order about all willy-nilly."

I snorted at that, picturing Alton becoming the drill sergeant of getting projects done around the house and Marla telling him to fuck off. The older Alpha might be feeling his mortality at the moment, but I doubted he was as ready to retire as he thought.

"Come on, Marius, we should be getting back," Spencer urged. "I'm positive they'll call you in, and you can't show up wearing jeans and a t-shirt."

Always the mother hen, our Beta, but he wasn't wrong. It was best that we returned to the house and got things settled so we had it ready when Cambrie was back home with us. Not to mention, I wasn't sure when the last time we ordered groceries was. Bodhi was in charge of that for the most part, and we just added our requests to the list on the fridge.

The drive didn't take long, but all of us were hesitant to step foot inside. We'd grabbed what we needed and spent the last three days at Alton's. Rafael was the brave one who entered first, flipping on the lights in the entryway. The day had been fairly overcast, as if it was going to rain but hadn't made up its mind yet. Spencer went to the decorative table set up by the stairs and picked things off the floor, placing them in their spot once more. Only one little figurine had broken, a small angel with its wings spread open, ready to take flight. Now it wasn't going anywhere with its wings broken off.

I refused to believe it was any sort of sign about what Cambrie was going through right now. Savo was with her, watching out for our sweet Omega, making me so thankful she wasn't alone. Heading up to my room, I had just started to change when my phone rang. Looking down at the name on the screen, I groaned. It was my mother. We had monthly check-ins, and I'd all but forgotten it was the fifteenth of the month. The obligatory day my mother picked when I left for boarding school was when we would speak.

"Hello, Mother," I answered.

"Nixon, darling, how are you? I heard something awful on the news earlier today, something about one of the Officials being poisoned?" she prattled on. "You don't know anything about this, do you?"

Breathing a heavy sigh, I sat on the edge of my bed knowing this wasn't going to be a quick call. "No, Mother, I know just about as much as you do. Marius has been home the last few days, but we expect him to get called in to deal with this mess."

"Oh? Is he alright? Do I need to send anything over? Has he talked to his mother?" she asked, shooting question after question, not once giving me the chance to answer. "You know, I talked to Beatrice the other day, and she said she hadn't heard a word from him in almost two months. Is everything alright over there?"

This was a question my mother found a way of asking every single conversation. What she really wanted to know was if Marius and I were still with Spencer. While Marius's mother had no issues at all with who her son chose to love, mine had quite the opposite view. Not only was I in love with a man, but I was also sharing him with my best friend. Couldn't I find someone for myself? What about children? What would happen when we had an Omega? It wasn't right to have another partner besides them. A happy Omega is the most crucial thing in the world, and how could they be happy if I loved someone other than them?

"Everything is perfectly fine, Mother. In fact, they are better than they've ever been. We now have an Omega in our pack," I shared, not wanting to hide Cambrie anymore.

When we got our Omega back safe and sound, she wasn't ever

leaving again. Hell, I'd hire Savo on the spot to ensure nothing like this happened, move him into the house to keep watch twenty-four seven, 365 days a year.

"Oh, my goodness! When did this happen? Darling, you should have told us right away. This is a momentous occasion," Mother gushed. "How did that young fellow you were close with take it?"

My jaw clenched as I tried to keep from screaming at her. It wouldn't matter, we'd always gotten into knock-out, drag-out arguments time and time again, changing nothing.

"Spencer is over the moon, the two of them get along wonderfully. It's adorable to watch them together as they set up her nest. What I think I love most about her though, is how much she understands and encourages the love between Spencer and me. Not to mention, the same goes for Spencer and Marius. Between the four of us, there's more love than any of us know what to do with," I explained, feeling the truth in my heart.

Not once had it distressed Cambrie that we cared for more than just her. In fact, I think she enjoys watching us together as much as she likes to participate, not that I would ever tell my mother that. It might send her into cardiac arrest, and that is the last thing I need to deal with right now.

"Oh," Mother commented, before a long pause as if she was trying to figure out what to say next. "Just know that might change, darling. Omegas are known for being selfish when it comes to the attention of their Alphas. I only want the best for you and don't want you to be surprised if she requests that you break it off."

The fact that my mother was speaking that way about Cambrie caused me to snap. "That will never happen because Cambrie loves Spencer as much as I do, and once a Beta is bonded to an Alpha, there's no going back. So, I'd appreciate it if you got used to having a son who loves a man named Spencer Wells and used it when speaking about him. If you and Father can't do that, then I don't need you in my life. My pack has been more of a family to me than you two ever have been, and I won't hear you say one more word against any of them," I barked into the phone.

"Darling, what are you saying?" Mother spluttered.

"Was that too complicated for you? Let me break it down to one simple concept. Accept who I am, who I love, or don't and forget that I'm your son. It's up to you," I stated bluntly.

"Dar... Darling, you can't mean that," Mother sobbed. "How can you say that to me?"

"You have two other children who seem to disappoint you less than I do. Pin all your hopes and dreams on them instead of me because clearly, I'm not meeting the standards you've put in place. I love Spencer and Cambrie, and they love each other as much as they love me. How is sharing an Omega with the rest of my pack any different than sharing Spencer with Marius?" I demanded. "I'm my own man with my own pack, and you need to trust I'm doing what's best for me."

"I'm sorry you feel that way about me, but all I've ever wanted is what's best for you," Mother sighed.

"The fact that you don't see how your best is choosing to hurt me more by asking me to leave Spencer says everything I need to know. I won't be answering your calls anymore, Mother. If you wish to speak with me, then you can come to the house and spend time with us all," I shared before ending the call and tossing the phone on the bed.

Dropping my head in my hands, I thought long and hard about what I'd just said to my mother. As I said them, it made me realize, in some ways I had been acting like my mother when it came to sharing Spencer with Marius. How did I feel so comfortable with Cambrie being with all of us and so insecure about Marius? I've known that man my whole life, and he would never do something to hurt Spence or me. So, what made me feel that one day Spence would be asked to choose between us?

Shoving up from my bed, I headed to Marius's room, needing to talk this out with my best friend. No matter what's happened, he's always been there for me with sound advice, and right now that's what I needed. When I entered his room, I heard the water running telling me he was in the shower. Just as I was about to leave, I heard a moan that I knew had come from Spence.

Time to put up or shut up.

Heading to the bathroom, I entered and found Marius wrapped around Spencer's body from behind, slowly fucking him as the water poured over them. Spencer spotted me first and smiled, reaching a hand out to me without a second thought. This is what I'd been blind to until Cambrie entered the picture. You could absolutely love more than one person with all your heart at the same time. Spencer didn't take his heart and divide it up evenly between us; he gave all of it and himself to each of us. Just like Cambrie took my heart with her as much as Spencer held it in that very hand reaching out to me.

Stripping out of my clothes, I joined them. Marius looked up from where his face had been nestled in Spencer's neck and grinned. "Care to join us?"

"Abso-fucking-lutly," I answered, then cupped Spencer's face. "I've missed out on too much, fearing that one day you might choose not to be shared between us. I'm sorry I didn't understand what you've been trying to tell me, but I hear you now, my Prince."

The smile that lit up Spencer's face was priceless as I pulled him into a deep passionate kiss, letting him feel everything I'd been holding back because of fear. If only Cambrie had been here for me to thank her for helping me see what I was missing out on. Soon, soon we would have her back and I wasn't going to be afraid anymore and claim her as mine, ours, so we would never lose her again.

CHAPTER 43
Cambrie

Spinning around to take in Savo from head to toe, everything started to make so much more sense. The way that I responded to him, the need to please, be touched, and be unable to distance myself from him, was because he was an Alpha. He had been since the day I met him, but why had I believed he was a Beta? None of this was making sense.

"Who are you really?" I demanded. When he tried to reach for me, I darted back. "No, I won't let you cloud my mind with your Alpha scent and the magnetic pull you all seem to have on me. I need answers, and I want them *now*," I growled between clenched teeth.

The same feelings that had welled up in me when I thought Nixon was trying to get rid of me flared to life. *How could he do this to me? He said he would protect me, but all he's done is lie.*

"Cambrie, do not run away from me," Savo warned. The Alpha tone in his voice was hard to miss now that I knew what it was. He'd used it that first night he'd had his face buried between my legs. "We are going to finish cleaning up, dry off, and then we will sit and talk, allowing me to explain things."

"Why should I listen to you? You're not *my* Alpha," I snapped. Even as I said it, I knew it wasn't true. The moment he held me in my room he'd proven the kind of Alpha he was, caring for me when I didn't know I needed it. I was hurt and lashing out because I had no control over anything happening in my life.

Savo took a step forward and gently placed his hand around my jaw, forcing me to look into his eyes. "You and I both know that's not true, *Keksík*. I've already claimed you as mine, as much as you've claimed me as yours. So, let's both make a pact that we won't lie to each other now that all of this is out in the open."

"How do I know you're not lying to me just to get me to fall in line? Maybe they put you here with me so I would trust you, then you'd mark me and take me away from my pack," I said, unwilling to move on from this so easily.

All my life, people had been manipulating me for whatever purpose suited them, and I was sick of it. I'd thought Savo was different and had nothing to gain from this, but knowing he was an Alpha changed everything.

Savo let go of my face, turned off the water, grabbed a towel, and wrapped me up so my arms were trapped by my side as he stepped out of the shower, setting me on the counter next to the sink. Leaving me there tangled up in the towel, he slipped on a robe and picked me up once more. I squirmed and wriggled, trying to get out, but he'd done something to make it impossible. Back in the bedroom, he took a seat in one of the armchairs with me in his lap. Not saying anything, he just waited as I thrashed about until I gave up, panting, still not as strong as I'd like to be after my captivity.

"Are you ready to listen now, *Keksík*?" Savo asked, his tone neutral, not betraying any of his emotions.

Glaring, I shook away a piece of wet hair that fell in my face with a huff. "What's there to listen to?"

"Cambrie, this is not you. Stop acting like a brat, or I will treat you like one," Savo warned. "Be my sweet girl, and you will get all the answers you are looking for."

Pouting, I stilled and looked at him. "I'm listening."

Savo grunted and shifted me so I was straddling his legs and facing him. "First thing I need you to hear loud and clear is that other than not telling you I was an Alpha, I've never lied to you.

Having to hide who I am from the world is more than I'd like to manage, so I don't lie in any other area of my life, and never to you. *Keksik,* when an Alpha connects to an Omega, there is no changing the connection. You are like my heart beating outside my chest. I'd never let anything harm you, including myself."

I searched his face, desperately wanting to believe what he was telling me, and what I saw had me feeling ashamed for how I'd acted. "Why lie at all?"

He lifted a hand, stroking my cheek as his expression turned sad. "This is not an easy story to tell, my sweet girl, but you, of all people, deserve to know who you will one day be bonded to."

The need to wrap him up in a hug was more than I could bear, but with my arms wrapped up, I could only manage to lean in and give him a reassuring kiss. "I'm sorry for being a brat, and I'm ready to listen to whatever it is you want to tell me."

A smile that didn't reach his eyes tugged at his lips before he gave me another peck and loosened the towel so I could free my arms. Taking a moment, I secured the towel around my chest but didn't move from his lap. Something told me that being there for him through this was what he needed.

"I told you that I grew up in Asturg and that I didn't have any family left there. That isn't completely true," Savo started. "My father is still living, but we hate each other, and I've never been able to see eye to eye with him on anything. I had a little sister, the one who I used to sing that song to, but she died in one of the breeding houses. As a female, your choice was to either join the fight carrying a gun or on your back bearing more children to replace those that were lost. Anica was like you, sweet with a gentle spirit that could never fight on the front lines. So, Father made sure she did her duty and died trying to give birth when she was only your age."

Savo took a moment, tears shimmering in his eyes as he stroked my head lovingly. "You two would have been good friends, I know it. Both of you see the good in the world when there isn't much of it left. Anica was all I had left. Our mother died when I was twelve leaving me to look after Anica, who was just seven. I tried to do everything I could to protect her, but our father wouldn't have it."

He took a deep breath and refused to meet my gaze. "Remember how I told you that there are two leaders in Asturg? Well, my father was one of those men, General Rasvan of the Northern Asturg army. He leads our people's battles and is also in charge of enforcing the laws of our people. Which is why he couldn't let his daughter receive any kind of special treatment. Southern Asturg is ruled by President Dragomire, who is trying to fight for peace between our two groups, even though my father is one of the cruelest generals the north has ever had. He doesn't care how many die as long as we gain ground and take back what's ours. The thing is, no one knows what that actually is, but he's so addicted to power, and father wants all of Asturg in his grasp."

I wrapped my arms around his neck and hugged him as tightly as I could, kissing along his neck feeling how much this was a struggle for him to tell me. "I'm so sorry, Savo, you've suffered so much losing your mother and sister like that. It makes sense why you had to leave. What I don't get is why you needed to pretend to be a Beta?"

"My father had planned for me to take over after him, training me in everything I needed to know to be the next general. That's why I'm so good at my job, it was beaten into me since I was able to walk or hold a gun. If the government knew who I was, with the knowledge that I have about my people, they would lock me away. Being a Beta means, I get overlooked. I can blend in with the crowd and no one's the wiser," Savo explained. "As a Beta, I was given this job, allowing me to look after you. Something an Alpha would never have been permitted to do for fear of what's happened between us."

Sitting back, I looked at him, scrunching up my face. "What do you mean?"

"Once an Alpha has decided an Omega is theirs, there is nothing that can be done about it. The Alpha either bonds with the Omega or they will forever long for that Omega. Either way that Alpha is no longer objective, they will do whatever is necessary to protect their Omega," Savo elaborated. "You are my one and only concern, *Keksík*. Everything else can fuck off as far as I'm concerned."

I felt the tears fall down my cheeks. "Forgive me," I begged. "It was wrong of me to doubt you after all you've done to take care of me."

"Shh, *Keksik*," Savo soothed, pulling me against his chest as he started to purr, soothing my worries. "Don't be so hard on yourself. I'm proud of you for standing up for yourself and getting mad at me. People who have been through what you have often struggle with being able to tell someone no or to push back in fear of getting hurt again. Cambrie, you are so much stronger than you realize, and it makes you all the more loveable."

Sniffling, I nuzzled into his neck. "I don't feel strong."

"That's alright. Your pack and I will be here looking after you until you do," Savo murmured, kissing my shoulder. "Now, let's get you properly dried off so we can get some sleep, hmm?"

"Okay," I whispered as he carried me into the bathroom.

Bodhi had been the only other person to do my hair for me, but Savo seemed quite practiced with it. It made me wonder if he'd done the same thing for his sister when she was alive. The feel of the warm blow dryer and his sure steady touch had me falling asleep where I sat. Once he was finished, Savo slipped the towel off me and we curled up under the covers with him cuddling me to his chest, purring me into blissful slumber.

EVEN THOUGH I'D only been here a few short days, Arthur kept us on such a strict schedule that it was hard not to adjust. After breakfast, I was back in the schoolroom, working on the skills that I'd been found lacking in. Having spent most of my life teaching myself, it wasn't that hard or different from before my designation presented itself. The hardest part was if I didn't understand something, having to approach Arthur about it.

"This is simple, Miss Cambrie. I'm not sure why you're struggling with it so much," Arthur grumbled. "Grammar is the foundation of communication. What does it say if you're writing a letter and constantly using the wrong 'there'? No one will take you seriously, and your new pack is in a position of power. You can't disgrace them."

Arthur's rant was interrupted when a knock sounded at the door. Frowning, he answered it, only to be handed a cell phone. Lifting it to his ear, he greeted the caller and then listened to whatever the person on the other end had to say.

"Understood. When will they be arriving to procure her?" Arthur asked. "Tomorrow, that is much too soon, Alpha." The butler flinched at whatever the response was, rubbing his forehead. "As you command, *Alpha*, but you better hold up your end of the deal. I won't be blamed if they find her lacking when I've only had four days to work with her."

Gritting his teeth, Arthur hung up and threw the phone against the wall so it smashed into pieces, making me gasp.

When he turned back to face me, his expression was blank, but his eyes were alight with fury. "It would seem that certain events have forced your father's hand, and you will be joining your pack tomorrow. We have the rest of today to get you as ready as I can before an escort comes to take you in the morning."

Dread started to claw its way into my heart. *This couldn't be happening. They can't take me away. I already have a pack!* My hands started to shake so badly that the pen I was holding slipped through my fingers. I didn't even bother to pick it up, feeling this whole thing was pointless. I was being sent off to a group of men I didn't know, by a man who claimed to be my father. How had everything been so perfect, only to fall apart in a blink of an eye?

A hand rested on my knee, drawing me back to what was happening around me. Savo was kneeling in front of me, concern radiating off him as he handed me back my pen. "You dropped this."

Reaching out, I grasped it, but he took the chance to take my hand and bring it to his lips. That one simple gesture, that could have cost him so much if Arthur had been paying attention instead of pacing furiously, gave me the strength I needed to calm myself. Savo wouldn't let anything happen to me; he was here right by my side as he promised.

"I need to step out of the room for a moment and reach out to the man who hired me," Savo explained. "You will stay right here in this room. I don't care who comes for you, you will not move from this place without me, understood?"

"Okay," I whispered.

He kissed my hand once more before leaving without so much as looking back at me. I trusted Savo, if he felt that he needed to leave right now, then it was important. Now it was my job to keep out of trouble and be here when he returned, no matter what.

CHAPTER 44

Marius

I assumed it would be chaos when I arrived at the Capitol building, but what shocked me more was the overabundance of security. A guard greeted me at my car as I handed the keys to Thomas.

"Good afternoon, Official Stone. I'm Rick Jones, and I'll be your bodyguard for the day," Rick explained. "Seems that arresting Official Alton's fellow packmate hasn't gone over well with the people. There's already been one attempt to rush the Capitol demanding his release."

My brows shot up at this. "I had no idea Eric had such a loyal following."

"Oh, this isn't for Eric. Alton has far more of the people's favor than anyone realized. They are out for blood if the accusation is true," Rick explained as he escorted me through security. "Official Dubois asked me to bring you into the council room when you arrived."

We rounded the corner and headed down a hall only accessible to us Officials. I nodded to the guards as we passed, their guns at the ready. When we got to the door, I noticed it was fully locked down, requiring me to use my handprint and code to let me in. Typically, it just took keying in my personalized sequence, but evidently things were bumped up a level.

"Before you head in, I have a message for you," Rick said, keeping his voice low. "Savo doesn't ask for favors, but he begged me to tell you the delivery is being sent early. The cookies leave tomorrow morning, but he can delay it if he knows there is more coming."

Fuck! Of course, this would cause Yoram to move faster with his plan.

"Thank you, is he able to receive a message back from you?" I asked.

Rick rubbed the back of his neck, looking down at his feet. "Look, I'm not wanting any trouble from the CoF, and I know Yoram is the one who hired him. Just tell me this is worth risking my life over, and I'll make sure to get a hold of him."

I reached out and gripped Rick's shoulder. "Helping us will save someone else's life who never deserved the fate they are being given. Truthfully, I need what Savo has in order to save us all."

"Fair enough. Tell me what I can do," Rick said, a determined look in his eyes. "Savo is a good man, and so are you. If you're working together, then I trust that whatever this is helps everyone."

"I won't be able to be a part of this, but the rest of my pack is waiting for this information. They need to know when to be there and how they can help. If he needs real backup, then we might require the help of any of your men who might not agree with how things are being handled right now. If we can get our hands on the right information, I can bring this whole farce of a government down," I explained, knowing it was risky to trust this man. However, there weren't many options left, and time was running out, according to Savo's message.

"There is one other man that I know I can trust, who can get in contact with Savo. He's one of the guards they took from me and placed him there indefinitely. I don't want to tell you his name just in case something happens, so it gives you deniability," Rick explained. "I know you don't know me, and it's crazy for us to trust each other off the bat like this, but something has to change. Our city is dying, and it's because of that man. So, you say you can get him out of power, then I'll take my chances putting my lot with yours."

He took a step back and saluted me as I placed my hand on the sensor and the door clicked open. Only Officials were allowed in here, ensuring that whatever was discussed couldn't be leaked, and if it was, we'd know who might have done it.

"Marius, took you long enough," Yoram barked as he paced the room. "The city is in chaos, and you're waiting for the call before you come in? What does that say about your commitment to this country?"

Never before had I seen Yoram exude anything other than calm confidence. This must have rattled him, finding out just how much backing Alton had even after being out of the limelight for two months.

"I'm sorry you see it that way. I was trying to understand what was going on, so I spoke with Alton to get first-hand knowledge," I answered, walking over to the coffee machine and making a cup.

Coffee was the last thing I needed right now, but I had to put on the show of not being worried about any of this. It was known in the building that I drank large amounts of coffee throughout the day since I didn't get much sleep.

"Oh, is that right?" Yoram questioned. "You weren't already at his house?"

"Alton is a good friend, and my pack decided to spend some time with him. Being cooped up at home for a month isn't something he's a big fan of," I said, taking my seat. "Setting that matter aside, what do you plan to do about this situation? There is no way you can slap a government verdict on this. He'll need to go through a trial."

Yoram stopped and whirled around to glare at me. "You don't think I realize that? I've been an Official of Oscad for nearly thirty years, I don't need *you* telling me how to do my job."

"That wasn't what I was trying to do at all, merely stating facts," I countered. "None of us had any idea people would be so up in arms about this. Eric hasn't been in the public eye for some time, choosing to distance himself from Alton. I don't have to tell you how vast the distance was between them. The only reason they live in the same house is because they're bonded to the same Omega."

"This is why you shouldn't bond with them. They just need to be breeders," Fredrick interjected. "Asturg might constantly be at war, but they understand how things should be. Use the breeders to get what we need, which is adding to the population. I bet they also use the drugs we banned to increase their chances as well."

I'd known that Fredrick sided with Yoram on this matter, but it was the first time I'd heard him spewing this nonsense. If anyone but the two of us heard him, he'd be under attack by the people in seconds.

"I don't think now is the time to bring that suggestion into play," I reasoned. "The public is already furious, and what we need to do is calm things down. Let them know we are going to have an outside group look into the accusations. Then they have no grounds to stand on saying we manipulated things."

Yoram harrumphed as he took his seat. "We control all law agencies, laboratories, and other such facilities. In the end, it doesn't matter, they will give the answer I want them to. As their leaders, we need them to see we are taking steps to investigate this. Ultimately, we must do what we need to in order to protect our city from those who would destroy it."

Frowning, I leaned forward. "I'm sorry, forgive me for being a little slow, but are you saying that Alton is trying to destroy Oscad?"

"What else would you call it when he refuses to let us expand our resources? Shearia's new leader reached out to us and wanted to foster a friendship, yet Alton blocked it every chance he got," Fredrick challenged, slamming his fist on the table. "Our country needs to expand outside our own borders to grow beyond what we already are. There isn't enough of a population to do the work, so we need to outsource it. Shearia was willing to work with us if we were willing to give something in return."

Utterly confused, I had no idea what they were referring to. The talks we'd had with Shearia's new leader Vikas had gone well. Alton didn't like the man, but the old bastard didn't like many people, so I didn't take much stock in that. Of course, I knew Cambrie was taken from us to be sent to them, so clearly, they'd had other conversations but I couldn't just say that outright.

"Fredrick, you make it sound like you've had more conversations with Chancellor Vikas than I'm recalling," I said, trying to push him into admitting to the secret meetings.

The portly man opened his mouth to speak but paused, glancing at Yoram as if worried he'd spoken out of turn. When he didn't get what he was looking for, he just muttered under his breath and narrowed his eyes at me. "You've only been an Official for a short time and attached to Alton's tit, so there might be some things that you've been left out of. When it comes down to it, we know whose side you're going to take when it's time to make a decision."

Shoving back from the table, I stood glaring at the buffoon. "When I make a choice, I do what I think is best for the people who live in this city, not what will make the most profit. Besides, you're one to talk about being on someone's tit. Everyone knows you'll do whatever Yoram says, no questions asked, and you expected me to fall in line right beside you. Too bad for everyone, I happen to have a mind of my own and can choose where to put what weight I have behind a choice."

"Gentleman," Yoram cut in. "Enough, we have important matters to discuss. Marius, if you would please take your seat."

Gritting my teeth, I sat knowing right now I needed to be in this room. The longer I stalled, the better. Not to mention the information I was finding out. Our people's reaction to this move was unexpected and had thrown them off their game. Right now, I needed to play into that and let them dig their own graves.

"Has Eric said anything other than what he announced on live TV?" I asked, directing us back to the main topic.

Yoram let out a sigh, pinching the bridge of his nose. "No, he was out there on the steps of his home spouting off for the world. Once we got him back here, he's been as tight-lipped as a monk."

"I didn't listen to his statement, but what information did he have to pin it on you?" I ventured.

Asking this put me in a precarious place, it would tell me if he knew more than he was saying about my time at Alton's, or it could put me in a cell next to Eric. Before I could move forward with a plan, I needed to know what information was known and what I had to bring to light.

Yoram dropped his hand and pinned me with a look that told me he was more worried than I'd realized. "The bastard claimed that I sent Alton a Get Well basket once a week with a tea that seemed to help with his illness. Everyone knows I hate the bastard. Why would *I* send him something like that?"

"It came from the PR office with a tag saying it was from us," Fredrick added. "They have been doing that for years to make sure the appearance of us all getting along is there. None of us have any clue what they send in those baskets. So, if something was poisoned, that's where I think they should start looking."

"We need to get ahead of this somehow," Yoram muttered. "The Chancellor is already getting cold feet after hearing about this. No one wants to get dragged into a situation, and if we can't calm everyone down, this could be blown way out of proportion."

Fredrick cleared his throat aggressively, as if trying to signal to Yoram that he'd slipped up in his anger. "What's the matter with you?" Yoram barked, shooting to his feet, and started to pace once more. "Are you getting sick as well? Coming down with a myste-rious illness that you plan to blame on poison? How could everyone believe a hack like Eric? He gave up his position in the world of science to deal with herbal remedies. If you ask me, it would be quite simple to turn this all on him."

I needed to turn this around fast, before Yoram settled on that course of action. "All that needs to be done is for the public to know we are looking into the situation. Staying silent isn't going to gain us any favor. Why don't I handle this press conference and explain our plan to launch an investigation into the matter, before we choose to do anything? Eric will remain in custody until the events have been evaluated for his safety as well as ours."

Fredrick was nodding his head, agreeing with me, which I found odd. Did he realize that Yoram wasn't thinking clearly right now?

Whatever the case, if we outvoted Yoram it didn't matter why he chose to do it.

Yoram stopped pacing to face me. "You."

"It has to be me," I reasoned. "If they are siding with Alton, it's common knowledge we are friends. If I say something is being done, they will believe it since I want what's best for him and his pack. The last person they need to hear it from is you. Forgive me for being blunt, but currently they view you as evil."

Fredrick puffed up his chest and pointed to himself. "Why not me?"

Both Yoram and I simply looked at him, and he deflated. "I know, I know, what Alpha gets stage fright and passes out in front of the cameras. He's right, though. If it can't be me, it has to be him."

The world must be spinning backward. There is no way Fredrick would side with me so blatantly in front of Yoram.

"Fine, you can be the face of this, but I will look over whatever script you are going to read. I'm not going to have you use this to screw me over because we are making you give up your Omega," Yoram announced. "Even though you put on a brave face, I know that wasn't the answer you wanted. So don't even consider using the public while they are this fired up to force our hand."

Slowly, I stood and brushed my hands over my suit, trying to calm myself before I spoke. "No matter what happens in my personal life, I am an Official of Oscad and my duty is to the people. Right now, they need someone they can trust to make the right choice when it comes to people's lives. Never would I manipulate the people just so I can get something I want. There is more than one way to handle things; I'm not you. Now, if you will excuse me, I have a press conference to prepare for. I think it would be best to do it at five o'clock and have you all there as well. Keeping a united front will be crucial, even if it's just for show."

Before either of them could stop me or give me more reasons to go against what I just said about manipulating the people, I left the room. Rick was waiting outside and walked me back to my office, where I closed the door and switched on the scrambler.

"Did you get a hold of Savo?" I asked.

"Not exactly. I got the message to my other guy, who is there now. It's just if he can get the message to him," Rick answered. "What might work best is if you keep me updated on the plan, then I can get things rolling the second I hear back."

Taking a seat at my desk, I studied Rick. "Why does Yoram use your men, your company, for almost everything? It seems odd to me that you would be so willing to turn against him when you profit so greatly."

Rick let out a bitter laugh. "You think I'm profiting? Damn, I must be putting on a better act than I thought. Yoram uses my company because he has dirt on every single one of us, and we will do whatever it takes to make sure he can't use it against us. Yes, we get paid from government funds, but the cost for the work is higher than any of us are truly willing to pay."

Everything I feared that might be happening right under my nose was coming to the surface. Yoram wasn't lying when he said he had control over everything to do with law enforcement. He'd single-handedly managed to manipulate the whole system to be under his thumb. Yoram didn't realize that all it took was one man standing on the steps of his home and being brave enough to say enough was enough. Once people saw they could stand up for themselves, the tide would turn faster than anyone, including myself, thought was possible.

"How far are you willing to go if it means you're free of him?" I asked, leaning forward as I waited for his answer.

Rick took a seat across from me, pulled out a picture, and set it in front of me. The photo was of a pregnant woman holding a toddler on her hip, who resembled Rick in many ways. "If it means my son and soon-to-arrive daughter can grow up in a world where they don't dread their sixteenth birthday, I'm not sure there's anything I won't do."

I picked up the picture and was amazed to see that the possibility of more than one child being born to a couple was real. "How?"

"Sasha is an Omega," Rick answered. "We met when I was on a

diplomatic mission in Shearia. A military unit is as close to a pack as you can get these days when you know the chance of having an Omega is zero. The five of us fell for her almost as instantly as we saw her. Our team was there for a month and ended up bonding with her. In that country, the bond is sacred and considered a forever commitment, dead or alive. So, there was nothing they could do about us bringing her back with us, even though they have fewer Omegas than we do."

"That's what Yoram has on you, that you broke our laws, even though you were in another country?" I realized. "Is he threatening to take her away from you? Because he can't now that she's had your children."

"No, not her, my children," Rick corrected. "In Shearia, Omegas can be born male or female, and his threat has been to remove them from our home and raise them in one of the Care Centers."

Just when I didn't think Yoram could be a more heartless bastard.

"I'm so sorry, Rick. It must be awful to have something so special in your life and fear every moment it might be taken away," I said, handing him back the picture. "I know what that feels like, and I wouldn't wish it on anyone."

Rick looked confused. "Your pack has an Omega?"

"We do, although because of my morals and wanting to do right by the law, we haven't bonded with her. In doing the right thing, I set myself up to lose her and didn't even realize it. While my pack and I were here trying to get proper approval from the CoF, Yoram sent a team of men to my home and stole her right out of her nest," I explained.

Understanding flashed in Rick's eyes. "Savo has her, doesn't he?"

I nodded and leaned back in my chair, looking up at the ceiling. "The heavens must be looking down on us for something like that to have happened. Savo and my Beta, Spencer, are friends, so Cambrie has met Savo before. It gives me some peace to know she isn't alone, unprotected, and suffering." Looking back at Rick, I could tell by the look on his face that he was wholly committed to helping us. "Yoram is trying to sell her off to the Chancellor of Shearia to gain some alliance. The message you passed on to me earlier was saying they are coming for her in the morning. We don't have much time, Rick. We need to do whatever it takes to bring her home."

"You said before that she's the key to destroying Yoram. How is that possible?" he questioned.

I rubbed a hand over my face, trying to figure out the simplest way to make sense of the whole thing. "She's proof that his Omega might not have died as he said she did. Cambrie is his daughter, and one of his female packmates smuggled the child away from him so she wouldn't end up in the situation she's in now. If we can find the other two pack members and get them to tell us what they know, or even if the public knows who Cambrie is, they will demand that he's removed from office."

"Wait, we can do that?" Rick challenged.

"It's an old law, one that's never been used, but if there is a vote of no confidence from a majority of the population, there has to be a re-election," I shared. "When they first started this concept of the Council of Four, it was to ensure it couldn't be controlled by solely one person. They also included a failsafe if there was a situation such as now. Yoram is one hundred percent as guilty as Eric claims. I'm the one who figured it out and brought the matter to him."

"Holy fuck," Rick gasped, sitting back in his chair heavily. "Okay, so we need to act tonight while you're all doing the press conference. Yoram will be busy and unable to do anything if he gets alerted to what's happening. You'll be there to stall him just in case something changes and he can get away. At the residence, I only trust Savo and my other guy, so I'll need to bring a team with me to deal with others stationed there. The biggest perk is that I know how many and roughly what the layout of the property is. No clue about the house, but if my guy can get to Savo and let him know what's going down, then we might not need to worry.

"The rest of my pack will want to be somewhere close so they can secure her as quickly as possible. I would love for them to take her back to the home she knows, but I think it would be best to have her in another location just to be sure," I said, reaching for my phone. "I'll give you their contact information and let them know what's going down."

Rick stood and held out a hand to me. "It's an honor to be working with you, Official Stone. If I had a say in how things go after this, I'd gladly call you our sole leader. We need a man who sticks to his morals and thinks about the country as a whole."

"Thank you, your words humble me, and I'm not sure I deserve them," I responded, shaking his hand. "How selfless am I if all of this was discovered because of a woman?"

"The fact that you're even asking me that, should answer your question. I know it will be hard to do but leave the rescue to me. I'll make sure your Omega gets returned to your pack safely. You just need to focus on our people and tell them as much of the truth as you can. Trust them to take the rope when you offer them a way out," Rick urged before leaving my office. "Oh, and I'll have one of the men I trust come to look after you for the rest of the day," he called over his shoulder.

Sitting there in my office, I took a moment to process everything that had just happened between Rick and me. Then, I called Nixon and gave him the much shorter version of our plan to have Cambrie in our arms by the end of the day. Now, I just needed to figure out what the hell I was going to say in this press conference.

CHAPTER 45

Cambrie

Something was going on. I could feel it in the energy of the room as I tried to concentrate on my history books. Arthur had me forgo all other books that didn't pertain to Shearia and their past until the present. It was an interesting country, focusing on education for all people, but their views on Omegas were subservient. While Oscad didn't have a fair system for Omegas, we weren't considered less than other designations. If anything, we were overvalued. Which made them control all aspects of our lives, even though we still weren't expected to be seen and not heard.

Could this be where they're trying to send me? My thoughts drifted to the one-sided conversation I heard Arthur having earlier. Whoever he'd been talking to said they would come for me tomorrow. His argument had been that he didn't feel I was ready, and now here I was focusing solely on this country.

Savo had returned a short while ago and seemed restless, not the silent sentinel he'd been the last few days. Between his agitation and Arthur's irritation, I was left in the middle feeling lost at what to do, so I studied. Learning was something I enjoyed, and it usually could distract me from the problems whirling around me, but not today. Today felt different, almost like I was on the edge of a knife and with one wrong move, I might get cut.

"Miss Cambrie, are you even paying attention to what you're reading? You've been staring at that page for over fifteen minutes," Arthur snapped, startling me into dropping the book on my desk with a loud *thump*. "Seems the history of a wise and noble people isn't to your liking. How about we work on something more physical and see if we can keep you on task? I'm going to get the tea service, and we will work through that. It will be one of the most important tasks you do for your pack, so you must master it."

Arthur walked over to the door and spoke to the guard outside before he returned to me. "Stand," he commanded.

Rising to my feet slowly, I watched his every move, feeling like I might get hit for some reason. The anger pouring off Arthur was almost palpable and had all the warning bells in my head going off.

"Morning tea is a ritual that happens before breakfast is served. It is the one task that must be performed by the Omega for her Alphas. Doing this shows your humility, willingness to serve, and gratitude for all they provide for you," Arthur droned on. "When you are serving, you must never meet your Alpha's gaze as a show of his dominance over you. While waiting, I want you to stand up straight, drop your head, and clasp your hands together, but keep them relaxed."

I did as he requested, but we were once again back to the stage of him using a ruler to poke and prod at places I needed to adjust. I could feel Savo's gaze heavy on my back as he watched. So far, Arthur hadn't done anything that caused me harm besides his cruel words. Something more was going on besides the fact that I was leaving tomorrow. That wouldn't have made Arthur so volatile after having kept such a cold exterior this whole time.

"Don't look so scared. Your Alphas are your protectors and providers," Arthur grumbled, using his ruler to tap the side of my cheek. "You should always have a serene gaze. Many would wish to be in your place, knowing they will never need or want for anything in their life. These men you will be given to are leaders of the highest level, and the actions of their Omega reflect on their ability to attend to your basic needs. Looking like you might cry at the drop of a hat would make people believe you are not being looked after."

Closing my eyes, I took a deep breath in, counting to three and letting it back out like Rafael had taught me. It helped slightly, except when I heard the loud banging knock on the door, I flinched. My heart was racing in my chest waiting for retaliation from Arthur, but when nothing happened, I looked up to find Savo standing next to me, glaring at the Beta. If looks could kill, the butler would be dead on the floor with the rage simmering in Savo's gaze.

"That must be the tea," Arthur muttered and turned on his heel to fetch it.

While he was distracted, Savo turned his gaze on me letting the back of his finger brush along the cheek Arthur had touched. He didn't say anything, only he didn't need to because the possessive anger was written all over him. Whatever he'd been doing to come across as a Beta didn't seem to be doing much good at the moment. I gave him a soft smile trying to reassure him, but he wasn't having it.

Instead of going back to his normal spot, he took a seat at the table. "It will be better for her to learn with two people, since I'm assuming the pack will have more than one Alpha."

Arthur's jaw clenched, but he nodded and sat in the seat opposite him. "Now, Miss Cambrie, in Shearia they use loose-leaf tea, so you will need to scoop one spoonful for every cup of tea you are pouring. As there are two of us, put two scoops in the teapot."

Looking over the tray, I found the glass jar of dried leaves. I tried to unscrew it, but the lid was on too tight, and I had hardly any strength to speak of, even though I was building stamina. I tried, but no matter how I maneuvered the jar, it wouldn't budge. My hands got sweaty as my anxiety rose, knowing that Arthur would be upset with me but I didn't know what else to do. How could I fix this if I wasn't strong enough?

"Hand it to me, Cambrie," Savo directed.

Arthur all but growled at the order. "No, she has to do it herself. This whole process is for only the Omega to perform. It defeats the whole purpose if any of the pack assists."

"You said it was the Alpha's place to provide for her needs. Wouldn't opening this when she can't fall under that line of thinking? Or are they solely concerned about her basic needs and nothing beyond that?"

"It's a jar. How is opening a jar providing for her? She's incompetent, and there's nothing any of us can do about it. Look at her, she's standing there shaking like a leaf, skin and bones, and not a trace of lady-like grace to her. We are sending her to be our representation of what Oscad has to offer Shearia, and this is a disgrace!"

Savo shot out of his chair, knocking it back with a roar. He grabbed Arthur by the neck and yanked him up so his feet dangled in the air. "How *dare* you speak about her like that while I'm sitting here. That Omega is *mine,* and you will never utter another disrespectful word about her, or I'll remove your tongue."

Arthur's eyes went wide as Savo's scent changed and his dominance filled the room. It was clear to me that while I knew Savo was an Alpha and could recognize the energy in him, I hadn't seen his true self. If I'd felt this before I trusted him, I would never have allowed him near me. The anger and violence rolling off him in Arthur's direction was overwhelming.

"Y... you're... Alpha," Arthur choked out.

Savo snarled in the man's face as he spoke. "Yes. She's *mine.*"

"How," Arthur rasped as Savo let up on him slightly.

"That isn't any of your concern right now. What you should be worried about is whether or not I'm going to kill you," Savo threatened.

Gasping, I grabbed the arm that was holding Arthur aloft. "No, you can't kill him. You're better than that. It's why you left everything behind you. I know you're a good man, Savo. Having his death on your hands will only hurt you later when you calm down."

My Alpha looked at me, his green eyes wild with the need to protect me. "He'll hurt you, that's been his goal all along, to punish you for being born."

"What?" I asked, completely confused by the change in topic. "What are you talking about? Arthur has no idea who I am. We only met when I came here."

Savo shook his head as he dropped Arthur to the ground. "Tell her, tell her the truth of what your Alpha did. She deserves to know why she's been put through hell her entire life."

"Hell? What does she know about hell?" Arthur spat, once his coughing subsided. "That bitch ruined everything when she stole Yoram's daughter and ran away. It was bad enough that her weak-willed mother couldn't withstand the drugs her own family made, leaving us with her spawn to raise. All we had to do was wait for Yoram to gain control of Oscad, then we could be free. He wouldn't need a pack to put on appearances, all he needed was the baby to barter with, and we were home free. Then, they disappeared."

It was as if a bucket of cold water was poured over my head as I started to make sense of his ramblings. "Are you saying that Official Yoram Dubois is my father and the woman who raised me *wasn't* my mother?"

"Seems you're not a complete idiot," Arthur taunted. "The woman who stole you was a Beta in our pack, Aria. Now it's just me and Laura, Aria's sister, left to clean up the mess she made. The three of us were with Yoram from the beginning, but he needed an Omega to give him a child. When he found the perfect one, he bonded her to him just like my Laura and her sister Aria. Bastard knew leaving me unmarked did him more good, threatening to separate Laura and me. He never loved her, he never loved any of us. All we did was get him what he really loved... power."

My heart beat wildly in my chest as panic, betrayal, and hurt slammed into me at his words. My real mother was dead, my fake mother was also dead, and the man who beat and abused me my whole life wasn't even my father. No, the man who held that title was even worse if what Marius and Spencer had told me was true. They called him evil, the devil, a man who cared about no one but himself. Arthur was only confirming that with this new revelation and how he abused his own pack.

Darkness started to seep into my vision as my legs collapsed under me.

"Cambrie," Savo called, catching me before I hit the ground. My sight was fuzzy as the stress and panic made my head pound.

My Alpha held me in his arms and started to leave the room.

"Where do you think you're going, Alpha?" Arthur snarled. "If you think I'm going to let you take my last chance for freedom, you're not the man Yoram told me you were. No wonder you had to run from your home. If your father knew the kind of man you turned into, he'd kill you himself for being such a disgrace."

Savo growled. "You don't know a damn thing about my father or me. If you'd been a stronger man, you'd never have let yourself be trapped here in this house. Aria was brave enough to run. What held you back? Seems to me like you let yourself be caged here in this place all your life because you were too scared of Yoram to do what a real man would have done for the woman they love."

"We'll see about that. I'll set off the silent alarm," Arthur announced, his maniacal laughter filling the room, making me shiver. "You'll never be able to fight off that many guards and keep her safe. No one is that good."

Savo clutched me tightly to his chest as he bolted out of the room. All the motion made me sick to my stomach, so I buried my face in his neck and held on tight.

"I've got you, *Keksík. I* won't let anything happen to you," Savo whispered.

"There they go," a man shouted. "Don't use your guns, we can't risk hurting the Omega. Switch to the tasers."

The sound of booted feet running down the hall after us had me peeking over his shoulder. Ten men with murder in their eyes were chasing after us. Each of them held an odd-looking gun that must be the taser he was talking about. Savo was fast, and we were keeping the lead, but how far could we get before they cornered us?

"Savo, you need to let me go and get out of here," I whispered harshly. "They won't hurt me, but they'll kill you if they catch you. Please, you have to stay alive. Let me go. I'll make sure I slow them down. You can even throw me at them, and they'll have to stop. Please, Savo, I can't lose you," I begged, my throat tightening as I spoke.

He ignored me and picked up the pace, gaining more of a lead. He paused long enough to kick down a door and I found myself plopped on my bed. Twisting so I could see what was happening, I saw Savo slam the door closed and shove furniture in front of it to slow them down. Once satisfied, he jogged over to me and cupped my face, kissing me so fiercely he stole the last bit of breath from my lungs.

"*Keksik*, I'm never going to abandon you. We will get through this together. There is a plan in place, we just have to stall long enough for help to come at five o'clock."

"What time is it now?" I asked, looking around the room for a clock.

Savo looked at his watch. "It's four-thirty, but I have an idea."

"What's your idea?" I questioned, flinching when the door started to rattle as people banged on it. "You didn't block the other door from your room." I cried when the sound of another door getting kicked in was heard close by.

"Cambrie, I need you to look at me," Savo said urgently.

Meeting his gaze, I tried to stop my hands from shaking as my already frayed nerves only worsened.

"Do. You. Trust me?" Savo asked gravely.

I knew the answer to that the second he asked. "With my life."

He searched my face as if trying to make sure I meant what I was saying. "I need you to know that you are everything to me, Cambrie, and no matter what happens, I will do whatever it takes to keep you safe."

"I know you will," I answered, kissing him softly. "You're my guardian angel."

He scooped me up in his arms like a child. I wrapped my legs around his waist, not caring that it made my skirt rise to just cover my butt as I clung to his neck. Walking over to the bookshelf by the fireplace, he hit a lever and pulled it away from the wall revealing a stone path.

"There's no light in here so just keep holding onto me tightly, alright?" Savo instructed.

"Okay," I answered, resting my head on his shoulder.

When the bookcase was back in place, the world went dark. While I wasn't afraid of the dark after spending so many years trapped in the basement, I didn't relish the idea of spending time in it. Savo moved with confidence as he ran a hand along one wall, leaving the other to cup my butt holding me to him. Voices from my room echoed and then a glow of light told me they'd found the entrance.

"Savo, they're coming," I hissed, trying to keep my voice low in my panic.

He paused for a second, switched hands supporting me, and started to jog down the tunnel. With the soft glow, we could see a little better, allowing him to move faster. Then he paused when we came to a door and tried to find the latch that would open it.

"They can't have gotten far," a voice said, echoing down the tunnel.

A whine escaped my lips, making Savo tense as he held me. Then he shifted his hold, pushing me up and over his shoulder. A hand trailed up my leg pushing the fabric of my skirt out of the way, leaving my butt exposed, only wearing my undies.

"What are you doing?" I demanded.

"You said you trusted me with your life. What about your heart?" Savo asked.

I frowned, wiggling in his arms. "What are you talking about?"

"To trust someone with your life is one thing but to trust them with your heart is a completely separate matter. Could you see us together? Would you be happier with me in your life or out of it?" Savo pressed as the voices got closer, and I saw flashlight beams bobbing as they ran.

"While I don't understand why you're asking me this now, I'll answer," I huffed. "If you left me, my heart would break, and I'm not sure I could bear losing you or any other member of my pack. You're all mine, and I want us to live a happy, loving life together. So if you have a plan to get us the hell out of here to do that, I'm all ears," I snapped, feeling scared and frustrated.

Every thought going through my head came to a screeching halt as teeth pierced through the skin of my butt cheek. A euphoric sensation flooded my body as I felt a connection; a link between Savo and me clicked into place. The feel of his tongue running over the mark he had just made had me moaning, because it felt like he was licking my clit instead of my ass.

"You're mine now, *Keksik*. They can't send you to Shearia anymore," Savo stated as he shifted me lower in his arms and turned us to face the oncoming men. "You hear that, assholes? This Omega has been marked and bonded to an Alpha. Lay a finger on her, and I will rip out your hearts for such an insult."

The sound of feet came to a stop. "Fuck."

CHAPTER 46

Cambrie

Savo marked me.

I was now a bonded Omega to Savo. *Oh my god, what were the others going to think? Were they going to hate me? Will they still want me if Savo now has to be part of the pack?*

"You bastard, how did no one realize you're an Alpha this whole time?" a man demanded. "We still can't let you leave. Once a person enters this house, they stay until Yoram decides they can go, and she was the first person that was ever going to walk out of here."

Savo adjusted my dress, so my butt was now covered and tucked me close to his chest. "I don't really care what you or Yoram think. That man is on borrowed time as it is, or didn't you hear the news?"

Turning my head slightly, I watched the guards and their confused expressions. Then the door behind us opened and a woman was standing there. At least, I think it was a woman. She was so frail and gaunt she could have been a ghost. Then as I looked at her longer, she reminded me so much of my mother— the woman who claimed to be my mother, that is. This must be her sister that Arthur had mentioned.

"What's going on here?" she questioned, then spotted me. "You!"

I yelped as she lunged at me, but Savo maneuvered me out of

her way and away from the guards. "Hold on tight, *Keksík*. We're going to make a run for it," Savo warned before he darted into the room the woman came out of, slamming the secret door behind us.

We were now in a room that looked like a hoarder lived in it. Stacks of newspapers were piled on any flat surface, with clippings pinned to the walls. Black marker was used to write around all of them with nonsensical phrases, but it didn't take a genius to figure out what they meant. This woman hated Yoram and Omegas with a burning passion. It's almost as if she believes that if *all* Omegas were wiped from the earth, her life would be better.

"What happened to her?" I whispered, fearing if I spoke too loudly she might pop out of some dark corner and attack me.

I could hear her screaming on the other side of the secret door, banging on it to let her back in, but Savo was already heading for the door that should lead us back into the house. He let go of me with one hand and pulled out his gun, the cool metal chilling my skin where it rested on my thigh.

"Are you really going to kill them?" I questioned as I tucked my face against his neck.

"Only if they leave me no choice, but if it's them or us, it's always going to be them," Savo said with a finality to his tone, telling me I wasn't going to change his mind.

"Savo!" a man hollered down the hall. "Hurry up, I don't know what you did, but shit hit the fan, and we gotta get a move on it. Rick is in place. We just need to be ready at the exit point."

I peeked out and saw a young man closer to my age waving Savo to hurry. "It's alright, *Keksík*, he's a friend who's been helping me get in contact with your pack. Help is coming, and we'll be out of this slice of hell soon. Just keep your head down."

We made it down to the first floor without any trouble, but as we made our way down the hall, five men appeared with guns at the ready. "Stop right there," a man ordered. "Put the Omega down and step away from her."

"Sorry, guys, that's not going to happen," Savo answered. "I would rather I didn't have to kill you since it's going to upset my

Omega. So, when I ask you to let us go, I'm doing it for her, not because I have any hesitation about killing you where you stand."

"We both know that if we let you leave, he's going to kill us anyway," another spoke. "This is a lose-lose situation, but there are two of you and five of us. I like our chances."

Savo grunted and kissed the side of my head. "I'm sorry."

Before I could ask what he was talking about, three shots went off in quick succession, making me flinch at the sound and my ears ring. Before I could even make sense of what was happening, another volley of shots echoed in the hall as Savo charged forward and ducked into a room. Two more shots and the sound of glass shattering made me cry out as Savo vaulted out of a window into the night air.

The weather was still cool and the sun was starting to set, making the sky a bright orange bleeding into pink. Normally, I would have appreciated the view, but all I could focus on was the metallic scent of blood. I knew I wasn't hurt, so it had to be Savo.

"Are you alright?" I asked desperately as I clung to him.

He didn't answer as he ran through the yard toward a low stone wall. Just when I thought he might need to slow down or turn to avoid the wall, he pushed harder. To keep myself from screaming, I bit down on Savo's shoulder, trying to stifle the sound as he hurdled over the stone wall. He used a hand to propel us further, but what I saw on the other side had me closing my eyes and squeezing his neck so hard I was worried I might be choking him. The drop on the other side of the wall was much steeper, and I wasn't sure how we would land without one of us getting hurt.

Savo wrapped his arms around my body as we landed and immediately started to roll down the rest of the hill. I could hear twigs snapping and Savo grunting every now and then until we came to a stop. When he didn't start moving right away, I wriggled out of his arms to look him over. There was blood seeping out of a wound in his leg, and he was covered in cuts everywhere his skin showed. He lay there on his back ensuring that I was safe, eyes closed and breath shallow.

"No, no, no, no, Savo," I cried, clutching his face, willing him to open his eyes. "Please, please wake up. You need to get up. We aren't safe yet," I begged. "You got us out of the house, but I don't know where we're supposed to meet the others. Savo, I need you. Wake up!"

Leaning down, I kissed him because that's what all the fairy tales I read said to do. He was my guardian angel who promised to never leave me. This had to work. When he still didn't wake, I got up and tried to move him, but he was far too heavy for me to even budge. I looked around wildly and spotted that we were near a road. *Could that be where he was trying to get us to?*

"I'll be right back," I whispered, placing another quick kiss on his lips.

Keeping low and trying to stay in the brush that littered the edge of the road, I crept forward. I spotted a black vehicle parked with the engine running, but the lights were off. *Do I risk it? What if it's more guards watching the road in case we left?* Then the door to the van opened with six men emerging, all giving each other silent signals. I almost turned to head back to Savo when I spotted Rafael emerge from the van.

"Please remember, if Cambrie is scared and you try to grab her without explaining, it will trigger a panic attack," he warned. "I understand there might not be time, but if possible, just tell her who you are and that we sent you."

"We'll do our best. If she's with Savo, then it might not be an issue. Our guy says he hardly ever leaves her side," the apparent leader answered.

That was all I needed to hear before I burst out of the brush and screamed with all my might waving my arms. "*Over here*! Please help, Savo's hurt!"

Rafael's head snapped in my direction and he was off running to me. Seconds later, I was scooped up and my face was buried in my Alpha's sandalwood and vanilla scent, making me sob with relief. Everything I'd been holding back for the past few days burst, and I sobbed into his neck as he covered me in kisses.

"Little One, oh my precious Little One, you're really here in my arms," Rafael muttered over and over, clutching me to his body.

He started to walk toward the van, and that had me pulling myself together. "No, we need to go back for Savo. He's hurt. We need to rescue him."

"It's alright, Cambrie, the others will grab him. You're my priority right now. We need to get you safe, the others are waiting for you," he answered, trying to soothe me.

I struggled in Rafael's arms, panic filling me at the thought of being separated from Savo. "You don't understand, I *can't* leave him, Rafael. He needs me, they shot him, and he wasn't waking up," I said hysterically.

Rafael stopped and loosened his hold to look me in the face. "Cambrie, what do you mean you can't leave him?"

I bit my lip but released it the second Rafael frowned at the nervous habit. "Do you promise not to be mad at him? I'll understand if you don't want me anymore after what happened, but I can't stand the thought of him getting hurt when he did it to save me."

"Shh, Little One, take a deep breath," Rafael urged, cupping my face and using his thumb to wipe away my tears. "There is nothing you can say to me that will make me turn away from you, Cambrie. I love you, and whatever happens, we can work through it no matter what it is."

"Do you mean that?" I asked with a sniffle. "No matter what it is?"

"On my honor as an Alpha, whatever you tell me will not change how I feel about you," Rafael vowed, his face serious, readying himself for whatever I was going to tell him.

"Savo and I are bonded. He's really an Alpha," I blurted out.

Rafael's whole body sagged in relief, as if he'd been expecting me to say something much worse. "While that is a big deal and not something I expected you to say, nothing about that changes my relationship with you."

If I hadn't already fallen for this man, who has always gone above and beyond to treasure my heart, this moment would have solidified my feelings.

"I love you too, Rafy, with all my heart," I shared, leaning in and kissing my Alpha, trying to show him just how much he meant to me.

Having found my pack and then being torn away from them, showed me just how much I loved them. Each of these men was a part of me, and I needed them to feel whole. While Savo kept me strong and sane through all that happened in that house, I needed the rest of them just as much.

"Little One, you honor me with your confession, and I will always do whatever I can to deserve that love. Now, let's go check on your Alpha," Rafael said, pressing a kiss to my forehead as we headed the way I'd come.

Three men were hovering around Savo, who was thrashing about. "Get the fuck away from me. Where is Cambrie? What have you done with my Omega? *Keksík!*" he bellowed.

"Shut the fuck up, you idiot," a man snapped at Savo. "Look, I get you're upset, but calling out our position isn't going to help anyone, least of all your Omega. Also, since when have you been a goddamn Alpha?"

My anger at the way that man was yelling at Savo had me all but growling. "Don't you dare talk to him like that," I shouted. Everyone's heads snapped to look at me in Rafael's arms. "You have no idea what he had to do to keep me safe and I don't like your tone, mister."

Rafael snorted, trying to keep from laughing at the soldiers blinking at me, but Savo just grinned, grabbing the guy who yelled at him. "You heard the lady, watch your tone and help me the hell up, boss."

"Yeah, I heard her. Sounds like she's the perfect woman to handle your bossy bullshit," Savo's boss muttered, helping Savo to his feet. "Looks like they got you in the leg. Any other injuries we should know about?"

"I think I hit my head on a rock when we rolled down the hill, which knocked me the hell out, but other than that I'll be fine," Savo answered.

His boss gave him a look that told me he didn't believe my Alpha in the slightest. "We need to get her to safety. Then I'm dragging your ass to our guy to have you looked over. I know you can't go to a hospital right now, but I would be the world's shittiest boss if I didn't make sure you weren't going to die."

I tensed in Rafael's arms, and Savo's gaze locked on mine as if he knew I was worried. "I'll be fine, *Keksík.* He's just being overly cautious." Then his eyes shifted from mine to Rafael's. "She tell you?"

Rafael nodded. "Let's worry about that after we get you both somewhere safe and looked over. The others are waiting for word at the safe house we'll stay at until the rest of our plan can be put into play, removing the real danger."

"Sounds good to me," Savo agreed.

We headed back to the van where they loaded the three of us in, along with the driver. When none of the others joined us, I looked at Rafael, confused. "Aren't they leaving now?"

"Not quite. Getting you was the main objective, but there are still other things they need to deal with," Rafael explained.

Savo groaned as he sat on the floor of the van, which was empty in the back except for simple benches along either side. It would seem they used it for jobs like this when they needed room for their gear and men.

"Make sure you locate the butler Arthur and a woman named Laura, they're Yoram's packmates. They know everything you could possibly need to take that motherfucker down," Savo informed his boss. "Laura's a bit unstable, so just be careful. She's unpredictable."

"Got it, now I'm sure you won't go to the clinic, so I'm gonna send Doc to you. No, don't say shit. Your Omega needs you to be looked after, so do it for her," his boss reasoned, pointing at me.

Savo glanced at me then shut his mouth and nodded, sliding the van door closed, and we were off to wherever the rest of my pack was.

Oscar

Glancing at my phone again, I saw two minutes had gone by since Rafael messaged us to say he had her. All of us had wanted to be there to get her, but there was no way that could have worked. When we talked about it, we thought that if my Little Star was traumatized, Rafael was the best person to be there for her. None of us had a clue what she might have gone through in the past four days, but I had a gut feeling it wasn't going to be a happy tale. The Beta, Savo, would be there to keep an eye on her, but would he have the ability to keep her safe?

I started to chew on my thumbnail as I paced in the living room of the safe house Rick sent us to. It was out east on the far edges of the main city, where hardly anyone lived these days. They were either in the city limits or further east in the country, where our farmers were with open land to grow food and keep livestock. The middle ground seemed to die off when things become too dangerous, not having people closer around you. Of course, with our situation, we needed to be away from people, a place no one would notice our comings and goings.

Arms wrapped around my waist as a body melded itself to my back. "They have her. She's on her way here as we speak. Everything's going to be fine," Bodhi reassured me.

Closing my eyes, I took a deep breath and let it out slowly, knowing he was right. Cambrie was with Rafael, which meant she was out of Yoram's clutches. Turning in Bodhi's hold, I looked into his hazel eyes that held as much concern as I'm sure mine must. I wasn't the only one who lost someone important to them, our whole pack did. I cupped his cheek and leaned my forehead against his, allowing his presence to help settle me.

With everything that happened since Cambrie went missing, the two of us haven't had a chance to talk. We'd finally been honest about our feelings and acted on them, but I didn't want it to be a spur-of-the-moment thing. I had to make sure he understood that I hadn't just lusted after him, that my feelings were so much deeper than that. Yes, finally, being able to wrap him up in my arms and feel his body accept me in every way possible had been mind-blowing. Since that happened, we'd been sleeping together at night, comforting each other, but neither of us had pushed it past that.

Now that our Omega would be back safely in our arms again, my next priority was to ensure Bodhi understood I *wanted* him. Not just for a night or for a fling, no, now that I've seen what things can be like between us, I craved more of it like a drug. Lifting my head, I kissed him, needing to reassure him, and myself, he still wanted me and that I wanted him.

Bodhi responded right away, letting one of his hands slide up my back to pull me closer as the other groped my ass. I couldn't help but smirk at the cheekiness of the man as eager for my attention as I was his. Deepening the kiss, he opened for me and I took my time exploring everything about him I could. A moan escaped him and it had me grinding up against him. God, I wanted to steal him away to one of the bedrooms and take him right here right now, but this wasn't the time.

Slowly I pulled back, pressing a final soft kiss to his lips and purring at the sight of his glassy-eyed expression. I'd turned him on just as much as he'd turned me on. "*We need to find time to talk, you and me. I need to know what you're thinking, feeling, and wanting between us before I assume too much,*" I said, feeling a slight twinge of panic that he might not want the same things I did.

"I would like that as well, but to be clear, what I want is you to be my Alpha and Cambrie to be our Omega. For this pack to be a family, fully bonded, the way it should have been before we ever left the house to tell the CoF about her," Bodhi stated, a slight tone of anger in his voice. "If Marius had let any of you bond her to us, then none of this would have happened."

Cocking my head, I searched his face, curious as to where this anger was coming from. *"Do you blame me for not marking her when I had the chance?"*

Bodhi let out a frustrated puff of air. "No, Oscar, I don't blame you or any of the others, if I'm being honest with myself. I'm mad because we could have done something to prevent Cambrie from going through any of this, but it wouldn't have stopped the problems. Who knows, going that route might have made things worse."

A sudden noise of a door being slammed caught our attention as feet thundered down the steps, and Spencer rushed for the front door. "They're here!" he called on his way past.

The house we were staying in was two stories with three bedrooms all on the upper floor, while downstairs was the living space. On the lower level were the kitchen, family room, dining room, and living room, where Bodhi and I were. The reason I'd been pacing here was because I could see out the front window to the driveway, but clearly, I'd missed the black van pulling into the driveway.

Bodhi and I were hot on Spencer's heels, with Nixon bounding down the stairs behind us. Marius had to remain in the city to deal with things, but we hoped that tomorrow he could find a way to sneak out here to see her. I knew it killed him to remain back at the house, but with the press conference being what we needed to get Cambrie out and Yoram distracted, he was making all this possible. This was why he was the man I chose to follow and let lead our family down the road we've been traveling. Honor and sacrifice for the good of all was not an easy choice to make when we all wanted to be selfish in this situation.

As the van door opened, we spotted a rather roughed-up Savo, making my heart seize at the thought my Little Star might be hurt.

"Would one of you mind helping me get up, fuckers shot me in the leg."

Nixon stepped up as did I, since we were probably the only two who could handle his bulk. Then my world once more became whole as I saw Cambrie's teal-haired head as she made her way to the exit. My cursory sweep of her told me she was relatively unharmed, if a little haggard looking, with her stiff, dowdy looking dress covered in debris. Spencer and Bodhi caught her up in a group hug, making me comfortable enough to leave her with them to get Savo inside.

"Do we need to get you to a hospital?" Nixon asked, leading the way to the kitchen, where the floor was tile and easier to clean.

A few blood droplets landed on the carpet but can't say I cared all that much. The house was decent and would keep us safe, but by no means was it anything for us long term. The furniture was basic and simple, most likely found secondhand. It was a place to stay as things blew over and didn't draw attention, which is what we needed.

"No, Rick is sending over our guy, Doc, and he'll look me over. It would be too risky for me to go to a hospital, and I won't leave *Keksik* until I know this whole thing is settled," Savo answered with a groan as he sat in the chair.

"*What happened? Did something go wrong for you to get shot?*" I asked, confused because the plan sounded fairly straightforward when Rick explained it.

Savo rubbed his face with a hand, hissing as he caught the large scrape on his cheek. "Fuck," he swore. "I think we need everyone here to be able to answer that question."

Nothing about that statement put me at ease, so I went to find my Little Star. If he was in such rough shape, I could only imagine what might have happened to my Omega. The front door was open, and I saw her walking in with Spencer and Bodhi holding her hands with Rafael right behind them. I caught his eye, knowing he would tell me the truth. "*What happened?*"

"Where did you put Savo?" Rafael asked.

Why were they all so concerned about this Beta? Yeah, he watched over Cambrie, but his job for the moment was over while she was with us. I knew Marius wanted to hire him to stay on after this, but we needed time as a pack.

"*He's in the kitchen since he was bleeding everywhere,*" I answered, jerking my thumb back the way I came.

"Cambrie thinks she's alright, but Savo told me she'd hurt her knees a few days ago, and if we are going to have a doctor stop by then I think he should look at them. Why don't we all head to the kitchen." He brushed a hand down Cambrie's hair drawing her attention. "Are you hungry? Thirsty? We have plenty of food in the house, even some hot chocolate, if I'm not mistaken."

"Oh, hot chocolate sounds delicious," she answered excitedly. "The house we were staying in was always so cold. Something hot sounds nice."

That was all Bodhi needed to hear before he took off for the kitchen to make our Omega what she desired. Unable to wait any longer, I walked up to my beautiful Little Star and scooped her up in my arms. With my face shoved in her hair, I started to purr, unable to tell her just how much I missed her. Nuzzling until I found her ear, I steeled myself for the pain even though I had to tell her. She *needed* to hear it from my lips.

"I love you," I forced out, cursing my broken voice. This woman, and a certain man, when it came time, deserved to hear those words but I wasn't able to do that for them.

Cambrie pulled back and held my face between her small hands staring deep into my eyes. "I love you too, Oscar, so, so much."

Using one of my hands on her back, I pushed her forward so I could kiss her tempting lips, relishing the taste of her. Although it had only been four days, it felt like I'd been missing a part of myself, and now that she was here, I was whole again. No more holding back, no more questioning if this was right or needing to follow the rules. This woman was ours, and I'd be damned if I ever let anyone take her from us again. She was the glue that turned our pack from a group of friends into a family. Without her, I wouldn't know how

Bodhi felt or have had the courage to take that step. Seeing how brave someone so small could be gave me the confidence I needed to take the leap and find even more happiness than I thought possible.

Releasing her lips, I started to kiss over every inch of her face, peppering her with love and affection until she giggled. God, her giggle could make me melt in the best way; I never wanted to go a day without hearing it.

"Come on, let's head to the kitchen," Rafael encouraged as Cambrie snuggled into my embrace, resting her head on my shoulder, content to stay right where she was.

Heading to the back of the house where the kitchen was, Spencer pulled out a chair for me to sit with Cambrie. He let his finger trail through her hair before he stood next to Nixon, wrapping an arm around his waist. Nixon looked down at Spencer with such a raw look of love I felt a little like I was intruding even seeing it.

Being a man who couldn't speak left me with large amounts of time to observe the people in my life. Something between them had changed, for the better, I believed. We all knew they loved each other, but there was an odd tension between Nixon and Marius when it came to Spencer. None of us saw it coming between them as friends or lovers, but whatever happened earlier had broken down that wall, leaving behind love and trust at its finest.

"Where's Marius?" Cambrie asked.

Nixon turned his attention to her as he answered. "He's back in the city. He should be finishing a press conference right now, and we hope he can join us tomorrow." Cambrie must have pouted at this as Nixon's lips twitched trying to hold back a smile. "We needed someone to keep Yoram from being able to stop us rescuing you, so Marius did what he needed to, and now you're home with us."

"But he'll be here tomorrow?" she questioned.

"We hope so, but only if it's safe to do so. None of us are going to give anyone a chance to steal you away again," Spencer added.

Cambrie nodded, sitting up in my arms, and looked over Savo, who had his leg propped up on a chair and his head tossed back. He looked like he was sleeping, if that was at all possible in such a position.

"Savo," she called to him.

He cracked an eye and looked at her worried face. "I'm all right, my sweet girl. Once Doc looks me over and I get some sleep, I'll be just fine."

"Why don't I believe that? Your boss seemed to think it was worse than you were letting on," Cambrie sassed back.

All of us were a little shocked at her response, only having caught glimpses of this side of our Omega. It seemed that Savo brought out the feisty side of Cambrie, and it was nice to see.

"Sweetheart, don't be rude. He saved your life after all," Nixon warned with a chuckle, stepping out of Spencer's hold to squat in front of me. "I realize I don't know the friendship you two have built with each other, but typically that isn't how wounded people should be reasoned with. Not to mention, men don't like to admit when they're hurt in front of a girl they like."

Cambrie turned till she was sitting with her back to my chest so she could face the others better. I missed not being able to see her face as easily. Watching all the expressions she made told me exactly what she was thinking, even if she didn't say it.

"There's something you all need to know, but I don't feel right saying it without Marius here," she announced, then looked over at Rafael. "Do I wait?"

"No, Little One, this is not a matter that you should wait to tell them," Rafael answered, making me worry about what she needed to tell us.

Giving my hand a squeeze, she slipped out of my lap and went to stand next to Savo. Instantly, he reached out and intertwined their fingers, letting his thumb brush over the back of her hand. "Let me, *Keksík,* I need to take responsibility for what happened and explain to your pack. There is a right and a wrong way to go about what I did, and under normal circumstances, I would be in the wrong."

Everyone in the room seemed to tense, as if bracing themselves for something we weren't sure we could handle. Cambrie had been through so much already, and our worst fear was even more awful things might have occurred while she was trapped in that house.

"First, I would like to say that I have the utmost respect for all of you and what you are doing for this country and especially Cambrie. This is going to take me a moment to explain, so while I don't deserve it, I would request that you let me share everything before making your judgment on me. I'm an immigrant. I came here from Asturg many years ago, trying to escape my country and my father, General Rasvan," Savo explained and paused a moment, letting us all absorb the bomb he'd just dropped in our laps, but he wasn't done.

"He wanted me to be his right-hand man, to one day take his place leading the Northern Faction when he passed. I couldn't do it. There was no way I could stand behind and fight for a country that killed both my mother and sister in the name of our people. Since the day I left my home, I took dampeners to hide my status as an Alpha, choosing to live life as a Beta. I got hired by Rick for security and knew that wouldn't be a life that would attract a pack or an Omega, leaving me to live my life. Then Cambrie appeared in my life out of nowhere, a chance meeting that showed me no matter how many pills I took, I would never be a Beta. After I left your home, I didn't think I'd ever see her again, but when the government told me I had a job to protect an important man's daughter, I couldn't refuse. Yoram knew who I was but not *what* I was, something that was his biggest mistake once he told me I'd be guarding Cambrie," Savo continued.

Bodhi cut in, pushing off the wall of the kitchen, looking frustrated. "What does this have to do with anything? You made it sound like you did something to her, and I want to know what that is. I don't give a shit about who you are or how you ended up in that house, so cut the crap and spit it out already."

Cambrie scowled and opened her mouth to scold Bodhi, most likely, but Savo tugged her to his side and caught her chin in his grip. "No, my sweet girl, he has every right to be upset, and I feel he won't be the only one in a moment. Let them process however they need to. It will help in the long run."

Nixon's face clouded with anger as Savo spoke. "Don't you speak to her like that. She isn't your Omega."

Savo closed his eyes and let out a heavy sigh. "Actually, she is one hundred percent my bonded Omega."

CHAPTER 48

Cambrie

The sinking feeling that twisted my gut had me bracing myself for them to scream, yell, or curse me for what I'd allowed to happen. Savo wasn't pack; they didn't know him as I did, the good man he was who did everything to keep me safe. My Alpha asked me to let them feel what they needed to feel, so I kept my eyes on the floor and waited for the backlash.

Savo's arm wrapped around my waist, pulling me to his side as he started to purr, trying to comfort me. I wasn't sure I could bear it if these men turned their backs on me. I knew Rafael told me it wouldn't change anything, but that was before he knew who Savo really was. Marius was an Official, there was no way he could allow the son of General Rasvan to be part of his pack. My heart begged me to trust them just as strongly as my mind contradicted that feeling.

"I'm sorry, there's been so much going on tonight I think I might be hearing things. Did you just say that you're bonded with Cambrie?" Bodhi asked.

Knowing they wouldn't believe it until they saw it, I hiked up my skirt and showed them the mark on my butt. "He did it to keep them from sending me off to Shearia. They had guns, so many guns. The guards didn't care. They would have shot him dead right before my eyes and stolen me away to another country. I don't know what happened or what changed, but the pack they sold me to was coming for me in the morning. Savo attacked Arthur, who was going to hurt me, and the guards figured out he was an Alpha. He saved us. He saved me, and he did everything possible before it was our only option."

Tears streamed down my face as I looked at all the men I loved so much. My heart felt like it was going to burst. Their expressions were full of shock, confusion, and surprise. Rafael gave me an encouraging smile but I knew I'd hurt them all, even if they were willing to forgive me.

"I betrayed you all. I'm so sorry," I sobbed, dropping to my knees and hiding my face in Savo's side as I wept. "I don't deserve to be your Omega."

Savo's purr turned into more of a growl as someone approached. "You better not be gearing up to tell her this bullshit she's saying is right. If anyone fucked up, it was me, and I'm not talking about the bonding because that would have happened no matter what. I'm the one who bonded with her before seeking pack approval, and I'll own that, but none of this is her fault."

"You don't think we know that?" Nixon's voice snapped from right behind me, making me flinch.

Savo's warning growl became deeper. "Watch yourself, Alpha. I might be wounded, but nothing will stop me from protecting her from anything or anyone who might hurt her."

"While I respect that, I would never do anything to hurt her intentionally. Out of all of my pack, I've made mistakes with Cambrie and given her the impression I wasn't all in, and I vowed I would never let her think that again. What's happened, happened, and by the sounds of it, you were doing it to ensure she could come back home to us," Nixon said in a serious tone.

Even though he was saying he wasn't upset with me, I couldn't bear to see the look of hurt I must have caused on his face. When arms wrapped around me and gently shifted me from clinging to Savo, I was enveloped in a scent of smoky tobacco and sweet scotch. Nixon started to purr as he wrapped me in his arms, tucking me close to his heart and letting me cry. I realized that I wasn't just crying about the bonding and how they would take it. No, it was a mixture of finally feeling safe, of being back with my pack, and allowing myself to acknowledge all the feelings I'd buried while I was trapped in that house.

The whole time I'd told myself I had to be strong, that they couldn't break me. Arthur's words had cut deep so many times, almost as if he knew right where it would hurt the most. Savo being there was probably the only thing that had kept me sane and not turning into what Laura had. Having one person in my corner was a shield, but it didn't mean that things didn't slip past and leave their mark. Now I was free once more and in the arms of the men who were my everything. It was amazing and terrifying to feel this way about people, knowing how much power they had over me. Yet I knew deep in my soul they would never use their power to harm me. They would always offer their love and protection as a family should.

"Sweetheart," Nixon murmured, pressing his lips to my head in a gentle caress. "Tell me what I can do to help you. I feel like you're drowning, and I want to save you but I'm not sure how."

I lifted my head from his chest, and he brushed my hair out of my face and tried to wipe away the tears still leaking from my eyes. "I almost lost everything," I croaked, my throat tight from the crying. "Only in my dreams did I think I could have people I loved and who loved me, then you all appeared. Yet, in the blink of an eye, it was snatched away from me, and I was once again trapped and locked away for someone else's gain. It was so hard to be strong. Without Savo, I don't think I could have done it."

Nixon's eyes were full of understanding and heartbreak as I spoke. He didn't interrupt me, he just let me ramble as I shared what happened in that house. Savo added his view on things or added a detail or two I hadn't remembered, bringing the tale full circle to finding Rafael on the street. While I was speaking to Nixon, I knew the others heard it all, but it was easier to explain focusing on one person. My emotions were so raw, and I felt like all the bandages they had put over them when I first showed up had been ripped off.

This was my cleansing, my purge of the lies I'd been told during my abduction. These wounds might not be as apparent on the surface like before, but they were just as damaging.

"There are no words I can say to magically make things better or to help you understand that what he told you was false," Nixon explained, pulling me back into his lap as he sat cross-legged on the kitchen floor, holding me tightly. "What we can do, no, what we will do, is remind you each and every day for the rest of your life how loved and cherished you are, Sweetheart. I know the pain of what you're experiencing. My family has done what Arthur did to you almost my whole life. If it hadn't been for Marius, Spencer, and the others of my real family, I never would have become the man I am today. It's taken me a long time to see the truth, to realize that what I'd been told to believe about myself by my family wasn't actually who I was."

I shifted my head to his shoulder to look up at him as he spoke, his voice was so soothing to listen to as I soaked up his words like a sponge.

"Did you know that I'm the oldest of three children?" Nixon asked, and I shook my head. I remember someone saying he had siblings at one point, but I didn't know their ages. "My family is from a long line of lawyers who worked in or alongside the government. They became judges, doling out justice and becoming important figures in the community. That's what I also went to school for, only to discover I hated it. The law itself was interesting to learn, but when I saw how it was practiced in our world today, it made me sick. Marius is the one who convinced me to break out of the mold my parents had set for me, and I came up with the idea for the shelter."

"My law degree helped in many ways making sure I followed the rules and guidelines while making sure others didn't screw me over. When my father found out I wasn't going to complete my law education by taking the final test to be able to practice, he stopped talking to me. My mother, on the other hand, decided that she would do whatever it took to convince me I was wrong. It was almost like she believed her words had a magical power to change me into what she wanted. Then, when Spencer entered my life, things only got worse, and my whole family turned on me. That's when I started to realize they weren't my family, my pack was. Without each and every one of them combating the lies that had been poured into me all my life, I never would have fallen in love with two amazing people. Or gained brothers who care enough to speak the truth when I'm being an ass," Nixon said with a grin looking over at Bodhi for some reason.

Then Nixon looked down at me with a soft, loving smile and with hope glimmering in his eyes. "Our pack was founded on the right things, and the people who needed to be a part of it found each other, yet we were still missing something. You, Cambrie, we were missing you. The glue that pulls us even closer, something that connects us on a deeper level than just comradery or shared ideals. That glue is love. Each of us loves you just as much as you love us. So, with that being said, if you love Savo and were willing to let him mark you, then who are we to punish you or be upset for giving him what you give to us? Cambrie, you are unlike any Omega I've ever witnessed before. You're able to ensure each and every one of us knows that you give all of us the same love. No one is more, and no one is less in your eyes, which is not what the world teaches us these days."

Spencer dropped beside Nixon and took my hand in his. "Little Dove, forgive us for reacting the way that we did. The past four days have been hell trying to figure out how to get you back, and most of us are running on little sleep. I promise we will figure this out together as a family, Savo included, because if *you* love him, then I trust your judgment. You picked us after all, so how can we say your radar is skewed?" Spencer teased.

A sudden knock on the door had us all on alert, but Rafael checked his phone and set us at ease. "Rick just texted saying Doc should be here any moment, so I'm going to guess that's him."

Spencer stood and offered a hand to me, pulling me to my feet and into a hug. "Oh, Little Dove, what are we going to do with you? Always driving us to reach deeper within ourselves to see the truth of the matter."

"I don't do that," I mumbled against his shirt.

"Hello, everyone, I'm Doc," a man greeted, causing me to lift my face from Spencer's shirt.

Doc was an older Alpha with salt and pepper hair, a kind face, and glasses that rested further down his nose than I felt was normal. He was dressed casually but had a medical bag in one hand, and Rafael was behind him with a duffel.

"If you could set that on the table for me, I would be grateful," Doc instructed. "Now, who am I looking at first?"

"Savo."

"Cambrie."

It would seem out of the whole room, I was the only one who felt that the bleeding man should be looked at first.

Doc took a moment to look at my pack and then down at me. "Ah, I see. Well, little Omega, they aren't going to let me look at your Alpha until I've checked you over. We'll be quick about it so I can set you at ease as well as the rest of the room."

I nodded and begrudgingly shuffled over to take a seat in the chair Oscar got up from. He reached into his bag and pulled out a few instruments I'd never seen before. "Can you tell me your name?" Doc asked as he checked the light on one of the tools.

"Cambrie, sir," I answered.

Doc looked at me over his glasses with a gentle smile. "No need for that. Call me Doc. When was the last time you were looked at by a doctor, Cambrie?"

"Um, I broke my arm when I was twelve. They put it in a cast," I answered.

The older Alpha paused with a frown. "And before that?"

"I really can't remember. I've always been healthy and never needed a doctor," I offered, knowing it was odd that I'd never been allowed to be seen by a doctor.

Doc cleared his throat and moved to the side with the device in his hand. "What I'm going to do is a quick overall examination since it's been a little while. It's best to make sure that nothing from this event you've been through caused any issues or made something worse you might not have known about. Now, this tool is going to let me see inside your ears. I'll look at one then the other, it might feel a little funny but shouldn't hurt at all."

The moment Doc's hand touched my ear, I froze, struggling to take in a breath. I knew that Doc wasn't a danger to me, but I was still too raw after everything that had happened. "Here, Cambi, take my hand and we'll get through this together," Bodhi offered.

I smiled at him, grateful for the offer, and gripped his fingers like they were the only thing that could keep me sane. Doc worked fast and was incredibly professional, yet my body and mind were still on high alert, not allowing me to relax. After my ears, he checked my eyes, listened to my heart and lungs, then had me pull my dress up so he could look at my knees.

"Looks like Savo did a good job cleaning the wounds. Knees are just tricky to heal with how much the skin moves around. My suggestion would be to keep ointment on them to keep the scabs softer so they don't keep cracking open and bleeding," Doc instructed. "Now, do you have any questions for me or anything else you want me to look at for you before I move to Savo?"

Shaking my head, I stood and wrapped my arms around Bodhi, unable to be touched by anyone but my pack right now. As if Doc understood, he nodded and pulled the chair over to Savo and plopped down to look over his glasses at the man.

"Alright, tough guy, when I ask you what happened, I expect you to tell me every detail. None of this macho bullshit where you tough it out because that's what Alphas do," Doc warned, holding Savo's gaze until he nodded. "Great, so other than the obvious, what do I need to look at?"

Savo shifted slightly, clearly not pleased with being cornered. "I jumped over a wall, twisting my wrist when I vaulted over it. The drop on the other side was steeper than I expected, and I cracked my head on a rock as we rolled down the hill. I haven't had a chance to look over myself to see if there are any other cuts that might need stitches. The bullet wound is through and through, so I don't think there's a bullet to worry about."

"Thank you for being honest," Doc shifted to look at the rest of us. "I know you want to be here for your packmate, but it would be best if I could have the room. I need to strip him out of his clothes to check him over and I feel everyone is entitled to their privacy."

Nixon nodded, and with an arm around Spencer's shoulders, the two of them walked out with Rafael trailing after them. I looked at Bodhi and gestured for him to give me a minute before walking over to Savo. I placed my hands on either side of his face so he was looking right at me.

"Be good, let Doc help you, and don't growl at him, please," I instructed.

Doc chuckled as he opened the duffle and pulled out the materials he would need. Savo tried to glare at the man but didn't fight against my hold. "I'll let him do what he needs to, *Keksik*, but I don't have to like it."

"I can work with that," I said, kissing him softly before I stepped back and let Bodhi and Oscar escort me out of the kitchen.

"Found yourself a good one, didn't you, tough guy?" Doc commented. I didn't hear Savo's response but I already knew what he'd say and that made me smile.

Bodhi led me into a room with an oversized suede couch that the others were already sitting on. Nixon was on the phone, but he crooked a finger, calling me over to him. When I reached him, he offered me the phone showing me the screen, which told me Marius was on the other end.

I snatched it from his hand and held it to my ear. "Marius!"

"It's me, Princess," Marius answered. "God, it's so good to hear your voice."

"I miss you," I blurted, not really knowing what to say first when I had so many things I wanted to share all at once.

"Not nearly as much as I miss you, Cambrie. I'm so sorry I couldn't be there tonight to welcome you home, but I will get there tomorrow," Marius explained.

Clutching the phone tightly, I nodded then remembered he couldn't see me. "There is nothing you need to apologize for. Nixon told me what you did so they could get me out. I'll be here waiting for you whenever you arrive," I promised.

"That is the best news I've heard all day, Princess. I won't make you wait too long, but I want you to know that what I'm working on will hopefully protect you from this ever happening again," Marius shared.

"I never doubted you'd come for me. You promised, after all," I said, trying to reassure him I understood he had things to take care of. He was one of our country's leaders, which meant looking after more than just me. "I love you."

"I love you too, Princess. I've got to run but I will see you as soon as I'm able," Marius assured me before hanging up.

Handing the phone back to Nixon, my body started to droop with a wave of tiredness. It had been one of the longest days with so many emotions, both high and low, and my body had reached its max. A yawn snuck up on me so big it made my eyes water.

"Come here, Sweetheart," Nixon directed, tugging me onto the couch next to him.

He urged me to lie down with my head on his lap and my legs resting over Spencer's. With the combination of Nixon purring and Spencer gently rubbing my feet and legs, I couldn't fight against my fatigue. It was fine to rest. I was home, in the arms of my family where I belonged.

CHAPTER 49

Cambrie

The feeling of lips brushing across my forehead, cheek, and then my lips had my eyes fluttering open to see a pair of bright green eyes. The scent of bergamot and clove wrapped around me like a warm spicy hug that had me reaching out to draw the scent closer. I nuzzled my face into his neck, needing to bathe in the fact that my final pack mate and Alpha was here with me.

"Marius," I whispered. "You're here."

"Nothing would have stopped me from getting to you, my Princess," Marius's voice rumbled through his chest that I was curled up against. "I'm sorry it took so long, but it sounds like you've been sleeping for a long time."

I peeked up from his body to look around, realizing that I wasn't in the family room anymore. Instead, I was in a simple bedroom and the clock on the nightstand told me it was the middle of the afternoon. Seeing the time, I started to wriggle out of his arms feeling that I needed to get up. It wasn't right for me to still be sleeping.

"Princess," Marius warned, tugging me down against him. "You desperately needed sleep, so we all agreed that we would let you do just that."

Someone shifted behind me as lips moved up my neck and a

hand ran up my leg, making me aware that I was naked under the sheet. "Little Dove, you didn't even stir once until Marius arrived in the room. That, to me, says you needed all the sleep you just had," Spencer murmured in my ear.

Spencer's hand moved from my hip to splay across my stomach, pulling me against him. A moan slipped out at the feel of their bodies trapping me between them. Marius started to purr as he cupped my cheek and tilted my head to kiss me. I opened for him willingly, letting my body melt against Spencer as he kissed along my shoulder, up my neck, to nibble on my ear.

"Say the word, Little Dove, if this is too much. We want you, but not at the cost of your health," Spencer said, causing Marius to pull back, which drew a whine out of my throat at the loss.

My Alpha brushed the back of his fingers along my jaw staring into my eyes. "I need more than a whine, Princess. Tell me what you want," Marius ordered.

"I want you. I want you both," I answered, pressing my ass against Spencer and my chest into Marius. "I want any of my pack that might find us in here reveling in the love we have for each other."

Marius's purr erupted from him as he caught my lips in a fierce kiss, pushing me against Spencer so I could feel his hard cock ready and waiting for me. Leaning back, Marius yanked the blankets off us, revealing my naked body to him. With a quick kiss on my lips, he drifted lower to my breasts, wrapping his mouth around a nipple. A gasp burst out quickly followed by a moan as I threaded my hands into his hair, holding him to me. Spencer turned my face to him as he kissed me deeply, groaning as I arched my back, rubbing him where his cock landed between my cheeks.

"Little Dove, you have no idea what you do to us," Spencer muttered as he nipped my ear, then pulled back. Desperately, I reached out for him not wanting him to leave me. He caught my hand and kissed the back of it. "Oh, trust me, I'm not leaving this bed, but I've been craving this certain taste, one that can only be found between your beautiful legs."

Marius followed as Spencer shifted my hips, so I was flat on my back and spread me open to him. My Beta looked down at me like I was one of the most precious things in the world. He grabbed Marius's head and pulled him in for a kiss, and Marius was more than happy to indulge him. The sight of the two of them was mesmerizing. I'd seen Spencer with Nixon a few times, and it had been just as amazing to watch. Where Nixon was in complete control with Spencer, Marius treated his Beta as more of an equal, with lots of give and take.

The two of them broke apart and turned their gaze toward me. "Look at her, Spence, could you ever imagine a more perfect Omega to share?" Marius asked.

"It's not possible. Cambrie was made for us, for this pack. She completes everything, pulling us together and creating a pack that's stronger than any I've ever seen before. That kind of magic can only happen when your souls are tied together as well as your hearts," Spencer shared as he let his hands drift up my leg, making me shiver. "Now, let us take care of you the way only a pack can, my Little Dove."

Without skipping a beat, Spencer lowered himself to his stomach, slipped his hands under my ass, and feasted on me in a way that made me moan so loud I'm sure the house knew what was happening in here. Turning my head to Marius, I reached out and grabbed the edge of his pants and gently pulled him to me. I needed to taste him as Spencer was tasting me.

"Let me take care of you, Alpha," I requested, looking up at him. "Let your Omega show you just how much she wants to please you."

Marius slipped off the bed to strip out of his clothes, then returned to me, kneeling where I had the best access to his cock. I let my fingers glide down the silky skin feeling it pulse under my touch. Grasping it, I pulled it down so I could lick the tip and the bead of pre-cum that had appeared.

"Do you see that, Princess? I want you so badly I can barely hold back from coming at your touch," Marius murmured as he brushed a hand through my hair.

I couldn't help but hum in pleasure as I took him in my mouth, loving the knowledge that my Alpha craved me as much as I did him. Spencer shifted me slightly as he slipped his tongue inside me, making me cry out around Marius's cock. My hips rocked as Spencer lapped at me like I was his favorite treat.

So distracted by what was going on between my legs, Marius started to thrust into my mouth as I relaxed into his movements. "Good girl, taking me so deep while our Beta eats out that perfect little pussy." This elicited another moan from me. "Yes, Princess, use your voice. Let us know just how much you enjoy our attention."

Never in my wildest dreams did I think I would crave such praise from my Alphas. Now that I'd gotten a taste of it, I was utterly addicted.

"Spencer, make sure you warm up both holes while you're down there. I have a feeling it won't be the two of us for long, and I plan on leaving my cum in her sweet ass," Marius instructed.

As if his statement had summoned him, Nixon appeared in my field of vision, looking down at me with hunger. "What do we have here? It looks like someone decided our Omega was on the menu for lunch."

Marius didn't slow down his movements, leaving me unable to answer him so I just hummed, making Marius groan. "Damn, it feels so good when you do that."

Spencer lifted his head, licking his lips. "Are you joining us, Nixon?"

"Hmm, am I going to join in on the naked fun with two people I love and my best friend? Seems silly not to, doesn't it?" Nixon chuckled. "But I'll need you to take the edge off, Spencer."

"Oh, I'm more than happy to provide that service, Alpha," Spencer all but purred in excitement, then lifted his ass and wiggled it like a puppy wagging its tail.

Spencer just had on sweatpants, which Nixon tugged off as Spencer resumed his work on me. He switched from my pussy to my second entrance, letting his tongue work over the sensitive skin, coaxing it to relax. Marius reached out and played with my nipples, making me writhe with all the sensations happening to me. My mind felt like it was going to short circuit, but I wanted to feel and experience everything my pack was giving me.

"Do we have lube?" Nixon asked.

With that question, everything came to a halt. "We have to have something we can use," Spencer said, his voice tinged with worry.

"How many times do I have to tell you, Spence, you don't leave home without lube?" Marius scolded as he pulled out of my mouth and snuck in for a quick kiss. "Don't you worry, Princess, I'll be right back. I won't leave you wanting."

I tracked him as he walked to the other side of the room and rustled through a duffle bag I assumed he had brought. Lying here and getting a perfect view of his naked body was nothing I'd complain about. His sculpted back was something out of a museum and his ass was firm, leading down to muscled solid legs.

"He's fucking hot, isn't he?" Spencer asked as he stretched out on top of me, kissing up my neck. "I never get tired of watching either of them naked, it's one of the most erotic things, and they could simply be brushing their teeth."

Shifting, I looked up into his bright green eyes that shone with heat and affection. "All of my pack are stunning to look at naked or clothed. I love watching the small things that happen between us. To me, that's the best thing to watch."

He smiled at me before cupping my face as he kissed me, letting his cock run through the slick leaking out of my pussy. Instinctively, I wrapped my legs around his hips, trapping him against me. Both of us moaned as the tip caught my entrance, but he didn't enter, just shifted back to glide over the surface again.

"You all really need to stop teasing me," I panted, feeling frustrated at the fire inside me that was getting stoked higher and higher.

Spencer moved off me, and I was left looking at Nixon standing naked at the end of the bed. "Goodness, it seems our little Omega is getting impatient." He reached out and grasped my ankles, dragging me down to the end of the bed so my legs hung over the edge. Bending over, he caged me in his arms with a smirk. "Tell me, Sweetheart, what do you want?"

"I want someone to fuck me," I answered.

Nixon shook his head. "I'm going to need more than that. How do you want to be fucked, and where? Give me every detail of what our beloved Omega needs from her pack to feel fulfilled."

A shiver raced through my body at his words and the eagerness in his eyes. This was the first time Nixon and I had interacted like that. From what I'd seen, out of all my men, he was slightly more aggressive and demanding. There wasn't a glimmer of fear or trepidation, but before I'd been taken everyone was concerned about how he would react being on the verge of a rut.

"Is this our moment, Nixon? Are you here with me this time?" I asked, reaching out to his face and letting my fingers trail along his jawline.

He shifted to kiss my palm. "Yes, Sweetheart, I'm all in, ready to commit and start a life together with you, Spencer, and our pack. Before, I didn't understand things clearly, but thanks to you, my eyes have been opened. My fears, while still there, don't have the same power they once did."

"Then I want you, Nixon, my Alpha, to fuck me," I stated. His face instantly became unsure, but I grasped his face and drew him down to me, putting all my love and trust into that kiss. "It's going to be fine; you won't hurt me because you love me. Your love will win out over your fear, and as you all keep telling me, I'm not as fragile as I look."

"Cambrie, what I enjoy in bed is being in control, pushing my partner's boundaries allowing them to experience new things," Nixon warned. "You've just come home to us, so that's not what you need. Right now, you should be showered with love, cuddled, and made love to, not fucked by a dominant rutting Alpha. Let Marius have you first while I fuck Spencer to help take the edge off."

"I'm more than happy to submit to you, Nixon, you're my Alpha," I answered, trying to get him to understand. "Have you ever been with an Omega?"

Nixon frowned at me. "No, before Spencer there was only one other person, another Beta."

"I hope this isn't wrong of me to say or talk about with you, but Savo is also an incredibly dominant Alpha," I started, licking my lips nervously. Only when he didn't react or say anything, I continued. "Even though he was clear in his orders, his physical interaction with me was never something I feared or felt was too much. Alphas protect Omegas, they can't help it. Instinct will take over, and what you enjoy with Spencer might not be what you find you need from me."

"Sweetheart..." Nixon said hesitantly.

Lifting my legs, I wrapped them around his waist and pulled him closer, feeling his cock brushing my pussy. "Trust me, then trust yourself as I do. Everything will be fine."

He dropped his head to rest on my shoulder and his breath became more labored as his cock sat right at my entrance. All I had to do was tilt my hips, but this was his choice, he needed to trust himself and I couldn't make him do that. Then ever so slowly, Nixon let his cock slide into me, inch by inch, until his hips met mine.

I threw my arms around his neck and rocked ever so slightly to encourage him. Nixon lifted his head and looked down at me with so much love I knew everything was going to be fine. "I love you, Nixon," I whispered.

"I love you too, Cambrie," he answered. "Thank you for trusting me more than I trusted myself."

A smile grew on my face as I nuzzled my nose against his. "That's what packs are for, to be a family who takes care of each other."

"How did we ever end up with someone as amazing as you?" he questioned, kissing the tip of my nose.

"Nixon," I ventured.

"Yes, Sweetheart?"

"Will you please fuck me?" I asked, the need roaring in my veins now that I'd been filled with one of my Alpha's cocks.

Nixon caught my lips with his as he pulled back, almost making me think he had changed his mind but then he painstakingly slowly entered me again. It was like the most painful torture of my life for him to move so arduously that I shifted my legs and drove my heels into his ass and lifted my hips, slamming myself on his cock. The feeling of it filling me so quickly had me moaning.

"If you want me to fuck you differently, you're going to have to use your words, Sweetheart," Nixon warned. "I trusted you. Now you have to trust me when I tell you asking for what you want isn't being selfish. As your Alpha, I want to give you all that you ask for, but I won't know what that is unless you tell me."

"Please, Alpha, I want you to move faster. It's too slow," I whined, my Omega needs and instincts overriding my normal trepidations.

Immediately Nixon started to move his hips faster, but it still wasn't fast enough or deep enough. "More, I need more. Faster, deeper, I want you to fill me, knot me, and never let me go."

The frenzy of my emotions made me feel like I was in heat again, but it was something else. There was something else I was craving. I needed Nixon, but even as we were intertwined in the most intimate way, it wasn't enough. My Alpha fulfilled all my wishes pounding into me and grunting as we clung to each other. He picked me up off the bed, and my back landed against a wall, it was abrupt but I wasn't hurt since he had a hand guarding the back of my head.

"I told you, you'd never let me be hurt," I murmured as that hand placed itself on the wall next to me as he thrust upward.

The weight of gravity pushing me down on him as he moved made it so much deeper. I could feel him starting to swell, and if we kept this up, it would be the deepest knot I'd ever taken. My hands held onto his neck, keeping myself steady as I used the wall for leverage to change the angle. Now he was hitting that sweet spot, sending shocks of pleasure coursing through me. I heard a noise and when I opened my eyes, I found Marius with Spencer trapped under his body as he pounded into the Beta.

Spencer's eyes rolled back as his body bounced under the loving assault. There was something so right about seeing my pack sharing love. I knew Savo and Rafael didn't feel the need to have anyone else in their life but me, and that was fine. Each person needed a certain amount of love to give or receive that required more than one lover.

That's where the difference was, there was love flowing equally in this room. I found joy and love in seeing my other packmates loving each other.

The world would be a happier place if people didn't feel constrained in how they loved. My family showed me every day the different kinds of love there could be. Now it was time for me to claim my role and allow that love to grow deeper between us as a pack. The need I'd been feeling that I couldn't figure out, I knew what it was now. Savo had flipped the switch, and there was no turning back now.

Nixon's knot started to swell rapidly as he buried his face in my neck, nuzzling into it as if he could sense my desperate desire. "Nixon, claim me. Bond me to you as your Omega. That is what I want right now. I want you to place your mark on me so no one can ever tear us apart," I said into his ear, baring my neck to him.

His movements became erratic as his hips rutted into me, his knot starting to lock in place. It was time. Deep in my soul, a small voice was crying out to my Alpha, begging him to complete the connection that had started the day he rescued me in the city. The day he saved my life and brought me to the family I never thought I'd have. It was fitting that out of these men, he would claim me first, it was time.

With one final thrust, he slammed so deep into me that I thought I felt the tip of his cock meet the end of my womb. As his knot expanded and locked me in place, his teeth pierced my skin, sending me into a screaming orgasm. Much like with Savo, I felt the connection snap into place, but it was stronger, more solid, as it hummed between us. The wash of love and triumph I felt through our bond was incredible.

As my body went limp in his arms, pure satisfaction and contentment made me feel like I was flying as Nixon brought us back to the bed. He managed to lie down on his back with my body draped over his soaking up all the purrs. Then he began to torture me in the best way possible. With every stroke of his tongue over the mark on my neck, I orgasmed around his knot, squeezing every drop of cum out of him.

CHAPTER 50

Spencer

It happened. Cambrie was ours, officially bonded to Nixon in addition to Savo, and I'm sure the rest would soon follow. I couldn't help but watch our Omega curled up on Nixon's chest basking in the newly formed bond, as Marius wrapped himself around me next to them.

When Cambrie decided that she wanted it to be just her and Nixon, I couldn't have agreed more. The two of them needed the chance to experience the first time together, allowing that connection to deepen. Marius and I had been too worked up from the attention of our Omega to just walk away or appreciate the view. Thankfully, I knew that our sweet Little Dove enjoyed watching, leaving me with no shame as I coaxed my Alpha into fucking me as Nixon fucked her.

Now all of us were sated and enjoying a moment of closeness. Four days might not seem like all that long to be separated, but it was more the not knowing if she was alright or if we would get her back, that made it seem like an eternity. So being able to just lie here, watching her be cradled in the protective arms of a man I loved as much as I loved her, while another man who held my heart nuzzled the back of my neck, was incredible.

"What are you thinking about so hard?" Marius asked.

Shifting so I was looking at my Alpha, I kissed him, just needing to share the feelings that were bursting out of my heart. "I knew one day we would end up with an Omega since that was something we all wanted, not to mention it would be easier with your position in the government. What I didn't allow myself to dwell on or dream about was being bonded to you and Nixon. Many Omegas don't like to share, and they are taught everything should revolve around them. I know you and Nixon love me, not a superficial love but a deep forever love. Yet, there was always some doubt that when we did bring in an Omega, if she didn't want me she'd make you choose."

Marius brushed a hand down the side of my face, sadness and understanding in his eyes. "This is one aspect I truly hope will change once Omegas are given back the freedom to choose who their pack is. It's not fair to anyone Alpha, Beta, or Omega alike, to be forced into a relationship they don't really want. If it hadn't been Cambrie, who clearly loves you as much as we do, I'm not sure I would have been able to bond with them. You are mine, Spencer, and an Alpha doesn't give up what is theirs."

A hand brushed down my back, and I twisted to see Nixon watching us, clearly having heard what I'd said. "Please know that if I ever gave you that feeling because of my own fear, that was never my intention. You kept trying to tell me that love could be shared and equal between partners, but I didn't believe any of you."

Reaching out, I took his hand, giving it a squeeze. "No, it was never something you did or said, because I knew in time you would see the truth. Everyone has fears; I don't have many, but I've had to fight that one for a long time. The curse of being a Beta and the lies they feed us as children about our place in the world."

Nixon sat up and lifted Cambrie off him and handed her to Marius over me. Rolling away from Marius, I ended up with my back to Nixon as he pulled me tight against his chest. "Just as Marius said, Alphas don't give up what is theirs," Nixon murmured, his lips brushing along my neck. "We claim those that hold a treasured place in our lives, placing a mark on them and showing the world they belong to someone and they better not touch."

His hand drifted down my chest to my stomach, hand splayed wide, covering as much of my skin as he could. The other hand gripped my jaw and twisted my head to the side so I was looking into Cambrie's gaze as she watched our Alpha claim his second bond. I thought the bite would hurt, since typically it was done in the heat of passion. Except the second Nixon's teeth marked me, I went from limp to rock hard in two seconds.

"Holy fuck," I gasped, my hips bucking forward.

Cambrie smiled as she pulled away from Marius to kiss me as her hand wrapped around my cock. I moaned into her mouth, loving the feeling of my Alpha cleaning his mark sending me to the edge of my control. Groping for Cambrie, I pulled her leg over my hip and slipped inside her pussy. I knew I wasn't going to last long, but I wanted us to be connected physically as we were with the bond humming between us, bouncing everyone's pleasure through us.

Nixon shifted, and I felt his hand working lube into my ass, but I had a feeling he wasn't going to need much with how badly I wanted him inside me. Marius had warmed me up and left behind his mark, adding to the ease Nixon entered with. Unable to hold still any longer, I rocked my hips pushing into Cambrie then thrust back on Nixon's cock. Just when I didn't think this moment could get any better, Marius closed the distance between him and Cambrie.

A soft gasp followed by a moan sounded as she pressed into me while Marius entered her from behind. Here was a situation I never in my wildest dreams thought I would experience. Each Alpha took their time alternating who thrusted as they fucked Cambrie and me together. This was everything, the bond and people I loved, all together in one happy fucking puppy pile of unadulterated passion. None of us lasted long, but it was enough for now. We would be able to explore this new level of our relationships for the rest of our lives.

I came first as Nixon locked his mouth around my mark and sucked as he slammed his hips against me, sending me shooting off into Cambrie. She followed and tossed back her head leaving plenty of room for Marius to leave his mark on the opposite side of her neck from Nixon. Her pussy clamped down around my already sensitive cock, making me come again as I felt another shoot through her in the bond.

Fuck, that was going to take some getting used to.

Knowing that an Omega's sex drive was higher than the average, I felt like we'd all need to figure out how to manage moments like this. I could just picture it, I'd be at the shelter and getting hit when Cambrie climaxed. Thank god Nixon worked with me, or I might end up embarrassing myself.

It took me a moment to realize that Marius had grabbed my arm and was bringing my hand to his mouth. He held my gaze as he bit into the fleshy part of my palm, then let his tongue run over it, making me cry out as yet another orgasm slammed into me. Now it was to the point I had nothing left to release. I was simply left in a perpetual state of euphoria as my body didn't understand what to do with the assault of endorphins.

"Please, my Alphas, no more. I can't take anymore," I mumbled as Marius kissed the palm of my hand before tucking it to Cambrie's chest between her breasts.

My Little Dove's forehead landed on my shoulder as her breathing started to slow back down to something slightly more normal. Here I was, worried about what it would be like with three of them connected to me, but soon Cambrie would have six people feeding into her. Thankfully, Omegas were built to be the conduit, and their minds were able to withstand that much input all at once.

"I know I just woke up, but I think I need a nap," Cambrie murmured as she nuzzled against me.

Marius kissed the back of her head, brushing a hand down the length of her body, soothing her as he started to purr. "Rest, Princess, I can feel how tired you are. We'll be here when you wake up."

With the cutest contented sigh, she drifted off to sleep without a second thought. This adorable woman was ours, was mine, to hold and love for however long our lives might last together for this life-time. If there was reincarnation and our souls ended up being reborn, we would find each other again. A love like how I felt for these men and our woman couldn't be for just one life, it was too strong. I let my fingers comb through her hair, brushing it out of her face, and kissed her tiny nose.

"How could the government keep this experience from people?" Nixon asked once we felt Cambrie had slipped into a deep enough sleep. "There has to be more to it than Yoram wanting to line his wallet. He's getting older and already has control over our country. What more does he want?"

"It's clear he wanted to build a connection with Shearia, but I agree it seems odd. Once he sent her off to them, he wouldn't have much else they would want," Marius mused aloud.

They were right, we were missing a piece of the puzzle.

"Nixon's right, though," I commented. "There has to be a reason why Yoram needs the connection to Shearia. If all he had to do was give them an Omega, why did it have to be Cambrie? He went to so much trouble to find her and was even willing to buy her from her fake father. Savo said one of Yoram's Betas said something about Cambrie's birth mom dying like the rest of them. Could he have done something that made it imperative that it was Cambrie who was given to another country?"

"Rick has both Betas in custody and will be interviewing them with the promise that if they give us what we need on Yoram, we'll let them live. From what little I've gathered, the two Betas are in love, and all they've wanted is to be able to be together," Marius shared. "The woman was more than happy to give up everything she knew. We're just not sure what if they are ramblings of a broken mind or fact."

Nixon pressed a kiss to my shoulder and slid out of bed, padding into the bathroom. Soon, I heard the shower running and figured he was getting restless. He wasn't a man who could lie about forever, and it seemed we'd reached his limit. If we weren't going to bed right after, I got about a solid half hour then he was itching to move on to other things. A man of action, something that made him so incredibly good at his job.

"Hey," Marius said, drawing my attention. "You know it has nothing to do with not wanting to be here with you, right?"

I smiled, realizing that Marius had picked up my disappointment at Nixon leaving. "Yes, that's been something he's worked on for me. He knows I could cuddle with any of you for hours and he just can't handle it. We've worked up to something I can accept and not feel like he's rushing off, but he will never be a man who could ever be counted as slothful."

"That has been true his entire life," Marius chuckled. "I hated sleepovers with him because we would be up so early and he'd have some plan for our day. Truthfully, I don't know what he'd be like on vacation or if he even understands the meaning."

"Do you think if we trapped him on a deserted island with no cell service and his only entertainment was us, he'd be able to relax?" I questioned, rolling on my back to stare at the ceiling as I let my fingers drift through Cambrie's hair.

Marius chuckled. "Hell no, he'd have us making tools so we could build a raft to get off the damn island. That or building a house or something, so he felt like we'd accomplished something with our time there."

I grimace. "That sounds awful. Now I'm not so upset we haven't ever taken a vacation."

A hand settled on my head, turning it to look at my Alpha. "I think we should leave him behind, and the three of us go someplace fun. After all this is over, I could go for some uninterrupted time with my family. If the others think they can have a good time and relax, they can join us."

"You know you haven't said anything about Savo," I mentioned.

He shrugged. "What is there to say? It was clear that the moment he met her at the mall, there was a connection. I'm just pissed I didn't see it sooner. You might be able to change your scent, but there's no way to hide your reaction to the right Omega. Plus, we were going to hire him as a live-in guard to look after her anyway."

"I suppose we don't have to pay him for looking out for his own Omega. Win-win situation if you ask me," I teased.

Marius grinned but shifted to sit with his back resting against the headboard. "When Nixon and I started to build our pack, we knew anyone we brought into it needed to follow two criteria. First, they needed to agree with our viewpoint on the government needing to change. If they didn't see how important that was, then I'm not sure they would agree with anything we'd planned for our future. Second, the pack needed to be a safe haven for those who needed a place to call home. None of us planned on Bodhi joining our group, but he was exactly who needed us. Later, we find out he was precisely the person Oscar needed. The two of them healed each other in many ways, preparing them for the truth of their feelings, and for Cambrie."

"That's what I find so fascinating about all of this. Each of us needed her in our own way; we'd managed to progress only so far as we had. Then she came along and pushed us the rest of the way, revealing things about ourselves we didn't know. Savo was different, while he needed us, the person who it was vital for him to meet was Cambrie. He was placed in our path for her, to be there when none of us could. After Nixon told me everything, and Savo added his take on things, she might not have made it through without him in her corner," Marius shared as he tugged the sheet over her and looked toward the door.

Lifting my head, I saw Savo leaning in the doorway. *How long had that blasted ninja been standing there?*

"Maybe next time you should make a sound or something, so we know you're there," I muttered.

Savo shrugged and sat at the end of the bed. "I felt her resting, so I figured it was safe enough to come in."

"My family warned me new bonds were demanding," Marius commented. "Thank you for allowing us time with her when I'm sure it was tough on you."

Savo just stared at Cambrie for a moment before speaking, as if he needed to soak in the sight of her. "I knew from the start she wasn't just mine. You all found her first and protected her until I could get here."

"Speaking of that," Marius ventured. "I don't want to assume your plans from here on out, but there is plenty of space in the house for you to join us if you wish."

"I'll be wherever she is, without question, but thank you for giving me the option," Savo answered, meeting Marius's gaze. "What's next? Rick has Yoram's pack, and you have the proof of Alton being poisoned, plus the knowledge that Cambrie was going to be sold to Shearia."

Grabbing a pillow, I covered my junk as I sat cross-legged in the bed. "We're missing something. There has to be a reason behind why it had to be Cambrie."

"I agree," Savo said with a nod. "If I had a secure computer, I might be able to do a little more digging than any of you could."

Nixon exited the bathroom with a towel around his waist and was drying his hair with another until he spotted Savo. "Is there news?"

"Nothing new," he answered. "I was just saying if I had a computer they couldn't trace, I could see what more I might be able to learn. Our best option is for me to reach out to Rick and see if he can get one of the encrypted laptops to us."

Cambrie started to stir, so I reached out and petted her head until she settled. "Maybe we have the others switch out with us so you guys can talk elsewhere?"

The expression on Savo's face looked like that idea pained him, but he nodded. He started to get up, but I grabbed his arm. "Wait, Savo, if you need to be with her, then stay. I didn't mean to dismiss you from being here if you require time with her. Marius and I have to shower, so why don't you stay? Nixon can reach out to Rick and tell him what you asked for."

Relief was evident in Savo's body language as his shoulders sagged. "That sounds like a good plan."

"Now, close your eyes," I ordered. Savo frowned in confusion. "Look, we're friends, but I don't typically parade around in the nude for all to see. We're new packmates to each other, so give me a little time to adjust, will you?"

Savo chuckled and crawled up the bed and curled up with Cambrie, hiding his face in her hair. The second he started purring,

I knew I was safe to get up. Marius caught my eye, his gaze full of mirth as I'm sure he could feel how uncomfortable I was at the moment. My Alpha just waved for me to follow him and I quickly sprinted across the room, only for Nixon to slap my ass as I passed.

"Run, boy, run," he called after me, and I just flipped him the bird. *Alphas.*

CHAPTER 51

Cambrie

This time when I stretched after waking up from my nap, I felt a body shift with me, and I knew instantly it was Savo. I could feel his contentment and happiness at having me in his arms through our bond. In the background, though, I could sense something was bothering him. Not enough to take him away from me, but more so a lingering need that would be dealt with at some point.

"Did something happen?" I murmured as I turned to face him.

"Hmm?"

"I was asking if something happened while I was asleep," I reiterated.

"No, *Keksik*, there isn't anything you need to worry about," he answered.

Frowning, I took my finger and booped him on the nose. "That isn't what I meant, and you know it. Now that we're bonded you can't hide how you feel. There is something bothering you."

Savo took a deep breath and let it out. "I don't have enough information to figure out what's bothering me. That's part of the problem, I suppose."

Just as I was going to ask him something else, my stomach rumbled loudly. My cheeks flushed at the sound and I clutched my stomach. "Goodness, it makes it sound like I haven't eaten in days." I giggled.

Savo was already in action, scooping me out of the bed and carrying me into the bathroom. "It's time for you to get up anyways. Almost a whole day asleep. We'll never be able to get you to sleep tonight at this rate."

Fisting my hands on my hips, I gave him a scolding look. "I'm not a child who needs to be put to bed. I'm more than capable of deciding that for myself."

My Alpha cocked a brow at me, then caught my chin. "My sweet girl, I'm sure there is something we can do to entice you to come to bed."

Heat trickled through my body at his words, and I knew he felt it as his eyes dilated and he took a deep breath. "No, *Keksík*, you need to shower and then eat. You are leaving this room and joining the others downstairs. While I love the idea of spending the rest of the day in bed with you, we have things to settle."

Pouting, I watched as he turned on the shower and then ushered me under its spray. "When someone comes back up here with clothes, you better be washed and not purposely trying to cause trouble."

"I don't cause trouble," I shot back as he headed out of the bathroom. He paused and looked over his shoulder with a knowing expression, then left. "I don't," I muttered to myself.

Knowing that Savo wasn't one to test, I set to washing. Having gone right to sleep after my romp in the sheets, I was glad for the shower. Plus, there was something wonderful about being able to wash off my experience at that house and know I'd never go back there. When I was done with the shower, I searched the bathroom, but there weren't any dry towels. Dripping all over the place, I headed to the bedroom and found Oscar entering. Stopping abruptly when he saw me, he cocked his head to the side and looked at me questioningly.

"There are no more towels in the bathroom," I commented.

Oscar gave an ah-ha expression, then gestured for me to wait a moment as he turned back the way he came. Not wanting to drip on the carpet, I returned to the bathroom and shivered at the cool air against my damp body. Moments later, Oscar returned and wrapped me in a towel before herding me to sit on the toilet seat. He grabbed a brush and started to work on my hair. This was a new thing a few of my pack did for me, and I loved it. There was something so intimate and caring about having someone brush your hair. When he finished brushing, he grabbed a blow dryer and used his hand to comb through it as he dried it.

Closing my eyes, I just enjoyed the time with Oscar, allowing my Alpha to care for me in a way that didn't need words to show he loved me. When the dryer turned off, I opened them again and swiveled to face him with a bright smile. "Thank you," I said and used the sign he had taught me.

He beamed at me and returned the sign.

"Why are you thanking me?" I asked.

Oscar paused, but then the answer came from the doorway. "Typically, in sign language, there isn't the same response as when speaking," Bodhi informed me. "When signing thank you, they also respond with thank you, fine, or no problem."

"That's good to know," I said absently as I pulled my lip between my teeth.

There was a tap on my nose that surprised me but had me looking up. Oscar gave me a scolding look and waved his finger no and pointed to his lip. Instantly it popped out, and I blurted out. "Sorry, it's such a habit."

Oscar used another sign and then looked at Bodhi gesturing with his chin to me. "He said it's alright."

Oscar repeated the sign and indicated I should repeat it back to him. I did since it was a simple gesture, and he flashed me two thumbs up. Then his hands started to move slowly, allowing me to see his movements as Bodhi spoke. "He wants you to know that depending on the situation, that sign can mean a few different things, the context of the situation and conversation help to clarify."

This time when I signed thank you, Oscar leaned down to kiss me before pulling me off the toilet and back to the bedroom.

"Bodhi, how long did it take you to learn sign language?" I asked as he set clothes on the bed for me from a suitcase.

He paused to think about that for a moment. "Since I spent almost all my time at the house with Oscar, it was almost like I was fully submerged into that culture. It made me feel like shit that he had to take the time to type everything out when he wanted to say something, so we divided the time between language and music lessons. I don't remember when I reached the point of just *knowing* what he was saying. There was just a day he didn't need to type anything out. There are times when I don't know a word or phrase, but when he breaks it down, I figure it out."

"So, I need to have everyone use only sign language around the house until I get it," I announced, and got dressed. "All of you know it, and Savo does as well, right?"

"That would be one way to get better at it faster, but I think since you have all of us who can help, we can take more bite-size pieces. Let's start with the alphabet. Once you know it by heart, you can spell whatever you don't know how to say. It's not efficient but it's a good place to begin," Bodhi suggested.

My stomach announced its hunger again and made both men snap to attention. "Sorry, Savo might be making me something, but I was instructed I had to leave the room and join everyone downstairs. Do you think he's holding my food hostage?"

Bodhi scowled and stormed out of the room. I glanced at Oscar, and then we dashed after the fired-up Beta. Unsure where I was going, Oscar guided me with a hand on my lower back until we reached the stairs.

"Savo," Bodhi snapped.

The house wasn't really big, but it was large enough that it shouldn't sound like Bodhi was around the corner. I could feel Savo's surprise at the sudden appearance of the angry man. If Savo answered, I couldn't tell since he was probably speaking in a more appropriate tone. Bursting into the kitchen, I found Savo holding a spatula in one hand and a frying pan in the other.

"Did you say Cambrie couldn't eat unless she came downstairs? Do you have any idea how hard we've been trying to make sure she eats? You think she's skinny now. It's nowhere near how bad it was. Food is one thing we never restrict from her, because her body is too comfortable with going without. We don't want her falling back into that pattern," Bodhi scolded the Alpha.

The rest of the pack wandered into the kitchen, taking in the scene of a furious Beta and one incredibly confused Alpha.

"What the hell are you talking about?" Savo demanded, setting down the frying pan. "I told her to take a shower, then come down and eat. Why in the world would I ever withhold food from her, let alone anything else she might need?"

Bodhi pointed at me, where I stood with Oscar's arms around me, as I watched wide-eyed at the exchange. All of them knew I didn't like it when they yelled at each other. In fact, I believe I'd berated Bodhi for doing it once before. Then I remembered what Rafael told me about how arguing was healthy as long as things resolved themselves in the end.

"Then tell me, why did she think if she didn't come down she wouldn't be allowed to eat?" Bodhi snapped.

Savo rubbed his face with a hand and muttered something under his breath. The feelings I got were how confused and irritated he was, but he was trying hard not to yell. "Bodhi, I need you to lower your voice and take a deep breath. If you keep shouting at me, I will do the same, which will upset her more than she already is. Now, I understand that I'm the new guy on the team and you don't know me yet. One thing you need to understand and *never* question me again on, is Cambrie's well-being. She is my Omega, and I will do anything and everything in my power to keep her safe, happy, and healthy. Do you believe me when I say that?" Savo pressed, holding the Beta's gaze.

Bodhi frowned and looked down, then over at me. I wasn't sure what he was searching for in my gaze, but whatever he saw made him sigh. "On that, I suppose I believe you."

"Not good enough," Savo barked, making me jump in Oscar's hold.

My Alpha started to purr, rubbing his cheek on my head in comfort. Then Rafael appeared before me, kneeling to meet my gaze. "Cambrie, remember when I told you sometimes conflict is good and healthy for people to have?"

I nodded. "That's what's happening right now. Savo is a new Alpha entering our family. While he's gained your trust and respect during your time together, it's going to take some time for everyone else to find where they fit. It's just our family going through growing pains, no one is going to leave or hate each other at the end of this. Those two need to test each other's boundaries and know how far they can push. Bodhi did it with all of us when he officially moved in and learned to live with others who cared about him. You, Little One, are beyond important to Bodhi. Right now, he feels Savo didn't have your best in mind."

"Savo would never do anything that would hurt me," I defended.

"I absolutely believe that, but Bodhi doesn't. Those two need to learn to trust each other, and this is the first step," Rafael assured me. "Come, let's leave them to work this out without an audience watching them."

Oscar turned us around and gave me a little push to get me moving forward. Marius and Spencer led the way into a different room than where we gathered last night. This one had a lovely picture window showing the wild front yard and the waning sun. No one spoke right away as I took in my surroundings in this strange house. It reminded me of the area I grew up in, making me wonder if we might be close. *Would Peggy still be working at the library?*

"What town are we in?" I asked, turning to face them.

"Lower Crossbend, I think is what this is considered, but we're also on the edge of Riken Grove," Marius answered.

I perked up hearing this. "I grew up in Riken Grove. Well, that's where Father moved us to once Mother passed away." None of them seemed to be as pleased about this information as I was. "What?"

"Out here is where you lived until you came to the shelter?" Spencer inquired.

"Yeah, I mean, I spent most of my time at the Riken Grove Library when I could. There is a wonderful woman named Peggy who used to help me while I was studying for my GED," I shared. "Do you think she might still be there? Could we go check?"

"I don't want to make you any promises I'm not sure we can keep, but if we have the chance, we will try," Marius said, reaching out to me. "Come sit with me. I have a few questions that I think you might be able to help me with."

Curious as to what I could possibly know that he didn't, I let him pull me onto his lap. "What questions?"

"Tell me what you know about the parents you grew up with. You said you moved, where did you used to live?" Marius asked.

"Near the mall, actually, where that man ran into us. I used to attend Forest Grove Elementary school before Father pulled me out to move," I shared. "Mother used to tell me that she and Father met when she needed him the most, saving her from a life she didn't want. She never went into more detail about that, but sometimes I wondered if Father really cared about her at all. When she got sick, he just got mad that she couldn't do everything around the house like she used to. Any time I brought it up or questioned her, she would scold me and tell me it wasn't proper to question someone else's relationship."

Marius seemed hesitant, and I could feel his reservation about whatever he wanted to ask me next. This made me worry and start to fidget. Nixon, who was sitting next to Marius, pulled my legs onto his lap and wrapped his hand around my ankle in support.

"Do you know what made your mother sick?" Marius finally asked.

It had been so long since I'd thought of those days she was in the hospital. I'd hardly been allowed to see her since Father had to accompany me as I was so young. That was the same time things at home started to get worse. If I had any bruises that could be seen, then I knew we wouldn't go. When we got to see Mother, she was so sick she didn't stay awake for long but always told me she loved me and told me to be brave.

"When we would go visit, doctors always pulled Father aside and would talk to him in the hall so I couldn't hear. The nurses weren't so worried, feeling I should be prepared for her to pass away.

I knew Mother was never coming home once she entered the hospital. She hated them, saying only bad things would happen. Once, while she was in her last days, she didn't really know who I was, she kept calling me by another woman's name. Told me that what they'd done to her was finally catching up," I murmured, letting myself stay in my memory as I shared. "She said something about the drugs still not working and the baby was a miracle."

Pausing, I scrunched up my face, trying to remember the name she had called me. It had been so long ago, and I was so young, scared, and afraid to be alone in the world without her. "Isabelle," I exclaimed. "That was the name, she called me Isabelle."

"That is your birth mother's name, or at least, that's what we believe," Nixon said, rubbing his thumb along my ankle. "We're still putting the last pieces of the puzzle together, but from what we've gathered, it's highly likely that's the case."

"Then who was my mother?" I questioned.

"Maybe we should start at the beginning," Rafael suggested. "That way, we can put everything we know together, and if Cambrie has something to add, it might make things clearer."

Marius shifted me off his lap and stood, pacing as he spoke. He told me about Alton, his friend and fellow Official, being sick and how that connected to Yoram. Somewhere about the time he was explaining about who they believed my birth mother was and who my grandparents were, Bodhi and Savo joined us. Bodhi headed right for me, picked me up, and then sat back down with me in his lap. Savo then handed me a plate with a perfect looking grilled cheese and chips.

"I'll wait a moment," Marius commented. "She's not going to hear anything we have to say now that she has a grilled cheese."

It took a moment to register what he said, and the sandwich was already almost to my watering mouth. Pausing, I looked around to see everyone was watching me, but the need to taste this amazing sandwich had me brushing it off. Chomping down on the buttery, crispy bread, I hummed as the melted cheese coated my tongue.

"You weren't kidding when you said that was her favorite food," Savo said with a hint of laughter.

Bodhi rested his head on my shoulder and kissed my cheek lovingly. "That's why I couldn't let you give her that burnt hockey puck you claimed was a grilled cheese."

"It was not *that* burnt," Savo grumbled. "Also, you should all know about the obscene amount of cheese he put in that thing."

"Yeah, even if we did know, none of us would ever take away her favorite food," Rafael countered. "Seeing the joy a simple sandwich can bring her, no matter what her mood is, that's worth its weight in gold."

"Guess I can't argue with that either," Savo agreed with a face that made the room laugh.

CHAPTER 52

Cambrie

As I ate my sandwich, Marius finished the story just in time for the same man who yelled at Savo last night to show up. After introductions, I realized Rick was Savo's boss and had been looking out for him since he came to Oscad.

"I know you wanted a computer to look into things, and I had information to share with you all, so I figured I'd deliver it myself. What I have to share would be far too great a risk to share in any other fashion," Rick explained, taking a seat in one of the armchairs.

Savo sat right in front of the couch where I was, while Marius chose to take up position behind me. "Whatever you need to say, you can say to all of us. Cambrie has been brought up to speed, and since it's her family, she should be kept in the loop," Marius announced.

Rick nodded and turned to me with a smile. "It's nice to meet you properly this time around."

"It's nice to meet you too," I greeted with a nod.

"Let's get down to business, shall we?" Rick said. "First off, I would like to confirm that Cambrie is one hundred percent Yoram's daughter, and her mother was the late Omega, Isabelle Neenan. We had a DNA test done just to be sure we covered all our bases on this, since that will be the first thing they'll fight. Secondly, Cambrie was smuggled out of that very house by Laura's sister, Aria, the night before the funeral."

In a matter of seconds, Rick had blown up everything I knew about my life without a shadow of a doubt. The man who claimed to be my father, who beat me for ten years of my life, had no ties to me whatsoever. Instead, one of the most evil men in our country was my father. I was not sure which was worse.

"What does that mean for me now?" I asked.

"Nothing," Rick answered instantly. "You are now a bonded Omega. Any ties you had to your family have been severed, and now your Alphas are responsible for you."

Relief about that flooded through me, and I had the sense it wasn't just me feeling it either.

"That's the easy part. The rest is a little murky and hard to prove, since most people involved are dead," Rick warned. "It would appear that Yoram was using the drug created by Isabelle's parents on all the females in his pack to help encourage the chances of an Omega child. Isabelle was the only one to carry a child to term, but the drugs killed her in the process. It's my belief that's why Aria got sick and passed, and it is the reason Laura is in the state she is now."

My heart twisted at the idea of these women having to suffer for the whims of a man who didn't care about them at all.

"Is there any way to prove that was done?" Rafael inquired.

Rick ran a hand through his hair before gesturing to me. "It's clear in her genetic makeup. There are markers of the drug. He wasn't using the original formula to help increase the chances, but the one that would alter DNA to ensure they would be born an Omega. There are two men who were part of the team that researched the incident with the EQ and have data on their findings. In the information, it shows a matching pattern or something science-y that I didn't get, if I'm being honest. When we showed them a copy of Cambrie's results, they confirmed that was the formula that had been used."

"That's it," Spencer blurted, shooting to his feet. "That's the piece we were missing." Through our bond I felt him practically vibrating with excitement and fear. "Yoram needed it to be Cambrie so he could send her off to Shearia to prove that the drug still works and bring it back. He got all the rights to the intellectual and physical property of that project. It might be outlawed here in Oscad, but why not branch out into another country?"

"I agree with you, Spencer, and we are looking into that, among other things Arthur alluded to." Rick paused and cleared his throat like he was nervous about this next part. "Marius, we need you to sign an executive order allowing me to take a team to one of the biggest Care Centers, to take a physical count of how many Omegas are there."

Rage flashed through me from Marius, making both Spencer and I turn to look at him. His face was unreadable, but his eyes betrayed just how furious he was. "Are you telling me he's been selling off Omegas to other countries?"

"That is what's been suggested, but with the laws we have in place, there is no way for me to confirm that. The staff in those places are appointed and they train their own people to work there. Once they are inducted into the Care Center, they don't leave. They claim it's for national security," Rick explained. "If I have a signed order, they can't deny me access."

Marius gave a curt nod. "You'll have your order. I'll even do you one better. I'm going to come with you. They won't be able to say anything if an actual Official witnesses the discrepancy. I also checked out all the records from the past thirty years to the current day on how many Omegas we should have in our Care Centers. If it's true that Yoram has been selling or bartering our country's Omegas, he will suffer the consequences and be denied a trial."

Rick sighed, his shoulders slumping as he hung his head. "I should be put on trial for all that I've let him get away with. I was far too concerned about my own family that I didn't fight for everyone else who might be going through the same thing."

"If that were the case, half our country would be on trial. All we can do is hold the man who instigated all of this responsible and learn from what happened. The current government isn't working, there aren't enough checks and balances. If one man can take over so easily, with no one standing up against him, what does that tell us?" Marius asked, but I got the feeling he wasn't really expecting an answer. "Is there anything else we need to know?"

"Not really, we know that Isabelle's parents were poisoned, and Arthur confirmed it was a tea he made. The same goes for Alton, so the bastard can't fight that charge, either. What they couldn't tell us, is how far the conspiracy goes. They have been trapped in that house since the funeral and Aria escaped with Cambrie. Yoram knows he will face death with or without his admission of guilt, so I doubt he will tell us who else he's working with," Rick grumbled.

"One thing at a time," Rafael encouraged. "Once they see we've taken Yoram out of power and have revealed what he's been doing, they'll understand they don't have him to hide behind. Knowing Marius and Alton, the two of them will comb through every file in the damn Capitol Building to discover what else he might have been doing under their noses."

I reached out to Marius and placed my hand over his as it rested on the couch, drawing his attention. "When can we go home?"

He smiled and used his other hand to cup my cheek. "Soon, Princess, I promise we will go home soon. If we do the checks of the Care Center tomorrow, then we will have everything we need to put an end to Yoram's control. The second that happens, I will feel better about you being back out in the world. We lost you once, and that was a harsh lesson I don't plan on repeating."

"Okay, I'll be patient," I replied, leaning into his touch. "Can we have a movie night? Rick can join us too if he wants, right?"

Marius chuckled. "I think Rick wants to get back home to his own pack. Maybe one of these days, we'll invite them to the house and have a cookout or something?"

I whipped around to look at Rick. "Would your pack be willing to do something like that? It would be really nice to meet another family like ours."

"Sasha would be thrilled to spend time with another Omega, and what makes Sasha happy makes us all happy," Rick answered with a chuckle. "Marius, I'll send word to Savo through the encrypted computer what the plan is for tomorrow. Until then, have a good night and enjoy your movie." Rick waved and left us all with lots to think about.

The rest of that night, we spent cuddled up together and watched movies until the others started to drop off and head to bed. Soon I was left with just Oscar and Bodhi, but Bodhi was dozing as he rested his head on Oscar's shoulder. We'd decided to watch the Lord of the Rings series, and we were almost finished with the second movie. I was hooked from the start and pushed for us to watch the second because I couldn't wait.

"Didn't I tell you you'd be up all night? Be good, and don't force them to watch the third movie. There are plenty more nights for that," Savo teased as he kissed me good night in the middle of the second movie and headed up to bed.

When the credits started to roll, I just sat there stunned for a moment. "They can't leave it like that!" I cried. "How am I going to sleep when there is so much I don't know?!"

Oscar looked at me with a surprised expression, and Bodhi jerked awake looking incredibly confused.

"Is Frodo really alive? What happens now that they have won the battle at Helm's Deep? Will Sam find him in time? What about Gollum?" I rambled, waving my arms about.

"Okay, that's it," Bodhi muttered, getting up and shutting off the TV. "I'm cutting you off, Cambi." He looked at Oscar as he scooped me up and tossed me over his shoulder. "Remind me next time I pick a movie that it can't be an epic fantasy. Otherwise, we have to have the time to watch all of it."

Oscar's shoulders shook as he laughed and signed.

"I can too, tell her no. I'm telling her no right now because we're going to bed," Bodhi huffed and marched up the stairs.

I laughed as he tossed me on the bed, and I bounced before Oscar pounced on me and started to tickle my sides. Peels of laughter burst out of me as I squirmed and wriggled in an attempt to get out of his hold.

"Guys, you need to quiet down, or you're going to wake everyone up. This house isn't that big," Bodhi chided.

Oscar rolled his eyes before snatching me up and rolling me so I was under him. His whole body caged me in as I grinned up at him, loving the joy in his eyes. Then his lips were on mine and I was moaning as his hips settled between my legs. The leggings I was wearing didn't create much of a barrier between his jean-covered cock and my needy pussy which was getting slicker by the second.

He started to purr as my perfume filled the air so strongly, even I could smell it. The bed jostled as Bodhi joined us, causing Oscar to lift his head and grab our Beta to him in a kiss just as fierce. I reached for Oscar's shirt and started tugging it until I couldn't get it off without his help. Bodhi saw what I was up to and slipped it the rest of the way off our Alpha. Seeing where this was going, he yanked his off as well, leaving me the only one fully clothed.

"Should we unwrap our Omega together?" Bodhi asked, heat flickering in his eyes.

Oscar nodded and shifted down my body, leaving the top half for Bodhi. He pushed up my shirt enough to kiss down to my stomach. As he reached the waistband of my leggings, he peeled them off slowly, kissing every inch of revealed skin. My breath quickened as he got closer and closer to my center.

Tilting my head back, I found Bodhi watching the whole process with hunger. Reaching out, I ran a hand down his arm feeling his muscles twitch at my touch. Breaking away from watching Oscar, he looked down at me and then let me pull him down into a kiss as our Alpha had my leggings around my knees and tugged them off the rest of the way. Splaying me open, Oscar let his fingers trail through my wetness, making me gasp into Bodhi's mouth.

Bodhi deepened our kiss, letting his tongue explore every part of me. When he pulled back, he shifted to the side and kicked off the rest of his clothes, leaving him bare to me. Then he lifted me up so we could get my shirt off, and Oscar hopped off the bed to shed his pants. Once we were all back on the bed, Oscar placed a pillow under my hips, lifting me, so it was easier for him to devour me.

A mewling whimper escaped me as Oscar added his fingers to

the mix. As his tongue worked over my clit, he stroked the spot inside that made me feel like my body was on fire. Bodhi urged me to turn my head, and I opened, more than happy to take his cock in my mouth. I hummed at the taste of him, reveling in this moment of pure intimacy between the three of us. Oscar pulled out his fingers then twisted my hips so I was now lying on my side. He lay behind me, lifting my top leg over his hip. This gave Bodhi a clear view of our Alpha working his cock inside me.

When Oscar seated himself inside me fully, I moaned, making Bodhi hiss at the vibrations it caused. "God, Cambrie, you're going to make me come too fast. The sight of the two of you together is so goddamn sexy. Look at you taking his cock down to the knot, letting it fill you completely," Bodhi praised as his fingers sank into my hair and he started to fuck my mouth.

I placed a hand on his thigh to hold me steady as Oscar thrust into me. My Alpha moved slowly, taking his time to enjoy the feel of me, his hand gripping one of my breasts as he kissed along my shoulder and neck. Then he started to purr, sending a shock wave of vibrations through my body. This added sensation made every stroke of his dick so much more impactful; it made me writhe with pleasure pushing back against him, needing to feel him deeper.

Sensing what I needed, Oscar took his free hand and placed it over my pelvis and pushed slightly, holding the pressure so all the sensations doubled in intensity. I cried out around Bodhi's cock, which was his undoing because he came down my throat with a grunt.

He pressed my head to his body and held me there as his cock released his cum. "Ah, fuck, yes, Cambi, your mouth feels so good. I can feel you swallowing down my cum like a good little Omega."

My eyes began to water a little as he pulled out, having been so deep down my throat. Cupping my chin, he wiped the cum and spit off my face then kissed me, humming his approval. "God, you're perfect, absolutely fucking perfect," he whispered, pressing a chaste kiss to my lips before pulling back.

Oscar paused in his movements to sign to Bodhi, who just grinned at whatever he said. "What did he say?" I questioned.

Bodhi shook his head as he lay down in front of me but placed his face right where Oscar and I were connected. "You'll find out soon enough."

Now that Bodhi wasn't using my mouth, Oscar picked up the pace, and I realized he hadn't wanted me to choke. These men never ceased to amaze me with how they took care of me, even when I didn't realize it. Twisting slightly, I kissed my Alpha, needing to show just how much I was in love with him and everything he did for me.

I cried out, but Oscar stole it away as he kissed me deeper. Bodhi was now sucking on my clit as Oscar pumped in and out of me. This had to have been what Oscar told him to do, and it was amazing. As Oscar pulled back, I felt Bodhi's hand pull him out of me, making me whimper at the loss. Breaking from our kiss, I turned to see what had happened and saw Bodhi sucking on our Alpha. Oscar growled in pleasure, thrusting his hips, then Bodhi helped to guide Oscar's cock back into me. Bodhi alternated between sucking on each of us until Oscar's knot started to expand, and he couldn't remove it from me anymore. It didn't keep him from lapping at whatever he could of the both of us.

His added stimulation had me coming multiple times as Oscar's knot stroked all the right places. Then as yet another orgasm rolled through me, Oscar's teeth bit down on the upper part of my ear. Another bond shimmered into place, leaving me in a haze of warm feelings of love, joy, and contentment as he marked me with his cum as well as his bite. I lay there, a twitching puddle of happiness and bliss, as Bodhi came to cuddle, wrapping Oscar and me in a hug.

"My Little Star," Oscar rasped. "Love. You," he added. His voice broke under the forced use, making me want to cry at the pain I felt it caused him to say those words to me.

"I love you too, Oscar, and that will never change," I assured him, cupping his face and kissing him. "Even if I never hear those words again, I will carry them in my heart forever."

Oscar started to purr deep and loud, and I was sure Bodhi could feel it through me. I took Oscar's arm and settled it between my breasts, then found Bodhi's and added it, so the three of us were connected as we slept. I knew the relationship between Oscar and Bodhi was new, but I never wanted there to be a moment they doubted we all belonged together.

CHAPTER 53

Marius

Having to leave Cambrie after only half a day with her sucked, but if this could end all the problems and give us our life back, it was worth it. Seeing her snuggled between Oscar and Bodhi, clutching their hands, made me feel a little better knowing the others would be with her. Oscar had been awake when I came in, and I silently told him I was leaving but would call the moment I knew anything. He nodded and assured me he would keep her distracted so she wouldn't worry.

How anyone couldn't see the benefit of a pack for everyone involved astounded me. Having a group of people to support each other made life so much more fulfilling. I knew Spencer would have Nixon to keep an eye on him today, but like Cambrie, the whole pack would care for one another. When Rick brought up going to the Care Center and taking a headcount, Cambrie didn't realize it was a mutinous act for me to sign the approval without the rest of the CoF agreeing. If we were mistaken and there was no foul play, Yoram might finally have what he needed to not only get me removed as an Official but he could also potentially call for my death.

As I pulled up in front of Rick's company's base of operations, I took a moment to really think about what I was doing.

Spencer, Nixon, and I got into a fight when we went up for the night, knowing this was a monumental risk. If it was true, it made me wonder if the black market problem for Omegas was tied to this as well. Knowing that was a possibility, people were more willing to give up their children to the Care Centers. It was rather brilliant in the way only someone with purely evil intentions could create.

Letting out a deep breath, I shoved out of the car and headed inside. I found Rick with a group of fifteen men dressed in black tactical gear like the night before. "Ah, Official Stone, just in time," Rick greeted. "You didn't get a chance to meet the crew, but these are the same men I sent to get your Omega. Three of them are also my packmates," Rick shared.

I shook each of their hands, thanking them. "I appreciate all you've done for my family and me. What we're going to do today might save those trapped in the Care Centers and protect those who might have ended up with their fate in the future. Before we go, I need to make sure you understand the risk of this mission. I am an Official, but to do something like this, it needs to be approved by all its members."

"Well, then it's a good thing you at least have half the vote now, isn't it?" Alton spoke as he walked over to me from an office he was waiting in. "I might not be able to go on this raid, but when Rick reached out to ask for my support, it was given without question. It's harder to fight two of us than just one, don't you think? Especially after one of our own tried to kill me," Alton added.

Grinning, I hugged the man, clapping him on the back. "You crazy old fool, I thought you were going to retire?"

"Bah, there's still time, but right now, what's best for our people is for you and me to be partners in this crime," Alton said, waving me off him. "Now, you better get going. The longer you wait, the more chance someone will leak the mission. There are eyes and ears everywhere, my boy. Just you wait, I'll prove it before this is all said and done."

"You heard the Official, let's roll out," Rick ordered. "Not you, Marius. You have to put this on first. I'm not taking you into this without some sort of protection," Rick stated as he handed me a bulletproof vest.

He made a valid point, so I removed my suit jacket and strapped it on then replaced my jacket, making it less noticeable. While I wanted to be safe, I also didn't want to draw attention to what we feared might happen. "Alton, are you staying here?" I asked.

"I'll be in the command center watching and listening. Rick, I'm told, will have an earpiece so we can communicate in case you need help with something," Alton shared. "I know you're wise to most of the laws, but there are a few obscure ones we haven't had a chance to change yet. Some can help, and some can hinder, depending on what they know. Though, to be honest, if they truly have been selling Omegas, nothing will save them."

I reached out and shook the man's hand before leaving with Rick. The primary Care Center wasn't all that far from the Capitol Building. It was the newest out of them all, being only five years old and the most state-of-the-art. Their reasoning had been that it was better to have it close by for security purposes, but now it made me wonder if Yoram wanted it close to control it easier. Rick motioned to the armored Humvee, with his men already in the back, guns at the ready. This wasn't going to be a subtle mission, but it would be one of the most important.

"You sure you want to come with us?" Rick questioned.

"If I don't, then none of this can be used against him. It needs to be me that sees what's going on, so he can't sweep it under the rug," I said, bracing myself as Rick started the vehicle.

Without another word, we left the fenced-in back lot and were out on the road. The public knew when they saw a vehicle like this that something was going down. My hope was that it wouldn't spread to Yoram too quickly. Everything about this needed to go by the rule book as much as possible.

The Care Center itself didn't seem like anything special from the outside, but that was by design. We didn't even put the name on the building to ensure no one knew what it was. All there was to show you were in the right place was a simplistic logo of two Cs. Rick pulled right up to the front door, and even before he came to a full stop, his men were out and entering the building. Through the glass, I saw a woman at the front desk screaming and leaping out of her seat.

Shoving the vehicle's door open, I headed inside and slapped the official letter on the counter. "My name is Official Stone, and I demand that we be allowed to inspect the Care Center and its inhabitants."

She gaped at me like a fish, her eyes so wide I feared they would pop out of her head.

"Ma'am," I barked. Since she was a Beta it didn't have the same effect as it did on an Omega, but it typically got an immediate response.

"Yes, sir, I need to call the Head Caretaker and let him know your request before letting you into the facility," she answered.

"No, you don't. By law, when an Official requests admittance with a signed, sealed letter, they are permitted access. Now, I'm asking you again nicely to allow me and my men to enter the Care Center," I explained, trying to keep my irritation out of my voice, knowing she would be instructed incorrectly to cover Yoram's ass.

"Sir," she pleaded. "I could lose my job."

"Ma'am, if you don't let me back there, you'll lose your job anyway," I stated. In no way did I want to be cruel, but right now bigger things were at play. The woman finally nodded, entered the code and the doors swung open. "Rick, I want some of your men to go around back just in case anyone chooses to avoid meeting with us."

"Yes, sir," Rick answered and motioned to three men. "Radio if you catch any stragglers."

Charging forward into the center before the woman could change her mind, I found myself in a waiting room of sorts. Couches and chairs were set up in various ways for people to use as they waited... for what was still to be determined. A woman exited a door with a clipboard in hand and looked up when she heard us.

"I'm sorry, sir, but we don't have any meetings set up for today. You'll have to reschedule with the front desk," she said, clutching the board to her chest.

"I'm Official Stone, and we're doing a check of the facility. I want to speak to the Head Caretaker as well as gather all the Omegas that are here so I might speak with them," I ordered.

The woman's face scrunched up in confusion. "We don't have any Omegas here. They were dispatched about two hours ago to be sent to their pack in Asturg."

"What?" I bellowed. "Why the hell would you be sending Omegas to another country when we need them right fucking here?"

She paled as my Alpha nature kicked into high gear. "I... I don't understand. We were told last night to send the bus this afternoon. Did something change?"

"Who communicated that to you?" I demanded.

"The Head Caretaker," she said.

I tried to take a deep breath so I didn't scare the woman, but my anger was reaching new heights and I wasn't sure I wanted to control it. "Get him. Now." I bit out.

Her head bobbed up and down before she scurried off. Turning, I faced Rick. "We need to find that bus and stop it from crossing the border. Call Savo and get his ass on that right now. I will not let our people be sent into that world to be used as baby-makers for a pointless war."

Rick pulled out his phone and dialed as I paced.

"You know what, fuck this," I snapped and stormed over to the door the woman exited.

Tossing it open, I entered the inner portion of the Care Center. It looked like a hotel with a lobby, and a grand piano in the corner played softly, even though there was no one there to listen to it. A set of stairs led to the second floor, where I assumed the rooms were, but I wanted to see the main part before ensuring there were no Omegas left in the place.

Pushing through a set of double doors, I found myself in a dining hall with a buffet line set up. A woman was cleaning up, so I assumed they fed them before shipping them off to a starved country. The place looked clean and well looked after, with nothing to tell me the women were being treated poorly.

"What do you mean they are doing a search of the building? No one is supposed to be here *ever*," a man grumbled as he and the other woman I sent after him entered the dining hall.

I stood tall and crossed my arms, waiting for them to realize I was here with reinforcements.

"You shouldn't have told him about sending off the Omegas. That information is strictly to be shared with Official Yoram and no one else," he carried on, then halted when he spotted me, and panic filled his eyes.

Slowly, I approached him holding his gaze. "Don't stop. I would very much like to know why it is that only Official Yoram is privy to this information. I believe that all the Officials should know about this as well as our people, wouldn't you say? How do you think they will take it when they find out what you've been up to?"

"Official Stone," he exclaimed, then whipped his head to look at the woman. "You didn't say it was another Official, you idiot!"

He lifted his hand like he was going to strike the woman, but I grabbed his wrist and yanked him away from her. "What the hell do you think you're doing?"

"She's killed us. She's killed us all!" he shrieked.

The woman looked terrified as she backed away from the raving man. Two of Rick's men came and grabbed him from me, holding him as another cuffed him. "Don't you say another word, Kim. They have no proof."

"Get him the hell out of here," I ordered, then turned to Kim. "Don't listen to him, I'm not looking to kill anyone. I just need some answers."

Holding my hands out at my sides, I tried to show I wasn't going to harm her. "Please, will you sit with me and help me understand a few things? Somewhere along the way, communications have been crossed, and no one is sure of how things are working right now. This is why I'm here, to ensure that the best is being done for our people." Kim gave a jerky nod and walked over, pulled a seat out, and sat. "Rick, I would like for your men to sweep the building and check every nook and cranny of this place. It also might be best to keep all the staff together so we can speak to them."

"Yes, sir," Rick agreed, and issued instructions.

I pulled out a chair across from Kim and leaned back, crossing my legs, trying to help convey that this wasn't anything serious. The more relaxed I could make her feel, the more she would tell me. "Now, how long have you been working here in the Care Center?"

"Three years at this location. I came over when they closed down the one in Cresswater," she answered. "Sir, have I done something wrong?"

Letting out a sigh, I shook my head. "I'm not sure, Kim. However, the more honest you are with me, the better things will be. Something tells me that you did something at the request of your boss without him telling you the whole story. If that's the case, then it wouldn't be fair to hold you responsible now, would it?"

She shook her head and set the clipboard down. "Where would you like me to start?"

"Tell me the basic process. A young lady comes to you at sixteen, then what?" I coaxed.

Nervously, she licked her lips and took a deep breath. "When we get new intakes, they are looked over by our medical team, and if they are in good health they are sent to the general population. If not, they are kept in the medical wing until they recover. Most of those are children from rural or outer city limits that don't have the help they need. We give them a day or two to settle in and get used to the routine of the Center." She paused and looked at me questioningly. "Is this the information you're looking for?"

"Yes, you're doing great," I assured her.

"While many come into their designation, the only ones we get right away are the poorer kids. I truly think it's because their families view it as a better chance for their child. They get three meals daily, a warm bed, and an education until they are twenty-one. Well, that was the case until the past two years. Now, they stay here until they are eighteen and then get sent to Asturg or Shearia once a quarter," Kim explained. "The only time we keep an Omega here is when Yoram picks them out personally. Then they are sent to another Care Center."

"I'm sorry, I'm going to pause you there," I interjected, leaning forward as I signaled Rick. "What was that about a second Care Center the ones picked by Yoram went?"

"He comes once a month and meets with all the Omegas, checking on their education and well-being. Then if he feels they will be a good fit for a pack he's been chatting with, he'll move them to a Care Center further in the city. Actually, it's close to the old Neenan Pharmaceuticals building," Kim said, looking at us both questioningly. "Why do I get the feeling you know nothing about anything I've said."

"You're correct, I don't know much about what's been going on here, and that's what we are trying to change. Do you know how many Care Centers there are active?" I questioned.

"Just this one and the other Yoram oversees," she answered. "The others have staff there to take in new Omegas, but they all get sent here. This is where we have all the medical and educational things we need. Every other location is just a place for them to wait if we don't have room here, but that hasn't been a problem since we've been sending them out of the country."

"Thank you, Kim. I truly appreciate you being so honest with me," I said with a smile as I stood. "I'm going to have you and the other staff members be escorted to an alternate location for now. We have more questions, but I think it would be best if we made a stop at the other location as well."

"Of course, though we have no contact with that Care Center, only the Head Caretaker and Official Yoram interact with the staff," Kim informed me.

Reaching out, I shook her hand before she was escorted out by one of Rick's men.

Running my fingers through my hair I let out a frustrated growl. "What do we know about the bus?"

"Savo located it and sent word that it's not to be allowed to cross. That we are in a state of emergency, and the border needs to be shut down. Protocol should be that they return here since they can't continue. I'm sending out a team to escort them back and to ensure my men can keep an eye on them," Rick shared. "I've called in more men. At this point, there is no way that Yoram isn't going down for this. How the fuck did he think he could get away with selling our own people?"

"The bastard is far too comfortable in his place at the top, figuring that no one would want to challenge him with all the strings he can pull," I growled as we headed back to the Humvee. "We need to get to that fucking center now, because if what I think he's doing is really happening, I'm going to murder someone."

Rick grabbed me by the shoulder before I got in the vehicle. "I get it, man. I do, but remember that woman you have back home? The one you have to look in the eye and tell what happened here today. Don't let it be you having to tell her that there's blood on your hands. Trust me when I say this from experience. You don't want that."

My shoulders sagged, and I nodded. "Yeah, I hear you and I don't want that, but fuck do I want whatever other retribution I can get."

"Now that I can stand behind," Rick agreed. "These people need to pay for their transgressions, but to the letter of the law, so no one else tries to take matters into their own hands. Just imagine what it will be like when the people learn their child is in another country. They are going to need a person they can trust and lean on. Right now, it's going to be you."

That reality slapped me in the face. "There's going to be riots in the streets. Hell, I wouldn't put it past them to burn the Capitol Building down."

"One step at a time," Rick warned. "We'll go to this center, deal with what we find, then we'll manage the rest. If we have answers to give, a person to blame, and actions already being taken to right this atrocity, we're ahead of the game."

"Right, well, let's go find out what else Yoram's been up to," I urged. "Not that we need another nail for his coffin at this point," I muttered as we headed off.

CHAPTER 54

Cambrie

The guys spent the morning doing everything they could to distract me while Marius went off to deal with things at the Care Centers. All I could do at this point was wait to hear word and pray that it would all be over. Nothing I'd learned about my birth father gave me hope that whatever was going on would be good.

We finished the last movie for the Lord of the Rings, and now Rafael, Spencer, and Bodhi were teaching me how to play Speed. I quickly learned that Spencer was far more competitive than I ever thought. He was normally so selfless that to see him standing by the table throwing down cards left and right was a surprise. When he lost, he didn't take it well either, always challenging a move or how something had been played.

"No, you can't put them down like that," Spencer snapped. "You have to lay them down one at a time."

Bodhi scoffed and narrowed his eyes at the fellow Beta. "That's a load of crap, Spency-boy, and you know it."

"Would you like me to google it?" Spencer challenged.

"Yeah, actually I would, and that other thing you yelled at me for in the last round. Personally, I think you're changing these rules so you win," Bodhi countered.

Rafael chuckled as Spencer pulled out his phone and started to type. "Just you wait."

"Hey, if you can prove it to me in three different sources, then I'll believe it. The internet lies so we need a few opinions to suss out the truth."

Not wanting to get in the middle of their fight, I got up from my chair and sat in Rafael's lap. He nuzzled into my neck, purring. "Hello, Little One," he murmured. "Are you having fun?"

"When we actually get to play the game," I answered. "Is there another one that might give us a better shot at playing longer before this happens?"

"Hmm," Rafael pondered, resting his chin on my shoulder. "I suppose there is Go Fish, Bullshit, or maybe we can see if the house has Uno or something like it."

"What's Bullshit?" I asked.

"It's a game where the object is to get rid of all your cards, but you have to lay them down in sequential order. If you don't have the card, you lie and put down something while saying it's what you need. The other players can call bullshit if they think you're lying," Rafael explained. "Do you want to give it a try?"

I shook my head furiously. "No, I can't lie at all."

"I suppose that would make the game challenging," Rafael agreed.

Feet pounded down the stairs, and I got a wave of anger from Savo as he appeared in the kitchen with his laptop. "You're never going to believe what that mother fucker has been doing."

I flinched at the venom in his voice, even though I knew it wasn't directed at me.

"Savo, please, watch your language," Rafael chided.

"Sorry," he muttered, then plunked his laptop on the table. "Seems Cambrie wasn't the only Omega he was trading off to other countries. He just sent a busload of Omegas to Asturg. I shut down the border and had them redirect the bus back to the Care Center, but that doesn't fix what he's already done."

My jaw fell open. How could this man, evil or not, be shipping off innocent people to other countries? What if they had a family that cared about them? Would we ever be able to get them back?

"What do we do about those already gone?" Rafael questioned.

Savo ran his hands through his hair and growled in frustration. "That's the thing, there are no records. We know who was brought into the Care Centers, but we don't know which country they were sent to or how long ago. What I don't get is what is Yoram getting out of this? I've been over his financials with a fine-tooth comb, and I can't see anything that would make sense."

"What if it's not money but power?" Bodhi suggested. "He's got as much power as he can here, but what if he was trying to take over Oscad completely? As in, making himself king or something?"

"What doesn't make sense to me is that Yoram isn't a young man," Rafael pointed out. "Why put all this work into becoming so rich and powerful when he's sixty and isn't going to live but for maybe another twenty years?"

"You're looking at this like a rational person," Savo commented. "If he's anything like my father, then it doesn't matter, power is power, and he'd rather die knowing he got all he could while he was alive."

Hearing him talk about his father made me wonder what might happen if this ended up causing a war between our two countries. Most start when one person promises something, and then they can't provide it anymore. If Yoram made a deal for Omegas and we cut them off, would they come after us?

"That's fair," Rafael admitted. "I wasn't thinking with that frame of mind."

"Why would you? Why would anyone? It's pointless," Bodhi muttered.

"What's pointless?" Nixon asked as he rejoined us.

He'd stepped out to deal with a few matters for the shelters. While I loved that they were all here with me, I knew they had things to take care of. When I mentioned this to Nixon, he just gave me a disapproving look and didn't bother to give me an answer.

"Power-hungry people and the way they look at the world," Spencer interjected, answering Nixon's question.

The Alpha blinked at us for a moment then cocked his head. "What brought that up?"

"Yoram," everyone at the table answered.

"Ah, I suppose I should have guessed," Nixon said, taking a seat at the table. "I take it you got word from Marius then?"

"In a manner of speaking," Savo mumbled as he typed away on his computer. "I had to divert a bus full of Omegas from being smuggled out of the country. Now, Rick and Marius are going to a Care Center that Yoram uses for Omegas he picks out personally."

"Why does that sound terrifying?" Spencer said with a shiver. "I would never want to be someone that man singled out."

"If I told you it was conveniently located near Neenan Pharmaceutical, would you be surprised?" Savo added, looking over his screen at Spencer.

"No," Spencer gasped. "You can't think he's trying to revive the program, do you? Hasn't it been twisted enough to kill off almost all the Omegas? When will people learn to leave well enough alone?"

Rafael let out a heavy sigh and slid me off his lap as he got up from the table. "Never. It's in our nature to keep pushing limits. If we could actually learn from our mistakes, then that might be one thing, but so far mankind has been found incapable of doing that."

"Deep," Savo said, nodding his head in agreement.

Rafael cupped my chin, lifting it, so I could gaze into his eyes. "Would you mind grabbing Oscar? I thought it might be nice to make lunch and have a picnic in the backyard. While we need to keep out of the public eye, I don't think that means we need to be trapped in the house. The backyard is fenced in, no one will see us out there."

I smiled brightly at him. "That sounds lovely. I'll go find him right now."

Oscar had work that needed to be completed, so he was taking the morning to work on it. I entered the bedroom without knocking and found him with a pair of headphones on, staring intently at a screen as he adjusted the music he'd finished. Through our bond, I could feel how intent he was, but the moment he became aware of me he paused and turned. With a smile, he removed his headphones and reached out for me.

I let him pull me onto his lap and capture my lips with his in a sweet kiss. Warmth and love flowed into me from him, and I wasn't sure there was a better feeling in the world than knowing how he felt without having to use words. "Rafael wanted to have lunch outside in the backyard and asked me to come get you."

He nodded, but instead of getting up he just wrapped his arms around me and nuzzled into my neck. Longing and relief swirled between us, and I realized that he'd been having some withdrawal being apart from me all morning. Twisting, I tossed my arms around his neck and kissed him deeply. Marius had mentioned that Alphas took a little while to adjust to new bonds, making me wonder how he was doing. Nixon had been around me for most of the morning, and Savo had been as well off and on. Whereas Oscar and Marius were the only two that had been more distant because of other obligations.

"Tell me what you need?" I asked, leaning back to see his face. Oscar just smiled and tapped a finger on my chest. "Me? That's it, just to have me here?"

He nodded and hugged me as he purred in delight.

"Well, that makes this easier then, doesn't it?" I said with a laugh. "Come on, we can see what the others are making for lunch, and I'll sit with you while we eat."

Oscar all but pouted when I slid off his lap and tugged him to get up, but he did and followed me downstairs. Rafael and Bodhi were hard at work making sandwiches while I spotted Nixon outside with Spencer laying out blankets on the grass. Savo was still at his computer. When I reached out to him, I felt his frustration and anger at the situation. The second he felt me though, his gaze snapped up to meet mine.

"Are you checking in on me, *Keksik?*" Savo inquired with a smirk.

Blushing at being caught, I just shrugged. "Still learning how this bond between us works. You seemed irritated, and I was curious if I could feel your true feelings."

"And?" he asked.

"You're incredibly frustrated mixed with how mad you are at this whole thing," I shared.

Savo got up and walked over to me, cupping my face. "All I keep thinking is that if your bastard of a fake father hadn't locked you away like he did, then you might have ended up like one of those women. If you'd been sent to a Care Center, then I never would have found you, and that pisses me off. What if those Omegas had people here waiting for them, only none of them realized it? I won't let that tyrant get away with this. I'm going to nail his ass to the wall."

Before Rafael could even say anything, Savo turned and pointed a finger at the man. "I know, but sometimes swearing is the only way to get your point across. I realize she doesn't like it, but it's going to happen from time to time if I'm around."

Rafael just looked at him with raised eyebrows as he paused in the process of spreading mayo on the bread. "I wasn't going to say a word because you're correct. Sometimes there is only one way to refer to a person, and that was right on the money."

"Alright then," Savo stated, then stroked my cheek before he returned to his computer.

"Little One, can you take this tray of sandwiches outside?" Rafael instructed. "Everyone else will be right out with the rest."

I gaped at the pile of food on the tray I picked up. It was so ladened down that I needed both hands to ensure I didn't drop it. Oscar opened the door for me and went back to grab something as I made my way to the blanket.

"Where do you want me to set these down?" I asked once I reached Nixon and Spencer.

Spencer sat up from where he'd be sprawled out in the sunshine and scrambled to his knees. "Here, Little Dove, let me take that."

I allowed him to rescue me from the weight, feeling frustrated at how weak I was at this moment. Who couldn't carry a tray of sandwiches? That was a simple enough task that anyone should have been able to perform.

"Sweetheart," Nixon called to me with a soft voice. "Come here, please."

Shame flooded me as I realized all of my bonded Alphas were feeling my defeat.

"Cambrie," Nixon said with a little more command.

Sinking to my knees, I shuffled over to sit beside Nixon, who wrapped his arms around me and rested his head on mine. "Talk to me, remember I want to know everything that's going on in that head of yours. The good, the bad, and the in-between, I want you to share it all so if I can help you."

"You're just going to tell me I'm being silly," I mumbled.

"How do you know that?" he chuckled.

"Because I *feel* like I'm being silly," I shot back.

Both of them looked a little taken aback at my sassiness, but I was feeling insecure and mad about it. "Do you know how ridiculous it is that I can't carry a tray of food from the house to here without my arms starting to shake? Back at the mansion where Arthur was trying to teach me, it was physically draining to do everything he pushed on me. None of it should have been that difficult but it was making me do stupid things that would upset him. If I wasn't so weak and pathetic like I am, then I wouldn't have had so much trouble."

Nixon stood up and pulled me up with him. He grabbed my wrist and slid back the sleeve to reveal my arm, that while it had more fullness to it, was severely underdeveloped. "Do you know how to flex?" Nixon asked.

"Do what?" I asked. I'd heard the term and read it in books, but I can't say I'd ever attempted the feat.

"Hold your arm up like this," Nixon directed and poked the skin of my upper arm. "Now, I want you to just focus on tightening this muscle. Turn your hand into a fist, and as you clench down think about using that muscle."

Feeling doubtful about this whole endeavor, I did as he instructed and closed my eyes, thinking about that one muscle and squeezing my fist super hard. When a hand gripped my upper arm and gave it an inspecting squeeze, I flinched, opening my eyes. "What are you doing?" I questioned.

"You said you weren't strong, so I wanted to check out your muscles just to make sure they were still there." Nixon informed me. "See, the interesting thing about muscles is that you can make them stronger with time, effort, and patience. Here, feel mine," Nixon encouraged.

Spencer snorted. "Wow, could you be any more Alpha right now?"

Nixon just gave him an irritated look and offered his arm to me. "I've been working out about three times a week for the past few years. Working at the shelter means I need to be ready to pitch in however I can, so I make sure my body is able to do that."

I reached out and gripped his upper arm and when he flexed the muscle bulged, as did my eyes. His arm doubled in size and forced his shirt to its limits. "Are you saying I can get this strong, too?"

"No," Spencer interjected. "There is no need for you to be *that* buff. What we can help you with is regaining and improving your strength from where you're at now, to someone who can easily carry two trays of food if you want."

"Now you're making me sound even more silly," I muttered, dropping onto the blanket. "What would I do if I didn't have you guys around?"

"When would that ever happen?" Nixon asked as he joined us back on the blanket. "Cambrie, do you believe we see you as weak or a burden?"

"I'm both of those things," I pointed out.

Spencer and Nixon both looked at me, stunned. Then Nixon shook himself out of his surprise and pulled me onto his lap, so I was facing him. "Sweetheart, I'm sorry, I should have realized where this was coming from, but I didn't."

Now I was the one who was confused and scrunched up my face.

"Cambrie, you are an amazing woman who has survived so much in her life already. You're going to have to give your body a chance to catch up to what you need from it now. We'll be more than happy to help you and show you simple ways to become stronger, but this won't change the fact that we all *want* to take care of you." Nixon shared, reaching out and tucking my hair behind my ear. "Did you know that all men have a strong desire to be needed by their partner? It helps us know that we're being useful and shows how much we care. Allowing us to do little things for you gives us a chance to do that. None of us see you as a burden, but I know you know that already."

A mixture of understanding and guilt battled inside me as I processed what he was saying. "So, you're telling me I should let you help me because it makes you happy and you aren't irritated by it?"

"In a manner of speaking. You are still finding your independence, and we all want to encourage that as much as we can. If we see you struggling and want to help you, don't let your first thought be we don't think you're capable of doing it someday. Right now, you need a little more help, but that won't be forever. Soon, we're all going to be fighting over the chance to do something for you," Nixon explained.

I nodded solemnly. "Okay, I'll do my best to remember that. I just want so badly to take on things by myself that I get mad when I find I'm not at that point yet."

"Give it time, Little Dove. We are always on your side cheering for you," Spencer added. "Once we get back home, we can show you where the gym is and come up with some simple things to start with. Right now, I think we all need a little grace in how we are dealing with situations. It's been a wild few weeks, and none of us have really found our groove."

The sound of the back door banging open and Savo charging out with a wave of rage slamming into me, had me gasping.

"What happened?" Nixon demanded.

"Yoram's been arrested but not before he took out Fredrick and Willem," Savo informed us. "The rat bastard tried to kill himself as well, but Rick's guys stopped him. They were all at the second Care Center where he was using the modified fertility drug, but it turns out he'd been working on fixing it without success. Cambrie is his only living child that turned out to be an Omega."

CHAPTER 55

Cambrie

Looking at the two men dead lying at my feet, I didn't know how to feel. The whole thing was a whirlwind of events that happened so fast my brain was finally catching up to what I was seeing. While I'd never been a fan of either man, I never would have wanted a death like this for them. They should have been given the chance to speak and share their sides of the story. It wouldn't shock me one bit to find out that Yoram had manipulated or promised them things from the beginning.

Did I believe they were blameless? Not in the slightest, but Yoram wasn't judge, jury, and executioner. Clearly, there were things these men knew that he couldn't risk getting out into the world. Thankfully, Rick's men were so well trained they were able to disarm the man before he could blow his own brains out. It stunned me that he would rather take his own life than let us catch him. Granted, there was nothing he could say to make us disbelieve what we'd already witnessed.

Could it be that he was trying to cover his tracks now that we fucked up his plans to send Cambrie to Shearia? This man would never be someone I could relate to. Although, when I thought about it, what else was there if he didn't have his power? He didn't have a single person that truly loved him. His own pack sold him out to get happiness the only way they thought was possible.

"Marius," Rick called, pulling me out of my thoughts. "We found the girls, and it's not good."

Fuck, did the bastard have to ruin more lives before we could figure this all out?

"Have you called for help?" I asked as I followed him out of the back room.

"There are five ambulances on their way, along with some extra medical staff to take samples of whatever they think will be helpful," Rick answered, shaking his head. "Why the fuck would he be messing with this stuff? None of it makes sense. Seemingly, it's killing more than it's helping. Why can't he get it through his head?"

"God, I wish I had an answer for that, but I'm struggling with this myself." I sighed. "At least we won't need a trial and can just pass judgment on crimes that have been committed in front of us."

"I hope you don't mind, but I had one of the guys reach out to your pack to let them know that Yoram is in custody. I thought it might help them feel a little more at ease."

I clapped him on the back in thanks, only to freeze as we entered a room filled with cots. Five women lay on cots, some looking like they were on death's door. What made matters worse was they were all pregnant.

"No," I cried, my voice coming out in a cracked whisper. "Please tell me this isn't real."

"Believe me, I'm going to have nightmares for a long time after this," Rick murmured. "I looked them over, and they're all still alive, barely, but we'll do everything we can, Marius. The least we can do is find out who their families are and contact them."

Rage that had been bubbling under the surface broke free of my control and whipped around me like a snake, ready to snap at anyone who dared to come close. "I swear on my honor as an Alpha, I will make sure something like this will never happen in this country again," I growled. "If I have to burn our government to the ground and rebuild it, then that's what I'll fucking do."

"You've got my vote," Rick agreed as the sound of booted feet came pounding down the hall. "That would be my men leading the medics here," he warned, pulling me away from the door so they could enter.

Soon the room was flooded with people, men yelling for medical supplies and other things I didn't recognize. It was clear they needed space and I could be useful elsewhere. Glancing at Rick, I jerked my head for him to follow me as I left the room. The women were in the best hands, and I had to trust they would do everything in their power because I was of no help.

"Where did you take him?" I asked.

Rick paused as if unsure he wanted to give me that answer. "You can't talk to him alone. Let's get Alton, and then I'll take you to where we're holding him. Everything about this must be above reproach so you don't get dragged down by this."

My Alpha side screamed at me to make Rick take me to him *now*. That bastard deserved what was coming to him, and I felt like a right hook to the face was the least of his worries. Yet I knew Rick was right. With all that we've discovered, knowing there were at least two of us following the law was the better option.

"Fine," I grumbled and followed him out of the facility. "I don't mean to step on your toes with this, but your men are gathering all the information they can from the place, right? I don't want there to be a chance of someone destroying anything with all the chaos."

"I made sure my own pack was hunting that stuff down. They are the only ones that I would trust with something this important," Rick assured me. "Believe me when I say there is nothing more that I want but to make sure we can save those women and hopefully find those that have been sent elsewhere. Hell, even our Sasha is still in contact with her family, even though Shearia told us we couldn't come back."

Instead of hopping back into the Humvee, Rick headed for a black SUV that was parked right out front. Seemed this was what the backup had arrived in, and they had left the key in the ignition as they came to our aid. "Any word on the bus headed for Asturg?" I asked as we headed back to their base.

"Nothing more than the escort found them and are ensuring they return to the Care Center."

I grunted my acknowledgment of the information and pulled out my phone to call Savo. I needed to hear from him myself that we'd managed to do some good today.

"Marius," Savo said when he answered. "Is there something else I can do for you?"

"Not as of yet. Rick said he told you we have Yoram?" I asked, needing to confirm.

I could hear talking in the background and Cambrie's laugh, making me yearn to be home with them. I wanted to hug each and every member of my pack to prove to myself they were alright and everyone was safe.

"Yeah, he called and had me hack into their computer system. I'm downloading all the data I can get my hands on from those computers, as we speak. It's taking a while with how much they have stored, but I'll get it all, don't you worry," Savo shared. "You doing alright? Rick mentioned you got there just as Yoram took out the other two. I'm sure that wasn't what you expected for your day."

"None of this is what I expected for my day, Savo, it's so much worse," I answered honestly.

Savo gave an understanding sound, and the voices got louder. "Hold on, I know something that will help."

There was some muffled talking and the sound of the phone being handed over. "Marius?"

Cambrie's sweet voice filtered through the phone, a hint of concern in her voice. "Hi, Princess. I just wanted to check in and let you know I'm safe, but there are some more things I have to do. My hope is that I'll be back for dinner, or better yet, I'll meet you back at home now that the all-clear has been given." There was silence, and I worried that she might have hung up or I'd lost signal with her. "Cambrie?"

"I'm here," she said. "Savo told us about what happened, I'm sorry you had to see that. I feel selfish asking this after everything that's happened and all you've learned, but does this mean it's over?"

My heart broke for so many reasons at that one simple question that had so much meaning behind it. "I believe so, Princess. Once I come back home to you tonight, I'll have a more confident answer. My gut tells me that the worst is over, and yeah, we might have a few more days or weeks of struggles as we move forward, but it will be toward a new beginning."

"I like the sound of that," she agreed. "I love you, Marius. Go rescue a few more princesses before you come home, okay? There are so many of them out there that need someone to fight for them."

"I love you too, my Little Princess," I said, knowing that even if I helped hundreds of Omegas today, the most important one would be the first princess I had the privilege of saving.

Hanging up, I realized we'd just pulled up to Rick's headquarters. "Do you mind going in and grabbing him?" Rick asked. "The old bastard doesn't like me all that much. I made the mistake of offering him tea when he arrived earlier."

A bark of laughter burst out of me at that, just imagining how Alton would take such an offer. "I'm amazed you're still alive after a comment like that."

"Let's just say it's a good thing I'm quick on my feet and lucky he's not as fast as he used to be," Rick muttered.

Chuckling, I headed in but found him already coming out to meet me. "Told you I could listen in on conversations, didn't I?" Alton reminded me. "It wasn't the offer of tea that had me ready to clobber him with my cane, it was the sight of the wheelchair sitting by the door. If Yoram's poison couldn't slow me down enough to need anything more than a cane, what makes that idiot think I'd be willing to use a wheelchair?"

"Did he actually suggest you use it?" I asked, feeling that was out of character from what I'd seen of Rick.

Alton frowned at me. "He didn't have to. He put it there, making it an implied suggestion."

"You know what, old man? I think you're making far too much of this than you need to," I scolded. "Come on, I'm going to pay a visit to the sick bastard, and Rick said I had to bring you along so I don't kill him. We need answers, and I doubt he will give them up willingly."

"Well, why didn't you say so earlier? Let's get going," Alton urged, waving for me to get a move on.

I headed for the door then paused, looking over my shoulder. "If you could listen in then, how come you didn't know this already?"

Alton looked chagrined. "Let's just say I got nosy and turned on the sound when you pulled up to the door. I only caught the last bit of what he said."

Shaking my head, I held the door for the old coot as he exited and offered him the front seat. "I'm not sitting next to him, he thinks I'm an old, crippled man."

"Cut the act, Alton, and get in. How Marla doesn't smother you in your sleep, I'll never know," I muttered.

Alton tried to look offended but gave up and climbed into the front seat. I got in the back and we were off to whatever secret location Rick's men were holding Yoram. When we pulled up to the Capitol Building, I was confused, but he kept going to the back side, which I'd never seen before. We unloaded and were led down a flight of stairs into an underground area that seemed to be where the main security office was.

Men at stations were looking over monitors that had video feeds on them, which made me nervous. Alton always told me not to trust any room of the building, and now I could clearly see why. None of the offices were watched as far as I could tell, but that didn't mean there weren't other ways they were keeping tabs on us.

"Are you sure it's safe to have brought him here?" I questioned.

Rick just waved off my concern and kept going deeper into the space past the offices. Now we were in an area that felt more like a dungeon, with holding rooms and glass windows that I was sure the other person couldn't see out of. This was where we found Yoram handcuffed to the table, with guards on either side of him and one outside the door.

"Any problems, Seth?" Rick asked.

"Still trying to kill himself any chance he gets, but he hasn't been successful yet," Seth informed us. "The two in there with him are also on the medic team, so if he does do something stupid, we have the right help ready."

Rick clapped the man on the shoulder. "Thanks, man. We're gonna talk to him for a bit, but I want you all to be right outside this door just in case."

"You got it, boss man," Seth answered, swiping a card to unlock the door.

Rick signaled for the other two to leave the room as we entered until it was just the three of us and one pissed-off Yoram.

"I should have guessed it would be you two that fucked this up," Yoram grumbled, sounding completely and utterly unlike himself. "After I got word the mansion was raided, I should have guessed that bastard of a Beta would sell me out. He's never been loyal to me, only that bitch of his."

"That's some way to talk about your pack," Alton murmured before he sat down and faced off with the devil himself. "It's a wonder they didn't have any sense of loyalty with that kind of loving care showered upon them. Tell me, did you even like any of the people you brought into your pack? Or did they just serve the purpose of making you look like you have a heart?"

"What do you even care? You got what you wanted. Just leave me be so I can die and leave this godforsaken world. None of you will see what I've done to make this country great. All you'll look at is the perceived evil you stumbled across today," Yoram accused.

Alton sat back in his chair, crossing one leg over the other, while I was ready to leap across the table and throttle the bastard. I felt Rick as he shifted at my side, probably getting ready to ensure I didn't do that very thing.

"Now would be a good time to tell us all the wonderful things you've done, because none of it makes sense to any of us," Alton pointed out. "Let's start with why you felt the need to steal Cambrie."

Yoram's face clouded with rage at the mention of her name. The need to defend my Omega rode me hard, but I managed to hold myself back as my hands balled into fists.

"What I do with my own offspring is none of your concern. In fact, you have no right to take her from her family home. She was born in that house and should have been raised in. Instead, one of my own pack betrayed me and ran off with her to a man worse than I'd ever been to any of my people," Yoram announced as he slammed his fists on the table with the slight slack the cuffs gave him.

"Now, why on earth do you think she would feel the need to do that? If you treat all your people with respect, why is it that you think a woman would steal a newborn away?" Alton pressed.

Yoram didn't seem all that willing to answer as he picked at his thumbnail, not looking at us. He wasn't going to answer that. I could just tell from the way he closed himself off to us. We needed to try things from a different angle and see if that worked better.

"Yoram, you were testing the drug again," I stated, knowing that was a fact, having had Cambrie's blood tested. "Did you really think that was the best way to help boost our chances at more Omegas?"

This seemed to pull the man out of his funk. "It did before, we all saw it. Before the EQ tried to destroy all the Omegas with that blasted attack, there were record numbers. It's in the data. Why wouldn't we want to revisit something like that?"

"Because it killed your own Omega," I countered.

"Bah, she was sickly as it was. The only chance I had to guarantee that I'd be able to provide the world with another Omega was to ensure it with the drugs. Her own family made it, but they refused to do anything with the power they had. Instead, they hid away in their country manor and just made fools out of themselves," Yoram ranted. "They had the science and money to start over, but they were too scared, so I had to do it myself. Cambrie is proof that it still works."

I scoffed at him, seeing how delusional he was under his carefully crafted mask. "You and I both know that from an Alpha and Omega joining, Cambrie's chances of being an Omega were fifty-fifty if Isabelle managed to conceive. Why not give her the normal drug just to help her fertility? Why mess with the DNA?"

"I didn't want a chance, I needed to be sure. Even before I'd been voted into the Circle of Four, I had plans for this world. I was going to single-handedly unite Oscad and Shearia. Bridge the two countries that had been working together since the beginning. We are so similar but struggled in different ways, so it would be possible for us to help each other. Their infrastructure is far superior to ours, while our women are more fertile," Yoram explained. "Did you know that in their country, males could also be Omegas? What is the purpose of that? They can't reproduce, and the female Alphas are so infertile there's hardly any chance they will become pregnant."

While Rick had told me about his son, I didn't realize how that was viewed in Shearia. It made sense why he wouldn't ever want to take his family back there. Yet, I wasn't all that convinced Shearia was better off the way Yoram did. I'd seen the numbers our peace-keeping teams had brought back with them. That was one reason I hadn't been all that keen on making a trade deal with them. Although it seems it didn't matter since Yoram did it on his own.

"What about Asturg?" Alton questioned. "That country is never going to be of value to anyone, so why send our women to them?"

Yoram let out a bark of laughter. "Do you think there won't come a time when they turn on us? No, soon they will realize they can't win against the other side and turn their gaze onto another target. By doing what I did, I ensured we gave them value and brokered an agreement with General Rasvan. Oh, speaking of, you might know his son, Savo. He was Cambrie's bodyguard, and I heard from my people he bonded to her."

Figures the bastard would want to get in his hits where he could, but too bad for him I knew how to be part of a pack. To share someone I loved and to know that if it made them happy, nothing else mattered. I had zero doubt that Cambrie loved me just as she loved us all, equally.

"Yes, Savo and I share Cambrie as bonded Alphas to the same Omega. In fact, he shares her with Nixon and Oscar as well, but I doubt Rafael will wait much longer to claim her. My bet is he's waiting for us to get back home, so we might all be able to take some time and spend it as a pack should once they bring an Omega into the fold," I informed the bastard. "This is how a true pack works, since you've never experienced it yourself."

Yoram's face turned bright red before he exploded on me. "How fucking dare you! They would have still taken her with the bodyguard bonded to her, seeing it as a bonus. What the fuck am I going to do now that you all sullied her? The Shearian are superstitious and won't accept an Omega that's bound to others, dead or alive. You've fucking ruined *everything*."

Frowning, I cocked my head. "You're talking like there was a chance in hell that we were ever going to let her be taken from us again. Don't you get it? Yoram, you lost. It's finished. The time you had in power to make these threats or choices is no longer. Not only did you kill two other people of the government, you fucking traded our *people*," I snapped.

"Ha, the people will never let you get rid of me. I know too much," he shot back. "I can ruin them with one phone call."

It was at this point I realized that Yoram might actually be out of his mother fucking mind.

CHAPTER 56

Cambrie

Our lunch didn't end up being as relaxing as Rafael had hoped, especially now that all of us were a mixture of excited that we could head back home and saddened by what Savo and Marius told us. As much as I wanted this to be over, I never wanted others to lose their lives in the process.

"Dove?" Spencer said, letting his fingers trail through my hair as my head rested on his lap. "What's with that face? You should be happy we're all going home."

I looked up at him and shrugged. "Seems like we shouldn't be excited. There are two families out there that aren't going to have someone coming back home to them."

"My sweet, sweet, Little Dove," Spencer murmured. "That big heart of yours is something this world doesn't deserve, that's for damn sure. Okay, so excited might not be the right word, I'll give you that. But how about being relieved that we can start to find a new normal now? Savo said they were supposed to pack up his belongings to send to the mansion so that would make it easier for him to move into the house with us. That's something to feel happy about, at least."

Letting out a heavy breath, I sat up and twisted to face Spencer. "Life might start to be normal for us, but I can't stop thinking about all those Omegas that have no idea they were about to be sent off to a country that doesn't value them as people. What about those that have already been sent to Asturg? I feel like those sent to Shearia have a better chance, since they will be looked after, if not respected as a person."

"That is something that will absolutely need to be dealt with, and I'm sure it will be a priority for what happens with the government next. Right now, we need to gather all the facts, learn what has been going on, and then develop a plan to help support those who have been sent to other countries. Thankfully, you have a team of Alphas who are well versed in dealing with matters like this, thanks to the shelter and being part of the government," Spencer reasoned as he shoved himself to his feet. "Come on, Little Dove, let's get our pack home and settled first, then we can work on saving the rest of the world. This conversation needs ice cream, I think, something to sweeten the bitter reality we're going to learn."

No matter how hard I fought against the urge, I smiled at the idea of saving the world over a bowl of ice cream. I placed my hand in his as I let him pull me to my feet, and we headed back into the house after folding up the blankets.

Since everyone brought the bare minimum to this place, it didn't take long for us to be packed and heading out the door. Savo had left a little earlier, heading back to get his truck from the mansion and then going to his place to see if they had really packed his things or not. Before he left though, he made sure that someone came to get us since none of the guys had vehicles here.

The whole thing was over in the blink of an eye as we entered the gated community and pulled up to the house. Only this time, I wasn't entering this home as a guest or a fugitive. No, I was a bonded member of this pack and wherever they were was now my home. The room upstairs that housed my nest was officially my room, the space that held all the things that belonged to me. One that I wouldn't have to give up one day if they got upset with me or decided they didn't want me anymore. While I still had fears and doubts about my life, none involved any member of my pack. These were the people who showed me what it meant to love and be loved in return.

Everyone piled out of the vehicle and headed for the front door. Oscar held one hand while Bodhi held the other as we walked down the path, but I hesitated the closer we got. Flashes of memories started to flit before my eyes as I remembered being abducted. I'd been in bed reading, snuggled up in my nest that lingered with each of the scents of my pack. My bedroom door had burst open and men wearing all black, with their faces covered in black ski masks, had grabbed me.

"Cambi," Bodhi called loudly, making me believe it wasn't the first time he'd tried to get my attention. "You're shaking."

A hand gently cradled my face and urged me to turn, so I was looking into Oscar's crystal blue eyes. Through our bond, I felt his concern and knew he could feel how terrified I was. "Can we go in through the garage? I'm not sure I can make it through the front door," I whispered, hoping he would feel my desperation and not question my request.

His eyes softened and turned a little sad as he nodded, then looked over my shoulder at Bodhi.

"Don't worry I got it. You stay here with her, and I'll open the garage," Bodhi said before I heard him jog off.

Oscar pulled me into a tight hug, where I was met with a wave of love and comfort. I could hear the whirring of the garage door as it lifted, but I couldn't see as I was wrapped in my Alpha's arms. This is what I wanted for every Omega, to understand that what we are isn't a curse. People should feel blessed to learn the level of love and trust a bond like this can create.

Maybe that was something I could do? When I first arrived here with my pack, Marius had talked to me about going to school and finding something I wanted to do with my life. What if I could somehow help change the world's perception of Omegas? After the attack by the EQ and how the CoF chose to protect what Omegas we had left, it was just ingrained in all our minds how evil or bad it was to find out you were on Omega. There had to be a way to show that Omegas were created a certain way, that yes, they did require slightly more attention and reassurance, but with the right pack, it should be natural.

Was I different from others when it came to the Betas in my pack? Did others not love them just as much as their Alphas?

These would be things I'd need to learn if I was going to make a difference, which is precisely what I planned on doing. If there was ever a time to change the world's mind, it would be now, seeing as what we'd been doing wasn't helping anyone. Omegas went from being the envy of all to being the one thing no one wanted to ever end up being. *If my pack had been able to change my mind, would I be able to do the same for others?*

"Cambi, the garage is open," Bodhi called, pulling me out of my thoughts.

I tilted my head back so I could see Oscar's face, curious to see what he might have gotten from that revelation. He just bent down and cupped my cheeks, holding me still as he placed soft kisses all over my face with a final one on my lips before tucking me into his side, and we walked into the garage.

Bodhi gave us a curious look, but I just shook my head. I wasn't ready to share my thoughts yet. Like Spencer had suggested, I wanted to hear the rest of the information about what was going on.

I shouldn't have been surprised to find Rafael waiting just inside the door for us. He wasn't one to ever miss details, especially when it came to me. "Are you alright, Little One?"

"I'm fine now. I just couldn't walk through the front door," I shared. "They didn't drug me until I fought against them and clung to the front door. The memories were too much right now, so I thought the garage was a better choice."

Rafael smiled and reached out a hand. Oscar urged me forward, assuring me he was fine as he signed, *"I love you"* before heading up the stairs. Rafael took my hand and led me into the living room, where we'd all gathered the first night I came to the house. He sat in the large, overstuffed armchair and before he could even ask, I sat in his lap, resting my head on his chest and listening to his heartbeat.

"Are you sure you're okay being back in the house?" Rafael

asked as he wrapped his arms around me, resting his head on mine. "I feel like I should have foreseen that you might have some trouble being back here, when they stole you right out from under our noses."

"No, this isn't your fault, Raffy," I countered, pulling back to meet his gaze. "This is our home, and it's where I want to be. I didn't know I was going to have any challenges but with all of you around, I know we'll figure out how to work around them. Being here doesn't make me feel unsafe, quite the opposite, actually. It feels so amazing to know I have a home here with all of you."

Rafael tucked away a lock of hair that fell on my face and brushed his thumb along my cheek. "You're one of the most remarkable women I've ever met, Cambrie."

"I highly doubt that. You've told me before that you used to work with all the rich and famous people before working at the shelter," I argued. "How can I be more amazing than any of them?"

Rafael laughed at that. "Oh, with ease, Little One, you have more grace and resilience in your little finger than they'll ever know in a lifetime. See, those people didn't want to be better. Though, I shouldn't say that. Those of the rich and famous don't realize there is a world they can live in where they can be better. All they witness day in and day out is their fellow man struggling with the same things they are. The real problem is they aren't willing to do the work to break out of the cycle, they think it's too hard and have to give up too much. They wouldn't have found an alternate way to enter the house. No, they would have sold the house with everything in it and started over."

I gaped at him. "Why in the world would they do something so drastic? That doesn't make sense at all."

"This is why I'm saying you're far ahead in the game than they are. People pay for my help to learn how to do what you did naturally. For you doing the hard work just makes sense. You've lost so much in your life before now, if something stands in your way you'll do whatever it takes to keep what you have," Rafael explained. "To me, this makes you absolutely remarkable. In your situation, most would come out of that experience with hatred in their heart and a chip on their shoulder. What I would love to know is how, after everything, you remain this sweet, kind, caring woman who chooses to see the good in this world."

I thought about his question, and it brought me back to Peggy, her fiancé, and Charlie, the man at the newspaper stand. "I've seen what anger and hatred do to a person and experienced it firsthand. During that time, I've also seen what kindness and a simple, selfless act can do when you need it most. Those are the people who changed my life, made it better, and kept me alive. Why would I want to become someone so jaded and angry that I can't help anyone else? How does that ensure what happened to me doesn't happen to someone else?"

He just looked at me for a moment as a smile tugged at his lips.

"What?" I demanded, feeling like he was trying not to laugh at me.

"Oh, I was just thinking that you might be a great therapist someday. It takes people a whole degree to understand something like that, and even then, I'm not sure they grasp it quite the way you do. Maybe instead of a therapist, a teacher, because if one of them had explained it in such simple terms, I think we'd all be better equipped for our jobs," Rafael informed me.

His comment had me thinking about how I could help other Omegas. "Is it a lot of schooling to become a therapist?"

"Well, it took me about seven years since I went for a doctorate, but depending on what you're doing with it you don't need to go that far," Rafael shared. "Cambrie, just because I said that doesn't mean you need to do that. Granted, I think you would be a phenomenal therapist with the skills and background you have. Either way, whatever you choose to do with your future, even if it's not going to school at all, what we want, as your family, is for you to be happy."

I wrapped my arms around his neck and hugged him tightly. "Thank you. I appreciate hearing you say that, it means everything to me. Right now, I don't know what I want to do, I have a few ideas but I think there's still some more exploring of the world around me that I need to do before I can settle on something."

"That sounds logical and wise if you ask me. Too many people jump into things before they really understand. Granted, I know a few people who truly thought they wanted to be in my field of work, but when they got into it they found it wasn't for them. Sometimes, you don't know until you start that it isn't going to work. Even better yet, if you have a few ideas, take a class or two on each of them and see how you like the fit. There's no need to commit to something if you want to explore," Rafael decided with a nod.

I snickered at his complete turnaround. "I'll keep that in mind for when I'm ready to work on that, but I think I should get my GED first."

"Yes, I think that would be a good place to start," Rafael chuckled, then turned slightly more serious. "There was one other matter I wanted to talk to you about."

This had my attention sensing it was something far more serious. "Okay..."

"It's about bonding," Rafael started, then paused. "I know I'm the only one who hasn't marked you yet, and I don't want you to question my intention, Little One. As I've said before, you are *mine*, and I have every intention of leaving my mark on you. It's just... I never thought I would have an Omega. Yes, I knew this pack would bring one into the fold, but if I'm being honest, I didn't think I would be an Alpha that was picked."

My nose scrunched in disapproval at the way he was talking. "Why would you say a silly thing like that? You're amazing, kind, loving, patient, handsome, and someone I've come to love immensely."

A slight pink hue shaded Rafael's cheeks. "Thank you, Cambrie. You have no idea how much hearing you say those sweet words mean to me. Most would have turned their nose up at my age, you being *so* young and myself being twenty years your senior."

"Why does it matter how old you are? Have we done something wrong?" I questioned.

Rafael shook his head. "No, not at all. There is no legal reason we can't be together. It's more people's perception of us that might not be viewed well."

"It's not their relationship. If they don't want an older man, then they can have someone younger. I picked you. That's all that matters to me," I announced.

"Fair enough, Little One, if you're not worried about it, then I won't be either," Rafael agreed and settled the matter with a breath-stealing kiss. "Will you humor me and let me walk you through the house and make sure you don't have any other triggering moments? It's better to know now than when you want to go to bed later."

"That sounds reasonable to me," I agreed and slipped off his lap.

Together we headed upstairs, and I took in the rooms, curious about which one Savo would choose. I'd been shown two of them, and neither seemed to fit, but I noticed another door near Rafael's room. Grabbing the handle, I looked at him but he just nodded for me to continue.

"This is your home now, Little One, you are free to enter any room you wish at any time. I know all of us will gladly welcome you into our space. Correction, we want you to be in our space whenever you feel like it," Rafael informed me.

I frowned at him. "You can't mean that. Surely there will be a time that you want to be alone."

"I suppose in a rare situation that might be true, but I'm not certain that will apply to *you*. See, to an Alpha, an Omega is an addition and the bond only makes it stronger. I suppose it can be the same for a Beta if they are bonded to the same Alpha as the Omega. Things leak through the bond between all parties," Rafael rambled on as I stepped into the room.

The space had light gray walls and was completely empty, not even a curtain over the window. Almost as if someone had been in this space then left, taking everything with it. "Was someone using this room before?"

"Oh, Oscar started out in this room but then, about a month in, moved upstairs with Bodhi. Those two are the night owls so I guess it makes sense, they can be up as late as they want on the third floor," he answered. "My guess would be this is the room

Savo will pick, but I could be wrong. He might have a secret love for yellow."

A giggle burst out of me as I thought about Savo in that bright flowery room. For me, it had been all wrong, but it was pretty, just maybe not for a man. We exited the room and headed the rest of the way down the hall and up to the third floor. Bodhi was already on the couch with Oscar next to him, arguing about what movies to add to the list for us to watch.

"No, I won't take *Shaun of The Dead* off the list," Bodhi defended. "I know that humor isn't for everyone, but how is she going to know unless she tries it?"

Oscar clearly didn't agree by his expression and the agitated movements of his hands.

"If she gets scared then we'll turn it off," Bodhi reasoned. "Oh, come on, you can't seriously mean that?"

Curious and slightly worried about how heated things were getting, I felt like I needed to step in. "What are you arguing about over here?"

"Cambi, just the woman to settle the matter," Bodhi greeted, his face instantly changing to a happier expression. "This list of movies we have keeps growing as we all add things to it. So far, we have it divided into two categories, ones that we feel you can watch now and enjoy with no problem and others that might scare or upset you. Scary movies are a huge category in general, and I was thinking of starting you off with a humorous scary movie when the time came. Oscar doesn't think we should show you any scary movies, ever. If you ask me, it's the bond talking and the fact that you were triggered earlier."

Oscar's hands flew a mile a minute, and I couldn't even attempt to guess what he was saying. Rafael and Bodhi understood it and seemed to have differing reactions.

"He's not wrong. Adding that sort of imagery to her imagination could make things worse," Rafael said.

Bodhi glared at the older Alpha and crossed his arms. "Great, now I have you against me, so that means it will never happen."

"Guys," I yelled, instantly gaining their full attention. "This is stupid to argue over, and you know I don't like it when you all fight. Even though I'm learning that some conflict is good, I feel confident in saying that this argument is not one of those cases, and you're all being stubborn."

"You know, I think I'm beginning to like this new bossy side of our Little Dove," Spencer interjected as he joined us. "Now, what are you three getting scolded for?"

Bodhi opened his mouth to answer, but I cut him off. "Nothing we need to worry about now. We just got home after being apart for far too many days for my liking. All I want is to enjoy this moment of knowing my whole family will be safe at home, where they belong. Now, I'm going to my room where I might read for a bit. If anyone would like to join me in relaxing, they may."

Oscar signed something I didn't have the first guess on, but the rest nodded in agreement.

"That's it, tomorrow Oscar, you, and I are doing a crash course on signing. I hate the fact I can't communicate with you properly, and I feel silly asking someone what you just said," I grumbled.

Arms wrapped around me from behind, and I felt my bond to Nixon hum with delight at the contact. "He said, Spencer's right. My Little Star is sexy when she gets bossy."

I leaned my head back to look up at him. "Are you sure that's what he said?"

"Would I lie to you?" Nixon questioned.

"No, but you would tease me," I countered.

"No teasing here, Sweetheart," he assured and kissed me on the forehead. "That's truly what he said and I have to agree with him. Maybe not about Spencer being right, but seeing a glimpse of the strong, confident woman you're becoming is breathtaking."

My cheeks flamed, and I nibbled on my lip.

"Little One," Rafael warned, my Alpha's command making me instantly stop.

Nixon gripped my chin and kissed me, sucking my lower lip into his mouth and licking it before he released me. "You'll learn one day to be nice to your lips, but until then, it's fun to remind you."

CHAPTER 57

Cambrie

Bodhi, Rafael, Oscar, and I went to the grocery store after I learned they hadn't been home most of the time I was gone, leaving the house with no editable food. With my father, I'd been the one in charge of doing all of that, but the difference was I'd been given twenty to fifty dollars to buy enough to last for two weeks. The rest of the money Father earned went to buying his beer for home or out at the bar.

"Are you sure we need that much?" I asked when everyone just started throwing things into the cart. "Do you already know what you're planning on making for the week or month?"

They paused as the two Alphas looked at me confused, while Bodhi placed four trays of meat into the cart.

"Yeah, I get where you're coming from, Cambi, but they don't work with the same budget we're used to. I typically know what everyone likes to eat and have default meals I make, but until you came into our lives none of us really ate together," Bodhi shared. "My plan when I go shopping is to get ingredients we can easily put together, no matter who's making what."

Oscar waved to get my attention and signed to me slowly as Rafael translated so I could see what gesture meant what word or phrase. *"Now we'll need to learn your favorites, Little Star."*

"Besides cheese," Bodhi interjected. "That's already well established. What about fruit, vegetables, or meat?"

I looked around the vast grocery store with its fancy signs telling me what the produce was and where in the country it came from, like that would make a difference. "Really, I enjoy most food. We didn't get a lot of meat since it was so expensive, unless I could find it on sale. Even then, I didn't typically get much of it."

"Bastard," Bodhi grumbled under his breath. "Alright, so what that means to me is our new mission is to discover foods that Cambi likes and loves. Maybe you can go through the cookbooks with me back at the house and we can see what sounds good to you."

"Oh," I exclaimed excitedly when I saw a particular vegetable. "I really love mashed potatoes. That was always something I could make and add to a meal. Father got tired of them, but I snuck them in when I could."

Rafael handed me a plastic baggy and I grabbed four of them. "Little One, I feel like I should remind you that your family now consists of seven men plus yourself. We might need more than four potatoes unless you want them all for yourself, which I totally understand."

My eyes went wide at his comment. "No, I would never keep food just for myself, that would be silly."

"Really? What if there is a food you love but no one else does? Are you planning on giving it up forever?" Rafael inquired.

This got me thinking. "Now that I'm officially your Omega and there's a little less danger, can we go out for dinner every once in a while?"

"Clever, Little One, very clever," Rafael chuckled. "Leave it to you to find the one loophole in my argument. Maybe you need to be a lawyer and defend those who can't defend themselves."

"I'll add it to my list of things to try out," I said, adding a bunch more potatoes to the bag.

We wandered slowly around the aisles of the store, which I didn't know I'd ever done before. I'd always been on a mission and it made the hunger worse the longer I looked at all the food I couldn't have. Now, if I lingered on something too long, it magically appeared in the cart.

"I think we might need another one," Bodhi muttered to himself, looking at the overflowing cart.

I gaped at him, horrified. "Absolutely not. There is more food in there than any of us will be able to eat before it goes bad. Why would we add even more?"

"Yee of little faith," Rafael tutted. "Remember, we like to cook large amounts and eat the leftovers, not to mention we use them for lunches. We've taken more time off since you arrived than I've ever witnessed, but things will need to return to normal."

Oscar tapped Rafael on the shoulder and said something.

"You're right, a new normal," Rafael agreed. "I don't think everyone will be working such late hours or over the weekends as much with Cambrie at home."

"What will I be doing?" I asked as we headed to the checkout. "If you're all going to be at work and Bodhi is doing schoolwork and helping Oscar, what's my job around the house?"

"Hmm, I feel like that will need to be a family discussion," Rafael suggested. "Savo will now be in charge of your safety, but I suppose we need to work out what that looks like. Is he home all the time with you, or only when none of us are there as well? Everything might change in the near future too, as Marius and Alton decide what to do with the government."

That had me realizing that one of my bonded Alphas was in the perfect time and place to create real change in the world like I'd heard them all talking about. *Would things stay the same, or would they bring it all down and create something new out of the rubble?* As horrible as things had been, it's still amazing to think what's come of all this.

"Do you guys mind if we stop at the shelter? I have a patient trying to get a hold of me, and I want to check in on him," Rafael asked.

Oscar shook his head as he slid into the driver's seat. Bodhi sat in the back with me while Rafael claimed shotgun and made a phone call to the shelter. "Good evening, Clara. Is Mike still there? I know he's been looking for me and I was going to swing by and speak with him."

I tuned out the conversation and gazed out the window taking in the city. Then out of the corner of my eye, I spotted a little newsstand on the side of the road. "Stop!" I yelled.

Oscar slammed on the brakes, jostling us all in the SUV and making other cars honk as they tried to avoid crashing.

"What, what's wrong, Cambrie?" Rafael demanded, twisting in his seat to look at me.

"I need to speak to that man," I said, pointing at Charlie.

The tension in the air seemed to break at this announcement. "Damn, Cambi, were you trying to give us a heart attack?" Bodhi questioned as he rubbed his chest. "I seriously feel like I just lost years of my life."

Oscar turned down the next street and then turned around so we were on the right side of the road for him to pull over near the newsstand. I crawled over Bodhi, who just chuckled at my determination. Shoving open the door, I climbed out with Rafael right behind me, a hand resting on my lower back.

"Charlie?" I called out, not seeing him in the stand. Then I remembered he was hard of hearing. "*Charlie!*"

"What? Who's there?" the older man demanded as he stood up. "The stand is closed. You'll have to come back tomorrow."

"Then it's a good thing I don't need to buy anything from you," I said once his gaze finally landed on me and his brows shot up.

"Hold on," he started, then squinted his eyes at me. "I remember you, you're the young lady who was looking for the shelter, all beat to hell." Then his gaze shifted over to Rafael. "He's not causing you any trouble, is he?"

A smile grew on my lips at how protective he was being right now. "No, this is Rafael, one of my Alphas that's part of my pack. Because of you and your kindness in helping me get to the shelter, I was able to find them and my new family."

"Is that so? A pack, you say," Charlie commented as he stepped out from behind the counter and came to stand in front of me. "Holy mother, you're an Omega."

"Yes, she is," Rafael confirmed. "One that is loved and treasured by her whole pack."

"Well, I'll be damned. You told me you'd come back and tell me how things turned out, but I never would have expected this." He paused and looked a little closer at Rafael. "Wait, do I know you?"

Rafael had a small smile on his lips as he shook his head. "Not personally, but since I'm part of Official Stone's pack, you might have seen me on TV attending a few events. That, and I also work with Nixon Hayes, who owns Open Arms."

Charlie's jaw dropped open as he looked at Rafael and then at me. "I... I don't even know what to say to this. Never in my life did I think helping a person out would have this sort of outcome."

Rafael grabbed his wallet and pulled out a card, handing it to Charlie. "If you're ever in the same situation again, feel free to call my personal line and I'll make sure the situation is handled. Would you mind if we send one of our team out here to give you some bus passes to hand out, as well as flyers for the shelter?"

Charlie took the card and just stared at it like he couldn't believe what he was reading. "You can send me whatever you like. I try to do what I can for those that want the help, but my stand isn't doing as well as I'd like it to. The world is going to shit, and no one wants to read about it anymore."

"I have a feeling that is going to change very soon, Charlie," Rafael commented and reached out a hand to the man. "There are no words to be able to thank you for what you did for Cambrie. We will always be in your debt, so don't hesitate to let us know if there's anything we can do to help."

"Just doing my part, sir, but I appreciate your words all the same. If more people could help like your pack is with the shelters, we might be able to make it through this until the tides change in our favor," Charlie shared, shaking Rafael's hand before returning his attention to me. "Now you listen here, young lady, while I'd like to believe you're in good hands, know that if you need anything, I'll do what I can."

An urge that was entirely out of character came over me, and I took a step forward and hugged the man. "Thank you for saving my life and helping me find my family."

Charlie returned the hug and then took a step back with a sniffle and a cough. "Alright now, go on home and don't go causing your Alphas any trouble. They are important men."

"I won't, I promise," I agreed, then waved as Rafael guided me back to the car.

Bodhi had moved over, so when I got back in I had the empty seat. "Everything okay?" he asked.

"Better than okay. Charlie, the man who owns the stand, is who also gave me a pair of wool socks so my feet didn't freeze and the change I needed to make the call to the shelter," I informed him and Oscar. "In a way, he's the reason I got to meet all of you."

"Hmm, I feel like we need to talk to Marius about giving him an award or something. Maybe naming the street after him? What do you think, Oscar?" Bodhi asked.

When we came to a stoplight, Oscar gave his answer and the other two nodded in agreement.

"No, he's right, those ideas were too small. He needs a holiday in his honor," Rafael commented.

I laughed and leaned my head against Bodhi's shoulder. "You guys are crazy. I think what would make him happiest is to know that his business is safe and that he's making a difference. Rafael is already going to help him do one part of that. Now we'll just have to see if we can get Marius or Nixon to find a way to keep his business safe."

"We'll add that to our list of things to cover in our first family meeting," Bodhi suggested.

"Oh, is that something we're gonna do?" I asked excitedly. "I think it's a great idea that we keep a family calendar, so we always know when to expect each other to be at the house or not. I feel like that will be super helpful for me, because I can already tell I'm going to be anxious not knowing where everyone is."

Bodhi wrapped his arm around my shoulders and hugged me close. "That sounds like a perfect idea. It will also help us know who is with you or if Savo has to be around or not."

"I hope I don't have to take him away from work. He didn't say it outright, but I know he loves working for Rick," I said with a sigh. "No matter what, I don't want anyone to give up what they love on my behalf."

"I don't think you need to worry about that. I bet if you asked him, he would say that he loves you more than anything else," Rafael interjected. "Nonetheless, I hear what you're saying and can understand the sentiment."

A few moments later, we pulled up to the shelter and followed Rafael inside. Clara spotted me right away and waved her greeting as she spoke with someone on the phone. Not wanting to bother her knowing just how important those calls were, I headed off to the side where a set of bookshelves were.

To my surprise, a bunch of people called out a greeting to Bodhi. I should've remembered the staff and others from the shelter would know him, since this is where he became connected to the pack like I did. Rafael had worked with him and brought him to the house, where he started lessons with Oscar. As I think of it, most of our pack had connections to this place in one way or another.

"There you are, you little bitch," a voice I never thought I'd hear snapped through the air. "Where the fuck have you been hiding, Cammy? Do you know what you put me through with that stunt?"

My whole body froze as terror consumed me when the man who claimed to be my father charged up to me. None of my pack were super close as they'd spread out to talk with people. Unable to move, I just watched as he grabbed my arm, causing me to let out a cry of pain.

Rage filled me as Oscar understood what was happening and rushed over to me. Bodhi and Rafael were hot on his heels but not fast enough to stop Father from grabbing my hair and yanking my neck to the side. I knew what he'd see there, proof that I no longer belonged to him, that I belonged to my pack.

"Son of a bitch, who the hell marked you? Damnit, answer me, Cammy. Who the fuck did you whore yourself out to?"

He didn't get to say much else after that, as Oscar's fist slammed into his face sending him crashing to the floor. Seconds later, I was in Oscar's arms as he held me tightly against him. My brain couldn't catch up to what was going on; my body was still frozen with fear as memories started to replay. Every instance he hit me, each cruel word he hurled at me, and the pain my body endured because of him overwhelmed my senses.

"You dare lay a hand on our fucking Omega?" Bodhi snarled, kicking my father in the ribs. "Let's see how you like being beaten within an inch of your life, you sorry sack of shit."

Rafael grabbed Bodhi and hauled him off, shoving a phone in his hands. "We need him alive long enough to prosecute, and I need you to tell Savo what's happening. The man is about ready to burn the world down, feeling her fear."

Oscar started to purr and tucked my head under his chin as he moved to stand next to Bodhi. I watched Rafael squat down and say something to Father. However I couldn't hear him and he was facing away from me so I couldn't try to read his lips either. Whatever he said made Father's face pale before he looked over at me for a second, then he returned his attention to Rafael. When he was done talking, my Alpha grabbed Father by the shirt collar, hauling him to his feet, and marched to the front door. There were two cops standing there, ready to take the man who'd caused me endless amounts of suffering off in handcuffs.

Bodhi stepped in front of my line of sight, making it so he was all I could see as he smiled. Slowly, he reached out and wiped my cheek with his thumb, making me realize I'd been crying. "Cambi, Savo really needs to hear your voice. Do you think you could do that, hmm?"

He held the phone to the side of my head so I could hear what was happening on the other line.

"That rat bastard better be dead by the time I get there. If there is so much as a hair out of place that he caused, I'll skin the bastard alive," Savo raged.

"You're coming here?" I whispered.

"*Keksik*," Savo gasped. "My sweet little *Keksik*, I'm almost there. Just hang tight. Did he hurt you? Did he lay a hand on you?"

"He pulled my hair," I said, my voice devoid of all emotion. "I think he might have bruised my arm... Why would he grab me so hard? I wasn't doing anything or trying to get away. I... I froze."

"It's okay, my sweet girl, just stay with the others. I asked the cops to just hold him until I got there. I'm two minutes away as long as someone doesn't try to stop me," Savo muttered. "Can you tell Bodhi I want to talk to Rafael?"

I nodded, then realized he couldn't see me. "Okay, I'll tell him."

"I love you, *Keksik*," he added. "Now, hand back the phone."

"Love you, too," I said in response, then looked into Bodhi's eyes. "He wants to talk to Raffy."

"Okay, I'll hand over the phone and be right back," Bodhi explained, then strode over to the older Alpha.

Rafael took the phone and put it up to his ear, only to flinch and pull it away again. He frowned down at the phone and hit a button, stuffing it back in his pocket.

"I think Rafael just hung up on Savo," I murmured.

Oscar hummed his agreement and carried me to one of the couches. The common area must have cleared out when the excitement happened since I couldn't see anyone else around. I curled up into a ball in Oscar's lap, hiding my face in his neck, taking in the warm caramel and cinnamon scent that was my sweet loving Alpha. He rubbed a hand soothingly up and down my back as he purred, lulling me into a state of welcome numbness.

CHAPTER 58

Savo

Being slapped upside the head with Cambrie's terror nearly had me driving off the side of the road. Thankfully, the streets were quiet in the area I was in, or I would have run someone off the road. My truck was jam-packed with boxes and my bed, knowing I needed something to sleep on tonight. I yanked my phone off its stand on the dash and called Spencer.

"Hey, I was wondering when you'd check in," Spencer greeted. "Do you—"

"Where's Cambrie? I need to know right now, don't fuck around with me, Spencer," I barked.

There was a pause then I heard Nixon bark an order as well. "Answer him."

"What's wrong?" Spencer demanded. "You two would only act like this if something was wrong."

"Damn it, man, tell me where my goddamn Omega is," I bellowed.

"Fuck," Spencer muttered. "She's not here with us. Call Rafael. They went to the groc—"

I didn't bother listening to the end of that sentence, having the name of the person I needed to call. "Hey, it's Bodhi," was the answer I got after three rings. "We're at the shelter. Cambrie's fucking dad showed up and found her."

"Is the bastard still alive?" I questioned.

"Unfortunately," Bodhi grumbled. "I hope I broke a few of his ribs though with one of the kicks I landed, and I'm pretty sure Oscar broke his nose. Rafael said he had to stay alive long enough for us to prosecute."

"I suppose I see his reasoning. Is she alright?" I asked as I whipped the truck around, tires screeching as I slammed on the gas. "I'm on my way to the shelter. I know you have security there that better have fucking called the cops, but I want to speak to that sonofabitch."

"We'll see what we can do, but I'm not sure they'll listen to me," Bodhi pointed out.

I let out a growl of frustration, slamming my fist against the wheel. "I'm going to hang up and call you right back once I'm done talking to the police, got it?"

"I won't put the phone down," he said.

Hanging up, I called the main switchboard. "Oscad Capital City police, how may I direct your call."

"This is Savo Bakal. I need to speak with Lieutenant Provenza," I ordered.

"One moment while I transfer your call."

The line rang twice before Provenza answered. "Savo, what can I do for you and the CoF today?"

"Official Stone's Omega was attacked today at the Open Arms shelter, their main location. I believe uniforms should already be there or on their way. I need to speak with that man before they take him away and charge him with kidnapping, assault, child endangerment, and concealing an Omega from the government."

Provenza didn't speak right away. "Official Stone has an Omega?"

"Yes, he does. They just bonded with her this weekend and she just went to the shelter with some of her other Alphas, Rafael, and Oscar, where she was assaulted. Do you have more questions, or are you going to call your men and hold the man there for me to question?" I snarled.

No one but the pack and Rick knew what I truly was, and for right now I wanted to keep it that way until the announcement. Things needed to be handled with Yoram first. Then, we could give the public a dose of happy sharing that the beloved Official now had an Omega.

"Let me put you on hold, and then once the message has been relayed, I'll let you know," Provenza offered.

"No need, I'm almost there myself. I just didn't want to cause more chaos when I demanded to speak to the man," I explained.

"Very well, I'll make sure they understand the situation," Provenza promised, then hung up.

I called Bodhi back, and he let me speak to Cambrie, who sounded completely shell-shocked. If I could have driven any faster to get to her, I would have, but getting myself killed wouldn't do anyone any good. Finally, I arrived at the shelter and saw the cop car out front with the lights flashing and two men chatting outside as I reared into the parking lot.

Tossing the truck into park, I got out and stormed up to the vehicle that held the one man I wanted to kill with my own two hands. Yoram was a piece of shit, but this man had nearly broken my *Keksík,* and for that, he would suffer. "Open the door," I barked.

"Are you Savo?" one of the men asked, unable to meet my gaze, letting me know I wasn't controlling my Alpha energy.

"Yes, I am, now open the goddamn door and walk away until I tell you it's time to take him to booking," I ordered.

There was a click of the locks, and the two cops went to stand a few paces away, but still close enough if I needed them. Yanking the door open, I slid into the car next to the bastard who dared to use the name Father for my *Keksík.*

"Who the hell are you?" he demanded.

I gave him a toothy grin that I'm sure came across more as baring my teeth. "Why, I'm one of Cambrie's Alphas, Savo Bakal. I also happen to be the son of General Rasvan, who taught me all sorts of ways to torture a man."

Reaching out, I grabbed one of his hands and broke his pointer finger, making him howl in pain. "You fucking lunatic, you can't treat me like this."

"Oh, so it's fine to beat and abuse a little girl, but I can't break a grown man's finger? Tell me, how does that math work out in your head? That beautiful angel did nothing but look after you and take her lumps, never once selling you out when she could have with one simple word to the authorities. No, I think you're a lunatic and I'm going to break every finger in your hand. Maybe the other, just so you'll never forget what hurting a woman feels like every time you try to do something with your hands," I informed the bastard.

His eyes grew wide and panicked as he fully understood that he was at my mercy and nothing was going to stop me from exacting my revenge. His screams grew louder and more frantic as I got done with one hand. I felt like now might be a good time to find out a few answers.

"Tell me, why did you keep her after her mother died? You didn't have to, hell, why would you even want to?" I asked.

The man sobbed like a baby, snot dripping from his nose as tears trailed down his cheeks. "On her deathbed, that bitch told me whose child she was. Mentioned that if she turned out to be an Omega, I had to make sure he never found her. What I heard was she'd be worth a lot of fucking money to the man. I had to wait until she was sixteen to know if she was gonna be an Omega or not. When her designation came in, she tried to run. I would have sold her to him sooner, but I couldn't get close to him. It wasn't until I started putting her up on auction sites on the black market that he reached out. Apparently, it's known that he's the biggest buyer when it comes to Omegas, uses them for some fucked up type of experiments."

"So, what happened when she ran away?" I pressed.

"Yoram told me I had a week to find her, or he was going to kill me. Then out of the blue, he told me it was over and I wouldn't get any money, but I'd live. Two nights ago, I got a call saying she was gone and that he needed to find her but couldn't look for her himself. He told me where to start and said to come look here," he answered, letting the words flow out of him like a geyser.

Taking his right hand, I gripped the pointer finger. "Thank you for being honest. I, too, will let you live. However you won't be able to touch anyone else, let alone yourself, when I'm done with you."

No longer needing information, I worked quickly until he passed out from the pain and slumped in the seat. Getting out of the car, I waved over the two cops. "He's good to go. The Lieutenant already knows what his crimes are, but if you have any questions contact Official Stone's people and they will get you in touch with us."

News of Marius having an Omega was going to spread much faster saying it so casually to these people, but I didn't have time to care. Knowing who she was bonded to would offer more protection, and she needed every ounce of it until Yoram was killed. I wouldn't put it past that man to have backup plans to the moon. Son of a bitch was crafty, and I wasn't going to allow myself to be surprised or caught off guard.

Entering the shelter, I noticed the lobby was cleared out and only the staff and my pack were left. It was odd to think of them as my pack when I never thought I'd have one. These guys were good men, and at least I knew most of them, having met them at events and other government functions. Spencer, of course, was good people and we'd become friends of sorts. Bodhi and Oscar were the two I didn't really know at all, but it didn't take me long to figure out that Bodhi and I understood each other on a certain level. The silent Alpha was the one who was hard to figure out and it had nothing to do with the fact he couldn't speak. In some ways, I envied him because the moment he needed to say something everyone shut the fuck up and listened.

The one thing I knew without a doubt was that he loved my *Keksik* as much as I did. Really, that's the most important thing, the rest can be figured out in time as we all get to know each other. Panic started to rise as I saw Cambrie curled up in a ball on Oscar's lap, with Rafael on one side and Bodhi on the other. She didn't move and if it wasn't for her breathing, I might have thought she was dead.

Slowly I approached, unsure of what reaction I was going to get from her. She could still be in shock, or her body could be on the defensive, ready to run at the perception of danger. Not wanting to speak and knowing everyone here knew sign language, I used that. "*Is she okay?*"

Oscar looked at me with sad eyes and shook his head. "*She won't talk. Since you hung up with her, she hasn't said a word, just sat here almost as if she's waiting for you.*"

"*Did he hurt her? Say something to her?*" I pressed, trying to understand what I might be dealing with once I let her know I was here.

Rafael shifted and pushed up the sleeve of her shirt to show a bruise the size of a man's hand. "*This is the only mark. He grabbed her hair, but Oscar got to him before anything worse could happen.*"

"*You gave him the broken nose?*" I asked. Oscar nodded solemnly. "*Good, I broke his hands for good measure, but I don't feel like it's enough.*"

"*It's a start, he deserves far worse,*" Oscar commented.

"I agree," I said aloud to see if Cambrie would perk up. "*Keksík,* I'm here. Can you wake up for me?"

Her eyes slowly opened, and I gazed into their shining crystal blue color that didn't have the same life to them as they normally did. "There you are."

She shifted and reached out for me, and I squatted so I could pull her off Oscar's lap and hug her tight. "It's over, Cambrie, he is going to jail for the rest of his miserable life and won't ever be able to touch you. You're finally safe, my sweet girl. We got them all."

Cambrie wrapped her arms around my neck and squeezed so tightly I was afraid she might actually cut off my airflow. "It's over? You promise?" she whispered in my ear.

"I can't promise that all danger is gone, but the ones we know about have been dealt with. You know what else I know?" I asked.

She loosened her hold to lean back and look me in the eyes, shaking her head.

"What I know is that no matter what, your pack will always protect you. Plus, now that I have the important stuff, I'm not going to leave your side. I'll be with you wherever you go, like your guardian angel," I vowed. "As long as there's breath in my body, I will love you and keep you safe. Do you believe me?"

"Yes, I believe you," she answered.

"Good. Now, we're all going to go home, make dinner, and start our lives together as a pack. This night marks the end of the old and the beginning of the new," I explained, setting her down. "Now you went to the grocery store, so did you have a plan on what we should make?"

"No, they don't make plans, they just make whatever they feel like," Cambrie shared. "That seems silly to me, but I was willing to see how it goes."

"I agree that does seem silly, I guess we'll just have to unload it all at the house and see what we come up with," I decided. Reaching down, I cupped her face and pulled her into a kiss. "We'll get through this together, tonight was unexpected, but we'll do better. We'll always do better by you."

CHAPTER 59
Cambrie

When I went to sleep, I was tucked into my nest with my whole pack surrounding me. Marius had joined us just as we were getting settled. He didn't say much other than it could wait for the morning. No one seemed to argue, having had enough excitement for one day. Just as Savo had said, my pack would always be there for each other, and I think Marius needed a cuddle puddle as much as I did. They let him pull me to his chest, and I burrowed as close as I could get to him. Our bond seemed to let out a sigh of relief now that we were together. Seems that issue was going to need to be addressed, but it, like everything else, would wait until later.

My night was full of fitful dreams, ones that I hadn't had since coming to this home, although seeing Father had rattled them loose. I'd thought having my bonded Alphas with me would have kept them at bay, but they were determined to remind me of all the awful things that had happened to me. Each time I woke up, one of my men was there to comfort me. Purring echoed through the mattress, with all of them using it to calm my nerves. It would take me a little while, but I would eventually fall back asleep.

When the sunlight shone through the skylight into my room, I watched through the shroud of gauze that surrounded my nest as puffy clouds passed by. I didn't know how long I'd been awake, but

I was content to lie here wrapped up in the arms of my loved ones. Savo had wiggled his way between my legs, so his head was on my stomach. Rafael had decided I would use him as a pillow and my head rose and fell with his steady breathing. Nixon and Marius ended up in an odd formation, with each of their heads close to my body as they angled away. Oscar had my other side, but he was sprawled on his back with Bodhi resting on his chest, his arm flung across his Alpha to hold my hand.

The one person I couldn't locate was Spencer, but I was too afraid to move and wake anyone. So, I reached out through our bond finding he was indeed here, probably hidden by one of our Alpha's large bodies. I'd given them all a restless night, the least I could do was give them a few hours of sleep. My mind wandered as I watched the clouds, replaying everything that happened from the moment I heard his voice call my name. *Why did I freeze?* I could have run away or just headed for one of the guys. What was it that made me unable to do anything? Even with Arthur, I could have stood up for myself and not turned into a statue. Why, why was he different?

Lips caressed my cheek, alerting me that Marius was awake. He kissed along my jaw and down my neck until he reached his mark. This time, instead of kissing it, he let his tongue run over it, making me shiver as pleasure ran through my body. "Good morning, my Princess," Marius purred into my ear. "I could feel the weight of your thoughts and figured it might be a good idea to distract you."

Turning my head, I looked into his bright green eyes that shone with love and hunger. "I don't think it's just me who could use something else to think about," I countered, quirking up an eyebrow.

"You might be right about that, but who could resist when you wake up to such a stunning woman as yourself?" Marius commented, letting his hand run down my neck and over my pajama-covered breasts.

"Better not be talking about me," Savo muttered, cracking open an eye to look up at us. "I know I'm good-looking and all, but I'm not sure princess is the right term."

I giggled, imagining anyone calling Savo a pretty princess made me laugh harder.

"Okay, *Keksik*, I don't think it was *that* funny," Savo grumbled as he pushed up on his arms and crawled closer to my face. "You don't think anyone would call me princess?"

Shaking my head, I tried to hide my smile, but the laughter kept finding its way back onto my lips. "I think if anyone called you princess, they would get tossed out of the room. No, to me, you are more of a gallant knight or brave soldier defending the one he loves."

"Oh, let me guess, you think that's you?" he taunted.

When I didn't answer, he started to tickle me and shoved his face into my neck, where he blew raspberries, making me squeal in laughter. Thrashing around, I tried to get away from him but the nest and all the bodies around me kept me trapped.

"I give, I give," I panted when he let up.

"You shouldn't ever surrender when you know you're right, and you, my sweet little Omega, are absolutely the woman I love," Savo whispered before stealing the breath I just got back with a kiss.

My body melted under his attention and didn't stop when he pushed up my nightgown and slipped inside me. While Savo was the first to bond with me, we hadn't crossed this step yet. However, our bodies knew we were meant for each other, and I took him in with ease. He clung to me, his nose right behind my ear, as he told me with each and every thrust how much he loved me. Nothing about this was rushed, as we took the time to enjoy being connected physically as we were emotionally.

My brave commanding Alpha, who turned into a giant teddy bear for me, cradled my body against his massive one as we made love. He sat up pulling me with him so I was seated in his lap, allowing me to take over, rolling my hips, working him in and out. A moan slipped out as I tossed my head back, his hands gripping my ass where he left his bond mark.

I heard shuffling in the bed and it took my fuzzy brain a moment to remember that everyone else was still in bed with me. My eyes flew open and I saw all my other men stripping out of their clothes, more than willing to participate in what Savo had started. Part of me worried how Savo would react not having experienced this with us, but he just grabbed my chin and paused his movements.

"*Keksik*, you need to stop worrying about me," Savo ordered. "I'm a grown man who understands what it means to be part of a pack, even if I didn't think I would be in one. You are mine, but you're also theirs. If I expect them to share you with me, how can I not do the same in return? Now be a good little Omega and ride my cock until the knot I'll put in you keeps you from moving."

A whimper burst out of me as he grabbed my hips and helped to push me down, taking him in as deep as possible. I could feel the ridge of where his knot was and how it was already growing. Moving with his assistance, I gasped when a set of hands kneaded my breasts. The scent of sandalwood and vanilla told me it was Rafael.

Gripping the bottom of my nightgown, he helped remove it so I was now bare. Savo wasted no time taking one of my nipples in his mouth, letting his tongue lap over the peak. Rafael slid his hand into my hair and turned me to face him as his lips found mine. I faltered in my movements as I was overwhelmed with the sensations around me, but Savo was more than happy to take back control. Shifting, he lay back so I was sitting and had better leverage to move. Rafael pulled back, freeing my head so I could lower it and take his cock in my mouth.

Feeling Savo's knot growing, I moved faster as I swallowed Rafael down. I truly loved being able to share pleasure with any and all of my pack, but there was something so amazing when more of them shared me at the same time. It made me feel like I wasn't leaving anyone out, that they didn't question whether I wanted them just as much as the others. Taking a quick glance around, I saw Spencer going down on Marius while Nixon was at the other end warming his Beta up to take him. Bodhi and Oscar were parallel to each other, using their hands and mouths to pleasure each other. This is what a nest was for, to be filled with love and the expression of that love in whatever form it took. This morning it was all of us indulging in the pleasure that our bodies had to give. Some might think I was silly for this kind of thinking, but it didn't matter. This was my family, my home, and my men. We were the rulers of this moment, and it was perfect.

Savo's thrusts became more intentional as his knot started to lock me to him. As he thrust up, he'd push me down, ensuring I was well and truly knotted as he roared his completion. His hot cum shot into me, making me moan as my body squeezed around him, milking all he had to give me. Not finished with me yet, he used those short rocking thrusts to hit all the spots that drove me wild and had me screaming. Rafael groaned as he forced me down on his cock as he came. I swallowed, gulping down every drop of what came shooting out, making me moan even more, knowing by the expression on his face how good it felt.

I pulled off Rafael and slumped to Savo's chest, my breathing heavy as my pussy twitched with the pleasure of being knotted. Gentle hands kneaded my ass and when my bond mark didn't react, I realized it wasn't Savo. They spread my ass and a tongue ran over my back entrance, making me writhe, but I couldn't get away. Peeking over my shoulder, I found Bodhi was attempting to get me ready to take his cock while knotted. Oscar was right behind him, offering the same service.

Was Bodhi going to fuck me in the ass while Oscar fucked him? Why did that sound like the most sensual thing in the whole world?

"Does my sweet little Omega like getting all the attention?" Savo asked, well aware of my reaction to what Bodhi was doing. He brushed the hair out of my face as he waited for my answer.

"Everyone likes getting attention from the people they love," I shared. "What I love is all of you and seeing those who also love others being together."

"Does it bother you that Rafael and I only love you?" Savo questioned. "Do you feel a pack needs to love everyone?"

I opened my mouth to answer, but Bodhi slid a lubed-up finger into my ass. "Oh god," I whimpered. "It feels so good."

"Maybe it's best if we leave the deep conversations for when this is over and she can concentrate," Rafael suggested with a chuckle.

Savo just nodded and decided to help distract me as Bodhi started to insert his cock, by kneading my breasts and rolling my nipples between his fingers. "Relax, *Keksik,* let your Beta take that perfect round ass I marked."

Moaning, I pushed up on Savo so I was at a different angle, and this seemed to help Bodhi as he slid inside me. I felt his warm breath on my ear as his body sank the last few inches inside, filling me to the point I wasn't sure I could hold any more cock. "God, Cambi, you're squeezing me so tight I don't know how I'm going to last," Bodhi panted.

Then he groaned into my ear, letting me know Oscar was claiming his Beta behind me.

"Oh fuck, that's so much to take," Bodhi swore, resting his head on my shoulder. "How do you take two of these, Cambi?"

Savo chuckled under me, which had his knot vibrating and moving, causing me to come again as I gripped both cocks tightly. "Shit, man, you can't do that. I thought she was going to take my cock clean off my body. Jesus, I'm not sure I'll be able to do this with him fucking me into you."

"Don't you dare move," I ordered. "I want to know what it feels like for Oscar to fuck us both. To know it's him setting the rhythm and we just have to follow."

"Damn, Savo, have you been teaching our Little Dove dirty talk?" Spencer asked.

I didn't hear Savo's answer as Bodhi was slammed into me from Oscar's thrust. A chorus of moans and whimpers from the two of us filled the room. This did nothing but spur Oscar on, setting a steady pace that had me bracing on Savo's chest or getting flattened. Having a knot keeping me in place helped, but it also added a hint of pain to the pleasure as Oscar's movements kept trying to shove me off it.

Savo must have noticed the problem and shifted his hand to brace my hips. That eased up on the discomfort and let my body soar in sensual bliss as I wrapped an arm around Bodhi's neck and pulled him down to kiss me. Our tongues caressed each other, as did our bodies seeking the next level of stimulation. Now that Savo had freed up my breasts, Bodhi took over the work. So when we broke from our kiss he licked and nipped down my neck. As I felt Savo's knot start to relax, I pushed back on Bodhi, urging him deeper to fill the void that was being created. The feeling of being full and locked to your Alpha was unlike anything, and it was addictive.

Bodhi cried out as he came, clinging to me as he was thrust into me once more, but then Oscar paused and let his shuddering Beta have a moment before he pulled out of me and off Savo. Bodhi's eyes were glazed in euphoric bliss as he lay down next to where Oscar was kneeling.

"Cambrie, come help our Alpha so he can knot that amazing ass of yours," Bodhi mumbled, making Oscar smile at him.

He grabbed his Beta's face and kissed the hell out of him until Bodhi melted onto the bed, happy as could be. I could feel Oscar's worry, and I hoped the two of them would talk soon. I knew Spencer never takes his Alphas knots, so I didn't think that's something Oscar should be concerned over. I reached out through our connection, sending him soothing reassurance. Not being able to take a knot wasn't a failure on either end. Omegas were built to accommodate, but that didn't make us superior.

Oscar's bright blue eyes met mine as he reached out a hand to me. I took it and he tugged me close, pulling me onto his lap with my back to his. Using my own slick, he made sure his cock was able to glide as easily as it could into my ass. I'm sure Bodhi's cum also helped and added to the point that we were all in this together.

Seated like this, I could see Spencer being fucked by Nixon and taking Marius in his mouth, the three of them moving in perfect rhythm. Those three were meant to be together, to share loved ones between them. Who better to be able to share with than your best friend? I was learning that love came in all sorts of ways. Marius and Nixon did love each other, it wasn't a physical love, but they would do anything for each other. This pack was that way, even with Savo being new and everyone learning where they fit. It sort of seamlessly started to happen.

Oscar shifted us slightly, so I was splayed open to the others as he slipped his finger into my pussy. He fucked me with his fingers as he took me in the ass, making me scream in pleasure as we both came. He'd been so close before but held back, knowing Bodhi couldn't take his knot. So once I clamped down on him, he was gone. This time, I came so hard I was seeing stars and lay there limp against Oscar's chest, the only thing keeping me upright. He lay us down and started to purr, which sent tantalizing shockwaves of bliss through my body. There was nothing I could do when my eyes started to close and I fell into a deep, dreamless sleep.

CHAPTER 60

Cambrie

"Why did you let me sleep so late?" I demanded as Spencer herded me into the bathroom. "It's late afternoon."

"Yes, I'm well aware of what time it is and that you didn't get much, if any, sleep last night," Spencer pointed out. "Dove, when you passed out in Oscar's arms, you didn't budge when the rest of us got up. Clearly, your body needed to compensate for what it lost out on. Obviously, next time you have nightmares, we'll know you just need to be fucked to sleep."

I gaped at him as he turned on the shower. "Spencer."

He just grinned and cocked an eyebrow at me. "Tell me I'm wrong? Don't bother, because I know I'm not wrong, having needed it done a time or two. Sometimes, my anxiety gets too much and I can't for the life of me calm down enough to sleep, so my Alphas see to it that I'm too fucking tired to worry about a thing. Now, into the shower with you."

Stepping in, I gave him a dubious look. "Is there something going on I need to be warned about?"

"No, once you're done getting showered and dressed, we're feeding you. Then we are having our family meeting to cover all those pesky questions we've all been mulling over," Spencer answered. "Do you care if I pick out something for you to wear?"

My first reaction was to grimace, having had that done to me at the mansion, only these were all clothes I'd picked out with Spencer and the others. "No, that's fine, but I don't want any skirts or dresses. It's all they let me wear."

"Dove, if you'd rather pick something out yourself, that's fine. I only wanted to be helpful," Spencer offered.

Reaching out of the shower, I grabbed his shirt and pulled him to me kissing him soundly. "Thank you, Spencer. I'd love to wear whatever you pick for me."

He searched my face for a moment and returned my kiss before pulling away with a wet handprint on his shirt. "Come down to the dining room when you're ready. Rafael has been making his famous pasta sauce but won't let any of us try it until you get the first taste."

"You guys haven't eaten?" I asked, but Spencer had already left the bathroom.

Savo's reminder that they were all adults echoed in my brain, and I tried to set aside my worry that I'd been holding them back while sleeping. I moved through the motions of my shower but slowed as I enjoyed the scent of the shampoo and conditioner, reminding me that I was home. These were my things, and I didn't need to fear that anything would be taken from me or that someone was coming after me. Yoram was in custody, as was Father, leaving me free to start my new life with my pack.

Hopping out of the shower, I dried off and braided my hair, not wanting to take the time to dry it. On my bed was a pair of trendy ripped jeans, a simple sky blue T-shirt, and an oversized long-sleeved cardigan in a rusty orange color. Spencer was kind enough to let me gather my own undergarments, which I appreciated. Dressed and ready to face the day, I skipped down the stairs and used the momentum to swing myself around the corner right into Nixon's arms.

"Well, hello, Sweetheart," he greeted, smiling down at me, then pressed a tender kiss to my lips. "You look like you're feeling much better after some solid sleep."

"I hope I didn't keep you guys from doing things today," I said, letting him take my hand and lead me into the dining room.

"No, we all decided that we needed a day to figure out the best way to move forward with our life the way it is now. So much has changed. We can't just return to the way things were. Besides, Rafael decided to make his homemade sauce and that took like six hours, so he wasn't going anywhere today," Nixon shared.

The second Bodhi opened the kitchen door into the dining room and the aroma of the sauce filled the air, my stomach woke up with a vengeance, letting out its excitement at the scent.

"Seems you woke up at the right time since he just declared the sauce done, but he said you needed to taste it first," Bodhi said as he placed a huge bowl of pasta on the table. "Come on, I want to eat, and the smell of this has been killing me all day."

I hurried after Bodhi as he returned to the kitchen, where I found the rest of my pack. They all stood huddled around the island, watching Rafael stir a large pot. When I entered, they all cheered and Spencer brought over the step stool for me, placing it next to Rafael.

"Here, Little One, you need to be the official taste tester on this," Rafael announced, holding a spoon with a sample of the infamous red sauce.

Leaning in and seeing the steam wafting off it, I blew on it and then wrapped my lips around the spoon. The flavor exploded on my taste buds so strongly that it took my brain a moment to process all the herbs and spices mixed into the bright tomato-based sauce.

"Wow," I blurted. "That's amazing!"

"You sure, you're not just saying that to be kind?" Rafael challenged.

I shook my head vigorously. "No, that has to be one of the most delicious things I've ever tasted."

"There she said it. Can we please eat now?" Bodhi begged.

Rafael took a taste of the sauce and closed his eyes as he swallowed. "Okay, I think she's right, it's good enough."

"Quick, hand him the ladle before he changes his mind," Marius whispered loudly.

Rafael glared at him over his shoulder. "What's the point in cooking something for six hours unless it's perfect?"

"No idea, since I would never make anything that would take six hours," Marius pointed out. "Now that everything is on the table, can we please eat?"

"Who would have known that a simple sauce could make grown-ass men act like children?" Savo chuckled. "You'd never guess that some of the most powerful and influential people were right here in this room."

Spencer just flipped him the bird as he passed with a basket of garlicky-smelling bread. "Just wait till you taste this, and you'll understand everything."

"Yeah, we'll see about that," Savo muttered under his breath as he scooped me up, nuzzling into my neck. "How are you, *Keksík*? You had a rough night."

"I'm fine, I promise," I whispered, rubbing my cheek along his. "I had all of you to look after me."

"Fat lot of good that did. If I'd known we'd be better off wearing you out with a good fucking, I would have done that right away," Savo reasoned.

I scowled at him. "No, I'm glad you didn't. That would have been an awful first time for us to be together. I rather like how things turned out."

"Can't say I minded either, finally getting to be inside my sweet little Omega, feeling you clenched so tightly around my knot as you milked me dry," Savo said, adding his purr to make things even more elicit.

Wiggling out of his hold, I smacked him on the arm. "What is with all of you? Did I go into heat and not realize it or something?"

Marius just chuckled, and he urged us both out into the dining room. "It's the bond, it makes Alphas a little extra randy for a time until the bond settles. It's one reason why some packs take two weeks to a month when they have a newly bonded Omega. It's too hard to keep your hands to yourself."

"Wait, but all of you have been running around dealing with all sorts of problems," I reasoned.

"Yes, and this morning is a perfect example of what happens when you deny it for too long. You just can't hold back anymore. I will expect more occurrences of that nature to happen if we're home with you," Rafael warned.

My eyes went wide as I looked at all the men seated at the table, looking at me like I should be the meal dished up. Part of me was worried that I wouldn't be able to keep up with them, but the other wasn't so much, sending a shiver of anticipation down my spine.

"Come sit," Rafael instructed. "You haven't eaten all day, and we can't have that."

Spencer dished up a serving of pasta as Oscar plopped on some bread and Rafael finished it off with some sauce. The plate was deposited in front of me, and the others dove in, putting heaping mounds of food on their plates. While my appetite had grown, I wasn't sure I would ever be able to eat as much as they did. The table fell silent, except for the sound of silverware on plates and moans of pleasure as we ate.

Once everyone was done with their first serving, Nixon started the family meeting. "First of all, I feel like this needs to be something we do weekly, if not more, so we can make sure we're all getting to say our peace."

"I agree, also Cambrie brought up a really good idea to have a combined calendar of all our schedules, so she knows where we are and when we'll be home," Spencer added. "This should also help us know who will be home or if we need Savo to be here."

"Why wouldn't I be here?" Savo asked. "She is my Omega and I'm her bodyguard. Wherever she is, that's where I'll be."

I reached across the table and grabbed his hand. "I don't want you to stop working with Rick if you don't want to. You've told me how much you enjoy the work, and if Bodhi and Oscar are home, it gives you time to do your own thing."

"*Keksik*, I don't think you've quite grasped this yet, but *you* are my full-time job now. There is abso-fucking-lutely nothing more important than making sure you are safe and sound. The only way that is going to happen is if I do it myself. Rick, of all people, will understand this," Savo stated.

Letting out a sigh, I sat back in my chair. "If that is what will make you happy, then I won't argue. But you say the word and we'll figure something out to give you free time."

"Not gonna happen, but thank you all the same," Savo said, then looked at the others. "I do like the idea of the calendar. It will help me know if something happens, who is where, and how to get a hold of you."

"Trust me, if you're calling me, I don't care if I'm talking to god himself, I'll hang up on him," Marius informed us.

Nixon started to say something, but I cut him off as I blurted my thoughts. "Why are you all talking like I'm still in just as much danger as I was before? They're both gone, right? What has you all so afraid?"

Everyone turned to Marius, making it clear he was the man to give me my answer. He rubbed a hand over his jaw, almost as if he was nervous to tell me. "Cambrie, with Yoram removed and Fredrick dead, that leaves only Alton and I alive as the interim government. The country found out last night, when someone leaked it to the press, that Yoram was under arrest. They don't know the extent of his crimes, but in a few hours I have to tell them. I fear that they will retaliate against Alton and myself, not believing we weren't involved."

"In retaliation, you think they will come after our pack," I surmised.

He nodded. "The other reason I wanted to have this meeting is because we all need to be on the same page for the future. I believe it's time we restructured our government completely and held an election for one leader, with a group of three to five men who look over all the laws and proposals the leader wants to make. The people would also elect these officials, and everyone would have to be re-elected every five years. This way, if the citizens of our country aren't happy with what's going on, they have the power to change it."

The table fell silent, making me realize he hadn't said any of this to anyone before now. Oscar raised a hand to draw our attention and asked his question.

"Yes, Oscar, I'm hoping to be the leader they elect. I would love it if Rafael and Nixon ran for the position of advisors, but I understand if you feel that's a conflict, being part of the pack. You both have been that for me through all of this. I think as a team, we could make this country come back to life," Marius reasoned.

Rafael crossed his arms with a contemplative look. "I'll have to take some time to think that over. It would mean giving up working with patients and I'm not sure I'm ready for that yet."

Marius nodded before his gaze shifted to Nixon. The man grinned back at his best friend and let out a huff of laughter. "Did you think I'd forget the promise we made to each other when you first said you were going to be part of the CoF?"

"No," Marius answered. "I just wasn't going to hold you to it if you felt your place at the shelter was more important."

"Nah, Spencer could easily run that place without me. Hell, even if Bodhi came to help him part-time, they'd be fine without me," Nixon scoffed and waved off the concern. "Of course, I'll put my bid in for the position. We said we were going to change the world one day at a time, right? You got elected, and I promised if the time ever came when you needed me, I would step up."

Spencer shot up out of his seat. "Hold up, I didn't agree to be the new CEO of the shelter? Was anyone going to ask me if I was okay with it?"

Both of our Alphas looked over at him with questioning expressions. "Well?" Nixon asked.

Spencer turned to Bodhi. "What about you? Are you just going to sit there and let them decide this for us?"

"Dude, do you have any idea what I'm going to school for?" Bodhi asked, a smirk on his face.

Spencer frowned. "Music, something or other, right?"

"Music education with a minor in business management," Bodhi announced. "I wanted to work at the shelter helping to teach people how to deal with life through music. Figured it would also help if I could do more than that, since classes wouldn't take up my whole day. Oscar let me help him with things, but he didn't *need* me, it was just an excuse for us to be near each other. Now that we're together and family, I don't have to worry about him falling for someone else if I leave him alone for part of the day."

Oscar grabbed Bodhi by the back of the neck and pulled him in to kiss him in a manner that was not meant for the table but was magical to watch. With a growl, Oscar pulled Bodhi onto his lap and wrapped his arms around his Beta's waist.

"Okay, well, that just happened," Bodhi commented with a goofy grin on his face. "What were we talking about?"

I covered my mouth trying to keep from laughing, but I couldn't help it when Oscar looked so pleased with himself. Dropping my hands, I let out my laughter and it filled the air, soon to be joined by the others. This is how a family should be, sharing in the hard choices, watching the tender moments, and sharing joy together. Every time these moments happened, I couldn't fight against the desperate need to share this with the world. Now I just needed to find out how to do it.

"Fine, if Nixon ends up in this new position, then if Bodhi's willing to team up with me, I could manage running the shelters. Just know that I'm going to be blowing up your phone for months as I figure all this shit out," Spencer huffed.

Nixon wrapped Spencer up in a hug and kissed him on the cheek. "Hey now, where's the man I fell in love with that told me he was far too overqualified to be front desk admin? Besides, nothing is settled, and there will need to be a vote. I would never just throw you to the wolves. I love you too much to do that."

"Ha, we'll see about that, mister," Spencer grumbled, trying to pull away, but Nixon just attacked him with kisses until he laughed. "Get off me, you weirdo. God, this bond thing is getting out of hand, you sex-crazed fiend."

Rafael cleared his throat loudly, bringing everyone's attention back to what we'd been discussing. "As I said, I'll take time to contemplate things, but I think that means we really need to know how we want to move forward. Savo will be with Cambrie around the clock. For the next few days, it might be wise to stick close to home and not look for trouble. As for the rest of us, we need to get back to work and show the country that just because the government is in a state of change, that we aren't worried."

"Cambrie has also asked what her duties will be while she is at home. The two of us had a conversation briefly, but I believe getting her set up to get her GED and then looking over some college classes might be wise. As for additional duties, I personally would like to see how things play out and what happens with the change in schedules. If Bodhi isn't at home as much to help with cooking and groceries, it might be a simple switch of responsibilities between them. Savo is also here to assist if there needs to be a run to the store or what have you," Rafael shared.

Marius nodded his agreement while Oscar once more tried to share his thoughts. No one interrupted him this time. *"I agree that Cambrie needs to work on her education, but I also feel it's important for her to know that there are many opportunities out there in the world that doesn't require her to do schooling if she doesn't want to. My Little Star shines so bright that no matter what she does, it will attract those who need her."* His gaze fell on mine and he smiled sweetly. *"Follow your heart, I can see the wheels turning in your mind, and you've thought of something already. I trust you to come to us when you're ready and we will do our best to support you in any way we can."*

My heart burst with a combination of his love for me and mine for him as I signed my thanks. "Oscar's right, I do have some ideas rolling around in my brain but I'm not sure what to do with my ideas as of yet. When I figure out what it is that I truly want to invest my time in, you will all be the first to know."

Marius looked down at his watch and grimaced. "I'm sorry, I've got to go. Alton and I are holding a press conference in two hours and we need to prepare. I asked to push it as late as possible so I could be a part of this. I'm not sure when I'll be back tonight, so don't stay up."

He rose from his seat, cupped my face, and gave me a quick kiss. Then he went to Spencer and did the same before heading out. The lightness of the meal seemed to vanish as we knew what this press conference meant. Yoram would be sentenced for his crimes, and the only fitting end would be his death. I knew they wouldn't have another option and that I shouldn't care after all he's done, but I would never wish death upon anyone.

"If no one's going in for seconds, can I take the last of the pasta?" Savo asked. "That sauce is fucking good."

Bodhi whipped out a hand and pointed at the large Alpha. "What did I tell you? Now you understand why we were all acting that way. Just you wait, the next time he makes the sauce you'll be begging and drooling right alongside us."

Savo flipped him off and grabbed the bowl, dumping the last mound of pasta onto his plate. "It's a damn good thing you don't make this often, I'd get fat in a heartbeat."

We all laughed, easing the tension once more as we chatted about various things while we finished our meal and cleaned up.

Bodhi

The kitchen was clean, Cambi was with Rafael looking at options for her GED, and the others were helping Savo get his room set up. I knew Oscar had gone out to his studio and I was just finding reasons why I shouldn't go out there and speak with him.

Groaning, I ran my hands through my hair trying not to second-guess everything that'd happened so far. The other night when he'd marked Cambi and didn't even spare a questioning glance at me, my heart sank. *Did he really want me? Was this just lusting after each other? Fuck, I feel like an idiot for even questioning any of this.*

"Man up and go talk to him," I muttered to myself. "He said he wasn't going to do anything until we talked, so just fucking do it."

Balling my hands, I took a deep breath and charged out the kitchen door. Bursting into his studio, I startled him to the point he almost fell off his stool and nearly dropped the guitar he was holding.

"Fuck, I'm sorry," I apologized as I grabbed him, making sure he didn't fall. "I just got all up in my head and wasn't really thinking."

Oscar set down the instrument and twisted to face me. "*What's wrong?*"

"Nothing's wrong, it's all fucking perfect, and it's freaking me the fuck out. I don't do happily ever after, Oscar. I'm not built that way, and right now I feel like I'm in a fucking fairy tale." I reached out and grasped his shoulders. "Tell me this isn't just a fling, you and I, because if it is, I'm not sure I can do that. Everything about this scares the shit out of me because I want it so badly. I'm in love with you, Oscar. If losing Cambrie told me anything, it's that this pack and all of you mean so much to me, and I can't fucking lose it. No matter how many times I tried to be a prick to you, chase you away, or do things to make you abandon me, you didn't. I—"

Oscar surged to his feet, grabbed my face, and pulled me into a kiss that felt like he was sucking all the air out of my lungs, only to breathe life back into me. I clung to him, desperate to believe this was part of the happiness Rafael always talked about. He used to tell me that I ran from anything that made me happy because anything could be taken from me, so better to have nothing to lose than lose it all.

He pulled back, breaking the kiss but didn't let me go as he urged me to sit on the couch in the studio. Countless days and nights I had slept on this thing, watching Oscar as he worked, just wanting to be in his space. Now here he was holding me, kissing me, and it was terrifying in the best way possible. Once seated, he knelt before me so there was nothing I could do but look into his face.

"Bodhi, I need you to take a deep breath for me. If you keep going as you are, you're going to hyperventilate and we'll get nowhere," Oscar instructed, his face firm in his order.

As slowly as I could, I took a deep shuddering breath and held it for a moment, then let it out once more. He signed for me to do it again, so I did it three more times until he was satisfied. Something about having Cambrie around had brought out the Alpha side of Oscar, and it was hot as fuck. The combination of the caring man who would give you the shirt off his back and mixing it with the commanding presence I was now facing got me hard as steel.

"Good, now let's start this conversation over. I can see it's clearly been weighing on your mind and I'm sorry I didn't carve out the time sooner to have this talk with you. That was unkind of me," Oscar apologized, making me open my mouth to argue, but he cut me off with a look. *"This is not a dream or a passing fancy on my part. I, too,*

am in love with you, Bodhi. I don't know when or how it happened, but there came a moment when I couldn't picture my life without you. When I risked it all during her heat, I wasn't sure how you would respond. However, when you did with just as much enthusiasm, it was one of the happiest moments of my life."

"You mean that?" I questioned.

He frowned at me. "*When have I ever lied to you? If I won't lie to you about your piano skills, what makes you think I'd lie to you about something vastly more important?*"

"That was a dick move, by the way, but I see your point," I said as I rubbed the back of my neck. "Why... the other night. With Cambrie... you... did you... God, why can't I fucking spit this out?" I growled in frustration.

Oscar grabbed my chin and forced me to look at him as he searched my face. I knew I couldn't hide my thoughts from him, and he'd see my insecurities written all over my face. Everything about this was new, and yet it was almost like we'd been together forever as our friendship turned into something more. He knew my flaws just as I knew his, yet somehow we still fucking liked each other enough to risk it all.

"*You want to know why I didn't bond with you as well when I marked Cambrie?*" Oscar stated. I nodded and held my breath as I waited for his reasoning. "*It would have been wrong for me to claim you when I haven't even asked you if that's what you want. Bodhi, you and I have been swept up in this amazing whirlwind, and I don't regret a second of it, but I had no way of knowing if you felt the same way. Once you're bonded to someone, that's it, and I wasn't going to do that until we talked. You mean far too much to me to find out later you never wanted to be bonded and then have you hate me.*"

I let out a huff of laughter. "I don't think anyone could hate you. Hell, I tried to hate you so I wouldn't like you, and I clearly failed epically at that."

"*Yes, well, I think that worked out well for both of us now, didn't it?*" Oscar pointed out. "*So, is this the point where I ask you if you would do me the honor of being my bonded Beta?*"

"You're making it sound like a marriage proposal," I countered with a frown.

"Isn't it? I'm asking you to share your life with me, to form a connection that shares our innermost feelings. Personally, I would say that it's even more serious than a marriage proposal," Oscar reasoned. *"The question is, do you want to be with me, with us, for the rest of your life, or do you want the freedom to leave at some point?"*

My jaw dropped as he asked me that. "Why would I want to leave you or the others? We're a family, even more so now with Cambrie here. This pack and you have saved my life. I don't know who I would have become if not for all of you." I cupped Oscar's face and leaned my forehead against his. "Also, I'm pretty sure I already told you that I couldn't see my life without you in it. One way to make sure that never fucking happens is to be bonded to you. So yeah, this would be the time to ask me that question, and my answer is hell fucking yes, I want to be *your* Beta."

Oscar pounced on me, forcing me back onto the couch as he crawled on top of me. He leaned in and put his lips to my ear, and whispered. "You're mine forever, Bodhi."

Without warning, Oscar bit into the skin of my neck making me cry out in pain, but it quickly changed to pleasure as the bond snapped into place. Each flick of his tongue over the mark had me panting and squirming as if he was licking up my shaft instead of my neck. It was torturous, like I knew I could come just from this but was brought right to the brink then stopped.

"Please, Alpha, I need you," I begged, my hands fisting the back of his shirt as I rubbed my jean-covered cock on his leg. "I need you to fuck me like the Beta I am, pleading for his Alpha's cock."

Oscar started to purr as he kissed up my neck, along my jaw ,and finally my lips. One of my hands wrapped around the back of his neck, holding him there afraid he might move when I needed him so badly. I felt a hand tugging at the button of my jeans and I quickly hurried to help him. The second the button was free and the zipper down, his hand was wrapped around my cock stroking it slowly as he swirled his thumb around the tip.

"Oh fuck, yes, God just keep touching me," I cried as he broke our kiss.

In an effort to help, I kicked off my shoes and tried to get my pants off, but it wasn't working with him on top of me. A frustrated growl leaked out of my mouth, making Oscar chuckle as he moved off me. He grabbed the end of my jeans and yanked them off me in one go. Then he grabbed the t-shirt and didn't bother pulling it over my head he just ripped the thing down the middle. I wriggled out of it and then grabbed for him, but he shook his head, pressing me back down on the couch.

Confused, I did as he asked then gasped as his hot mouth enveloped my cock. It was harder than I'd ever been before and the feel of his tongue on the sensitive underside of my dick had me clutching the couch. "Fucking hell, why did it take us so long to get here?" I blurted out as he gently stroked my balls.

The combination of sensations had my eyes rolling back in my head. Everything felt ten times more than it had before and all I could think was how fucking hot it was knowing how much Oscar was enjoying this. Through the bond came wave after wave of love and possessive hunger as my Alpha devoured me. My breathing started to quicken as I got closer to coming, but having sensed this, Oscar shifted gears. Using his hand to stroke my cock, he switched to teasing my ass with his tongue, making me arch up off the couch groaning in pleasure.

"Lube. tell me we have lube," I mumbled, cracking an eye to look at Oscar.

He paused and lifted his head to grin at me. Reaching behind him to the side table, he pulled open a drawer and snatched up the bottle showing it to me. *I took Marius's advice seriously. Always have lube close by.*

"Thank fuck," I sighed.

The cool feeling of the gel hitting my skin made me jump, but it was quickly followed by a warm hand working over the tight entrance. Never in a million years did I picture myself as a bottom begging for some cock, but goddamn if it wasn't the best feeling in the world. It wasn't because of the sex, it was the person I was doing it with. Yeah, so Oscar was a man and so was I, but love was love, and it was strong enough for us not to give two shits what gender we were. Just like with Cambrie, it didn't matter to me that she was a woman or an Omega. I fell for her the moment she tasted the first grilled cheese I made her. Both of these people who held my heart in their hands had me falling for them because of who they were, not what they were. The world may have their opinions, but I say fuck 'em all, they're missing out.

A shifting of the couch had me looking at Oscar, who was now naked, stroking his cock, and looking down at me like he knew everything I'd just thought. Fuck, maybe he did through this bond of ours. That was going to take some getting used to, but it was a small price to pay for all the other perks it brought with it.

"I'm going to fuck you now that I've claimed you as mine with a mark. Now, I'm going to own this ass and fill it with my seed, marking you as mine in every way possible," Oscar informed me with a dangerous glint in his eye as he pressed the head of his cock to my entrance.

Spreading my legs as wide as they could go, I tried to relax as he worked his way inside me. I wanted to watch as every inch of him entered me. All I'd wanted in life was a place to belong and people to belong with. Now, I had all of that and the love of this amazing man and a woman who still didn't realize the potential and power she had to do anything she set her mind to.

I tossed my head back as the last inches slid home, and his hips met mine. "Fuck me, Oscar, I'm yours to do with as you please," I said, running a hand down his arm as he leaned forward over me.

He caught me in a kiss that was all tongue and teeth, not holding back from our urges to possess each other. His movements were slow and steady letting me adjust to him, and then once I started to loosen and allow for more speed, he picked up the pace. Determined, he took my legs and pressed them to my chest, so my feet were over my head. Thank god I was flexible, or this wouldn't have worked, but fuck, did it hit all the right spots.

A sheen of sweat coated our bodies making it harder for him to hold me down, so he switched it up. Sitting back, he pulled me up so I was sitting on his lap, my knees under me, allowing me to help set the pace. I could feel his knot starting to swell and at first I was concerned, but I ignored what Spencer had said and trusted my own body instead. Oscar gave me a questioning look but I just kissed him, grabbing the back of his neck, and slammed myself down on him as far as I could take.

His knot didn't make it all the way in, but I'd managed about half of it and it had me roaring in pleasure as I felt Oscar coming inside me, causing my own climax. He bit down on my shoulder as he struggled to not thrust into me like he would with Cambrie. Where his knot was, was exactly where it was going to stay, there was no change of movement with my asshole. He clung to me, holding me tight to his body as he made noises of pleasure.

Slowly and carefully, we shifted so we were lying on our sides, a tangle of sweaty limbs, heavy breathing, and tender kisses. "I love you, Oscar. Thank you for never giving up on me when I was such a prick."

Oscar nuzzled into my neck and kissed his mark, making me moan as a spark of pleasure ran through my body. "I love you too," he rasped, his voice full of love and pain.

As we lay there enjoying the silence and intimate time together, he started to purr and combed his finger through my hair. Now I could absolutely understand why Cambi loved this so much. It was addictive to have someone's undivided attention. This was just the beginning for us and our pack as we charged ahead, leading this country into a new way of life. If there was ever a time when our country needed new hope, it was now.

CHAPTER 62

Cambrie

My eyes started to blur as I looked over yet another list of classes and requirements. Rafael had placed me at his desk and pulled up five different sites that offered GEDs. Picking the program had been easy, and the sign-up was simple enough. Where I'd run into trouble was when he'd shown me the list of classes I could take at the local community college.

"I just want you to see what's out there," he explained. "It's hard to know what you might want to learn if you don't know all the options. Like Oscar said though, if you don't want to go to college right away, or at all, that's perfectly fine, too. My goal is just to show you all the different avenues so you don't miss something that might be perfect."

Now I was finally in the L's section of class names. I'd written down a few things that sounded interesting, but I had no idea if they paired together at all. A knock came on the study door, and Rafael looked up from his book as Nixon entered.

"The press conference is about to start if you want to watch," he offered.

Needing the break, I pushed back from the desk and followed Nixon out of the room and up to the third floor. Rafael joined us with Spencer on his heels, his face bright pink.

"Um, I don't think Oscar and Bodhi will be joining us," Spencer shared. "They're otherwise entwined."

As he said that, I reached out to my bond with Oscar wanting to make sure he was okay, and realized what Spencer had meant. It appeared that I could feel Bodhi as well through my bond with our Alpha, making me smile. My family was almost complete, one more bond had to be established, and I would have all my loved ones connected to me.

"That's alright, we'll just fill them in when they rejoin us," I commented and plopped myself next to Savo, who was sprawled out on the couch.

Immediately, he wrapped his arms around me and turned on his side so I was using him as a backrest. The rest found their places before Nixon turned on the TV. Apparently, it didn't matter what channel you turned to, all of them were broadcasting the announcement. There was a backdrop of our country's flag and the seal of the CoF with a podium in front of it. A sharply dressed woman I didn't know stepped up as Alton and Marius entered the stage and took a seat just off to the right of the podium.

"Tonight, we come to you with an important announcement regarding the allegations brought against Official Yoram Dubois. I will give a brief statement, and then I will hand it over to Official Stone and Official Banks to answer your questions," the woman announced. "Two days ago, it was brought to our attention that Official Dubois abducted an Omega and hid her away in his country home with the other members of his pack. His intention was to sell this Omega off to Shearia in an alliance of power."

"This is an act of treason per the law of Oscad and has brought about his arrest and those of his pack. In exchange for immunity Official Dubois' pack shared all the information they knew, connecting him to various murders of his own in-laws, as well as other members of government, including the attempted murder of Official Banks. When a team of soldiers was sent to arrest him, they discovered he'd set up a base at one of the decommissioned Care Centers near the Neenan Pharmaceuticals building that had been shut down after the attack. Using the data, private medical staff, and researchers, he began to explore using the drug once more to increase the chances of the baby being an Omega." The woman paused as the crowd of reporters exploded in front of her and shouted, "Lucy," which I assumed was her name, trying to get her to answer their questions.

She waited them out calmly, not flinching at the words hurled at her so viciously from the people around her. My gaze shifted to Marius, who was the picture of calm confidence as he sat there with Alton. Closing my eyes, I reached out to him, and even though the echo was faint, I sent all my love and support in his direction. He was stronger than anyone I'd ever known, and he was exactly what our country needed right now—a fair and just commander who wanted what was best for *all* his people.

"Please, I understand this is all shocking and you have many questions but there is still more that I must go over. The list of his atrocities is long, and we are still uncovering more as we go," Lucy said as she tried to gain control of the masses. "This is not something we as a country will get over easily, but revealing what has been done behind closed doors is the first step."

This seemed to get everyone to simmer down enough that she could speak and easily be heard. "There were women found in the Care Center, and they were rushed to the hospital. They are receiving the best care we can give them in the hope we can save them and the babies they hold. As the soldiers raided this Care Center, Official Dubois shot and killed Official Fredrick McCoy and City Magistrate Willem. They stopped him before he could take his own life, and he was placed in protective custody, where he's currently being monitored to prevent any further attempts to escape justice."

"While all of these egregious events alone give us cause to strip him of his title along with pursuing the death penalty, there is a greater transgression that has occurred. During the raid of the largest Care Center in our city, we were informed there were no Omegas left in the building. They'd been sent in a bus to Asturg as payment to keep General Rasvan from turning his attention onto us here in Oscad. Thanks to the heroic efforts of our soldiers and Official Stone, who led this whole mission, they were able to stop the bus from crossing the border, and all our people are safely back at the Care Center under security supervision." Lucy concluded, allowing the stunned media to absorb what she'd just said.

It didn't take long before they started shouting, demanding answers, and hurling insults at the CoF for allowing this to happen. My eyes watered as I thought of those poor women who'd been trapped and forced into an experiment they'd never asked to be a part of. Then there were those who were back at the Care Center, clueless about what happened or what they were saved from. Finally, I prayed that all those who'd been sent to those other countries weren't suffering a terrible fate due to the greed of our leaders.

"There has to be something we can do," I whispered. "Someone has to find them."

Savo sat up and pulled me onto his lap, drawing a blanket over me, and wrapped me up tightly in his arms. "We will, *Keksik*. I promise we will do everything we can to find them, even if I have to talk to my father to make it happen."

Hearing him promise that told me just how serious he was about standing behind his word. Talking to his father could get him killed as a traitor, but he was willing to do whatever it took, and that meant everything to me.

"Now, Official Stone will answer your questions first since he was witness to it all, then we will bring up Official Banks to discuss what will happen next," Lucy informed the crowd before stepping aside, letting Marius take her place.

We watched as Marius artfully handled each and every question tossed his way. Many wanted to know the state of the women he found or how this could have happened without anyone knowing. True to the man of honor that he was, Marius didn't shirk the blame or claim to be innocent of any wrongdoing. After what seemed like an hour, he'd answered enough questions to pacify them to the point that they would allow Alton to speak.

While I'd never met the man, I got the sense from his poise and command over the people that he was a good leader. It made me sad to think that Yoram had tried to kill him simply because he disagreed with his plan.

"Please, please, I'm an old man and don't have the energy to shout at all of you," Alton spoke into the microphone.

Nixon snorted. "That's a big fat lie. I've seen him and Marla go at it. He could whip those idiots into shape if he wanted to."

"Oh shit, has it already started?" Bodhi asked as he joined us, pulling Oscar to sit next to him. "Why didn't you guys say anything?"

We all looked at him without saying a word, allowing him time to figure that one out on his own. A blush colored his cheeks as he cleared his throat. "Right, fair enough. Did we miss anything important?"

"Not anything we didn't already know, but Alton is going to announce the upcoming changes and Yoram's sentencing," Rafael informed them.

Bodhi reached for the remote and turned up the volume as Alton began to speak, refusing to project his voice. Almost instantly, the crowd quieted, eager to hear what the man had to say about the future of the disgraced Official.

"I would just like to state that even though I was a target in Official Dubois' plan, it saddens me that it has come to this decision. As the senior member of the Council of Four, with the support of Official Stone and in accordance with the laws that we were charged to uphold, we have no choice but to sentence Yoram Dubois with the stripping his title. His finances and other assets will be put into a trust, and he will be charged with high treason against the country of Oscad. As well as charges for taking bribes, using our own citizens as collateral in negotiations with other countries, and for the harm of an undetermined amount of Omegas." Alton paused to take a sip of water, and I noticed his hand shaking. Setting the glass down, he straightened and finished the sentencing. "The final act that this government will enact is to command the use of the death sentence. It has never before been used, but due to the vast nature of these crimes, we feel it is the only course of action befitting the harm done to our people and nation."

Hands shot into the air as they called out their questions in a much more controlled fashion than they had been for those before him.

"You said this is the final act of this government. What do you mean by that?" one reporter asked.

Alton nodded and leaned on the podium casually. "This whole situation could have been avoided if the structure of our current government had been built differently. Right now, all that's left is Marius and myself, and let's be honest, I'm getting too old to deal with the changes that need to be made. We will have more information for you in the coming days, but suffice it to say that this is the end of the Council of Four, and we will be creating a new government that will serve the people's needs. Marius and I want to give more control to the people, enforce term limits for those in power, and create a task force that will work on locating all the Omegas that have been smuggled out of our country. We owe it to them since we failed the first time, letting them be sent off in the first place."

"I plan to bring in brilliant minds from all across our amazing country and hear what will serve our people best. What I want is to know that when I step down and make way for the new generation, I'm leaving it better than I found it. It will take us time to unravel all that Yoram had done but know this, all deals, offers, or blackmail that occurred in secret will be null and void. Don't expect to come to me and ask for the same bargain because you won't get it. Instead you'll be slapped into cuffs and thrown in jail. It's time we cleaned up this goddamn mess and bring back the nation I know we once were." Alton had to pause as the whole audience erupted with cheers, whistles, and clapping their excitement over the changes that would be coming.

Once they settled, Alton resumed. "Lastly, we will be abolishing the Care Centers as they are being used now to create something that will actually help our citizens. No one should fear being a certain designation or being forced away from their families into a pack that isn't the right fit. Packs should never have become a thing of the past. They are the heart of our being. Packs are how we were genetically wired to function. This will be brought back into practice, and the Care Centers will be renamed and revamped into a place where packs can meet and interact with Omegas in a safe environment. I believe with all my heart that this will change our nation in the best way possible. Packs that have been able to bond with an Omega the way nature intended to have much higher reproduction rates, but more than that, they are happier and live more fulfilling lives. Help us do what's best for our country, and trust us as we make changes for a brighter future."

By the end, we almost couldn't hear what he was saying. The cheering was so loud that Bodhi had to turn down the TV. I knew Marius was concerned about the people's reactions, but I think he underestimated just how much this change was needed. We'd been suffering in silence for so long it was joyous to hear that hope was on the horizon, even when mixed into it was sadness. Lives had been lost, women had been sold, and so many have been forced into situations they would never have dreamed of, just to survive. Now there was a real chance for change.

CHAPTER 63
Cambrie

We stayed longer to watch a movie and just be together after the meeting. No one would admit it, but we were all trying to wait for Marius, even though he asked us not to. When he finally got home, he greeted us all, ate something, then kissed me and Spencer goodnight before heading to his room.

"No, Sweetheart," Nixon said, blocking me as I tried to follow. "I know you want to be there for him, but right now he needs some space. He gets like this when he's forced into making a choice he doesn't want to. Marius knows there is no other choice but to be the first and the last to use the death penalty. Tonight, he needs to wrestle with that side of himself, and he can't do that in front of anyone."

I looked at Nixon, seeing the worry on his face. "Are you sure?"

"Yeah," he answered with a heavy sigh. "Sometimes, you need to be able to look in the mirror and battle your own inner demons before anyone else can help you."

"He gets one night," I declared. "One night to fight whatever he needs to on his own, then that's enough. We're a family, and part of that means we help each other in our battles."

Nixon hugged me tight and kissed the top of my head. "Sounds like a good plan to me."

"Little One," Rafael said, pulling my attention. "Can I ask you to spend the night with me? If that's all right with the rest of you?"

The others all shrugged.

"That's all you, Dove," Spencer decided. "You are the master of your body and time, no one will ever tell you how you need to share it. Actually, I kind of like the idea of getting you all to myself on occasion. Maybe Raffy is onto something there."

"I agree it's nice to have time together as a pack, but having one-on-one time is also important. We need to strengthen our individual bonds as well as the packs'," Oscar added.

Nodding, I looked at the others. "Okay, then it's decided. If anyone is in need of some individual time with me or their other partner, then we speak up and ask for it. No hard feelings and everyone accepts, with no complaints."

"Someone is getting incredibly bossy and I kind of like it," Bodhi fake whispered to Savo. "Pretty sure that's your fault. She wasn't like this before she met you."

Savo shoved the Beta playfully and grinned. "It's fun to see her standing on her own two feet against all seven of us, isn't it?"

Everyone laughed and headed their separate ways while Rafael held a hand out to me. "Do you want to run up and get settled for bed, then meet me in my room? Or you can bring things down, whichever you're more comfortable with."

"I'll get ready in my room. I know you share a bathroom with Spencer, so it will be easier," I said as we headed up.

Rafael let out a huff of laughter. "In theory, I share a bathroom with him, but he never uses it since he's always in Nixon or Marius's room at night. I can't remember the last time all three of them have slept separately, if they're not arguing, that is."

"Then why don't they just combine rooms?" I questioned.

Rafael looked at me, humor shining in his eyes. "Two reasons, Spencer is horribly messy, and he has far more clothes than any man should be allowed to have."

I snickered. "I suppose that makes sense."

"Go take your time. No need to rush. I'm not going anywhere, and I need to get ready for bed myself," Rafael instructed as he waved me off when we reached his room.

Popping up on my tiptoes, I kissed him on the cheek and headed up to the next floor to my room. There were butterflies in my stomach as I brushed my teeth and changed into a pretty lavender silk nightgown Spencer had snuck into the bags during our shopping trip. This was my first time staying with one of the guys in their space, and I couldn't place why this felt so different, but it was. I brushed out my hair and braided it to the side; the teal color was the perfect contrast to the lavender.

Not feeling confident enough to wear just this while walking through the house, I slipped on my simple white silk robe and then padded down the stairs. Savo was leaning in the doorway to his room and heat flared in his gaze as he spotted me. "Maybe I shouldn't have said the old man could have you to himself tonight," he teased.

"Don't call him that, he's not old," I chided.

Savo just smiled and wrapped his arms around me. "Did you think you'd get away without giving me a goodnight kiss?"

"I'm sorry, I didn't know you were waiting on me for that. Is that a new rule you're imposing? I know how you love all your rules," I quipped.

"Careful, *Keksík,* you're on the verge of being a naughty little Omega," Savo warned, the rumble of a purr in his tone. "Good little Omegas are the ones who get the rewards, remember?"

"Hmm, I remember quite well how that works," I agreed as I grabbed his shirt and pulled him down to me. "But tonight, since I'm Rafael's, I don't need to worry about how good I'm being."

I gave him a quick nip on the nose and tried to dart out of his arms, only to be pressed up against the hall wall.

"Oh, *Keksík,* that was a foolish move. You want to know why?" he asked, nuzzling against my ear. "Come tomorrow morning when they all go to work, you're all mine."

Heat crashed through my body, and slick started to seep out of me at his words. There was something about Savo and his commanding nature that had me acting so cheeky. Yet when he pushed back like he was now, I turned limp and needy, begging for him to make me his good girl.

"While I'd love to know what exactly you did to turn her on like the flick of a switch, I'm not sure it would work the same for me," Rafael said, cutting into the moment. We both turned to look at him where he stood in the doorway to his room, wearing no shirt and silk boxers that showed just how turned on he was. "My apologies for interrupting, but her perfume is hard to resist when it's coming off that strong."

Savo gripped my chin to turn me back to him before he kissed me and pressed me into the wall, his leg rubbing between my legs. "Sweet dreams, *Keksík*."

Stepping back, he guided me over to Rafael and grinned. "Let me know if you can't keep up, old man. I'll help you out with her."

"Thank you for such a gracious offer, but I believe I'm more than capable of taking care of my Omega's needs. Remember, with age comes practice and skill, which can more than make up for in stamina," Rafael countered before slamming the door in Savo's smirking face. "Seems he's feeling far more comfortable around here."

I burst out laughing at that comment, having enjoyed the verbal sparring between my two men. "A real family should be able to poke fun at each other, don't you think?"

"If it's in good humor, I would agree with you. My fear is that Bodhi is going to figure out that Savo is more of a kindred spirit with his sharp wit and verbal sparring skills. Then, we're all going to be in trouble," Rafael muttered, and he pulled back the covers, scooped me up, and dropped me in the bed. "No, I don't want to talk about the others. I want to focus all my attention on you instead."

Grinning, I sat up and slipped off the robe, handing it over to him. He froze, seeing my nightgown, and missed grabbing for the robe the first time but managed it the second. Turning, he draped it over a chair then crawled into bed but didn't stop until he loomed over me, eyes bright with desire. "You, Little One, look stunning lying here in my bed, where I get to have you all to myself for a time." He bent down and nuzzled my neck, which I bared for him. "No, Little One, we are not going to rush this moment. I want to savor every inch of you before I mark you as mine, ensuring your body is well aware of my claim."

I hummed in delight at his words, letting my hands run down his chest feeling his muscles and the softness that was just *him*. "Rafael, you know you've already claimed my heart."

"Yes, but I want more than that. I want the world to know that you belong to us, to me and that if anyone dares to take you from us again, we will destroy them," Rafael announced, his voice gruff with the growl that lingered in it.

My hands slid up his neck to grasp his face, and I pulled him down to me, kissing him tenderly at first, but soon it devolved into something far more passionate and desperate. He settled between my legs and rolled us so I was now lying on his chest, as he let his hands wander down my back to grope my ass. I loved the feel of the silk against our skin, making it feel like there really wasn't much between us. The bottom of the gown bunched up, and he paused as he realized I didn't have any underwear on.

"Little One, when did you get so bold?" Rafael asked with a smirk.

"It's because of all of you," I whispered. "You make me believe I can be brave and take risks. Of course I would never do something like this outside our home. That would just be foolish."

"It would be life-threatening for anyone who found out about it besides us," Rafael muttered.

Sliding off him so I was more on my side, I ran my hand down his chest to the waistband of his boxers and slipped my hand in. His cock was hard and already leaking some pre-cum, making me lick my lips as I sat up and pulled the fabric off him. His dick popped up, eager for me to notice it, as if I might have missed seeing it. Grasping it in my hand, I licked from base to tip making sure to get all that had leaked out so far.

"Fuck, Cambrie, that feels so good," Rafael groaned, hands fisting the sheets. "This was supposed to be about you tonight."

I settled myself over one thigh as I worked his cock in and out of my mouth, using the motion to rub myself on him. Pausing at his comment, I released him to answer. "Then you'd have no problem letting me do this, since I love to make my men feel the same amount of pleasure as you give me."

Rafael wanted to argue, but I resumed my work, cutting him off as he moaned, jutting his hips into my mouth. My slick soaked his leg, allowing me to glide over the skin easily, giving me the needed friction. Using both hands, I squeezed the base of his cock as his knot started to grow, knowing he needed the pressure to get the most out of his climax.

"Oh God, Cambrie, the things you do to me," Rafael gasped as he exploded in my mouth, and a moment later, I came all over his leg.

I let myself slump to the side as we both panted, taking a moment to collect ourselves. Rafael sat up and pulled me so I was nestled against his chest, listening to his heartbeat as he purred. "How lucky I am to find someone like you, Cambrie," Rafael murmured into my hair. "The love you have to give and how you take the time to ensure everyone knows they are cared for equally is unlike anything I've ever seen."

Tilting my face to meet his gaze, I was stunned by the love and adoration this man was directing at me. "I just refuse to let anyone I love or care about doubt my feelings for them. Having a life like this was always a dream for me, something I read about in books, because the world we live in now doesn't support that way of life anymore."

"This is something I believe Marius and Alton are hoping to change," Rafael added.

I pulled myself up further on his chest so we were at eye level. "I don't know how to do it or what I need to study, but I want to be part of that change. We need to teach other Omegas what it means to truly be part of a pack that is meant for you. If they are giving us the freedom to make that choice once more, people won't know what to do with it. Being around all of you, I was able to learn what a happy, healthy pack is. You were one even before having an Omega, which was shocking. All of you chose to be together because you had a common goal and a vision, and you became friends. The foundation of the pack was rooted in all the right reasons. That is what people need to understand."

"They said they wanted to change the Care Centers into a place where it's safe for Omegas to interact with packs. What if they were also for education? I don't know what they teach in school since I wasn't part of that, but how much did all of you need to teach me? Something I'm not sure anyone knows about but another Omega. What it feels like to be in heat, how a bond affects you, and the huge emotional drop you can have when you start to emotionally bond with a pack. Tat's just a few things I can think of off the top of my head. Each of you does amazing and important work, I want to be part of that too," I explained, my heart beating so fast as I talked about the dream that's been growing inside me.

Rafael cupped my cheek, letting his thumb caress my skin. "This world doesn't deserve you, Little One, but I'm so fucking glad you're ours."

"So, you don't think it's a stupid idea?" I pressed.

"No, Cambrie, I think this is exactly what is needed. I would bet everything to say that we are one of the few packs that have found true happiness in how our biological needs are met. Packs have been formed for power, influence, and what would give them the best chance to be awarded an Omega. As you mentioned, we created our pack on an idea, a hope to change the world. Little did we know it could actually happen. Then we met you in a surprising manner, but our connection grew how it should naturally," Rafael pointed out. "That is what people won't understand right away. The need for a relationship to develop naturally. Scent is a large factor in helping Omegas to know who is compatible or not, but we've taken trusting our instincts out of the equation. Now we need to put it back in, and who better to teach that than someone who's experienced it?"

"Exactly," I blurted, sitting up excitedly. "Then I also want to start a community or organization whose sole purpose is to find Omegas who have been sent to other countries. If they are with packs, then we will create a way to establish communication with their families back here so that connection isn't lost. For those who might be in trouble or in an abusive pack, there has to be a way for us to save them. They didn't choose that life, it was forced on them and I won't let that stand."

Rafael chuckled and sat up, resting against the headboard.

"What?" I demanded, crossing my arms.

"Nothing, I'm just wondering if I should give Marius a heads up that he's going to have his hands full with one incredibly determined and visionary Omega. Part of me thinks it will be more entertaining to see his reaction firsthand," Rafael pondered aloud.

"Are you teasing me? I can't really tell, but I feel like you are teasing me," I challenged.

Reaching out, he tucked a strand of hair behind my ear. "No, Little One, I am most certainly not teasing you. These ideas and plans are big, bold, and exactly what you should do. Since the moment I met you and looked into those brave blue eyes of yours, I knew that deep under that scared, abused shell of fear was a warrior. It was just going to take time for you to realize it, and now there are cracks in that wall and the true Cambrie is starting to peek out. I'm just not sure the world is going to be ready for you, but that is a problem for another day."

Grasping Rafael's hand, I held his gaze. "Will you help me do this? If I'm going to get there and do what I want to, I'm going to need all of you to guide me in the right direction. If I need to go to school, help out in the shelter, or even work with Marius at the Capitol Building, I'll do whatever it takes so I can be the person I so desperately needed before I met all of you."

"It would be my greatest honor to help you achieve your dream, Cambrie," Rafael said, and pulled my hand to his mouth and kissed the back of it. "I will always support you and offer what wisdom I have to give to the woman I love with all my heart."

My cheeks heated at his declaration, allowing him to draw me closer and be pulled onto his lap. His lips found mine, and in another moment, my nightgown slipped over my head and was tossed aside. "Now, it's my turn to shower you with love, so you have plenty to share with those who don't know what it looks like," Rafael whispered before taking my nipple in his mouth.

I sighed as his tongue swirled around it, then moaned when his teeth scraped gently over the tip. Grabbing his shoulders, my nails bit into his skin as he shifted me up and then settled me down on his cock. Letting gravity do the work until I was fully seated on his cock, I wrapped my arms around his neck and moved my hips at the urging of his hands. Rafael set the pace slow and deep while our hands and mouths wandered over whatever skin they could find. We lost ourselves in each other, the room filled with the sound of our moans and heavy breathing as we made love.

Rafael turned us so I was on my back, with him rutting into me as we hurtled toward our climax. His knot swelled, locking me in place, but it didn't stop us from milking every ounce of bliss from the situation. He growled as he came, latching his mouth around my nipple and sucking in as much of the skin as he could before biting down. I cried out as I was hit with orgasm after orgasm from him marking me and continuing to work his knot over the sensitive spots that only an Alpha could find. Wrapping my legs around him, I forced him to stop moving and torturing me with an overwhelming amount of stimulation as he continued to pay careful attention to my newest bond mark.

"Please, Rafael, I'm not sure I can take more," I pleaded. "The bond makes everything so much more intense."

At that, he released my breast and kissed the mark once more before settling himself on top of me. I loved when he did this, covering my much smaller body with his large one until I wasn't sure I could be seen. Our bond was flooding me with all his emotions and I let my hands wander over his skin, giving him time to adjust.

"This is incredible," he whispered in awe. "I can feel you, like there is a part of you in my mind letting me know just how you're feeling. Is that how it is for you?"

"Yes and no," I mused. "When the bond is fresh, it's hard to ignore anything that's going on, but after a little while it settles into the background, and I can reach out to it when I want to know.

Which is good, because I'm not sure I could handle this all the time for eight people. The Betas are different, it's like they are another level or extension of the Alpha they are bonded to."

"A miracle, that's what this is. To think we are blessed with something so amazing and integral to having a healthy pack," Rafael mumbled as he reached down and pulled the blankets over us. "This is nothing like people describe. If they did a better job of it, I think more people would jump at the chance. Now they just fear the bond, believing there's no privacy or autonomy once it happens."

Yawning, I nuzzled his cheek. "I'll add that to the list of things to teach in my new program."

He chuckled, kissing me a few more times before we drifted off to sleep.

CHAPTER 64

Cambrie

The next week was a blur of activity within our household. Marius spent long hours at the Capitol Building as he and Alton restructured the whole government. They had meeting after meeting with advisors and other people of power within the current system, trying to find what would be best for our people. He would come home and flop into my bed with whoever else was there, or with Spencer if he couldn't make it up the second flight of stairs.

Nixon, Spencer, and Bodhi were working hard at the shelter. The Alpha was getting them set up to handle things while Nixon geared up to help Marius once the new system was in place. Rafael split his time between working at the shelter and helping me navigate a plan to earn my GED. Savo was my ever-present shadow, but when it came to history, he was rather helpful in sharing what he knew of Asturg and Shearia. Oscar was catching up on all the projects he'd been pushing off for the last few weeks.

All of this made it somewhat challenging to have quality time with my pack, and I knew they were just as bothered by it as I was. Family meals had been put on hold, and we ate when we wanted, but I tried to make dinner and keep it in the oven or on the stove waiting for them when they returned home. During my downtime,

Savo and I worked on projects to help streamline life together. Things wouldn't always be like this, and when it slowed down, what I was working on would be implemented fairly easily.

"*Keksík*," Savo called from the base of the stairs. "Hurry up, we're going to be late."

"We're not going to be late. You just want us to be there crazy early," I grumbled as I took one final look in the mirror.

Today was the day Marius was going to announce the new government system and I would officially be presented as his Omega. Why I needed to be presented to the remaining government leaders made no sense when we were just going to change the majority of it.

The dress was a beautiful shade of lavender with a sweetheart neck, capped sleeve, and a skirt that hit just above the knee. The skirt was pleated to give it some extra fullness and movement as I walked, which I loved. I had on low white heels that just made the whole thing so much classier. My teal hair was up in a soft braided knot, with some of my wavy hair escaping around my face to give it a carefree look. Not being an artist with make-up, I'd done the best I could but kept it simple.

"You've got this," I told myself. "If you want to change the world, then you have to let the world know you exist."

With a final nod, I grabbed my white coat off my bed and headed downstairs, where everyone but Marius would be waiting. It was Sunday, the day we were supposed to have together, but it seemed the country had other plans for us. In a way, I guess we should learn this might become more of a regular occurrence if Marius gets elected to the position of our nation's leader. They hadn't revealed the title yet, not even to us, keeping it all incredibly hush-hush. The news had been criticizing how fast this was happening, but I wasn't really sure how long they expected the nation not to have a functioning government.

A whistle pulled me out of my thoughts and I found all my men gawking wide eyed at me. Oscar nudged Bodhi. "*Are we sure we have to do this?*" he said a few more things but I was having trouble understanding it all.

Oscar, Savo, and I spent a good chunk of time each day working on my singing skills. I was making great progress, but then again it was a whole new language to learn. There was so much to know, all the slight nuances or expressions, but it was absolutely worth it.

"Yeah, I agree we should just make a run for it now. How long do you think it will take Marius to find her with his bond connection?" Bodhi asked, looking at the others.

"What are you talking about?" I questioned, frowning at them all.

Nixon stepped forward and offered me his hand. "Only that you are going to be the most stunning woman at this event and none of us want to have to stab anyone for looking at you too closely."

My jaw dropped. "You wouldn't really stab them, would you?"

"That all depends on how respectful they are," Savo answered. "Because I have zero problems making an example out of someone."

I whacked him in the chest with a glare. "Don't say things like that, people might take you seriously."

Savo caught my hand and kissed the back of it. "Good, it will keep them alive longer."

"Alright, you cavemen, let's get in the limo before they leave without us," Spencer announced, opening the front door.

Rafael and I had worked on various parts of my PTSD, especially when it came to the front door. I still had some trouble going out the door but if I closed my eyes and let one of the guys guide me, it was easier. Today, Savo wasn't taking any chances and scooped me up so I could hide in his neck as we left. In the street was a beautiful white limo with a man holding the door open for us.

The guys all climbed in first then Savo maneuvered me in skillfully, where Spencer took over, pulling me to sit between him and Nixon. "There we are, step one complete."

"Did you really think it was going to be that big of a struggle to get us all out of the house?" I asked with a chuckle. "I can't imagine why you would think that, when you're the worst of them for running late."

"Cheeky Little Dove," Spencer said, catching my chin and

planting a kiss on my lips. "Lucky you're cute so you can get away with things like that."

Grinning, I rested my head on his shoulder as I took Nixon's hand and placed it on my lap. "Okay, go over this once more?"

"First, we are meeting with the current government leaders, and we are just going to introduce you and put your name in the book of records as being our bonded Omega. Then we will move to the steps of the capitol, where Marius will address the country. Once that is done, I believe there might be a dinner we have to attend, but I'm not sure about that. I think that is being left up in the air until we see how everyone takes the news of the new government," Nixon explained.

The drive didn't take long, and I was surprised to see how close we were to the Capitol Building. When we pulled up, there was already security waiting for us and blockades set up to keep the gathering crowds from getting too close to the building. There was a large grassy area that people seemed to be camping out on, only the second they saw us exiting the vehicle, they shot to their feet. Cameras started to flash, and news reporters spoke loudly into microphones and faced video cameras.

"I'm coming to you live from the Capitol Building, where in just a few short hours Official Stone and Official Banks will be sharing their new government proposal. Official Stone's pack has just arrived at the Capitol and this is the first time we are getting a glimpse of their newly bonded Omega. It's rumored that she is the Omega that the late Yoram Dubois kidnapped and tried to sell off to Shearia. Do any of you have a comment? Can you tell us your name?" a reporter shouted at us.

Many more asked various questions, each wanting to know some detail or information about me or the pack as a whole. The security kept them off us as we headed up the steps and into the building. We made it through security without any trouble, but Savo kept me close to his side. While I'd made a lot of progress from when I first escaped, I still wasn't great with people I didn't know. This whole day was going to be full of moments with people I didn't know, and I was trying to reason with myself that I couldn't act like a scared child.

"Breathe, *Keksík*, I won't let anything happen to you," Savo assured me as we walked down a long hall into a reception room.

Marius was waiting for us in a sharp-looking pinstripe suit with his hair styled to perfection. His gaze fell on me immediately, and he smiled, his eyes lighting up with love and happiness. Savo let go of my hand just in time for Marius to grab my waist and pull me toward him.

"Look at you, Princess," Marius murmured as he ducked down for a kiss. "You look radiant, and I couldn't be prouder to introduce you today. What lucky men we are to have you as our Omega."

The heat my blush put off could have started a fire with how embarrassed by his words I was. "Thank you, Marius, you look dashingly handsome yourself."

"Well, when we have you at our side, I doubt anyone will notice," Marius teased.

"Oh, don't worry, that's what I'm here for," Spencer called out, giving us both a wink. "I'll always make sure our Alphas don't go unnoticed."

I chuckled and turned back to Marius. "Remind me why we have to do this again?"

"Because until I share our new plans with the country, we are still under the legal obligations of the old law. So, if I'm going to go out there and tell them I made sure to follow the letter of the old laws, I can't make myself out to be a liar now, can I?"

"No, I would never want that for you," I agreed with a sigh. "So, do we just go in there and get this over with?"

"Patience, they will come to get us when they're ready," Marius chided, but gave my hand a reassuring squeeze. He held me against him as he turned to face the others of our family. "I wanted to thank you all for being so supportive and understanding during this past week. Once this part is over, things should become steadier, and I won't have to work so late. It's always been my goal that once we had an Omega in our pack, I would ensure I was home every night for dinner. That is something I plan to make happen as much as I can. After you hear the announcement, I'm sure you'll understand things are going to change but I promise you my family is just as important if not more than my dreams for this country."

Savo snorted. "The man's already making speeches, and he hasn't even been elected yet." Everyone laughed at this. "Don't worry, Marius, we all have our roles, and I have no doubt that over the next month or year each of us will have a purpose that pulls us away for a short time. Whether times are good or bad, the packs are there to support one another."

The others murmured their agreement as Marius clapped Savo on the back. "It still amazes me how it feels like you've just always been part of the pack. Guess our girl knew best when she picked you."

"It's all about learning to trust your instincts," I interjected.

With everything going on, I hadn't had a chance to tell everyone my plans for the future and I was hoping tonight might be the time to share.

"Official Stone," a woman I recognized from the press conference called when she opened the door. "They're ready for you."

"Thank you, Lucy, we'll be right there," Marius answered, then looked down at me. "Ready?"

Nodding, I squeezed his hand, and we headed into a vast room with the seal of the Council of Four on the marble floor. There was a table with a group of seven men seated, watching us with warm expressions, setting me at ease. In the middle was Alton, but I didn't recognize the rest of them.

"Welcome and happy greetings on this joyous day," Alton greeted, rising from his chair. "I promise this will be painless and, as I'm sure you're aware, just a formality. Typically, this would be done prior to the Omega receiving the bonding marks, but under the circumstances, we've all agreed it was done to safeguard the Omega in question."

The rest of the men nodded in agreement.

"I won't bore you with telling you all our names and titles since many of us will be retiring today, but we are thrilled that the last act we have is placing an Omega with her forever family and pack. Cambrie, if you would please do me the honor of stepping forward," Alton instructed.

Trying not to glance at Marius, I clenched my jaw and released my hold on his hand and headed to the table. There was a large book with names, dates, and various other information written in a ledger of sorts.

"Would you please write your full name where it says Omega? What this is acknowledging is that you are accepting this pack of your own free will. No one has forced you into this union, and you accept these men to be your Alphas," Alton informed me.

I took the pen then paused. "I'm sorry, sir, but I'm not sure what last name to put down. I've always used my mother's last name, but as I'm sure you know, she wasn't really my mother."

"Hmm," Alton pondered, then seemed to decide on an answer. "Cambrie, if it's your mother's name you've used, then Neenan would be the correct name to use. She was a lovely woman, and I'm so sorry you never got to meet her or your grandparents."

"Thank you, sir," I said, unsure how else to answer.

It felt odd to write that last name, but in a way I was happy to have the truth of it. My mother had raised me with love and kindness, but knowing she wasn't the person who gave birth to me changed things slightly. My love for my mother didn't, but knowing someone else gave me life left me wishing I'd known who she was.

"Excellent. While I have you here, I wanted to also inform you that you are the sole heir to the Neenan estate. Everything that was once your mother's is now yours to do with as you see fit. A lawyer will get in touch with Marius and set up a time to discuss things with you. We know of your past and feel that it's only fitting that you receive this," Alton informed me.

My eyes went wide, and I looked back at the others, completely unsure what any of this meant but Oscar just signed that we would talk later. I answered him and then faced the men in charge once more. "Is there anything else I need to do?"

"No, my dear, that is all we need from you," Alton said with a smile. "Next, we will need the Alphas of the pack to sign the book."

They did that without any further question or fanfare, passing the pen to the next until Marius was the last to write his name.

"With these signatures before witnesses, we acknowledge your pack and the benefits that are granted such unions by the law of Oscard. May your pack be fruitful and prosper in the years to come," Alton announced and snapped the book shut. "Well, now that we've gotten that drivel out of the way, shall we make history?"

The change in the man from the formal Official to the casual sweet older man was sudden and incredibly welcome. It set everyone at ease as they stood and shook hands with my men, greeting each other.

"Come, Cambrie, I would love to introduce you to my pack," Alton instructed, gesturing for me to follow him.

I paused but saw that Savo was right at my elbow, ready to accompany me.

"Goodness, you big brute, I'm not going to cause any trouble with your Omega. The poor girl has been through quite enough, don't you think?" Alton huffed as he crossed the room with us trailing after him. "I just thought it would be good for her to meet other pack members who have lived life with someone in the political office. It's not something that life just prepares you for," Alton rambled as he entered a room where three men and a woman sat chatting.

"Oh, done already?" one of the men asked, raising to his feet, signaling everyone else to do the same.

"Everyone, I would like you to meet Cambrie, Marius's Omega. This is Marla, my bonded Beta, our Omega, Phillip, his other bonded Alpha, Eric, and his bonded Beta, Keith," Alton introduced.

I smiled and greeted them all but paused when I met Phillip. "I hope this isn't rude, but I've never met a male Omega before."

"No, it's not rude at all. We are around but incredibly uncommon here in Oscad. My parents were from Shearia and came to this country to work, then never left," Phillip explained.

"Well, it is a pleasure to meet you," I said with a little curtsy, remembering from my time with Arthur this was the proper way to greet people.

"Aren't you simply charming?" Marla cooed. "Come sit, we have some time, and I'll bet those two workaholics will disappear to go over last-minute things, leaving us to entertain ourselves." So, we waited and chatted.

CHAPTER 65

Cambrie

Marla was surprising in every way, and Phillip was the perfect counterbalance to her when she got heated about something, which seemed to be often. My other men chatted with Eric and Keith, who were I learned, renowned scientists and doctors helping the women Yoram had been experimenting on.

The time flew by, and the nerves I had faded as I enjoyed listening to everyone. Then the call came for us to head out to the steps, and the fear came roaring back. All my Alphas snapped to attention and stopped what they were doing to find me.

"What is it, Little One?" Rafael asked, running the back of his hand along my cheek reassuringly.

I licked my lips and tried to swallow. "There's going to be so many people," I blurted. Emotions fluttered in my stomach, making me queasy. "What if something happens? Everyone is going to be out there. What if they hate their ideas and come after us?"

Nixon squatted in front of me and took my hands in his. "I know we might have scared you with the need to keep Savo around and keep your ventures outside the house minimal, as we were unsure how people would take things. To be honest, I think that was more for our benefit. We lost you, and it shook us more than we like to let on, so we used this as an excuse to be overly cautious.

People have been incredibly open, if not excited, about the changes. The news likes to make everything out to be doom and gloom, but it isn't the reality. Our city has always stood behind Alton and he's put his backing toward Marius, ensuring he's well received. I can't promise nothing will happen, no one can, but what I can tell you is they've done everything in their power to make us as safe as possible."

"Okay, I trust you. None of you would let me do this if you didn't think it was as safe as you could make it," I said, giving him the best smile I could.

Nixon gave me a quick kiss and stood, still holding my hand. Oscar reached down and took the other while the rest of my pack created a semicircle around me. When we stepped out into the setting sun, the thousands of people before us cheered as Marius and Alton stepped up to the front. The noise was deafening, but I was relieved to hear it was excited cheering and not screams of hatred or booing.

"Thank you all for joining us here tonight as we share the future of our country," Alton announced into the microphone. "This will be my last act as an elected Official, and I couldn't be more honored to hand over the responsibility to someone younger and smarter. Please know that the choices we made weren't made lightly. We've spent countless hours, days, and sleepless nights going over every inch of this plan. Today is the announcement and the beginning of the plan. Things will change over time, but we hope that in six months, everything will be running at full speed. Now, I leave Marius to share with you the vision of our future for Oscad." Alton stepped back, clapping and ginning at Marius, who smiled and gave his thanks.

"Good people of Oscad, our nation has been rocked with a shocking truth and betrayal by those who we voted to lead us," Marius said, silencing the crowd. "In our efforts to make this new government into something that couldn't be manipulated, we've found that might be impossible, but we plan to do our damndest to ensure our people will be protected. We will no longer have the Council of Four; instead, we are making way for a role we named

Head Speaker. The purpose of the Head Speaker is to speak for the people of Oscad."

"The Head Speaker will be elected by the people and will be allowed to stay in office for five years. They will then have to be reelected to continue serving the people. If they are not elected, they will be removed from office and the people's choice will take over the role. Under the Head Speaker will be five governors, who will each have an area they oversee, as well as advising the Head Speaker. These members will be elected every four years to prevent any interference with or from the Head Speaker in the vote. The Head Speaker will not be able to vote for these members since it's their job to ensure the Head Speaker is doing his job." Marius paused for a moment, letting people absorb this information.

"As Alton shared, as of tonight, the role and power given to those of the CoF are no longer. By a final vote of all remaining government leaders, it was decided that I would act as interim Head Speaker. This will only be for the duration it takes to elect our first official Head Speaker, but we need our government to continue working. It is my intention to run for Head Speaker, in the hopes that I might be able to continue helping this nation in its change and growth into a prosperous nation. All other positions will currently remain the same until the Head Speaker is put in place. At that point, we will be doing a hefty investigation into all areas to ensure they are being properly run by those best suited to the job. Changes are coming, and I hope we will become the nation our grandparents told us about, the glory days they remember. There will be more announcements regarding the Care Centers and the guidelines for packs searching for an Omega in the following days. A nation can't be changed overnight, but we are doing all we can, as fast as we can, to fix all that has been broken."

Marius had to pause as the crowd's roar overtook what the speakers could put out, drowning him out with their exuberance. I gripped tighter to my Alphas' hands, feeling the rush of emotions from Marius as he felt so much pride and love for the people of this country. If there was a way I could share this with them, so they understood what he wanted to give them as a leader, they'd be idiots to choose someone else. Once the people had calmed down, Marius gave his closing remarks and took a step back.

Lucy took his place and started going over how people could register to ensure they could vote. Many had stopped doing this when CoF members stayed in office for so long but now everything was going to change, and this was just the start. Marius walked over to Spencer and kissed him sweetly before taking his hand and then reaching out for me as we exited back into the Capitol Building.

"We're going to hang here for a bit for things to settle down outside, then we can head out," Marius informed us. He looked at me, glowing with excitement at how things had gone. "You're the only one who hasn't been here before. Do you want to come up and see my office while it's still my office?"

"I would love to see where you work," I answered right away, swinging our hands as we walked.

We headed up a few flights of stairs, then down a hall where Marius paused to unlock the door and ushered us in. Glancing around, I took in the beautiful office with its ornate wood accents and stately desk that I could picture Marius working late into the night. Turning, I discovered it was just the three of us and Spencer had closed the door.

"What's wrong?" I asked, suddenly concerned.

Marius walked up to me and cupped my face. "Nothing is wrong. Everything is absolutely perfect, my Princess."

Before I could say anything else, Marius's mouth was on mine, kissing and nipping at my lips until I opened for him, allowing him to deepen the kiss. Now that he had my full attention, I could feel his *need*. Marius had gone too long without being intimate with Spencer or me, and our bonds were not having it. To my amazement, Marius had managed to push it off to the point that he was almost in rut.

"Please, Princess, I need you so badly." Marius whispered against my lips.

I wrapped my arms around his neck when he picked me up and set me on the edge of his desk. "I'm yours, happy to give you what you need."

Marius looked over at Spencer, who joined us. "Tell me what you need, Alpha."

"What I need is for you to fuck me as I fuck our Omega on this desk. Right here, where I've slaved night after night to make this new reality happen. It's kept me from you both, and right now it's gonna give back," Marius announced.

Spencer grinned as he dropped to his knees and removed Marius's pants. In turn, our Alpha shoved up my dress and without even bothering to remove my underwear, he shoved them aside and began to devour me. I gasped but slapped a hand over my mouth, afraid someone would hear me.

"It's okay, Princess, no one is up here. Savo wouldn't ever let someone hear your cries of pleasure, not even security." Marius chuckled before he went back to work on my pussy.

I couldn't see Spencer from my position, but I could hear him working Marius's cock with his mouth. Within minutes, the regalness of this office was destroyed by my moans, Marius's growls, and Spencer gagging on our Alpha's cock. Marius slipped in two fingers, stroking my sensitive spot making my hips buck as he sent me over the cliff into an orgasm.

"Yes, Princess, let me hear you come. I want to know I'm making up for lost time with you both," Marius encouraged as he thrust his fingers into me.

Spencer rose and walked over to the desk and pulled open the third drawer to grab a bottle of lube. I met his gaze, and he winked. "This isn't the first, nor the last time something like this will happen. Personally, I love the change of scenery and the excitement of knowing we're doing it where he works. Our scent will linger, driving him crazy for days, making you and I very happy partners."

I laughed as Marius straightened and used the hand he's been fucking me with to wet his cock with my slick. "Oh, is that why you always talk me into fucking here when I've been working too much? You shouldn't share your secrets, now I'll know what you're doing."

Spencer pulled Marius into a kiss that had them both moaning as they stroked each other's cocks. I pushed up on my elbows so I could get a better view of my men, so desperate for each other.

Marius broke the kiss first and turned back to me. "Are you ready for me, Princess? I'll apologize for it now, but this isn't going to be gentle and sweet. We have places to be, but I won't last if I don't have you both."

"Take what you need, Alpha," I answered, letting my legs fall wide as I lay back.

Marius grabbed my hips and pulled me until my ass hung off the desk and he slammed into me. Crying out in pleasure, I groped for something to hold on to as he pumped into me. After a moment, he paused only to let out a groan I'd never heard from him before. He bent forward, and I saw Spencer behind him pushing his cock in.

"Fuck yes, this is exactly what I needed," Marius moaned. "Don't take it easy on my Spence. I want to know I've been fucked."

Spencer grinned and gripped Marius's shoulder, giving him the leverage he needed, and got down to business. He was moving so hard and fast he was fucking Marius into me, setting a quick and brutal pace that felt amazing. It wasn't something I'd always want, but I could see the appeal every so often. Clinging to the edge of the desk to keep myself from being shoved off, I watched Spencer fuck our Alpha. At one point, Marius took control swinging his hips in a way that had him fucking us both at the same time. When I felt his knot starting to form, he pulled back not allowing it to take hold. Instead it just bumped on the outside, knocking my clit, which sent me into a screaming climax just as Spencer roared his.

Marius wasn't quite there and rode us both until he also found his completion. His cum filled me and because he didn't knot me, I felt it seeping out as he continued to thrust into me. Now his desk was going to have a stain on it, proving Spencer's reason for fooling around in the office.

"Ah fuck, now I'm going to need to buy this desk," Marius muttered as he hid his face in my neck, kissing his mark. "Can't leave your intoxicating scent around for just anyone to enjoy."

Slowly, Spencer eased out of Marius and then my Alpha did the same. Spencer stepped into the office bathroom and reappeared with a washcloth. What shocked me was that he handed the cloth to

Marius and dropped to his knees, and proceeded to lick the cum right out of my pussy. I was so sensitive that each stroke of his tongue had me writhing on the desk, begging for more.

"Just look at the two of you. How the fuck did I get so lucky?" Marius purred as he watched his Beta eating me out and cleaning me up all at the same time.

My underwear was ruined, and even if I wanted to wear them again, they were soaked with my slick and scent. I wouldn't be able to walk anywhere without someone scenting me.

Cleaned up as best as we could manage, the three of us left Marius's office. Now here I was, walking through the Capitol Building with no underwear on, making a liar out of me when I'd told Rafael I'd never do it outside of the house.

"I think we should go out to dinner to celebrate," Nixon announced.

Upon everyone agreeing, my mouth went dry, knowing I'd have to go bottomless. Thankfully, my skirt was plenty long enough and the fabric was thick enough that no one would know but the two people who looked far too pleased with themselves. Bodhi wrapped an arm around my shoulder when the others started to leave and I was still rooted to where I stood.

"Come on, Cambi, most of the people should be gone by now," he reassured me thinking that was my reluctance. "Nixon called and made a reservation at this amazing steak restaurant that is super hard to get into. They got us in right away and had a private room for us to use. Guess Marius being the leader of our country, for now, gets us some perks," Bodhi added, grinning down at me.

Hearing this made me breathe a little easier. I wouldn't be in a crowded room with people who might guess my secret. "That sounds awesome. I can't remember the last time I had a steak."

"You know who's pretty amazing at grilling, Oscar. Never would have guessed it, the man isn't so good with the stove, but you give him a grill and damn, those are some of the best burgers I've ever eaten. He cooks a lot during the summer, so I'm sure you'll eat more meat than you ever have before," Bodhi said, chatting along happily.

Spencer looked over his shoulder with a wicked grin telling me whatever came out of his mouth next would be filthy. "Oh, I'm pretty sure our Little Dove has already earned herself more meat than she thought she'd ever had."

Nixon smacked him on the back of the head and scowled. "Not out in public, you never know when reporters might be listening in. That's the last thing we need running around in the papers."

"Fuck, you're right," Spencer said, looking chastised.

This time we didn't take the limo, instead there were three blacked-out SUVs that they split us between. Marius had me with him and Nixon, which meant Savo came as well while the others were in the second vehicle.

"I'm sorry, this is going to be the new routine if I'm with you. All of you will have security details with you, but now that I'm the sole leader of our country, there are extra precautions," Marius explained. "There will be some freedoms we give up, but that's a price I am willing to pay to help change this world for the better."

"It's fine, Marius, it makes sense. If they lose you, then there's no one to handle things," I agreed.

The restaurant was in an area I'd never ventured to before, but it was deep in one of the more well-off neighborhoods my pack lived in. Security went in first, and we were escorted right into the room we'd be eating in. People gawked as we passed, but many cheered and yelled their encouragement. Only a few people seemed unhappy, but they kept their mouths shut, only glaring. I had a feeling those benefiting most from the deals with Yoram would be the most resistant.

"We are so honored to have you and your pack dining with us this evening, Official Stone. I'm sorry, I believe the new position is Head Speaker, my apologies. If you would give us the pleasure, my chef has asked that he might be able to prepare a special four-course meal for you all," a man in a fancy suit greeted us once we sat down.

Marius smiled at the man then looked at all of us. "Does anyone have an issue with that?"

"As long as we can still order our own choice of wine, then I'm fine with that," Rafael said with a smile.

"Of course, sir, I'll make sure to get you a full list of what we have to offer. Are there any allergies or other requirements our chef should know about?" the man asked.

Everyone shook their heads, and with that, the man gave a little bow and left the room.

"Can I just say that makes things so much easier," Bodhi said with a sigh. "I couldn't decide what I wanted and now I don't have to make a choice."

Laughter filled the room, and I couldn't help but agree, not to mention I didn't know what the things listed were. By no means was I a picky eater, I just wanted to know what it was I was eating. Drinks were ordered and salad was served before they left us in peace until the next course.

I cleared my throat nervously and used my spoon to clink my water glass like I'd seen in movies to get people's attention. Instantly, I had all of their attention and I blushed. "I know today has been a big day already, but I've been doing a lot of thinking about what I want to do in the future, and I said I would share them with you when I am ready. After talking it over with Rafael and looking into classes, I think I know what I want to do."

"Tell me, Princess. I would love to hear what dreams you have for yourself," Marius encouraged as he folded his hands on the table, giving me his full attention.

My gaze flicked to the others and they, too, were fully invested in what I was about to say. "There isn't a degree or specific classes that will help me get to where I want to be, but counseling and social work of sorts are the closest Rafael and I could find to what I needed to spend time learning about." I bit my lower lip only to stop instantly, knowing better, and shifted in my seat feeling uncertain about this next part. "Marius, I know you said there were plans in the works for the Care Centers and what you wanted to change them into. If you haven't already set things in motion, I have a plan I think might be the best solution to help Omegas as well as others who want to become a pack."

Marius smiled and nodded for me to continue as he took a sip of wine.

"I know my education wasn't normal, but I still believe they haven't been teaching us Omegas what it truly means to have this designation. I want to change the Care Centers into something that helps packs learn how to be a cohesive unit, while also educating Omegas in their role. We need to change our perception of both pack life and structure, as well as including an Omega into the mix. Both have been looked down upon, manipulated, and misunderstood for so long that no one knows what it's supposed to look like," I explained.

Nixon nodded his agreement as he leaned back in his chair. "It's true. Our pack in fact was viewed as odd since we built it around an idea and people we felt a genuine connection and friendship with instead of what value each person brought into the mix. Seeing so many packs formed purely for their advantageous nature makes me wonder what their home life is like. Do they even really have a pack, or just people who live in the same house tolerating each other? It's also highly uncommon in recent years for Betas to be brought into the mix if they aren't a lover of one of the Alphas."

"I agree, so many people found it shocking that you guys took me in when I had nothing to offer, and at that point, wasn't with any of you," Bodhi added.

"*Re-education is going to be vital for this new era, and I couldn't think of anyone better to pave the way than our Little Star. She's seen it all, the best and worst of the system as it is now. It would be interesting to work with already existing packs as well if they want counseling,*" Oscar shared.

"I suppose this is when I should tell you, Marius, that I won't be running for any of the Governor positions. I feel it's going to best serve our people for me to work with Cambrie on this effort, offering counseling and support as Oscar mentioned," Rafael announced. "But that is something we can discuss later. I believe there is more our Omega wishes to share with us."

"Yes, there is a second half to this. Whatever we turn the Care Centers into, that will only be part of what I want to do. The most important thing for me is to head up a team that will locate all the Omegas that have been sent to other countries. Savo and I are going to team up with Rick who is, under your direction, I believe, setting up a task force to investigate this. I'm not sure what can be done, but I would like to bring back those who no longer wish to live in the other country if they aren't bonded or committed to a pack. Those that are, I would like to establish communication between them and any family they might have. I can only imagine the parents who trusted that the Care Center was the safer option are devastated to know their child is gone. We owe it to them to do all we can since we failed them," I declared.

This idea seemed to catch all of them off guard, besides the two who already knew. Marius turned to Savo with a curious expression. "You're in support of this idea?"

"One hundred percent," Savo answered. "I feel as strongly about this as she does, which is why I suggested we work together. Rick's Omega is from Shearia and can help us with that connection, and as we all know, I have ties to Asturg. It's not lost on me that there will be a lot of political red tape to pull any of this off, but I think if we make welfare checks a concession at first, it means we can locate them and it won't ruffle too many feathers."

Marius rubbed his jaw in contemplation. "This project will take time, but I think we can absolutely make this part of the overall agenda. If I inform the public about it and use it as a major part of why they should re-elect me, it's a win-win for everyone across the board."

"That was my thought, plus it's the right thing to do," Savo agreed.

Spencer reached across the table and took my hand, which had been nervously plucking at my napkin. "Little Dove, I think these are brilliant ideas and something to be proud of. It will take some time to get these up and running, but what about if you started some small classes at the shelters? Start small, find what works, what people want to know or don't know already. This can help direct you. An education is important, and if you feel that needs to be part of it, then do it. Just don't let it stop you from setting things in motion. There will be political hoops no matter who's in charge, but if you get the ball rolling, it's harder to stop it."

I smiled and squeezed his hand. "Thank you, Spencer. It means a lot to me that you're already so invested in this idea. I think you're right that education is not going to be the thing that holds me back, but I want to at least have my GED. For me, that's been a dream to accomplish for three years, and I'd like to do it for myself."

"Then that's what will happen," Rafael assured. "You're already in the program and it's a go at your own pace, so if you want to finish it as fast as possible, then we'll get you there."

My heart swelled as I felt all their love and support through our bonds, bolstering me for the hard work that was to come. "This is just the beginning, I see all of us doing our part to change the world in our own ways. As you always tell me, this pack was founded on an idea and look how far you've all come. I'm so excited to see what the future has for us all."

"Here, here," Nixon cheered and raised his glass. "To the future of Oscad."

"To Oscad," we all said, raising our glasses.

Marius stood, holding his wine glass and looking at all of us. "I know another speech, but I promise it will be brief." Everyone snickered, but we held our glasses waiting for his toast. "To the pack of misfits who saw how broken the world was and decided to change it. Little does the world know the power a unified pack full of love and friendship can have. Thank you all for being my family, and I have no doubt our future will be unlike what any of us expected. Here's to you, because without you all, I wouldn't be here today."

"Cheers!" I cried, thrusting my glass of water into the air, knowing our adventures were just beginning.

Cambrie

THREE YEARS LATER

The world around us had changed in so many ways over the past few years. Marius was officially elected as Head Speaker, and Nixon was elected as Governor of Citizen Welfare. Fitting if you asked me, since he was in charge of making sure all of our citizens had the support they needed to build better lives for their families. Spencer and Bodhi were now the directors of the Open Arms Shelters and Education centers. They were a fantastic team and have used their skills to help so many get back on their feet; finding jobs, homes, and finishing education they might have missed out on like I had.

Oscar was still producing music, but he was also working with Bodhi in his music classes at the shelters. They became so popular they were overwhelmed and had to bring on more help. People didn't see the point in learning a skill when it couldn't put food on the table. Now that life was a little easier, it allowed them to find joy in hobbies and other activities they'd been forced to set aside.

The biggest change was, of course, no longer forcing Omegas to be sent to a Care Center. They were free to be with their families and grow up with all other designations. Once they reached eighteen, they were able to file with the Pack Support Organization (PSO) that they were open to finding a pack of their own. Of course, many packs developed naturally between people of all designations, and they just had to register their pack with the PSO to receive support and guidance whenever needed.

With Rafael's help, I founded the Omega Education Initiative with my inheritance, and we had decided instead of making classes for people to go to, we held them at schools. It didn't take us long to figure out it was the new generation we needed to focus on first. Helping them understand how all designations were equal yet had biological differences and some needed more attention than others. It was simply magical to witness children driving the change and teaching others how to respect and care for each other.

As for the work Savo and I paired up to do, that wasn't progressing as smoothly as we'd hoped. The Omega Recovery Project was up and running with Rick's amazing support. Sasha, Rick's bonded Omega, joined our team as well, assisting us as the Shearian ambassador. Through her connections, we got their government to allow us to send in teams to check on the health and wellness of those Omegas that had been sent there. Asturg wasn't so open to having anyone step foot in their country, especially since we were no longer going to send any Omegas to them like Yoram had.

Most of Marius's efforts were dealing with the fallout of breaking deals made with Yoram. There was a tense time when we thought we'd have to go to war with Asturg, but by some miracle, they managed to figure something out between them. It was hard to adjust to the fact that Marius and Nixon couldn't always tell us what was going on when it came to national security, but it made sense.

"Mrs. Neenan," Sheela called through the intercom. "There is a Mr. Tibble to see you."

I looked across my office to where Savo's desk was. He flat-out refused to let me have my own space when I was meeting with so many *shady* people, as he called them. Really, they were different connections and underground workers who helped us locate the Omegas we were looking for. Since there was a massive crackdown on the black market sellers, I came up with the idea that they could switch sides and help us if they didn't want to go to jail.

"Send him in, please," I instructed.

Savo got up from his seat and took his place behind me, watching my back as I spoke to our newest recruit. Mr. Tibble was a black market smuggler who dealt mostly with Asturg, where we needed the help. Most of the Omegas that got sent over there were placed in breeding houses and I'd made it my sole mission to get them all out of there if I could. An incredibly small number of women had found a pack and seemed to be happy enough. I had offered them the same chance I did all the others if they wanted out, but most refused. Only one had accepted, and we'd smuggled her back into Oscad and into the safe house I'd converted the family mansion into. So much heartache had taken place there, so I wanted to use it for good. Now that it had been gutted and remodeled, it was a safe house for all the Omegas we smuggled out to receive treatment for their physical and mental wounds.

"Ma'am," the anxious man greeted me as he stepped into my office. His hand nervously twisted his hat in his hands as he stood there.

"Please take a seat. I was told you have information for me?" I instructed, gesturing to one of the chairs in front of my desk.

He sat but refused to look at me. I wasn't surprised by that, Savo had that effect on pretty much anyone. "Yes, ma'am, I located another group of girls in Southern Asturg. I'm not sure how they got there since the North is careful to keep an eye on all the Omegas they have. Many are chained to their beds in the breeding houses so they can't run."

"Yes, I'm well aware of this," I said, fighting back the bile that was threatening to come up at the mere thought of these poor women suffering. "What is the importance of them being in the South? From what I understand, their views on Omegas aren't that much different."

"Well, you see, there is one thing they do differently. They only place them with the military, and they are trained to fight as well as to be bred. These women are in a training camp and I'm not sure we can get them out. President Dragomire pairs them up with a unit, kind of like a pack that they train and serve with. It's one reason their Omegas live longer; they can fight and are guarded around the clock by their unit. These aren't just normal units either, only the elite are awarded an Omega," Mr. Tibble explained.

I sighed and rubbed my forehead, feeling a headache coming on. "Thank you for the update. I'll reach back out if I need any other information."

"Thank you, ma'am," Mr. Tiddle said with a bob of a bow and scampered out of the room.

Large hands started to massage my neck, making me groan at how good it felt. "Don't be making sounds like that, *Keksik,* unless you want me to take you right here right now."

I glanced up at him. "We already had sex this morning."

Savo shrugged. "Doesn't matter. I'm pretty much ready to knot you any chance I get."

I laughed, leaning into his touch. "You say the sweetest things."

He bent down and kissed me until I was breathless. "Only to you, my sweet girl."

"How about we head home? He was the last meeting I had, and I'm exhausted," I sighed.

"Didn't we all tell you that working while you're pregnant wasn't the best idea? I mean, if it were up to Marius and me, you wouldn't leave the house ever again, but we also don't want to be kicked out of the nest for the rest of our lives," Savo muttered as he helped me to my feet.

I ran a hand lovingly over my swollen belly I'd been waddling around with for six months. "I'm glad you realize the consequences of your actions. Now, I need a nap and like ten grilled cheeses. Do you think Bodhi will be home yet?"

The next second, a phone was placed in my hand, with Bodhi's name on the screen. I lifted it to my ear. "Hello?"

"Let me guess, you mentioned grilled cheese and now I'm getting a phone call," Bodhi chuckled. "I don't know what you did to scare Savo so badly that he won't make another one for you, but I kind of love it."

"He burnt it. The man tried to hand me a burnt grilled cheese," I stated, glaring at the man in question. "That is as sacrilegious as it gets in our household. Anyways, we are on our way home and I wasn't sure if you and Spencer were going to be back yet."

"Don't worry, Little Dove, I'm bringing the grilled cheese master home right now," Spencer called out, telling me I was on speakerphone in the car. "How hungry is our little guy?"

"Well, he's one of your sons, so I'm guessing at least three will be needed. God, if I wasn't already the size of a whale, I would be with all I'm eating," I muttered into the phone.

"None of that," Spencer scolded. "We worked long and hard to get meat on those bones, and I, for one, love that you're a little extra squishy to cuddle."

I rolled my eyes at his comment. "Alright, we'll see you at home. I know Oscar is already there, and Rafael texted he was leaving ten minutes ago. Has anyone heard from our supreme leader?"

Spencer snorted. "God, the face he made when you used that the other night in the middle of things was priceless. I wish I had a camera to capture that moment and be able to show it to our little man when he arrives."

"I had no idea he would like it so much," I sighed. "He had me knotted for almost an hour, and I had to pee so badly."

"Hey, I offered to get a bucket," Spencer teased.

Having had enough of that conversation, I hung up the phone and handed it back to Savo. "They're on their way home."

Savo grabbed the door as I waddled my way out of the office into the main hall of the Capitol Building. Imagine my surprise when I found out this was where Marius wanted me to have my office, making the Omega Recovery Project government-backed. The people had spoken, and they wanted action about this situation. It became so much more of my main focus, that Rafael had taken over the education part of things. I was sure once this little man made his appearance, I'd have to hand off more things, but I wasn't going to allow them to push me aside. This was my idea, and I was going to run it.

"What are you planning to do about the girls in the South?" Savo asked as we waited for the elevator.

I leaned into him, resting my head on his chest. "I don't know.

There isn't much we have to go off in the South. The North borders our lands so it's easier to have access, but it seems we might need to shift some of our people to learn about the President and the way he runs things. Even though it's bad they're chained to a bed, at least they're taught to fight."

"What if we were able to get to one of the girls and get them to help us?" Savo suggested. "If it's too hard to get them from the South, we convince them to go North again. Then we'll have a team there to bring them home."

"That's a smart idea. We just need someone who can get in contact with the girls. Plus, how do we know they will believe who we send? Asturg is known for keeping their people in the dark about what's happening outside their country," I pointed out as we stepped onto the elevator.

"If I told you I had a connection, someone I trusted to help us in the South already, would you let me reach out to them?"

I turned and looked at my burly overprotective Alpha, who felt just as passionate about this program as I did. "Who?"

"I have a childhood friend, we haven't spoken since I left Asturg. I didn't want him to get in trouble with his father for us being friends when it was spread across the nation that I had abandoned my people," Savo explained.

I placed a hand over his heart. "Tell me."

"It's Sorin, Dragomire's son," Savo shared.

"Wow, that was not what I expected, but if you think you can pull that string, then I'm all for it. If we can get the President's son to help us, then we might be able to foster a real friendship between countries. Wouldn't it be amazing if we could help end the war?" I gushed as we headed for the building's exit.

"Now, Princess, isn't it enough to overthrow one government, let alone two?" Marius asked from where he was waiting for us.

Clearly, Savo had told him we were leaving for the night, even though I'd told him not to. "Hey, a girl can have big dreams, right? That's what you keep telling me anyways. Also, why are you here? You have a huge meeting tomorrow for the tax reformation thing."

Marius walked up to me and pulled me into a hug, kissing my

forehead. "Yes, I do, but we made a deal when we found out you were pregnant that family was more important and I would be home every night. Our child is going to grow up knowing all of his fathers love him and make time for him, no matter how important running a government might be. So let's go, I hear you've already demanded grilled cheeses be made."

"I did not demand," I countered.

Savo and Marius both looked at each other over my head, making me smack Marius in the chest. "Stop it right now, you're making me sound like a cheese tyrant."

"You said it, not me," Marius stated, tossing up his hands in surrender. "Come on, Princess, let's get you home before you get too hangry."

Each of my Alphas took a hand, and we walked out of the Capitol Building together. I looked over the city that had changed so much in the past few years and knew we had a long way to go, but it was heading in the right direction. Was it wrong of me to wish everyone could live in a place that fought to value its people? That we didn't see any designation as property or as livestock to be bred? In my mind, we were just getting started and if I happened to help change the rest of the world along the way, so be it.

"Make the call, Savo," I said as I climbed into the SUV. "We aren't going to leave anyone behind."

"I'll make it happen, *Keksik*, but after that, you need to let me handle it. Your job right now is this little guy," Savo said, resting his hand on my stomach. I could feel a little kick right where the hand was, making me groan at the thought of him being a daddy's boy.

"You know we're going to have to try again. There is far too much testosterone in our house. I need someone on my side," I grumbled.

Marius cupped my chin and turned to look at where he sat next to me. "We're always on your side, Princess, forever and always."

The end!

About the Author

International Best Seller Elizabeth Knight, has been writing and telling stories as a hobby for years, but wasn't sure it would make a living. After her other job was shut down due to the pandemic she was encouraged to take her writing more seriously. So she published her first reverse harem Discovering Synergy April 2020. Since then Elizabeth has written prolifically and is constantly exploring new genres and ideas, putting her own twist on things. It's incredibly hard work, but she's never been happier than when she sits down at her desk with new imaginary best friends to share with us all.

If you'd like to stay in the know, then sign up for her newsletter:

Sign Up Here
https://geni.us/EKLinks

Also By

Sunshine & Rainbows Omegaverse

<u>Bailey-Rose Duet</u>:

Clouds & Daydreams + Petals & Promises

<u>Lyra Duet</u>

Knot Now Knot Ever + Yes Now Yes Forever

Caprioni Queen - Complete Series

Glitter & Guns

Blood & Heartache

Revenge & Truth

Love & Power

Gun Runner Princess

(Caprioni Queen Spin off)

One For The Money

Two For The Show

Omega Assassin - Complete series

Dual Nature

Hidden Nature

Perfect Nature

Knot All Omegaverse

Knot All Is Lost: Part 1 & Part 2 (Complete)

Knot All Is Ruined: Part 1 & Part 2 (Complete)

Hidden Empire Series - Complete series

Two Tricks

Three Tricks

Four Tricks

More Tricks

Our Tricks

Hidden Empire Novel

(Suggested to be read after Four Tricks)

Harper's Renegades

Standalone Books

Nicolette: Ladies of the MC

Lying Lainey: Underground Omega Syndicate